W9-CMH-469

ONE SHOT, THREE KILLS

An MBC Omnibus Edition

ONE SHOT, THREE KILLS

An MBC Omnibus Edition

THE SCOPE OF JUSTICE: BOOK 1
TARGETS OF OPPORTUNITY: BOOK 2
CONFIRMED KILL: BOOK 3

MICHAEL Z. WILLIAMSON

THE **MILITARY** BOOK CLUB ★★

THE SCOPE OF JUSTICE Copyright © 2004 by Michael Z. Williamson. ISBN: 0-06-056524-1. First Avon Books paperback printing: July 2004

TARGETS OF OPPORTUNITY Copyright © 2005 by Bill Fawcett & Associates. ISBN: 0-06-056525-X. First Avon Books paperback printing: March 2005

CONFIRMED KILL Copyright © 2005 by Bill Fawcett & Associates. ISBN-13: 978-0-06-056526-8. ISBN-10: 0-06-56526-8. First Avon Books paperback printing: September 2005

First Military Book Club omnibus printing: March 2006

All rights reserved, including the right to reproduce this book, or portions thereof, in any form.

This is a work of fiction. Names, characters, places, and incidents are products of the author's imagination or are used fictitiously and are not to be construed as real. Any resemblance to actual events, locales, organizations, or persons, living or dead, is entirely coincidental.

Published by arrangement with:
AVON BOOKSPAN
An Imprint of HarperCollins Publishers
10 East 53rd Street
New York, NY 10022-5299

Avon Trademark Reg. U.S. Pat. Off. And in Other Countries, Marca Registrada, Hecho en U.S.A.
HarperCollins® is a registered trademark of HarperCollins Publishers Inc.

Visit our website at www.militarybookclub.com

ISBN-10: 0-7394-6549-X
ISBN-13: 978-0-7394-6549-3

PRINTED IN THE UNITED STATES OF AMERICA

CONTENTS

THE
SCOPE OF
JUSTICE

To Ray Chatterjee:
Thanks, Dood.

"YOU WILL USE TEN KILOGRAMS OF SEMTEX, WHICH will be provided to you by another. Messages regarding it will be delivered to the safe house," Rafiq bin Qasim said to the man before him, concluding the briefing. "Are there any questions?"

"None, sir. I go with God!" replied the man. His name wasn't important. Allah knew his name. Soon he would be dead, then others would know it, too.

Bin Qasim's office was unusual. The brand-new computer and flatscreen monitor, fax, several TVs and radios, all wired into uninterruptible power supplies, set on modern desks and static-reducing mats, were in sharp contrast to the poured-concrete walls and hazed glass in the single, small window. Woven mats covered the rest of the floor, lit at present by the four-tube fluorescent can overhead.

"Go with God, brother," he agreed, dismissing the man to his fate. He was neither bright nor highly trained, but he was dedicated to the cause and that was enough. If all he could do to help was die, bin Qasim would send him to die.

There were others like that. There were also those who didn't want to die, who had to be led to believe such plans were nonlethal. But martyrs were necessary to the cause, and it was annoying that so few of them were intelligent enough to bother with. Some were the type to accomplish great deeds, and others only served as role models. This man was just bright enough for the latter.

That done, he watched as his three assistants, the only ones allowed to be armed in his presence, escorted the future martyr out of the building. A car would take him to the airport, he'd fly a circuitous route through increasingly more respectable countries until he reached Egypt, then Germany.

Shortly thereafter, an explosion would destroy a nightclub. A place filled with sexual music and rutting, filthy women, alcohol, drugs, and best of all, American tourists and soldiers. Bin Qasim would see to it that as many of them as necessary were blown up to force them out of the Islamic lands.

Perhaps he could arrange for a day-care center next. Any American who didn't grow up was a good American. Pondering that, he looked over the office, and focused on the pliers atop the toolbox. He'd been too distracted earlier to finish. Now, perhaps.

He rose, retrieved the pliers, and said to his guards, "I shall be some time. You may leave."

They nodded and filed out, grinning in amusement, but not in front of bin Qasim, for his temper was legendary.

Bin Qasim took the pliers with him into the back room, where the British woman reporter still waited, whimpering. He'd taught her her place, in fear and suppliant to God, then Man. Now to let her show her enthusiasm for that place.

"Sergeant Monroe, right face," came the voice on the radio. Sergeant First Class Kyle Monroe did so, and waited for further instructions. He knew what they'd be: the sniper trainee was clearly visible. But he was damned sure going to be letter-of-the-regulation fair to the student who was about to fail this exercise. The observer at the end of the range had to make the call, Kyle was only a marker for him.

But this kid was as obvious as a hooker in church.

Kyle sighed, feeling old again. He had fourteen years of service, and still felt physically capable and flexible. He hadn't slowed down when he hit thirty, the way everyone said happened. Inside he felt worn, though. It wasn't the years getting to him, but the mileage. But he had all his hair and none of it gray, a taut physique and clear eyes. After tours in Bosnia and the first Gulf, Ranger and Airborne Schools as well as Sniper, and a few miscellaneous radio courses, he felt that his physical condition was still decent and quite an accomplishment. He'd feel a hell of a lot better if he could lose the guilt over that event in Bosnia, which was something everyone said wasn't his fault. It felt that way to him, though. It didn't help that he had been an instructor here at the school since then. It was mere coincidence; they needed some of the best snipers to teach others, and everyone said he was that good. But he couldn't escape the timing. It felt like a punishment, no matter how much he really did like teaching the kids.

"Three meters," he was told, then, "left face," which he did, leaving him facing the boots of Corporal Samuel Merrick, clothed in a shredded burlap ghillie suit and hidden in deep weeds.

At least he imagined he was hidden in deep weeds. "Two meters forward and tell Merrick he's a corpse," was the next radio transmission.

"You got 'im," he confirmed for Staff Sergeant Dick Rogers, who was one of the "targets" the students were trying to "shoot."

"Stand up, Merrick, you're dead," Kyle said. Merrick sighed, heaving himself up as if a pile of weeds suddenly assumed human form. "Figure out what you did wrong?" he asked.

Merrick said, "The sun came out."

The boy was exasperating. "Sun came out, my ass. Relying on the light is luck. If you rely on luck here, you'll rely on luck in combat. Dead! Get me? Dead!"

Merrick looked slightly chagrined, but Kyle was still talking. Merrick likely wasn't cut out to be a sniper. He could shoot, he could hide, he could observe, but he just couldn't coordinate them with the patience required to be a true professional. He even took it lightly, wearing a grin.

"I'm not smiling, Merrick," Kyle said yet again. "Look there!"

The kid was a bit more attentive now. He turned to look behind him, where Kyle was pointing. Predictably, he let his heavy M-24 rifle—a highly modified Remington 700 in 7.62mm NATO—swing across his legs as he turned. It tangled with his right boot and his ghillie suit. He hopped, recovered, and stood.

"See that?" Kyle snapped, pointing at the tall growth of the range. "There's a very clear Corporal Merrick-shaped rut through the weeds there. Anyone can tell you crawled through here. And it's a *straight* line. Prey don't move in straight lines, only hunters. So what will anyone seeing this think?"

Without waiting for an answer, he continued, "Then, you shifted the branch you used as a rifle rest. And when you shot, you blew that stalk in two. See?"

Merrick looked, and finally gave evidence of remorse. That had been really stupid. Any one of the errors was bad. All of them together were inescapable. He'd screwed up.

Kyle's problem student nodded, turned, and headed for the trucks. He was done for the morning, and the loss of points wouldn't help his final class score.

Kyle wasn't sure if the kid needed a girlfriend, a thousand pushups, or just a couple of years to mature. He was all hyped on the glamour of being a sniper, and didn't want to hear about the slow, boring infiltrations. Those were in bad weather, bugs, dirt, and with the risk of being discovered and shot.

Kyle Monroe knew about all of that personally. It hit him again right then, that pain that wasn't fading. Bosnia. He and his spotter had been a bit too eager to advance on a target. End result, Sergeant First Class Jeremy Reardon dead, a Serb sniper's bullet through his head. The funeral had been closed casket, and Kyle really hadn't cared to discuss it with Reardon's pretty young wife and seven-year-old son, who was old enough to understand death, but not old enough to understand why.

He snapped back to reality. This time it was nausea, washing over him as he massaged the scar on his right arm. Other times it was fear, sweats, anger. And he'd be drinking tonight, fighting with himself over whether to not drink, drink enough to relax, or just burn brain cells with alcohol.

In the meantime, Captain Schorlin, the school commander, was over there watching, and the expression on his face indicated he wanted to talk. Kyle hitched at his load-carrying harness and headed in that direction. The other instructors and the French observer were looking at him, too, and he knew why. Normally, everyone snickered and laughed at inept movements, strange twists of fate, or sheer forgetfulness. There was enough stress in the class, and they tried to be relaxing when counseling. Kyle had been rather brusque.

Schorlin looked at him levelly. It wasn't unkind, just appraising. As Kyle approached, the blond-haired young man—he was only thirty—said, "I think you need to ease off just a bit on the kid, Kyle."

"He needs to grow up, sir," Kyle replied. "Or he'll wind up dead and taking people with him."

"We have time," the captain said, sounding relaxed and unperturbed. "And you know I won't let him graduate if he can't hack it."

"So I'm helping him with that."

"Yes," Schorlin agreed, "and making him think he can't hack it. At this point, we've gotten rid of the bad ones. He just needs encouragement and some sarcasm. Remember when you could be sarcastic without being mean?"

Kyle had to grin at that, though it was a sickly grin. "Yes, sir. So what's up?"

"We've got a meeting tomorrow. It might mean an assignment for you."

Kyle was immediately defensive. Were they trying to shuffle him off? "But I like it here, sir. Is something wrong?"

"Yes, but not with you. It's TDY only, I'm told, which is good, because we need you here. They want you to help with a problem elsewhere. But General Robash has the details. So be at the classroom at 0900. Look sharp. BDUs and beret," the captain said, pointing at Kyle's headgear, which, like his own, was a standard Battle Dress Uniform cap. It worked better in the field than the beret, and both men, despite being Ranger trained, took it as a point of honor not to wear the Monica, as it was deprecatingly called, unless they had to.

"Yes, sir," Kyle agreed, controlling the slight grimace he felt. He resented how the black beret he'd earned the hard way was now being worn by everyone and his brother . . . and sister. He realized it hadn't always been a Ranger symbol, but it had become one, and then it had been taken away and trivialized.

He turned his attention back to the broad terrain and work. There was a twitch of grass. It was Sergeant Brendt, moving too eagerly. From the radio came Sergeant Rogers's voice, "Sergeant Monroe, left face, ten meters." Rogers had spotted another one. Kyle sighed and went back to the task at hand.

It was a pleasant spring day, at least, though the ground was damp, making it cold and squishy for the students. The undergrowth was thick and plentiful. Apart from daylight, it was the thickest concealment a sniper could ever reasonably hope for. If the students, all trained infantrymen, could get past the sharp eyes of the target/observers, they should be able to get past anyone. And "anyone" would be an enemy who was trying to kill them, not merely humiliate them.

For this exercise, Rogers and McMillan were seated at a desk in the bed of a truck, portraying driver and passenger. The students infiltrated the 1,000-meter range, trying to get under 800 meters from the targets and as much closer as necessary for a clear shot. Upon doing so, they would fire a blank and call the target. An instructor on the range, like Kyle, would report the shot, and the target would hold up a placard with a letter. The students would call off the letter, proving they had a clear view of the target through the scope, and the shot would be scored. They would then take a second shot. In the meantime, the targets were scanning with binoculars. If they caught sight of the students as they approached, or after they shot, indicating spoiled concealment, those students failed.

If the students had paid attention, they should easily be able to do it in this Southern pine forest, full of red clay, brush, rolling ground, and deadwood. If they couldn't do it here, there was no way they could do it in the desert or on open fields.

And right now, three of them were lined up about five meters apart, line abreast. So if one of them fired, it was likely that the spotters would catch all three of them. They were all infantry trained and should know better. But eagerness and carelessness brought them to this.

Then, there was Sergeant Favrot, who'd decided that 400 meters wasn't good enough for a shot. He was nearly to the 200-meter mark. He'd certainly get a clear shot from there, but he'd also be much easier to find. The point of being a sniper was to keep hidden and distant, getting as close as necessary, not as close as possible. Still, Favrot was good enough that he might pull it off. But he needed to be cautioned against excessive exuberance. They were here to shoot, not make records.

Kyle chewed an MRE for lunch, just as the students would when done. They'd have time for lunch between now and the afternoon shoot, which would be in a concrete building, one group sniping from it, and the other countersniping from outside. There was no time to drive off range, down long, rutted and washed-out roads, to the cantonment area of Fort Benning. But he knew he needed to eat, and wasn't in the mood for fast food or the chow hall, anyway. His lingering depression, anger, sadness about the Bosnian screwup he'd been involved in didn't encourage a good appetite. Neither did MREs for that matter, but he had one and chewed at it component by component. He washed it down with water from his CamelBak, the gallon capacity soft canteen he wore on his back, with a drinking tube running up the shoulder strap to his mouth. They were finally standard issue rather than just a nifty accessory, and he used it without even realizing it was there, which was the mark of good equipment.

After Favrot got in his shot, along with two others who'd pushed the time limit, the students climbed into the back of their truck and rolled off. Kyle followed behind in the stake truck, the jolting ride down gully-washed trails clearing his mind slightly.

The concrete training "house" used for the next exercise was also used by various units practicing assaults. Expended flash-bang grenades and blank rounds joined cobwebs and deliberately placed furniture and debris. While movie snipers would shoot from near a window, professionals, or those training to be, found contorted positions well back against inside walls, with several feet of space to absorb muzzle flash and dull some of the report of a shot.

Merrick picked a good spot, atop a sturdy table, out a curtain-shrouded window facing south. He could see through the sheer fabric *out* with his scope, but it would be near impossible for someone outside to see *in* to the comparatively dark room. His position was solid, his view clear, and took in the large drainage culvert that was an obvious hiding place for the infiltrating team. And being obvious, one of them would invariably take it.

The kid was shrewd when not in a rush. Kyle simply watched silently from the doorway to the adjoining room, where he could watch Favrot, calm and imperturbable, set up a low position through a loophole and across what would seem like a safe zone.

Just as when doing the shooting himself, the wait hypnotized him into calmness. He watched and waited for twenty minutes, until Merrick said, "Permission to shoot, Sergeant?"

"Stand by," he said. He grabbed his microphone and asked, "Rogers, Monroe, do we have permission to shoot?"

In moments, everyone confirmed readiness—hearing protection was necessary in the tight confines, against echoing high-decibel reports, and it was polite to warn the cadre and any students who didn't have plugs in yet. "Go ahead," he said to Merrick, who nodded and squeezed. The muzzle blast echoed tinnily around the concrete structure.

"Where?" Kyle asked. He passed Merrick's instructions on to Rogers, who walked to the culvert and retrieved a student who was probably disgusted. Kyle couldn't make out who he was from where he stood, but Merrick had done a creditable job. "Way to go, Sniper," he said in encouragement, a grin on his face.

"Roger that, Sergeant!" Merrick replied.

Two minutes later, another student bagged Merrick, who'd snuck a peak through the "curtain." Kyle sighed. Getting off a shot wasn't the end of the mission, and didn't make the area safe.

Outside, he waited for the end of the exercise. He wondered again about the possible TDY, both because it represented a pending upheaval, and because it took his mind off Merrick. He stared at nothing, face tight, until Rogers said, "Hey, Kyle, cheer up. You okay?"

"Yeah, just stuck in the past," he said. "And wondering about the future."

"Could be worse," Rogers said. "Could be raining."

As if on cue, the steady overcast dropped a few beads of rain on them.

"You jackass," Kyle said, smiling despite himself. Rogers just laughed aloud and walked back over to the mockup house, where half the students waited patiently for the other half to get within range and become visible.

The day ended eventually, and Kyle finished documenting the day's activities and logged off his computer. He wondered what the possible TDY—temporary duty—was about, and why a general was coming to see him. But Schorlin either didn't know or wasn't saying. So he climbed in his truck and joined the exodus toward the dorms, base housing, and off-base living. He drove without thinking, pulled up in front of his dorm, and parked his Chevy S-10.

Kyle had never been married, though he'd had a few girlfriends. Currently, however, he was single; Rebecca had gotten frustrated with his odd schedule and left the month before. She'd objected to a few other things as well, like his drinking to relax, drinking to forget. In fact, Kyle was pretty sure he was drinking too much to be healthy, and had been working on lowering his intake. Since she left, of course, he was drinking to forget her, too.

His mind focused on Merrick. If the kid would just slow down and not expose himself, he'd be great. As it was, he was heading for a violent screwup where people would die, just like that one in Bosnia.

Dammit, why did everything have to remind him of that flubbed mission and Jeremy's death? Kyle wondered as he grabbed a bottle of cheap bourbon from the cupboard. He poured three fingers and took it to the recliner with him. As a single NCO, he didn't bother with much furniture, just the recliner and the couch, both good for sprawling across. He had the TV on, but wasn't paying much attention. He sipped at the whiskey while staring into the glass. Screw up for two minutes, regret it forever.

It ran through his mind again. They'd been in good concealment, thick alpine scrub that was a sniper's dream. Then Kyle had decided to crawl out for a better view of the battlefield, because that same brush restricted vision to narrow apertures.

"I don't know that we should do tha——" Jeremy had said from beside him, the last word drowned out by a *Crack!* and his head exploding. Some Serbian sniper had seen movement in the brush, scoped them, and fired.

Then dirt fountained right under Kyle's face, up his nose, in his eyes, a *Crack!* and a soft, moist sound of the exploding soil inter-rupting his shock. He threw himself on hands and feet and scooted back behind a heavy bush, then farther to place an outcropping of weathered basalt between him and his opponent. Then he noticed the burning pain in his arm and the running blood.

The sadistic bastard had taken Jeremy's body apart with perfectly placed shots, while Kyle tried to call in helos for support and extrac-tion. Three days of sneaking and his spotter's life wasted because he'd been too eager to grab a good shot.

It hadn't made him feel better that the Army had refused to place blame and dropped the investigation with no fault to him. He knew whose fault it was. So did the Reardon family. His assignment to the school was a step up for his career. It still felt like punishment some-times.

It was then that his focus moved to the TV, which was showing a documentary on Bosnia. He punched at the remote until the screen went dead, and slugged back the burning liquor. He stood quickly and put the glass in the sink before he threw it, and decided to call it a night, dinner be damned.

KYLE WOKE GRITTY-EYED AND HATING IT. HE WANTED to sleep in another two hours, but that wasn't going to happen. He'd never been a morning person, but fourteen years of service had conditioned him to rising early. Even that didn't make up for the night before and the lousy sleep.

But a general officer didn't want to hear excuses, so Kyle would just have to deal with it. He showered, shaved thoroughly, and put on his "dress" BDUs. They were starched and ironed, in violation of regs, because starch and heat defeated the anti-infrared treatment of the fabric and made it shiny and reflective. The pockets were stitched flat, in violation of regs, because stitched pockets were as useless as tits on a boar. Still, that's what the Army bureaucracy required to look "professional." It was one more way the pencil pushers forced style over substance. He felt ridiculous, but it was supposed to be impressive. He still had his old black Ranger beret, but instead would wear the new one, blocked to look pretty, that the Clinton administration had crammed down their throats to make everyone feel special, whether they were or not. He understood his predecessors had had similar complaints about Lyndon Johnson and SecDef McNamara's changes back in the 1960s. It was always the same. None of it helped his mood.

He arrived at 0600 and grabbed a cup of coffee. That in itself was an indication of how tired he felt. Caffeine caused shakes, which were bad for shooting, and he never touched it if he could avoid it. It was generic coffee, good enough for keeping people awake or scouring sinks and not much else.

Schorlin was already in his office with the door open. The office reflected the man. It was neat enough to use as a backdrop for press releases. Books were perfectly aligned on the shelves, desk dusted. His computer was on but idle, the screensaver showing a scope reticle over a black screen, the last image visible within the panning crosshairs. He had an I Love Me wall that was impressive. It started with Ranger school, covered West Point after that, direct commissioned, and wound up in Kuwait, Bosnia, and Afghanistan. There were certificates from the Marine and SEAL sniper schools, too, as well as foreign ones. Schorlin was the kind of officer Kyle respected, because he'd been there and done that. He was a pleasure to serve under.

Schorlin looked up and said, "Morning, Kyle. You look like hell."

"Morning, sir. I feel like hell." He threw a salute that was casual enough for their relationship, sharp enough to show he meant it and that he was ready for a general to arrive.

"Well, try to cheer up. The general will be here shortly."

"Yes, sir," he replied.

"How's that problem child of yours?" The question was conversational, but interested. Good commanders kept track of such details.

Merrick had done much better in the afternoon, patient and steady in the house. He'd scored a good kill. "He'll work out eventually, sir. But for now, the boy needs a serious asswhuppin'. He could shoot for the Olympics. He can quote the book better than I can. He's got eyes like a cat. But he's too damned eager." Aggravating. That's what the boy was.

"Hmmph. Sound like anyone we know?"

Feeling sheepish, Kyle said, "Yes, sir. Me when I was that age."

Nodding slowly, he said, "So there's how you approach him."

"Yes, sir," Kyle agreed. He hadn't made the connection in those terms, though he had recognized the annoying attitude. He'd forgotten that it had taken him fourteen years to get where he was.

Right then, the phone rang. Schorlin grabbed the receiver and said, "Yes, Joe? Great, don't let him wait. We're ready." He hung up and said, "He's here."

Kyle nodded. It was unusual for a ranking officer to come to the soldier. Usually, the reverse was true. He wondered what was going on.

They stepped into the hallway and Kyle checked over his uniform. Good enough. Then they walked out the door, down the broad metal steps, and down the hill to the classroom.

The Sniper School's facilities were rather spartan. There was the office building, a maintenance building with a bay for cleaning and repair of the rifles, a basic barracks with racks and lockers and a small classroom, all inside a barbed-wire-topped chain-link fence. That was it, and it surprised the rare visitor with its spareness.

It was that classroom, a bare twenty by thirty feet, that was their destination. With the students on the range, it was very private. Kyle held the door for Schorlin, followed him in, pulled a chair off a desk and sat down.

"Relax, Kyle," Shorlin said. "No one's in trouble."

"I know that, sir," he said. "I'm just not a morning person." He winced at the fluorescent lights overhead.

Very shortly, booted steps arrived on the landing outside. Kyle rose to his feet with Schorlin, and awaited the general's appearance.

General Robash was alone, which was unusual for someone of his rank. He wore old but serviceable BDUs, and a standard BDU hat in lieu of the beret. He looked as if he were ready for the field. He was tall and broad, with a slight bulge in the midsection from too much office work. His presence preceded him as he paused at the door and knocked.

"Come in, sir, please," Schorlin said. "Welcome." He saluted and offered his hand.

"Thank you, Captain," Robash nodded. "This must be Sergeant Monroe. Good to meet you, Sergeant." He stuck a bear paw-sized hand over, and Kyle took it.

"Good to meet you, sir," Kyle replied. He saluted after they shook, not worrying about the breach of protocol if the general didn't. No doubt about it, General Robash was huge, and his demeanor even larger.

Schorlin asked, "Coffee, sir? It's not the best but it's fresh."

"No coffee, thank you. Too much already. That's why my eyes are brown, no matter what other rumors you may have heard." There were chuckles. "But let's step outside so I can smoke a cigar."

"Yes, sir," they both agreed, and followed him back through the door.

"Thank you," he nodded, as he drew one from a tube in his pocket. It passed under his nose for inspection as if it were on parade. A small, pearl-handled Case knife flashed from pocket to teeth to cigar, then closed and disappeared as the snipped tip bounced off the steel railing and onto the ground, and he used a badly scuffed Zippo lighter to breathe fire into it.

Through a rising cloud he said, "Good Dominican."

"Wish I smoked sometimes, sir," Schorlin said, eyeing the brown cylinder.

"No, you don't, but it's polite of you," Robash said. He stood easily. The cigar was an affectation. He wasn't an Academy grad, but maintaining that image was good for dealing with the network who were. Though like a lot of the younger ones, Captain Schorlin didn't smoke.

Robash spoke. "Well, officially I'm here to inquire about using some snipers in an upcoming field training exercise. We'll discuss that later. Right now, I need to impose on you."

Schorlin replied, "No imposition, sir. We're at your disposal. How can we help?"

The general smiled and said, "I need to talk to Sergeant Monroe for a few minutes. Privately."

It was obviously for show. Schorlin clearly knew what was going on, even if he hadn't officially been told. He saluted again and walked back to his office. That gave Kyle a slight chill. What kind of mission was this for, if deniability was an issue?

As soon as the captain was gone, Robash said, "At ease, relax, son. This is where I ask you if you can handle the TDY, and you impress me with your coldhearted expertise and gung-ho attitude. Then, when the BS is done, we'll talk for real. So start by telling me why you're wearing a stitched and ironed clownsuit."

Kyle was taken off guard by the attitude. "Ah, I was told to look neat, sir, so I wore a tailored uniform."

"That's not what you wear every day, then?" The general was an experienced cigar smoker, and puffed to keep it lit, then waved the cloud clear.

"No, sir," Kyle admitted.

"Good," the general blew another cloud of smoke as he spoke. "So don't waste any more time on that crap. The BDUs are supposed to be *used*. Class A's are for impressing generals. And this general isn't here for a beauty pageant. I need to know three things. Can you shoot?"

Nodding, he said, "Yes, sir. Well enough to teach here, at least." He was still snickering inside at the general's agreement with his perception of dress.

"That says a lot, and I knew that. Can you kill?"

"I have, sir," he agreed, a bit reluctantly.

"Not what I asked, son."

"It's my job, sir." He had a few reservations, but dammit, he was a soldier.

"Good. Will you bag an al Qaeda terrorist asshole for us?"

Kyle paused for just a second as that sank in. "Yes, sir!" he replied. His stomach was twitching in eagerness or nervousness or both, but that was an honest mission.

"Outstanding. You may know there've been a few mixups over in Afghanistan, and al Qaeda don't have the people they used to. Nevertheless, they're a real pain in the ass, and we're going proactive on them. The current number three man is a real sadistic piece of work, and we plan to use you to shut him up for good."

Kyle was startled. "Isn't assassination a CIA mission, sir? Or Delta?"

"Normally, yes," the general agreed. "This isn't normal. Delta is busy, and there's enough press and sympathizers watching them that they aren't as discreet as we'd like anymore. The CIA has only limited means, and this guy, Rafiq bin Qasim, is a paranoid freak who won't let anyone get close enough to do a proper job. So it's got to be a good, reliable shooter from a distance, who they won't know is in theater. You." He crushed the cigar against a raised boot, tossed it into the weeds, and opened the door.

Kyle hesitated for a moment, then preceded him in. "Why me, sir?" he asked.

"Why not you?" Robash asked, door closing behind him. "Airborne and Ranger qualified, two real world kills in a war zone, proven to be solid under fire. We've got most of our good shooters tied up in Iraq and Bosnia, and we've kinda let Afghanistan slide. We want this done quietly, and we need someone good, reliable, who can operate alone. You."

"Thanks, sir, I guess," Kyle replied. "Though I lost my spotter on the last mission because we got eager. I got eager," he corrected.

The general lowered his voice slightly. "I know about that, son. It was a mistake. A bad one. But things like that happen, and you're aware of it and won't do it again."

"You're right about that, sir," he agreed, nodding. "I suppose I should take the mission. Though I would like a few more details before I jump aboard."

"Fair enough," Robash nodded. "Give me a second." He whipped out his phone and punched a couple of buttons. Whoever he wanted to talk to was on speed dial. "Sergeant Curtis, come on in."

A minute later, the person in question arrived at a brisk walk. Kyle had met him previously, the sniper community being small. Wade Curtis was a black man with coffee-colored skin and an expressive face built around deep, thoughtful eyes. His build was muscular but not overly large, and he matched Kyle's six feet in height. He had been an instructor when Kyle arrived, had left shortly afterward for the 10th Mountain Division. He was a staff sergeant, who'd also graduated Ranger School and had done a training stint with a British sniper section with the 42nd Royal Marine Commando. Despite that, though, he'd never actually been in combat. Still, he'd only been in the Army seven years, and there was a first time for everything.

"I believe you two have met," Robash said.

"Sir," they both replied at once. Kyle continued speaking as he rose to shake hands. "Staff Sergeant Curtis. Yeah, we've met at the club and on the range. Only for about a month last year. Been a while, Wade."

Wade shook hands back, firmly but with no macho-grip games. "Kyle," he nodded. "So, what are we going to do?"

Kyle looked over at the general as they both sat. He wasn't sure himself, and waited for enlightenment.

Robash nodded to both of them, took a deep draw on his cigar. "The mission is to go into the tribal area of Pakistan and take out bin Qasim. Obviously, that's the sticky point here. Not Afghanistan, but Pakistan. Technically, that's friendly territory. Actually, it's riddled with rats. Those rats have connections within the government, so anything we do officially they'll hear about. The plan is to give you orders to get over there, cash to operate, and only inform the Pakistanis if something goes wrong."

He leaned forward and continued, "Please note that distinction. This isn't a covert operation, exactly. We will be telling the Pakistanis, and we know Musharraf will be okay with it, as we hinted to him already without any specifics. So you can't bust up a lot of locals to do this, not innocent ones, anyway. It will be semiofficial afterward, even though it will likely stay SCI for a good long time, in case we decide to do it again."

Kyle thought for a few moments. Actually, that wasn't too bad. He wasn't expendable or deniable, he was simply going to be a secret weapon. He looked over at Wade, who was nodding appraisingly, his mouth and brow twisted in thought.

Kyle asked, "Why this way, sir?"

"Remember rumors back in ninety-one that we had a sniper placed to take out Saddam?" Robash waited for nods, then continued, "Those rumors are true. But the press got a leak and had to open their goddamned yaps about how it would be illegal to target a foreign head of state. So now we have the screwup before us. So for this one, we don't want any press and we don't want any leaks. As to why, same reason we've got the Special Operations guys running around doing what they were trained to do at long last. While we've got a leadership that will let us, we're going to hunt. We want to do it fast, the backlog's too much for the spooks, and there's always leaks. A couple of good Rangers who are also snipers is the prescription for this little disease, and one they won't see coming."

Cautiously, Kyle said, "Sounds worthwhile, sir. What kind of gear and backup?" He looked over at Wade.

Wade asked, "Or is there any?"

Through another puff of fumes, he replied, "Oh, there's gear. We'll be flying you out there civilianwise until you hit theater, then you'll take transports. You'll have Iridium phones, radios, orders to let you requisition stuff in theater and such. Use your government credit cards as needed. Your orders will be secret and just authorize you to ride along with no questions asked. You'll also have cash in U.S. dollars, Pakistani rupees, and afghanis. You'll take whatever gear you want, but it'll have to be stuff you can hump. Once on station, there'll be locals to meet you and help you find this jackass. You bag him, call in on the radio and we'll send air support and choppers. At that point, as long as the press doesn't know, we don't give a flying fuck who else does. Better if they do, in fact."

As they started to digest that, Robash asked, "What do you know about the border area of Afghanistan and Pakistan?"

Wade replied, "Damned little, sir."

"Me either," Kyle admitted.

"No problem," he nodded. "We've got people to take care of that. We'll get you briefed and up to speed. Can you leave in a week?"

The two looked at each other, considering. It wasn't a question to answer lightly. "Gear's not a problem," Kyle said.

Wade grimaced slightly and replied, "Training is going to be a bitch. We've got to be briefed, then you and I have to run at least one rehearsal if we're going to shoot together."

"That, and I need a refresher on radios. A week's tight."

"But doable?" Robash asked. "We've got a window we need to exploit."

"Doable, sir," Kyle agreed. He felt nervous about committing to such a deadline, but it didn't seem there was much choice.

Robash smiled. "Good! Once there, look as ratty as you can. Got to look the part. Don't bother with any more haircuts or shaves," he said, pointing at their closely cropped heads. "Though it's not as if you're going to look shaggy anyway. Still, we work with what we've got. Now, let's talk about training and prep. Hold on."

Robash drew the cell phone again from where it was clipped inside his BDU shirt, and thumbed buttons as he raised it. "Yes, we're ready," he said. He waited for a response. "Roger," he nodded, and disconnected. Turning back to the two snipers he said, "I took the liberty of bringing the personnel with me." They all chuckled, though there was a nervous tinge to it. He'd been ready, and wanted them overseas ASAP. This was a serious operation on a tight schedule, not an administrative deployment.

Twenty minutes later the two of them were ensconced in a briefing room manufactured on the spot. It wasn't hard. The classroom was set up to handle computer projection and had classroom seats, a dry-erase board and a phone. There were much cushier and more secure facilities on post proper, but, as Robash pointed out, "There's going to be rumors either way. Fewer people will hear them here, and less significance attached to the event."

Time was short. For two solid days they would be educated as to terrain, the political situations in several regions and villages and the people they'd be dealing with, expected weapons, and languages.

The civilian language instructor came in first. He was portly but seemed to have good muscle tone underneath. He was roundfaced with graying hair, slightly balding, very alert and cheerful. He was lugging a laptop case and several books. "Sergeants," he said in greeting, holding out a hand. His grip was firm. "I'm Bill Gober. I'm here to tell you about the languages you'll encounter and give you some basics."

"Mostly Arabic, right?" Kyle asked, nodding.

Gober gave him a look that was faintly annoyed but mostly amused. "No, probably no one you meet will speak Arabic, except maybe some scripture from the Quran. The predominant language of the area is Pashto."

Kyle looked confused and said, "Never heard of it." Wade looked taken aback, too.

"Which is why I'm here," Gober smiled. "Pashto and Dari are the official languages of Afghanistan, and Western Panjabi and Urdu are very common, but there's about a dozen languages in the area. Even Farsi from Iran is not unusual. But we'll mostly concentrate on Pashto and its Pakistani variant, Pakhto. They're both very similar, almost interchangeable, and Dari isn't much different. I've got phrasebooks you can take, CD-ROMs you can study en route, and some audio to familiarize yourselves with the tonal qualities."

"Okay," Kyle agreed. "I'm not very good with languages, though."

Gober said, "Probably you are good enough, you've just not been shown the right way. It isn't hard to learn a few basic vocabulary words. Rather than perfect grammar and style, you need to hear threats when they're mentioned, or pick up key words. That's what we'll focus on. The hardest part is going to be learning the written language, as it's a variation of the Arabic alphabet, hard enough to read as is, and these languages aren't very close to Arabic."

They spent the entire morning and afternoon until two, munching takeout from the chow hall as they familiarized themselves with a hundred basic words. Gober had been correct; reading the street signs was going to be much harder than speaking. The entire language was curlicues and squirming lines and dots.

He gave them one easy-to-remember hint as to structure that had them laughing as he used a querulous voice. "Pashtuns the verb at the end of the sentence put. In this they like Yoda are. Silly it is; but likely you are, Yoda's speech patterns to remember, and remembering the whole point of this is. It in good health you should use and enjoy."

At three, Gober rose to depart. "It would be good to have a few more days to practice, but I'm told we have no time. Do make sure you spend a couple of hours a day at it, though."

Wade answered for them, "Will do, sir, and thanks."

There was one more thing piled on that afternoon: maps. Relief and political maps of the entire Afghan/Pakistani border area in question, with smaller scale maps for some of the towns and border crossings. "Ideally," they were told by yet another briefer, a Lieutenant Vargas, "you'll just drive across one of the existing crossings. There are some manned by U.S. forces that shouldn't pose a threat. However, if something causes suspicions or closes the border tighter, you'll have to infiltrate some distance away over the mountains."

"I can handle mountains," Kyle said. "Wade?"

"Climb, actually," Wade joked. "Been there. But I'd rather drive than hump those ridges. They look ugly."

"Can we get a practice run in? Hills, shooting?"

"You likely won't have time over there, and we really don't want to announce your presence," Vargas said.

"What about here? Out West somewhere? Nevada, say?" Wade suggested.

"That's possible," Vargas agreed. "We could fly you out West and hop up into the hills. Be a chance to practice a helo extraction, too, just in case. I'll talk to the general and set it up. But you're looking at a day, tops."

"We'll take it," Kyle said, wondering why the government always waited until the last minute, then began a panicky juggle of hurry-up-and-wait. These things really should be planned out. Idly, he wondered which Pentagon whiz kid had come up with this, then decided he probably didn't want to bother.

THEY CERTAINLY WERE GETTING EVERYTHING THEY
asked for. Early the morning after next, they were aboard a flight
from Benning to Nellis Air Force Base near Las Vegas. Their gear
was crated and palletized with them. Once at Nellis, the sun barely
up, they were urged aboard a USAF Pave Low helicopter, and taken
out somewhere in the middle of nowhere. "We're going to use you
as a search-and-extraction exercise," the master sergeant Pararescue
Jumper told them. "I understand you're doing a mountain exercise?
Shooting?"

"Something like that," Kyle agreed over the assorted turbine
noise, blade beats, and wind. "We'll be most of the day."

"No problem," the PJ agreed. "You'll call for extraction, we'll
come and get you. They briefed you on flares and smoke?"

"Sort of," Kyle agreed. "They gave us photocopies from the manual."

"Good enough. You practice your thing, we'll practice ours.
Hopefully we'll get all the bugs ironed out. If not . . ."

"That's why we're training," Wade supplied.

"Yup."

Soon, they were flaring out over a relatively flat, high plateau.
Wade and Kyle dropped out, turned in the whipping wind and
grabbed their bulky gear, turned back and trotted away, low to
avoid the downdraft.

Then they were alone. The bulky helo was away and disappearing fast into the cerulean sky.

"Well," said Wade, "the good news is, it's friendly territory and
we have GPS and a computer. Not to mention cell phones."

"Right," said Kyle. "The bad news is, we have no idea where in hell we are, and it's as hot as hell already." It had to be ninety-five degrees if it were anything.

"At least it's dry," Wade said, looking for any shade. There was none to speak of.

"And dusty," added Kyle, as the wind wafted more grit in his eyes.

"And hot."

"I already said that."

"So I'll say it again."

"Yup. Let's find a place to start shooting. Then we can take a hike north, according to this map, and we'll be met about there," he pointed.

Wade looked and grimaced, "Ten kilometers? That's going to be a hell of a hike."

Kyle looked around at the bleak terrain. "Yup. But it'll be cool this evening. Or cooler. For now, let's just amble northerly for a good spot until it's too hot to bother."

The day went adequately. Both were trained for harsh climates, and apart from the heat it wasn't bad. Besides their rucks and full CamelBaks, they had an M-107, the Army designation for the Barrett M-82 .50-caliber autoloading rifle. Kyle carried it, Wade the spotting scope, radio, and extraneous gear, along with an M-4 carbine with grenade launcher. He wouldn't use it here, but it was part of the equipment they'd deploy with, so he was carrying it to make the exercise more realistic. They made about three kilometers before they found a good place to shoot. By then, both were sweating, though their clothes were quite dry, the desert air evaporating the moisture as fast as they exuded it.

Looking around at their chosen position, Kyle said, "Think we've got about three thousand meters clear?" Kyle asked.

"I'd say so," his partner said. "That would suit me fine as a range to nail this guy. No reason to court counterfire from his buddies or those Russian howitzers they might have."

"Yeah, though getting more than a thousand accurately is a problem."

"I know that," Wade said. "Maybe we'll get lucky and we can nail some explosives near him. You're the one who insisted on the fifty."

"So spot me," Kyle said. "And we're taking this because it was suggested, because our target might be in an armored vehicle or behind cover." The Barrett was a huge piece of equipment, though it did have slightly better range and much better penetration than the 7.62mm M-24.

They each took ten shots, slowly and methodically. Precision shooting is as much science as art, and they recorded every shot and its impact for later review. The brass would go back with them. Not only was it good discipline for concealment, but the gunsmiths— "small-arms repairers"—liked to examine them for wear to ensure the weapons were performing to their utmost.

The weapon was already adjusted for good accuracy. Wade called, "Reference: upright rock. Base. Small boulder with yellow striations. One one five zero."

"Got it," Kyle said. He squeezed, and God kicked him in the shoulder.

A puff of dust erupted back from the left of the rock. "Again," he said, placed the reticle on center, squeezed, and fired.

"Both to the left, twenty inches," Wade said.

Kyle made two minor corrections to the scope. "And again," he said.

"Same target?"

"Sure." They had similar climatic conditions to what they could expect, so they'd keep shooting until they were happy.

Kyle's next shot chipped the boulder, the fragments spinning off into the air. The fourth missed to the left again. There were limits to the accuracy of the weapon, and Kyle thought they were reaching those limits. He could hit reliably with a .5 minute of angle weapon or better. The Barrett was only a 3 MOA weapon. But for armored targets or vehicles, it was what they needed. He would have preferred to take a 7.62mm M-24 as well, in case they could get a closer shot, but there were weight limitations. Three weapons cases would be a royal pain in the ass, as well as obvious. He'd made the decision, but he wasn't very happy with it.

"Slight adjustment to the right should do it," Wade said.

"Yeah," Kyle agreed, coming back to earth. A trickle of dust blew into his face as the wind eddied, and he spat drily.

Two more shots hit the small rock and reduced it to a pile of sharp-edged pieces of rubble. A .50-BMG round delivers better than 13,000 foot-pounds at the muzzle, more than twice that of most elephant guns and five times that of the 7.62 cartridge. It was better than a jackhammer for demolishing rock.

"We could tweak it more, but it's not going to get appreciably better."

"Agreed," Wade replied. "So take a few more, let me at it, and then let's get that other seven kilometers done."

By the end of forty minutes, twenty rounds had screamed down the barrel and delivered better than 200,000 foot-pounds of energy to what was now a sad-looking little splinter amid a pile of sand, sitting in front of a badly chipped boulder.

Seven kilometers isn't a bad hike. When lugging basic gear, an AN/PRC-119 radio, spotting scope, and a forty-eight-pound rifle, up and down stark, hard terrain, it's a serious workout. The snipers climbed and scrabbled up steep inclines, slid down others, passing the gear back and forth to keep it safe, and were abraded, dusty, and exhausted by the time they finished.

"Glad we brought the extra water," Kyle said, dousing his throat again. They both knew it was necessary to stay hydrated, and were drinking frequently. Besides, the more water in the body, the less there was to carry as gear.

"This should be about it," Wade said. They were on another plateau. He checked their position by GPS, then by compass and three peaks as landmarks. That done, he fired up the radio.

In short order, the Pave Low appeared as a large, intimidating insect to the southeast, and dropped in for a landing. They scurried in close, shoved the gear aboard, and clambered in.

"Good hike?" the PJ asked them.

"Good enough," Wade agreed. Kyle just grunted.

Yes, it had been a good hike and shoot. But how would it be in hostile territory, surrounded by witnesses and without close backup?

Kyle suspected the real mission was going to be quite a bit tougher. And he still had his own doubts to fight, too.

The next morning was their last before deploying. They were both short of sleep, after the grueling fifteen hours of flight and ten hours of climbing the day before. They'd snoozed on the planes each way, but were still groggy. The general was sympathetic, but didn't offer any slack. Nor did they expect it. Lack of sleep and food was the Army way, and they were both experienced with it.

"I've arranged cash," Robash told them. They were in the same classroom they were so familiar with. "And I brought a staff with me to take care of all this at once. I'd rather cut TDY orders for people to come to you, than have you shuffle around playing games." He nodded, and the staff sergeant in the corner came over.

He said, "Fifty thousand dollars, gentlemen. It's split into two packages of three currencies each. Sign here and count it. Please note that it's expendable, and spend what you need. We'd like it back if there's any left over, but don't sweat it."

Kyle was glad of that phrase, officially attached to the document.

Many covert soldiers had later been busted for "embezzling" funds that had been issued to them. It seemed Robash was the straight shooter he'd shown himself to be already. They weren't going to get screwed over this. Of course, they still might die.

The money was ten thousand dollars worth each in Afghan and Pakistani currency and the balance in good American cash, useful almost anywhere on the planet. They each counted their half. "Try to keep the nonlocal stuff hidden," Kyle said to Wade, "and stash it in several places to minimize loss."

The finance sergeant left right after he checked their signatures. As soon as he was alone with them, the general resumed his brief. "Now, guys, let me give you your contacts. You can write this down, but lose it before you cross the border into Pakistan, and lose it well. You'll meet with General Kratman at Qandahar Airport and give him this letter." Robash handed them each a sheet, and they both stuck them in their increasingly bulging folders. "It authorizes you to take any routine equipment and charge it to the mission. Vehicles, ammo, small arms, anything reasonable. Though I'd think very hard before taking U.S. vehicles, as you'll stand out like a hooker at a Madison Avenue wedding. Kratman knows you're coming, but not what you're doing. My phone number is on all these documents. If there's any questions, call. If I'm not there, my XO and my civilian assistant are briefed on what to do, and can be reached by cell phone twenty-four seven. You're both on my call-through list. I'll bitch like hell if it's not important, but I'm here to support you on this mission. Use me if you need me."

"Yes, sir," Kyle and Wade agreed together. It certainly seemed as if he meant it, and that by itself was a huge morale boost. General Robash apparently knew what a lot of officers had never learned, that troops who feel they have support will do almost anything for their commander.

"Once in theater, you'll meet with a local tribal leader named Qalzai. He'll take you in and spot your target. He doesn't speak English, but he has a translator. He's very reliable on intel and anti-Taliban operations, so you're safe with him, but we have no idea who's in his unit. If you feel compromised, abort and exfiltrate, either on ground or by chopper. But get the hell out of there. We want you alive and our target dead, not the other way around."

"Right," Wade said. Kyle simply considered that. There was a hell of a lot of risk in this operation. But it was too late for second thoughts. They were just nerves anyway, he thought.

"The chain of command for this is Kyle, Wade. You're officially commanded by a colonel in the Pentagon, but I'm the Operations guy, so it's very odd, but very simple.

"Now, we go see Lieutenant Bergman for flight arrangements. From what I understand, you're going to be in the air a long time."

"Yes, sir," they agreed. That last wasn't unexpected; they were going halfway around the world.

"The last item," Robash said, "is that commo is going to be a bitch. I'm sorry guys, I tried, but there's no way to get the radios working properly. You'd need forty batteries for ten days, and there's no way to ensure you can recharge."

"Hell," Kyle said. It was the handicap of modern radios. They scrambled by shifting across 280,000 frequencies, but if they weren't powered in to the net from the beginning, they wouldn't be synchronized with the scramble code, which changed daily. They either needed a constant supply of charged batteries to maintain contact and scramble, or else any transmission would have to be in the clear. Neither was good. The batteries were three pounds each.

"'Hell,' is correct," Robash said. "You'll have a one-nineteen for final call to the helo, because they can't handle Iridium phones. But you can call direct to the AWACS with the cell phone, and to me in an emergency. You've got a whole list of numbers for backup. But final extraction is going to require that you coordinate through the AWACS, then use the radio at the last minute. And be brief, because some of those Taliban bastards have radios and translators."

"Oh, lovely," Wade said.

"Yeah, it sucks to be you," Robash nodded. "But you have my thanks, and I want it to be a good mission."

By lunchtime, they had orders, more disks for the laptop, more documents to hand out en route, extra maps, and all the miscellany they'd need. With nothing else to do, they parted ways and headed back home to rest up and finalize personal gear.

The logistics experts at the transportation office would crate all their weapons and heavy equipment up in form-fitting expanding foam surrounded by wooden frames and sheathing, if it wasn't already packed in hard cases. Everything was receipted and accountable. It pained Kyle to hand over his personal stuff, and he was nervous in case anyone complained about his personal weapons. But no questions were asked and he accepted the receipts for file.

There was the M-107 Barrett .50 caliber, scoped and bipoded and with twenty rounds of match-grade ammo in a sealed pack. Its case fit tightly around the disassembled components, cradling them in foam. It probably wouldn't need to be resighted when they arrived in theater, as the scope was zeroed to the weapon and attached to a precision rail. They'd do a check when they could, of course. The scope was actually more important than the weapon; it could be transferred, and it could also gather intel. Everything that could be done to protect it was a good thing.

The M-4 carbine, a shortened M-16 with provisions for attachments, which Wade would carry most of the time, was in there, with its emergency folding sights flat and taped, and the Eotech Holosight encased. It was the backup weapon. It wasn't likely they'd use it beyond 100 meters, and the iron sights and the Eotech were good for 400. It had GGG Corporation's side-sling mounts at gas block and the rear of the receiver, so it would hang across the shooter's front, ready to deploy. Spare batteries for the Eotech were in a rubber plug in the pistol grip. Batteries were often more important than ammo in the modern army. It had an underslung M-203 grenade launcher for social engagements. It didn't seem like much, but it was likely they could get 5.56 ammo in country, and this was supposed to be a sniping mission. One shot, one kill, as the cliché went. It was Kyle's experience that it almost always took more than one shot, and sometimes a lot of suppressing fire, too. At least they would have a claymore and fragmentation grenades and smoke, once they drew them in theater.

In addition to his two pistols, Wade would have one, also. It was a standard issue M-9 Beretta 92F. "Standard GI everything, huh?" he'd asked.

His partner shrugged. "I like other stuff better. But issue stuff is easy to get parts for. And if it goes missing, Uncle Sam can weep, not me. I'd hate to lose that lovely piece of yours," he said, in reference to Kyle's Ed Brown custom .45.

"Me, too," Kyle said. "But it makes me feel safe," he joked. It should. The 1911-style frame had the mainspring housing contoured into a rounded, easy-to-conceal shape. The magazine well was welded and flared to make reloading easy. The expected palm-swelled thumb safety, Commander-style hammer, and deeply cut front strap let it sit low and securely in the hand. It had low profile, almost guttersnipe sights. The barrel was conical for a tight lockup. Then the mechanism was ramped, polished, and the ejection port flared. Outside, it was smoothed and phosphated with Pachmayr grips. It had cost two-thousand-and-nevermind dollars, but it was easy to find ammo for, accurate, reliable, and Kyle's best friend. It was going with him. He'd had it in Bosnia last . . . which wasn't something to dwell on.

His backup to that was a little nickeled Colt Mustang .380 that he could fit in a pocket. He never thought he'd use that on duty, but it was the ideal gun for the situation. It wasn't much of a distance weapon, but if it came down to that, things weren't good anyway, and it would reliably put out bullets.

Then it was home and a last night to prepare. If this had been a unit deployment, the unit would go out on a riotously fun drunk and decorate a bar or club. As it was supposed to be a TDY for an exercise, it was officially no big deal. So he'd sit at home, Wade in billeting, pondering the future and going through whatever rituals they wished to keep calm and thin the tension. Beer seemed the logical choice.

Kyle sorted through his personal gear and checked his list of what to take, making additions. Actually, there wasn't much debate. He'd take a couple of uniforms for blending in on military installations, one each three-color desert and woodland. His ID and the cash they were issuing him. They were shipping the weapons. A CD player would get lost or stolen or confiscated by some foreign security goon, so he didn't bother. There'd be no time to listen to music, anyway. He hated reading airport bestsellers, so he'd take a couple of cheap paperbacks to read while traveling. He was amused by the amount of action the characters in books could experience within the first hundred pages, and was glad that his own life was far less exciting. So it was down to underwear, socks, toiletries kit, and the essentials.

"The Essentials" evolved over time, but basically stayed the same. He had the large CamelBak for keeping hydrated, and he worshipped the man who'd invented it. He took his own small GPS to back up the one crated. He had the SOG Powerplier pocket tool he preferred to the issue Gerber, but had an old Gerber Predator BMF he'd carried for years. Sometimes, nine inches of steel was what you needed to do the job, whether that job was prying open a door, cutting a stretcher, or, theoretically, killing someone. He'd never been close enough to worry about that, but it could happen. Then he had the Sebertech pocket tool on his keychain and the Benchmade automatic with the four-inch Tanto blade in his pocket. He took an extra Lensatic compass for last-ditch escape. His sidearms were already crated. He had burlap and tan canvas sewn to a desert uniform to make a functional ghillie to blend-in in an arid mountain environment. He'd used the same ratty pair of gloves for shooting for fourteen years; everything one could do to make the conditions of every shoot predictable improved the odds of success. He had a calculator and measuring tape, and the M-22 binoculars. A laptop with ballistics information, language programs, and tech manuals. Parachute cord was always useful, whether lashing sticks, building a stretcher, or tying gear down. An empty sandbag that could be filled and turned into a rest was stuffed in. He carried extra triangular bandages to use as head covers or "do rags," as camouflage, slings and, well, bandages. A compact of makeup, in earthtones and greens was in there, rubber bands and a sewing kit for repairs and to improve camouflage, as well as a lighter and matches, and an eyepatch to let the off-eye muscles relax during long pauses, pencils, and an AA Maglight. Then there were the necessary chocolate chip cookies, Cajun beef jerky, a couple of six-packs of caffeine-free Coke and a box of shoestring potato snacks, which tasted almost as good as chips and wouldn't crush into powder when carried. All told, it was about thirty-five pounds, which was light enough to not be a hindrance, but packed enough tools and weapons to save his ass. He had permission for personal weapons this time, or more accurately, it wasn't an issue, this being a clandestine and deniable mission. Even had they forbidden it, though, he would have tried to smuggle the stuff through. You could never rely on dear old Uncle Sam to have what you needed, and a good soldier took his own supplements. The whole load when added to his issue gear would break 200 pounds.

Wade would have the M-49 spotter scope, AN/PVS-6 laser range finder, AN/PRC-119 radio set and blade antenna, night vision for both of them, a field surgical kit, a roll of 100 mph tape, a small toolkit, cleaning kits, and his own issue plus personal necessities like toothbrushes.

The guns were already loaded along with the issue gear, radios, and scopes. The rest packed, and set to go with him as luggage. All that was left was the waiting.

He could spend the night out, seeking entertainment or women, but he really wasn't in a sociable mood. He didn't want any emotional entanglements, and a bar quickie near base wasn't worth the effort. He could drink at home.

But he wouldn't, he decided. There just wasn't much point. And he wouldn't be drinking in Pakistan, so he should minimize the booze now. Heck, it would be good for him. He'd fallen into a rut of teach class, NCO club to be seen by the sergeant major for brownie points, then home to eat and drink. It had been a year. Time to get out of that cycle.

He crawled into bed and turned the light out. Eventually, he slept.

4

THE ALARM JARRED KYLE AWAKE AT 0330. GRUM-
bling, he shut it off, got up and staggered to the bathroom. A hot
shower helped him wake up, and as it might be his last for some
time, he enjoyed it. He finished, left the door open to let humidity
vent, and called for his ride. By the time he dressed, grabbed his bag
and locked up, doing a final check on his list for anything he might
have missed before tossing it in the trash and walking downstairs,
the car was waiting for him. The driver, a cute female PFC, way too
alert for such an early hour, opened the trunk for his bags and the
door for him, then got in and waited for him to fasten his seatbelt.
All by the book. Good. He wasn't up for socializing much. Wade
was already in back, sprawled across the seat and with a flat cap
over his face.

"Airport, correct, Sergeants?" she asked to confirm.

"Correct, soldier. Mind if I take a nap?" His question, like hers,
was rhetorical. He wasn't going to nap, but he didn't want to talk.

"Go ahead, Sergeant," she agreed.

He lay back as far as the seat allowed and closed his eyes to think.

It was a good mission, and he'd agreed to it, so why was he so jittery? It wasn't just Jeremy, he tried to reassure himself. It was also
that this thing seemed so haphazard and last minute. Actually, it
very well might be Jeremy. That, and being in a country where he
didn't know the language, alone with a spotter and no friendly fire
support on the radio. Jitters did mean he was thinking and sane, he
thought. If he wasn't worried about this, he'd be a fool.

So much for fairytale heroes.

The first leg of the flight was from Columbus aboard a small
Army transport plane. It was a twin turboprop job, and the sway-

ing of the wings as it landed at Atlanta's Hartsfield was disconcerting. They could see ahead through the cockpit, over the pilots' shoulders, and the horizon swung up and down as the little craft bobbled in the drafts.

Military personnel traveled in civilian clothes to keep a low profile, and they were already a bit unkempt after not shaving. Still, their bearing made them soldiers, and they both knew they'd have to work on appearances and body language. The idea was to be nondescript. How a tall, white male and a tall, black male who didn't speak the language were supposed to blend in in the Middle East and the 'stans was beyond Kyle, but he wasn't going to question anything else. It was obviously going to be a screwed-up mission. Then he tried to recall a mission that hadn't been screwed up. He couldn't recall one.

All their gear had been checked through ahead on transports with official paperwork to clear it through the DOD Courier Service. It would arrive still crated and undisturbed, they hoped. The two of them were flying like any other civilians, except they were using their military IDs and orders as passports. The orders identified them as "surveyors" from the Army Corps of Engineers going to Kuwait to do a construction survey at Camp Doha.

Kyle hadn't flown commercial since before the terrorist attacks. He knew security had been tightened, but had no idea how it was at the current time. He'd left everything except his keys in his checked bags, just to be sure.

"Final destination, sir?" the clerk at check-in asked him.

"Kuwait City," he said, because it was true enough for airline purposes, and "The ass-end of Asia to kill someone," just wouldn't be politically correct. She was too young and cute to freak out in that manner. Nor did Kyle need the probing that would certainly follow.

"Would you like to check your bags straight through?" she asked.

"Yes, please," he said. He'd been cautioned to ask for that anyway. Otherwise, the bags would be held for customs in London first, which could take three days or more. Checked straight through, they'd only be inspected at destination.

That done, he took his small carry-on, which had a change of shirt, socks and underwear, toiletries, a notebook, and a garish scifi paperback with an exploding spaceship on the cover. What the heck, it looked like a good read. It was going to be a long flight.

He walked through the metal detector with no hassle. Considering that, he was a bit annoyed when some jackass came over with a wand and waved it over him. He remembered there'd been more threats, and an elevated security level.

"Raise your arms," the "Security Officer" said, then poked and prodded his pockets and belt before patting him down. Amateurs pat when searching. Professionals slide their hands to catch things. Nor did this punk kid check the small of his back or the collar of his jacket.

He sighed slightly and dealt with it. Americans were now being treated like criminals in jail, in case they might be Muslim terrorists. Certainly, that mother might have a bomb in her diaper bag. Better check the diaper, too, pal. That baby poop might be rigged to explode.

The annoying part was that the hassle was all for show. Kyle had seen the reports of testers smuggling guns and knives past the security at many major airports. This farce wasn't going to stop a determined terrorist, and was a pain for all concerned.

"May I check your bag, sir?" he was asked, as if he could say no. At least this guy looked competent. He was wiry and young, but had alert eyes.

"Sure," he agreed.

It was simple enough. A chemical pad was run over his bag, looking for reactions that would indicate drugs or explosives, he assumed. It made him nervous. Not because he had anything that would trigger it, but the whole atmosphere was one to cause paranoia in the honest person. A trained terrorist, of course, would blithely bull his way through, unconcerned.

While doing this, the man spoke to the kid with the wand. "Moore," he said, "don't worry about the small children and the old folks. They don't need to be kept standing around. And check ankles and wrists, too, okay?"

"Uh, yes, sir," the kid replied.

Kyle's bag was returned, and the man said, "Sorry for the hassle. I've got to check a quota per shift. It's late."

The sudden change in atmosphere was palpable. "No problem, sir," Kyle said, meaning it.

"No need to call me 'sir,' Sergeant," the supervisor said with a grin, as he handed Kyle's wallet and keys back from the conveyor belt. His military ID was in the clear front. "I worked for a living. Semper Fi."

The Marines. Marines had no trouble stomping on idiots. "Thanks, Marine. Rangers Lead the Way."

They all chuckled as Kyle and Wade headed for the jetway, except

Moore, who looked confused. Everything went back to what seemed to pass as normal these days. Kyle heaved a sigh as Wade joined him and whispered, "You know, I thought we were the good guys. Nice to have the government agree."

"Yeah. Hell of a world, huh?"

There was still one more hassle. Along the jetway stood people in sports jackets and shirts with badges on neck cords. The badges read DEA and U.S. CUSTOMS. One of them waved at Kyle, the next at Wade. Sighing, Kyle went over.

"Can I see your passport, please, sir?" the man asked. Kyle handed over his ID card and orders. It took a moment for the man to track, then he smiled under his graying moustache as he asked, "Are you carrying more than ten thousand dollars in cash today?"

Kyle smiled back. "Yeah, right."

"Have a good trip, sir," the man said as he handed the card and sheet back.

Kyle waited until he was in the plane to sigh. He was carrying $25,000 in three currencies. So was Wade. But it wasn't anyone's business but theirs right now. Certainly they could have explained it with a phone call, but it wasn't supposed to be an issue.

There were actually only about twenty people aboard the flight. Kyle didn't know if that was due to the economy, the "enhanced security," or the early hour of the flight. Maybe all. But it did mean that after takeoff he could loosen his collar, flop across six seats in the middle, and crash for a couple of hours. Wade did the same two rows back. The cloth seats were a bit rough, the gaps between them not comfortable, and a seat belt end jabbed Kyle in the kidney. Still, it was better than being stuck in tight quarters sitting upright.

The purser left them alone. The only noise intruding was the steady whining roar of the engines.

He woke much refreshed if a bit stiff over the Atlantic, and stretched as he sat up. The smells of food had woken him. He had the chicken, precut and cardboardy. Still, it was hot and it was lunch. He dug in. Wade moved up next to him and had the fish.

"Is there anything to drink?" Kyle asked as they were served. He wasn't going to get drunk, but one to take the edge off wasn't the same as drinking himself into depression.

"Certainly," the flight attendant replied. She was likely near forty, well tanned and slim with a few faint lines just forming around her eyes. Nice-looking lady, he decided. "We have a very nice red wine, and Budweiser, Heineken, or Sapporo."

"Better make it the Heineken," he said. "And thanks."

"You're welcome," she said, plunking two iced and sweat-beaded bottles down in front of him. Wade took the red wine. Kyle hated most wine and wasn't curious enough to try it to see if this was the exception. He expected to be charged for the beer; airlines always did. But nothing was said. Whatever had happened, it was a pleasant error or courtesy after—and before—many other less pleasant screwups.

Next to him, Wade said, "I'd offer to run through vocabulary, but they'd likely freak."

"Yeah," Kyle said. *They'd think we were terrorists.* He wasn't going to even think that word where it might be heard. Someone would panic. "So tell me about your career," he said. He wasn't sure he wanted to get friendly with another spotter. There was a loyalty issue, which was silly, because Jeremy was gone, and because he needed to be familiar with the man he was going to be working with. They needed to talk. Besides, there was nothing else to do for the next twenty hours . . . or for the month after that.

"Not much to tell," Wade admitted. "Grew up in the horrible ghettos of Bloomington, Illinois. My father's a doctor. You can imagine how rough a life that was."

Kyle laughed quietly. "Yeah, sounds rough. My old man's an engineer. So how the hell did we wind up here?"

"I wanted adventure and money for college," Wade said. "After I kept scoring expert, and went to a couple of unit competitions, they asked me if I wanted to crosstrain. So I did. Then I reenlisted and applied as an instructor. I figured it would be useful when I got to college."

"Never got to college," Kyle observed.

"Not yet," Wade admitted. "But I still plan to, eventually. And this is all useful for a degree in sociology."

"Sociology," Kyle mused. "From shoo . . . dealing with bad guys." The environment felt so hostile he didn't even want to say "shooting." What had America come to?

"Yeah," Wade said. "Ain't it a kicker? What about you?"

"Oh, I thought about college, but, really, I don't have the mindset. I learn by doing. The Army treats me decently, I guess, even if I do bitch up a storm—"

Wade cut in, " 'A bitching GI is a happy GI.' "

"About right," Kyle agreed. "So I'm still here. If I take retirement at a reasonable age, I guess I see if L.A. or some other city needs me for a special police team of some kind."

"Or coach the Olympic team," Wade suggested.

Kyle was silent for a moment. "You know, I hadn't thought of that, but it actually makes sense. Thanks."

"No problem."

They got back to the business of sipping beer, reading trash, watching movies, and running through things in their minds. International flights could be very long and tiresome. Kyle figured they'd learn to hate them on this trip. If he didn't already.

There was a four-hour layover in London, which was just long enough for a bite to eat and paperwork.

Heathrow was scary. Kyle hadn't realized things were so bad in Britain. First, the plane had to park far back, as there wasn't enough terminal space. They were picked up in a scissor-lifted mobile lounge that dropped as it rolled across the apron. From there, they shifted to a train at the terminal. Kyle couldn't help but notice that they walked unescorted from one to the other, and that it would take only a moment for someone in a coverall and coat to run through the unlocked door marked AUTHORISED PERSONNEL ONLY and ditch the coat.

That wasn't the only risk. Once they left the train, they were crowded up an escalator through a passage with faded, yellowed, and cracking walls. It didn't look like a modern, western airport. Then there was a delay at the top. There was only one metal detector. Nor did the staff have wands. Britain was proud of the fact that almost no one carried guns legally. But it meant that a dedicated terrorist could rush this point and be among crowds in seconds.

There was a delay caused by a man who appeared to be Indian or Pakistani. He walked through the detector and beeped. Apparently, he wasn't a regular flier, as he kept walking and had to be ushered back. The guards explained by pantomime that he should take off his watch and empty his pockets. Everyone else was made to wait.

Kyle thought at first that they were doing that for security reasons, to avoid distractions. But as it went on, he realized they were just incompetent. It took the man four passes through the machine, as he unloaded pounds of change, keys, a camera, a watch, some jewelry, and a handful of paper clips. He was still beeping, and they pulled him aside and had him spread his arms and legs. Then they gave him a cursory pat and let him go.

Kyle was very nervous as he approached, and their treatment didn't help. Even with his pockets empty, he beeped, likely his belt buckle. But the attendant merely took the trench coat he was carrying, hung it over a rail, gave him a quick pat, and then handed his coat back, unsearched.

Wade was waiting, and Kyle followed. As soon as he was sure they weren't being overheard, he said, "I could have hid a Beretta and two grenades in that and they wouldn't have noticed."

"Tell me about it."

Then they had to stand in line for customs, even though they were passing through. That took only a few minutes, but was marked by the large Middle Eastern family in front of them.

The five kids ranged from ten down to two years, and the mother was obviously tired as she took a seat some distance away. Then one of the older kids ran toward the restrooms. The father wandered off to talk to an official about something, and then suddenly, both middle kids, who were playing, ran off. That left a large pile of luggage unattended.

Anywhere in Europe, that is not done, and the crowd at once started backing away from the bags. Wade loudly said, "Whose bags are these?" and the two kids came rushing back to stand by them, wide-eyed, followed at once by the father. Perfectly innocent, but it was that type of atmosphere. Trust nothing.

With two hours wasted, breakfast was the only real option, even though it was evening by their clocks. They found a shop that looked clean and modern, with the typical turned wooden railing and vinyl booths, and grabbed seats.

Ten bucks for breakfast, after conversion. Ouch. And a thick accent on the waitress, who asked, "Worr I git fuh ye genlmin?"

British bacon was meaty, with bits of bone. That was good. The toast was better than American restaurant toast. The fried egg was barely cooked. Kyle thought about sending it back but decided to skip it and just not eat it. He'd been through Britain once before and recalled that was how they did it unless told otherwise. And there was that grilled tomato he wasn't sure if he liked or not. The potatoes were cold and greasy, so he left them.

At that, it might be the last civilized meal for some time, or ever. He left a fair tip as they departed.

"What now? Duty-free or departure lounge?" Wade asked.

"Lounge," Kyle decided. "Better to be early."

"Right."

Kuwait Airlines, however, ran a tight operation. They had their own metal detectors, and wands, and staff searching people professionally. Wade said, "Excuse me," and headed for the restroom, so Kyle held his place as the line advanced.

Wade returned in time to squeeze past the large family from earlier. They were scanned, their kit bags opened and inspected right down to Kyle's paperbacks and Wade's CD player. Then they were searched thoroughly enough. Kyle wondered about asking the guy for a date, just as a joke. But the procedure made him feel much more secure. If you were going to have a security point, then by God have a security point.

The KA desk staff were Aer Lingus contractors from Ireland. Kyle slid up to an attractive redheaded young lady in a green smock, who smiled and said, "Pahsspoht, please, sah?"

He extended his military ID card and the orders that would take him to Kuwait. "That's foine, sah," she agreed with a smile, and in moments he was waved through. He took a seat near the jetway, and leaned back.

Wade joined him, and as he lowered his bag said, "Well, that was close."

"What?" Kyle asked.

Leaning in close, Wade whispered conspiratorially, "I had one of those Cold Steel nylon-bladed Tantos. Just in case. But that check-point made me take a detour and drop it deeply in a trash can, wrapped in paper towels."

"Jesus, man," Kyle replied, grinning slightly. "All those searches and no one noticed?" He was bothered that Wade had brought it, and, bothered that no one had found it.

"Who checks a man's tie?" Wade asked with a smile as he flipped the end of it.

He was right, Kyle thought. One could tuck a slim item in there and it would be unnoticed.

The lounge wasn't crowded, but quickly became so. Based on their headdresses, many of the passengers could be Muslims or Sikhs, and Indian women in richly brocaded silk saris were numerous. Kyle wasn't familiar enough with their caste marks to place them. Judging from some of the nomadic-looking bunch, they could expect camels, goats, and sheep in the back. Not really, perhaps, but there was a huge spectrum of culture and societal levels represented.

Shortly it was standing room only. "Where are they all coming from?" he asked quietly.

"Well," Wade drawled, "it occurs to me that if you're flying from Europe to the Far East, there's only three main routes. Through Russia, through Iraq, which is almost impossible and inadvisable, or through the emirates or Kuwait."

Kyle nodded. That made sense. So this flight was going to be seven hours with their tall frames crammed into airline seats and elbow to elbow with other passengers. The flight from Atlanta seemed a wistful dream.

Shortly, they were boarding. "Well, this is *nice*," he commented.

"Very," Wade agreed. Kuwait Airlines was state owned, and like everything else with the Kuwaiti stamp, was brand new, gleaming, and perfectly maintained. The Boeing 777 still smelled of the factory. Every seat had its own personal LCD TV screen on the chairback in front, and pillows on the seatbacks. They were both nodding as they stowed their carry-on bags and sat. They couldn't know that they'd shortly come to loathe those screens.

The standard preflight safety briefing started even as the last passengers were being helped to their seats, and moments later, a tug shoved the plane free. "That's fast," Wade muttered and Kyle nodded. Apparently, the pilot was in a hurry to keep his slot. The briefing was in English, Arabic, and some Indian dialect. Kyle didn't hear anything resembling Farsi, Dari, or Pashto.

In short order they were airborne and winging southeast. The default on the screen in front of him showed the plane's direction, velocity, and expected arrival time on a continental map, then on a regional map, then flashed to a screen with the direction of Mecca. He knew Mecca was important to Islam, but this drove it home with a dozer blade. It was vital to the devout Muslim to know where Mecca was five times a day for prayer, and at other times for reassurance. More so than Jerusalem or Rome, that one city was crucial to how a large number of people lived. It would be smart, he thought, to study more of Islam. He'd just exhausted most of his knowledge of the faith. He had a feeling it could be important knowledge in the future.

He was wiped out from the trip already. It was noon local time, 6 P.M. by his internal clock, and he'd been up since 0330. It was already a full day. It would be almost twenty-four hours by his clock by the time they arrived. Not wanting to watch prerecorded TV or a fluffy movie, he turned off his screen and reclined against the pillow, hoping to nap.

That's when he started hating the screens. His neighbor was elbow to elbow with him, and his screen was still on. He couldn't see the flatscreen well at an angle, but it *was* on and it was annoying. It flashed and moved against its dark background. Farther over was another. The other way, Wade's was off, but the next one was on. He had four screens within ten feet of him. And he couldn't shut them off.

Growling silently, he closed his eyes and pretended TV didn't exist. But that left him with his own images. Those weren't pleasant.

5

HE AWOKE AS THEY DESCENDED INTO KUWAIT CITY. Wade nudged him, he stirred and pulled his seat upright, and responded to his partner's, "Look at the map," with a grunt.

He flipped the screen on and stared. Yes, that was interesting. He nodded.

Kuwait Airport's main runway ran north-south. It was so close to Iraq that landing from the north was all but impossible, so all flights approached and departed from the south, contorting their routes along the border. That had to be a pain. Perhaps that would change shortly, if Iraq could be turned around.

They landed and cleared the plane into a new terminal, all white and chrome and huge hanging billboards. The ads were similar, except that the American Express Card display bore the name ABDUL ALI MUHAMMAD, whoever that might be, and the gorgeous women staring back from the banners were covered to the necks. Still, their elegant arms and piercing eyes were sexy, and being used to push product. Some things never changed.

The security were Kuwaiti soldiers with rifles. If they weren't oppressive, they weren't smiling, either. Doors that led to secure areas had lights that blinked when they were unlatched. The customs and passports people were more soldiers, behind bulletproof glass. And they were too helpful.

A sign above the booth warned travelers in a dozen languages to HAVE YOUR PASSPORT AND VISA READY. Kyle slid his military ID card and orders under the window when he reached the front.

With only a moment's glance, the moustached sergeant replied in rough English, "Ah, military. Gohead, gohead," and waved him on. Kyle wanted to ask a question or two, but the man's attention was already on Wade and saying, "Yes, yes, you, too. Gohead. Welcome."

There was such a thing as too much courtesy, Kyle reflected. They'd been helped so thoroughly they didn't know what to do next.

"Baggage claim," Wade pointed, and Kyle followed him over that way. Yes, folks, we're a tall white guy and a tall black guy with short hair and good muscle tone, picking up duffel bags and flight bags. Nothing suspicious here.

A hungry-looking porter eyed their bags and his cart, but Wade shook a negative and they shouldered their loads. "Got to be someone here who speaks English," Kyle mused aloud.

"As long as we don't use those other languages yet," Wade joked in caution.

Butthe soldier at the door just smiled and waved them through. It was dark, and warm and dry, the air flowing over them as the door opened.

"Welcome to Kuwait, what the hell do we do now?" Kyle muttered. "Either someone's waiting for us, or we call that number on a pay phone . . . where the hell *is* a pay phone?" He looked around the spotless pickup loop, but saw nothing resembling a phone. Would they have to make a scene just to be found?

Moments later, an olive-colored Chevy Suburban rolled up in front of them. An obvious American stood up from the driver's step and said, "Al Jaber Air Base?"

In relief, Kyle replied, "Yes, that's us."

"Then please come around here," the man waved. He was blond, in civilian clothes, and had a Midwest accent, and it was *good* to hear that accent.

"Tech Sergeant Henderson," he introduced himself, holding out an ID card.

Kyle examined it, nodded, and carefully drew his own. "Sergeant First Class Monroe."

As soon as Wade identified himself, Henderson nodded and said, "Sounds good. Load your gear in the back, and climb in. I'll inspect the vehicle." He popped the hatch.

Henderson walked around, eyeballed all the wheel wells and the bumpers for potential bombs, nodded, and got back in. It was a formality, as he'd not left the vehicle, but a necessary habit in the Middle East. Kyle and Wade slammed the back and climbed in, Wade riding shotgun. Kyle let him so he could stretch across the back.

The trip to al Jaber was at near eighty mph. Every so often, the vehicle would hit eighty-one and the dash would whine, a warning sound to indicate excessive speed. It didn't stop, either. "Yeah, it's annoying," Henderson said. "But that's how they cut down on speeding." As he spoke, a Mercedes coupe whipped past them doing at least a hundred.

The freeway was as modern as anything else, and brilliantly lit. Signs warned in Arabic and English that CARS MAY MERGE AT ANY TIME by driving straight in off the desert, and that SPEEDING CAUSES DEATH. The locals seemed unworried about either. A car merged from the sand, bouncing lightly straight onto the freeway, and Henderson slid over a half lane. "Sorry, but this is how they drive here."

"No worse than L.A. or Chicago," Wade assured him. "Hell, I'll bet some of them even have AKs." They all chuckled.

"What are those tents?" Wade asked. "Part of the oil facilities?"

"Those are houses," Henderson said.

"Houses?"

"Yup."

Kyle had wondered, too, and looked them over. Each was a compound of tents about the size of GP mediums, on concrete slabs with generators, air conditioners, and fluorescent lights. Chevys were preferred, and Suburbans abounded. Considering the temperature never got much below fifty degrees Fahrenheit, it was a cheap and practical way to live.

They turned off the freeway onto a well-paved road that had sand drifting across it like snow during a Great Plains winter. It was a familiar but strange sight. The road here was dark, but the windshield was clear as soon as Henderson turned on the wipers to clear dust. No crushed bugs, no water spots, just dust. It was pervasive. Arabian sand is in reality very fine clay, desiccated to powder.

They drove past a camel-racing club that took a few minutes and jokes to explain, then off the major road onto a narrower, potholed one, then through three perimeters of guards, the first merely a warning to civilians to stay away, the inner ones increasingly stiffer, until the innermost was USAF Security Forces.

"No photos, no cameras out of your luggage," Henderson warned them. He spoke to the sergeant at the gate, exchanging passwords buried in the talk, though not very hard to spot. The military was so predictable, Kyle thought. All their IDs and orders were checked, the vehicle exterior inspected. "Has the vehicle been out of your control?"

Henderson replied, "I haven't left it at all." Then they were waved through.

"So where are we taking you? Billeting office?" Henderson asked.

"That's a hell of a good question. We're supposed to board a cee-one-forty-one here."

"So let's call Ops and find out."

Twenty minutes later, they were in a large Quonset-type hut near the runway proper. It was one of the Air Force's nifty modular things, with actual windows that were covered by solid panels against light leakage or bomb damage or both, air conditioning, and proper lights. Although there were lots of curious stares, no one asked who these guys were and what they were doing. They did collect a couple of sly, casual nods, though, after they changed into uniform. They'd change out again after leaving the base, but the idea was to appear nondescript to the U.S. forces en route. Apparently though, everyone had figured out they were doing something clandestine.

They were provided cots, and dossed out to nap for an hour. Better to rest here, under bright lights and with generators roaring in the background, occasional aircraft up close as A-10s, F-16s and Kuwaiti F-18s flew patrol over Iraq, than aboard a plane, vibrating them slowly insane.

Kyle was just getting comfortable, his mind a warm haze, when his shoulder was shaken. "Sergeant Monroe, Sergeant Curtis, flight's here."

"Roger," Kyle groaned. He stretched, ignored the dead-mouse taste in his mouth and sat up. Well, he'd gotten fifteen minutes of snooze, which was better than nothing.

They wore their ID in pouches on the left arm. Everyone on base had to have visible ID, and the guards weren't shy about asking for it. They were IDed again as they ascended the ramp. They were both very familiar with cargo aircraft and lashed themselves in on the troop benches, backs against the webbing. As it appeared there was plenty of room, they propped their feet up on their duffels and, after inserting earplugs, thought about sleeping further. Whether or not the thought became reality would depend on several factors.

The flight was for three pallets of unidentified gear and the two of them. The loadmaster was briefly friendly, then left them alone.

It was 900 miles to Qandahar Air Base, Afghanistan, as the crow flies. Detouring around Iran made it 1,200 miles. For more than two hours they tried to sleep, existing in a precarious fugue state between unconsciousness and awareness, joints stiffening and aching, ears ringing despite the hearing protection, from the engine noise and frame vibration. A trip to the latrine at the front that was basically a porta-potty and small sink were the only chance to stretch and unwind, though the loadmaster did let them walk a couple of laps once they were at altitude. It was cold even with their Goretex on, and even the bitter, rancid Air Force coffee was welcome against the chill.

Kyle remembered a brief stay at an Air Force training site when he'd first enlisted. The coffee came from a machine in paper cups emblazoned, THANK YOU FOR USING UNLEADED GASOLINE. The quality was what one might expect. It seemed some things didn't change. Heck, this might be that same coffee, recycled.

They arrived near dawn, and there was no welcoming committee. They walked stiffly down the ramp and looked around in the gray half-light.

Qandahar Air Base was also Qandahar Airport, which had obviously been modern in the recent past. It had a huge, arching, terminal, all white concrete and broad, darkened glass. But a closer look showed it to be chipped and peeling. There was no real firefight damage, but it had clearly seen better days.

They were expected, sort of. They identified themselves and were greeted with "Oh, right," and then shuffled off into a corner for the sin of violating "the process." They were patient, and it was only fifteen minutes before a specialist with a Humvee arrived to take them into garrison proper.

Once outside the flight line and terminal area, literally thousands of troops were billeted in tent cities and transportable barracks. It was a logistical marvel, Kyle thought, that they'd moved so much stuff halfway around the world and set it all up in the middle of nowhere.

Ten minutes later they were reporting in to General Kratman. He didn't look thrilled.

"So," he said, swigging coffee as he spoke, "I'm supposed to extend support to you two gentlemen, to do something I can't be told of, somewhere I can't be told of. You aren't in my chain of command, or even an attached unit, you're just sort of tourists packing personal weapons, looking scruffy and with two crates I'm not supposed to look at. And they tell me you're Army, not CIA." He was lean, healthy, and had an I-take-no-crap presence.

Kyle didn't need to be polite, but it seemed a good idea to not ruffle feathers. "We are Army, sir. And this is secret, but nothing to be ashamed of or illegal. It's just low profile. If I could tell you, I would."

"All well and good, Sergeant," Kratman replied. "But I've got an orderly operation here, and I don't like rumors. A squad of Delta came through here a couple of months back, and basically helped themselves to anything not nailed down. I don't mind support, but I'll be damned if it's charged against my operation. My troops need that stuff, too, which is why we brought it. So tell me what I do need to know and make it quick."

"Sir, we're departing the post with the predeployed gear and some extraneous equipment such as MREs, in civilian clothes. We will accomplish our mission. There may be calls for support from above, if we run into trouble. After accomplishing said mission, we may depart through here or another route. We don't intend to interrupt your operation. It's just a staging area."

After a few more minutes of talk, Kyle being the solid, reliable NCO, Kratman was mollified somewhat. "Fair enough. You do your mission, I'll give you what I'm supposed to. Nothing more. I don't need my command or my ass getting entangled in stuff I'm not authorized to do myself. So list what you need and I'll see it's delivered. You'll be clearing post when?"

"Daylight tomorrow, sir."

"Good. Hopefully this will all make sense in the end. Staff Sergeant Morrow at the end of the hall will get you bedded down and fed, and see to any gear you need. And gentlemen," he ended with a pause.

"Yes, sir?" Kyle asked.

"Good hunting, whatever the hell it is." An almost-grin appeared on his face.

"Thank you, sir." Kyle grinned despite himself as they turned and left. He could understand a commander in this hole being a bastard about equipment, and the man was no-nonsense enough to make exceptions when needed. But he did need to see a reason.

Once they'd paid their respects, plugged into the chain of command, and grabbed a bite, they sought out their gear. If all went as planned, it was supposed to have been waiting for them. A couple of inquiries got them where they needed to go, and they approached a warehouse that was functional and solid if stark. As they were climbing the steps up to the door, a First Sergeant opened it briskly and exited. Flipping his hat on his head, he looked them up and down. "Gentlemen, is there some reason you aren't shaved?" he asked.

"Mission orders, First Sergeant," Kyle said at once. "We'll be out of uniform very shortly and off post right afterwards."

"Ah," the grizzled old NCO replied. He smiled faintly. "Good luck, then."

"Thanks, First Sergeant," they chorused. His question had been professional and his response appreciated, but the sooner they stopped getting such interest, the happier Kyle would be. Once in civvies, everyone would just assume they were Delta or CIA—or manufacturer's reps for some of the deployed equipment—and stop hassling them.

Inside, the blocky building was unpainted, as it had been outside, but not bleached by sunlight. The office area was neatly kept and all papers were stacked. The computers were tactical models and in use. Wade murmured, "At least they're organized. Hopefully everything's here."

"It better be," Kyle replied, "or we're not going."

A specialist arrived at a run. "Sorry, Sergeants, we're short on manpower. Can I help you?"

"SFC Kyle Monroe," he said as introduction. "Here to pick up transported equipment and some additional gear."

"Yes, Sergeant," the specialist nodded. "What are you needing, and do you already have the documents executed? Or do you need some?"

"You do have a crate for us, I hope?" Kyle asked. He felt queasy, and it wasn't just over his personal weapons. That Barrett was his baby.

"Oh, yeah," the specialist agreed. "Big, long thing. Heavy, too. Almost took Jacko's toe off when we dropped it."

Kyle was cringing, even if it didn't show much on his face. Wade spoke up and said, "Well, Specialist, I hope it *did* land on his toe, because the contents are far more valuable than a soldier's foot."

"Oh, it wasn't damaged," the kid said hastily. "It had one of those shock cartridges on it that would break if it dropped more than three feet. It never did."

"Good," Kyle said. "Still, that's a *maximum* allowable drop, not something to be attempted."

The specialist realized he'd better shut up and get to it before he admitted anything else. They were taken through tunnels of boxes at once, to where the crate lay near a receiving door. Wrecking bar in hand, he pried the top loose. "Here you go," he said. He started reaching in before Wade said, "That's good, soldier. We'll take it from here if you don't mind."

"Sure thing, Sergeant," he agreed with a nod. "But I have to observe the contents to ensure it's all accounted for."

"No problem," Kyle grinned back. The kid was going to have an orgasm when he saw this haul.

Getting the stuff out was a bitch, though. The kid—Leo Darcy was his name—had to pry all four sides off. Then he helped them, carefully, under their direction, to cut away chunks of foam with a knife. He was warned that a scratch would cost him his testicles. "Doesn't seem worth it," he commented. "What's in here, anyway?"

"You'll find out," Wade said. "Then you'll keep your mouth shut."

As the contours were revealed, the kid almost drooled. "Jesus H. Christ! What are you guys going to do? Bag the Taliban's head goon?"

Well, thought Kyle as he gritted his teeth, it was rather obvious why two lone snipers were here in country with a crated .50-caliber sniper rifle. "That's really something we and you aren't going to discuss with anyone, okay?"

"Sorry, Sergeant," Darcy admitted. "I'm cleared, and I won't say anything. But whatever you're shooting with *that*," he said, pointing, "is going to be a shoe."

"Shoe?" Wade asked, beating Kyle.

"S, H, U," the kid said. "Severely Hurting Unit."

Chuckling, Wade nodded, "That they will be. Now don't mention it again."

"Mention what? All I do is open boring old crates of crap all day."

"Very good."

Shortly, the gear was all uncrated, cleared of dust and staticky packing foam. Everything appeared to be in good shape.

It only took a few minutes to fill out the appropriate documents for the shipment. "We need a few other things, too, Specialist Darcy," Kyle said. "Ammunition, grenades, claymores, batteries, usual stuff like that."

"Not a problem," Darcy replied. "Sergeant Korkowski's the armorer, and he's not here, but I can do the paperwork and he should be back at 1800. I'll need to see orders authorizing you, though."

"No problem," Kyle said, pulling out a spare copy of his blanket letter. "Here." He handed it over.

Darcy looked surprised, and a bit disturbed. "Holy crap,

Sergeant, I've never seen one of these!" He gave the letter another quick read and said, "Okay, when do you want it by?"

"We can come back tonight, as long as the stuff is ready."

"Okay," Darcy agreed. "It'll be waiting for you right after chow."

"Thanks," Kyle said.

In a few minutes, they were back outside, festooned with radios, GPS, sidearms, rifles, and loaded rucks. "We need a vehicle," Kyle said. The load was staggering.

"I think we need to fire a few rounds in this terrain to help break us in," Wade said.

Kyle thought for a moment and replied, "That's a damned good idea. We've got a day, we've got the weapons, they need to be checked out anyway, so let's find a mountain."

It wasn't quite as easy as that. The motor sergeant was reluctant to sign out a vehicle, especially to just two soldiers. He wanted to see orders for an operation first. "It's not safe, gentlemen. And I can't lose vehicles on someone's word. I'd be paying for the damned thing."

Kyle agreed, angry. He reassured himself that the motor sergeant likely hated paperwork as much as he did. Still, it was aggravating.

"What now?" Wade asked.

"I suppose we find a patrol and tag along," Kyle offered.

That wasn't easy, either, although patrols were leaving all the time. A number of them were aboard choppers. Those in vehicles were going a considerable distance for several days. Some were in tracks. None were suited to the task in question.

"I've got an idea," Wade said. "Going to cost us some ammo."

"Fair enough," Kyle agreed. "Lead on."

Nodding, Wade reached out and took the Barrett from Kyle. "Watch this," he said. He led the way down a dusty street between tents. It was classic Army architecture and hadn't changed in centuries, barring minor variations in tentage.

"All we've got to do," Wade said, "is offer a bribe."

In a few minutes, they found a platoon that had returned from a patrol and was cleaning weapons. It was obviously a day-after affair, and they were stripped to T-shirt or skin in the warm sun. Jokes flew as they scrubbed their encrusted weapons industriously. One or two noticed the Barrett's blocky case and nudged each other. They had to be wondering what it was.

Wade's target was the lieutenant. "Sir, we've got a problem. Perhaps you can help."

"Perhaps I can," the fresh-faced kid replied. "Who are you gentlemen?"

Introductions were made, the bare bones explained, and the bribe offered. "If you can find us a few guys to throw a patrol together, we'll let you shoot a few."

Suddenly, fatigue and aches were forgotten. To fire a monstrous M-107 .50-caliber sniper's rifle, the troops would forego sleep and eat another MRE or two. There was no shortage of volunteers.

The lieutenant snapped, "Quiet," and was obeyed. He might have been young, but he was competent enough to be respected, and that said a lot. Turning back, grinning now, he said, "That sounds like a blast. I can get a squad or two together, but transport could be a problem."

"I've got that," Kyle said. The general wasn't going to like it. In fact, Kyle was making a career of pissing off high-ranking officers here, but it was all legal and kinda fun.

Twenty minutes later, a squad of infantry, the lieutenant, and the two snipers rolled out the crude gate. The rest consoled themselves with smuggled beer and pictures of women.

"So where do you sergeants want to go?" the lieutenant, Daniels, asked.

Wade said, "Anywhere safe, with lots of room and a good clear field of fire for a thousand meters or so."

Snickering, Daniels said, "Well, there's nowhere really safe, but this is the least unsafe area. And we can just go south to a mined and abandoned village and shoot at the buildings."

"Sounds good. Can one of your guys hold the target for us?" Wade suggested, holding up an apple he'd snagged at the chow hall. To the lieutenant's look of confusion and consternation he said, "I'm joking."

"Right. Sniper humor?"

"Dunno," Wade said. "My humor." Kyle snickered. It was good to be joking with a spotter again. The school had made him morose.

On a flat stretch of desert hardpan overlooking a collection of crumbling walls that could be called a town only by the most generous of definitions, Kyle and Wade set up as fast as they could, treating it as a timed range exercise. Behind a very slight lip, Kyle scraped a groove for the bipod, dropped the bipod down into the depression, flopped down behind the rifle and pulled off the scope caps. He drew a ten-round magazine, loaded two rounds, inserted it and worked the bolt. Wade already had his scope out, M-4 laid aside in easy reach. As Kyle worked the action Wade called the target.

"Reference: tall building, large gray stone construction under peak at forty degrees left. Target, yellow protruding ledge, eight seven zero."

Kyle wasn't sure it was 870 meters, but he'd trust Wade. "Sighted," he said, and squeezed the trigger.

The world exploded. The Barrett went "*Blam!*", the stock shoved back against his shoulder, and dust blew up from the gale out the sides of the muzzle brake. There were exclamations of "*Yes!*" from some of the spectators. They loved their M-16s, but the Barrett was a better hung weapon than most of them would ever handle.

"Up twenty," Wade said.

"Correcting," Kyle said, then fired again. Another kick to the guts came with the shot.

Wade studied the impact. "Looks good. Let's try a closer one, then a farther one."

"Right." Kyle extracted the magazine and loaded two more rounds.

Wade located another target. "Reference: patch of green, right of peak and under overhang. Target: lone tree between two large rocks, four six zero."

"Sighted." *Wham!*

"Good shot. Reference: roof peak. Target: bare patch underneath and right, lone broken concrete chunk near right, one two seven zero."

It took a moment, even with the resolving power of the scope, then he found it. "Sighted." Kyle eased the muzzle a few hairs, let the reticle align, controlled his breathing and grip, and squeezed.

As soon as the trigger broke past the notch he knew it was a good shot. The shove and the bang and the face full of dust were just treats. "I got it," he said. It was over a second later before dust kicked up at the rock, and three seconds later, while everyone was silent, before a faint, echoing, anticlimactic crack came back.

The troops were both eager and hesitant. None of them approached, but they all clearly craved to. Kyle cleared and safed the weapon, extracted the magazine and handed it with two rounds to Lieutenant Daniels. "Want to give it a try, sir?"

"Thanks, Sergeant," he replied, looking like a Boy Scout at his first day on the range.

Daniels slipped easily down behind the Barrett. He still had a young man's flexibility and eagerness. He had enough familiarity with weapons and had watched carefully, so he had no trouble sliding the magazine in, cycling the action, and preparing to fire. Wade read him off a target, he squeezed and *Blam!* "HOO*ooly Shit!*" he grinned, looking up from the massive recoil.

"Give it another one," Kyle encouraged.

After that, there was no hesitation. The entire squad lined up to take their two shots. Kyle noted one with particularly good technique. "You shoot expert, soldier?" he asked.

"Three years in a row, Sergeant," he replied.

"Good. If you can learn good scouting and concealment, you could do this."

"Really?" the young man asked. He looked positively elated.

"Really. Call the school and ask about class schedules. Tell them SFC Kyle Monroe referred you."

"Will do, Sergeant Monroe, and thanks!"

"No problem, soldier. We always need more shooters."

It wasn't long before they were heading back in, jolting over the uneven ground. It seemed as if, thrills done, the drivers wanted back on post as fast as they could manage. "Don't bump my scope," Kyle said.

"Sorry, Sergeant," their driver, the same one who'd shot so well, said, and slowed. They were just taking a curve in the road and Kyle was shoved against the door. The cased rifle on the hump between the seats slammed into his shoulder, twisted and fell and banged his knee as the other end almost bashed Wade in the head.

"Oh, sonofabitch," he said, exasperated.

The driver said, "Ah, hell, is everything okay?"

"Yeah," Wade said. "Everything's cased and we'll heal." He untangled the rifle.

"Good," was the reply, but he did slow a bit more.

"Are we expecting to get shot at?" Kyle asked.

"Er . . . no, just to not miss chow," the young man replied.

"I'll make sure we get fed," Kyle promised.

"Okay. Understood, Sergeant."

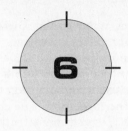

6

BIN QASIM SAT BEFORE THE COMPUTER AND CHECKED
for messages. It was brilliant and poetic the way it was done.
One of the billions of pornographic websites the Satanic Westerners
loved had pictures modified with encoded dots. He downloaded the
images in question and ran them through for decoding. It was obscene the things the Godless enjoyed. Two scrawny, half-fed women,
their loins shaved, licked perversely at each other. Somehow, this
abomination was considered exciting.

But of the billions of sites, it was statistically impossible for the
security forces to find this one, deduce the algorithm for the code,
and crack it. Even then, it was a positional notation of numbers that
had to be fed through a proper matrix of the Arabic alphabet to
make sense, and code words were used. No code was unbeatable,
but this was very secure. And very ironic to make their technology
a weapon to be used against them. Especially when it generated
some tens of thousands of dollars a month.

While the program worked on the series of images of *Jana and
Laurie, the Teen Sweatbox Lesbians,* bin Qasim pondered other issues.

The newspaper woman was becoming jaded. No longer was she
reacting with terrified eagerness. She knew what he expected, and it
seemed she no longer really cared. It was always that way. They
learned fear and obedience, then they learned contempt, then they
had to be dispensed with, like a dog that would no longer follow
commands.

Still, he considered, that meant he could strangle her, slowly. That
would elicit a response. She'd quiver and gasp and thrash around,
and that would be exciting. He understood, he thought, why West-

ern men liked responsive women. But allowing them to join the world of men was a dangerous way to get a thrill. Far better this way.

Yes, she'd gasp and moan and her muscles would tighten under him. It was time for that final thrill before he moved on. And he'd be relocating his headquarters within a day or two anyway. There was no need for excess baggage.

The system was done. Turning his attention back, he opened a window. The information there made him smile. Another revolting club was about to feel the wrath of Allah, if not through Osama, his chosen instrument, then through bin Qasim, his messenger until the grace of God returned Osama to them from hiding. From bin Qasim the progression led to a lesser courier, to the man who would plant the bomb. Thus did Allah light the way for dozens of the Faithful to fulfill His commands.

He typed a reply that would be uploaded later that evening, with a "new" series of images. The photographer through whose camera eye these disgusting pictures were captured had no idea of how useful he was being. Nor would he be killed. His sins were, for now, of use. It would be just to gouge out his eyes, but punishment often waited for Allah, as was proper. Only certain actions in the mundane world were justifiable. Lesser evils would have to wait, and patience was one of the virtues.

Bin Qasim had been patient. Now he would take that bitch by the throat and enjoy the justice he would deliver. It was a small justice, but it gave him pleasure, and if Allah was thereby served, that pleasure was not a sin.

So far, so good, Kyle thought the next afternoon. Of course, all this, with stuffy bureaucrats, paperwork, jet lag, and crowding had been really minor compared to the leg ahead of them. Any deployment was like that, on the way in and the way out. The closer one got to the objective or home, the worse the trip became.

But they had all their gear prepped and ready, a TEMPER tent to themselves to rest in, the weapons sighted in and cleaned, then stuffed into soft cases wrapped in rags. If they could only get some rest, they'd be good to go at 0400.

Kyle had a problem, however. He could never sleep well the first night anywhere. Or, right before a major move. So more fatigue was in the cards for him, despite the nap he'd caught in the stuffy heat of the day. He sighed and lay still, comfortable enough in borrowed blankets on an issue bed frame, and focused on a spot on the side of the tent, hoping to zone himself asleep.

It didn't work, but somehow he got an hour or two of honest rest anyway.

They were up at 0400, and out the gate at 0600, chauffered by two MPs in civvies, one with an M-4 and the other with a pistol. They rode in a civilian Suburban rather than a CUCV, so they could pass as press or other foreign visitors, as long as no one took a good look inside the vehicle. The troops on gate control had been warned to expect them, and made no comments, only nodded.

Then they were in the streets of Qandahar, stomachs full of butterflies. Kyle was regretting the oily coffee he'd had to warm him and wake him.

It was a city that was alive. Dirty it might be, with culture ranging from medieval barbarous to twenty-first-century hi-tech, from donkey-drawn carts with produce, textiles, and livestock, to the occasional cell phone and computer. But it was unique and interesting. The wandering armed men, burqa-clad women and rag-clothed children clashed with business people in Western-style suits or fine jellabas with kaffiyehs, turbans, or local hats. Persians, Indians, Afghans, Tajiks, South Africans, Pakistanis, Indonesians, Chinese, and almost every other culture were represented in some degree. Despite the early hour, a respectable portion of the populace was awake and about.

The driver sought the designated meeting place, weaving through tight, narrow streets that had been built with no thought for automobiles. They squeezed past a truck that looked to be seventy years old, with green plywood framing the cab and bed. It was stacked fifteen feet high with goods. It was well they had a Suburban, because a Humvee wouldn't have fit. In fact, a smaller Toyota would have been large for these routes, and less conspicuous. The roads were what an American urbanite might call alleys, like those behind 1920s houses for garage or delivery access, except that shacks and buildings with raised wooden porches butted right up to them, with barely enough sidewalk for vendors. Merchants and foot traffic spilled right out into the street. Everything was a dun, dusty color.

Finally, the driver stopped. "Okay, we're here. Now what?"

"We wait," Kyle said..They were supposed to meet their local escort and guide, and be driven over the border quietly. It had all been arranged ahead of time, and by messages he was assured had been received. He'd feel better if he knew who had sent them, and what method had actually been used. Phone? Radio? Messenger snail?

"Okay. But can you help keep an eye out? I'd like to still have all four hubcaps when I return."

"Sure." Heck with the hubcaps, Kyle thought. They'd be lucky to hang on to their boots. Children were scraping at the doors, holding up food, jewelry, trinkets, even spare car parts. He'd forgotten what it was like in the third world. Bosnia had been much the same, as had Egypt during that training mission.

He was startled from his musing by loud honking from behind. The horn was flat and wheezed, but it was obviously intended to get their attention. Then the vehicle with it, a shabby old Toyota that might be twenty-five years old, pulled around them, close enough that Kyle expected sparks.

Sergeant Fleming, the driver, carefully rolled down the window to the gestures from the passenger, and a torrent of Pashto came through. There were four men in the crew cab, and three more in the bed. In the Suburban, the specialist riding shotgun was clutching at his M-4 and looking very nervous.

"Hold on!" Fleming said, gesturing.

Kyle in back tapped his partner on the shoulder and said, "Wade, let me over," and began to scramble in the tight confines. The web gear they were wearing didn't help. Wade squirmed underneath, Kyle on top, and they managed to swap places. He got the window down and said, *"Ta tarjumen larey?"* Do you have a translator? What was wrong here?

In response he heard a long but slow and enunciated phrase in Pashto and caught only "translator," "dead," "soon" and "sorry." He thought he heard "Taliban" in there, too.

"Great," he said to Wade. "Do we still want to go?" The irregularity was not reassuring. Frankly, he wasn't convinced it was a good idea. So far, the whole thing seemed cobbled together.

"I think we should," Wade said. "It's not tripping my ohshit meter yet. But let's keep an eye out for other irregularities."

"Yeah." Kyle thought about calling in on the Iridium, but there wasn't much anyone would be able to tell him. He'd have to make the decision.

Suppressing a mental image of things going to hell and them getting shot, Kyle indicated the gear in back with his thumb, and pointed at the back of the other truck. Grinning wide teeth through his beard, the driver pointed forward, indicating they should follow. His teeth were dirty but intact. He probably didn't get a lot of sugar here, but he likely didn't have a toothbrush, either.

Fleming followed the truck into an alley, whereupon the passenger in the bed indicated they should reverse in. Fleming nodded and pulled them around, while the specialist riding shotgun kept a firm grip on his weapon and scanned every face he saw.

But there were no incidents as Wade clambered into the back cargo area, climbed through the back window and dragged the fabric-wrapped rifle case and two old battered rucksacks behind him, with Kyle bringing up the rear. Kyle relaxed his grip on the little Colt in his pocket, and hopped over the side of the bed to get in the empty front passenger seat.

"*Sta noom tse day?*" he asked. What's your name?

"Qalzai," was the answer. Good. That was who he had been told to meet. At least the names matched. Now he just hoped they hadn't been compromised. Though it could still be a Taliban setup to kidnap or murder them. Kyle was flushed, and his pulse was likely over 100 beats a minute.

"Okay," he shouted back to the MPs. "Follow us until we're out of town, and I guess we find a new translator as we go." He was still prickly. He wanted a translator.

"Are you sure you'll find one, sir?" Fleming asked. He hadn't been introduced to Kyle until that morning, and to him, any American in this region in civilian garb was a "sir." Delta, CIA, whatever, they were above his level.

"No, but it's likely. We all want the same thing, so I expect some cooperation." Kyle just wished he felt as confident as he sounded.

"Very well, sir." It was clear the driver wasn't very happy with the idea.

Turning back to Qalzai, Kyle said, "*Lar,*" and hoped it meant "go." Whether it did or not, his meaning was clear and Qalzai grinned, nodded, and slipped the clutch.

The ancient vehicle's gears ground and caught and they pulled away quickly. The Army driver followed at a reasonable distance as they wove through the streets. While it was clear Qalzai wasn't trying to lose them, he was cheerfully and carelessly buzzing along.

"Um, ah," Kyle said as he fumbled for the right phrase. Dammit, he needed to calm down. He was dwelling on the past again, not paying attention. He was a shaking bundle of nerves.

Wade spoke from the back, "*Mehrabani waka pa karar kooz sha,*" straight from the phrase book by rote. Please slow down.

With a quizzical look, Qalzai eased off the gas.

In a few minutes, they were at the edge of town, the shacks looking more and more bedraggled until there were none left. The ground was reminiscent of western Texas—slightly rolling, scrubby and fertile enough for a few hardy crops. The shacks were gone,

Kyle noted, but occasional wide tents with sloping sides were visible here and there. To the south were the hills they'd have to cross.

With all the formalities taken care of, they waved a clear signal to the MPs that everything was as it should be. At least, they hoped so. Kyle felt suddenly very alone.

Shortly, they pulled over to the roadside.

"What's happening?" Kyle asked, suspicious at once.

"We're cool," Wade said. "Clothes."

"Ah. Good," Kyle agreed with relief. From behind him came a local "chappan" jacket in bright cotton, a hat and head cloth, and a rough shirt for later. He got out, swapped jackets, climbed back in, and they were off once again in their Central Asian Plateau limousine. He was reassured. If they hadn't been shot and dumped here, it was likely as it should be. But he was still nervous.

Trying to get names, Kyle turned toward the truck's bed and introduced himself. "I am Kyle," he said, thumbing his chest.

Qalzai chattered and pointed while Kyle and Wade wished he'd keep his hands on the wheel and eyes on the road, though there wasn't much to hit on this plateau. Except boulders. Herds of goats. Maybe the occasional unexploded Russian bomb or land mine or Taliban artillery shell. But from the gestures and a few snatched words, they gathered the gist. Behind Qalzai was his son, Khushal, twenty something and not yet aged beneath his beard. Behind Kyle was a nephew, Shamsuddin, who looked about fifteen and skinny, though not naïve. In back now with Wade were Ustad, Mirza, Qalendar, Bait, and Ajmal. They were all cousins or nephews of Qalzai, and varied from Ajmal who also looked like a teenager, through Bait, about thirty, who had leering, weird eyes, to Mirza who was about forty, though well worn for his age. They were all skinny, leathery, and with ragged hair. Their garb was boots, trousers, coats, and wool hats. Mirza's coat was an old Soviet armor NCO's overcoat.

With nothing else to do, and hoping to improve relations, Kyle pointed at the coat, back through the glassless rear window and over Shamsuddin's shoulder. "Coat?" he asked, indicating his own jacket.

It worked. Mirza launched into a long story that almost certainly started with the Pashto equivalent of "No shit, there I was, thought I was gonna die . . ." He talked loudly, to be heard over the vehicle noise, for a good fifteen minutes, to chuckles and jeers from his fellows, while Kyle and Wade picked up local intonation and rhythm for the language, and got an ear on phonemes. As to vocabulary, they only caught about one word in ten or fifteen, but that was enough to confirm that he'd fought the Soviets as a boy and was quite proud of his trophy. And the story was a familiar social interaction to Kyle. It helped calm him down.

The road across the plateau was fairly decent by local standards. It was dirt, but marked with rocks periodically, and signs put up by some residue of government long ago. Most of the signs had been salvaged as building materials long ago. Debris was mostly cleared to the sides, and picked through for anything useful. They rumbled along to war stories from Mirza and Qalzai, punctuated by grinding gears, occasional backfires, and a clatter from the rusted exhaust.

Kyle learned to loathe the vehicle in short order. Sure, it had character, with its chipped and faded paint, exposed and crumbling foam in the seats, the hole rusted in the floorboard, and the missing roof, replaced by a sheet of tough canvas attached to the pillars.

But then there were the ticking valves and the cylinder that kept missing, the carburetor that backfired whenever the engine revs changed substantially, grinding gears, and howling differential. The combination made conversation impossible. That "tough canvas" over the cab was full of pinholes worn by age and flapped and snapped in the wind. And there was a spot on the seat worn to bare metal, which kept jabbing Kyle in the spine and right kidney, even through his jacket and load vest underneath it. They jounced over a potholed strip that could only charitably be called a road and every bump and shimmy caused him to be stabbed again.

And that shimmy . . . he could swear a motor mount was broken, and perhaps an axle mount, too. He was just glad they were not yet riding the edge of those mountains. This was a hell of a way to travel. He almost wished for a horse, though he'd only ever ridden nags at fairs or on his uncle's neighbor's farm.

It was a long trip, even as short a distance as it officially was, less than 200 miles. Besides the worn vehicle, there were detours around flocks, holes, burned or broken vehicles. Those last were quickly stripped of anything useable, and were mere hulks. It seemed as if any car parts were quickly scavenged, and it didn't take long for even engines to be pulled. He'd seen a couple of truck beds used as wagons, too. The materials were too valuable to waste.

He wondered how much money he could make by opening an auto parts store.

They ate on the road, cold goat and rice and beans. It was mostly bland under a sauce that provided heat but little flavor. Goat was close to lamb, of course, but stringier. Still, it seemed sanitary enough, and was nutritious if boring. Water was from their own CamelBaks, and they'd filter everything they came across. While it was supposed to be a short mission, Kyle didn't crave screaming diarrhea while he tried to take a shot. There were at least three rivers on the route, and they'd crossed the Tarnak and Argestan Ruds already.

The trip was dusty. It had started chilly in the morning, was warm at midday, and quickly cooled again. The local clothes were stale and smelled of dried sweat, but kept him warm. The hat and head cloth were actually quite comfortable and practical, and would mask his features. He hoped no one noticed Wade. Height might be overlooked, but black skin was very out of place here. On the other hand, Wade was a good sergeant, a great shot, and very steady and reliable. It was an Army thing that Kyle wasn't going to dig into. He was quite sure Wade had his own musings on the subject.

They passed through several small villages, drawing gasoline from 1950s-style pumps, from rusty gravity-flow tanks set on scaffoldings and from cans they carried in the bed. It seemed precarious, especially as the gas gauge didn't work. None of the instruments worked, in fact, but their host was cheerful and unconcerned. He acted as a tour guide, pointing at sights and waving and gesticulating. Kyle nodded back, made "yeah" sounds now and then and tried to feign interest in little huts, rocky ridges, and bends in the road. He couldn't tell if the stories were "we fought a great battle here" or "here's where my youngest boy's son was born" or "best breakfast in the country, until they got shot up." Still, he tried to be polite.

By later afternoon it was chill as they rose higher into the Toba Kakar Range toward the border, then turned to follow it east along a very crude track that could only charitably be called a "road." They wished to avoid the refugee camps at Chaman, and to the west was lifeless desert. Toward the mountains was their best route. Traffic was almost nonexistent and what there was was animal drawn.

The road had been built in the 1970s, as a U.N. project. The U.S. had built a modern, two-lane road around half the perimeter of Afghanistan. It had been a good road in its time, but thirty years of weather, wear, and abandonment had reduced it to rubble. It was a pity. To the north and east, the Soviets had outdone themselves and built a modern, multilane highway. Everyone had wondered why, until their tanks had rolled in by that route a few years later.

Kyle mused until they pulled off into a draw that paralleled the road, apparently in search of shelter.

A canvas tarp was stretched out from poles set into crudely welded rings in the truck's bed, and stretched out with thin nylon twine and metal stakes forged from rebar. They were done in time for sunset, and prayers were chanted, everyone facing southwest toward Mecca. After that, Shamsuddin and Mirza lay down in the truck bed, across fuel cans and spare tires and went straight to sleep. Bait and Ustad, mean and worn-looking, walked off a few feet with their AKs and lit up cigarettes while they stood watch. Wade commented, "Think we should tell them how badly that screws up their night vision?"

"Nah," Kyle replied. "We're taking turns on watch. I don't trust anyone with our package," he said, referring to the cloth-wrapped, cased Barrett.

"No problem. Four hours?"

Kyle nodded, "Yup. I got some bad z's in the cab. How about you?"

Wade smiled, teeth white in startling comparison to the locals. "That's the most comfortable bed full of sharp metal, spares, guns, rotten boots, slimy muck, gas cans, trash, and assorted crap I've ever slept in."

"Well, good. I'll swap off with you tomorrow."

"Don't worry about it," Wade said, shaking his head. "I'd be cramped as hell in that tiny cab. The honor is all yours."

"Right. Goodnight, then," Kyle said, pulling a thin GI blanket from his ruck and using it and his poncho as bedding.

"Sweet dreams, don't let the bedbugs bite."

Kyle did sleep well. He didn't realize how comfortable he was until Wade woke him at 0200.

"Rise and shine," he heard, and shook himself awake. It was chill out, and he realized he'd been clutching the poncho liner around himself. It was like camping again, as it had been when he was fourteen. Only that had been his uncle's farm and this was a range of mountains where unfriendly strangers would try to kill him.

"I'm up," he said, standing, stretching, and taking the M-4. He made a quick and automatic chamber inspection. "What's up?" he asked.

"Just you and our two teenage chaperones," Wade said, indicating the two boys on watch. "Though they seem reliable and not too nervous."

"Good," Kyle said. "Not nervous is good."

"Right," Wade agreed. "See you in four hours." He had his own poncho in the truck with his gear, but it made more sense to just swap off as they had weapons. Less packing was less time wasted. He lay down and was snoring before Kyle had walked out to the patrol point manned by the two locals.

"*Assalam u alaikum,*" he said in Pashto. Peace be unto you, the local equivalent of "Good evening."

One of them replied, "*Wa alaikum u ssalam.*" And upon you peace.

"*Saba hawa tsanga da?*" he asked. What will the weather be like?

"*Rokhana,*" he heard. Cloudy. Then a bunch of what was gibberish.

"*Ze ne pohigam, wobakha,*" he said. I don't understand, sorry. They shrugged back and all three resumed silence. He'd used what little Pashto he had to stay in practice. It wasn't enough, even with a laptop and phrase books. There was no time for that while shooting. So they'd still need an interpreter to get anything done. But hopefully they'd find one soon.

The teens were quiet. They stayed still and didn't fidget, and didn't smoke at the post, taking turns to go back behind the truck and shielding their eyes. Decent discipline, for what were essentially militia. Kyle was reassured. At least they weren't bumbling amateurs, even if they were largely illiterate tribespeople.

It was a good watch, which is to say a boring one. Absolutely nothing happened before 0600. No animals stumbled across them, no one attacked, no stray rocks dislodged and fell. Nothing created any disturbance. Kyle was relieved to see dusk grow from gray to purplish blue overhead.

They drove as soon as everyone was awake and prayers said. Breakfast was bread and a few precious cans of soup, heated over the engine during a few moments' rest an hour later. Kyle and Wade settled for MRE spaghetti, also heated against the block.

Looking over, Kyle asked, "Got enough hot sauce there?"

Wade grinned and finished emptying the tiny bottle. "I carry extras. Always useful. Makes the stuff edible, at least."

"Yeah, they're pretty bland," he agreed. "But some of the new ones are decent."

They dug in with spoons, stirring to mix the hot and cold areas of the packets into something resembling warm food. It wasn't really breakfasty food, but it was familiar and nourishing. "You did bring extra toilet paper, I hope."

"Four rolls," Wade agreed. "Dunno what they use here. Leaves, sand—"

"Skidmarks," Kyle suggested.

"Thank you," Wade said. "That goes so well with spaghetti."

"You're welcome," Kyle replied, smiling. He reflected it was a good thing he wasn't a coffee addict. Coffee here was almost non-existent, thin and bitter, the imported Arab beans not the best. Of course, heating it on the engine didn't improve the flavor. Though likely some of the glop that passed as engine oil would. Some of the men were grumbling about not having any tea, but they'd have to wait until lunch.

While they stood around the opened hood, their escorts jabbered back and forth. A couple smoked unfiltered cigarettes down to bare stubs, which they saved for reuse later. Unlike Western cigarettes, they came in bundles, not packs, and were slightly conical rolls. Kyle had wondered at first if they were joints, but they did smell like tobacco. The smoke was fragrant. "Indian," Wade said. Kyle took his word for it. He sucked down a few cupfuls from his CamelBak to stay hydrated. They had spare canteens along, but would still have to find a well or river soon.

Then they were back on the road as the shadows shrank and the few brave drops of dew lost their battle with the arid environment. A dry wash was to their right and south, weathered and old. Farther west, it became a stream.

Shifting in the seat, Kyle tried to get comfortable in some fashion, back at an angle against the seat, feet toward the drive hump, elbow on the window ledge. It didn't work, though he could have been much more uncomfortable, he thought. The bench seat was far enough forward for Qalzai, who might be five feet six. Kyle broke six feet and was much longer limbed. He wondered how Wade was managing in the back, crammed in with junk and five militiamen. Plus their very expensive and very precious rifle.

Ahead, he could see what was the peak of this particular ridge of the mountain range. There were likely others beyond it. Wade had been right; it was much like Nevada, only more lawless and desolate.

He didn't realize that he managed to doze. His body had adapted to the inevitable, head on hand, and the steady bouncing had a hypnotic effect. That combined with the warmth, the very short sleep plus the fatigue of the trip zoned him into a nap.

He was still out when the rickety old vehicle braked and stopped. "What's going on?" Kyle asked, shaking himself awake. They were alongside a vehicle that was coming the other way, and Kyle was disturbed that he'd been asleep. If it had been a threat . . .

But it didn't appear to be. Qalzai spoke to the other driver. They rapid-fired words at each other, loudly and with furrowed brows. Gestures passed back and forth as both troops grasped at pistols, just in case. Kyle opened up the laptop, keeping it in the footwell for now. He had a feeling the dictionary was going to be useful.

As the other vehicle drove off with waves all around, Qalzai spoke to his son. Kyle handed him the laptop, and the boy brightened. A computer was a neat thing to him, and after a quick explanation, he scrolled through the words on screen and said haltingly, "Border ahead. Guarded American Marine soldiers."

"Oh," Kyle said. It was the smartest thing he could think of to say.

Wade asked, "Bypass it?"

"No," Kyle said. "We've got ID, we'll go through. Let me handle it." He turned back to Khushal and said, "Approach slowly and let me talk." He used his hands a lot to get the point across.

"You're the boss," Wade agreed, sounding unsure.

As they reached the peak of the rutted pass, the road split. To the left was the road to Ghazluna, which they wanted to avoid. Not only was it a visible area, but there were solid border patrols. Instead, they curved off to the right and south. Ahead could be seen a checkpoint, clearly guarded by Marines in Humvees mounting M-19s and M-240s, and a Pakistani detachment with an M113 APC. Apparently, something was expected to cross the line that the Marines wanted to take a look at. But they'd be easier to deal with than Pakistani guards in a populous town, with no U.S. presence, had they taken the other route.

One of the armored and helmeted figures waved them forward, palm flat to indicate they should slow and stop. Qalzai eased the grinding clutch in and crept up. Everyone had his hands visible. The tracking guns helped keep everyone's attention.

As they stopped, the M-4-armed Marine spoke in halting Pashto. Kyle drew back the cloth over his face and said, "I'm American, Marine. So's my assistant."

"Who are you, sir?" the kid asked. He might be twenty-two at most, but he spoke the language, was dusty and dry and had eyes too wise for that age. He might be surprised but he wasn't impressed. Across from him was another youngster with an SAW.

"Army. Intel. Monroe, SFC, and Curtis, Staff. Here's our orders and our ID," he replied, handing forward the documents as Wade uncovered his own face. His dark skin actually helped here, as further identification. There were almost no blacks in Afghanistan, and almost certainly none who weren't American or French. "We need to talk to your commander."

The Marine read over the orders a bit haltingly, strange acronyms giving him pause. But they were clearly U.S. Army orders, and the accompanying letter said to extend any requested facilities or equipment to the two soldiers identified. "Gunny Reagan is in charge. Come with me, but leave the weapons, please."

"Can do," Kyle agreed, and climbed out the back slowly. Wade would stay to guard the gear.

Gunny Reagan was obvious. He had a slight grizzled look, a demeanor that bespoke confidence and command. This was a man who wouldn't need to raise his voice. He extended a hand for the orders, and said, "Gunnery Sergeant Reagan, and you are?"

"Kyle Monroe, SFC, U.S. Army. Pleased to meet you."

"What's the deal?"

" 'Fraid I can't say, Gunny. Sergeant Curtis and I are cleared to cross the border, and we may or may not be back this way. In the meantime, I need to ask that you and your men forget I was ever here."

Reagan nodded that he heard the statement, but not that he agreed. He looked over the letter, flipped back to the orders again, scanned them, and said, "Then let me call in this code here and see what I'm told." He looked at Kyle for any evasiveness.

"Go right ahead," Kyle agreed. He didn't blame the man. Documents could be forged easily enough, and the two could be reporters, spies, drug dealers, sympathizers, or anything else, even antiwar nutcases wanting to make headlines. The Marine strode briskly over to the nearest Humvee, climbed in the passenger side but left a leg dangling, and reached for a radio.

It could be a few minutes, with relays through various air and ground stations, so Kyle dropped into parade rest and waited. It was a comfortable enough position and it wasn't likely to make anyone nervous. He was glad of the cloth over his head in the hot sun. He hoped no one lost a file and left him with the Marines. It would be embarrassing.

Shortly, Reagan came back. He handed over the dusty sheets and the ID and said, "Forget what?" There was a perfectly rehearsed confused look on his face. He gave a thin, tight-lipped smile, extended his hand to shake and said, "Good hunting, whoever the hell you are and whatever the hell you're doing."

"Semper Fi, Gunny," Kyle grinned back.

"Semper Fi. No problem. Good day." He turned and said, loud

enough to be heard but not shouting, "Let this vehicle pass." One of the troops repeated it in Pakhto to the Pakistani squad. The two and their guides were scrutinized curiously, but they weren't hassled with further questions.

They resumed their jolting, dusty progress. The only good thing, apart from the few minutes of respite, was that the gunny's call had confirmed their whereabouts for the chain of command and made the next call-in less urgent. Still, Wade dialed in and reported their position. Things got lost in passage, and it was better to contact directly. "We're good," he said as he disconnected. "Spoke to his exec."

Kyle had thought downhill would be less nerve-wracking. He'd forgotten that the truck's brakes were as bad as the rest of it. They squealed and slipped and pulled to the right, while Qalzai ground the gears to torque-brake against the engine, and pulled on the hand brake, too. Hopefully, it wouldn't be necessary to use feet. Once, when they met a car coming the other way, also overloaded with gear, they seemed to hang in empty space. Kyle held tightly to the door handle, clutched at the seat and said nothing. Somehow, the thought of a roll down the mountain was less appealing than that of being shot. He reminded himself that Qalzai had done this before, likely for his entire life, and that it should be safe. While he did so, the wheels slipped for just a moment on a slope that was a bare hairsbreadth from the cliff.

Kyle was only too glad when they hit a wide spot with rock on both sides, and took a break. He had to pee very badly, and Wade did, too.

They continued up and down sharp ridges and escarpments, the road cut at steep angles and worn. The wind and the weight of vehicles and even the centuries of animal hooves and human feet had worn things down. Many of the routes had never been intended to take motorized vehicles, and had been damaged further. Sometimes, the truck would scrape one side or the other on rocks as they negotiated a narrow stretch. Qalzai could be heard to mutter what could only be curses.

That was scary, Kyle thought. If the local guide was worried, he probably should be, too. He began to wish they'd simply parachuted in where they needed to go.

But they were stuck with this, and it had only been two days so far. Two long, aching, sweaty, gritty nerve-wracking days.

It was dusky by then, making the descent even more interesting. Kyle heaved a sigh of relief, as did Wade, when Qalzai leveled them out at the bottom of the slope. They stopped again for the night on this local plateau. It gave them good visibility against incoming trouble, but less protection against wind. As dark fell fast and hard, Qalzai pulled them off into the scrub and picked a spot where they should be slightly hidden. They were behind a slight rise that would also give them the tactical advantage if attacked.

"We shouldn't be at risk," Wade said. "Pakistan is friendly territory and a civilized nation."

"Do you really believe that?" Kyle asked. The two were standing back as the Pashtun pitched the canvas tarp.

"No, but I sound convincing, don't I?" Wade grinned.

"Yeah," Kyle said. "Keep that thing loaded and a sharp eye out."

"Right," Wade agreed with a nod. He was still smiling, but serious underneath.

The night chilled rapidly. Ustad and Qalendar unpacked a salted haunch of goat, which they roasted over a small, smoky fire of scrub stalks. Along with beans and rice, it made an adequate meal. The beans and rice were so much cardboard to the Americans, but the goat had a rich aroma and the salted flavor was welcome, if a bit strong. It was stringy, chewy meat, too. Still, it was meat, and the smoke from the fire added to their hunger, even if it was a bit astringent and harsh. Kyle had brought a box of rations, and decided he'd break them out within the next day or two, to boost morale and pull favors, though the idea of pulling favors with MREs was hysterical.

Once done eating, Kyle slipped down into his poncho liner and blanket, ruck as a pillow, and was soon in that warm state between dreams.

Then a shot crashed nearby.

He kicked off the covers automatically as he snatched for his .45. Wade was already dropping down behind him, safety coming off the M-4 with a *snick*. Kyle's heart was thudding as his body temperature soared and sweat beaded on his skin. He wished for something heavier than a pistol, but the Barrett was too heavy and there was only one M-4. None of the locals had a spare AK, or if they did, now was not the time to be asking.

"What happened?" he asked Wade. He was shaking. The shot had his nerves fried.

"I dunno," Wade said. There was yelling, and another shot as everyone else finished scrambling out and for cover.

Recalling what had happened so far, Kyle asked, "Were both shots outgoing?"

Wade hesitated, and said, "Yes."

"Okay. So let's not do anything sudden."

"Agreed."

Qalzai was yelling out at one of the others, who was yelling back. Then he went out into the dark, shouting as he did so.

"Who's out there?" Kyle asked.

"Er . . ." Wade said, "Ajmal and Qalendar."

Shortly, Qalzai returned with Qalendar. Qalzai held both rifles. His face was a cross between amused and disgusted.

"What was it?" Kyle asked.

Qalzai said something that was hard to comprehend, but included "fighting" and "sick." Turning to Wade, Kyle said, "Near as I can tell, the man suffers from PTSD." He could see that. He had some of it himself. And right now, it was very near the surface.

Wade said, "Post traum—well, I guess that's understandable."

"Yup. And we're not in any danger. So why don't I take over on watch and you sleep?"

"Sleep? After that?" Wade replied. "Funny. But I can hold your hand and sing you a lullaby until you calm down."

They both laughed nervously. It had been terrifying for a few moments there.

"We're both staying up, I assume?" Kyle asked.

Wade nodded, "Yeah, for now. Hell, we don't need sleep anyway."

It was cold, near freezing, with frost and hoarfrost and gelatinous dew clinging to every patch of green amidst a sinking, swirling mist that was starting to settle.

"If we'd had this fog when we woke up, I think I would have crapped my pants. This is *creepy*," Wade said.

"Tell me about it," Kyle agreed. "Isn't it amazing how a mission so simple on paper can turn to shit at every stage?" Their mission was very simple in theory: go in, meet up with locals, find target, eliminate target, withdraw. He still doubted it would go that smoothly.

"The Army way. Has been since at least the Romans."

"Yeah," Kyle replied, his nod unseen in the dark. "Want me to get out NVGs or warm up something with an MRE heater?"

"Save the goggles," Wade advised. "But yeah, something warm. Cocoa? Coffee?"

"Sure. How about a blend of both with extra creamer to create a nice Italian mocha latte?"

Wade grimaced at the thought. "You can really be a sick son of a bitch, you know that?" They both chuckled and he said, "Just co-coa, thanks."

The MRE heater was a calcium carbide grid in a plastic bag. Adding water made it churn out hydrogen bubbles and lots of heat. There were also ways to use them as small incendiaries, but Kyle hoped mightily they wouldn't get that far down the drain on this mission, no matter what went wrong. He dropped one plastic heater package each into their canteen cups, risking minor contamination and bitterness, which got the water boiling. He decided cocoa did sound preferable to coffee, and doctored his with extra sugar. Wade kept up a small patrol area, with the rise, the truck, and a rock dome as cover, while Ajmal and Shamsuddin watched the heaters in amazement. Their whispered conversation was unintelligible, but they were obviously awed by the technology. They knew of radios and small arms, artillery and aircraft, even chemlights. But there were many very basic military items they'd never encountered.

7

KYLE AND WADE WERE BOTH STILL GRITTY-EYED AND exhausted when dawn turned to a boiling oil sunrise oozing over the ranges. They hoped to reach their destination today and start the mission proper. Aching and stiff, still chilled from the night, they crawled back into the truck.

Qalzai turned the heater on, and it worked after a fashion. The fan had long since burned out, but motion created positive airflow. With the windows closed and the broken back glass wide open, all they succeeded in doing was drawing hot air past the boots and up their legs, but that helped immensely. Kyle shivered in his Goretex parka and pants and Nomex gloves, and wondered how Wade was managing in back. The day was warming slowly.

Amazingly, he did manage to sleep, head lolling forward. He awoke like that around eight, and had an excruciatingly stiff neck to go with the acid stomach and headache. Sighing, he drank water, that being all that was currently available. He longed for the one thing he couldn't have: bacon and eggs.

Qalzai said little, but he did mention "*Da sahar chai*" and "*rasturan.*" Breakfast tea something restaurant. Kyle agreed and nodded.

They splashed across a shallow ford of the Pishin Lora River. What was here might have been a road and proper crossing at some point. Now it was just a wide spot with flat rocks. The vehicle tilted and swayed at a steep angle, but they were across soon enough.

Their first destination became visible as they cleared a rise beyond the bank. Berishtiya was a sizeable town, which surprised Kyle, it being located in the ass-end of nowhere. It was likely a center for what passed as trade and government out here. "Not even a Mc-

Dogfood's," he quipped to Wade, who chuckled. They could see all of it easily from here. It was all block and bleached tin roofs packed in closely.

Wade leaned close and whispered, "Not even a bar or whorehouse. No wonder some of these guys are mean." They both stifled laughs from that.

Khushal was giving them an odd look as Kyle turned back around. "Just a joke about the terrain," he said, figuring to be vague. "It's similar to some of our Western desert." Then it took ten minutes to use the laptop to assemble the sentences into something understandable. By then they were near the town.

"I think America is green?" Khushal asked, looking quizzical.

"Oh, no," Wade cut in. "Desert, mountain, arctic cold to the north, wet forests, plains, swamps, some of everything. We just don't have time to visit a lot of it."

Kyle added, "And we don't often fight in the mountains. More often in the woods or cities." They picked out enough words to get the points across.

Khushal studied the screen and nodded. "All mountains here. Pretty, yes?"

"Sure are," Kyle agreed. *If you dig bleak, cold, and lifeless.* But he wasn't going to insult a man who was his host, brave enough to fight the bloodthirsty freaks who were not anxious to relinquish this land, and who was necessary to keep him alive.

Berishtiya was in a high valley. There actually was quite a bit of greenery there, compared to the stark cliffs. Flocks and herds of sheep and goats munched here and there, and they had to slow to get through them. The roads were dirt mostly, though there was one section that had been paved sometime in the last century, and some graveled areas.

Traffic wasn't heavy, but the streets were as narrow as they'd learned to expect. Donkey-drawn carts, VWs, rattly old Mercedes cars, and unknown Indian cars fought for space, drivers cheerfully shouting and waving fists at each other, demanding Allah bless or curse the obstacles in front of them, depending on mood.

Among the shanties and shacks were a few better buildings. Some appeared to be civic centers. There were nicer houses, in that they had land, block walls with pierced concrete, and stone walls around courtyards, sheds, or garages and balconies. One had a worn fountain or pool, now dry and choked with dust. The mayor and chief of police lived here, Kyle surmised. Or perhaps some local warlord or black marketer. He didn't need to know and wasn't going to ask.

Small shops were scattered, and small was the operative word. Some of them might be a hundred square feet, a ten-foot hut with an awning, open in front. Some were more spacious. Kyle didn't understand that. With all the empty room they had, why not make use of the space?

Then his thoughts were distracted by the smells of food.

They pulled up near a clutch of small buildings with a courtyard. A fire was going in a brick stove, and pots were crowded on the surface, with other things in the oven area. Two women in long dresses and veils were bustling about tending the food, and several children, better fed than their northern neighbors, scurried about, helping and hindering and being chastised.

Qalzai and Khushal hugged another man and swapped greetings, then laughed loudly. Shortly, they were all hunkered down around a low table, drinking at hot, sweet tea and tearing at bread, with jam and goat milk to spread and dip. It wasn't the most appetizing breakfast the Americans had seen, but they managed.

Kyle grabbed the laptop from his coat—he'd been carrying it alongside everywhere, figuring it was harder to replace than a rifle, and easier to steal. He opened it up and grabbed the dictionary program, so they could communicate more.

At once, he was surrounded by a mob of children, who were highly impressed and very excited. They'd likely never seen anything like it, heard only stories, and here was a screen with images on it. They were delighted.

Kyle swore, and heard Wade mutter, too. The last thing they needed was publicity. While it wasn't an obvious connection from computer to assassin, it was certainly a hint of visitors from the West, and that combined with a shot or two would be serious intel for their target, the Pakistani authorities, or anyone.

He closed it at once, shooed the children away, and Qalzai said what was clearly, "You children go play and leave the adults alone."

"Phrasebook for now," Kyle said to Wade.

"Apparently our best choice," Wade nodded.

After eating, they sat back as the men pulled out a tall vaselike ceramic container with a narrow neck.

"That can't be what—" Kyle started to say as Wade said, "Hashish pipe."

"Oh, great," Kyle said.

"Typical here," Wade said. "Hash has been used in Central Asia for at least three thousand years. Just smile and ignore it. If they make a stink, fake a hit."

"I'm sure the Army will love this in the after-action review," Kyle said.

But the man charitably offered to share, and simply smiled when Kyle and Wade declined. The others each had a few good lungfuls, and seemed to mellow out. It didn't appear to be an addictive habit for them, merely a social thing like a drink. But Kyle hoped they didn't plan on driving again soon.

He was relieved when Qalzai said, "We stay here," or something close to it, with, "Friends help." So they were waiting for allies, or spies or something. Fair enough, as long as it wasn't too long a wait. Kyle and Wade both knew they were nervous, and kept eyeing each other, waiting for one of them to express their distrust. It wasn't that their guides were unreliable, it was that the locals were well networked and they weren't. The word would get out sooner or later, and that would make their stalk and shoot much more problematical. Best to do it quickly, shoot and scoot, before anyone had any suspicions. But if they needed more intel, they'd have to wait.

They spent all day in the compound. At least it felt like a compound. Wade explained the reason it felt that way.

"The home is all-important. So the buildings look in on the courtyard. It's part of why they're so clannish and have so little nationalism. Comes from early times, and was reinforced when Alexander stormed through here; they built to provide defensive walls. And since then . . ."

"Since then they've been at each other's throats in some fashion," Kyle offered.

"Yes," Wade said. "Mongols, Moghuls, the Afghan empire, the Kazakhs, the British, the Soviets, always someone."

"Wonderful," Kyle groused.

"They're a very proud people," Wade said. "Unfortunately, they're stuck in the Middle Ages."

"I wondered," Kyle said. "They seem to have bright cotton fabrics, lots of horses, all stuff that would have made them rich five hundred years ago."

"It did," Wade nodded. "But they haven't changed much since. And the Taliban influence took them back even further. The burqa used to be a mark of a high-class lady who didn't need to show her face. Now it's a prison."

"So let's get our shot and leave them in peace," Kyle said.

"Suits me."

They passed the day reviewing manuals mentally, looking over maps, practicing the language, handling gear and discussing it, talking tactics, and swapping war stories. Lunch was brought to them by a very pretty young girl, perhaps ten, in bright diamond-patterned cloth with a scarf over her chestnut hair. She smiled and blushed and gave them a flat bowl of mutton and lentil pies. "*Sta na shukria,*" Kyle said. She giggled and left.

The only odd part of the day was the constant prayers. Five times a day, everyone bowed to the southwest where Mecca was and prayed.

"That's a lot of time used up," Kyle said.

"And keeps them subservient. The nutcases make use of that."

"Yeah. Remember the plane flight and the map?"

"Exactly," Wade said.

Kyle leaned close and spoke softly, "Do you notice anything odd about Bait?"

"You mean that he's always watching us and has beady eyes?" Wade replied.

"So it's not just me."

"No, I see it, too. I think he's the real contact here."

"So why isn't he open about it?" Kyle asked.

"Dunno. Bears watching though. Or he could just be curious."

"Could be," Kyle admitted. He didn't believe it. The man looked at them every time he passed by. Either he'd never seen Americans before, or he wanted something.

Or maybe he was just eager to have the shot taken. Perhaps he'd lost family in the war? Many had.

Kyle and Wade were busy enough reviewing maps and texts, and Qalzai and his men returned around dinnertime. They couldn't converse much. Khushal gave them what he could. They would rise early, and then would travel again and work on the shot. That seemed reasonable, and they nodded agreement.

As it grew dusky, the sun leaving violet streaks over the plains to the west, they rolled out their bedding, set their gear for easy access, and tried to sleep.

The hut they were in was crude but weatherproof. The blocks were tight against wind and the corrugated sheet-metal roof kept potential elements at bay. The floor was earth, but packed hard enough from years of use to be almost concrete. There was a faint smell of goat. Still, they decided to swap off on watch, cradling the loaded M-4. Kyle paced quietly, far back from the lone window, occasionally sneaking a peek through a chink in the back door. That way were mountains and nothing else. Out front was the courtyard, plunged in deep shadows with little going on, except the occasional person walking through to the latrine out back. An occasional passing vehicle overheard outside—he counted only three in four hours, and one of those a donkey-drawn cart—was the limit of activity. He scratched at his scraggly, growing beard. It was one more minor annoyance that wouldn't go away.

When he swapped off with Wade at 0200, he was drained from the tension, and managed to sleep easily.

Still tired and aching, they cleaned up with baby wipes and headed out. Qalendar nodded from across the small compound where the others were, and soon Qalzai and Khushal joined them. Qalendar stayed behind and the four walked into town. Kyle was nervous as hell about leaving the weapon unattended, and said so to Wade.

"Yes, but we've got to show some trust. Besides, I've got the bolt and the ammo," he said.

"Yes," Kyle said. "But I signed for the damned thing. This is very nonreg."

"So it is," Wade agreed. "So's the whole mission. But if we make a point of always leaving one of us by the truck, everyone will figure out in a hurry that there is something there of interest to the Americans. Guarding the truck is good. Only us guarding the truck is bad."

"You're right," Kyle admitted. "But I still don't like it."

"Neither do I," Wade said. "I've got to keep the radio with me. That's even more accountable than the rifle."

"True." The encryption hardware for SINCGARS was something any foreign government would pay a fortune for. It wasn't excessively large, but had to be carried at all times. Wade had a small, nondescript canvas bag to tote it in.

Dawn had brought activity, and the townspeople were bustling with their day's activities. There were cries from peddlers, occasional curses from teamsters wrestling carts or trucks through the narrow accesses, and smells of animals and food. "Very Middle Ages," Kyle commented.

"Except for the Mercedes diesels, yes," Wade replied with a wry smile.

"I dunno. Looking at the shape that sucker is in," Kyle said as he pointed at one such, "I could believe it's five hundred years old."

"Nah, not more than two hundred. It still has unrusted sections."

"That's due to the dry climate," Kyle replied. This was fun.

"You win," Wade conceded.

Indicating with a tilt of his head, Kyle said, "Those hills are just as impressive from this side."

Wade said, "Yeah. Greener than Nevada, about like northern New Mexico. Or maybe parts of the Arizona desert, but more bush and less cactus."

"What's that sound?" Kyle asked.

"Hold on," Wade said, and cocked an ear. It was a repetitive, rhythmic droning. "I think that's a classroom."

As they walked the noise grew, and became discernible as a chant of children. It did sound like a classroom, not a mosque.

Wade said, "Yup, right in there," and pointed with a head tilt. They'd both become very good at not waving fingers around in just a very few days.

Through the open door they could see the stereotypical schoolmarm, except dressed in a full dress and with her head covered. Like many in the region, she wasn't subtle. Her dress was purple with a shawl of checked blue and yellow, and her sleeves were embroidered as well. She was scribbling squiggly phrases on a blackboard and coaching young children through them.

"That's a good sign, in this area," Wade said.

"Yup. Best chance to end the paranoid theory that the Religion of Peace has to blow up every other group on earth."

"It's weird," Wade said. "Since we got in theater, everyone has been kind, generous, decent. No one has mentioned you being white or me being black. We're Americans, we're not Muslim and they know it, and no one treats us badly because of it."

"Yeah, it only takes a few assholes to make an entire nation look bad. Like this scum we're going to bag."

"Or Congress," Wade added.

Kyle laughed, deeply but quietly. "We aren't supposed to think seditious thoughts like that, my friend."

"What sedition? I'm talking treason."

"As long as it's just talk," Kyle said.

"Oh, sure. I'll trust the political process. But I'm sure you agree there's a few honorable members of Congress who'd look better as a billboard ad for the benefits of life insurance."

"Yeah, and if we all did that to our own tastes, we'd have no Congress left."

"I don't see what your problem is," Wade replied, deadpan.

This time they both laughed.

They found an actual restaurant, and had scrambled eggs for breakfast with fresh flat bread. The tea was strong and very sweet.

It was better than coffee, Kyle thought. Tasted lighter and cleaner, had caffeine but it wasn't the kind that gave shakes nearly as much. He remembered in time not to insult the staff by leaving a tip—it implied that they weren't paid enough. He did pay for all of them, and Qalzai hugged his thanks.

Back out on the street, the day was in full swing. There were numerous and varied people running around, some locals, some obviously transported refugees from Afghanistan. They were identifiable by the scrawny children. There was a boy of possibly five who might manage twenty pounds. Sad. And propaganda aside, the blame for that was purely on the Taliban for not letting the nation advance out of the Dark Ages. There simply wasn't enough food, distribution, or education to operate. Reading scripture was a good thing, in Kyle's view. Reading nothing but scripture, and doing nothing but read it, was a waste of life.

Back at the farm, while the men went out with their local cousin to ask questions, Kyle and Wade slept in shifts all afternoon, catching up from the draining travel. It was comfortably warm in the hut, if dusty. The little farmstead had a well and cistern that gave enough pressure to shower with under a bronze head well encrusted with scale and green with verdigris. But there was real soap, and they got clean. The women and children washed their clothes and kept them fed.

They used the well to fill up the five-gallon can they'd brought for the purpose. Once done, they siphoned the water through a filter and decanted it to their CamelBaks and canteens, then refilled the can for later use. They weren't about to risk untreated water here, even after typhoid shots. If necessary, they had water treatment tablets, but those didn't improve the taste any. Filtered was their choice.

The men all returned in time for dinner, and curried chicken over rice was served. They'd smelled it all day.

"You know," Wade said, "if these people opened a restaurant in New Orleans, they'd have people flocking."

"Yeah, it's good," Kyle agreed, throat worn rough from cumin and eyes watering. Holy crap, but it was hot. He'd had south-Texas ass-burner chili that didn't come close. But Wade was packing it away with ease. Kyle consoled himself with the thought that it would come out as corrosive as it went in, and Wade wouldn't be so calm then.

But he did thank their hostess, Noora, and her daughters. He'd seen the scrawny old chickens they had to work with, yet the meat in the dish was tender and juicy. They had to have been stewing it for a week to get it that soft. And under the heat it had been tasty, far more so than the beans and rice they'd boiled or had cold en route.

That evening, they went out for another walk. The town rose up from the valley floor to the hillside where they were. Everything was dun and brown under pale green and straw growth. The buildings were amazingly like Southwestern adobe buildings. Form followed function, Kyle guessed. They were roofed in tile, sheet metal, or occasionally wood.

The streets weren't in a grid, but wandered around. Between rickshas, carts, wagons, horses, donkeys, occasional Bactrian camels and pedestrians, even the late evening quiet kept them alert.

Something made Kyle stop for just a moment. He cocked his head and listened. "What was that?" he asked.

"I didn't hear anything," Wade said.

"Wait," Kyle said.

Wade nodded silently.

"There it is again," Kyle whispered. It was a hissing crack followed by a muffled, whimpering cry.

"Down the alley. Watch it and stay clear," Wade warned.

They stepped past the dark tunnel carefully, peering into the darkness. Then the noise came again. Suddenly, the shadows resolved as an image, and Kyle flinched.

He wasn't sure exactly what was going on, but he did know that hitting a woman was unacceptable to him, and, as far as he knew, unacceptable to Muslims. As far as flogging and kicking and punching and ripping at her robe was concerned, he wasn't going to stand for it no matter the local customs. He sized up the terrain quickly. It had trash cans, piled crates and pallets, some cardboard boxes, and a heap of something. There was enough room to maneuver, and it looked clear enough otherwise.

He slipped down the alley quietly but with haste, grabbed a good position behind the short, little asshole, and went to town.

Kyle knew how to "fight like a man." He also knew it was usually a good way to lose, and that this punk didn't deserve it. His first punch slammed the man in the kidney enough to make him stagger and cry out. He smashed his boot toe into an ankle, then spun the figure around and caught him a stiff hook up into the guts.

His victim dry-heaved and his eyes bugged out. Kyle took that as a sign, and pasted his left fist into the right eye, knowing it would bruise his knuckles and not caring. He followed with a right across the jaw, and a symbolic kick to the groin. He had near eight inches on the man, probably fifty pounds, and was in top shape. The snaggle-toothed little cretin tumbled back and struck his head on the wall and collapsed unconscious, broken and bleeding in the dust and grit.

"*Tsanga ye?*" he asked to the shifting form on the ground. How are you feeling? "*Ye doctor larem?*" He knew it was atrociously ungrammatical, but it was the best he could do.

A woman's voice replied. He caught "okay," "Allah" and "You (something) good." Then she continued in accented but clear English, "Are you English?"

Wade hissed behind him, "Dude, this isn't our fight!" and he laid a restraining arm back.

"We speak English," he said. It wasn't as if they could really deny it, but there was no need to admit a home country. There were Aussies and Brits here, not to mention a lot of Indian and South African traders who spoke English. It wasn't much of a cover, but it wasn't an admission.

"Thank you," she said simply. "I am grateful to you."

"What was that about?" he asked. He got a look at her now. Her face was red over the right eye, and would swell. Her lip was cut slightly, and had an ebon drop clinging. Other than that she was disheveled and dirty. Her attacker was still unconscious, though he wiggled slightly and moaned, so was obviously alive. That was Kyle's only concern.

"I am a schoolteacher," she said. "Some of the more . . . conservateef immigrants and refugees object to me teaching modern things. I've been harassed before, but never attacked." He recognized her then. It was the woman they'd seen in class the day before.

"Do you need a doctor?" he asked. She was rising now, and he gave her a hand up.

"I have only bruises," she said. "Besides, most doctors won't touch a woman, and I have no man to allow it."

It took a moment for that to sink in. If she wasn't married or a daughter of someone, it would be hard for her to do anything. The Taliban-imposed customs required permission from a man, and without that she was not human, not to be dealt with. Kyle got angry all over again. The Taliban were officially gone, but their stink remained. Even across the border in Pakistan.

"We can find you a doctor," he insisted. He wasn't sure where, but he'd find one if he had to jam a pistol up someone's nose.

"Really, I am okay," she said. "I am bruised and sore, nothing else."

A scheme began to form in Kyle's brain. "Do you speak other languages?" he asked.

"Yes," she agreed. "Hindustani, Pashto, Dari, and French. I went to college in France. Before the Taliban I was a professor of economics. Now all I can do is teach children, but I will do that no matter the beatings. They must be taught!"

The shock was getting to her at last. She was babbling and shaking. That was actually a good sign.

"We need a translator. Could you help us?" he asked.

Wade was covering the mouth of the alley, but overheard. "Oh, no way!" he hissed. "You're going to get us killed!"

"But it's perfect!" Kyle argued. "As a local woman, no one will notice her. And with a woman along, we're less obviously an aggressive force. She can help us get set up, then we can give her some money or something to help with the school."

"Translate?" she asked. "Don't you have a translator?"

Kyle agreed that it was an odd situation. "He died, apparently, before we got here, and our company couldn't find another one in time."

"I see," she said, slightly frostily. "An odd company that is so eager to do things that it can't wait for a translator." She sounded amused but disconcerted.

"Very odd," he agreed. "Will you do it?"

"For how long?" she asked. "I'll need to let the parents know, and find someone to teach, and someone to protect them. You'll need to pay for that."

"We can pay, we're on an expense account," he said. He wasn't sure how much she had in mind, but it couldn't be much in American money.

"Very well," she said. "I am Nasima."

"I'm Kyle Monroe," he said. He was about to stick out his hand to take hers, but realized she hadn't offered it. Instead, she bowed very slightly, eyes cast down. Right. No touching of women at all.

"Wade Curtis," Wade said, and she bowed to him, too.

"Can you meet us at the inn tomorrow morning at nine?" Kyle asked. "And we'll head out from there." He gave her the name and street.

"I can," she said. "Don't mention me in public, though. Modesty is essential, especially with my position."

"Sure, we try to be sensitive to local customs," he agreed. "Can we help you home?" he asked.

"Thank you, but no," she said firmly. "I must not be seen with men unless properly escorted. Especially now. I will see you tomorrow, Kyle and Wade."

"*Shpa dey pe khair,*" he said.

"Goodnight to you, too, dudes," she said, smiling. The effect was spoiled by the blood on her lip.

After she left, Wade said, "I think it's a mistake."

"Wade, we need a translator. She's available," Kyle said.

"I'm sure if we ask around we can find a man who won't be so obvious, and who won't bother the locals. How did we meet her? Oh, yes, she was being beaten by a man for the crime of existing." The sarcasm was clear in his voice.

"So we'll cover for her. It doesn't seem to be a big deal in the cities, it's just the hicks who are the problem."

"Yes," Wade said, "and it's those hicks we have to deal with."

"Well, for now, she's who we have."

8

THE ARGUMENT WAS IN REMISSION, THOUGH NOT
gone the next morning. They walked across the street for breakfast, not sure if she'd actually be there. She might have decided to
simply avoid them.

But Nasima was there, and cleaner than the night before. Her
dress was vertical stripes of black and purple, with a black-edged
head scarf printed in geometric reds and yellows. Whatever the re-
quirements of dress here, they didn't let themselves be drab. Her
black hair was clean and hung over her shoulders past the cloth, and
she rose to meet them, bowing slightly.

They nodded back and sat. With her was a man, fiftyish and lean.
His hair was largely gray, bald on top, and all of it kept short, including his beard and moustache. "This is Kamgar," she said. "He
owns the school."

"*Assalam u alaikum,*" Kyle said with a nod.

"*Wa alaikum u ssalam,*" he replied with a broad, friendly grin.

"I will need money," she said, "and you must pay Kamgar, or
some of these people will think I am a prostitute."

"Right," Kyle said. "How much?"

"Five hundred American dollars," she said. "Or afghanis or rupees to equal it." She looked ready to defend the demand.

Considering the standard of living here, it was a high rate, but
reasonable for professional consulting, Kyle decided, especially in
light of the risk involved. And hell, Uncle Sam could afford it.

"Sure," he said, and waved his hands a bit. "But let us pretend to
make small talk first. Can I get you some breakfast?" he asked in
English, pointing at food and making an open-armed gesture to the
table.

Kamgar agreed, grinning comfortably. Everyone was as they said they were, and they all relaxed. Kyle was still glad to be armed. There was no way to know who people were around here, with assorted tribes, the war with India to the east, Afghan refugees, black market dealers . . .

Shortly, they had all eaten, cash had been exchanged, Allah praised, and a letter provided introducing Nasima as the servant of the school's owner, working for the two Americans and an honorable Muslima. She should be treated as a lady and given leeway to speak for the foreign guests. It seemed professional enough and clear for the local customs, and everyone was happy. It didn't quite seem like Kyle was renting a mule.

They walked back across the street to the hotel, Nasima following. She was short, Kyle realized, maybe five feet two. A slip of a woman by Western standards, maybe a hundred pounds. More of the poor diet, he presumed. But it hadn't affected her mind, if she had a PhD in economics from a Western university, nor her looks. She was a gorgeous combination of Indian, Caucasian, and Persian with a hint of Chinese. Her almond eyes were deep and mesmerizing.

Khushal was waiting for them. "He's one of our party, and watches our gear," Kyle said.

"I understand," she said. At once, she introduced herself and chattered away. Khushal looked confused, then a bit disturbed. He replied slowly.

"He says he's glad for a translator. But I feel he's not thrilled with the idea. His father is in charge?"

"Well, that depends," Kyle said. "I'm in charge, he's the local guide for our project. I do take his advice."

"I see. By the way, what is your project here?" she asked.

"It's a military mission," he said. He'd decided he had to tell her that much. "We're looking for some specific information for a study."

"I understand," she said. It was clear she wasn't going to leave it at that, but would for the time being.

A few minutes later, there was a familiar knock at the door. Wade nodded, Khushal opened it, and Qalzai came in with Bait, his assistant. At once, they spoke. Qalzai looked up at Nasima, at Kyle and Wade, and started to speak.

He made it clear he wasn't happy with a woman along. Nasima translated easily for him. "He says I'm a woman and have no place in the battles of men."

"Well, tell him if he can find us a good English speaker, I'll leave you behind, but I'm not doing this mission unless I've got someone who can help us," Kyle replied. What was the problem? It seemed to be more than the gender issue. They seemed uncomfortable that he was showing initiative.

Nasima turned back and rapid-fired Pashto at Qalzai. She held her body so as to indicate she was the poor, meek feminine underling he expected, but there was steel in her voice. She'd play the local game to get the job done and teach her kids, but it was only a game to her. Kyle was developing a lot of respect for this young lady. There was no way in hell he'd play the slave for these people, or for anyone else.

He realized that she'd have a much easier life in one of the larger cities, which were much more modern and Westernized, and that she liked where she was and what she was doing.

His musing was interrupted when Nasima turned back and said, "He says I can come along until the last part of the mission and then must stay behind, and that you are responsible for me. The word he used isn't 'father' or 'husband' but more like 'keeper.'"

"Isn't that so thoughtful and modern of him?" Kyle muttered. "Agreed," he said. "So let's stock up on food and supplies and get to it."

"Very well. Kyle?" she asked, "what is it we are to do?" She'd already asked, but he'd clearly been evasive.

"Oh, I'm leaving that one to you, boss," Wade said, chuckling nervously.

Feeling a flush of embarrassment, Kyle said, "First, we're going to find someone."

"And then?" she asked, looking curious and distrustful.

"And then I'm going to shoot him," he said. He realized he had some defiance in his voice. What about it, lady?

She paused for only a moment. "Very well. So long as I know."

They were saddled back up within the hour, and rolling west. Nasima sat in back on one of the spare tires. The others introduced themselves, gave her nods of acknowledgment that were a mix of surly, friendly, and gallant, and then kept quiet.

The hills would continue through the area around Quetta, a sizeable town, where they hoped to get some intel. They'd avoid the town proper and hit the outskirts. There was no need to court official notice by the government.

It was very disturbing, Kyle thought, that Qalzai was their only source of information. They had nothing current from American sources. Who had ultimately planned this mission, and what were they basing it on?

Sighing, he leaned back in the cramped seat and tried to relax. Hopefully, it would all make sense afterward.

He wasn't really asleep, more just zoned, when he heard what was obviously a curse from Qalzai, then from the others.

"What?" he asked.

Qalzai steered the truck off the rocky road in a hurry, shouted something, of which the soldiers caught, *"Lar!"* Quickly. There wasn't really anywhere to hide, the hills steep and straight, the growth low. Kyle moved for what concealment there was, trying not to jump to frightening conclusions.

They were urged out, and Shamsuddin, Mirza, and Ajmal joined them. All their gear was tossed over the side, everyone gathered up an armful, and they ran for cover in the rocky terrain. As soon as they were clear, Qalzai took off, tires spinning on the shingly surface. Nasima was with him.

"What the hell?" Kyle asked.

"I think," Wade said, "I saw the edge of a tank over the next ridge. Might be a convoy."

"Ah, hell," Kyle said. "Last thing we need." He could hear a rumbling and the clank of road wheels. The occasional revving diesel confirmed that it was a line of military vehicles.

Mirza was saying what was obviously "Quiet!" as they ducked low behind rock.

Kyle looked around. Wade had the .50 and the M-4 in addition to his ruck. Kyle had his ruck and someone's old Russian rig and an AK. Shamsuddin had Kyle's briefcase and laptop. Ajmal was invisible behind a pile of valises and bags. It appeared everything threatening was accounted for.

They sat there silently, not daring to speak, while the convoy rattled past. Qalzai and Khushal had driven on, with Bait, Qalendar, and the others. And Nasima. Kyle assumed they intended to return after the convoy was gone, but still felt very lonely all of a sudden.

The convoy was a tank, a couple of M-113s, four cargo haulers, and two jeeplike technical vehicles. The troops were professional, but bored, and apparently hadn't seen fit to stop Qalzai. Of course, finding two Americans along would likely have changed that.

Once it had passed, they all sat facing each other, waiting quietly until the valve clatter of the truck returned, and Qalzai's voice called out. They rose, trooped down the hill lugging their gear, and clambered back aboard.

They rumbled along in the cramped vehicle for several more hours. It was near dark when they could see the glow of a city ahead. It wasn't bright, but it was definitely civilization. It was something familiar to Kyle and Wade, and helped them relax.

Quetta was large enough to have modern conveniences, including hotels. It also had an Army base. They detoured wide around it, with a glimpse of a perfect turquoise lake in the middle of desert mountains to the east. Once clear around to the west of the city, they sought a smaller town, Bemana'abad.

While small, it was modern enough. There were modern signs, paved roads, and some light industry. There was working electricity and lights, and quite a few more cars, though most were old and rattly and animal power was still very common. Small stores were scattered along the street as they headed in, mixed with houses and small industrial shops. There was a major marketplace, with gorgeous tile work in blue over the arches and columns of obvious Islamic architecture. The blue was lapis lazuli, which was native to the area and not many other places. Street vendors pushed their way through the evening crowds. As they drove through, Kyle thought longingly about a proper shower and clean clothes. But they had to blend in, so he killed the idea.

"Let's spend some money for good will," Kyle decided on impulse. "Qalzai, *ghuaram kheh otel.*" Nice hotel. He flashed the corners of a handful of rupees, keeping it low and discreet. "Was that correct?" he asked Nasima.

"*Ah, hoo. Sta na shukria!*" Qalzai said, all grins. The rest of them lit up, too.

"No," said Nasima, "but I understood your intention. Money translates universally."

They were a sight. While remote, Bemana'abad was a town, it had a government and business. They were hillbillies in Des Moines, and looked very out of place. And weapons were not encouraged here. Still, they made it inside, Kyle paid for two to a room, with a room at the end for Nasima, and they headed down a long bricked walk to their lodgings.

The water was cold, but clean, the heater lacking the capacity for a large crowd. There was a lamp in the room. No TV, of course, but there was a radio, all in languages the two didn't speak. The facilities were shared with the entire hallway, and were typically Eastern. But the mattresses were clean and modern, and Kyle and Wade were both able to stretch out, sleep unfettered, and their only sop to security was to sleep with loaded pistols and the M-4 between them, there being only one bed. "Just don't grip that trigger late at night," Kyle joked.

"It won't be the trigger I grip, trust me," Wade replied. But he pointed the muzzles at the foot of the bed, rather than the head, just in case.

The next morning they were all much refreshed. Khushal sat down with them at the laptop, while Qalzai stood behind them. Nasima arrived, and they left the door open for reasons of "modesty."

Nasima looked furtively around to make sure no one was in the hallway, moved in close and said quietly, her eye on Khushal's back, "The man whose name in English is what you use to fish is an Afghan, not Pakistani. He moved here a few years ago."

"Okay?" Wade prompted while looking at the computer. "Hell," he said. "Not working." He examined the case, which had a huge ding. As it had been in a nylon carrying case during the rush out of the truck, it had been one hell of a smack.

Kyle sighed and jiggled the battery. He tried the external power. Rebooting, sliding drives out and back. "Near as I can tell, the hard drive is damaged," he said. "No way to get that fixed here."

"Or rather," Wade said, "there might be, but not quickly, and it would make it *very* obvious that two Americans are here, and all the data on the disk would be unsecure while a tech looked at it."

"Right. So we can't fix it here. Dammit, must have been when we bailed out of the truck. Was it that rough a landing?"

"Oh, yes. We hit the ground pretty hard," Wade said.

"Hell. So we smash the drive and dispose of the pieces . . . okay, Nasima, what about that man?" Fish with Bait. Right. And she didn't want to say his name where it might be overheard.

"I don't trust him," she said. "He's not part of the clan, and he's very condescending, even by local standards."

"That's disturbing," Wade said, while doing another check of the laptop, just in case. "We'll keep it in mind. Anything specific?"

"No," she said. "But I have a feeling he's not right. I know it sounds silly."

"Not at all," Kyle said. "We work that way, too. Thanks for the input."

"You are most welcome, and do be careful," she said.

They tried to hash out what details they could. They were waiting here for more info, apparently, no more than a day, then they would go west again. They had an approximate area for their target, and Qalzai was sure that was the right place.

"Well," said Kyle, "it's only money, we might as well stay right here until we hear more. We can afford it."

"Sure," Wade said. "I think we might have been a bit obvious when we showed up, but staying won't hurt anything, and might give the impression we're U.N. types or reporters. Next time, let's bring cameras to use as cover."

"Good idea," Kyle agreed. He thought for a moment and said, "Very good idea, actually. We should suggest that."

"Let's suggest they send an entire squad, or better intel, or just bomb the hell out of somewhere instead," Wade said.

"True," Kyle nodded. They were discreet, certainly. But he wasn't sure how effective they could be. And two men alone in hostile territory was still bringing back memories he didn't want.

"Whatever," he said finally. "Let's get Khushal to sit the gear, and take a look around. We need to get acclimated, and not just be trained monkeys for these guys." Dammit, he wanted more intel. Nasima was helpful, but it still felt as if he was a hireling to the locals, not a soldier with an independent command.

"There is that," Wade agreed. "Okay, let's do it."

Khushal was agreeable, and they promised to bring him back a Coca-Cola. He might be a militia fighter, but he was also a teenager, and travel into this part of the country was an adventure to him. He had a small camera he'd bought earlier that day, and intended to record the mission. Both Qalzai and Kyle had cautioned him not to take photos of any of their people or gear, only of the surrounding areas.

The two men dressed in cleaned clothes, had Khushal help them wrap their lungees and drop the tails across their faces, and headed out into the nightlife of Baluchistan Province.

The city had a liveliness to it. Even late at night with the vendors gone, there were tea houses open, and restaurants. Parties here and there celebrated weddings or births, some buildings decorated with colored lights like those for Christmas trees.

It was becoming familiar. That brought its own dangers, of course. Familiarity breeds contempt, and there were hundreds of cultural cues the two of them would miss. Much like tourists learn to feel safe in New York, London, or Havana, only to be caught by a mugger or gang by missing obvious local hints. Still, the look around helped them acclimate further. They were trained enough to stay cautious.

Kyle decided he'd never acclimate to the beard. It was still itching. Sighing, he scratched at it as they walked.

THE NEXT MORNING, BAIT AND QALZAI KNOCKED ON
their door early, excited. Soon, the entire clan was gathered
around. Nasima arrived at a run, in a long skirt and sweater in dark
brown. Practical for the terrain. "They say we are ready," she said.
"We head northeast again, very close to the border, and into lower
hills. The man we seek is in a village there."

"Sounds good," Kyle said. "Wade, call and tell them."

"Right," Wade nodded. He dialed a number and reported in, location, destination, current conditions.

They loaded up the truck again, and rolled out. They did, in fact,
look like yokels, even in this small town. It was obvious to all that
they were poor farm folk on some kind of errand. Good, Kyle
thought. Better to be thought hicks than killers. There'd been a lot
of creepy and scary happenings so far, but no real pucker factor.

He hoped it stayed that way.

The ride took all that day. On the plus side, they'd bought a
cooler in town, and filled it with fresh food, including apples, ba-
nanas—imported at some expense—and sandwiches rolled in the local bread. Everyone was much happier, and grinned at their guests
as crumbs fell from their beards.

"They say you can join their missions anytime," Nasima said, "if
you arrange the hotels and food."

"Tell them they're welcome, and we're glad to be able to do them
a small favor for all the help they're giving us," he said.

After the meal, they resumed the aching, bouncing ride. It was
near dark when they stopped and pulled behind some concealing
scrub. At once, the men emptied out the cab and laid cloths over the
windows.

"I will sleep here," Nasima said. "They're being polite."

"No problem," Kyle agreed. It did make sense socially. He just hoped they didn't need to leave in a hurry, with gear left piled in the bed to fall out. "Can you ask Qalzai for a mission update?"

"Yes," she said, and turned and chattered. Qalzai deferred to Bait, who seemed to leer. He had odd expressions, sneers, snarls, and leers, that didn't match his pleasant demeanor. Or pleasant enough to the Americans. Nasima apparently wasn't finding him so. But she turned back and said, "We're in the area. We will look for him tomorrow," she said.

"Got it, and thanks. Wade, call up and update them. We'll let them know after we get the kill."

"On it," he said, whipping out the phone. He was through and back off in moments.

As they prepared a sleeping area, the air chilling quickly in the dark, Wade asked, "What I want to know is why they need us? They're brave enough, have the weapons and intel. Why can't they wax this jerk?"

"I dunno," Kyle replied, pondering. "Maybe Uncle Sam wants the credit. Maybe they're afraid of some feud. Or maybe they can't get close enough for a good shot. It is unusual, though."

" 'Ours not to reason why,' " Wade said.

"Right. Time to sleep."

They were up before dawn, and patrolling on foot. Tired from little sleep, weighted under their rucks, the two men cursed silently as they followed the locals into the "lower" hills. Kyle and Wade were trained and experienced, but these people moved like mountain goats. In short order, they were wheezing and huffing.

"I'm going to cheat," Kyle said to Wade. Turning to Nasima, he said, "Call a break. We need to report in."

Everyone squatted down to wait, while Wade took his own sweet time about making the call, and reported to the AWACS on station that they were commencing their recon of the target. After that, he faked it for a few moments, asking about Yankee scores to a dead phone. Nasima grinned but didn't say anything, and after catching their breath, they stood to continue.

Their breath steamed out in front, as if puffed from locomotives. It was dark, in the forties, and while they had lots of experience hiking, it was harder in local garb over terrain that was so unfamiliar.

They broke at sunrise, and brewed tea over a small British trioxane stove that might have been fifty years old. Kyle and Wade were glad of it, and wrapped their hands around their canteen cups. It was tasty tea, with sugar and some undefined spice. Cardamom, perhaps. Qalendar was a gourmet. It refreshed and revived them, and a few nibbles of sweetened bread helped immensely.

Then they were back to it, as the sun bled over the hills and dripped down on them. Ghostly wisps of mist arose from the dew, and burned off as the temperature rose.

Bait led out in front, looking for signs of patrols and other threats. Qalzai brought up the rear. Nasima and the snipers were safely ensconced in the middle, which did relieve some of the worries, of loose rocks, discovery, and other threats.

They scrambled up and down slopes, across old, wind-weathered sheets of rock, and past jutting shards. As the sun rose, it became warm enough for them to unbutton their coats. Then it got warm and sweaty. The wool and cotton breathed, but still insulated. That was fine when it was near freezing, but not above fifty degrees while exercising hard.

Straps cut into their shoulders, adding aches to the mix. The rigs were comfortable certainly, but seventy pounds plus each was a staggering load. They were glad to have left the extraneous gear at the truck.

"Doing okay, buddy?" Kyle asked between breaths.

"Passable. You?" he replied.

"Yeah." It was all the reply Kyle could manage.

They ate dried goat en route, and Kyle passed around the last three MREs. He still wasn't keen about sharing germs with this crowd—they all dug their spoons into the same package—as none of them had bathed recently, and didn't seem worried about it in general. But they were all in the same unit, so it was good for morale. The dried fruit and gorilla cookies went over well, and the coffee was shared at lunch. They were all hunkered in a small ravine against discovery. Though if they were sighted, it was crap for a defensive position. Bait walked off during lunch, waving as he did so. They finished without him, and the men lit cigarettes.

Bait returned within the hour and conferred with Qalzai. Nasima translated from Qalzai, "The man we want is in this camp. We'll have to wait for a good time to get a shot."

"Excellent," Kyle said, a feeling in his stomach like that of a giant rat scrabbling. This was what they'd come for. So why did it seem so problematic?

Probably because there hadn't been any problems.

It still could be a setup, to embarrass America, or to put them in a bad political position. Kyle realized he should have asked more questions Stateside—how had this mission come about, and who had set it up?

"He says he'll take you up there in time for the shot," Nasima said, interrupting his thoughts.

"Tell him I need to reconnoiter the area first, so we know what our escape routes look like."

They argued over a plan. Kyle found it annoying. While these men were more local to the area than he, he was the professional. They didn't seem to grasp that a good escape was dependent upon knowing the local map, surface, and features. They actively fought against preparation, saying they were worried about discovery. Kyle told them that was the point of having Wade and him along; concealment was what they did. It took nearly an hour to get the point across. Apparently, the local method of fighting was to take cover, throw as much lead as possible until one side or the other quit, and leave. Their bravery and dedication were excellent. They weren't strong on tactics or discipline.

Luckily it was a warm day, over sixty degrees. Considering the altitude of nearly a half mile, and the fall season, it was a blessing. Of course, it was also of use to their target. Kyle preferred cold, wet weather, mist, and calm air. But you worked with what you had.

While the debate took place, Wade slipped off to make a map anyway. Khushal went with him, grinning. Kyle saw it from the corner of his eye, and smiled inwardly. The man was a pro who needed only a hint. It was a pleasure to work with him.

But Kyle also needed that information himself, first hand. Finally, he got them to agree that they had to do it his way. He opened the case and assembled the Barrett while he spoke, hoping the sight of the massive rifle would encourage them.

Nasima argued his point while he turned to Wade and discussed their observations. They picked three routes down the mountain they felt they could handle. "We'll each take a different one up," Wade said. "You on one, me on another, Qalzai on a third. According to the map," he shuffled through the sheaf of them until he found the one they wanted, "there's a saddle right about there," he pointed up the slope, "that should give us a good position."

Grumbling, they split into three pairs, Kyle and Khushal, Wade and Mirza, Qalzai and Bait. Qalzai could read well enough to follow a map, and had a watch. They each tightened gear, dumped excess equipment, and prepared to ascend the rough slope, Kyle lugging the long mass of the Barrett in its tough bag. Nasima returned to the truck with the rest.

Kyle contented himself during the rough scramble with the thought that the mission was about to reach completion. Shortly, they'd be overlooking a camp and Kyle would take his shot. They'd extract quickly from a good range, find a place to recross the border, or call a chopper and be done with it.

The mission couldn't be this easy, he thought. On second thought, the terrain was anything but easy. They constantly slipped on dust-covered shelves. They were sweating and panting. It was dry, and the sun cooked moisture out of them as sweat and the wind sucked it off their skin. It kept them cool now that they'd removed their coats, but greased them with dust and parched their throats.

He was having second thoughts the whole way. Good thoughts, then bad. He took several slow, measured breaths to refresh himself. This was a bitch of a climb.

A big part of it was the scrubby terrain. Almost any other terrain like it would have tree roots and such he could grip. Here, it was scrub with very shallow, thready roots, and rock. He was glad they'd split up, and he hoped the others had an easier time. They'd need a fast descent against incoming fire.

When he finally reached the saddle and peeked over, he could see Wade already there. Or rather, he couldn't. Wade was a shapeless lump of dun and dusty burlap in his ghillie suit. Kyle crawled out farther and saw Qalzai's element, too. He was last. That was fine, that meant the other routes were easier. He started dragging his own camouflage out.

Wade said, "We'll take my route down. Easy descent with a gully and lots of grip."

"Glad to hear it," Kyle said, panting. He sucked down some more water.

"No problem. And I found a spot to shoot."

"Even better," Kyle agreed. "Show me."

Wade had found a fine location. It was just below the military crest, in a dip between two rocks, and had a panoramic view out across the plain. The sun was to their left, so there'd be no reflection off a scope. All in all, it looked good.

And two thousand meters away, in a long, lazy arc, was the camp they sought.

"That is a long-ass shot," Kyle commented. At that range, he'd be shooting a two-meter circle. Getting the human body in that two-meter circle was going to take several quick, precise shots and some luck. Otherwise, they'd have to extract and do it again.

"Will be," Wade said. "Are you up to it?"

"I think so," he said, squinting and taking in the whole scene. "Good weapon, good rest, plenty of time. But we've got to get him to hold still long enough, or in a vehicle I can nail."

"Right, so let's set up our exfiltration."

The two looked back along Wade's route. "If we're going down there, we've got good cover. But we'll need supporting fire in case of disasters."

"I see a spot," Kyle said.

Qalzai was quietly jabbering away. Wade shook his head. "I don't think he understands the concept still."

Growling in frustration, though under his breath so their host wouldn't be offended, Kyle turned with what he hoped was an eager look on his face.

"We aren't just going to blaze away," he told Qalzai. "*Delta intazar?*" he said, trying to say "wait." "*Ghuarum arama loya tiga.*" That was as close as he could get. *I'm looking for a quiet rock.*

As they started reconnoitering the area, Qalzai seemed to understand. He pointed out several well-hidden areas. Though that wasn't quite what the two snipers wanted. Qalzai looked confused as they seemed to retreat slightly from the area, along the route they'd be departing.

"There," Wade said. "Easy to reach and solid cover."

"Good," Kyle said. "And we can keep it under fire from there."

"Right. Now to explain to our host. Any ideas?"

"I think so," Kyle said. He turned to Qalzai and indicated several areas in turn. "*Yau negdey loya tiga. Yau porta korner. Dua pe manz ke.*" One at the rock, one above the bend, and two inside the cut in the cliff. It was amazing, he reflected, how much one could convey with fewer than fifty words.

He couldn't remember the phrase he wanted, and the closest in the ratty, dog-eared phrase book in his pocket was, "*Lutfan lag saber waka.*" *Please wait a while. We need to be patient.*

Qalzai seemed to be with the program now, and indicated the lower positions to the three men. He would take the nearest. Bait was apparently unhappy at being at the bottom. He wanted to see. Sighing, Kyle relented. "I think he's got some kind of grudge," he said to Wade.

"Seems like."

They snuggled close to the rocks and looked through binoculars and scopes. Bait had an old Russian pair that had seen better days, but whose optics were still good, even with a scratch or two. Kyle used the Schmidt binoculars, Wade had the spotting scope.

They waited in the sun for six hours, watching and learning. Kyle and Wade switched off on the scope to gather intel. They kept a log of comings and goings and drew a map. They estimated weather and atmospheric pressure, calculated what trajectory the bullet would describe, and what the sight picture should look like.

The camp was all men, so it was a militia operation. The tents were arranged in a box around a central area. That central area had a review stand. All the men were armed with AKs, and there were a few RPK machine guns, rocket-propelled grenades, and a mortar in evidence. Wade thought he saw what might be a recoilless rifle stashed under an awning. The vehicles were pickups, four-wheel drive, and two of them mounted machine guns, Russian 12.7mm heavies. The men moved around in such a way as to suggest they planned to move within the day. There was no immediate activity, but the vehicles were being checked, and some packing was taking place.

"So we wait more," Kyle said. "If they plan to move, they'll rally around the vehicles at some point. And if he sits and has to wait for a driver, even better." That would be an ideal shot, in fact.

Or what was happening now. The men pulled the trucks back from the cleared area, and gathered on foot. That left one truck with a clear bed. They formed a rough semicircle around it, and one man climbed up to stand erect and address them.

"That's him, he says," Wade confirmed.

"The tall guy in the blue turban with the brown coat?" Kyle asked. He wanted to be sure. The man didn't look a lot like the photos he'd been shown, but at this range, clothes and a beard change could easily mask features. He was clear enough in the scope, just small and distant.

There was another exchange and Kyle heard, "Yes, man, shoot," among it.

"Dammit, are we really sure?" he asked. He didn't like this at all. Something seemed wrong. He kept his eye to his scope and his stance easy and ready to shoot. If this was the wrong guy, they'd have a fight for nothing, possibly screw things up worse than they already were. If it was the right guy and he didn't shoot, they might not get another.

"Yes, do it," Wade said. "They're sure that's him and I showed them through the scope."

"Okay," Kyle said. He sighed, got as comfortable as he could, and zoned into his shooting trance. You had to trust the other guys to know their job, even if you thought they were idiots. If for no other reason than you couldn't do their job for them. He steadied down, aligned the reticle and calculated lead by eye. Breathe . . . squeeze . . . *Blam!*

Flight time was over a second, sound would take three seconds. There was time to take several shots, and Kyle did. In an instant, he had the reticle aligned again and shot dead center of mass on his target, then again, align and shoot, then three more rounds through the space filled by his body just to make sure. As he squeezed that last one, the first round hit.

Even at that range, the .50 packed more punch than most cartridges intended for cape buffalo or elephant. On a human figure it was overkill. The second round that hit the torso and the one that caught a waving wrist were redundant. He was blown into three pieces, all hanging together by bits of flesh, and collapsed in a gory heap.

His followers, troops, cheerleaders, whatever the hell they were, wasted no time in reacting.

They scattered, ducked, and began spraying with their AKs in seconds. One of them ran over, took a look at the shattered body, and squinted uphill. He yelled something undiscernible, but it was clearly something about large-caliber weapon and the ridge. "Right, let's move!" Kyle said. He'd seen enough. Kill was good, reaction was fast. It was time to leave posthaste.

The Barrett was a bitch to lug. Kyle took it, banging his knee hard as he hefted it and singeing hair off the back of his hand. He stuffed it into the long drag case, not worrying about any possible heat damage. Wade grabbed the scope. As they passed Qalzai, and Bait, the two fell in behind them. They passed Khushal and Mirza, who brought up the rear.

The locals were in hot pursuit, though. While they were well out of range still, that didn't stop fire from the Russian machine guns from ricocheting past them. Then someone opened up with one of the recoilless rifles. It was loud, potent, and blew chips from the hill.

Luckily, they were heading down fast, and the fire was well above them. But if anyone made it through a cut in the ridge, they'd have superior position to shoot down at them. Kyle felt an itch between his shoulders that he knew was psychosomatic. He was scared even if he didn't want to admit it aloud. Inside, however, he knew he was terrified. Bosnia all over again. The itch became a tickle, then an empty, exposed feeling all over. He slipped and the rifle landed atop him, knocking his breath out. He swore, stood carefully, despite a burning sensation in his thigh from sliding in gravel, and continued, breathing deeply and deliberately to avoid doing it from panic.

The run downhill was a roller-coaster ride without the roller coaster. As they hit the cut that would take them down, a mortar shell exploded behind them. The explosion rocked them with a *bang!* and threw rock around, the shockwave tugging at their breath.

Kyle swore as a rain of stinging pebbles came down, accompanied by a cloud of dust. The rifle was long and clunky and didn't fit well between the walls of the crevice they were descending. It was straight, but straight is a relative term when speaking of fissures in cliffs.

But he made it. They skidded and skittered over the sandy surface, suffering contusions and abrasions. Kyle skinned a knuckle and swore, banged his head and swore again. Then they were on a spreading slope and running fast, digging their feet in as brakes.

It would have been good, Kyle thought, to have had vehicles closer. But this would have to do. It was to be a high-speed sneak and exfiltrate across rough terrain.

The fire stopped for the time being, but would resume as soon as their pursuers hit the high ground. It would be wise to use that time to get away. Not hidden; knowing they were there would cause a search that would lead to discovery. This wasn't a fight they could win standing up, it was a fight to run from. They'd already made their kill.

For ten minutes, they scrabbled across the ground in the failing light. Dark would be good, though they couldn't assume the enemy didn't have night vision as well. Heedless of throats chilled by drafts of air, burning lungs, and aching guts, they pushed on. Any distance now was a good thing; there was little cover and no support to rally.

Then the enemy cleared the ridge and were shooting at them.

The fire was grossly inaccurate, but there was a sufficient volume of it. While beyond effective range, it was shot from a clear, elevated position. Kyle had thought himself worn out and unable to go faster, but suddenly found a burst of energy he hadn't expected. Incoming fire does that to a person, he thought, as a round cracked off a rock ten meters away. He was glad at that moment that Nasima wasn't along. Small and untrained, she'd be a liability and none too safe. He wondered why he was thinking about that now, as he grasped another ledge and swung over and generally down. He was still half exposed, but it would help.

He saw movement, realized they were bunching up and making

an inviting target for an area effect weapon. He was about to say so when Wade shouted, *"Shindel!,"* scatter, which was not in the phrase book, but had been on the CDROM of useful military phrases. Glancing around, the others fanned out and staggered their line.

Ahead, they could see the sharp bluff that led back to the road. They were safe, as long as they could make it there. Again urging speed into his burning thighs, Kyle swallowed between breaths, the spit cold and hard in his throat after the extreme effort.

They took the ledge far too fast. Wade was just ahead of him and slipped, grazing an elbow and abrading through his shirt. Blood seeped through whitened, raw skin, but he cursed a single word and kept on. Kyle slowed for that spot, and avoided injury with the exception of a toe jammed inside his boot. It was uncomfortable, but not really painful, especially in light of the dings to knuckles and knees, the strained shoulders and rasping throat he already had.

Shortly, they were tumbling to the ground, leaping into the back of the trucks, and Qalzai and Khushal were gassing the engines. They took off amidst roostertails of dust, heedless of the obvious sign they were leaving. Kyle yelled, *"Wro wro!,"* slow, and they did, but the panic had done its damage. It would be obvious where they'd started from.

The only thing to do now was to get onto a road and drive fast, far, and out of range. Then they could call in for extraction.

They were done.

"How was the shoot?" Kyle asked. He knew, but wanted another opinion.

"Clean, fast, and solid," Wade said. "A bit high, likely due to the reduced atmospheric pressure at this altitude."

"Yeah, I thought about dropping the aim a minute or so."

"It was fine. Clean kill. So scratch one asshole and let's get out of here."

"Yeah," Kyle agreed. Over. Done. No one hurt. Yet.

Despite the immediate fire, there was little pursuit. They drove insanely for fifteen minutes, but there was no visible threat after that.

"We should go as far as we can before stopping," Kyle said. "Tell them, Nasima." He was again glad she'd stayed behind, because he knew he would have worried about her.

"Okay," she said, and relayed the message.

Qalzai agreed, and they drove, while Mirza capped off a few bursts at their increasingly distant pursuers. Or maybe he was doing it in defiance, like ceremonial fireworks.

After another ten minutes, Wade said, "Relax, Kyle."

"Huh? Oh," he said, realizing he was still white-knuckling the cab and holding his breath. He let out a sigh. "We got away with it."

"Yeah, done," Wade said. He seemed elated, but was as ragged as Kyle. They swapped glances, and began sorting gear and packing their camouflage away.

They stopped for the night in yet another small farm that was linked by blood somehow to Qalzai's family. This one had an outer wall that had once been sections of building, and an inner courtyard that had once been a smaller house. It was on a dark green-mottled hillside with scattered sheep, and the oddest-looking goats Kyle had ever seen. Their asses stuck out about a foot past the hind legs, like the tailcone on a plane. He wasn't sure if it was a genetic trait, or a medical condition, but he decided he wouldn't eat goat here.

He needn't have been concerned. As they arrived, greeted by dozens of people he wouldn't remember, amid cheers and shouts and soon dancing and instruments, he was handed a bowl of curried lentils and rice. It was tasty enough, with fat, crisp lentils in a sauce with some vegetables, and rice pilaf underneath. Though he longed for meat, he avoided the goat. They were served naan bread to dip into the bowls, and served Coca-Cola, goat's milk, and tea. He passed on the milk, decided a Coke was in order, even if it did have caffeine.

Some man started to ask a question. It seemed to be a standard, "So, how was the mission?" inquiry, with a big curious grin breaking his beard. Qalzai made surreptitious shushing motions, laid an arm over his shoulder, and led him away, waving an arm and talking.

They got some odd looks, and Kyle chalked it up to them being foreign. But eventually, he decided the stares were more than that. They weren't threatening, but they were not just curious. And some of the grins looked familiar. He'd seen them in high school when someone had staged an elaborate prank.

He might be overreacting, though, he thought. He'd be ready in case of some local ritual or hazing, but he'd be cautious. It would be bad manners to respond to a local jape with gunfire.

"I think they're planning something amusing and degrading to the naïve Americans," he said to Wade.

"Yeah, I noticed," Wade replied. His hand was in his coat, obviously near his Beretta. "I won't do anything brash, but I'm ready in case of an issue."

They all gathered in the main room, which was roomy enough at twenty feet across, but cramped with so many men jammed in. But the conversation was not elated. There was satisfaction, certainly, and some grins, but the atmosphere definitely made Kyle think they were about to be set up for an elaborate practical joke.

Nasima had been banished to the kitchen with the women and girls. She slipped through the door and gave Kyle a look that seemed to ask for help, while asking him to keep quiet. Wade caught it, too.

"I don't like what I'm feeling, Kyle," Wade said softly, big grin plastered across his face as camouflage. "We got that son of a bitch. How's it feel?" He made a big show of high-fiving Kyle.

"And now all we have to do is get out. Soon," he continued. He was still grinning, and emphasized his meaning with a nod.

"Sounds good," Kyle said. "Creepy, yeah."

Nasima came through then, and served them, Khushal and Qalzai with curried chicken, tender and richly sauced, with rice. Under Kyle's platter was a note on a tiny slip of paper. It said, in block letters, NOW WE SHOULD LEAVE.

That did it, Kyle decided. If two trained troops and a local all felt nervous, something was up.

Except there was no way *to* leave that wasn't obviously a bug out. They'd have to play this for a few more hours, and sneak out by night.

As they lay down in a guest room, they were glad to see an outside door. They'd be through that when things quieted. "I'm on first watch," Wade said.

"Asshole," Kyle replied. "As if I can sleep now."

"I know the feeling," Wade said as he turned out the light. Both men were fully dressed and had their hands on their pistols under their coats.

The house quieted bit by bit, but it was past 1 A.M. before the last of the clan settled down. And the women would be up around five, to shoo the boys out to herd and milk and to start cooking. There wasn't much of an aperture there.

There was a scuffling at the door. Kyle clutched for his pistol.

"Who's there?" Wade asked in a whisper.

Nasima was speaking very softly. "It is I. We have to leave at once," she said.

"What? Why?" Kyle asked, nodding to Wade to open the door.

She came in, heedless of any customs of propriety. "There's no time to explain now. We must be out of sight by dawn, and I'll explain as we go, but there is danger for you both."

Kyle hated situations like this. Still, he did trust Nasima and his own instincts, and if there was a threat, they should get moving. It had to do with Qalzai and Bait, and he figured they were safer off alone with her as translator than with those others and no translator. "Grab your gear, Wade," he said, above a whisper but not much. "We'll do as she says."

"Understood," Wade agreed. He had his ruck in seconds; it was already packed, and the three of them started walking. Kyle carefully maneuvered the cased Barrett through the door, and they were off into the dark. They eased through the courtyard, and Kyle was glad that dogs weren't common. They bumped brick or stone twice, but didn't make any major noises.

As they slipped out the gate, Nasima said, "It is good we are near a town, so we can find a place to hide."

"Right," Kyle agreed. "Now, what's going on?"

She looked at him and said, "Kyle, the man you shot was not who you thought it was."

"What? How do you know?" he protested. She didn't even know who he had been shooting at, as far as he was aware.

"Because I heard Qalzai talk about settling a grudge. It's a man he's been fighting with for twenty years."

"Okay, so it's an old grudge, so what?" he said, but her comment was setting off alarms in his brain.

"Kyle, he shouldn't have known him in that case. The Taliban haven't been around that long, and al Qaeda even less," Wade said.

"Yes," Nasima nodded. "He said you'd done well for him, and he was glad to have American money. He doesn't know where your target is, and doesn't care. That kill was for him."

"You mean we're in the middle of a hillbilly feud here?" he asked. Things were spinning, and he shook his head to clear it. Dammit, they should have had more intel.

"If I understand your idiom, yes. Tribespeople killing each other over old hatreds," she said.

"Ah, shit. Sorry," he apologized to her.

"It's okay, I'm familiar with the term. Also *merde, scheisse,* and a few others." There was a twinkle in her eye as she swore in multiple languages. "And it fits," she said.

"Okay, so we get hid and figure out what we're going to do. Though under the circumstances," Kyle said, hating what he was thinking, "we better abort the mission and have them try something else."

"Right," Wade said. "But first, we have to get out of this area and into another town. Any ideas?"

"Nasima," Kyle said, "We have money. Is there a discreet way to get a ride?"

She thought for a moment. "There are always vehicles that will carry people. But the word will be told. There's no way to stop people from talking."

"So we need to be on the first vehicle anywhere, and hope the rumors are behind us," he said.

"That is correct," she said. "But there are few vehicles this late."

"Hell, I'll buy one if I have to," he said. But he knew that wasn't a practical idea in the middle of the night.

"So we keep walking and grab what we can," Wade said. "If we need to, you can pass off as a local better than I can," he held up his coffee-toned hand as emphasis, "and I can stay hid while you get us space."

"We should avoid a public bus," Nasima said. "Do you want to go to Quetta? Or somewhere else?"

"Right now," Wade said, "we just need somewhere quiet, so we can call and report in. Then we can call for a helicopter if we have to."

"Very well," she said. "And what of me?"

"We give you a ride home," he said. He wasn't sure of Army policy, but he wasn't going to take "no" for an answer. They owed her.

"Thank you," she said, sounding honestly relieved. Well, with the way the government dicked everyone around, including him, he couldn't blame her.

10

THE NIGHTCLUB WAS LIKE MANY OTHERS IN GERMANY.
This being Oktoberfest, it was packed with revelers, even if they weren't celebrating in traditional fashion. Dancing and drinking and fumbling gropes were still ongoing at 2 A.M. local. A number of American airmen from Rhein-Main Air Base were mixed among the crowd, and a platoon of soldiers fresh from Iraq were taking a couple of days to unwind while the military sorted out travel arrangements. Rough German industrial music shook the structure, low guttural voices amplified to almost painful levels. It was unfamiliar to some, but to the soldiers it was definitely Western and definitely a sign of civilization. That in itself made it good. Add a few pitchers of rich German beer and tall, blond women in tight leather and spandex, and they loved it.

Where the bomb had been planted was a mystery that would take days to solve. Its size was easy to estimate. It had been fifty kilograms of Semtex, somewhere toward the rear of the building, behind the steel cage and grated floor that served as a DJ booth. At 2:01:06, it detonated. The stylish metal cage, the grating, chunks of speaker magnet, cabinet, and grille all served as shrapnel. Not that they were necessary. The blast was sufficient, and contained by the walls for a mere fraction of a second, it propagated forward into the open dance floor.

Seventy-nine people were pulped or crushed to death by the explosion. Two hundred and six others would bear scars from minor scratches to missing limbs or shattered faces. It was headline news on the Web and TV within minutes.

• • •

Kyle, Wade and Nasima were still walking at dawn. There wasn't much else they could do. Luckily, all three were used to hoofing it, and their spirits were adequate. Though all three were nervous at every little sound in the desert.

"If we can get back to Hicheri, I know the area," Nasima said. "We can get transport anywhere. But how can you cross the border?"

"We have papers," Kyle said. As long as he could hang on to them. They were now rolled in a metal tube in his ruck, and he wasn't putting it down. The briefcase could go, so could the weapons. But the radio, phones, and the papers were their link to home.

"Okay," she said. "Then we will try to ride with a truck."

Kyle broke out one of his hoarded MREs and the tub of shoestring potatoes. They shared them around, including the freeze-dried fruit salad and crackers. It wasn't much for the gourmet, but it was calories and filling.

They lucked out shortly when a truck came by.

It was a truck like none Kyle had ever seen.

The bed had canvas over arched metal bows, like a military carryall, but they were high-peaked and arched. Another bow angled forward half over the cab, jutting up like the peak on a Nazi cap. There was no hood, and the engine stuck out in greasy mechanical contrast to the rest. For the rest of it was painted in lime green and garish geometric art.

"Pakistani hippies?" Wade asked.

"Hippies?" Nasima replied, confused. "Oh, no. Just as with the bright colors of clothes, people are proud of their vehicles." She waved an arm and the driver slowed.

It took her less than a minute, while Wade held his lungee over his face and squinted. She turned and said, "He agrees to carry us for fifty rupees."

Fifty rupees. Less than a dollar. Kyle would have paid a thousand times that to put distance between them and their former allies. "Done," he said.

They were ushered into the back, which was covered with plywood and had a plywood door with a brass knob set into it. The wood had faded from green to a contrasting black and straw as the wood aged. Inside was obviously someone's store. There was a narrow walkway, perhaps eighteen inches wide, and the rest was bundles and bureaus of assorted stuff—textiles, spice jars, hardware, and more they couldn't see. Wade scurried in first with the rifle case and his ruck, then Kyle with the rest of their gear. Nasima came in last, thanking the driver and paying him. The door was closed, leaving them in virtual darkness, the weak dawn entering through a window eight inches square.

Kyle squatted with his arms around his knees. "Well, it's cramped, but private," he said as the gears clashed and jolted them forward.

"He will get us to the next town," Nasima said. "From there, we can find some way to Hicheri."

"I don't suppose we can rent a car?" Kyle asked. He'd feel much safer with the minimal privacy of doors and a roof over their foreign features.

"No," she said. "But it may be possible to buy one. How much money do you have?"

Kyle tried to look at Wade over his shoulder, realized it was impossible, and said, "Almost forty-nine thousand dollars in afghanis, rupees, and dollars."

"Forty—!" she started. Then, "I think I should have asked for more money as your translator."

"Nasima, you can have whatever's left when we leave. It's an asset we're supposed to use," Kyle said, trying not to sound desperate. He didn't want her feeling put upon.

"That's generous of you," she said, "but not necessary. I will work for my pay. It was an honest price." Her smile was faintly visible in the growing half-light. "But we should be able to buy a car with that easily. Perhaps with far less." She chuckled.

It was a disconcerting ride, jolted and bounced in the dark, hanging on around bends as the old truck swayed. The springs were shot, and the shocks of course, and the differential howled. It reminded Kyle of the duct tape and baling wire monster of a pickup he'd had in high school, except that this was a twenty-foot Mercedes that was likely older than he was.

The light improved, their hunger increased, and the bouncing and squatting didn't help bladder pressure. It was late morning before they arrived back in Bemana'abad. It wasn't too soon to suit them. The weather was mild, but under the dark, musty canvas of the truck, it had been stifling and sweaty.

They nodded to the driver and started walking, following Nasima's lead. Eyes turned and followed them.

The problems were obvious. Either Kyle or Wade alone could have managed to have stayed discreet. But they were both very tall, well-built, and had obvious American weapons. To avoid that, they'd wrapped them, but it was still clear they had large hardware. The natives noticed them.

It wasn't the curious glances that were bothersome. Those were to be expected. But some of the looks were puzzled, mean, or offended as people deduced who they were. Clearly, the word had got out about their shoot. Not one person in twenty belonged to the tribe in question, but they'd talk. Eventually, the word would get back.

"Nasima," Kyle said softly, "we need to become better hidden, or get out of here fast."

"Yes," she agreed. "So let us find a vehicle. There's a merchant over that way. I assume the first one will do?"

"As long as the car works, yes," Kyle said. "Wade, how good a mechanic are you? I'm used to big American cars, not the little foreign ones."

"I know enough to spot a lemon," he said.

"Good."

Nasima asked, "Lemon?" and looked quizzical.

"Slang for a sour, bitter, lousy car," Kyle said.

"Ah."

It wasn't much of a lot, being simply a cleared and graded corner with weeds poking lazily through the dust and a shed as an office. It contained several vehicles ranging from three years old to ancient. Rust wasn't bad in the dry climate, but all were abraded and bleached to some extent.

Nasima swept up and engaged the dealer in rapid-fire Pashto. They smiled and gestured and occasionally he'd nod his balding head. Kyle and Wade smiled as they exchanged glances, and sidled up on an old Toyota. It looked like a Camry.

The cars were actually cheaper than the trucks, and it took some thinking to figure out why. The farmers needed trucks. Only urbanites would have cars, but they'd prefer a newer one. Anyone buying basic transport would get a truck or van first. But this would be fine for their needs, and when Wade popped the hood, it was obviously worn but functional. There was a dent on the right-rear corner, which was hardly surprising the way people drove here. "Chaotic" was the politest word for it.

The dealer would know who they were anyway, so they spoke in English. Wade started the engine with the provided key, revved it, and listened. "Smooth enough," he said. "Let's haggle over the body, the nonworking air conditioning, and the clutch."

Nasima bargained for them. She was animated, pushy, and

seemed quite confident. The man feigned disgust at her offers and jabbered back. It took only a few minutes before she turned back and said, "One thousand dollars, and I suggest another two hundred to keep him silent about us."

"Done," Kyle said. He peeled out rupees and passed them over. A few minutes took care of title in Nasima's name, and they filled the trunk with gear and piled in. The wrapped weapons went with them.

"Who's driving?" Kyle asked.

"I am," Nasima said. "When we get out into the country, you might need to take over. But for now, I know the way."

"Got it," he agreed.

It was frightening driving through town. They were almost used to the insanity of the drivers by now, but the additional risk of being recognized caused them to keep glancing about. "Where are we going?" Kyle asked.

"Hicheri," she reminded him.

Once on the road, Kyle punched for General Robash on his phone. This was important enough that he wanted to talk directly.

"Robash here," was the answer on the first ring.

"Kyle here," he said. "General, I hate like hell to say this, but we've failed. We're heading out." The admission was nauseating, painful. He hoped it wouldn't be taken too hard back home.

"What happened, son? Talk to me," Robash said.

"Sir, our so-called allies were playing us as patsies. We assassinated some other local gang leader for them. They're very happy. The other tribe is not. The word is out, and we're being watched."

"Shit," Robash said.

"Yes, sir. We've secured transport and a translator, and are heading for the border. Do you have any specific orders for us?"

"Stand by," was the reply. Kyle waited, looking nervously out the windows as Nasima took them swiftly out of town. He listened to nothing as Robash did something, with the expensive line open.

Shortly, he was back on. "Status report, please."

"Sir," Kyle said, "we are uninjured, all equipment except the laptop accounted for—it's broken—in control of the situation, and with transport and a translator. We have broken contact with our former allies, whom I judge to be uninterested or potentially hostile at this point. We have over forty thousand in cash left, and are heading for a safe zone before retreating across the border. Several local tribes are seeking us, and I judge the risk to be moderate at this time."

"Right," Robash said. "We need you to stay if you can. Is there any reason not to?"

Kyle thought furiously. "Other than the local search, I guess we're still clean. But we're known now, and our target is likely to get word."

"There is that," Robash said. "But we've had a car bombing, three hundred casualties in a club in Germany and several other threats. As we tighten the noose on these assholes, they're getting desperate. We can't get another team in anytime soon, and they'll be watching. It's good that you're making noises of retreating; we want them to think that. But if you can regroup and push on, you're still the best shot we've got at doing this."

"If you tell me to do it, sir, we'll do it," he said. He turned his head and Wade nodded. "There's risk, but I understand your point." A nightclub. Lovely. Likely one he'd been in less than two years ago, too, if it was in Germany.

"I'm asking, not ordering," Robash said. "You're the man on the spot. Tell me you need out, we'll do it. Tell me you can push on, and you'll make a lot of people very happy."

"We'll do it," Kyle agreed, though he wasn't one of those who'd be happy. And "request" aside, it was an order. He'd have to justify bailing. He could, but it stuck in his craw, and Robash had to know that. It was polite railroading, but still . . . "There's risk, but we'll do it. But I'm not sure how to find him now. Suggestions?"

"Not yet," Robash said. "I'll get you intel as fast as I can. You get hidden and rest for a day or two. And thank you both. You're handling a bitch of a situation in first-class fashion."

"Thank you, sir," Kyle said. The compliment was honest. Other commanders might have complained, or been overly understanding. Robash was competently aware and let his people do their jobs.

"Roger that. We'll get you intel, you bag this dirtball, snipers."

"Will do, sir. Out."

"Out."

Turning to Wade he grinned and said, "We're fucked." He wasn't worried about offending Nasima anymore. The lady was tough.

"That bad?" Wade asked.

"I guess not," Kyle said. "Looking at it logically, we had allies we couldn't trust. We now have one ally we can, and familiarity with the area. But we have no intel on this guy at all."

Nasima asked, "Who is the man you're looking for?"

Swapping quick glances, Wade nodded and Kyle said, "Rafiq bin Qasim, one of al Qaeda's best people." There wasn't any reason not to tell her now.

She looked surprised for only a moment, then recovered. "He shouldn't be hard to find," she said. "He's bound to have local allies, and word always gets out among the tribes."

"Okay," Kyle said. "Then who do we ask? Lost and found?"

"First we get to Hicheri," she said. "Then we look."

"Okay," he said. "You keep driving, I'll think."

"Don't hurt your head," she said, smiling. He chuckled.

For several minutes, he said nothing, eyes closed, head back, letting his brain digest all the data. And also to ignore Nasima's driving, which was fast enough over the rough road that he wished for a helmet against bumps.

The biggest problem was the lack of intel. The biggest risk was that of discovery. The former required local sources, which Nasima might help them find. Nothing more to be done about that. The latter required better disguise.

Sitting up, he said, "One of the problems is that lovely piece of hardware." He indicated the trunk with a finger.

"The Barrett?" Wade asked.

"Yep. It's big, clunky, and obvious. Can't hide it. I'll bet everyone within a hundred miles knows about it and is scanning with binocs. And really, we're not going to need a thousand-meter-plus kill. Eight hundred, even as little as three hundred will do it. We need a weapon better suited to the environment."

"You aren't thinking what I think you are, Kyle?" Wade asked. He looked a bit wide-eyed and disturbed.

"Oh, I'm not going to sell it," Kyle grinned at him. "I do plan to stash it somewhere. We've got enough cash to buy whatever we need."

"You're going to buy an M-24 Sniper Weapon System in the ass-end of Pakistan?" Wade asked, incredulous.

Chuckling, Kyle said, "I probably could. But that would be obvious, too. I'm sure we can find a Mauser though. Or even a Dragunov."

Nasima was still driving, quietly. She'd heard everything, but hadn't offered any comment. "Rifles are available on the street where the metalsmiths are. I can show you," she said. They started bouncing over a rough spot in the road, and she jolted with the motion of the wheels and steering.

"Great," Kyle said. "I'll tell you what I need and you can buy it."

"I wouldn't know what to get, or how to bargain," she said. "I know weapons when I see them, everyone does. But not enough to talk about them."

"But, Nasima," he said, "We're obvious. You're a local."

"I suppose," she replied. She was clearly unhappy with the idea.

Kyle spoke to reassure her. "Fair enough," he said. "We'll try another approach."

"Like what?" Wade asked.

"I'm not sure," Kyle admitted. "But let's stash this sucker first. I'll think about it meantime. What I'll do is pull the bolt. Nothing they can do with it then. We'll keep that, and find somewhere to hide the rest of it."

"Makes sense," Wade nodded, though his tone made it clear he wasn't happy parting with the massive weapon. A lone M-4 and pistols against artillery, machine guns, and Kalashnikovs was not an appealing state of affairs.

"I know of a cave," Nasima said. "It's remote and very narrow."

"Sounds good," Kyle said. "Nearby?"

"Not far from Hicheri. We played there when I was small. Since I came back from Afghanistan, I haven't seen anyone go near the area."

"Sounds good," Kyle said. At the rate she was driving, it was less than an hour before they reached it. With all the convoluted routes, they'd come within twenty miles of where their failed shot had been, and were now heading back roughly toward Quetta.

No, Kyle decided, the shot hadn't failed. The shot had been good. The intel had failed, and that wasn't his fault.

11

THREE HOURS LATER, HE WASN'T SO SURE ABOUT THE hiding place. With the Barrett disassembled, he and Wade each carrying half, it was still an awkward climb through jagged outcroppings. The path was up a fissure between two large massifs, and was well-hidden from town or the plateau, but it wasn't a pleasant walk in the park.

"It's just up here," Nasima said, indicating to their right. "Come."

Tired and sore, they followed her. It was a bit disconcerting to have the slim woman radiate so much energy as they lagged behind. Kyle kept reminding himself that she was familiar with the terrain. It did make a difference.

Shortly, they were gathered around a long crack. "Here," she announced.

"Very nice," Wade said, looking at the convoluted opening. He shone his Xenon flashlight inside, and decided it was deep enough for their purposes, as well as being out of sight. "Just one problem," he said.

Kyle finished the thought. "Neither of us will fit in there," he said. It might be fifteen inches wide and there was no section long enough for legs or torsos for a six-foot male.

"It is smaller than I remember," Nasima admitted. "I think I can still squeeze in, though."

"Great, if you can," Kyle said.

"Okay," she said. For a moment she stared at him, considering. Then she said, "That means you'll have to turn around."

"Huh?" he asked, confused.

She blushed red and said, "I'll need to pull up my skirt and squirm in. It's not proper for a man to watch."

Of course. Muslim doctrine demanded she not show anything except her face and hands. "Oh, no problem," Kyle said. "Sorry, it's just that we're not used to these things. Here's the components," he said, unlimbering the filthy burlap package from his shoulder. Wade dropped his alongside. "We'll move down about ten meters and just keep an ear out for emergencies, okay?"

"Excellent!" she beamed. She sat there, legs folded demurely under herself, until they moved away.

Behind them were scrabbling noises. "Dammit, I want to look when I hear sounds like that," Kyle said.

Wade snickered. "And you want a glimpse of leg, too."

Kyle punched his shoulder and said, "Yeah, she's cute, what about it? I'm not going to piss off our only reliable guide to get a gawk at something I can't have anyway. No fraternization."

"Right," Wade said. "Let's hope she's done soon, and that none of the kids come out here hacking around."

Kyle gazed over the terrain. "Not a lot here to indicate activity. I'd say it's pretty dead."

"Yeah," Wade agreed. "Kids these days. No matter where you go, they're more urban, less adventurous, and listening to industrial music."

"Hey! I listen to rock on occasion," Kyle said.

"Great, old man. You must be a huge hit with the over-eighty crowd."

They joked quietly until the scrabbling sounds stopped, and listened carefully, ears twitching for signs, eyes alert for movement.

"Thank you, gentlemen," her voice said. "It's hidden, and I appreciate your modesty."

They turned. Her skirt was dusty and scraped, with a puckered pull of thread over her left hip. "We'll have to give you some money for more clothes. This is wearing out your wardrobe," Kyle said.

"I'll be fine," she said. "Besides, there are no clothing stores nearby and there's little selection in the marketplace."

"Speaking of which," Kyle said, "we need to get more local garb, and shift to another village where we can hide better. And where we can buy a rifle."

She thought for a few moments. "If we can leave tonight, I know where there is a road east. It will take us where we can find a rifle and allies. And we need allies."

"Let's leave now," he said.

Nasima drove again. Kyle was getting used to her Eastern style. It involved no philosophy or mysticism, it was simply based on being mean and rude to other drivers and pedestrians, and barreling along as fast as possible.

After so many direction changes, Kyle wasn't entirely sure where they were. He was glad they had a GPS receiver, because he was sure they'd be needing it before this played out. In the meantime, they were approaching another town, and even from the outskirts it was obviously full of small industry. The rust stains and metallic stenches said as much.

By now, they were less obvious. Between two weeks' worth of beard and dirt and sun they looked like any other peasants, so long as they were seen from ten feet away and kept their short hair hidden. Wade's facial features were still problematic, but a lungee and a stiff coat fixed that. His skin tone was unremarkable. The people here varied from tan to near-black in the sun, skin leathery and stiff on all but the very young. Like Nasima.

She'd been right about the town. He could see various children working at buffing wheels and using files on metal, and glimpses through curtained doorways showed revolvers, shotguns, even a few AKs. Whatever they might need should be available here. Quality would be debatable, but they could do some work themselves and pay for other aspects.

It was amazing, Kyle thought, how a few hours' travel and the disposal of the Barrett had made them invisible again. The lawlessness and lack of proper TV or Web gave them a camouflage reminiscent of the Old West. As long as rumors didn't catch up in a hurry, or any rumors were garbled by the time they got here, they'd be okay.

First a rifle, then intel. He really had no idea how to accomplish that second requirement.

They parked the car in a sunny, dusty street. The dust was pervasive, just like that in Arabia, and covered everything. It was worse here, as the road was mere dirt, gullied and with stones protruding from some ancient rain.

The stores they wandered past were a bewildering mix. There were restaurants, textiles, dry goods, a video arcade with twenty-year-old games from the U.S. and a handful of Russian machines, a dealer of plastic cases, and gun shops. Lots of gun shops.

Wade picked the store that seemed quietest, pointed, and they slipped through the translucent fabric. The walls were lined with rows and stacks of rifles of all kinds. A clutch of pistols sat atop a shelf behind the counter. The shopkeeper nodded. He and his son both were dressed lightly in cotton, neatly bearded and kempt, and carried AKs. There were likely other weapons handy. At least, Kyle would have weapons handy if he ran the place, so he assumed they did, too.

They all nodded and bowed, and Nasima handled greetings and small talk. Wade watched the door as Kyle sought the left side of the store, which seemed to have many grimy, dirt-encrusted examples. The son watched him firmly but not threateningly as he examined the merchandise. There were many old Mausers, some Russian Moisin-Nagants, some Indian-made Enfield #4s, a scattering of odd things like a Swedish Ljungman and a Parker-Hale .22 that had seen far better decades. There was a lot to sort through.

Then he stopped short. That looked like . . .

It was. A Short Magazine Lee-Enfield. World War I British surplus. Only this one had been worked over quite a bit. He picked it up and examined it.

The muzzle-length Mannlicher stock had been shortened to a reasonable modern length, and the stock cap that held the bayonet mount removed. It had been refinished and phosphated instead of blued. The length of pull was a bit short for a man of his stature, of course, but that could be fixed. Then he saw the stamp on the left side of the receiver. PROPERTY US GOVERNMENT.

It clicked in his mind. During the '80s, lots of these, cheap, familiar to the locals and easy to procure, had been cut down and packaged for the mujahideen. The SMLE or "Smelly" was a reliable, accurate weapon, almost as good as a 98K Mauser, and easy to maintain. With a bit of work it would make, as others had before, a fine shooting rifle.

"*Da pe tso dai?*" he asked. How much?

"*Zer rupee,*" the man replied confidently. Kyle figured for a moment. One thousand Pakistani rupees was sixteen bucks American. It was cheap, and ridiculously within his budget.

But it would be out of place not to haggle, and he couldn't have stories of a stranger tossing money around freely. "*Penza sawa,*" he countered. Five hundred rupees, eight bucks.

The man looked offended but clearly wasn't, and stuck to his price. Kyle pointed out the "defective" stock, how short it was, the grunge and dust, no bayonet mount. He didn't speak the language well enough, but didn't need to. All he had to do was point, shake his head, look grossly put upon and disgusted. Twice he put it down and walked toward the door, and each time the man countered with a slightly lower price. Kyle would turn back and they'd start again.

It took ten minutes, with much grumbling and complaining, gesticulating and shaking of heads, but finally they settled at twelve dollars, 750 rupees, with sixty rounds of match-grade ammunition included, twelve stripper clips to hold it, the rifle to be adjusted to his specifications, and a sling added, along with an abused but functional Dragunov bipod and better sights. He'd have to settle for iron sights, but they'd be good ones. The ammo made him suspicious. It sounded too good to be true.

"You bargain well," Nasima acknowledged.

"Lots of flea market trips as a kid," he replied. She looked confused at the term and he added, "I'll explain later."

Haggling done, he sought to explain the modifications he wanted made.

"What do you seek?" the man asked. He didn't seem bothered at Nasima translating. That was typical. As a woman helping a man, she was in her place. Besides, he was being paid.

Or possibly he was modern-minded enough not to care. Kyle decided he was being too harsh in his assumptions. So far, almost everyone had been very hospitable. Even Qalzai's people, while they screwed him over, had been polite and helpful. There was no reason to impute bad thoughts to everyone.

With a bit of conversation and a few gestures for technical matters, Kyle got his point across. "Ah, yes," the man said. "Ah, yes," when he understood the nature of the changes. "Ah, yes." It might be the only English he spoke, though Kyle wasn't going to assume so, and would watch what he said around him.

Kyle stayed on site while Nasima and Wade went to shop for food, more clothes, and assorted accessories. He watched and advised with a few basic words and hand signs as the smith cut off the remaining barrel band. He then dismounted the weapon and carefully placed the stock in a vise, padding the jaws with leather. He gestured for Kyle, who used a scribe and straightedge to carefully mark how he wanted it cut, then held up his hands to indicate it should be hollowed in a semicircle along those lines.

What he was trying to do was relieve most of the pressure of the stock against the barrel, free floating it. This would allow the barrel to oscillate with a harmonic resonance as it fired, rather than shaking the stock. It also prevented warped wood from humidity changes from affecting the barrel, and left a small air gap to reduce the effect of bangs and strikes against the barrel. A small amount of pressure at the front of the stock would make things stable and consistent.

Kyle almost jumped in shock when the craftsman grabbed a chisel and mallet and banged along the lines indicated. He was sure the stock was ruined from the rapid, careless striking. He held still, not screaming, jumping or reacting, trying to think of a polite way to address the issue. He'd be needing one of the Mausers now.

At a wave, he stepped closer to look at the damage, and paused. In actuality, it was a job almost as neat as a precision machine could do.

It came to him that this man was a craftsman in the old style. He'd be lost in a modern machine shop, but with a handful of files, a drill, and chisels, he could do any of the same precision work, it would just take longer. Though "longer" was in comparison to machine tools only. His work so far was faster than Kyle would dare try with a chisel.

Impressed, Kyle nodded agreement, and indicated that the foremost part of the stock should be left proud so as to support the barrel. The grimace the man gave him indicated he was well aware of that fact, and the arrogant foreigner should stand back and let him work. He selected a large riffler rasp from his rack and commenced to shave out long, paper-thin strips of the old beechwood.

Kyle simply watched. The man's hands were sure, his eyes squinty and clear. Stroke by stroke the well-aged wood was scraped and cut into a more modern shape. It took about an hour, which was surprisingly fast.

How to indicate fiberglass bedding? He sought a piece of plastic, found a Stanley chisel with a translucent handle, and indicated it and the inside of the stock.

At first, the old man thought he wanted him to use the chisel. Then after a few moments, the idea caught on and he limped over to a cabinet. He pulled out a can that contained a popular American brand of fiberglass resin for autobody repairs.

With that, he created a slurry of shredded fiberglass cloth and resin, pressed it down into the cut and smoothed it out. He used a rubber glove that had likely been used for a thousand other fiberglass jobs, crusty and crackly over much of its surface.

It took only a couple of hours to complete, including a wooden cheek piece shaved to fit and pinned in place with wooden dowels as a Monte Carlo-style stock, and another piece screwed in place on the butt to lengthen it to fit Kyle's long frame. It was a good three inches longer than the short British stock. Careful pegging and filing filled out the grip to something Kyle might hold more easily.

Wade and Nasima returned with meat-stuffed pies. The filling was mutton. Though if Kyle hadn't known, he wouldn't have asked. He'd learned to eat what he was given, enjoy it or reject it and not ask about pedigree or breed. But Muslims were strict on eating only mutton, goat, or beef as far as mammals went, and there were few streams here to fish from. He bit at the pie, and gave the spare one to their host, who hugged them graciously and plowed in as the fiberglass finished setting. Once he'd munched his meal, he returned to delicate filing and hammering on the bolt mechanism. After that, he drilled the rear of the receiver for a proper sight assembly. He actually had a small drill press that looked fifty years old and held a standard hand drill, but it cut straight holes, which he threaded by hand.

"That is one ugly-looking bastard son of a left-handed, red-headed stepchild," Wade said, eying the stock critically.

"Ain't it, though?" Kyle agreed, beaming. Yes, it was ugly, its soft old lines surgically altered to rakish angles and now converted to butchered curves. But it was purely functional. It should, if everything had been done correctly, and to Kyle's eye it had, shoot every time he squeezed the trigger, and put every bullet within a couple of minutes of arc of where he aimed.

After the glass bed had set, the smith smoothed it down with files and a metal scraper with better curves than a French stripper. There was no sandpaper in evidence anywhere; all finish work was scraped patiently to a fine, smooth surface.

Meanwhile, the trigger had been reshaped and the bolt reworked. Once reassembled and set into the stock, the man presented it to Kyle for examination. He wore a confident smile.

Kyle hefted it, liking the balance. The bipod had been screwed to the forestock and added just enough weight that it should help hold the muzzle down. The stock was long and tall enough for his arm and neck, the grip swelled to fit his large hand. He raised it, worked the bolt and safety, though he wasn't likely to use the latter much. Still, it was a good test of function. He drew the trigger, which still had a long, creepy draw, but was crisp at letoff and not mushy.

He nodded satisfaction. The man had done a fine job.

"Ammunition," he reminded the smith, and the man nodded. He spoke to his son, who slipped into the back. After a patient three minutes, Kyle asked Nasima, "Do we know what's taking so long?"

She spoke, the smith spoke back, and she said, "The match ammunition is hidden at the back of the safe. It will be here shortly."

"Okay," he agreed. But it was another five minutes before the son returned. He handed over a paper wrap that contained the rounds, and another that held the clips.

Kyle examined the rounds carefully. The case markings varied, and he wasn't very familiar with British ammo. This batch was stamped a 79 7.7ʀ 1ᴍ3ᴢ. 1979, 7.7mm rimmed? That seemed likely, but the rest meant nothing. But the cases were very even in shape and length, had faint turning marks on the necks, and the bullets were in nice condition. He had no idea where "match-grade" ammo came from out here, but he'd seen all kinds of stuff, including a titanium Taurus .357 that couldn't reasonably be here. He shrugged inwardly and decided to take them. A dozen tight, springy stripper clips let him load sixty rounds for easy feeding. One could carry extra magazines for the Smelly, but typically, the magazine was left in place and ammo fed from strippers into the top. The clips were phosphate finished and looked recent, though they were worn from use.

With that accomplished, they paid the man in rupees, thanked him profusely, and accepted both a modern sleeve for the rifle and a burlap wrap to hide that. Then it was back outside and into the car. It was time to test-fire the weapon.

They drove out of town and found a quiet area with rolling fields. On a broad, stalky-green area about 200 meters from the road, Kyle found a boulder, and propped two smaller rocks on it as targets. "Spot me," he told Wade.

"Of course," Wade replied. He uncased the spotting scope and got comfortable on the ground.

Kyle dropped prone, extended the bipod and set its length, checked the sling and stock in case he needed to shoot from rest, and did a full check of the weapon. His life would depend on it. "Good enough" wasn't good enough.

It snugged comfortably up against his cheek, and the bolt and safety worked very smoothly. He loaded one round. With curly green stuff against his face, he eased lower and closer. The Zen of rifle. It was a joke of his. Become one with the weapon. Be the bullet.

The trigger pull was still long, but steady. It fired crisply, and recoiled more than he expected. The .303 was a respectable round, and this wasn't a heavy rifle. The "*Boom!*" rolled out and echoed pleasantly.

He missed, throwing up chips from the boulder.

Wade was on it, though, and said, "Five inches low, three inches right."

"Stand by," Kyle replied. The original sights had been a mid-mounted tangential ramp and a post in front. They were adequate for battle, but not for precision. The new rear sight was mounted to the receiver ring and was click adjustable. It wasn't any brand Kyle recognized, but it ought to work well enough.

He clicked up and left, said, "Ready," and loaded one round. Consistency was essential to a good sight-in.

As that shot echoed and more chips flew, Wade said, "Barely low, one inch right."

"Stand by," he said. He corrected again, leaned in, and fired.

The rock shattered in bits.

"Second target," he said. One round.

That rock joined its neighbor in igneous heaven.

"Good enough. Your turn."

"Suits me," Wade said. He might have to take the shot, and they might wind up mixing weapons. He needed familiarity, too.

There was one small piece of the second target left. Wade flopped down, eased in, loaded, squeezed, and shot. The now-pebble jumped high into the air and disappeared. "Damn, sliced," Wade quipped.

"I'm happy," Kyle said.

Nasima had been silent. Now she said, "I am impressed."

"Thanks," Kyle said. "But we're trained for much farther than that."

"Yeah, do we want to resight for farther?" Wade asked.

"Adjust the vertical. Zero for three hundred."

Wade nodded, and whipped out a calculator and notepad. "Assuming one eighty grains and twenty-four sixty at the muzzle with a two hundred *yard* zero, which is the figures I have here, plus two point five inches at one hundred, sixteen point eight inches low at three hundred. Zero at three hundred."

"Right," Kyle agreed. The projectile would hit high on a closer shot, rapidly drop after three hundred, but would be within a human silhouette for the entire flight. After 350 yards, he'd need to aim higher, on the head or above it, for a center of mass shot.

They discussed some finer points of trajectory for a few minutes, and potential deflection from wind. "It should do the job," Kyle said.

"Hope so," Wade said. "Because I don't think this is 'match' ammo." He held up a round and indicated with his finger. "That turning on the throat was done with emery paper. The rim is a bit beat. And the shoulders are not fire-formed." That last referred to fitting cases to a chamber by shooting them, forcing them to shape. "Looks like standard ball."

"Ah, hell," Kyle said.

"Go back and complain?"

"Nah," Kyle said. "It should be consistent enough, if it's standard ball. The work was good. We don't want a scene. Let him keep the extra buck fifty."

"Sure, though it makes me itch," Wade said. "Bet that what took so long was the emery cloth and polishing?"

"No bet," Kyle replied with a shake of his head. "Now, we're using iron sights on this. I've got the scope from the Barrett to use for intel and spotting, but you're going to have to do most of the spotting for me with your scope."

"Roger that," Wade nodded.

"Are we done here, then?" Nasima asked. She'd been quiet through the technical discussion, but appeared impressed.

"Yes," Kyle said. "What now?"

"Now we try to find your target," she said.

"I'm dying to find out how," Wade said.

"We ask questions," she said. "The key element is to ask the correct questions of the correct people."

He knew that much. "I guess we're in your hands," he said. Because he had no idea where to start.

"I have an idea," she said.

They returned to the car, hid the weapons carefully in the trunk and climbed back in. Nasima started the engine and pulled back onto the road.

Shortly, she pulled over. Hopping out lightly, she asked something of a woman on the street. A pointed finger and directions were returned.

From there, they drove across town and sat waiting near a mosque. It was a stunning piece of architecture, and the two Americans gaped like tourists. Even in this backwater, the mosque had arches, minarets, rich blue tiles, and other exquisite decorations. Lunch came from a passing vendor with a rickety wooden cart, and Nasima disappeared inside for nearly an hour while the men sweated in the sun. She emerged, they climbed in the car, and off they went again.

They crossed town three or four times, Nasima stopping to ask questions. They circled a good piece of the outskirts and then headed west again, up into the hills.

"We're seeking a small village nearby," she said, "where three tribes have been fighting. One is known to have been involved with the Taliban during their reign. We will seek one of the others and ask of their enemies."

"Good, just ask carefully," Kyle said.

She turned and gave him a look that would freeze a blowtorch. "I have some experience avoiding trouble, Kyle." Her tone made it clear she didn't like being patronized.

"Right, sorry, nerves," he said.

"It is okay," she said, and softened slightly.

"How will we find the final information?" Wade asked. "I'd think we don't want to ask about it at all."

"And we won't," she nodded. "We'll see who is afraid, and hasn't been warring recently, or who is deferring to the others. The Taliban are bullies. Others avoid them."

They stopped at another ultramodern petrol station in a tiny town that was a scattering of huts. The station was the most modern building they'd seen all day, and was a local hangout of sorts. The Americans stayed in the car, Nasima went in. When she returned, she was smiling.

"I have another lead," she said.

"Oh?" Kyle prompted.

"I asked about safe routes for driving. I was told where to avoid, and why."

"Ah," he said. Yes, that was a classic way of doing it, and it wouldn't have worked if he'd tried it. Nasima was very useful to them. They'd gotten far more than their money's worth from her already.

It was evening when they rolled up into the hills proper. At dusk, they stopped at a convenient farm, paid a few rupees, and were bedded down in two rooms. Nasima had cautioned them against trying to leave the rooms and associate, and they stayed quiet. It wasn't easy, though.

"Dammit, Wade, I want to know what's going on!" Kyle fumed in a whisper. "She drives us around, asks questions . . . what happens when someone associates her with two strangers, and those two strangers with a dead leader in the area?" They sat in a room lit by a single candle, with bare dun walls and a packed earth floor. They'd rolled out ponchos and rucks as bedding.

"Chill," Wade said. "We're better off this way. We'll have more warning of any trouble, and we have transport we control."

"Yeah," Kyle said. "I had the illusion of control before. Now I have control, but it's limited, and through a young woman who doesn't know military matters."

"Not formally, no. But she does have a knack for intel. I think it's inbred here. So many factions and relations that you have to learn diplomatic ways of gathering data before you even greet someone at a party, in case you piss someone off."

"True," Kyle considered, sitting on his ruck. It sank under him, despite its fullness. "And I suppose I'd better sleep. Long day again tomorrow."

"Yeah, I've got watch. See you in four hours."

"Right," Kyle said. But sleep wasn't easy with ghostly enemies haunting his dreams, prepared to knock down the doors and shoot him . . . and under all that was an image of Wade, being shot by a sniper, screaming in agony. Then everything shifted and Nasima was the target. His mind was recalling old hurts with new friends and confusing the images.

It was a long time before he slept, and it was restless when it came.

12

SO, BIN QASIM THOUGHT, THERE WERE AMERICANS IN country. Or more accurately, more Americans in country. The CIA was getting tricky. This pair had not come to his attention through the usual sources. His informants in the Pakistani Inter-Services Intelligence had not mentioned them. He would have to caution them against contempt. The Americans were not to be underestimated. Their money and arrogance could not stand against faith, but it was still a threat, which is why jihad was necessary.

Whoever they were, the illiterate savages of the border were keeping them busy. Faithful, those tribes, if stupid. But it was their place. All who worshipped Allah were assured of the rewards of faith, but Allah chose which gifts to bestow upon His people.

It was also possible they were SEALs or Delta, those annoying thorns in his side. Or perhaps Marines or Air Force. The Americans had a bureaucratic mindset that caused every service to duplicate efforts, including commandos. That maze of paperwork often kept data hidden for months, even years. Of course, that same morass had kept the September 11th attack hidden at their end, so perhaps he shouldn't curse the inefficiency. It was also a blessing that he'd just moved his headquarters. Darting through the ground like an animal was undignified, but it was one of the many sacrifices he'd had to make for Allah's will, and he bore the burden stoically.

Either way, military or CIA, ISI should know. Pakistan had one security apparatus. It simplified working with them. So someone needed a reminder of his human failings, and urged to dig deeper. Perhaps Shujjat's daughter would serve to guarantee his future loyalty. And if he proved unreliable, she might be most entertaining.

Bin Qasim smiled as he picked up the phone.

• • •

After a breakfast Kyle didn't remember, bleary-eyed and nauseous with fatigue, they rolled again. Nasima had asked more gently probing questions the night before. It was reasonable for a traveler to ask about threats, and the local people were friendly and liked to chat. He did vaguely remember the herder and his wife talking about the tribes, how they had shifted over the years from bolt rifles and shotguns to captured Soviet and surplus Pakistani military weapons. The farmer had a well-worn Russian side-by-side shotgun in the corner that he had pointed to.

"All I have, all I need," he'd said. Kyle had picked up enough vocabulary to grasp the statement. The man was in his fifties, gray and lean, and seemed wistful and reminiscent.

They thanked the man and his wife, who had accepted Nasima's story that the men were mercenaries looking to set up a smuggling route. The government was a remote concept out here, and smuggling not regarded as a sin, only a crime on paper. It wasn't the safest story, but it was the best available to explain two foreign men toting rifles and radios.

They were on the road again, with curried rice and vegetables wrapped in bread for lunch. Kyle had left a little more money, offering it as a gift, not as pay. These were a very proud people, and he didn't want to offend them. Given better access to modern technology, he saw them becoming a major power in the world. They had far more independence and self-reliance than, say, the French.

"So what now?" he asked Nasima.

"We know who we are to talk to," she said. "Though it's difficult."

"Difficult how?" Kyle asked.

"One of the leaders mentioned is named 'Qalzai,'" she said. Their stunned looks must have been visible even with her eyes on the road, because she said, "Yes, it is the same man. He is not involved with the Taliban, but he will not be friendly to you. I'm told he is trying to avoid them, and has paid several bribes of weapons."

"Oh, great," Kyle said. "That's all we need. So he did know, but wasn't going to queer a deal he already had. And by using us to gap his local enemy, he was trying to avoid more trouble. That fucking weasel!"

"About right," Wade said. "And I assume that by now, everyone has heard of us?"

"Yes," Nasima said. "I'm also in danger. They are told of a

woman translator. So from now on, one of you must lie down in back and not be seen."

"At least," Wade agreed.

"Then there's the other tribe, under a man named Gul," she said.

"What about them?" Kyle asked.

"They were under a man named Rahman, who was shot only three days ago," she said.

After that sank in, amid fifteen seconds of silence, Kyle said, "Wade, how would you feel about bugging out right now? We're not that far from the border here."

"Tempting, my friend," he said. "Nasima, what do we do? Is there any way we can find out what we need safely?"

"Safely? Where the Taliban and al Qaeda are concerned?" she asked. "There is no safe in this."

"Not anymore," Kyle agreed. "What do we do, then? Pull out? Go elsewhere for allies?"

"We must meet with them," Nasima said.

"*What?*" Kyle asked. "You've got to be kidding!"

"No," she said, shaking her head. "Carefully, of course, but we must meet and explain, so they stop the rewards for you."

"Nasima, they aren't going to drop it with an apology, believe me."

"Believe you?" she asked, voice rising. "Who has lived here? Who speaks the languages? Who has traveled the world and learned the language of the other? What makes you an expert on the ways of my people?" She was panting when done, and clearly annoyed.

For a moment, Kyle said nothing. Everything in his experience said she had to be wrong. Yet, he understood intellectually that this was a different culture with different rules.

"Okay, Nasima," he said, "I'll listen to your expertise. And I'm sorry."

It was her turn to stare for a moment. Clearly, she'd expected him to argue more.

"Very well," she said. "And I shall explain my reasoning."

"Please," he said. "It's outside my experience."

Taking a deep breath, she began to lecture. "Nearly all these tribes have fought each other at one time or another. They shift sides and allegiances as Americans change musical tastes. Bitter enemies today might be allies tomorrow, and change sides in the middle of battle."

"Okay," Kyle said. "But I don't find that reassuring." He could see finding new allies who would also want him to settle a score. He felt like a cross between a mercenary and a charitable organization.

"Maybe not," she said, "but it is the way. That is why prisoners are so hard for your army. One group captures others, and a brother of a cousin of a stepson reminds one of an obligation, and gets his group set free, or offers to change sides if the loot looks good."

"Right," Wade nodded. "I've heard of that. You think we can exploit it?"

Taking a deep breath, she said, "I don't know. But we must try. You can't accomplish your mission otherwise."

"True," Kyle said. There was something else he needed to ask, and he hoped it wouldn't make her angry.

"So tell me," he said, "why are you helping us? We appreciate it, but what's in it for you?" The right phrase came to mind and he said, "I know it's not about money."

"No," she said, eyes glazed. "It's about my job as a professor, gone because I'm a woman. It's about other women treated as dogs, run over in traffic, dead from lack of proper medical care. It's about children blown up by land mines, because cards or games to teach them what to avoid are 'gambling tools' or 'distractions from the Holy Quran' or 'American Satanist capitalist attacks on our purity.' It's about our homeland, torn apart by tribes, armies, terrorists, religious extremists, and the Russians. The Taliban and al Qaeda are creating trouble where there was more than enough already, and turning families against each other. People are poor and starving already, now they are weeping with hopelessness. The people you hunt are demons, and if I can help you kill them, I will."

Both men sat silently for some time. Nasima was literate, well spoken, controlled, and mature and had the deadly poise of a coiled viper. Small and feminine she might be, but she was sharp-witted and determined. No amount of religious fervor would shake her foundation beliefs.

"Good," Kyle said at last. "So tell us what to do?"

"First," she said, studying her hands on the wheel, "we must find someone who will carry a message to them."

Another tiny village was ahead. Kyle was slightly smaller than Wade. Only slightly. So he agreed to be locked in the trunk, so long as he was armed. He could breathe well enough through a gap in the rear deck. Wade lay down in the rear footwell, covered with rubbish and an old cloth they found. That left Nasima to ask questions like a local, while they sweated from heat and fear.

Had I known all this when the job was offered, Kyle thought, I would have laughed and asked for a discharge. But he knew he wouldn't have. Men like him were soldiers because of the constant trouble. They'd be bored to drink by doing nothing.

With sudden clarity, Kyle realized that his assignment to the Sniper School, good as it was, was the wrong task for him at that time. What he'd needed was to be tossed back in, like this, to recover his nerve and work through the pain.

The door opened and slammed, the engine started, and as the car pulled back onto the road, he heard Nasima mutter something. Wade said, "Okay," and there was no further response, so he concluded that he should just wait.

"I have found where Gul is," she said loudly enough to be heard. The gap through the rear deck meant it was clear, just distant. The only muffling was from engine noise and the rattling exhaust under Kyle.

"Excellent," Kyle said. "I hope."

"Yes, it's good news," she said. "But the meeting is going to be tense and awkward. I'll translate, and you'll have to take my advice." She seemed nervous about that.

"Nasima, we'll do exactly as you say in this area. You're the expert," Kyle said.

"Good," she said, and there was a slight sigh. Egos here could create trouble, and Kyle and Wade knew that. Kyle regretted his earlier condescension to her, but it seemed best to simply ignore it rather than dwell on it. He'd offended her, and that disturbed him on a professional level, and on a social level below that where he really shouldn't go.

"You should not carry rifles," she said as she pulled over. Kyle gratefully squeezed out of the trunk and squeezed back into the rear seat, as Wade slipped up front. Chinese fire drill done, Nasima resumed driving. They'd have to hide again when they stopped, but for now, the fresh air was welcome.

"Yeah, that would seem to be provocative," Kyle said, thankful for the interruption. "I'd like to have a pistol, though. Just in case."

"Okay," she said. "But don't handle it or draw it. Just keep it inside your coat."

"Agreed," he said, as did Wade. No doubt, he'd carry his Beretta.

"So where are we going?" he asked.

"Another farm," she said. "The people we want to see are there now."

"Now," he repeated. "Well, I suppose there's no need to delay."

"You are nervous," she said.

"No," he said. "There are people who want us dead. People who betrayed us and now realize we're a threat and want us dead. Not to mention other people we've offended who are likely to want us dead. Not nervous at all," he said.

" 'Terrified' is, I believe, the word we're looking for," Wade said.

"Terrified," Kyle admitted. And his pulse, respiration, and body temperature agreed. Facing a threat across the battlefield was bad enough. Walking into the home of someone who had every legal and moral right to execute them for murder was an entirely new level of pucker factor.

It was less than an hour, while they sweated and worried and discussed their negotiations with Nasima, before they drove off the road onto a worn but maintained track on a low slope. Goats covered the area, cropping at what low greenery there was. They appeared well fed. Whoever this Gul was, he was considerably better off than Qalzai's bunch. He even had a Mercedes, ten years old but in good repair, parked outside the broad house.

A teenage boy watched their approach, and Nasima waved. He returned the gesture, but wasn't smiling. It was simply an exchange that acknowledged their arrival wasn't clandestine, but a public entrance. Nasima drove up near him and got out. She said, "You should stand against the car so you can be seen as not a threat." They nodded and stretched.

The pending meeting was enough to cause near panic, and both men kept glancing at each other as they surreptitiously checked their pistols. Rifles they'd agreed would be obvious, of little use in close quarters, and could be perceived as a threat. But both wanted to be armed.

"What do we do if they tell us to disarm?" Kyle asked.

Wade pondered, and said, "I say we do it. It's not as if we could do more than take a couple with us if they want us dead, and I don't see them waiting for us to get that close if they plan to."

"Right," Kyle agreed. "So why are we bothering at all?"

"Because there might be an impulsive idiot," Wade said.

"And it makes us feel five percent better."

"That, too."

Kyle didn't know what it felt like to face a firing squad, but this had to be close. And very well might be doing so.

Nasima returned a few minutes later. They climbed in and let her chauffeur them, hoping she was as competent as she was confident.

The house was spacious enough; Gul was definitely more prosperous than Qalzai. The trucks were newer, and there were several of them. Two Nissans were behind the Mercedes. The courtyard had tall plants arranged, and was neatly paved. The gateway actually had a gate, of wrought iron. The pattern of it was interesting, but they were through too fast to decipher it. Inside, the wind was the barest zephyr with a faint smell of flowers. It wouldn't have helped cool them, even if they weren't terrified and sweating, hearts palpitating all the way up their throats. Brave men can face death. But only fools are fearless.

The men within did not look friendly. Kyle was glad he had his pistol, but equally sure it was only a reassurance, and wouldn't matter squat if it came to a fight. They were crammed into a small common room with chrome chairs, like those from a 1950s American diner.

Nasima introduced the Americans. She never got a chance to introduce the locals.

The headman, Gul, stormed at her, while pointing at them. He didn't shout, but the deadliness came through his voice just by inflection.

There was fury, hatred, murder there. She spoke back, when he stopped for breath, in slow, measured tones. Then he'd rage some more. Kyle felt partly that he should step in and take the blame, and partly that he should stay the hell out of it. He might just get them all killed. And for now, the men were waiting for Gul, and Gul was still talking with Nasima . . .

Realistically, Kyle couldn't blame him. If someone had shot one of his friends from 2,000 meters, he'd be pissed as all hell, too. Still, that wasn't reassuring.

He noticed, however, that Nasima was getting in longer and longer phrases. Her exotic features were calm and unafraid, and she seemed to be holding his attention. *No wonder she can handle forty kids,* he thought. She had the poise of a master actor.

It took about a half hour, during which time he and Wade sat motionless and aged ten years, before the two were speaking in conversational tones. Kyle no longer felt naked and vulnerable, but he still let his fingers brush his little Colt. Things weren't good, but at least they weren't ugly.

He realized how far things had progressed when Nasima interrupted his musing. "Kyle," she said, "now is the time to apologize."

He stepped forward nervously in the small room, and stood before the short, wiry man. "Gul," he said, "*Wobakha.* I'm sorry about the shot." Nasima translated as he spoke. "He wasn't the man we were sent to shoot, and we have no quarrel with you. Our quarrel is with others, and with those who set us up to attack you. They're cowards, afraid to fight their own battles, but we won't fight for them. I just wish we'd known sooner."

Nasima's translation ended, and Gul replied. "I accept it as honest," she said for him. "Though I am angered in my heart, raging. Your truth doesn't change the event. But fighting you will not help us, and won't bring to justice the ones who were behind it. I forgive you."

"*Sta na shukria,*" Kyle said. "I will have my government make compensation, if it will help a family in need." He'd phrased that carefully. An offer of a bribe wouldn't go over well. But it was possible, even likely, someone had been widowed or orphaned.

"The family is in need," Gul agreed, "and it would help much if you provided compensation."

Kyle nodded to Gul and quickly flicked his eyes to Nasima. "How much should I offer?" he asked.

She replied at once, "Offer him five hundred dollars worth of rupees. I will tell him it is a personal gift from you, because you haven't spoken to your government yet. That will make it seem more of a sacrifice on your part."

He nodded and drew two stacks of money from his pocket. They'd been counted into wads before the trip, for easy bookkeeping. That way, he didn't have to flash any more than that.

Thirty thousand rupees. Five hundred dollars. That was a fair price for a human life out here. Part of him wondered what twenty million in the right place would do.

Likely screw things to hell, he thought. Money didn't solve problems. But it did occasionally make things easier.

Gul accepted the money gravely, then handed it back to another with what were obviously instructions on where to take it. As his assistant nodded and scurried away, Gul turned back to Kyle and said, "That is thoughtful and gracious of you," was the reply. "An honest man fixes his mistakes. Let us eat and talk."

And only then did Kyle take his hand off his pistol. An offer to eat was an important aspect of hospitality, and that meant they were safe. For now.

So they sat and smoked—Kyle and Wade faked it—and ate lamb with noodles and a ton of cumin. Between tobacco fumes, spicy aromas, and body heat, the air was quite thick. To clear the tears, they drank water and imported grape juice. Gul laughed at their discomfort, then had less incendiary dishes brought. It seemed he accepted them on some level, at least.

Kyle decided he'd run a gauntlet of paddles, tar and feathers, if it would ingratiate them to these people and not get them killed. The hot food was hardly a real test.

When he thought that, he was afraid their new hosts might see it that way, and devise something *really* rough.

It didn't seem as if their hosts had warmed to them. But they were at least now distant professionals who could collaborate, much like another tribe or faction. No one was about to shoot them, Kyle was sure, and honor was a significant factor here. With that in mind, he relaxed just a little, and looked at Wade.

"So far, so good," he said.

"We hope," Wade replied.

Nasima came over and sat with them. "Welcome back," Wade said. "And thanks."

"Yeah, you've saved our behinds. Again," Kyle admitted. If they'd had her along from the start . . . Part of him wondered if the CIA could use her. If they'd sought someone like her in the first place, this mission would have been a lot smoother. Trust the bureaucrats to act before thinking.

Another part wanted to get done and leave her in peace. She was a fine lady, dammit, and didn't deserve all this crap.

"We are all saved, for the time being," she said. "I am in the odd position of sitting in a man's meeting, from their view. I am needed as a translator, and to tell them about you. So if things seem a little strained, that's part of it."

"I'd be surprised if there weren't many more straining things," Kyle said.

"No," Nasima replied, shaking her head vigorously. "Changing alliances are the way, here. They are sad still, but you have acted honorably. They might be stiff, but that is their own discomfort, not any fear of you. Our situation is much improved," she explained.

"Good," Kyle said, believing her intellectually. He just wished his stomach would relax. He was still in fight-or-flee reflex mode. "When are we going to discuss the situation?"

"Soon," she said. "We can't impose on hospitality for long without a reason."

"Will they be receptive?" he asked.

"I think so," she said. "There's little love for the others here, and I've not heard anything that would suggest it with this tribe. Remember, these are working people. They have to do more than worry about religion. Religion is very important, but civil life also has its needs. Those are subordinate to God's, but they still exist. If they are offered something worthwhile, they are less inclined to stray. America is a place they only hear about, it's not real, so there's no strong urge to fight it."

"More money?" Kyle asked.

"Properly offered, yes," she said. "It must never appear as a bribe, but as a gift or contract."

That was fine, Kyle thought. Buying their way out bothered him morally, but they had the cash, and if that's how things were done here . . .

After they were done eating, and the cigarettes and pipes were puffing out smoke, Nasima prompted Kyle. "Now would be a good time to talk," she said.

Nodding, Kyle took a deep breath and said, "Gul, we're grateful for your hospitality. It's been a tough time for us all lately. Now I need to ask for your help with a task."

"What do you need?" Gul asked back, blowing smoke from his nostrils. It ringed his head as it eddied and rose, giving him a sinister look despite his almost smile.

"We are sent to hunt a man," Kyle said. He wasn't ready to throw a name out yet; he needed to feel his way. "We need help finding him and getting to him. The people we dealt with turned out to be less than honorable and clumsy, too. But from what I have seen of your people, you could help us. I want to persuade you to do so."

"Americans need our help?" Gul replied through Nasima. "That's a change from the past." He didn't sound unfriendly, but he did sound a bit put upon. The irony in his voice was clear.

"America has always needed your help," Kyle said. "You live here, and know more about this region than we ever can. Any soldier knows this. Our politicians just think they know everything."

"Much like ours," Gul replied with a grin a foot wide. He chuckled. "Who is this man, and why do you seek him?" he continued, serious again.

"His name is Rafiq bin Qasim, and he's an enemy of our people," Kyle said. And again, he was glad for the .45 under his coat. A wave of tension swept across the room. It was palpable, almost physical as it silenced everyone.

"Mr. Qasim is well respected by some," Gul said, waving his hand to calm those nearest him. "He provides money for the poor and helps with those wounded in our battles."

"Be careful, Kyle," Nasima added.

"Oh, I will be," he said. Facing Gul, holding his eyes, he said, "In some ways, he may be well respected. But that is an act. He wants to use your people as a shield, because he knows we won't bomb him that way. In the meantime, he was part of the attack against our people."

"I have heard of that," Gul said. "They crashed planes into your greatest buildings."

"Those weren't just our buildings," Kyle said. "There were embassies in them. Also offices for the poor. Very few soldiers were attacked, because these people are too cowardly to fight real warriors. They now hide among other women and children, afraid to come out. There's only the two of us," he indicated himself and Wade, "but they still won't fight like men."

That seemed to have some effect. "Coward" was a grievous insult here, and while the Americans were not held in high regard, the two snipers versus bin Qasim and his personal army were a David to Goliath. They could call him afraid, and only by meeting them would he be able to prove his courage.

The faces around them were full of conflict. People don't like having their values challenged, nor being taken advantage of, and the suggestion of both was causing turmoil and debate. At the same time, there was no doubt that al Qaeda was being generous in the region to maintain diplomacy. The Taliban were loved by some, loathed by others, but feared and respected as Islamic warriors with a mission.

Wade caught Kyle's eye. He had something to contribute, and Kyle nodded. The man knew his history and politics, and Kyle was glad to have the backup. Wade had been an excellent choice for the mission.

"The people they attacked were innocents," Wade said. "They were women and children, tourists and workmen, merchants and diplomats. The Quran says that such people should be left out of war. Some of the victims were American and Eastern Muslims. This was not an attack on our government, it was an attack against children."

Kyle took over again, "If they want a fight, we're here for them. I've already told you how sorry we are for our mistake. Imagine if we'd sent a plane to bomb the village. We pick our targets with care, because we don't want to hurt the innocent. These, Nasima, please find a word for 'scum,' preferably involving pigs in a crude fashion, want only to create trouble. They seek a martyrdom."

Gul had been listening calmly, with nods and gestures to prompt them on. He spoke at last. "What if they seek a martyrdom? It is their right, even duty."

"Gul, if they want to meet Allah, we are here to provide the travel arrangements," Wade said. "But it is not just they who will suffer. We've had people in America speak out against all of Islam. We know you are respectable, and Nasima, and the Kuwaitis we met on the way—" they hadn't really met any, but a global view couldn't hurt— "but our people at home don't. All they know is that they were attacked by men who claimed to speak for Allah. If you help with this, it will be a favor to our innocents, and let you . . . show the true face of your God to these corrupt idolaters. If everyone unites against them, they'll go away. Then we can devote our efforts to peace and farming."

Gul was nodding more often. "I think he sees the logic of our position," Wade said.

"Right," Kyle said. "Do you think they agree enough to help us?"

Nasima spoke again, her poise very submissive, almost begging. The exchange went back and forth for several minutes.

"Dude, we're still waaay up the creek here," Wade said.

"Don't I know it. And that bodyguard type looks nervous, so let's stop talking." Kyle didn't point at the man in the corner, arms crossed, who was a knotty giant by local standards.

Neither Kyle nor Wade said anything. Nasima talked on and finally turned back.

"He says he doesn't want a fight with America. But he also doesn't want a fight with the Taliban or other tribes."

"So tell him we don't want a fight, either. We haven't done anything over here since we sent weapons to the mujahideen, and we will leave as soon as we get rid of al Qaeda, because they are hurting our people at home," Kyle said. This wasn't easy, trusting to a translated phrase to carry the proper logic and emotion for the diplomacy he wasn't trained for anyway.

Nasima spoke again. He wondered how she did it. If this screwed up, she'd be killed out of hand, or worse. Kyle had an oath and a mission here, what did she have?

He thought and decided she had her own country to protect. And by getting rid of the Taliban influence, even on this side of the border, she had a better chance at a life. Probably her motives were better than his.

Nasima interrupted his thoughts. "He says that America didn't do anything to stop the Taliban from taking power, and forgot his people after the Russians were gone."

"Dammit, I was afraid he'd see it like that," Wade said.

"So you phrase our arguments. It's your field," Kyle suggested.

"I'll try," Wade sighed. "We don't make policy for our government. Our leaders are as fragmented and childish as the tribes here are."

She looked wide-eyed at him. "But that's insulting—"

"Yes, I know, but tell him that," Wade said. "Then tell him we came here because it's easier to talk to leaders here, who can clearly see their own interests, than to our leaders, who are interested only in money."

Kyle saw where Wade was taking it and nodded. That might be a better approach. Let the locals think they could do things the U.S. government could, which was true enough, and that they'd be heroes out of it, even if only they would know.

Nasima got both phrases out in a hurry, even if she seemed to protest a bit. *Don't blame me, I'm just telling you what the Yankee said to say.*

But Gul nodded very slightly, and turned his lined face back to Kyle. Nasima translated his reply as, "I am a man of my word. I feel sorry for you if your leaders are not."

Wade said, "Tell him we're sorry, too, and wish our government had done more. The people here are kind, generous, and we've made many friends. We're sorry Qalzai lied as he did, and we'll try to see that something is done. But that's not our mission. Our only mission, our jihad, is against al Qaeda and only al Qaeda. We have to do it, and we're going to do it."

As soon as she finished speaking he added, "But we'd like his help, because he is more trustworthy than our former allies, and knowledgeable of the area. We can't buy that kind of ally; we can only gain one through trust and faith."

Still thinking as he went, he said, "And if he'll do it, he'll have our gratitude, and will sooner see the day when all his enemies leave him alone to live in his own land." He motioned at his pocket. Nasima nodded, and he drew out another packet, containing almost $2,000 in rupees. "How do we offer it properly?"

"I'll tell him it is a gift with which to buy weapons and equipment."

"Not peaceful stuff?" Kyle asked. He didn't really care; he knew where it would go. It just seemed an odd way to offer it.

"That would imply he cannot take care of his people alone," she said. "But if it's offered as foreign aid for defense, so to speak, it's diplomacy, not charity."

"Right," he agreed.

Gul nodded at this, and accepted the money coolly. He didn't even bother to count it. Clearly, the money couldn't be perceived as a bribe. His reply was slow and measured. "You flatter him, he says. But it's honest and restrained flattery, and there's logic to what you say. He'll help you find your man. But in exchange, he expects that you will fight for him if he finds Qalzai."

"In a second," Kyle agreed. "As long as our first priority is our target. We'll nail Qalzai if we see him, or afterwards if there's time, but our mission is first. As Wade says, it's our jihad."

Nasima said to him, "I think you actually understand jihad, rather than it being merely a phrase to you."

"Damn straight," Kyle said. "We'll haunt him as ghosts if we have to. But I'd prefer a good, clean shot."

After another exchange, Gul started laughing. Nasima said, "I told him everything, including your last phrase. He says you are a hill man at heart."

It was late by the time everyone had agreed to work together. They were shown to rooms, Nasima with an eldest daughter, Kyle and Wade to a room along the outside wall.

They slept adequately. The beds were comfortable, with real mattresses. The room was lighted and heated, if small. And it had a poured concrete floor. All in all, it was about equivalent to a military barracks or cheap rustic motel. The facility wasn't the problem. The pending fight and the prickliness of new allies was what was still a worry.

They had tea and naan again for breakfast, with jam and butter. It was tasty, but Kyle agreed with Wade's comment that, "I can't wait to get back Stateside for bacon and eggs."

"Yeah, but they're better than MREs or T-packs."

"True," Wade said. "I'll stop the bitching."

13

THEY WERE ON THE ROAD AGAIN AT ONCE, IN THREE pickups. These, however, were in much better shape than the last one. They were dusty and faded, obvious working trucks, but everything worked and there were no sharp metal bits poking through the seats. Rested enough, with food and a full CamelBak of water, weapons, ammo, translator, and reliable (hopefully) allies, it seemed as if it was a real mission at last.

Just before noon, they turned off the road and angled uphill. It was a jolting ride, but the drivers were familiar with the area and experienced in the techniques needed. They'd done this a time or two.

Just how long had these feuds been going on? Kyle wondered. They were less urgent and intense than the Middle East or the Balkans, but they were remembered for just as long. A strange life, plotting and scheming and never being at peace. And there were people who insisted America was militant and violent. He smirked. A few of those whiners needed to spend a week here.

Or Bosnia. There were too many similarities, and he didn't want to go back there yet again. Dammit, the past was the past. And this future might not be too long, so he'd have to pay attention.

Shortly, they got out and started slogging on foot again. Gul had confirmed that the cell phones could call his farm, and at the suggestion, Kyle had taken another risk and given one of the two to Gul's burly bodyguard, herder, and deputy, Pir, who was far more perceptive than he looked. Nasima wrote out directions for using the phone, and he seemed familiar with them. So the vehicles could catch up later, when they were needed for extraction. For now, they'd move quietly.

The walking was a bitch. Kyle had a sore spot on his left foot he felt sure was a small stress fracture. It wasn't debilitating, but it was annoying. They were definitely getting their route marches in. He didn't think the Army would waive PT for the year, though. Pity.

"I wonder how much of a problem it's going to be to find this weasel?" he asked aloud.

"I don't think finding him is the problem," Wade said. "I think it's more that no one wants to screw with this guy."

"Yeah," Kyle agreed. "If he'll blow up children and torture women for fun, who wants to piss him off and see him when he's *really* mad?"

"Exactly. But that means we can hope it's not that hard of an infiltration."

"Except for that part about two Americans and a translator," Wade said. "I think he knows we're here."

"Yeah, it sucks to be us," Kyle said, "but I don't think a squad would be less noticeable."

"Right, he'd be gone. We're along because we won't scare him. Until it's too late, that is."

"That's the plan," Kyle chuckled. "I bet he crapped his pants after that shot I took."

"He should," Wade said. "He's only big and bad because we haven't found him yet."

"That's the idea. Keep in mind how cool we are, how efficient, and eventually we might believe it."

"Well, us and our allies," Wade said.

Gul had been good to his word. His tribe was also better equipped than Qalzai's had been. They had newer, cleaner weapons, including AK-47s in 5.45mm and even one AK-100. They clearly had better sources of intel and materiel. In that light, Kyle had reason to be thankful.

After jabbering around a map, Gul and his next deputy Nasrulah, who had no teeth and a bald head, pointed out a likely area. "We'll go here," he said, "and then over this way. We'll find them."

It was reassuring to the Americans to see a map. It was even a standard 1:50,000 military map. They brought out their own, newer copy and took a look at the area. They were trained professionals, and the contours on the map formed into peaks they could see in their minds. It would improve their navigation on the ground.

"You know," Wade said, slipping on another loose rock, "if I'd thought it was going to be this much of a pain, I wouldn't have been so eager. To hell with the enemies, this terrain sucks."

" 'A bitching GI is a happy GI,' " Kyle replied with mirth.

"Screw that," Wade said, though he smiled, too. "I'd say it could be worse, but I won't, because I can think of fifty or a hundred ways it could be a lot worse."

"We could be on an alien planet, tracking down some strange artifact . . ." Kyle said.

"Or just rain and incoming fire. That seems a lot more likely and real," Wade said.

The poor excuse for a road dove into a deep cut in the hills. Wind whipped occasional dust devils down it. It was foreboding, even though silent and empty.

At least it seemed empty. A burst of fire boiled sand from the rutted track in front. Everyone scattered for cover.

"Son of a bitch!" Wade gasped as he dropped down between Kyle and Gul behind a boulder to one side.

"Hey, you're the wiseass who mentioned incoming fire," Kyle said. Frankly, he was getting sick of it himself. He just wanted to take this shot, drop this freak, and get home. The universe seemed to be conspiring against him.

"Right, so what do we do now?"

"Nasima?" Kyle called after the next burst. She looked over from behind another rock, keeping low. "Tell them I want them to shoot where Wade shoots his tracers."

"Tracers?" she asked.

"Bullets that light up."

"Ah, yes," she said, and told Gul, because of course, she couldn't give orders, only he could, and she could only relay the request.

Luckily, Gul nodded agreement with a grin.

"Right, Wade, you light 'em up, they pour out the fire, I'll spot for you and hit anything that needs precision."

"You got it," Wade replied. He had already swapped out his magazine for one of straight tracers. He pushed the button to light up the Eotech sight and hunkered down around the little carbine.

It was noisy, Kyle thought. He hadn't expected this much fire from as few people as he could see. It took a few seconds before he figured out what was happening.

Their fire discipline, to put it mildly, sucked rocks. They were great at pouring out long bursts of automatic fire that did little but waste ammo and make noise. Some of the more experienced ones stayed on semi and banged off rapid fire groups that were likely yards across. Only two or three of the group were worth a damn.

Kyle reflected that that was often true in American units, too. But in an American, or any, actual military unit, there'd be an instructor to train the panicky kids out of that. Some of these guys had been shooting like this for forty years, and he wasn't sure how they'd lived that long, considering the real battles they must have been in.

Unless, of course, the people they fought against were equally bad shots.

Still, there was enough metal in the air that something was bound to hit sooner or later. A quick, decisive action would end this before that happened, or before their allies ran out of ammo.

Kyle sighted what looked like a vintage Russian RPK, from the snout protruding between two clumps of bedrock and the muzzle flash. Whoever it was was spraying with abandon. "Wade! Reference: twelve o'clock high. RPK."

"Sighted," Wade said. "Nasima, have them fire on my tracer!" He squeezed off a short burst that came close to doing the job itself.

This was a game to the locals. As the streaks appeared, they enthusiastically turned their weapons on target and actually *aimed,* at least as far as the start of their fire. Enough bullets hit to carve the outcroppings down some, and there were several dings against the weapon itself. Its fire stopped. Whether or not there was a casualty behind it was unclear. Either way, the incoming fire declined.

Kyle had already scanned and found a competent marksman. He called to Wade, who ended the problem by himself, his tracer round cracking center of mass as the man slipped from behind a boulder to shoot, and dropping him. Nevertheless, their friends poured out a sufficient volume to reduce the corpse to hamburger. That was of great psychological effect, as the incoming fire tapered off another order of magnitude.

But someone over there was shouting orders, and the copper-clad hornets picked up once again. One of their own allies had been hit and was screaming. Chips flew above Kyle and he decided it was time to duck. He pulled in close to the earth, shimmied forward just enough to get a peek, and sought a target.

Yes, there was Qalzai, that sneering, conceited jackass. It wasn't a good idea to mix business and pleasure, but in this case, Kyle would make an exception. There were rounds cracking close to him now, but he ignored them. He eased the SMLE forward, clicked off the safety, and sighted carefully. The range wasn't great, perhaps 100 meters, and that was an easy range for this weapon. As long as there was no sudden movement.

Qalzai ducked and shifted, to yell at another of his men. Kyle sighed, avoided letting it get to him, and resighted. It was only a matter of a second, though in battle, seconds of action could decide the issue. But calm and professionalism would win. He breathed, squeezed, and felt the sharp kick against his shoulder.

Qalzai came apart in a mess, half his face blown off. Better yet, from a tactical point of view, he wasn't quite dead yet. He screamed and thrashed and provided all kinds of gratuitous special effects to dissuade his buddies, who were now not firing, but running. They left their wounded and even some of their gear in their haste to retreat. Kyle wondered at the effect he'd had with that one shot, until he realized Wade had accounted for two others. That was five down out of twenty or thirty, a respectable casualty count and more than these people liked to see in thirty seconds of feuding.

Most of the kills had been by Kyle and Wade, or at least under their direction. That left far fewer wounded than could be expected. Kyle de-stressed with a long drink of water, ignoring the grit and slime in it for the cooling, cleaning wetness it provided. He tried to ignore the screams of the wounded, which were punctuated by cracks of fire as several were put out of their misery.

He and Wade at once administered first aid to their side's casualties. One man had a vicious wound to his shoulder, the bone nicked and fragments scattered through the flesh. He bandaged it as best he could and tied the arm in place. One man was dead, a bullet through the lung leaving a pool of blood two yards across. Wade had bandaged up a man with an excruciating shot to the hand, and three minor wounds where people had crashed into rocks.

While they were finishing, the patrol Gul had led up returned with loot, including the damaged RPK. Considering the local craftspeople, it was likely to be operational again within a few days. Gul was grinning a yard of teeth. Nasima translated his raucous comments. "He says you shoot with Allah, destroying the enemies. And he congratulates you on Qalzai. He doesn't say so, but you've proved yourself to him."

"*Sta na shukria*," Kyle said in thanks.

Several bodies besides Qalzai's were brought down. Mirza was one of them, and Kyle felt saddened by it. He'd been a good man. It was likely his only fault was in teaming up with Qalzai. Khushal had gotten away, apparently, or had not been involved.

"No Khushal. Good. He's a good kid," Wade said. They'd both been thinking it.

"Yeah," Kyle agreed. "And there's Bait," he said, pointing at another corpse. "I guess it wasn't a bad day."

"Glad to hear it, but we better hurry," Wade said. "We need to be well clear before dark."

Nasima nodded, repeated it, and Gul shouted orders. In moments, everyone had formed back up, the bodies left behind with some hasty dirt and rocks thrown over them. "They will bury them better later," Nasima said. "We are moving for safety. But it's not right to leave any Muslim exposed to carrion birds and wild dogs."

Kyle frankly didn't give a damn about Qalzai and Bait, but it would make sense tactically to have them better covered. Although it wasn't likely to happen before this mission played out. "That's decent," he said diplomatically, taking another pull of water and falling into line.

14

BIN QASIM WAS VERY HAPPY. THE NIGHTCLUB BLAST
had been perfect. Better yet, the soldier of God had not died in
the explosion, but had been captured by the German authorities.
Since decadent Westerners would never execute an enemy, except
for the Americans, and even they did it so rarely and after such a
long time that it was meaningless, he could be ransomed in exchange for reporters or diplomats. Perhaps Allah would smile and
some of them would be women, who could learn of God's hierarchy
from bin Qasim first.

Or, the bomber could be shot in custody, by another soldier, of
course, and turned into a martyr, creating greater fear. Already,
southern France's Muslim population had managed to close many
of the clubs, and impose decent standards of dress upon women. If
Germany could be brought along next, the new wave of Islam could
sweep the world.

And if America could not be persuaded, why, then she could be
raped like the whore she was.

The phone rang then, line number three. He picked up the receiver quickly but carefully.

"Yes?" he said.

"We are on our way," a voice whispered. "There has been a fight.
The Diversion Unit was hurt badly, but inflicted three casualties.
Here's our coordinates," the informer said. There was a pause as he
switched to text messaging, followed by a string of numbers on the
display.

"Thank you. Call when they are within five kilometers."

"Go with Allah," was the last comment before the line went
dead.

Bin Qasim marked the map. That was a convenient location, but he'd wait a while. When they were closer, he'd spring the trap. When they were too close to escape.

Grinning, he shut down the computer and turned to matters of the soul.

After which, those American snipers would be turned into a sign from God.

It was Wade who suddenly said, "What the hell?"

They were moving along a shelf that protruded from the hillside. Wade had casually leaned against the wall to adjust his ruck, and seen something . . .

"Does that man have a radio?" he asked aloud.

There was instant reaction to the tone of his voice, and Kyle turned. Sure enough, there was a short, shaggy man with what looked like a radio or cell phone just disappearing into his pocket. The expression on his face was of utter surprise, though a quick storm of other emotions rolled across. He clearly was embarrassed.

Nasima said something that included "Telepone," the word borrowed from English, and in seconds the man was surrounded and pinned to the wall. One of Gul's close henchmen held up the device. It was, in fact, an Iridium phone, similar to that the snipers carried.

There was shouting, curses, and accusations. Gul and Kyle both had to yell for silence. That left the man, Sidiq, standing surrounded by a semicircle of bewildered, angry people. He was relieved of his weapons in short order, but not without a struggle. He was pushed down, acquiring a bruise on the cheek along the way. Again Gul had to shout for order. This time, silence and calm prevailed.

"I can't think of a valid reason for this clown to have a cell phone. Can you?" Kyle asked, voice quivering with rage.

"No," Wade said. "Nasima?"

She was already speaking to Gul, and it was clear that he was not happy. Not only was this a threat to him, but it was a threat to his guests. The two together amounted to a major sin against propriety, the tribe, and what nationalism there was.

"How much did he talk? Do we need to abort?" Kyle asked. He hated like hell the idea that they might have to bug out, but if someone was waiting for them, it would be suicide to continue.

"I am asking," Nasima assured him, her tone snappish. Kyle breathed slowly and mentally backed off. He kept trying to run every detail himself, and he simply wasn't qualified for some of this. *Let the other guy handle his own MOS*, he thought. *Or woman in this case.* There was too much to do, and too much he didn't know, for him to throw his weight around.

Sidiq was defensive and outraged at the accusations. But when Gul asked him point blank, "Who did you call? Three numbers here. Who?" he didn't have a good answer. He shut up entirely.

While in an American court the Fifth Amendment would protect him against self-incrimination, this was neither court nor America. It was a battlefield, and they had to know what was going on, and act on that information quickly.

Gul punched Sidiq, a heavy, straight smash to his face that knocked him back against the rock. He staggered, eyes unfocused and head lolling.

When he recovered, with a shake of the head that threw drops of blood from his nose, his attitude had changed. He started ranting something about Allah. Kyle didn't need a translation to know he was justifying himself, but when Sidiq faced him, he spoke in English anyway.

"It is a holy honor to die for Allah," he said. His eyes had that look of the true believer. The nutcase who will endorse hatred, killing, socialism, or other religious idiocies, no matter how illogical or how often proved wrong, just because he believes.

Kyle had had enough. "An honor indeed," he said. He wasn't opposed to torture for information in this case, but it would take time they didn't have. He snagged a grenade from his harness, flipped the pin out with his left thumb, and stuffed it down the coarse shirt of the little troll. He gave him a heartfelt knee to the balls, driving his leg to his own waist, a good foot above the skinny little runt's crotch, then drove his heel into the man's chest. Sidiq grunted, "Guhhhhh!" with a terrified look on his face as he bounced over the precipice and down. Precisely at the three-second mark, a horrendous *Boom!* indicated that his body was splattered over the cliff face. "Bon fucking voyage. Say hi to Allah for me," Kyle said.

There was a slim chance someone might hear the boom, identify it, and come after them, but there were so many little engagements, uses of grenades for mining, celebrations, stray land mines, and fire for God only knew what else that he wasn't worried. And didn't care. He'd been a traitor, and he was dead. And with bin Qasim knowing their location anyway, it couldn't really hurt.

And, he reflected, killing the little bastard made him feel quite a bit better.

That done, fury and fear fighting inside, he drew out his own phone and called in.

On the second ring, it was answered.

"Gilpin." Gilpin was Robash's civilian assistant. His voice was deep, and he likely bellowed in person.

"Mr. Gilpin, Sergeant Monroe. I have a problem," he said.

"What do you need?"

"We've got a local infiltrator with an Iridium phone, who likely called our target. Can we check the numbers called and track the physical location of the receiving party?"

"Stand by, Sergeant," Gilpin replied. "Can you give me the ID from the phone that called, hold on air, and I'll get a rep to talk to me?"

"Sure," Kyle agreed. He read off the serial number, and the phone's ID from memory. "Holding," he said.

Kyle spent the pause twitching and fidgeting. It was only two minutes, then Gilpin was back. "Sergeant Monroe, the number belongs to a geologic survey company based out of Kazakhstan. The call was received within two hundred miles of your location. That's as accurate as they can say unless the user attaches a GPS option."

"I don't think the user is going to do that," he observed wryly.

"Neither do I. Sorry I can't be of more help on that."

"Oh, that helps," Kyle said. "It was definitely in theater, therefore it's a threat. One of our allies had a cell phone and was calling out."

"Understood. What do you plan to do?"

"I'm not aborting yet, if that's what you're asking. We'll take a different route in," he said. He probably should abort, but it had become a point of honor. He and Wade were going to get this rat bastard.

"Understood. We'll be here if you need us."

"Thanks. Kyle out." He disconnected. "Well," he said to Wade and Nasima, "that's that. They know we're coming. What do we do?"

"Hide in a hurry, and either evac or at least clear the area," Wade said.

Nasima spoke to Gul, who said, "If we get higher, we will have better position and visibility."

That was true, Kyle thought, and there wasn't much in the way of air support here. "Sounds good," he said. "Quietly and quickly."

The terrain wasn't that hard to climb; it had plenty of texture. Still, they were at altitude, and the air was thin. Adding huge rucks to the equation made it an athletic event. Gul's people helped carry some of the gear, but even so, it was crushing. The safest technique was to slither over the rocks, using hands and feet. Dust and sweat turned to mud on their skin, and they were all soon abraded and scraped.

They rested every hour, sipping water slowly and chewing at boring rations. As soon as their parched throats were comfortable, they were climbing again. The locals, Kyle thought, moved like mountain goats. Even Nasima was ahead of him, bouncing easily. He actually had caught a glimpse of ankle, and her muscle tone was rather attractive. Sighing, he pushed on.

They were still safe at sunset, and it seemed there'd be no more interruptions. Wade had suggested, and Kyle had agreed, that they should bite the bullet and travel around the village to another site. There was no need to risk setting up where their traitor had known they would be. Gul nodded at the suggestion, said, "Very wise," and led them widely around.

They pushed on in the dark until progress was impossible. The Americans had night vision, and Gul had an old Russian set that was twenty years old. But the rest had eyes only, and even with a half-moon, it was too dark for safe footing. They unrolled blankets and snuggled against the hillside, under a slight overhang that cut the wind. It did nothing about noise, and whistling whines announced gusts all night. Any audible approach would also be apparent, of course. Sometimes, the best shelter was in the open.

Underblankets, wool chapan coats and shirts, with their lungees wrapped down around their faces, it wasn't chill, but cool. It couldn't be above forty-five degrees outside, and the windbreak and clothes stopped them from getting hypothermia but not much else. But they'd trained for worse, and the locals seemed used to it. Or maybe it was just the lack of central heating most of them had.

Gul posted sentries, using his night vision and one of the American sets. Kyle felt as if he were loaning out his car to a teenager. But the young man took only a few minutes of fiddling to decipher the controls, and slipped off like a ghost. He seemed to know what he was about, so Kyle tried to concentrate on sleeping.

Oddly enough, he did. Exhaustion put him under, but there was something that lowered his suspicions. With Nasima along, and the effort Gul had made toward communicating, planning and tactics, it *felt* right. No yokels, these; they were competent guerillas.

They awoke at dawn, breath misting in the frigid air. There was some frost, and Kyle ached all over. He had blisters on his cold, stinging toes, chafing around his boot tops and on his shoulders, and a crick in his neck. His mouth tasted horrible.

There was no tea, but he brushed his teeth as they started walking again at once, out from the ledge they'd sheltered under and up the slope. A swig of water to rinse with made him feel five percent closer to human, and he shifted his gear around as he marched, trying to find the most comfortable arrangement. He forced himself not to favor his right foot, that being the worst-blistered one, because he could injure himself worse with bad posture.

"Man, you look as ugly as I feel," Wade said to him, catching up alongside as they crawled over a steep slab.

"Same to you, pal," he snapped back. "Enjoying that great fresh air and the huge paycheck that comes with it?"

"Oh, absolutely. I feel like singing," Wade said.

"You do and I'll shoot you first," he replied. "I didn't think you could get a hangover without drinking."

"Altitude," Wade said.

"Yeah, I know. Doesn't mean I like it, just because I understand it."

The verbal sparring stopped as one of Gul's men slipped back and extended his arm. He held the night vision goggles, cased and secure. "*Sta na shukria,*" Kyle said as he took them. It was more natural to him now than "thank you."

The terrain wasn't all uphill. They spent as much time angling obliquely across slopes down. That was sometimes worse, with slippery dirt over loose, scaly rock underneath.

Kyle estimated their progress at perhaps one mile per hour, with the rough ground and slope. Some areas were smooth and green, lush with growth from rain caught by the hillsides. Other areas were chaotic jumbles of bedrock. It certainly never got boring, he thought, as they clambered over a sharp, jutting point and lowered themselves.

Nasima was panting, but gamely hanging on. She'd started with youthful energy and flexibility, but in the long term, the veterans could push beyond the fatigue barrier. Even sheened in sweat with stringy hair escaping her hijab, she was striking. Kyle wondered again why she stayed here. With her drive, she could be very successful in the West.

Still, home was home. He'd do well here, with an American pension. He couldn't see himself doing so.

"Are you okay?" he asked her at a break.

"I am," she said. "Though my shoes are too stiff. But I will manage." She drank water from her canteen, a typical camping-style one slung over her shoulder, and then greeted Gul as he approached. She translated effortlessly as they chatted.

"We are in the area," Gul said. "I expect they are in the village over that next ridge," he pointed. "It's about seven kilometers, and we'll have height. What do you want to do?"

Wade spoke first. "We need to reconnoiter the area, and find a good route down and on. We'll have to get within about five hundred meters."

"Next time, I suggest the mortar," Gul said with mirth.

"Wouldn't we like to," Kyle said. "Or just spot for an Air Force jet. But we have to be discreet, and we have to avoid casualties. The press will cause trouble."

"Perhaps you should use the reporters for target practice," he said.

"We had that exact conversation," Wade said, "only with politicians."

They all laughed.

Gul continued, "We are on the far side from the road. We'll need to sneak around and across. If you can call, our drivers can be waiting to pick us up."

"Right. Where?" he asked. It wouldn't do to have vehicles close enough to take fire from direct-fire weapons and give away their position. They looked at the map and selected a location. The ridge they'd be on tapered off to the west, and a road hooked around from the south. It was about two kilometers away from the target, and would be concealed until pursuing elements cleared the ridge by going either over or around.

"Looks good. But if I were this guy, and knew we were coming, I'd have patrols all over these ridges," Wade said.

"Assume so," Kyle nodded. "So we can't have the vehicles show up until after the shot. We can do that with the phones easily enough."

"And meantime?"

"Meantime," Kyle said, "we need very good hilljacks to find where those patrols go."

Gul grinned, "I have three men who are perfect. They will tell you who made their shoes."

"I'll settle for the shoe size," Kyle said. "I hope they won't be disappointed."

Gul whistled up three of his men. All looked to be on the older side, though with their living conditions, that could be late twenties. They nodded, and slipped off in three directions; along the ridge, down behind it to the road to the south, and back to the east where they'd come from.

Gul said, "We'll want the trucks on the road, and traveling, not parked. No one will attach significance to them."

"Of course," he continued after a pause, "that little bastard Sidiq may have given them the license numbers."

"Risk we take," Kyle said. "But if they aren't close by, it shouldn't hurt us."

"True. Let's rest while the scouts search."

So they did, and Kyle actually got a precious hour of sleep. Wade woke him and they switched off. Nasima could translate, she couldn't make tactical decisions. One of them had to be awake for that.

After they were both awake, they fidgeted. Nothing would speed up the process, and Gul's patrols had binoculars but not radios. They'd report back in person when they had something substantial, and not before.

15

AFTER A LUNCH OF BEANS AND RICE WITH VEGE-tables, heated over a trioxane stove, Gul asked, "How do we approach this?" His scouts had come back and drawn a map of the area. The al Qaeda patrols were marked.

"It's not that hard, really, at least on paper," Kyle said. "We find a good spot for a shot, set up support, take the shot, and run. Once we're done, we can call support aircraft. We just have to hold out long enough to get a chopper in. Hopefully no more than an hour or two. If we run fast . . ." he tapered off.

"Running is not dishonorable when a task has been done, or to save soldiers for a better fight," Gul said. "How do we arrange supporting fire?"

That was an excellent question. The discussion was important, but Kyle was groggy and wanted a nap. He'd settle for sitting still while they talked tactics.

It was decided to make the shots in the evening. They'd be to the southeast of the target, which would give them shadows and illumination. There was a risk of reflection from the scopes, but long shrouds and careful use of fabric should avoid that. The sun wouldn't quite be in their eyes, but they might get some glare.

On the other hand, it would be much harder for them to be pursued at night, it would avoid another night camping, and would let them use NVG and then aircraft for overwhelming effect. There were no ideal conditions. But this was a good compromise.

With an improving grasp of the language and Nasima's assistance, it was a much easier infiltration. They moved up the ridge before dinnertime, flitting from bush to boulder. They kept below the military crest until they found a good site, and made a quick, surreptitious recon over the peak.

Yes, there was a village. And it had signs of being more than that. First, there was a twenty-meter radio mast. Also two surplus Pakistani army technical vehicles, guards at the door of one house, and patrols on Suzuki dirt bikes. "Looks like it," Wade said.

"Yeah," Kyle agreed. This was much more military than the last encounter, and the radio antenna was the key item. Almost everyone around here was armed tactically. But communication implied a strategic mind. And that slight arch behind the house was . . . yes, a satellite dish. "This be the place, I think," he said.

Gul eagerly took his directions, dispersing his men in groups of two and three to provide cover fire. Once Kyle or Wade took the shot, they were going to pour automatic-weapons fire and RPGs into the camp, then run.

"I'll wait here," Nasima said.

"The hell you will," Kyle replied. "We need our translator alive. I'll motion if I need you. Get down the hill where you're shadowed from stray shots."

"Yes, Kyle," she sighed, clearly not happy at being pushed aside again.

"Not sure if she's just eager to see the climax of all this, trying to be one of the guys, or afraid to be down there alone," Wade said.

"Dunno," Kyle said quietly. "I do know I don't want a civilian this close. And she's got a real life I'd hate to see wasted. I know it's cold, but I couldn't care less if two or three of these guys buy it."

"Yeah," Wade said. "She's got presence, a way of grabbing you. And she's a babe."

"I hadn't noticed," Kyle lied. Yes, she was stunning. He couldn't know her genetic mix was Pashto, Moghul, Turk, and Hazara. He did know she was exotically beautiful, and her temper, wit, and keen mind made her that much more exciting. And as a local, a Muslim, and a civilian support specialist, she might as well be on the moon for his chances of approaching her. So he wasn't going to go there. Anymore. He reached into his ruck and drew out his ghillie. He wanted the best concealment he could get.

" 'Hadn't noticed,' " Wade said with a snort. "If you say so." He reached for his suit, too.

"What's our range?" Kyle asked, ignoring the comment.

"About eight hundred meters."

"Not close enough," he said. The SMLE could reach that far . . . but it would be a high-arcing trajectory, and not reliable. Especially with the bogus "match" ammo he had. As near as he could tell, it was standard ball. Still, the smith had done an honest job on the rifle. And there wasn't anything he could do about it now. "Can we get closer?"

A brief exchange yielded the answer, "Five hundred meters. No closer." That was a very respectable range for the SMLE, but doable. It had been a mistake to bring the Barrett in the first place. It wasn't a weapon for extreme precision. It was a weapon for busting armor and vehicles. An infiltration with support was how it should have been played all along.

Next time, he'd tell them he wanted a weapons platoon.

"Three hundred," Kyle said as he donned the shapeless tan ghillie. There was nothing without risk. He'd prefer to simply call an air strike at this point, but that wasn't possible in putatively friendly territory with so many undefined people around. He wasn't going to call them "innocent," but he would give them the benefit of the doubt because his orders said so.

Gul sighed in exasperation as he answered, "Yes."

So they sought an approach down the rocks. It would need to allow them a swift retreat, heavy cover, good concealment, and a clear field of fire. The criteria were tough. Luckily, the ridge was long and geologically recent. There would be an appropriate place somewhere, they just had to find it.

It only took twenty minutes. While Gul and his boys might not be professionally trained, they were experienced enough to be patient and calm. One of the teenagers whistled softly for attention, and grinned a mouth of teeth as he pointed.

"Good enough," Kyle commented. It was. Bedrock with enough texture for traction lay down the hill, with tumbled slabs over it, slowly weathering away after their collapse from a vertical peak above.

He and Wade, with Gul and the teen, moved forward. Kyle would rather have had another experienced troop, but it was the kid's right as the finder to be along. Still, he seemed reliable. Above and behind them, the other six hugged the ridge, prepared to fire and under orders to do so only if incoming fire threatened the snipers. That left one driving each vehicle, and one each on the guns in case of pursuit.

The sun was angling down, shadows lazily falling across the landscape as they snuck down. "We might get darkness for cover, too."

"Excellent," Wade said. "Though I don't think we've got the only night vision."

"I bet we use it better," Kyle said. It was arrogant, he knew, but really, most of these guys weren't that well trained. Cunning, sneaky, intelligent, sure. But not trained and schooled. Education was key.

Education, patience, logistics, communications, adaptation . . . even on a mission with only two troops, he reflected, battle was a complex skill that took massive support. "An Army of One" might be a great PR tool for recruiting, but this mission depended on two snipers, their knowledge, local support, a chunk of cash, a radio, a computer, an orbiting aircraft, satellite intel, CIA-gathered intel, several transport aircraft, and four military installations. Two generals, their staffs, an infantry lieutenant, a whole chain of supply clerks, and several pilots and mechanics had put them here.

He shook himself back to the present, though the mental drift was good, as it meant he was in the mindset to do his job. One couldn't have a wandering mind if scared or overwhelmed, so he was calm. All he had to do was keep a focus on the operation, and zoom in where needed.

He found a good position, in shadow from the falling sun, framed by rocks and wide enough to pan across the entire village. Wade was right next to him.

"I'd call this three hundred and fifty-five meters to the near edge," Wade said, "three hundred and ninety to the antenna."

"Right. Far side?" Kyle asked.

"Eight hundred meters. But we're waiting for him to get near the radio, right?"

"I figure he's in there now. Hence the guards."

"Good bet," Wade agreed.

Next came the waiting. They stared in turns, taking time to rest their eyes. Sweat rolled down them, and the rock underneath was cool, then chill. As the shadows lengthened and swallowed them entirely, the temperature dropped. That left them dusty and sticky, then wishing for more clothes. The wool itched and scratched, as did Kyle's two-week beard. He might be less noticeable, but he was not comfortable.

But he'd been less so before, and this was the crux of the mission. He put it aside, and nibbled crackers from his ruck, letting the crumbs and the plastic packaging stay inside. No need to leave any traces. The weapon was placed, sighted, loaded, and safed. All he needed was a few seconds.

Wade jerked suddenly.

"What?" Kyle asked, but no answer was needed. Wade pulled out a vibrating cell phone. It was the one Sidiq had carried.

"What the hell do we do?" Wade asked, staring at the phone as if it were a grenade.

"Don't answer it," Kyle said. "It's bad, but answering it would be worse. If they don't know what's happening—"

"They might think he's surrounded and can't answer," Wade finished.

"Right. Still, it's a Bad Thing."

Everyone had clustered around, and was staring. "Let's not bunch up, folks," he said. He made shooing motions and the gaggle dispersed.

Wade said, "There's no number given. They're blocking."

"I think we're pretty sure who it is. Let's let him stew a while."

"Sure," Wade said.

The phone buzzed again at once. After that, nothing. Whoever was calling had apparently decided there wasn't going to be an answer.

"This just keeps getting more and more succulent," Kyle said. "Emphasis on the suck."

"Well, we can't turn around now."

"No," Kyle said, "But I'd really rather call an air strike. Why'd this bastard have to be in Pakistan? Just over the border, we could blow him to Mars and be done with it."

" 'Ours not to reason why. Ours but to punch holes at long range,' " Wade said.

"Yeah. Enough chatter out of me. Back to the task," Kyle said.

It was more than an hour before anything of further interest happened. Meantime, men wandered around, joked, swapped off on guard. Several vehicles drove by on the road, and were watched suspiciously from both sides. Yes, these guys were hiding something.

There was a smell of stewed goat and burning grain under the oily fire smoke. Kyle lay low on the rock, chin on arm, and cautiously twitched his toes in his boots to keep circulation going. He was too well trained to make large movements, but he needed to shift a little or his body would fall asleep from inaction.

"There," Wade said, interrupting his musing. At once, he leaned over the rifle, wrapped around it and eased up into a shooting position. Then he waited.

"What?" he asked.

"Someone opened the door, and one of the guards nodded. Not sure what's next, but it's the first action we've seen all day."

"Right," he agreed. "Tuck a dollar in my G-string." But he stayed on the weapon, waiting. With his left hand, he raised his scope and took a look.

Wade chuckled. "We'll see."

But the action was followed by more. A few minutes later, the door opened again. A figure came out and strode away. His face was in shadow, and Kyle cursed, begging for light to identify his target by. The dusk was making it a bitch to use available light or night vision. If need be, they'd stay here a day, two, a week, however long it took. But patience and eagerness are not opposites. Kyle could be patient, but he was eager.

Then the figure turned and the orange sun caught him in profile. It was a repeat of that first shot days before, only with, Kyle hoped, reliable allies. *This* face in his scope was quite similar to the provided photo. "Good," Kyle said. He put down the scope and leaned over the SMLE.

"That is him," Wade confirmed. "Three seven zero meters."

"Got it," Kyle said, and squeezed. The trigger pull on the venerable rifle was long and slow, but even. Patience was called for even here, as he held the reticle firmly on the man's chin, expecting the shot to take him high in the chest. Squeeze, squeeze, and then it broke.

It was a crisp, clean letoff, the rifle boomed and kicked, and the short stock had his hand close enough that he banged his nose with his thumb.

"Hit," Wade said. "Breastbone. I call him dead."

"Good," Kyle said, calmly cycling the bolt, lowering his aim and putting one through the brain to make sure. *Bang!* "So do I. Let's move."

Bin Qasim wasn't happy. Sidiq had reported on the Americans' location, but had not reported back. His phone was intact, but he was not answering. It could be that he was too close to report or reply, but in that case, he should be faking an injury and slipping off. Once they were within five kilometers, he could easily direct artillery and roving patrols to them.

It was also possible Sidiq wasn't smart enough to handle the situation. That was a common problem. Many of the smartest had died in the attack upon America, Allah praise their names. Many others with an intellectual bent were too . . . detached, reluctant for operations. Bin Qasim would call them cowards, but as he needed them, he tried not to think it too loudly.

None of the patrols had found any sign of the Americans or their traitorous peasant allies. They had likely been lost and slowed by the mountains. He couldn't rely on that, though. He needed concrete intelligence about his enemy soon.

Additional patrols were going out in an inner perimeter. It wouldn't do to appear nervous or afraid; there were two of his own people who might jump at an opening and do something stupid and criminal. But he did need the patrols.

It was time to send out another update. The lesser soldiers were often competent, but lacked the fire of the warrior of Allah. They needed to talk to a real leader in order to maintain their courage. Which was fine; it was why Allah, all glory to him, had placed people like bin Qasim on this earth.

After that, he would see about planning another relocation. The Americans were constantly biting at him, hordes of insects against the power of Allah, but even insects could be dangerous in number. Faithless, vile, but nonetheless a threat.

He looked up at the door of the communications center to see the guard snap to attention.

Then excruciating pain tore the breath from his lungs as a 180-grain .303 bullet smashed through his ribs, his heart, and out the back. He staggered, stepped, and saw the shocked look on the guard's face.

"Help me," he uttered, but it was silent, no air behind it. He knew he was on his knees but not how he'd got there, his memory fading. Then he was prone, nose and lips battered by the impact, but that pain paling in comparison to the mule kick to his chest. He breathed a choking mouthful of dust, and the cough that followed felt like the fires of hell.

He died too quickly to feel the shot that pulped his skull like a melon.

16

KYLE AND WADE WERE ON THEIR KNEES, THEN THEIR feet. Kyle slung the rifle, grabbed his ruck, and waited in a crouch. Wade stuffed the scope into his pack, scurried back, and took a defensive position. "Move," he said, and Kyle crawled back past him. Then Wade. Then Kyle. Gul gave them a triumphant grin and a raised fist as they passed his position.

The thrill didn't last long. It was less than ten seconds before massive fire came their way—14.5mm Russian, or perhaps Chinese. Either way, it was heavy, aimed with skill and vengeance, and lethal.

Splashes of splinters came off the rocks around them, and for a moment, Kyle lost it. He saw a repeat of Bosnia, saw Wade dead, saw fire blowing around him and himself bound for hell with the next burst.

Then Wade grabbed his arm and pulled him, and he was back to normal. "Come on!" Wade shouted. "We've got cover fire, let's move!" Then he lobbed a 40mm down into the square before retreating again. It was extreme range, but it couldn't hurt, and might keep people's heads down.

They ducked and crawled. The fire was heavy, but other than the one machine gun, it wasn't very well aimed.

It struck Kyle just like that. *These assholes can't shoot for shit!* It applied to both the enemy and his allies. They were enamored of long, raking bursts, but only the most experienced were using their fire wisely. To the untrained, automatic fire is better because it puts more lead out. But one crucial lesson in training is to see how widely a burst disperses after the first three rounds. A few minutes of angle leads to missing by yards, and that's what was happening.

Still, it wasn't fun to retreat while bullets lashed the hills around them. There were interspersed ear-shattering bangs from something larger, perhaps a recoilless rifle or grenade launcher. Hell, it might even be a small mortar. There was no telling what those jerks were firing, and the growing grayness, smoke, and dust made it impossible to look.

Nor did Kyle particularly care. He wanted out of there, and now.

He had no idea how they made it up to the ridge, but then they were over it and heading down. As they ran, he peeled off the ghillie. It had served its purpose, and was a hindrance now. He dropped it behind a rock.

At least the trip was easier than it had been with Qalzai's morons. The terrain was better, and the troops knew how to retrograde. They were shouting, joking, cursing while they burned through three or four magazines each in the growing dusk. *Give them this, they've got plenty of ammo,* Kyle thought. Wade wasn't firing at all; there were no targets. But he kept dodging past Kyle, low and fast, taking a position and covering him. No doubt, the man was professional. It might be his first time in a war zone, but he wasn't panicking, wasn't wasting fire, and wasn't freezing. Kyle couldn't have asked for a better spotter.

The slope of the hill was relatively gradual. They went down fast, but that meant the enemy would, too. There was no time to slack off. Every second of distance would improve their safety, and Kyle relished the pending ride in the trucks almost as little as he did the incoming fire. It was going to be brutal. But at least they'd bagged the right guy, and the Army's part of the mission was done.

Surviving and extracting was nice for the troop, useful for the Army, but secondary to the mission. If he died now, the Army would give him a medal and a nice funeral, and that would be all. The men and women of the Army would do everything they could to keep him alive on the way out so he could be used again, but the Army as an entity was done for the time being.

Not that it mattered. Wits were what were going to keep them alive for the time being.

The trucks were waiting, their tailgunners watching the rocks and panning back and forth. They weren't firing yet, and looked disappointed at the lack of targets. The drivers were waving and shouting.

Then they were skidding out on the scree slope at the bottom of the hill, and making a mad dash for the vehicles. At any moment, their pursuers might reach the peak and have a beautiful view straight down. It wasn't reassuring. The armor value of these vehicles wasn't enough to stop a BB gun, much less a 7.62 Russian round or any support weapon.

They leapt into the bed of the lead truck, Nasima clutching at their free hands while they tried not to crack her skull with the rifles. She shouted, *"Penza! Shpag!"* as they tumbled in. Gul was next, and she called, *"Owa!"*

Bodycount, Kyle realized. Then, *"Ata!"* as the last man came aboard. Five, six, seven, eight. Plus four on the trucks, plus Nasima. All accounted for. While Kyle was sorting that out in his mind, the driver nailed it.

He banged his head against the bed, falling on the rifle painfully. He stayed still for a few seconds, though the truck's motion continued as it turned.

Once oriented, he rolled and twisted carefully among the feet and weapons, until he was on his back. The bouncing ride was banging his head repeatedly and painfully against the bed, and he tilted up quickly, then heaved himself to a sitting position.

He was just in time for the incoming fire from al Qaeda.

At this distance, with those troops, small-arms fire was of negligible import. However, someone had an RPG on the ridge, with a beautiful field of fire down at them, and someone else had a heavy machine gun mounted on a vehicle. A quick glance, in fact, showed three of them. It also showed the RPG round incoming in a blur, the setting sun a boiling halo behind it.

Luckily, it missed. The explosion was in the dirt to the right front of the vehicle, which meant they drove right through the debris cloud. The explosion was horrendous, even from thirty meters away, slapping at them and beating them. Dust and dirt choked the air, particles got in their eyes, and a few chunks of rock crashed down. One scratched Kyle as it crashed into the bed of the truck. Wade cursed as a smaller piece hit him, dislodging his hat. Luckily, the thick wool cushioned the strike. There were curses in Pashto, and several bangs as rocks pelted metal or glass.

But they were through that one. The driver braked hard, the truck nosed down and stopped, and the gunner aimed a burst up that way. The range was about 500 meters, but Kyle took advantage of the bare few seconds to snug up the rifle, wrap his arm through the sling, aim and squeeze. He had just fired when the truck started rolling again, the recoil merging into the forward momentum as if he'd moved it all by himself.

His shot was good enough; the RPG gunner staggered and dropped his weapon. His assistant scampered back from the cover he'd taken from the fire and scooped up the launcher. But by then Kyle's crew were moving fast and the threat was greatly diminished.

The incoming fire from the machine guns, however, was getting closer. The men fired long raking bursts, but they had plenty of ammo and were walking the bursts closer. Even with the truck's evasive maneuvers, they were going to hit sooner or later.

Then three more vehicles pulled into the chase.

"This is not good!" Kyle said. He leaned over the back to try a shot on the fly, hoping to damage a vehicle or driver enough to reduce the threat. Wade leaned next to him and started rapid firing, the shots synched to the vertical movement of the oncoming truck. It wasn't made easier by the setting sun in their eyes.

One of them hit a radiator, and fluid sprayed. That vehicle wouldn't be in this chase for long, but it was still driving at present. Also, when it stopped, it would be a stable platform to shoot from as soon as the gunner figured it out.

"Nasima, have us stop again!" Kyle yelled. He knew the word "wadrega," but not enough grammar to get anything substantial across. "I can hit better if we stop for five seconds," he added.

She shouted, the driver stopped hard again, leaning Kyle and Wade backward. "Get the gunner," Kyle said. It had nothing to do with penetration. Contrary to folklore, 5.56mm rounds will handily punch through vehicle glass and metal. It did have to do with Wade being able to put out more fire against the gunners who could move easily, while Kyle would have only one shot against a driver who couldn't dodge in the seat.

Wade said, "Gunner," in confirmation, and they both settled down as the vehicle stopped. Kyle let the sights settle over the driver, squeezed, and watched a hole punch clean through the windshield. One. Above that, three rounds from Wade ripped through the gunner, tearing him and his clothes to shreds. Kyle cycled the bolt with his thumb, slipped it back in, and swung across at a second vehicle, just coming around the first. It was a larger, heavier truck, likely a Mercedes cargo hauler, but it still had a driver behind glass, and his snap shot was adequate, cracking the windshield as it entered at an oblique angle. He'd at least wounded whoever was in there, and Wade blew the second gunner's head open a moment later. Then Wade leaned back and fired a grenade. It was extreme range, but the explosion couldn't hurt and would make the enemy think twice.

Then they were moving again, the truck weaving and evading. It was that moment that the al Qaeda troops concluded they could use the same trick. They stopped, and the machine-gun muzzles pointed dangerously.

"Duck!" Kyle said, gathering Nasima close and dropping flat in the bed. Wade was alongside in seconds, and their own gunner poured out a burst, empty cartridge cases and belt links bouncing and stinging over them. Gul had climbed through the missing back window into the passenger seat, and was shouting orders while he fired.

At least, Kyle thought, we don't have any break in fire. Moving or stopped, we're shooting constantly.

But they were outnumbered, and the pursuit was dogged. Kyle fought a moment's panic. They were still alive, no mistakes had been made, and if they got shot, it would be because of the disparity of forces, not because of any errors he'd made.

A sharp bend in the road put solid ridge between them and pursuit for a moment, and shadow almost at once. Kyle heaved a sigh and then realized he'd been holding his breath. He inhaled deeply and said, "Sit up." He checked himself over for injuries, then glanced over at Wade and Nasima. She was panting, but appeared unhurt, though disheveled and scared. She certainly put out heat, too, he thought. It had to be the exertion, because he'd felt the heat off her in waves. Wade was sweating and panting as he replaced his partial magazine for a full one. That reminded Kyle to slip another five rounds into the SMLE, thumbing them hard and tossing the clip. He had limited ammunition anyway; there was no need to worry about a fifty-cent metal spring.

"We need to split up," Gul said. "We can attack them from the trucks if they dismount. Nasima should go with you. She will be safer."

"Is it that bad?" Kyle shouted back.

Nasima nodded even before she translated Gul's reply. "Yes. They will pursue us until they completely lose us or destroy us. They won't be discouraged by casualties. If they chase us, you are safer, if they stop to dismount, we can attack them. You'll have less pursuit, and so will we."

"Okay," Kyle nodded. "You're taking a hel . . . a major risk," he said, wanting not to even get close to religion. He didn't know the way the colloquialism would translate. "We appreciate it."

"It is an honor," Gul said. "You have shot well, and perhaps we can get rid of the rest of these dogs soon."

"I'm not thrilled at the prospect, I have to admit," Kyle said.

"I'd feel safer with you than chased by those thugs, Kyle," Nasima said.

Gul made one last comment and she translated it. "Gul says he hopes we can meet again some day, and extends the hospitality of his village to you or any relatives. That's a gesture of friendship, like a diplomatic offer."

"Sounds like it," Kyle said. Turning to Gul, he said, *"Sta na shukria, de kuday pe aman, assalam u alaikum."* He finished by hugging Gul and shaking with both hands.

"Out at the curve ahead," Gul said. He snatched a ragged map from his old Russian pack. "It's here," he said, pointing at the approaching bend. The road turned back out from the ridgeline, and they'd be visible again.

"Right," Kyle said. "How?" Were they going to roll or stop?

"We'll stop for Nasima for a moment. We'll drop any other gear as we drive off."

It was a measure of trust and respect that Kyle didn't think Gul would take the opportunity to abscond with the equipment.

"Good," he said. "Wade, carry the prick," meaning the PRC-119. Because trust aside, no SINCGARS encrypted radio equipment was left out of U.S. control. "We'll head for that outcropping and up from there."

"Got it," Wade said, shouldering his ruck. He clutched the SMLE and got ready to bail. Kyle grabbed the M-4, which he'd use for any needed cover fire, and his ruck could be dropped.

It was seconds only before the curve came up, and at a signal from Gul, the truck skidded with a roar as the driver slammed the brakes. Nasima was lifted out quickly but gently by Gul and a man whose name Kyle had never gotten. Kyle was out the back and ready to shoot from a low crouch. Wade dropped over the side to his knees and stood. They sprinted off as the driver peeled out, throwing up dust to add concealment, Kyle detouring five feet to grab his dusty, tumbled pack. Kyle again noted the professionalism of these people as he shrugged into it. Give them some proper training in fire discipline and radio, good support and equipment, and they'd be a very competent force. The Special Forces should look into it. He made a mental note. He followed the others up the hill, and dove behind a rise as soon as he saw movement to his left.

Then Gul and his people were manning the machine guns on the racks in their vehicles. They were off in a noisy clatter of gravel on undercarriage and with much banging of metal.

But the pursuit knew they had split forces. While the fire from

Gul's crew was plentiful, the maniacal idiots weren't being deterred. One truck stopped and spilled out men, then another.

"Shit, they've got radios!" Kyle said, seeing an old Russian rig.

"So we run and call the helos," Wade said.

While the al Qaeda troops were bent on pursuit, they had to pause against the fire from Gul's crew. One of his people fired an RPG round that took out a truck in a bright flash and bang. Taking the better part of valor, Kyle motioned for them to move low and fast up the hill, providing overwatch positions as they went.

"I feel like a rabbit," he muttered as he passed Wade on one movement. He dropped the M-4 in front of him.

"So find a hole," Wade quipped back, voice low. There was fire down below, close enough to be a sharp reminder. He passed the SMLE over.

Kyle found a hole. There was a crevice in a rock that gave him excellent cover and field of view. He took it, and Wade and Nasima hopped behind the outcropping it was split from. Then he scampered farther up and slid behind a scraggly bush that wouldn't stop a fart but would at least break up his silhouette. That let Wade and Nasima dart to a flat ledge and move back. Lying there, they were out of sight and protected.

"I think we may have lost them in the confusion," Kyle whispered. He crawled past and took a position in a gully anyway. He was panting for breath already. He was still carrying about a hundred pounds of gear, and while he'd trained for it, it wasn't a walk in the park.

"No, they are definitely split and definitely following us," Wade said. There was movement down below, and occasional pot shots.

"Oh, that's great," Kyle said, and threw out a string of creative obscenities he hoped Nasima didn't understand. It was bound to be considered sinful to a Muslim, he thought, entirely outside her experience, most likely, and he had no idea what she'd think of him for it. But dammit, it summed up his feelings.

"Yeah, well, if we can break a crest, you can call," Wade said.

"Right," Kyle said, patting his pocket where the cell phone was. Where the phone wasn't.

As Wade ran past, then Nasima, he clutched at all his pockets. No phone. He swore again, stood, and dodged. As he passed them, he said, "Unless it's in my ruck, we don't have a phone."

"That falls under the heading of 'sucks ass,'" Wade said to his back, as he slid behind more rock.

"Let's get over the crest and look," Kyle said. "But I'm sure it was in this coat pocket, and isn't. Must be on the road down there."

"Might as well be on Mars," Wade said.

"Yeah." It was true. There was no way they'd ever get down there. Damn, damn, damn.

"Well, we've got the radio. As long as the battery is good, we can call in clear," Wade said.

"We were going to have to do that anyway. But they've got a radio, too." Dammit, they needed that phone! It was the only reliable way to contact their support.

"Yeah. Sucks all around."

"I don't understand," Nasima said as she slid in with Kyle.

"The radio encrypts the signal," he said. "But we're out of the net and not encrypted. We'll have to transmit in clear. That means they can hear us and possibly find us with theirs."

"Oh," she said.

Wade was in cover, and Kyle and Nasima skidded out and up. They were near a saddle, now, and could be over shortly. That would give them some time to seek better position. "Looks like a valley with a bend to northwest. Heading that way gets us closer to the border, and gives us tactical position."

"Good," Kyle said.

Nasima said, "I have an idea."

"Yes?" Kyle prompted as they moved again.

"Once you make contact, do you have anyone who speaks French?"

"That's not a bad idea," he said, seeing where she was going. "Likely." And it was unlikely that any of the enemy spoke French. "But I don't know if we'll be transmitting long enough for that to matter. They know who we are. Any transmission helps them."

Suddenly, with a quick glimpse for trouble, they were over the saddle. The pursuers were temporarily stymied, but they'd likely have backup soon.

Kyle was surprised at how dark it had gotten. His eyes had adapted to the dusk, but it was now rather dark indeed. That was of use, as they had night vision. The al Qaeda might also, but would have the harder job of finding people who wanted to stay out of sight. The hunters had to move. The prey didn't.

Meanwhile, it was time to get backup. "Wade, get the battery in now."

"Suits me," he replied. "Means I get to drop my ruck." He unshouldered it, opened the compartment and pulled out the radio. He opened up the compartment and set the battery. He slipped the blade antenna in place and fastened it. "Here goes," he said.

He warmed it, set the frequency, and keyed the handset. "Bossman, this is Roadkill, over."

Nothing.

"Bossman, this is Roadkill, over."

There was still no reply. "I don't think we're in range," Wade said. "They're rather far north. Even at this altitude, we have mountains in the way. Have to catch them as they come over the horizon, or else get someone to relay."

"Right," Kyle agreed. "Meantime, we walk. It's only about forty kilometers to the border anyway." Only. The terrain wasn't inviting. He looked around at the steep shadows.

"I'm not sure this group will recognize that line," Wade said.

"I'm sure they won't. But it gets us closer to our people, away from them, and it gives us fresh air and exercise."

"All in all, I think I'd rather sit on the couch and watch football," Wade said.

"You do that," Kyle said, smiling.

In moments, they were up and moving again. The only support they had at the moment was position and distance. It was time to make the best of both.

For now, they moved on. It was slow going in the increasing darkness, but while they had the advantage, they'd take it.

"Wade, let's go to night vision. We can guide Nasima."

"Roger that," Wade agreed. They'd barely touched the NVGs. They had batteries to last a hundred hours.

"Going to be cold tonight," Wade said as he snugged his on his forehead.

"Yeah. Exercise will keep us warm. That's what they taught me in basic."

"Funneee," Wade said.

"I am tired and hungry," Nasima said. "And I need a toilet."

"Er . . . behind the rock, if that's okay. We'll wait here. I have a few nibbles." He tried to think what else he might have.

"So do I," Wade said. "Though I doubt any of it is halal."

"Under the circumstances, I think Allah will forgive me for eating unclean food. As long as it's not pork."

"Spaghetti with beef."

"That will be fine. Thank you. One moment." She slipped behind the rock to take care of business.

"Have we even bothered with GPS yet?" Kyle asked. It was a change of subject, and it was something he wasn't recalling.

"No," Wade said. "As far as maps and routing go, we've been fine so far. The batteries are good. Holler if we need them."

"If . . . when we get hold of support, we will need it. I want to give them a good grid from which to start a search if we lose the radio." There was no reason to actually lose the radio. But the batteries could fail. It might get shot. There could be other issues. After everything that had gone wrong so far, he was not optimistic.

"Yeah. This mission isn't getting any better."

Nasima came back. "Thank you," she said.

"No problem. It's not my rock," Kyle said. "Wade, quick break?"

"Yeah, in turns. Cover me."

Kyle had been about to say, "Try not to get it shot off," but decided not to. Nasima was at once very tough and easily embarrassed. He would keep the innuendos to a minimum.

Shortly, they were trudging again. Nasima seemed happy with the spaghetti, loaded with Tabasco. Wade had an extra entrée he was sucking from the pack, and Kyle stuck to a couple of strips of his hoarded jerky and a handful of cookie crumbs. Anything that lightened their load now was a good thing. Though there was little they could abandon, and nothing they dared leave to be found.

The terrain was easy to handle when moving at a comfortable walk. It required some care when placing feet, but there were plenty of things to grasp for support. They moved downhill steadily, hoping not to have al Qaeda hop over the ridgeline and start shooting. For all they knew, they'd been observed, and artillery was about to start dropping on their heads. The technology gap between the U.S. and al Qaeda and the Taliban was substantial. But the gap between them and the two snipers was just as vast, and didn't depend on technology, but brute force.

After hours of moving obliquely down into the valley, Kyle said, "It's after oh one hundred. Let's find a place to hole up for a couple of hours."

"You think that's wise?" Wade asked.

"No, but I think it's necessary. We need a break. And Nasima isn't complaining, but I think she's about dead. Nasima?"

"Yes, Kyle," she said. "I am too tired to go much farther."

"Two hours?" Wade asked.

"Three. Ninety minutes for each of us. A solid nap, then back to it."

"Okay. There's a depression there. It won't be visible from behind us."

"Good enough," Kyle agreed. He was so tired, he wouldn't even notice the cold. It was promising to be in the thirties again. Forties, if they were lucky. It wasn't that cold to people dressed and active, but the ground would suck heat out of people holding still. He wished now he still had the ghillie.

"My turn to sleep first this time," Wade said.

"Sure," Kyle agreed. He needed some time to think, anyway. About that damned phone. They could have been back on base by now. Should have been.

Maybe the enemy would assume so, and leave them alone. Though he wasn't betting anything on that, either.

Nasima and Wade wrapped in blankets and dropped down. Kyle stayed standing, because he was afraid of falling asleep otherwise. It had been a wise decision to rest, he thought. He could barely avoid hallucinations as it was.

He was sure of that when he looked at his watch. It was ninety-seven minutes since they'd called time to rest. He'd passed the time and not even been aware of it, it was just a hazy blur behind him.

"Wade," he whispered as he shook Wade's shoulder.

"Yo," Wade said, waking fast. "Got it." He stood, took the weapon and stepped out. "Anything?"

"Nothing," Kyle said. He dropped down, grabbed the blanket and rolled up. Nasima was very cute and very young-looking hunched down in her blanket. He started to move a rock that was jabbing him, and was asleep before he got hold of it.

17

HE WOKE QUICKLY WHEN WADE SHOOK HIM, AND RE-
alized he was somewhat refreshed. "We'll need more breaks,"
he said, "but they can wait until we have distance."

"I know that," Wade said.

"Sorry," he said, waking fully. "Thoughts coming straight out."

"Well, we haven't slept much the last month. Why start now?"

"Very Army thinking. You should get a job at the Pentagon,"
Kyle said.

Nasima woke easily enough, but still had huge bags under her
eyes. "I can walk," she said. "Let's go."

They were in the valley proper soon, and turned northeast, heading for the rocks ahead. "This morning is when I bet on trouble,"
Kyle said. "They have a radio, know our approximate distance and
direction, and can look for all the signs we left behind in the dark.
Then they'll call more people in from other directions. We're only a
few kilometers from the village."

"Do you have to be so optimistic?" Wade said.

"Sorry. But that's how I see it," he replied.

"Yeah, me, too," Wade said.

"If I were to guess, I'd say the same," Nasima said. "It's not the
first time they've stalked an enemy."

"So we all agree we need to get up that hill," he pointed at the
stark cliffs ahead, "so we can call for help and have good shooting
position."

The climb up wasn't easier than the previous one, though they
did have more time and less immediate threats. But they were underfed and exhausted. Wade's CamelBak was empty, Kyle's rapidly

getting so. Nasima wasn't drinking enough, and he had to force her to pay attention to hydration.

During their second break, Wade said, "That's it."

"Nasties?" Kyle asked.

"Yup. Movement on the hill." He rummaged for his spotting scope, and swung it up for a glance. Kyle eased slowly down behind the boulder he'd been resting against, to avoid silhouetting.

"Yes," Wade said. "I count six, with radio, rifles, and an RPK. Also, movement on the southeast, would be coming just about straight from that village. Unknown number."

"Great. Makes me wish we'd stayed on the vehicles."

"I don't think it would matter," Wade said. "They aren't going to back off until superior force kicks their asses. We'd have the same problem somewhere else."

Nasima said, "It would be worse in a town where we don't know who is trustworthy."

"I suppose," Kyle said. "I don't have to like it. We need elevation quickly, and a position to shoot. Try the radio, just in case."

Wade nodded, reached into his ruck and twiddled controls. He made two more calls. "Nothing," he said. "Higher is all I can suggest."

"So let's get higher fast."

It was none too soon. As they rose, dust burst from the hillside in a fountain, accompanied by a bang. It was two hundred meters away, but it wouldn't be the only shot.

"Mortar!" Wade said.

"Yeah, move!" Kyle added, digging in. He grasped Nasima by the hand and pulled fast. He doubted this bunch could adjust fire quickly. Lateral movement was what they needed; anyone could get distance right from adjusting elevation incrementally.

"Eighty-two-millimeter Russian or Chinese?" Wade asked.

"Yeah," Kyle said. "Everyone makes them now."

"Haven't they heard of gun control?" Wade quipped.

"Likely not, or they would have hit us," Kyle said, as a second round dropped farther uphill. It wasn't far below their elevation now. "Next round will be to our right," Kyle said. "What's the spacing on the shots?"

"That was about twenty seconds."

"Okay, so now's the time to start moving left!"

They dug in, turned, and headed back, angling uphill as they did so. The threat assessment, of course, assumed that this bunch could figure out how to adjust the mortar properly. It was possible they'd get directions reversed and drop one right on them. But that wouldn't hurt at all, so Kyle didn't think about it. Nasima was gasping next to him, because they were moving at a near sprint. Her legs weren't long enough for this.

Kyle suddenly remembered Bosnia. It didn't affect him anymore. It had just been a screwup, as this was a screwup, and there was nothing to be done about it afterward. He almost smiled at the sudden burden lifting from his mind.

Another round cracked rock. It was still distant enough not to worry about, but any incoming fire is bothersome. There are vets who can glibly watch it and not panic, but Kyle wasn't that experienced. He also hoped like hell he never got that much experience.

"Let's keep heading west," he said. That was to their left. "If we get past the curve of that hill, they'll have to come looking. Go lower!"

"Lower!" Wade agreed. The recent impacts had been about the line they were on now. Anything that forced the crew to adjust their mortar reduced their probability of hitting.

It was less than a kilometer to where they'd be out of visual range of the enemy. That kilometer was across rough ground, however, and would have been a serious race even without all their gear. As it was, Nasima was choking, and Kyle had a hideous cramp in his guts that blended with the pain in his lungs.

Worse yet, the crew had seen what they intended, and were concentrating fire at the edge of their visibility. Three rounds had landed in a vertical line ahead of them.

"We'll have to time it and dodge through," Kyle said.

"Expect them to lob a couple just past that line as we do," Wade said.

"Agreed. Wait for the next one . . ." Kyle said as they turned straight uphill, wanting to be moving anywhere rather than be holding still.

Just below them was an enormous bang. They should almost be used to it by now, Kyle thought.

"Now!" he said, and they turned left and downhill. It was a dizzying, slipping, skipping route, threatening to tumble them and break a leg at any moment.

It worked. The next round exploded far uphill, and none of them fell.

"Uphill now!" Kyle said. They were out of view, and needed to get into heavy cover fast.

It felt like a marathon. Kyle regretted not being twenty-two again, because it had been a bastard of a movement under fire.

"I think we have about ten minutes before they get a view over this way," Wade said. His face was purple.

"About right," Kyle panted, nearly sick. Nasima was dry-heaving on her knees. "Rest a moment," he said, "then sip water. Are you okay?"

"Uh huh," she gasped between heaves, nodding her head and letting it loll.

"We're going to take a position and shoot. Any comment?" Kyle asked.

"Sounds good," Wade said. "If we're hidden, we can try for the crew or the weapon as they get here, then take them as they advance uphill."

"Yes. You think ten of them?"

"Or more," Wade said. "I saw ten. I'm sure there were others."

"Okay, uphill while we can. We've got about five hundred meters to the top. Can you make it, Nasima?"

"I won't stay here," she said. "I'll walk."

They took the climb in slow, steady steps. Kyle placed his hands on his thighs and pushed with every step, using the extra leverage to help take the load. His gear balanced well, and wasn't hard to carry, but it was damned heavy, and that manifested itself worse when moving quickly or in awkward terrain.

"Once up there, we try the radio again."

"Okay," Wade said. "Got to work sooner or later."

"Yes," Kyle said, though he wasn't sure about that. Its range in these conditions was likely about 100 miles. They were about that from Qandahar. But the AWACS was operating more to the north. The other option was to try several frequencies and hope to find another unit, like that one along the border.

Otherwise, they'd have to walk out or fight it out. Neither option offered good odds. They were down to dregs of water.

Then they were at the crest of the hill, and over. It was a jagged, rocky top, and Kyle smiled. It had cover, concealment, and a good, clear field of fire. A quick glimpse showed the valley below in a clear panorama.

"Well, this is one bright spot," he said. He took a look around for the best sniping points. He had a choice of several.

"I'll take a good position there. You offset to the right in that notch, and call shots. When they get close enough for me to handle on the fly, you pick off a few in front, then at the rear to slow them,

then anyone who tries to flank us. And pour out fire while I reload."
He again touched the loaded five-round clips in his pocket, wishing
for more than eight of them. That and ten rounds in the weapon
were all he had. Plus two loose ones.

"Got it," Wade said, squinting through the harsh, reflected light
at the depths of shadow where Kyle had pointed. It was a short
climb, perhaps five meters from their present position. Yet it looked
foreboding in these cliffs. He made it up in seconds, leaned back to
make room for his ruck, and pulled the radio out again.

"What about me?" Nasima asked.

Kyle looked at her quizzically.

"I can shoot a pistol. They might get close. Show me one," she
said.

He gulped, said "Okay," to stall for time and rearranged his
thoughts. She was a goddamned civilian! But she was in the middle
of the fight. The best thing she could do was duck. On the other
hand, more fire going out would keep people's heads down while he
and Wade dropped a few. She was here; she might as well help.

He reached into his waistband and drew the Colt Mustang .380.
Start her small and work up as needed. He held it flat in his palm
and pointed at the controls. "Magazine release. Safety. Trigger.
Hammer. Slide. Slide release. Draw the slide, watch it chamber a
round. It will lock back when empty, press the slide release to close
it and rechamber from the fresh magazine. It holds five rounds. I
have only two spare magazines."

She took it, cycled it with only a little fumbling, ejected and replaced the magazine, and nodded. "Only close range or subversive
fire?" she asked.

"Suppressive fire," he corrected. "Yes."

She nodded. "How do you say? 'Let's do it'?"

"Let's do it," he agreed. Wade echoed him. "And take care of the
pistol. I can't get another . . . and take care of yourself."

She nodded and smiled. "I shall duck like a mouse."

Kyle crept up the rill and pointed out a good spot for her. It was
separated from his position slightly, had lots of rocks to echo the
shots and confuse an observer, and a good field of fire at an angle to
his, should anyone get close. It also put rock between her fire and
him. He'd seen enough Afghan "veterans" shoot to be leery of them
as allies, terrified of a half-trained woman raised in this culture. She
might be able to hit the broad side of a hill, if it held still. But even
unaimed fire would be a help. The enemy wouldn't know it was unaimed, and wouldn't expect her. Also, if they saw her, they'd be con-

fused and reluctant to shoot. It might last only a second, but he could kill two or three if they held still for that long.

Hopefully, she wouldn't get her head blown off in the process. He'd seen that, too. The thought of it happening to a cute young lady schoolteacher whom he liked wasn't something he wanted to dwell on.

He crawled up near Wade with only a few dings, and then tried to get comfortable on cold, sharp stone. Kyle was under a slight arch, his head and shoulders filling it and making it look like solid, shadowed rock from a distance. He'd be hard to hit at this angle, but could see adequately, though he wished for a better view to the right. He also wished the points stabbing him in the belly, hip, and crotch weren't there, but they came with the territory.

"No luck on the radio," Wade said. "I tried for other units, too. Nothing. We're going to have to get closer."

"Okay," Kyle said. "It sucks, but it's all we can do."

Nasima scrabbled up the slope to his right in her lousy shoes and goofy robe, making him wonder again at this pathetic waste of a region. He couldn't see, but could track her progress by skittering rocks, scraping sounds of flesh on basalt, and occasional invocations to Allah in Pashto. She needed jeans and sneakers at the very least. The VC women had had jeans and sneakers. So had the Bosnians.

After that, it was back to waiting. Still, it gave them time to catch their breath, sip a few precious drops of water to clear dust and phlegm, and cool from the burning endorphins. It really was an addictive high, Kyle thought. Or maybe that was just the adrenaline from being shot at so often.

"Hell," Wade said.

"What?" Kyle hissed back.

"Even more than we thought. I'm guessing at thirty. Entire platoon."

"Wonderful." No matter how well they shot, there were limits to the odds. There were also limits to ammunition.

"Yeah. And I think I see some on the hill across."

"They're too far to worry about," Kyle said. It was a kilometer or more across the valley. No small arms were going to make it that far. Unless, of course, they had another mortar. "They'll come down or go away."

"Or have a mortar, or spot for one," Wade echoed Kyle's thoughts.

"We can run."

"Sure. We've been doing that a lot," Wade agreed.

"Well, for now we shoot. Tell me when."

"Will do," Wade whispered.

"Are you okay back there, Nasima?" he asked.

"Yes," she said in a hoarse whisper. "What should I do?"

"Just stay there unless they get up the hill. You'll know from the cussing and shooting," he said.

"But Kyle, you've been cussing and shooting for days."

He had to chuckle. "Yes, but this will be worse."

"Worse language than you used last night? I'm impressed. One hopes you haven't done most of those things."

"Yeah. The Army wouldn't like it," he said.

"Nor would the goat, I suspect."

Wade was chuckling now, too.

"Right, let's keep quiet," he said. It was the best retort he could think of, and it was a good idea, too.

For minutes they sat, physical stress draining while mental stress built. There was nothing right about this part of the mission. It was a Giant Mongolian Clusterfuck, as the slang went.

He wondered how far they could walk if they had to. They might manage two days, if they dumped a lot of gear. That would get them close enough that even the border posts should be within range.

If they weren't, then they were going to have to find water. There wasn't much green this way. The prospects weren't good. They were less good back toward Pakistan, as they'd be running a hostile gauntlet.

Kyle didn't feel like a superhuman killer in a movie. He felt like a man alone and scared. It was one thing to shoot and be shot at, when you knew you had support, medics, radios, and food and water. It was totally different to imagine dying in the middle of a desiccated desert and never be heard of again.

Wade's whispered voice disturbed his thoughts. "Got 'em, Kyle."

"Right," he agreed, and hunched to shoot. He checked again the venerable rifle, flexed his hands to get more familiar with it, and got a good cheek weld. Shooting was a relaxing task, especially now. It was something he could do to improve the odds.

Wade called him his first victim. "Reference: Directly below the tallest spire ahead of you, left of the notch. Target: one asshole. Two hundred fifty."

Kyle had to smile at the ID. There. He was creeping along the cliff at the edge of the trail. Should he fire now, or wait for more targets? Now would bag one bad guy of thirty or so. Waiting might get three or four before they scattered, but would have them closer and more of a threat. "Got him sighted. Others?" he asked.

"Nothing."

So take the shot. He shifted just slightly, eased the rifle over until the man's turban was just above the post, took a breath and relaxed his mouth, then squeezed the trigger.

And squeezed. And squeezed. God, it was so creepy. Whole wars had been fought with this thing. It really was accurate. But the trigger sucked. Would it creep forev—

Bang! The shot took him totally by surprise. The recoil still wasn't bad, but he was wedged in tight and banged his skull on sharp points. Lacking room to shake his head, he squinted and grimaced, waiting for the flashes in front of his eyes to stop as he cycled the bolt automatically. Through his ringing ears he heard Wade say, "Hit! Right through the goddamned nose! Scanning . . ."

He resumed his sight picture, then glanced above the peep to see what was happening below. Someone somewhere was shooting at something, but it wasn't at him. No fire discipline and absolute panic. Should we duck out now? he wondered. No, better thin the herd a bit more first.

Wade called, "Reference and target: behind the first at one hundred sixty meters. Flush to cliff."

"Can't see him," he replied.

"Want me to take the shot?" Wade asked.

"Is he advancing?"

"Not right now," Wade said.

"Wait."

"Roger."

There were suddenly five figures down there, and he didn't need a spotter to see them. They shot as they ran, mostly suppressive, but with a few shots aimed in the general direction of Kyle's position. One of them pinged nearby, scattering dust. But Kyle was well hidden and they obviously hadn't marked him. He squeezed off another round that gapped the first one under his breastbone, eyes bugging wide as he tumbled. A second shot caught one in the hip and the man behind him in the foot. Nice! Then the other two dodged as the third shot smacked into rock. Kyle swore and closed the bolt, took several breaths to catch up and calmed down for more waiting.

He hadn't banged his head on these shots, but had been flinching to avoid it. He'd shot okay anyway, but he should have been able to get off at least one more round in that time. Damn. "Wade, shoot anything you see," he said. "I think it's about time to mov—"

A flurry of shots came in, including some automatic fire. Dust kicked up in his face and he shimmied back in a hurry, tearing cloth and skin on the lip as he did so. He was about to clutch at the empties he was leaving, then decided they didn't matter. They weren't any use as intel and the enemy knew who he was and where. They could stay on that mountain as a memorial for the bodies below, who would either be carried off or eaten by buzzards. Hell, maybe some archeologist a hundred years from now would find them and annotate the incident, if it was ever publicly admitted.

"Nasima!" he called. "Let's go!" Then he swore at himself. He'd just used her name where they could hear. Damn. Maybe they hadn't heard over the din of fire and the distance, but it was a bad thing, anyway.

Fire started coming from the right.

He yelped and rolled behind a boulder, slid down the slope, belly exposed as his shirt peeled up, and gratefully took several gouges rather than a bullet.

"Seven, about forty meters, just below the crest," Wade said. Damn, but the man had sharp eyes. Any movement at all was a cue to him.

Another fusillade came in, but Wade rapped off a few bursts in response, along with a canister from the grenade launcher. There was no chance of hitting anything at that range, in this terrain, on autofire, but it did make the enemy duck. The canister load might have done something, but it certainly let the enemy know the Americans still had teeth. There was no comparable Russian weapon.

Kyle shot and worked the bolt three times to voice his own opinion, and Nasima fired three times. She was about twenty meters away and running toward Kyle in a fashion to do credit to a sprinter. "I'm behind you," Wade said.

Good: All three together for best fire effect. Bad: All three together as one target. Worse: Seven bad guys at point-blank range, and more on the way. Dust and chips of stone flew, bullets ricocheted in cracks and whines, and Kyle raised the Lee-Enfield and shot three times. He nailed one, winged a second, and missed with the third. Wade was firing on semi as fast as he could pull the trigger and got two more. Nasima fired twice, the Colt running dry.

Someone had to be ready before Wade ran dry. That someone was Sergeant First Class Kyle Monroe. He had perhaps a second. The Ed Brown .45 came out of its holster, familiar and snug in his grip. He drew it, raised it, and then immediately had to shove it at a tribesman standing over him, shoving an AK at him in a parallel motion.

He yanked the trigger, let his arm ride the recoil rather than try to shoot center of mass again. The muzzle caught under the chin of the thoroughly surprised and pop-eyed native, then Kyle shot again. The man's head exploded out the back in red mist, his cheeks and throat jiggling like Jell-O as the hydrostatic shock tore through them.

Kyle looked around frantically to locate the rest. Wade had gotten another, and Nasima had somehow managed to reload while some idiot had tried to grab her. He lay in front of her, neat holes in chest and face. Kyle's first thought was that the stupid SOB planned to either capture her or rape her in the middle of a firefight. Either way, he'd gotten dead, and that was fine.

Everyone was panting for breath. The lone survivor, who Kyle had wounded in the side of his belly, was moaning away. Nasima jumped across two rocks as if they were stepping stones, pointed the little pistol at his head and said a phrase he recognized, "Go with Allah," as she pulled the trigger. She looked green and nauseous as she turned back around. Part of that might be due to a wound in her head, oozing through her scarf.

"Are you all right?" he asked.

"It is a rock chip," she said. "I'll be okay." It didn't look okay; it was a dark, spreading stain.

Wade had reloaded, and Kyle followed suit, topping the Enfield with a fresh clip. He couldn't find the one he'd dropped, but wasn't keeping track anymore.

"Let's move," he ordered, forcing his body to ignore the stings, dings, and chunks of bruised and torn flesh. They needed to get farther away in a hurry. He detoured to snag an AK from the nearest body. There was only the magazine in the weapon, and a quick check showed it to hold five rounds. By then, they were a hundred yards away and still running. It didn't seem worth it to lug the weight for five rounds, so he stripped it and scattered the bolt group as they ran. At least no one else would use it.

"Nine dead, two wounded," he said as they scrambled up and down the hill, glancing behind for signs of pursuit. "But I'm down to thirty-two rounds of three oh three and my pistol. Wade?"

"Five mags left. We'll be fine, boss. Nice shooting." Turning, he spoke to Nasima, "And you, too, young lady."

Nasima blushed and looked shocked, embarrassed, and ill. "I

only got one. And I used seven shots." She was examining the magazines.

Kyle said, "With that pistol, that's about right. It's backup only." He turned to his partner and said, "Wade?"

"What?"

Kyle made a pistol shape with his hand and held it up.

Wade caught on and said, "Oh, no!"

"Wade, you've got the M-4. It's plenty of firepower. I have a bolt and a pistol to save me from reloading in a hurry. Take the Mustang if you want, but let her have something worth using."

Sighing, Wade said, "Oh, all right! I suppose it makes sense. Now, or when we stop?"

"Better be as we travel."

"Right. Oh, Nasima!"

Wade handed her his Beretta and showed her the differences between the pistols as they moved, she nimbly like a goat, he more like a lumbering bear. She nodded and said, "I have no belt for a holster. I'll just carry it."

"Fine," Kyle said from ahead. "I'll loan you a belt when we stop. Will the spare magazines fit in that little pouch of yours?"

"Oh, yes," she said. "But I can't reach them quickly."

"If we get attacked, grab one and hold on to it. Then take cover. We'll do the shooting, you just defend yourself or make noise if we tell you to, okay?" he said.

"You are the expert in this field," she smiled. "I will obey."

"Touché," he said, and smiled, with a hint of blush. "So let's walk."

It was already well past noon. They'd had a busy morning, Kyle reflected. They were all still alive and unwounded, and the longer that was the case, the better. But there was no telling how many people were closing in on them, and it was becoming beyond imperative to make radio contact.

They stopped every hour for Wade to try a call. The second time, he announced, "I have static!"

"Good!" Kyle said. "Anything else?"

"No, but stand by," he said, and clutched the handset. "Any U.S. military unit, this is Roadkill, say again Roadkill. Contact Bossman. Inform Bossman we are three zero kilometers north of previous grid. Request Bossman contact us. Critical. Over." He ran through the spiel twice more. If anyone could hear them, they might get the backup they needed soon. "That's all I can do," Wade said.

"No sweat," Kyle said, trying to sound nonchalant. "It's better. It will keep getting better. Let's move." He wasn't sure it would, but he had to encourage his tiny command.

"Right," Wade said.

"As we must," Nasima said, trying to sound cheerful. She looked as if she'd been through a washing machine.

The distance between breaks got smaller, as they tired. They were in a fugue state beyond exhaustion, and kept going only because they had to.

"We haven't had any immediate pursuit," Wade said.

"No," Kyle said. "But I'm betting on a hot reception in Afghanistan. They've got a very good idea of our route, and roads to get there."

"Yeah. Once we get there, it's plateau, too. Nowhere for good cover," Wade said and indicated the map. "We're here," he said, pointing out the grid he'd taken from the GPS module.

"Right," Kyle said. The terrain ahead turned to rolling hills, a bit like the moors of Scotland or the high plains of Wyoming. It was warmer and dryer, though, with tough, stalky grass in clumps amid the rocks. They'd driven through a bit of it on the way here. Crappy terrain for a fight.

Around them, everything was still a dun color. Long rills of the mountains trailed off onto the southern Afghan plateau ahead. "We stay with the hills," he said. *And hope to get in radio range Real Soon Now.*

Three hours later, the sun was dropping quickly. "We need to find a cave if we can, or a hollow if not. And it's going to be chill again," Kyle said. The clear skies and unprotected heights meant any warmth was radiated away or blown off. It wasn't going to be really cold, but it would be cool enough by contrast to make things unpleasant and potentially dangerous.

"I'll look," Wade said, moving ahead. He was getting more sure of his footing as they traveled, but was favoring his left leg. Likely from some injury or other. Kyle would ask him when they stopped, but he'd likely deny being hurt.

They'd better check each other for injuries and not pretend, Kyle thought. That "rock chip" was soaking Nasima's scarf with a dark stain. Head wounds were bloody, and needed treatment. But when he mentioned it again, she said, "It's not necessary."

"Nasima," he said, "it needs to be bandaged. Really. You've got to let me do it." It had bled a lot, and could still have shrapnel in it, or worse, damage to the skull. Even if it were only a slice, it needed to be cleaned and dressed.

They'd been following one of the ridges, and it seemed to still have a feature or two they could use. Up on one granite cliff, there were pockets that could be caves, or at least overhangs to hold air still and reduce convected cooling. They trudged wearily up, slipping and tripping.

It was fully dark when they reached the pocketed area. The holes gaped like huge mouths, dark and foreboding. There was an instinctive fear of the black maws, but also a tactical one. Kyle's nerves were naked wires as he eased up to the first, the muzzle of the SMLE preceding him by a few inches. He held it close, not wishing to have it snatched or deflected by some waiting threat. Not even his NVGs showed him much inside other than a hole. It was that dark.

He used his Maglight with a red filter to take a better look. That was insufficient illumination to give their position away to an observer, but enough for the goggles to see the confines of the mountain. It was a cave a few meters deep, and not even bats were present. It was still eerie and tense, but with the goggles he could see well enough to know intellectually there were no threats present. Now if only he could persuade his quivering guts of that.

He stepped back out carefully, fearful of making a disturbance of rockfall. It was possible, even likely, they'd be surrounded by dawn, and have to stay hidden for some time. Or shoot their way out.

Or, he reminded himself, die a messy death. One RPG round into that cave would mince them to sausage.

Wade was waiting, muzzle down but ready. They nodded at each other, not a prearranged signal, but merely an acknowledgment that they were both okay. Kyle stepped down slowly, each foot in place before he moved further.

He crouched back with them. "It's safe, tight, and not too large," he said. "Let's get in and shelter. Nasima, I'm going to look at your head. It needs treatment."

Her face worked, mouth twisting. "Wade," she turned and said, "I must be rude. Will you stay outside?"

"Huh? Sure," he agreed. "Someone needs to be on watch anyway."

Kyle suddenly got it. For her to take her scarf off was a major breach of the modesty protocol. Even when hurt, she had an issue with it. Like an American woman taking off her pants or exposing her breasts. And it was just her head. He just couldn't understand it.

She led the way inside, and sat down facing him. Taking a deep breath, she unfastened and unwound her scarf as he held up a blanket. He needed lots of light for this, but couldn't risk it being seen. With the blanket tossed over his ruck and a protruding rock, they had a tent of sorts to shield the glare. He held his Maglight out, shaded with his hands for now.

Underneath, she was much prettier, her head and hair framing her face. That hair fell in wavy cascades down below her shoulders or longer, and was a lustrous blue-black in color. It would likely be even shinier cleaned of dirt and sweat and the dark, oily sheen of blood above her right ear.

It was as bad as Kyle had expected. He could see white edges to the wound. He might have to suture, and scalp wounds hurt like hell. But before that . . . "I'll have to cut away some of your hair," he said, feeling ill. It was gorgeous hair in contrast to an ugly wound. She was a tough young woman, and there was an electric tension to the moment that was disturbing and exciting.

She nodded slightly, then winced. "Yes, I thought so," she said.

"Hold the flashlight," he said.

She took it from him and held it still. "Where?" she said. He reached over and adjusted her arm and the beam and felt that tension again.

It was lust, plain and simple. She was pretty, young, self-assured. In this foreign wasteland, she was the only link to his world, by speaking his language, and they were both under a lot of stress. Add in not having been laid in weeks, and it was easy to explain.

He shook it off and continued. "Tilt your head to the left," he said, and she did. Carefully taking a small handful of hair, he raised it and held it clear of the scalp. "Hold still," he said.

The blade on his SOG Powerplier hadn't been abused and was razor sharp. He placed his hand against the back of her head for balance and moved the blade carefully in close. It sliced the strands off in a single pass as she winced only a little. He selected a few more and sliced, some more and sliced, and cleared the area around the wound down to a half inch or so.

The edges were raw and he'd have to do quite a bit. It was a small, triangular wound, but it was ugly and stale, blood congealing in shiny globs. "I need to shave it," he said. "This will hurt."

She nodded and clenched her teeth as he leaned in again. The blade was sharp enough, but the scraped off strands stuck to the bloody mass around them. Her breath came in hisses and her chest heaved. The light wavered as she gripped it tightly. Kyle barely noticed. He was intent on doing this safely and perfectly, and forgot the trouble he was having.

Leaning back and releasing a breath, he reached for his canteen. "Here," he said as he handed her a soaked bandage. "Pat it clean and away from the wound."

She nodded and took it. Gently she stroked it to the surface. Her hair looked odd now, with a wedge cut above her right ear. Her scalp was pale, then inflamed, then red as it got closer to the hole. And suturing was not an option in the field. The edges of the flesh were curled under and too wide to stitch.

"Can't suture," he told her. "But it's not bleeding badly anymore. I'll need to sterilize it though."

She nodded through what was already a wince, tears forming at the thought of the pain that was to come. She kept her eyes averted as he splashed merthiolate into a wadded bandage and closed the bottle. Then he raised it.

Her wince became a whine became a whimper and then a suppressed cry. Blood-tinged liquid ran from under the bandage, and she trembled. Head wounds are horribly painful, and this was traumatized, bruised, abraded, and now tortured with chemicals. Then she was crying, mouth open, keening to keep the noise down and let out the pain.

He caught her as she passed out from the agony. That wasn't unexpected. Kyle had had a thrown rock split his scalp in school, and could remember what he thought was terrible pain as two nurses held him down to clean it. This had to be excruciating. "Superficial" does not mean "painless."

Her head was in his lap and he reached over for the light, plucking it from her limp fingers. He stared into the wound. There didn't appear to be any damage to the bone, but it was going to hurt like unholy hell for weeks. There was no grit, the hair was mostly gone, and it would be fine until she could get into town. But there'd be a nasty scar there forever.

She stirred, and her eyes fluttered. Her first mutter was in Pashto, then she said, "I was passed out?"

"Yes," he said. "But you're okay now. It's clean at least."

She nodded just barely and said, "Help me up, please."

His arms were under her shoulders, and he lifted. In a moment, they were face to face, eyes reflecting the reflected glimmer of the flashlight from the rocks, and their lips were perhaps two inches apart.

Kyle knew he shouldn't. It was tactically, medically, morally, and politically insane. But those liquid eyes were drawing him and he leaned forward just a fraction, and she did, too.

Then she pulled away.

They stared for a second, eyes locked, and her hand was caressing his arm. "I can't," she said, and stopped stroking, too, as she averted her eyes. "I'm sorry you have been excited by me. But I am Muslim and unmarried and I can't. It would be a sin I could never repent."

Closing his eyes for a moment, Kyle said, "And I can't. Don't apologize, because it's not your fault. I shouldn't have even thought of it, because this is a mission." At the same time, her strength in her faith made her that much more unreachable and that much more of a prize. Jesus, it was a nightmare. He shuffled back to give her more space. And to get away from the attraction.

He pulled out a dressing, laid it carefully over the wound as she offered her head. He wrapped it and tied it securely but gently. "Is that okay?" he asked.

"Yes," she agreed. "And it feels much better, now that the burning is gone. And I thank you."

"I wish I could do more," he said, meaning it on several levels. Dammit. "I'd better go take a turn on watch," he said. "Do you need a clean covering?" he asked.

"I have another scarf," she said. "Are we done?"

"Yes," he agreed. In seconds, her scarf covered her head. It was as if it were a shield, and he felt the frustration retreat just a bit. He shut off the light and reached for the red filter again. He gathered up the trash and her ruined scarf and stuffed it into a pocket.

"I'm going to dig out all the remaining food we have," he said. "You eat what you need to, we'll finish it off."

"That's not fair to you," she said. "You're bigger."

"That means I can lose more mass and keep going," he said. "You're injured, we may need you yet, and even if not, I'm not leaving you for those animals."

"Thank you," she said. He could almost see her smile in the dark.

With the red filter in place, he dug through his ruck and turned up two more sticks of jerky wrapped in plastic, a handful of hard candies, one small bag of airline peanuts, and a stale apple. There was a packet of MRE peanut butter, but nothing to spread it on. It would have to be sucked out. It didn't appeal to him; the stuff tasted like cardboard. But it was protein and calories and they needed it.

It would be even worse with no water to wash it down. "Dig in," he said. "I'll leave the light on for you." She wouldn't get the joke, though.

As he found his way cautiously to the cave lip, he pondered the spookiness of that cultural issue, and how it could affect him, an unbeliever.

"How'd it go?" Wade asked as he came out.

"Messy and painful," he said. Then he realized he meant that another way, too.

"Going to be okay?"

"Yeah, it'll scar, but it's sterile and bandaged."

Wade chuckled and replied, "I meant you, jackass."

Kyle paused for a moment, flushed in embarrassment, then realized it was an honest question. "I'll be okay."

"Good. Let me know if you need to talk."

"Thanks," Kyle said. Wade was a hell of a decent man. "I think we just did. Go get some sleep. We're going to share whatever food is left now. Let me have the carbine."

"Sure," Wade said, unslinging it and passing it over. "Nothing so far. It's dark and still, and unless someone has infrared, we should be fine."

Wade slipped inside. Kyle had nothing to do but wait, worry, and watch. He decided now might be a good time for another attempt at the radio. He set it up on a ledge, set the frequency for the AWACS and hoped. "Bossman, this is Roadkill, over," he said, wishing he'd picked a different call sign. It had seemed amusing a lifetime ago. Was it three weeks?

Nothing. He set a frequency the Army should be using at the borders. "Any U.S. military unit, this is Roadkill. Urgently need relay to Bossman, over."

Nothing. There had to be units within one hundred miles now. Though if they were encrypted, they wouldn't really be looking for him on a single frequency. But the only way to plug into the encryption algorithm was to have another set do it remotely.

He'd try again around 0200, he decided. Or have Wade do it. If they couldn't get a good signal then with the nighttime atmospheric effects, it wasn't going to happen. But dammit, they had to be close! It was frustrating.

Carefully, he shut it off and disconnected the battery. The nominal eight hours in that battery was likely down to seven, minus any loss from not being used for two weeks.

That left him nothing to do but look at the sky. It was the prettiest sight he'd ever seen.

Stars by the millions, a sliver of moon that set quickly . . . and a moving light far overhead and to the south that had to be a satellite. A Satcom unit would have been great, he thought, but too bulky for this.

All those bright pinpoints made him feel even smaller and more insignificant. Just the thing while being chased by half the world's terrorists in the ass-end of nowhere.

About two, there was rustling and whispers from inside the cave. Wade came back out. "Your turn," he said. "We should pull out early."

"Right. How is she?" Kyle asked.

"That's one brave but crazy lady," Wade said, sounding bewildered.

"Oh?" Kyle prompted. What now?

Wade said, "She wanted to stand watch. Said it wasn't fair that she sleep so much."

"Dammit, she needs the sleep, and to be still, and she's not trained with the weapons!" Kyle said.

"Easy, pal. You think I let her?" Wade replied. "She's sulking but agreed with me. I fed her some more Motrin. Now go sleep."

"Right. Sorry. Long night. Check the radio. Thanks," Kyle muttered, handed over the M-4, then turned and felt his way into the cave. There was a dim glow from the Maglight, left on for his convenience. They'd left him the peanut butter. As he grimaced at that, he noticed a dried fruit component from the MREs and half a pack of chicken with noodles. There were four Oreo cookies, too. It was no banquet, but it would let him sleep more easily and last another day.

After eating, he turned the light off again, curled up in his blanket, and leaned against a naturally perfect hollow that was quite comfortable.

18

WADE WOKE HIM BEFORE DAWN. "LET'S MOVE." IT was just a voice in the dark, with a presence behind it he could just see against the stars.

"Right," he agreed. "Nasima?" he called softly, afraid of touching her.

"I'm awake," she said. "Can you step outside and wait?"

"Sure," he agreed. He and Wade went outside and relieved themselves into a depression between two rocks. Hopefully, no one would see the puddle, and it would dry quickly. Obviously, Nasima was doing the same in the cave in the dark. But it was one of those things not discussed between men and women here.

"We're ready," Kyle called as soon as he was done. In moments, she rustled out from the black mouth in the rock.

"My head is throbbing, but better," she said. "I'm ready to travel."

Wade nodded. "I think I should take point, Kyle, with you in back. Nasima, stay between us. Even if we get attacked, don't shoot until we're down on lower ground. We might dodge suddenly."

"I understand," she said. She sounded quite calm.

"Makes sense," Kyle agreed. Wade had more experience in the mountains, having just come from 10th Mountain Division.

The climb was tiring but not dangerous. They were careful of their footing, and slow at first. Twilight is hard to see in, but by scanning the eyes one can get a good image of the area, better than with the focal point of the eye.

Then the sky was gray. It hadn't happened suddenly, but it had reached a level discernible to the brain. Shapes began to resolve themselves as boulders, protrusions. Spiky spiderlike terrors became bushes.

The rest and food had done them a world of good, Kyle thought. They were moving more easily, and were alert and awake. It turned to proper dawn, crisp and cool with a hint of dew. All he needed now was bacon and eggs. How did these people survive without bacon and eggs for breakfast now and then?

By sunrise, the ground was flattening out. That was good, in that they could make better speed, but bad in that they were exposed to fire from behind.

"We just keep slogging," Kyle said. "Nothing else to do. And if we get far enough away, they may give up."

Nasima said, "They won't give up. But we may find territory they don't like, or a place you can call for help from."

"I figure we should be in range now. So if we can get a bit farther north and find a high spot, we should be able to reach the E-three. Assuming there's still an E-three up there. Of course, it could be on the far part of its orbit." An AWACS plane, usually an E-3 Sentry, was constantly circling or "in orbit" above the region, to provide command and control. They were primarily intended for aircraft control, but could be reached by radio from the ground, if the radio were in range and line of sight. The mountains were making that impossible at the moment.

"Right. Well, we work with what we've got."

Nasima said, "This is not good."

At once, Kyle asked, "What?"

"Listen," she said.

He did. Wade did also, and kept very quiet; his feet on the soil were barely audible. There was a faint sound that was familiar and disturbing.

"Dogs?" he asked.

"Wild dogs," Nasima confirmed. "Following us. They attack travelers in packs."

"Ah, hell. How many in a pack?" he asked, dreading her answer.

"Twenty to fifty. Mongrels, large but not well fed. They take goats, even cows, and people if they find them. Very dangerous outside towns."

"Right, and a dead giveaway to our pursuers," Kyle warned.

"Will they stop if shot at?" Wade asked.

"Yes," said Nasima. "Or if hit with rocks. But it takes several wounded before they understand."

"Rocks are good," Wade said. "But I've also got canister loads and HE." Kyle snickered, Nasima looked confused, until he patted the grenade launcher and the high-explosive shells slung from his belt.

"Ah," she said. "Yes, but very loud."

Kyle said, "I think we should save the grenades. At least until they're up close. For now, let's run. The dogs might get bored, at least."

"Dogs, al Qaeda assholes, what's the difference?" Wade said.

They all laughed at that, and broke into a brisk jog. The men could have gone considerably faster, but they weren't going to leave Nasima behind.

"We would be on flat ground by now, of course," Kyle said. "Oh, the hell with running. If we have to fight them now, let's get it over with!" He dug in his heels and stopped. "We're on open ground anyway, so why get tired?"

"It appeals to my sense of valor," Wade said. "But part of me wants to haul ass."

Nasima said nothing. She just looked scared.

"Keep walking," Kyle said, checking the loads on the SMLE and his Ed Brown.

He wasn't going to run, but there was no reason not to be at a fast walk. They needed distance anyway.

"Grab a couple of good rocks each as we go," he said, and reached down to scoop up a heavy chunk of something. "If we can cripple a couple fast, they may leave." He stuck the rock in a pocket of his coat, and watched for more.

The parade of canines drew closer, and the noise grew. If they could just persuade the dogs to bark away while they moved, it would be excellent cover, and their pads would obliterate any tracks the humans were making. Somehow, Kyle didn't think they'd listen to his plan. But at least the noise told them where the pack was. There was no need to look over their shoulders to gauge the distance. They did anyway, however.

"I will *not* ask what else can go wrong, I will *not* ask what else can go wrong," Wade chanted. Kyle had to agree. Armed pursuit. Phone lost. Radio not working. Ammo low. Food and water gone. Chased by dogs. Feet blistered to pulp. Beard tangled and itching and with a sweat rash underneath.

At least, he reflected, they had good maps and GPS, so they'd know exactly where they were going to die. It was a melodramatic thought, but it fit his mood.

Ahead was another valley. It seemed to be an ancient riverbed, or maybe a seasonal wash. Farther on, it deepened to cliffs. Eventually, it would all lead down to the rivers on the edge of the Afghan plains.

"I hate to suggest the low ground for cover," Kyle said, "but terrain features of any kind are what we need. It's too flat up here."

"May as well," Wade said. "Nothing else has gone by the book."

They were almost to the rills of the valley wall when the dogs caught up to them. They were well inside rifle range, even inside pistol range, and Kyle itched to take a shot. He didn't dare make that much noise unless they had to. He was pretty sure they'd have to, though.

The mutts were spreading out, closing in, and slowing. That meant they were doing a quick assessment of their prey before attacking. Kyle had never seen such ugly, scrawny, vile-looking dogs in his life. No wonder no one thought of them as pets.

"That's close enough," Kyle said, reaching into his pocket. "Hit 'em."

It was good, he reflected, that he'd never been a doglover. His first fast pitch smashed one of the mutts in the jaw, throwing strings of gooey drool and blood back over its shoulders. Nasima wasn't much of a thrower, but the dogs were skittering back from where her stones landed. Likely she'd never had much practice playing ball.

Wade, however, was doing brilliantly. Kyle recalled him playing for a local softball league, and the man had a snap to his wrist that was devastating. Three rocks landed smack, smack, smack, on a snout, causing one to roll on the ground in anguish, on a forehead between the eyes, braining the beast, and into a foreleg, shattering the knee. At that moment, Kyle nailed a second one hard in the ribs.

But the dogs were close now, and he could smell them. Their barking and yipping was a cacophony from all sides. He snatched at his pistol and started shooting. One dog was snapping at his leg, trying to nerve itself to close in. He kicked at it, aimed and shot, yanking his foot back just in time. He'd panicked and almost blown his own toes off.

The shot shattered the rear of the skull and upper spine. Wade pinged one with the .380, which had more than enough muzzle energy to drop it. Nasima was rapid firing, but seemed to have gotten two with five shots as Kyle literally blew the brains out of another. The skull shattered like a watermelon did when he went shooting back on his uncle's farm, and red, wet contents splashed.

Then the remaining dogs were retreating at a sprint, tails low and ears folded. In seconds, they were bounding back the way they'd come.

Which was where the men on horses were. They were galloping like a posse in a bad cowboy movie, only they brandished AKs.

"Kyle, we need to get into that valley now," Wade said. His voice was surprisingly calm.

"Amen, brother. Nasima, let's go. Hold your fire again. We'll need a lot of it when they get close, and the pistol doesn't have enough range for this."

"I understand," she said.

This time they sprinted, and it seemed wrong to Kyle to run from these scum when they hadn't from dogs. As far as he was concerned, the dogs were a far cleaner breed.

Kyle realized he should have expected horses. There were enough of them, and they were the best vehicle for this terrain if there was no road. He recalled a game played with a beheaded goat, which resembled polo. That summed up the mindset of the people they were facing.

Then the first incoming fire of the day slashed past them.

He didn't need to tell anyone to duck; it was a technique they all had down by now. They scurried downslope to the valley, and rose gradually to a crawl, then upright. Then they were below line of sight, and could run.

"Want to take a few shots as they clear the horizon?" Wade asked.

"No, I want to get into those rocks so they have to dismount," he said. He also didn't want to shoot the horses, though he would if he had to.

"First time I've seen horses with the assholes on top," Wade said.

"Good. I hope you plan to shoot like you crack jokes."

"Count on it," Wade assured him.

They plunged down into the ravine, cut, whatever it was, and scanned around for any good shooting positions. The ideal location would offer height, view, solid cover, and concealment. Right now, Kyle just wanted a tree or a rock. His back felt naked and exposed, and he was panting in fear. Would the first warning of them catching up be a bullet through his spine?

The ground dropped away. Grass grew in tufts, forcing its way between unyielding rocks. With little water for erosion, it was rough, raw terrain. It was the first good news of the day.

"Let's get up on that ridge," Wade said.

"Yeah, I see it, too," Kyle agreed. It wound its way along a strata break in the ground, with lots of hard cover and a view down lower. Any pursuit would have to be single file along it. Under the circumstances, it was the best terrain they'd find, and it was available now, so there was no need to push their luck hoping for better.

"Give me ten seconds," Wade said. He had the radio out and was setting it up.

"Okay, but hurry the hell up!" Kyle said back, panicky. Yes, they needed it, but now was not a good time. On the other hand, there wasn't likely to be a good time.

It was back in his ruck in seconds, warmed and ready. Wade grabbed the handset and called. "Bossman, this is Roadkill, over."

He started walking again, M-4 cradled low and sweeping for threats. Kyle brought up the rear, and tried to keep the pace. The urge to back along was powerful.

Wade unslung his ersatz radio pack long enough to change frequencies. "Any U.S. military unit, this is Roadkill, urgently need relay to Bossman."

Wade paused, and Kyle came up short. What was the problem?

Then Wade said, "Roger, Bouncer Five, this is Roadkill. Relay to Bossman. We are thirty kilometers north of our last grid. Urgently need contact, over." They had a contact!

Grinning, Kyle forced himself to pay attention to the terrain and threats. The radio was Wade's gig. He flashed Nasima a smile as he turned, and she grinned back, eyes crinkling in real happiness and relief.

They could still get very dead, though, and Kyle pushed his awareness to the limit. It would be ironic and suck royally to get clipped now.

Far back and higher up, there was movement. It was just discernible as a man on a horse. The question was, should he take the shot now and risk blowing their temporary concealment, or push on and risk letting them get too close?

Stealth, he decided. The cavalry would literally be here soon.

Ahead, Wade said, "Roger, Bouncer Five, Roadkill acknowledges. And we owe you many beers if soon we meet. Roadkill out."
He turned and said, "They had to relay through their battalion, to aviation, to Bossman, but the word is they're circling down this way and will have us in twenty minutes. They've got choppers warming now. They'll leave about the same time."

"Right, so how long?" Kyle asked. He was trying to estimate himself, but his brain was foggy from fatigue.

"About an hour after that."

"Eighty minutes," Kyle said, considering. That was a long time.

"We can do it," Wade said, sounding sure.

"Right, we keep walking," Kyle said.

It wasn't a hard walk, but they'd been doing it for days. The stress damage to his left foot, the blisters he could feel sheathing his toes, heel, and instep, and the increasing shin splints were not fun. They were hungry, thirsty, worn, and ragged. Still, they'd proven that two U.S. soldiers were better than al Qaeda's remaining best.

So had Nasima. He wondered what they thought of that.

She was looking out of it. Despite her earlier grin, she was a trifle unsteady, and her eyes had a thousand-yard stare that was obscene on a face so young and vibrant. They owed her a lot, and Kyle wished there was something beyond money they could do. Perhaps State Department could arrange for better school facilities? Or even just prod the Pakistani government into a bit of action.

Meanwhile, they were still slogging along. Afterward, Kyle would sit down with a map and figure out just how many miles they'd covered up, down, and over these mountains and plateaus.

"Down," Wade whispered.

Kyle dropped at once. Nasima was barely slower. He wasn't sure it was conscious reaction; it seemed as if he'd collapsed. "What?" he asked.

"We've got bad guys across the ravine, searching. Likely some above us, too."

"And some behind on horses, lower down," he said. "I would bet on some on foot on this ridge."

"So it's very prickly," Wade said. "Your call. Hide, find a position, or keep moving?"

Kyle made a quick scan. Up ahead, the valley widened. That would reduce the threat from across the way. They were also getting lower, the cliffs building above and to the northeast.

"We go a bit farther," he said. "Distance from any of them helps. Where it widens, we'll try to hole up with a solid front."

"Okay," Wade said, and crawled forward. He rose to a crouch and shuffled along.

The only good thing about being out of water, Kyle reflected, was that his gear was forty pounds lighter. Though given his raspy, parched throat and the throbbing headache that was coming on, he craved that weight. Food was one thing, and could be acquired most places. But water was the biggest logistical problem for covert operations. There was just no way to carry enough, and their pursuers likely knew that.

They knew about the lack of water, the lack of food, that a small civilian woman was along, and probably that they'd been calling for help and not finding any. Now that backup was coming, Kyle concluded, either this group didn't have a radio and didn't know, or didn't care and were determined to nail them before the choppers arrived.

So they should be expected to do something rash.

With that in mind, Kyle moved at the crouch, too. It was sheer hell on his lower back and knees, though it did take some load off his shoulders.

Up ahead, Wade whispered hoarsely, "This is Roadkill, Bossman. Go ahead, over."

Yes! Kyle thought. Just a few more minutes. Any good defensive position, or a hide, preferably, as he had no need to prove anything else and no desire to get into a pissing contest, and they could kiss this pimple on the asshole of the world goodbye.

"Roger that, Bossman. Our coordinates are—"

Not that it wouldn't be nice to see Quetta and that reservoir again, as a tourist. The art and culture was amazing. But these hills were worse than Nevada, and the natives worse than any Appalachian nightmare.

"Roadkill acknowledges, Bossman. Roadkill out," Wade said. He continued speaking back over his shoulder. "Sixty-two minutes until they get here, maybe sixty-five. We'll use flare and smoke to get their attention. And guess what? We're in Afghanistan. Friendly territory."

"And the bad guys are, too," Kyle observed. "And will see the smoke."

"We won't pop until they are right on top. At that point, we'll have fire support in seconds."

"Right. We've got a Blackhawk coming? Or an Air Force Fifty-three bird?"

"Well, my friend," Wade said softly, a chuckle hidden underneath, "it seems we rate the One Sixtieth Special Operations Aviation Regiment."

Kyle was silent for a moment, then said, "That's some serious fucking firepower. Sorry, Nasima."

"It's okay," she said. "Right now, I'd like to see this serious fucking firepower."

And Kyle tried not to laugh at the scene of this tiny, religious woman swearing like a soldier.

Wade spoke again, and his voice was soft but urgent. "Kyle, I estimate at least thirty hostiles. We've got ten down below that I can see, a dozen across the ravine, and I'm going to assume an equal number above. We've got to get somewhere safe."

"Yeah, I'm open to suggestions," Kyle said. Having bad guys above was very unappealing.

"Lower is all I can suggest," Wade said. "And close to one wall, so that squad, at least, can't get a clear field of fire."

"Well, twenty is less than thirty," Kyle agreed. "I can't think of anything better."

"We can angle down farther ahead," Wade said.

"Lead the way. How are you on ammo?"

"One twenty-three," Wade said.

" 'One shot, one kill' is the motto," Kyle said sarcastically.

"Right. You ever used only one shot?"

"I'm sure I have," Kyle said. "I just can't recall when right now."

"Here's a crevice. I can slide down."

"Go," Kyle said.

The cracked rock had a narrow chute that dropped perhaps twenty feet. It was a good start, and would cause the enemy to have to maneuver again. Wade squirmed and cursed, stuck in the tight confines. Finally, he looped his ruck's strap around his ankle and let it dangle.

"Please don't land on the radio," Kyle said, guts churning.

"I won't," Wade said, not joking for the time being.

There were scraping and slipping noises as he dropped out of view, and one slight bang of the carbine against the side. Kyle eased forward and looked over. Wade was scrabbling lower, the native garb hindering him somewhat.

Then he was down. "Nasima, you're next," he said.

She gulped and said, "Okay." She handed the pistol to Kyle. Shimmying around, she got over the split and paused, a scared look on her face. "What do I do now?" she asked.

"Hang your legs over, then press one forward and one back to hold yourself in place," Kyle said.

She nodded and twisted. An indication of her fear was that her skirt hiked well up her thighs, and she didn't seem bothered by the immodesty. She was too busy holding on. "What next?" she asked, voice tight but controlled.

"Move your rear foot forward and down below the other," he said. "Then just walk down with your back to the wall." Wade had been able to scissor across the gap, but Nasima had too little length for that.

He held her hand as she worked lower. It wasn't of any real use as support, but if it kept her morale up, it was a good thing. The friction pulled her robe up until it was past her head. It would be full of grit, too, though that seemed minor. Nor did Kyle have any time to bother with a great view of her body. He took one glance, pulled his eyes away, and focused on the descent.

She slipped past his grip with a look of panic but didn't fall. "Keep going," he said in encouragement. She nodded once and stepped down, down.

Wade called from below, "Almost here. I won't touch you, because that would make you fall."

"Okay," she said, and kept moving.

Then she was down, and leaning against the side in relief. Kyle started to twist around for his own descent.

That's when the fire started.

He swore, spun, fell rather than dropped into the crack and shoved both hands out. He slipped at once, caught with one foot, tumbled sideways and cracked his skull and shoulder. Eyes tearing up, he shoved both hands out to keep from falling farther, and worked his feet down. Three healthy steps that strained the backs of his thighs got him down.

"Where the hell did that come from?" he asked as he shook off the pain and jitters.

"Across," Wade said. They were all bunched up together. The crack was wider at the bottom, but still very cramped. It was hard to maneuver.

"They've got us pegged. Where do we cover?" he asked.

"Right here for now," Wade said. "We can clear the front, then move into those rocks below."

Kyle looked down where Wade was pointing as he handed Nasima back the Beretta.

"Okay," he nodded. "Nasima, we'll tell you when to fire, but if someone is within thirty feet, give them two shots. Only two. If they don't flinch, give two more. Ammo is low."

"Two shots at a time. I understand," she said. She was still rearranging her dress, but didn't seem flustered anymore.

"Target," Wade whispered.

"Where?" Kyle replied, unslinging the Enfield and raising it.

"Large outcropping ahead, up twenty degrees. Left and below. Man with AK. Two hundred," Wade said.

Two hundred meters. Kyle found the place, found the man, leaned against the cliff for support and worked the bolt. He squeezed the long trigger, and felt the shot kick him. The noise was deafening in the tight confines, but he rode through it.

The shot was good, and the man jerked and crumpled.

"I suggest we get lower right now," Kyle said. He dropped prone and slithered out onto a shelf.

"Yeah," Wade said. "Go, Nasima."

It was none too soon. As soon as the target's buddies figured out what had happened, they cut loose with everything. Automatic fire scythed across the rock face, and Kyle jerked as a spent, flattened bullet dropped in front of him.

"What an exposed place we have here!" Wade said. "There's rocks below. Over the edge, quick!"

Kyle was glad of the information, and rolled over at once. He didn't look. There wasn't time, and he trusted Wade implicitly. Wade was his spotter. Just as Jeremy had been. But Wade was still alive, and Kyle intended to maintain that state of affairs.

They were all down and hunkered in a cluster of rock, with thick, desiccated dirt underfoot.

"How's the time?" Kyle asked. He and Nasima had their backs to boulders and the enemy. Wade was sprawled low and facing them.

"Forty minutes," Wade said.

"I say we stay here for a few," Kyle said. "If they get nasty, we'll move lower. But there's a limit on how far down we can go."

"Okay."

Another flurry of shots hit the area above them. Kyle wasn't sure if the enemy thought they were still there, or were unable to get a better angle.

Two minutes later, he had an answer, as a round cracked right over his rock. Someone had either seen them earlier and told the others, or was seeing them now. If the latter, it was time to move.

Another round snapped between Nasima and him, making her flinch and gasp. Yes, someone had spotted them. Time to move down another layer.

"Wade, out to your right and down more."

"Sure, it's my pleasure to act as decoy," he said. He pushed with his feet, crawled over the lowest part of the rock and crawled down. As his knees cleared the edge, he dropped suddenly.

Nasima went next, Kyle holding her feet while Wade took her hands and swung her down. Another shot cracked overhead as he released her, and he dove over himself, ruck catching on something. He was hung by his arm for just a second, then it snapped free.

"Not bad," Kyle said. They had solid, tall spires of rock on three sides. The valley notched to their right, spreading out into a broad arc. To their left, it ran alongside, but one convenient tower of granite would block incoming fire until the enemy moved around.

There was the risk of being infiltrated from below, of course. Kyle wasn't sure what to do about that.

Fire started coming from above and to the right.

Kyle swung, found a target, and shot without waiting for Wade. Someone was leaning over a shelf with an AK. It wasn't accurate fire, but there was a lot of it. He put a round through the man and cycled the bolt.

A torrent of rounds came in reply. The snipers and Nasima ducked, shifted, and tried to find better holes to shoot from.

"Warn us before you do that again, huh?" Wade said, humorously brave in face of disaster.

"Yeah," Kyle agreed. He hoped the 160th SOAR was fast. This was beyond terrifying. Nasima was crouched in back, a good place for her, and clutching the pistol. Hopefully, they wouldn't let the enemy get close enough for her to need to shoot.

The fire from the above right wasn't slacking off. It seemed they were going to shoot until the rock was chipped to nothing. Every few seconds, a round would find one of the gaps between the spires and crack past. But Wade had found a small trough that led under and shimmied into it. He fired several rounds. Incoming fire paused for just a second as the onslaught hit them, and Kyle rose rifle first, leaned, shot, and dropped back down. He'd only had a moment, but a man's head had been in his sights.

"Miss," Wade reported as he came back out. "Close, but a miss. They'll think twice about standing up, though."

"Yeah, let's watch that side. Or do we split?" Kyle asked. "And how long?"

"I'll cover up, you cover down. There'll be fewer targets, we hope, and not expecting it. Thirty-two minutes."

"Good."

They shifted, and Kyle flashed a smile to Nasima, who was crying but trying to smile as tears streaked her cheeks. She was doing better than most recruits, and far better than he'd have expected. "Soon," he said. She nodded quickly.

The squad from the far side was working its way down into the ravine, intermittently visible. "Wade, spot now," he said.

Wade fired five rounds rapid and shimmied back over. "What?

Ah," he said, as Kyle indicated. "Start at top and back, I'll spot you down."

"Right," Kyle said. In a moment, he slumped over the rock, aimed, and squeezed. The man had been just stretching to place his foot for a step, and died with a bullet through the top of his chest.

"Outcropping below him, man to left hidden," Wade said.

"Waiting," Kyle said. Waiting. The enemy knew they were under fire now, and were being more cautious. Though the enemy now behind them were picking the fire back up. Kyle reminded himself he had solid cover, and steeled himself not to flinch.

Patience paid off. His target stood, and Kyle plugged one right through his skull.

Just as he did, Wade said, "Notch in rock below and right, one man," and Kyle swung and shot. Miss.

An explosion rocked them, shards of granite showering down. They stung and burned and cut the flesh.

"RPG!" Kyle shouted. His ears were ringing. "Move now!" he said, and reached back to clutch Nasima's hand.

Wade fired four short bursts on auto, then tossed a grenade down ahead of them. There was no need to risk a face-to-face encounter. On a count of three, it exploded, throwing debris back up. Kyle already had tossed a high-concentration white smoke grenade behind them, and amid the billowing, acrid cloud they jumped over.

It worked. They weren't shot. The smoke also seemed to confuse some of the al Qaeda, who fired furiously into it. Two of them were standing up as they did so. Wade got one, Kyle got the other.

"Where the hell is that RPG?" Kyle asked. What else was along? A mortar? Machine guns?

"Not sure," Wade replied.

Fire slacked off audibly. That set alarm bells ringing in Kyle's head. They might be leaving, but they also might be . . .

"To our left!" Wade shouted.

A handful of men were dodging through the rocks, and Kyle fired five times as fast as he could work the bolt. He hit at least one, who flinched and fell. He had no idea if it was a wound or a kill. Nasima fired two rounds, then two more. Wade was firing about once a second. He also nailed at least one.

"Close on them," Kyle said.

"Right," Wade agreed.

Kyle pulled Nasima forward. "Trust me," he said. There were no more than six or seven bad guys to their three, and their buddies were demonstrating that they wouldn't shoot into that crowd. Kyle just hoped that stayed true. He didn't like six to three odds, with an untrained civilian in the three, but it was better than the twenty to three or worse they'd been facing.

Nasima fired again at once. Good girl, Kyle thought. No one had told her not to. He fired twice more, then once again, while Wade tossed a grenade. "Fireinthehole!" he shouted and they all dropped.

The grenade banged like the devil on a trash can, the sound assaulting them from all sides. Wade had made a quick, dangerous battlefield calculation, and there was a bare lip between them and the grenade blast, that deflected the shock wave and only left an overpressure pulse to snatch at their breath.

Wade stood, leaned over and fired an antipersonnel cartridge from the 40mm. There shouldn't be much left interested in screwing with them, but they came over the ledge with weapons out. Nasima shot twice at a twitching body, and hit it at least once.

"Good girl!" Kyle said. He was starting to think they'd get out of this yet. Someone else moved, and Kyle put a round through him. It was amazing, he thought, how the rocks reflected and dispersed shock waves and fire.

The incoming bullets picked up the pace again. Wade said, "May as well use the HE now. Agreed?"

"Do it," Kyle said. Wade nodded and grabbed his four remaining 40mm grenades. He ducked low, picked a target that seemed to be a source of trouble, and fired. He opened the action, reloaded, picked another.

Massive fire came in retaliation, from a machine gun. Kyle spotted the puffs of dust around its muzzle and started methodical fire at it. On his third round, it stopped. He shoved another clip of five rounds into the Enfield to keep the magazine topped off.

"Better drop lower again," Wade said. "And twenty-seven minutes."

"Lower," Kyle agreed. He wasn't sure they'd survive that long, however, but was damned if he'd give up. He might wind up using the Enfield as a club before this was over.

They crawled downward, weaving through jutting chunks of rock. If the estimate of thirty bad guys was correct, Kyle thought, then they should be down to about fifteen. Of course, there may have been more, or they may have called for backup. It occurred to him that they could listen in on the enemy's radio, too, but that would take personnel and time they didn't have.

There was a sloping curve of granite, its surface fairly smooth.

There was nothing to do but slide feet first down it, and hope the drop at the end wasn't too high.

"Me first, then drop the radio," Kyle said.

"Got it," Wade agreed.

Trying not to think, Kyle slid up and over, and shoved to get moving. He got to vertical and fell about seven feet, landing hard. He fell backward, and would have cracked his tailbone but for his gear. It cushioned well enough, though the impact jarred his whole torso and neck. No additional damage was done, but his already injured foot flared in pain.

What he hadn't considered was how Wade would know when to drop his gear. Wade had figured that out. The ruck appeared, hooked on Nasima's right foot. He nodded and held up his arms, she released it. It thumped him hard in the chest, knocking his breath out, but it was a good catch. He laid it down carefully, held his arms back up, and Nasima let go of Wade.

She dropped, dress tangling, and it was a good thing Kyle caught her. There was no way she would have made the landing with all that fabric caught on her legs.

Moments later, Wade dropped down, too, staggering but not falling. "Okay, they'll have to acquire us yet again."

"Don't bet on it," Kyle said. "Look." Wade looked.

They were now in the very bottom of the ravine, with stark walls on two sides and a steep climb on a third. The way forward was fairly level, and would leave them exposed.

"Let's hope the choppers are fast," Kyle said. "This is as far as we go."

"So let's stall for time and then shoot when we have to," Wade said.

"What else can we do?"

19

IT GOT QUIET. AL QAEDA HAD FIGURED OUT THEY WERE hiding, and were controlling their shooting until they had a target. The silence was eerie after all the shooting.

Wade wordlessly mouthed, "Twenty-two minutes." Kyle nodded.

Nothing happened for long seconds, perhaps minutes. Nasima started crying again, her lips trembling. "I'm sorry I'm so scared," she whispered.

"It's okay," Kyle whispered back. "We're scared, too. You're doing great, and we'll be out of here in minutes." Then he held a finger to his lips. She nodded.

The tension was thick. No doubt someone hoped the pause would make them break. All it would take was one hint, and fire would pour in on them. That RPG was still out there, and the machine gun was likely still functional, even if Kyle had bagged the shooter.

But the longer it went on, the closer they were to rescue from the helicopters. Kyle focused on that and took a deep breath.

The reprieve lasted another minute. When it broke, it was with another RPG round just outside their little hollow.

Nasima shrieked as the round crashed. Kyle and Wade both shouted in pain and fear as debris whistled overhead. But that was as far as it went.

Wade said, "Behind you, ledge, protruding shelf." Kyle turned, drew up the SMLE and fired at a figure who was hastily trying to get back. The shot took him in the shoulder, and he cried, dropping the launcher. It bounced off the edge and out of sight.

"Good enough," Kyle muttered, but he thumbed the bolt and took another shot. The man was still squatting there, hurt. The second shot went through his right eye and exploded out the back. That should stop the pain, asshole, Kyle thought as he dropped back down.

He turned to see movement on another ledge, and fired over that way. He wasn't sure if it was good, but they were on the offensive for the moment, and they should press that advantage against these clowns while they could.

Shots were coming from all around now. Most were wide, a few close, and a handful were obviously aimed with intent. Figures were leaping among the rocks, and some were getting lower and closer. Kyle caught one as he stepped between two protrusions, and the man dropped like a sack.

"Targets of opportunity," Kyle said, amazed at how calm his voice was. "Ask for backup if you need it. It's been a privilege serving with you."

"And you," Wade replied.

"Yes," Nasima said.

The odds of surviving more than two or three minutes were pretty damned slim. Flitting figures presented themselves, but Kyle held his fire. They'd be closer and clearer soon enough. He gripped the Ed Brown in its holster, just to remind himself it was still there.

"We might as well be moving targets. They know where this spot is. Over toward that face there," he pointed. They nodded, and he said, "Go!"

They were up, and none too soon. Five figures were creeping over the rocks. Wade swung, pointed, and shot. Kyle picked the rearmost, but paused as the man threw himself behind cover.

They were just getting to the cliff, a solid backing they could rely on. Kyle was first, as he had only paused once. Wade was right behind him, having taken a moment to heave another grenade far out at someone hiding on the ground. It detonated about five feet up, and if his aim had been good, that person was scorched goo.

Kyle turned, prepared to give cover fire, and Wade crashed in alongside him, as if tackling the wall. Then a shot came from their right.

Nasima's body was tossed like a rag doll. It wasn't bullet energy that did it; small arms aren't that powerful. It was muscle reaction as her nerves convulsed.

Her robe tore open in a gout of red, chunks of rib flying free. She tumbled off her feet and broke across a sharp rock face, her gurgling scream becoming audible in a break in the fire.

"*Nasima!*" Kyle shouted, clutching at his ruck to get the medical kit, knowing it was too late. She'd lost a lung or her heart or both on that shot, and was dead where she lay, even if her hands were still trying to hold her ruined body together and tears were running down her cheeks as her mouth worked soundlessly.

Seeing that, Kyle came back to his weapon. There was nothing he could do but kill as many of them as he could until he ran out of ammo, so that's what he'd do.

Bolt action rifles are fast in the hands of professionals, and Kyle Monroe was not only a professional, he had been shooting them since he was seven. There was no one better, as these assholes were about to find out. He swung the Enfield up and fired, shooting a man right under the chin. His hand and the bolt shot back, then forward and he fired. Another one down, right through the breastbone. Work the bolt and fire, and another lost the top of his head. That was the last round.

Heedless of incoming rounds, standing, he dropped the clip he held between the fingers of his left hand into the open receiver, thumbed the rounds down with his right, then flipped the empty clip away and closed the bolt. Incoming fire tore past him, but he didn't notice, and Wade was doing an outstanding job with that little carbine, 5.56 rounds cracking past him and ripping holes through their aggressors. Kyle had his rifle back up in less than three seconds and fired again, and again. Five rounds on the clip, reach for another, and reload.

"*Kyle!*" he heard behind him and ducked behind rock before turning to glance at Wade. Wade said, "Grab that AK and stay the hell behind cover!"

Nodding, he snatched the weapon in question from the outflung hand of a corpse he hadn't seen while it was alive, and slung it over his shoulder. He still had a dozen .303 rounds and he wasn't going to leave a loaded weapon for the enemy. Besides, he'd been through a lot with the Smelly. If he could, he would keep it. He had no other souvenir, and his only local friend was now dead.

The survivors had taken cover now. The fifteen or so corpses in front of the two Americans had either scared them or wised them up or both, because they were not visible. That brought its own dangers. The fire was still coming in, but from concealment.

"Get us out of here," Kyle rasped, unable to speak in a normal voice. It was due to the breath burning in his throat, and too much yelling, and the cold, and a little bit was a combination of fury and pain at Nasima's death.

"Cover me," Wade said. He tossed the M-4 at Kyle as he ducked low and got the radio handset. "Bossman, this is Roadkill, over."

It made sense. The M-4 was not only familiar, it had the grenade launcher. The acquired AK was an unknown quantity. Kyle nodded. Wade had adapted very well to combat: calm nerves, cool head.

Right then, something stung his leg. He'd been shot, he knew. It couldn't be bad, he told himself, as he was still standing, leaning over the rock. He panned the M-4, both eyes open, seeking the telltale dust tossed by shots. There. He swung the muzzle until the illuminated reticle of the Holosight covered his best guess, then fired three rounds; one on that spot, one two feet to either side. He took a deep breath and shook his head to clear the splotches in front of his eyes before seeking another target.

"Roger that, Bossman. Roadkill out." Wade changed frequencies and said, "Nightstalker Seven, this is Roadkill, over . . . Roger that, Nightstalker, we are glad to hear your voice! Kyle, we've got choppers!"

"Good," Kyle replied. He wasn't sure he meant it. She was dead. Like Jeremy. Why?

He needed to ask Wade if there was a load in the M-203, and if so, what type. He didn't dare take the time to inspect the chamber. But Wade was busy with the helos, and he didn't want to disturb that golden hope. No matter how he felt, Wade deserved to get out alive.

He was down to one spare magazine plus a few rounds in the weapon. He counted five of the al Qaeda gathered behind an outcropping, based on muzzle movement. Worse, they were higher than he was. However, they had a slight overhang above them, and they were about sixty meters away, so they were outside the minimum range, even if it was risky. Hell, letting them shoot at Wade and him was risky.

But Kyle had never tried to *snipe* with a grenade launcher. Still, it looked like a good time to start. He hoped to hell it was loaded—it certainly hefted like it—and hunched lower, easing it forward. He checked the tangential sights, checked the Holosight, made his best guess along the barrel . . .

"Roger, Nightstalker, we will mark with flare and smoke. I'll be on air, but might be away from the mike a moment or two. Hope you understand. Roadkill, over."

. . . the fire was really picking up now, as he took another check of both sights, made his best, professional estimate—professionals don't guess—and drew the trigger.

Boonk! Slam! The HE shell impacted on the ledge right above the creeps. At that range, the explosion tore them to bloody mush. A piece of what he thought was a rock splinter whistled overhead, spinning like a boomerang, and Kyle realized it was a bent AK. Rocks were tumbling onto the ledge, crushing whatever was left, and a blood-soaked man ran screaming off into space. He'd been climbing up to join his buddies and had just enough cover to be alive. Whether it was his blood or another's Kyle didn't know. He'd automatically taken the snap shot as the body appeared, however. Between the explosion, Kyle's round, and the impact on the rocks below, the man was way dead.

Kyle had to admire their persistence. And what was it the manual said? "Break contact. Do *Not* engage in a drawn out battle with a larger force." He laughed, the manic gesture relieving some stress. He fired again and felt the bolt lock back, magazine empty.

The M-4 would be needed badly here shortly, with its one lonely magazine and the single canister round Wade had left. Then they had pistols and grenades. They'd never had a chance to use the claymore. This fight wasn't over yet. Pistols weren't much of a threat, but a scared enemy seeing a rifle he didn't know was empty, and hearing a pistol, would think twice about sticking his head up to do a comparison. Kyle laid the M-4 down where Wade could get it, and raised the Enfield again.

Moments later, Wade was shooting again. "Just stand by, they're en route. Maybe five minutes. Get ready to pop a flare and pop smoke."

"Roger," Kyle agreed, swinging up to his right and dropping a man who'd thought to flank them from the right by crawling through spiky scrub. His leg was screaming at him now. He'd forgotten he'd been shot. Twisting and putting weight on it was excruciating. He hoped it was a quick five minutes. It could be a goddamned long time with rounds coming in every second. And they were coming in like a swarm of angry hornets.

But he had seven rounds left for the Enfield, and he cycled them through quickly, seeking movement. As he drove the last clip down into the magazine, he felt pressure against his hip. It was the AK he'd forgotten about. "Wade, stand by for cover fire," he said. "Pick your targets." The M-4 was a far more inherently accurate weapon, and had much more consistent ammunition compared to the AK. But he could rapid fire or auto fire at exposed targets and keep them down while Wade took them out.

He took his last shot with the Enfield, slung it over his left shoulder as he unlimbered the Kalashnikov. "Fire!" he commanded, then stood and commenced shooting.

His leg was on fire, numb at the bottom, burning and freezing all the way up and making his groin twinge, too. But it was still supporting his weight. He aimed through the smoke and dust, hoping visibility was good enough. There was movement to the right, under a ledge at their own level, and he said so to Wade. "Fire on my impact," he ordered, leaned in and fired five rounds rapid. They chewed chips from the rock and worked down into the hollow.

There was movement under the overhang, and Wade put three rounds down into that shadow. There was no obvious response, but the incoming fire seemed to slow. Dropping back down by the simple expedient of taking the weight off his legs, Kyle grunted in pain. He rolled to the left, got low between two comforting knobs of rock and found another nest. "Fire on my impact," he ordered, and gave it five rounds. Wade cracked three sharp, barking 5.56 rounds between the crags in question, and seemed to score a hit; another rifle tumbled out.

But the Kalashnikov was empty, its firing pin dropping on an empty chamber.

"Flare now!" Wade yelled. Kyle dropped low behind the rock, discarded the AK, snatched the flare from his belt and let fly, pointing it generally upward and yanking the lanyard. It arced up into the air and lit, a bright red star even in daylight. "Sixty seconds, then the smoke!" Wade said.

Kyle nodded and couldn't tell if Wade had seen him. His voice was too ragged to speak, his throat dry and papery, tinny tasting from propellant and gilding metal. He pushed up painfully using his left foot, and leaned over to shoot at anything that moved. It was all he could do, as he was down to his Ed Brown, with two magazines plus three rounds. At least they were eight round mags.

But the bucking, kicking, roaring .45 was a comfort to him. He gripped it firmly but not too tightly, arm solid to support it and rocking slightly with every shot. It was an extension of his arm and he pointed at movement and shot, shot.

"Smoke now!" Wade reminded him. "I'm empty!" he added.

Kyle stuffed the .45 into his belt, grabbed the AN-M8 smoke, yanked the pin, and tossed it. The "Pop!" of the fuze firing was barely discernible, but billows of white gushed reassuringly from it. Ideally, one used a bright color smoke for extraction. White was what they had and would have to do. It also provided concealment. It also provided concealment for the bad guys. "Oh, shit, this is not *good!*" he commented. He had eleven rounds left with the fresh magazine he'd just slid in. The slide dropped, clacked reassuringly into battery, and he raised it to provide cover fire as they retreated to the left and away from their backing. It wasn't the best choice for superiority of position, but they'd have to hope that chopper was here shortly anyway. If smoke was out, they should be here. So where were they?

Behind him, Wade said, "Roger, Roadkill confirms white smoke." Just in case some bright boy on the other side had a different color going. It had happened before.

Kyle thought at first something was wrong with the pistol. He couldn't believe the noise and the pressure slapping at his ears. Then he realized it was an incoming helicopter. The choppers had arrived.

"One casualty, civilian. All element members healthy under the circumstances . . . Roger, out!" Wade yelled. "Danger close!" he said to Kyle, and they both ducked down close behind the boulders.

Then the world exploded.

Four choppers came in. Two AH6J Little Birds were hitting the area with their pods of 2.75" rockets. The craft came into view just after a huge multiple pressure front slapped the air. Kyle didn't know the danger close distance, but the pilots apparently did. Other than ringing, stinging ears and a thump to the chest, he thought he was okay. But rock was flying and the enemy suddenly was very disinterested in them. The little craft darted around like hummingbirds, firing as they saw fit.

It was best not to take chances, and the 160th Special Operations Aviation Regiment were not the type to let an enemy off easily. The doorgunners on an MH-60K Blackhawk were hosing the landscape with 7.62mm miniguns. Another MH-60 with M-240 machine guns was punctuating with "normal" automatic fire. They knew exactly where the friendlies were, there was no risk of collateral damage, and there was no reason not to shoot anything that moved. It was also daylight. Those were choice working conditions, and the gunners' enthusiasm was clear as they swept their mechanical bullet hoses back and forth, bursts chewing anything suspicious into dust.

Overhead was an Apache. It likely wouldn't be needed, but too much firepower is always better than not enough.

The smoke from the canister joined dust that was whipped up and blown swirling by the blades. A farting explosion blew a stream of fire through the smoke; a 7.62 minigun firing a burst of perhaps 200 rounds. At 6,000 rounds a minute, that was two seconds.

The MH-60 rocked over the draw, buffeting winds bumping back against it. But the pilot knew exactly what he was doing; it held position, even if it wobbled. Then a figure on a cable started winching down.

"You first!" Kyle yelled over the roar. "Take whatever you can. We ain't leaving dick for these assholes to play with."

"Understood!" Wade shouted back through the din.

Wade met the rescuer when he touched down. In moments they were winching back up fast. That left Kyle alone, looking over at Nasima's corpse and knowing he couldn't do a damned thing. Nor could he go over and say goodbye. His pickup was right here. He kept his attention on the rocks, wondering if some last, dedicated al Qaeda soldier would fire a suicidal shot to kill one more American.

Then the penetrator on the end of the cable was dropping back down and it was his turn.

The ride up was brisk and wind tugged at him. He dragged himself aboard the chopper's deck and nodded thanks. Then he cleared his throat of a cubic yard of dust and spat.

"Check on the woman!" he shouted, voice ragged and losing control.

"Kyle, she's dead!" Wade replied, taking his arm.

"*Check on her!*" he screamed, throat stinging from the force.

The soldier nodded. He said to Wade, "We'll check anyway, sir. Stand by."

The crew were professionals. The chopper lifted, swayed over to Nasima's location and hovered as the two gunners rapped out short, steady bursts at movement. There likely wasn't much opposition left, but one always assumed movement was action and shot to keep it at bay. The medic was out the side and down the winch almost as fast as it could unspool, the flight engineer watching the mechanism.

After a few tense moments, the cable started rising again.

The look on his face said everything. "She's dead, sir," he said. Hands helped ease her battered and bloody body onto the deck, wounds gaping blood everywhere. Her eyes had a vacant look, her mouth open in an expression of sheer agony. She hadn't died painlessly. Almost no one does.

Then the deck tilted and the chopper surged, vacating the area in a hurry. A silent streak to starboard as they broke the ridgeline resolved itself as a U.S.-made Stinger. It had missed. The Apache unloaded a ton of ordnance on that location. Whoever had fired wasn't around anymore, because half the cliff face came loose and slid down, the dust looking like oil in motion and the large chunks dropping straight, not tumbling.

Kyle bid a farewell to the rocky crags of the Toba Kakar range and followed it with a one-finger salute. It really wasn't a chunk of real estate he could justify fighting over. The deck tilted, Gs pushed at him, and then they were in level flight.

Then he looked down at the broken corpse and the empty eyes. She'd been a hell of a young woman. And the bastards who'd killed her had been her own people. That's what made it so disgusting.

In a moment, he knew what to do. "Wade, map, please," he shouted over the din of the thumping rotors. Wade nodded and drew the creased, stained, and tattered sheet from inside his shirt. It was a bit of an icon of their mission to hell, and he planned to keep it as a souvenir.

Kyle took it, flipped it over and around, jabbed his finger down, and said, "We're going here, first. Berishtiya."

"Sir?" the flight engineer asked.

"That's her home. We're returning the body." It was all he could do, but he'd damned sure see it done.

"Yes, sir," the sergeant agreed. It wasn't on their route, but there wasn't any reason not to, and they seemed to realize Kyle wasn't in the mood to argue. The map was passed forward for the pilots to compare to their charts.

The medical sergeant spoke to him from the other side. "Sir, I need to treat your leg. Please lie back and relax the best you can."

Kyle nodded and reclined, loosening the straps of his ruck and letting them ease him out and up to a litter. He winced slightly as his pant leg was cut away, but said nothing. As his sleeve was rolled up, however, he said, "No IVs! Not until we're done with Nasima."

Sighing, the man said, "Very well, sir. But this is going to hurt like a son of a bitch." There was a half smile on his face as he said it, from exasperation or amazement or both.

"Fine, get on with iiiit!" Kyle said, gripping his harness and restraining a cry of pain. He snuck a quick peek, then decided he didn't want to watch. The medic was debriding the torn flesh and sterilizing the wound. It was close enough to the surface to be a rip rather than a hole, but it still hurt worse than anything he'd felt before. "Superficial" did not mean "Painless." As he recalled that statement, he scowled.

Twenty agonizing minutes later, his leg was bandaged and he had some candy—Motrin. It wasn't much, but it took the edge off and he was alert, mostly. He washed it down with what felt like a gallon of water. Then they were landing at the edge of Berishtiya. He vaguely knew that the variation on the flight was a hassle for the

AWACS people, and had caused various other air assets to be standing by, just in case. He really didn't care. They owed him, and they owed Nasima.

A crowd started to form, only five or six people at first, but then more. Many of them were children. Wade and the flight engineer hopped out, Wade's weapon replenished with a fresh magazine, and more in his gear. The doorgunners stood ready. The crowd was only curious, not threatening, but there was no reason to let them get close.

Kyle stood on the deck, swaying a bit until his balance returned. He crouched and wiggled his arms under her corpse, which seemed so light now. She wasn't large as women went, and even as . . . dead weight . . . was negligible. He slid out, got his feet on the ground, stood and turned.

Several children cried out. They knew who she was even from there. He strode painfully toward them, every step aching and stinging, the dust swirling from the whipping rotors. In moments, four men came forward, jabbering away. He didn't know enough Pashto to handle this.

But one of them said, "She is dead," in English, and he nodded. "Nasima. Yes, dead. She was our translator and . . ." he wasn't sure what he should tell them. "She was very faithful. Pray to Allah for her." Dammit, there was nothing else to say. He tried unsuccessfully to restrain tears.

The man nodded. He and the other three were apparently parents of her students. They wore simple knitted hats over their bright vests, not the turbans of the more conservative. He trusted they'd treat her properly. They took her gently and laid her on the ground. One of them shouted out and he caught the word for "cart." The children were gathering around and crying. They'd seen death before, but this one was important to them.

He couldn't kiss her goodbye. Not only would she not have wanted him to, it would grossly offend these people. Then he remembered. He reached into his pocket and drew out her matted, blood-encrusted scarf. Gently, he laid it over her face. "Go with Allah," he said in Pashto.

"We have to go," he said. "But I will send a letter explaining." He wasn't quite sure how, but he'd do it.

They nodded, he nodded, someone said, "Go with Allah," and he turned. He wanted to leave this country at once. He limped back to the waiting chopper, and heard the rotors and turbine whine as the pilot prepared to lift. Everyone backed in, climbed aboard, and then they were lifting.

Kyle had expected to be debriefed in theater. However, no one in Afghanistan cared about anything except helping them leave. Kratman didn't meet with them, and the staff in personnel simply signed them in and back out. Kyle did make a point of providing a map with the location of the Barrett marked. Even without a bolt, the Army would want it back, or would want to destroy it. A .50-barrel by itself was too useful to the fractured clans and factions in the area.

Everyone was polite and helpful, but no one knew what to do with them, and the easiest thing for all concerned was to shuffle them out quickly. They dumped the native garb. The Army considered it to be its property, and would likely just throw it out. They surrendered and receipted the remaining cash. Weapons and gear were crated for transport. They wound up on the same C-141, same crew, and headed back for Kuwait.

"Shave now, or after we land?" Wade shouted from three feet away. They were back in uniform, and looked like hell with beards and hair brushing their ears. Even after showering, they were a mess, deeply tanned and lined from the sun, obviously sore and tired, ragged and wired.

"I really don't care," Kyle replied. "We'll be swapping back to civvies as soon as we land, so whenever we damned well feel like it. After all, we're done and we don't need to pretend we weren't here as long as we don't brag about it."

"Good enough. I'm going to crash back and nap."

But Kyle was already asleep, even if his face indicated he wasn't getting much rest.

Epilogue

TWO DAYS LATER, AFTER TIME TO SHOWER, SHAVE, sleep for a solid nine hours in a bed and get a good meal of pork chops, they were in a briefing room at Fort Benning again. This one was in garrison proper, and had more amenities, which they'd be using to debrief for the next few days. It wasn't an appealing concept, sitting and talking and typing, while everything was nitpicked by bureaucrats, but it was necessary. And they were Stateside. Kyle decided it was better conditions than he'd had two days ago.

Robash greeted them warmly when he arrived, and said, "Well, gentlemen, you done good. I'll sit on the complaints. It may not have been by the book, and there may have been a few liberties, but the job got done and nobody got hurt, as far as the Army is concerned. And as it never officially happened, it's hard to complain. You did a hell of a job, and a lot more than expected. Thank you." After a moment, he added, "I'm sorry you lost a friend, guys." He seemed to understand, without the weirded out or snide looks a lot of people had given them both, Kyle especially.

"Thank you, sir," Wade said first, Kyle echoing it just behind him.

"And, sir," Kyle continued. He waited a moment for Robash's attention. "I need to speak to Mr. Gober about getting something translated."

Robash nodded and said, "I'll email you his contact info. Congratulations again, gentlemen. And I told the debriefers you'd be starting tomorrow, not today."

They stood, saluted, he left, and that was it.

They continued standing. It had been only a couple of days, and they were both still wired from the mission, the trip home, and the pending debriefing. Hair-trigger nerves stuck out from them, and they were bristling even at each other. Finally, Wade said, "Come on, buddy, I'll buy the first round."

Kyle nodded. "Actually," he said, "I think I won't drink."

"Oh?" Wade asked.

"Later, I'm sure," Kyle said. "It's not that I'm turning Muslim on you . . ." and they both chuckled, though they each had a new respect for the good Muslims, as opposed to the nutcases who made the news . . . "but I don't think I should mix stress and booze. I did that for a year and regretted it."

"Good deal," Wade said. "So I'll buy you a Coke and you can overdose on mild stimulants. When you're destressed, you can buy the beer. Better deal for me."

Laughing, Kyle asked, "Club, or off post?"

"Hell, you can't really cut loose unless you're in town. Let's see if my car still starts."

Acknowledgments

I am indebted to numerous people for this project. Ms. Noreen Khan, as a native of Pakistan, was most helpful with details. As to technical expertise, I was taxed to the limit of my knowledge and I am grateful to many other veterans for input. Especially, I would like to thank Ms. Elsie Jackson, CPT Jason Kostal and the cadre and students of the U.S. Army Sniper School for hosting me and my barrage of questions, not to mention a photographer, for a day of research. I have taken liberties, I'm afraid, for the purposes of an entertaining story, and the responsibility for such inaccuracies is solely mine. After all, accuracy is their primary product.

TARGETS OF OPPORTUNITY

To PFC Gail Sanders,
enlisted at age 35.

A target of opportunity I'm glad I hit.

SERGEANT FIRST CLASS KYLE MONROE WAS DOING THE one thing everyone in the U.S. Army had to do: paperwork. Napoleon had said that an army moved on its stomach, but the twenty-first–century U.S. Army moved on piles of paper and computer files, liberally lubricated with red tape.

Kyle was an instructor at the U.S. Army Sniper School. At the moment, no class was in session. That didn't stop the paperwork. Nothing stopped the paperwork. It was an enemy more pervasive, insidious, and overwhelming than the Nazis, the Communists, Muslim terrorists, and the IRS combined. At least, that was Kyle's opinion.

His phone rang, and he was glad for the distraction. "U.S. Army Sniper School, Sergeant First Class Monroe, this is not a secure line, how may I help you, sir or ma'am?" The official phrase rolled off his tongue without conscious thought. Because to think about a line that long just to say hello was ridiculous.

"Sergeant Monroe, I'm wondering if we might discuss another assignment?" said the gravelly, powerful voice at the other end. Kyle recognized it at once. General Robash.

"I suppose we might, sir," he said, stalling for a moment to think. The last "assignment" had been a temporary one, a month of sheer hell in the highlands of Pakistan. The end result, however, had been a dead al Qaeda leader, a Bronze Star with Combat V, a Purple Heart, and a sharp reduction in terrorist activity in Europe.

And, Kyle recalled, a very pretty young local woman who'd hired on as their translator, gruesomely killed by a burst of machine-gun fire. That, added to the death of his spotter in Bosnia before that, was a heavy burden on his soul.

The general interrupted his musing with, "Good, let me give you the basics. We can talk more if you say yes."

"Go ahead, sir," he prompted.

"Romania. We've got someone staging through there with explosives for Europe, and it's causing sheer hell for the NATO forces in Yugoslavia, er, Bosnia-Herzegovina, or Macedonia . . . all over that Government of the Month Club, whatever the hell they're calling it now." Robash was joking slightly, Kyle could tell from his tone. The general was very familiar with that area and its geography and politics. He had a Ph.D. in international relations, after all.

"What's the game plan, sir?" he asked.

"Similar to last time. You and Wade"—that would be Staff Sergeant Wade Curtis, his spotter for the last mission— "with whatever gear you deem necessary. We'll insert you quietly, the CIA will furnish you with intel as to these assholes' whereabouts, and you eliminate the problem with a well-placed bullet or two. Or fifty. Whatever it takes, as long as civilian casualties are minimized."

Kyle thought for a moment. Romania was far better than the wastelands of the Afghan/Pakistan border, he thought. Europe had plenty of water, food he would be partially familiar with, phones, and—language trouble aside—the alphabets would have to be easier to work with than translating Pashto.

Still . . . "I'd like to consider it, sir. Can I let you know tomorrow?"

"Sure. I'll have an outline emailed to you. Will be coming through secure in about thirty minutes."

"Yes, sir. I'll be back with you ASAP."

"Rangers Lead the Way, Kyle." It was a friendly greeting and farewell from one Ranger to another.

"Roger that, sir," he said, and hung up.

Kyle finished his day's paperwork and drove home automatically. He didn't even notice the trip until he found himself opening his apartment door. Another assignment performing as what amounted to a role as an assassin. He had no moral qualms about shooting terrorists, but he didn't want to encourage the idea that he was a hired gun. Hollywood glamour aside, there were too many agencies with too many agendas for that to be a safe job. Sooner or later the odds would catch up with him.

He unlaced his boots and grabbed a Sprite from the fridge without taking off his shirt. At one time he'd been a light drinker. Then he'd lost his spotter and become a heavy drinker. Then he'd been a very light drinker after returning from Pakistan. Gradually, he'd stopped altogether. Heavy drinking made him morose and depressed, light drinking didn't do much of anything. There was no point in wasting money for the flavor of cheap beer, and expensive beer was not something he'd ever learned to appreciate. So he stuck to soft drinks.

He sprawled back in his recliner. It and a good used loveseat that didn't match were the only casual furniture in the room. He had a small desk and computer against the wall, with an office chair. If he ever invited more than three people over, he'd need to get some cheap plastic seats.

The TV was in front of him, but he left it off. Right now he needed to think, and TV and thinking didn't go together.

He stared at a place on the wall above it. On a cherrywood rack he'd built in the post hobby shop hung a World War I British Lee-Enfield rifle. It was uglier than hell, but had meaning for him.

The rifle had floated around for seventy years God knew where, then had been bought and refurbished by the U.S. government for the Afghan mujahideen during the early 1980s, with a shortened forestock and hard parkerized finish. After that, it had found its way into Pakistan, where Kyle had bought it in a hole-in-the-wall shop for local use. It was less blatant and bulky than the massive M107 .50-caliber rifle he had taken, and better suited to the environment. At Kyle's direction, a local smith had lengthened the butt and built it up for precision shooting. The wood didn't match, the finish was spotty, but it was an amazingly accurate rifle for something so old and abused.

Battleworn, ugly, and deadly. It matched Kyle's soul. Perhaps it was time to take it shooting again. Feel the kick, hear the roar, watch the bemused and bothered expressions at the old piece of crap the sergeant was shooting.

Or maybe it was time to shoot something new.

He sank back into his thoughts again.

A few minutes later, there was a knock at the door. He rose automatically, quite sure who it was, and opened it.

He'd been correct. It was Staff Sergeant Wade Curtis, a former Sniper School instructor and his spotter during the last mission. They were friends, despite being posted separately, and the fact that Wade was at Benning rather than his current posting of Meade meant that there'd already been some planning for this mission. Wade was grinning broadly, his mouth a yard of gleaming white teeth against his coffee skin. He carried a small cooler.

Kyle smiled, reached out a hand and pulled Wade into the apartment, into a manly hug and grip on his shoulder. "My man," he said in greeting.

"Back in action! Their most hair-raising mission yet! Can our heroes top their previous brilliant exploits?"

"Get stuffed!" Kyle laughed. Wade had a knack for humor that took the edge off.

"How ya been, Kyle?"

"Getting better, I suppose. Have a seat," he said, gesturing.

"Thanks." Wade dropped down into the couch, the cushions whuffing out air from the impact of his 180 pounds. Both men were tall, lean, and in formidable shape for their early thirty-something ages. They were "old" by Army standards, but still at the far end of the curve as far as physical fitness.

"So what do you think? Romania. Europe, at least. Theoretically Western and modern," Kyle offered to get things started. "We need weapons we can carry on the street that aren't obvious. Stuff that blends in."

"I'm waiting for them to figure out I don't blend in some places," Wade said.

Kyle laughed aloud, because he'd been thinking the same thing during their last mission. Blacks did not blend in in Central Asia, and likely not in Eastern Europe, either.

"Yeah, you laugh," Wade said. "Someday, we'll go to Zaire and I'll be the one amused."

"It might be one of those tribes who wear beaded skirts. You won't laugh then."

"Right," Wade said. "So assuming we're doing this, what are we going to use that's discreet?" he asked, bringing the subject back to the mission. "Unless and until they change the rules of engagement on us?"

"I was thinking of a Ruger Ten Twenty-Two. Have you seen the takedown kits for backpackers?"

"No," Wade said. "What about them?"

"Carbon fiber barrel, stainless liner. Slots in and snaps in with the fore end. Stock folds. Whole thing fits in a briefcase. Add a good scope, bipod and a silencer. We can use it near witnesses and no one will ever know."

"Such nifty toys the free market system comes up with. God Bless American Capitalist Greed," Wade said and they both laughed. "But how do we get close?"

"If it's city, we'll get a room or roof nearby and drop him. Cities are much the same tactically, whether it's Bucharest or Hong Kong.

And I did some in Bosnia." That brought up more memories, though they were just ghosts now. "If he's hiding in the mountains, then we either use a real rifle—the M Four will do fine—or we do a Ranger sneak and get close enough to bag him with the twenty-two or pistols."

"Given the choice, I prefer distance," Wade said. "It's neater."

"Sure," Kyle agreed. "I don't want another knife fight if we can avoid it."

"I'm not sure about the M Four, though," Wade said. "It's blatantly American and new. And I hope we won't need any forty millimeter this time. We can get a Romanian SKS or AKM or even an AK Seventy-four that will blend in much better."

"Hmm . . ." Kyle considered. "Don't they suck rocks, accuracy wise?"

"Yes," Wade agreed. "But from what I understand, that's mostly an ammo issue. If we work one over well and load some good ammo, it's discreet. We can fit it with a suppressor, and have something good for four-hundred-meter shots."

"I like it," Kyle said. "Good idea. But let's stick to seven point six two, not the five point four five." The older AKs and SKSs came in 7.62 × 39 caliber. The newer AK74 was in 5.45 × 39. That was a good battlefield infantry round, but fast and with a tendency to oscillate. The 7.62 was a bit more stable, and being older, more common and nondescript. Properly loaded, it would be better for long-range shooting. It lacked the power of 7.62 × 51 NATO, the .308 Winchester round; or .338 Lapua or 7mm Remington Magnum, the monsters of the precision-shooting world, but one had to use what was least obvious. The only good large-caliber round in the area would be 7.62 × 54 Rimmed, the old Russian round that fit the Dragunov sniper's rifle. But that was a large piece of hardware, and hard to hide.

"So, an old AK or SKS, and sixteen inches of barrel?" Wade asked.

Kyle nodded. "That should be accurate enough, if what you say is true."

"Good. The bottom folding stock is an inch longer than the fixed wooden, which will let us pack it down in luggage or under a coat, and we can get a cheekpiece that snaps on for better long range."

"You seem to know the weapon better than I do. You take charge of it, you carry it. I'll have the Ruger."

"Good division of force," Wade said. "I'll want some civvy ten-round magazines that are less bulky than the thirties, say two, with match ammo. Hell, it may as well all be match ammo. But we can load up with local seven point six two for suppression. Better sculpt the grips and stock, float the barrel, use a match barrel, the usual state-of-the-art precision modifications for which we, the world's best observers and shooters, are justly infamous for."

"You should switch to public affairs and write press releases," Kyle quipped, chuckling and rubbing his eyes. "Okay, so the gunsmith is going to be busy with your weapon, the contractors are going to be busy with mine, and Robash is going to be busy having his people write checks."

"You know, I think that's a *very* good division of labor," Wade said. "Meanwhile, we shall study the maps and drink beer. That way, when they change the rules on us yet again, it might make sense."

"Pistols," Kyle reminded him.

"Pistols, of course. I need a suppressor for the Beretta. Damn, this is starting to feel very James Bondish. Think I should carry a Walther PPK?"

"Thirty-two caliber?" Kyle asked, eyebrows raised.

"Right. Better stick to the nine. You going to leave that cannon of yours behind?"

"No way," Kyle said firmly, shaking his head once. Kyle had a highly customized Ed Brown 1911, smooth and easy to draw, accurate and reliable, with all the internal mods necessary to shoot any junk ammo that came along. Typically, though, he shot high-quality ball, or jacketed hollowpoints when allowed. "I can get a silencer for a forty-five. Brown will have to make a threaded barrel to fit. And Uncle Sam is paying for it. They'd have to, anyway. And this way their name isn't on the weapons."

"What about your three-eighty?" Wade asked. Kyle had a Colt Mustang stainless in .380 caliber he carried for backup.

"If it gets that bad, noise is the least of our problems. I'll take it as is."

"It could really suck to be us."

"Oh, Romanian jails can't be fun," Kyle said, frowning. They would want to check on that. They might be really unpleasant, and there was a strong if sporadic government presence to work around. "But the cops will have to deal with the government. But we don't want to be caught in the first place."

"We didn't want to get caught last time, remember?" Wade said.

"Yeah. Nasima." It was still a sore spot for Kyle, and would be for a long time. Especially the occasional half-snide comments he overheard about his "girlfriend." She'd been a remarkable lady. It had been a strictly professional relationship, though he'd certainly wondered what it would have been like romantically. He wasn't sure if the strict professionalism made it easier or tougher. All he knew was she was dead, and it was a waste of a good person. Then there'd been Jeremy, killed by that Bosnian countersniper. And why was that coming to mind now? Likely because they were going to the same part of the world again. What had Robash's joke been? "The Government of the Month Club."

Sadly, that was a fairly accurate statement.

His reverie was interrupted by Wade saying, "Sorry. Didn't mean to bring up a sore spot."

"It's okay. I'm not riddled with guilt. Just sad." He really was okay. But it still hit him now and then. In which case, it was good he wasn't a drinker.

"At least the alphabet is familiar," he said, to get back on track and not dwell on life. "And Romanian's not far from Spanish."

"Really?" Wade said. "I guess that makes sense, given the name. I would have figured it for some Slavic thing if you hadn't said anything."

"Yeah. I had four years of Spanish in high school. A few days listening to a Spanish radio or TV station should get me brushed off and cleaned up. We should be able to manage. We'll still need to talk to Mister Gober, though."

"Right." Bill Gober was a civilian contractor who seemed to know every language on Earth. He'd drilled them in Dari and Pashto before the trip to Pakistan, and they were assuming they'd meet him for this trip. "What else? This is essentially clandestine and more cloak-and-daggerish than front-line military."

"Yeah," Kyle agreed. They'd still need a lot of military hardware, but they'd have to trim the excess. "I suppose we can look like backpackers. Enough of them in Europe. We could pass you off as Algerian or Moroccan."

"Kyle, you don't know much about African history, do you?" Wade was chuckling and shaking his head.

"No," he admitted. "Why?"

"Because we all look alike to you," he said. His tone was friendly, though. "My ancestry is west and southern African. North African blacks have a lot of Berber, Arabic, and Mediterranean influence. I don't look like them. I look like an American."

"Oh," was all Kyle could say. He was too embarrassed to continue.

"No sweat," Wade said, breaking the pause. "We can be reporters. We can use a good telephoto for initial spotting, and get some intel with the cameras while we're at it. That will explain us having backpacks to travel with, and money . . . we are getting money, right?"

"I assume so," Kyle said. Last time, they'd been handed $50,000 in cash in three currencies for expenses.

"Check on it. We need the money for our tuxes and to impress the fine ladies of Eastern Europe. Assuming we can find a couple with less facial hair than you."

"Funny. I'd rather have it for renting cars, bribing petty thugs, and eating, thank you."

"Well, there's that, too," Wade agreed. "But I think we can pull off being reporters. We'll take a laptop, audio recorders, and all that crap. I wonder if we can get a good pair of walkie-talkies and justify it?"

"They all look the same. I think Motorola or someone has the military contract. It wouldn't be surprising for reporters to have them. And we'll have a satellite cell phone again, I'm sure."

"Good," Wade said. "Let's make lists and cross check. Mind if I use your computer for a few minutes?" He rose as he spoke.

"It'll be an hour, as slow as that dial-up relic is, but sure."

"No hurry. And at least this time, we're doing the chasing."

"We agree we're doing it, then?" Kyle asked, though he didn't think either of them had doubted it. All they'd had to do was get in the right state of mind.

"Sure. We're soldiers. It has an immediate, positive payoff. And it's what we signed up to do."

"Yes, that it is. Kill enemies. And these scum are everyone's enemies. I just don't want to lose any more friends."

"That's always what we want . . . but Kyle, even Nasima was a volunteer. It's painful, but better than kids in day-care centers or on buses." He stared levelly at Kyle.

"Yeah, I know," Kyle said. It was true. It still hurt like hell. "Yeah, let's do it."

Wade reached down and drew a bottle of Heineken from his cooler, went to the kitchen nook, popped the cap and poured a bare taste in a glass for Kyle. He kept the bottle. "Toast?" he suggested.

It was barely a mouthful of beer. Kyle decided that was acceptable. He raised it and said, "Sure. Absent companions."

"Absent companions," Wade replied.

"And death to terrorist assholes."

"Amen, brother."

THE TWO MEN MET WITH GENERAL ROBASH TWO DAYS
later, Thursday. As before, they all gathered at the Sniper
School's classroom. It was remote, quiet, and unobtrusive, and thus
a perfect place for the purpose. The twittering birds and sunlight on
red Georgia clay had always seemed to Kyle to be in ironic contrast
to the controlled death discussed within.

"Sergeant Monroe, Sergeant Curtis." Robash greeted the men as
he walked in.

They stood to attention. "Sir," they replied together.

"Please be seated. I'm informal, and we're here to talk business."

He fiddled with his unlit cigar for a few seconds while they relaxed their lanky forms out in chairs. Once everyone was comfortable, he said, "We've got a bit more lead time than last time, and
better data to start with, as I said. We'll go through what we can
here, and more in theater. Also, Romania is more Western, urban,
and modern, so it's going to be a different operation.

"What we've got, gentlemen, is a terrorist cell linked to al Qaeda
who's moving explosives from the east, across the Black Sea,
through Romania, into Europe and parts of the Middle East, and
killing people. We've linked them to bombs in Iraq, Bosnia, Germany, Israel, and Egypt. Likely the same group who supplied material for Spain last year and France this year. You're going to help
stop them the old-fashioned way."

"Well-placed shots," Kyle said.

"I knew you'd approve." Robash grinned, eyes twinkling, and
chewed on his cigar.

"The main pipeline is across the Black Sea through former Soviet
Georgia and Azerbaijan. They were going through Turkey, but the

Turks don't take too kindly to it and shoot them readily. So they come from Pakistan's fundamentalist areas and Iran, across the Caspian and Black Seas, into Romania and up into the rest of Europe."

"Why not stop them on the sea?"

"We're doing some of that, our SEALs and the Turkish Su Alti Taarruz, but there's a lot of ships and it only takes a few pounds of explosives here and there. That slows them down. To stop them, we have to nail the command and control, which is based out of the Carpathians. We have names, we have the general area. What we can't find is a base of operations. We're trying to get a live one for that information, or bag a few at meetings."

"How's the Romanian government on this?"

"It sucks, to be frank," Robash said, tapping his lip with his cigar stub. "We've made some inquiries, and they were favorable in response. But there's so many holes over there that we can't risk setting it up. Unlike Pakistan, there's no dictator we can talk to as sole source. We'd have to talk it over with the cabinet and defense ministry. That would mean leaks. All I can promise you is that I'll back you to the hilt if you get in trouble with the locals. But that does mean the mission is likely to be compromised."

"Mission, yes, but will the U.S. be in trouble?" Wade asked. Kyle understood what he was asking. Were they deniable and expendable?

"We've got a good cover story. Not that you wandered over the border, but something that will cause the whole incident to be forgotten in a couple of days. We won't leave your asses hanging out."

"Good. It's the only ass I've got," Kyle said.

"Beat me to it," came from Wade. He continued, "We'll be as discreet as we can until it hits the fan. I don't think we can promise after that, sir. Once we nail a bad guy, the rest seem to respond unfavorably."

"So we noticed last time," Robash said. He slipped the stogie back in his mouth. "If it's quiet, walk out. If not, we'll come get you. But you won't have to wait long for pickup, we hope. Air Force Pararescue will be ready in Turkey, about two hours away, to do a low-key extraction. If it gets really messy, just go to ground and we'll have some Rangers ready, too. We'll drop them in. Of course, that means we'll need permission from the Romanians."

"What if they don't want to give that permission?" Kyle asked.

"Then it's going to be ugly, so try to throw yourselves on any local official. We'll have the embassy and CIA take it from there."

It didn't sound very reassuring. Hope the locals played along and didn't shoot them, or weren't in cahoots with the terrorists, who likely spent much money locally for cover, or that it was quiet enough to allow them to sneak out or be roped by a chopper, or that some bureaucrat gave permission for a drop. Kyle said so.

"Yeah, it's your turn in the barrel," Robash said. "But we have set up a war game in that general time frame, forty to seventy days from now. If you can make this happen in that window, we can have an 'accident,' where a drop goes bad, and run you out in spare uniforms."

Kyle nodded. It wouldn't be quite that easy. Governments generally wanted passports and ID from any foreign soldiers coming in to play games—and again on the way out, just in case they were spies trying to infiltrate. Still, it had obviously been thought about in some detail. "This is getting a bit spooky," he said, referring to spycraft, not ghosts.

"Yes, it is," Robash agreed. "But you're the men we've got. It worked last time, even after everything turned to crap. It should work now."

"Yeah, it should. I agree. Wade?"

"Hell, it's why we're here. Kick ass and take names, chew bubble gum and drink coffee. Or some junk."

"We're on," Kyle confirmed with a nod, as team leader.

"Outstanding, gentlemen," Robash said. "Our intel people will find what they can, you get in close and observe, pull out all the details and photos possible, and make the shots. Done right, we'll severely cramp their planning and execution, which will make it easier for the locals to find them. We'll feed you, you shoot. Rangers Lead the Way."

"Roger that, sir," they both replied.

"Stop shaving now and grow some hair. Scruffy is good. Moustaches are good."

They nodded. That was expected under the circumstances, and thirty days was enough to get a bit shaggy.

Robash continued, "Now, as to transport, you'll fly in on the Rotator as far as Aviano, Italy, catch a hop to Rome, fly commercial to Bucharest. After you get your gear and meet with the embassy intel people, they'll brief you up to date and help arrange local accommodations as needed."

"You can't use SATO to book transport, obviously." SATO was the military's travel agency. It would be rather clear who they were. "You'll have to call a civilian company and get them to book any trains, taxis, and hotels. Your contact is Mister Mick Cafferty at the embassy, and he'll provide you with local links for more stuff.

"You'll rent a car, because you may have to travel some distance, and follow targets from the sea up to the mountains."

"Communications?" Kyle asked. "Anything special?"

"Will be available there," was the reply with a nod. "We're giving you both new encrypted satellite cells plus Motorola civilian jobs with headset radios to keep in touch with. They look like cell phones, because they're that, too." That was something Kyle and Wade had discussed, so it was one less thing for them to chase down.

"Good," Kyle said. "What about other gear?"

"Laptop, PDAs, anything you can think of for cover," Robash agreed.

"Cameras," Wade said. "And other stuff to make us look like reporters. We might even get some footage you can leak or even sell."

"Yes to the gear, maybe to the pictures, no to selling anything for cash due to conflict of interest, and no to the Army publicly admitting we did this."

"I suppose that's fair," Wade agreed.

"Two stars says it's fair, sergeant," Robash grinned while tapping his collar insignia. It was friendly. "But if you get a chance to get good pictures without risking the mission, by all means do. It's PR, it's also evidence and intelligence."

"Yes, sir," Wade said. He looked happy.

Kyle was fairly happy, too. It was definitely going to be a better mission than the last one. The Army did learn from mistakes on occasion.

"What about disposable assets?" Kyle asked, humor in his voice. Though the question was real and serious.

"Your mission cash is going to be U.S. dollars, euros, and lei," Robash stated.

"Lei? Like the Hawaiian wreath?"

"Same spelling, different language. We'll make sure you get leid," he joked.

"About time the Army took care of important needs like that," Wade returned.

"So we do have on-site intel this time?" Kyle asked.

"Yes. CIA has information from the Romanians, their own digging and whatever they get from our intel-sharing program. Of course, the Saudis and the Pakistanis only tell us as much as they think won't send the Wahhabis into a bombing frenzy, and there's so many holes in their intel that we have to double-check all of it. But you'll have in-nation backup. That was the big problem last time; we assumed the starting intel was accurate."

"Yeah," Kyle said. After a moment he added, "Sir." He didn't want to think about that last mission, or the one before it. Whenever there was a screwup, someone died, and there was always a screwup. All you could hope for was that it was someone else who took the bullet, and that the mission got accomplished anyway.

"Also, we've got a month to prepare. Gather what you need and train up. I've got you a language briefing, a political briefing, and some tourist books to read so you're familiar with the area."

"Good," Kyle said. Robash was a good man, and tried his damnedest to take care of his troops. He also accepted responsibility for mistakes and tried to prevent recurrences. In this cover-your-ass-and-pass-the-blame era, that was something to inspire confidence.

"Have you given any thought to weapons yet?" Robash asked.

"Yes, sir," Kyle said. "I've got a list."

"Good. Finalize it, find NSN numbers on everything you can, and push it through Colonel Wiesinger. You remember him?"

"Yes, sir," Kyle said. Wiesinger was the nominal intermediary between them and Robash, through 3rd Infantry Division, whom they had been temporarily assigned to for the last mission. Kyle remembered him as an overbearing ass more concerned with administrative details, most of which he got wrong, and throwing around his weight, which Kyle had heard was considerable and above Army standards, than with getting a job done.

Still, there was nothing in Army regs that said you had to like people you served with, or that they had to be competent. You just did what you had to and tried to keep a safe distance from idiots. Wiesinger was in Washington, only at the end of a phone line. That seemed a safe distance to Kyle.

After emailing his list in, he wasn't so sure.

He spent all morning the next day looking at National Stock Numbers, with their thirteen digits, all seeming to start with 8 and with a 00 or 01 in the fifth and sixth places. Everything in the military, from buttons and paperclips to tanks, had an NSN. At least Kyle could look them up on computer. He'd heard horror stories of the days when they'd been in huge binders.

The radios and other communication gear, the cell phones and PDAs, already were listed and numbered. The weapons were a bit trickier. Wade had read up and decided to go with an AK104, a later, better variant. A few did exist in the U.S. military for training purposes and clandestine missions, but were not readily available. The suppressors, on the other hand, were custom, and the takedown Ruger had never been issued.

It took some time to find a soldier at the post armory who could tell him which form to use to request custom-made weapons. Then he had to provide justification, in the form of a mission order. Naturally, being non-standard, those were questioned. If he'd ordered a bomber and a nuke, likely they would have flown in within the day, no questions asked; they had numbers. But try doing something different . . .

He knew there was a problem when the phone rang. He could feel it. Someone had seen the request, called in on the orders, asked for a decision from higher up, and now shit was rolling downhill. He also knew who the problem was before he picked it up.

He'd barely identified himself when the ranting started.

"Sergeant Monroe, why are there civilian weapons on this list? And mods for your personal sidearm?" It was Wiesinger, of course.

"Easiest and best way to handle the job, sir," Kyle said. He supposed it did look a bit funny, but he'd included a detailed write-up of what and why.

"You're wanting a militia survival-nut twenty-two with space-age gadgets, and a silencer for a very expensive personal pistol, plus extensive custom work to a cheap-ass former Commie rifle. Any idea how that looks to Uncle Sam, Sergeant?"

"Sir, I included an explanation for the request," he said. "It's—"

"Yeah, I read it. Nice try. But I'm not going for it. You can use standard Army issue rifles and carbines, or buy something locally with the cash you'll be issued. A local weapon which you will not attempt to bring back CONUS this time, you understand." CONtinental U.S. The man was too much an official prig to say "Stateside."

"Sir," Kyle started, then took a second for a very deep breath to get his anger under control. This pencil-pushing REMF was going to be a pain in his ass. "Sir, we need to be discreet, and we need accurate weapons for intermediate range. The two circumstances are contradictory in nature, and therefore—"

Wiesinger cut him off, which was a shame, as he thought he'd sounded properly bureaucratic.

"You're not going to be discreet with a God-knows-how-expensive pistol with a silencer on the end. You're a goddamned soldier, not James Fucking Bond!"

There was just no way this jerk was going to grasp what they were doing. He could try to explain that no one should see the pistol until too late to worry about it, that few people including soldiers would be familiar enough with the hot-rod gun market to identify it, and that it was backup only for close range in an urban environment, but it would be a waste of breath. "As you say, sir," he said.

"Just do your damned job and don't try to think too much, Monroe," Wiesinger said.

"No problem, sir. I'll leave it to you." He gritted his teeth and scowled. Ten more seconds. He just needed to hold on ten more seconds.

"You do that. Resubmit your list and I'll approve everything reasonable." His voice had a sneering tone that almost pushed Kyle over the edge.

"Yes, sir," he agreed, and waited for the click.

He placed the phone carefully down, dropped his fists to his desk, and clenched and shook. He hated what was going to happen next, but he was damned if some desk-warming bean counter was going to screw Kyle's mission over an amateur opinion of how it should be done.

Deep breath, he told himself. Deep breath. He let the shakes and the flush subside.

That done, he leaned back and smiled faintly. He punched another number into the phone and leaned back in his chair.

"General Robash? I seem to have run into a problem . . ."

When Kyle finished the call, he turned to see the school commander standing in the doorway, smiling faintly.

The current commander of the Sniper School and Kyle's immediate commander was Captain Schorlin. He was not yet thirty, but deadly competent and with a very sharp mind. "TDY again, Kyle?"

"Er, yes, I meant to tell you, sir. But we've been busy."

"It's okay." Schorlin smiled. "The general did brace me first. He's not stealing you from under me."

"That's good," Kyle said. He realized he hadn't thought about his chain of command and how his leaving would affect the training schedule. All of a sudden, he was back, his mind working on exercise problems and thinking about the weather and curricula. He shook his head to come back to the matter at hand. "We're not clearing post for about a month, but I'll be TDY at once, briefing and prepping. I'll be using my office here, if that's okay."

"Sure. If it helps you, and lets me claim the materials on our budget."

"Thanks, sir. As to mission, I'm not sure. I'd say at least thirty days. Maybe longer." He frowned slightly. This was rather open-ended.

"Just do come back, Kyle. We need you here."

"Planning on it, sir. I'm not looking for fame, just to do a job. Can you do me a favor and watch out for Lucas? He's overeager with the students, and . . ."

Schorlin cut him off with a faint smile. "We'll manage, Sergeant. Go kill terrorists."

Kyle smiled despite himself. "Yes, sir."

The weapons were delivered despite Wiesinger's complaints. No doubt he was shitting a brick somewhere in the bowels of the Pentagon, Kyle thought, smiling thinly to himself. Not that he gave a rat's ass.

Actually, he did. Anything that inconvenienced a bureaucrat was a good thing. It wasn't that most of them were bad, though most were, but that almost all of them got out of the habit of thinking. Choose an option A through G. Refer to manual 35-10. Fill out form NMS-2112 in triplicate. Why think, when one could refer the decision elsewhere? And when enough decisions got referred, nothing got done.

Although, Kyle thought, where the government generally was concerned, that might not be a bad thing.

He called Wade and they got together at his apartment. Technically, the weapon shouldn't be there. But it was a private place to meet and the weapon was perfectly civilian legal if a bit unusual in the configuration in question. Kyle made the decision, and there was no one to know he'd violated the reg. Except Wade.

The little Ruger and kit was as Kyle had said. It had been purchased new from Butler Creek, under the category of "training weapons," which wasn't entirely false; they *were* going to train with it. The receiver and its custom folding stock were one assembly, with the barrel separate. It assembled as a break action shotgun would, the fore end snapping in place, thanks to Ruger's clever wedge attachment for the barrel/receiver mate. The case also held a fine Leupold scope, two factory ten-round rotary magazines, and two twenty-five-round curved box magazines. The barrel was short, barely legal for civilian use, barely long enough for good velocity. It couldn't be shortened further, being a wrapped carbon-fiber sleeve around a stainless steel liner, with a screw adjustment for tension. "That's going to make a silencer hard," Wade commented. There was no way to thread the carbon.

"No," Kyle said. "G-Tech in Indiana is building one that slips over the front sight, from aluminum, that will muffle it down to nothing. Light weight, thirty-eight decibel reduction."

"Damn!" Wade said. "That's as close to silent as you get. Subsonic ammo?" With the muzzle blast dissipated and no supersonic crack, the weapon would be untraceable even in the dark.

"Yes, but also some hypervelocity," Kyle said. "I'll see if CCI can special-load us some even hotter than their Stinger loads. Damned near twenty-two-magnum energy. We won't always want close and quiet, after all, and pistols aren't the best for sniping."

"'Aren't the best,'" Wade replied, snickering. "Aren't you funny?"

"Anyway," Kyle said. "It fits in a standard briefcase with room to spare for ammo, we can carry extra in our pockets if need be, I'll fit it with a picatinny rail for the scope and whatever else, and I think with practice we can get down to thirty seconds to uncase, assemble, and shoot."

"That sounds like fun," Wade said. "The practice, I mean. Not that gapping terrorists is less fun."

"Remember to be professional," Kyle replied with a grin.

"Always," Wade said. "But there's nothing wrong with enjoying my work."

"Right."

"Going to use that scope?" Wade asked.

"We'll take it along. I'll also bring an AN/PVS Ten scope, in case we need to shoot at night. Actually, I'd prefer to shoot at night."

"Suppressed twenty-two in thick, cold, humid air in the dark would be ideal," Wade agreed. "So naturally, we'll have to do it in daylight."

"Yeah, Murphy's already packed his bags, I'm sure. Anyway, we're waiting on the suppressors at my end, and CCI's hottest ammo. How's yours?"

"Got the AK," Wade acknowledged. "The armorer is flogging it. It actually doesn't need much, because the barrel's the right length and it's already got fiberglass furniture. He's removing the bayonet lug and cleaning rod—I won't need those—and threading it. So we're waiting on a suppressor and some custom ammo. I ordered a thousand rounds from a civilian loader who insists that it won't possibly work properly. I told him it was for a custom hunting pistol. He seemed to buy that."

"Fair enough. Where'd you get the ballistics figures for the round?"

"I asked a ballistician at Natick Research Center, who checked with a physicist and with Olin. They offered to load some rounds up, but it would take four months and they have a two-hundred-thousand round minimum order."

"Uh . . . yeah," Kyle said. "So we'll need to test this ammo, then." It wasn't a question. Sniping was as much science as art, and everything was checked and measured before being tried in the field.

"I figure to use half the ammo for practice," Wade said. "Maybe more. I'm hoping not to shoot more than a magazine of the special stuff for keeps. Standard Eastern Bloc fodder can fill in the rest, and I'm taking some civilian stuff that I know is reliable, too. But I have a question."

"Yes?" Kyle asked.

"How the hell do we get the weapons there?"

"I'm told State Department will ship them to the embassy, and that it's done all the time."

"Oh. Reassuring. I think." They shipped special weapons into embassies all the time? How many operations like this were being run by the CIA, NSA, FBI, and God only knew how many other agencies?

"Yeah, that was my reaction."

3

IT WOULD BE SEVERAL DAYS BEFORE THE REST OF THE accessories and gear were ready. In the meantime, there were more briefings. Kyle didn't mind. He was a natural tourist, loved seeing other cultures, and was learning to appreciate Wade's fascination with the details and differences. The briefers seemed to know what they were talking about, and they didn't waste time. Facts and key items only.

Neither of them knew a lot about modern camera gear. They were brought up to speed in a hurry. Their instructor was a slim, dark-haired man with a faint Russian accent who was very engaging and informative.

"You've goht the three still cameras," he said. "Point and shoot. They've had the circuits disabled so they won't beep when you shoot. Fifty photos on each memohry stick, and you can carry extra ones."

"Roger." Wade was handling this, but Kyle took notes, too, so he could double up.

"Yohr best bet is the camcorder. With memohry sticks it can take passable stills. It can use digital tapes for up to two hours, and it has an IR illuminator good for about ten meters or so. Telephoto lens, and you've goht a two-hundred-millimeter lens adapted to fit it. Eastern European power supply and spare batteries. Make sure you carry the spares."

"Yeah, definitely," they both agreed. Batteries were the ammo of the modern army. Bullets could sometimes be done without. But batteries were essential.

"Now, the betacam is noht going to be used much, but it has to look like it is. I'll show you how to operate it, and how to look professional."

The man knew nothing of their mission, but he really knew cameras and photography. Wade was delighted to take a minor hobby and improve upon it with good lessons.

They spent a morning looking at the economics and social fabric of Romania, which hadn't fared well under the madman Ceaușescu and the Soviet Communists before that, and was still only slowly entering twenty-first century Europe.

Their briefer was a college professor. All he'd been told was that they were going over to act as liaison with the Romanian military for a training exercise and needed to know about the culture and people. As a result, there were important questions they couldn't ask him and would have to catch up with later.

"The economy is still in a recovery phase and social systems are in a state of flux," he told them. He was full of information, but much of that was hidden in heavy babble. He gave figures about GNP, GDP and relative worth, told them of the excesses of the former regime, and even described several amusing and informative misunderstandings he'd encountered on his own trip to the Universitatea din Bucuresti. They made notes.

When they broke, Kyle expressed an opinion. "You know, it's always some kind of goat rope. We've got all this support, so it seems, but they don't want to make it obvious to foreign intelligence that we're doing anything. So we can't ask State Department to brief us here, we can't take enough backup, and we can't even ask some questions, and have to hope they have someone on site who can help us. It's really, really . . . aggravating."

Wade agreed, "Ours not to reason why," he said. "Which is a damned good thing, because we'd go crazy trying to figure this out."

After a lunch of Taco Bell, cold but better than chow-hall takeout, they were ready for their language briefing.

"Greetings, gentlemen," Bill Gober said as he walked in. As always before, his arms were full of CDs, books, and notes. A bag slung over his shoulder was stuffed like Santa's pouch with more documents. He was portly and balding, roundfaced and smiling, dressed in a casual sport shirt and jeans. He wasn't a stuffy type, and had done an excellent job of prepping them on the basics of languages they'd never even heard of for the last mission.

"Mister Gober," they both replied.

"Let's talk about Romanian, which is, of course, a Romance language."

"I wondered about that," Kyle said. "They're in the middle of all those Slavic countries."

"Yes, and it's corrupted their language," he agreed as he sat down. "There's Slavic endings and vowels stuffed into the degenerate Latin. But there's good news."

"Yes?"

"You speak Spanish, I'm told. Spanish has better than seventy percent commonality, so you should be able to be understood. Of course, dialects can vary, and if they speak quickly, you'll be hard-pressed to extract more than a few words."

"Understood. I haven't used it much in some time."

"I've got CDs of Romanian and Spanish you can listen to that should make comprehension much easier. Anyone who wants to understand you should grasp the gist of what you say." He tapped the stack he'd arranged on the table.

"Yeah, that's the key," Kyle nodded. Of course, if someone who clearly understood most of what he was saying tried to pretend they didn't, he'd find ways to make them understand. "What about other languages?"

Gober took a sip of his water before replying. "The Gypsies speak Romani in various dialects. But they almost all speak Romanian. There's a smattering of Hungarian, Turkish, Bulgarian, and of course Arabic might crop up."

"Right. And the local alphabet is based on the Latin one," Wade put in, looking over one of the guide books.

"Yes. They switched from Cyrillic when the Soviet Union collapsed. Or rather, the Soviets imposed Cyrillic on them, but it's a Romance language, so it used a Latin base originally."

"So I read up, use Spanish as needed, and you, Wade?" he looked a question at his partner.

"Oh, I can pick the written parts up at least," Wade said. "Looking at this page, I see 'natura,' 'interiorara,' 'primul,' and 'arhitectura gotica.' Much of it looks easy to extract."

"Yes, much easier than last time," Gober said. "We've got more than three weeks before you depart, I'm told, so there's time to practice."

"Any chance of practicing with you, Mister Gober?" Kyle asked.

"I wouldn't be of much help. I'm not a linguist, I'm an ethnologist. I study the development and relationships of languages. I can handle basic grammar and vocabulary, and advise on pronunciation, but I'm not fluent in a great many."

"Okay," Kyle said. That cleared up a great many things. It would have been amazing had Gober actually spoken all the languages they discussed. This made more sense. Though he did wish the Army could dig up a linguist to work with them.

On the other hand, that would mean either flying to Monterrey, where the linguists were, or bringing one here, or trying to get a clearance for a civilian instructor of unknown loyalty. Any of which would make it obvious something was going on, and wouldn't be of substantially more help in a few days. Gober was likely more useful to them in that regard.

And Gober was cleared. He knew approximately what they were doing, and could give them military terminology and specialized language that most non-military experts wouldn't know, and would immediately get suspicious of. They worked with him three afternoons a week, the three days they weren't practicing shooting and spotting, just to keep the basics fresh.

Then there was all the research they did themselves. As with most military installations, Fort Benning had a decent amount of material in the post library, and both men knew how to use computers. They swapped links, dug through sites, made and compiled notes, and then sat down to compare. The problem with online information was deciding which was accurate, which was amusing fabrication, and which was ignorant hearsay.

Wade came over every couple of nights and they discussed their findings. One of the first things he'd looked at was the religious background.

"It's not far from what used to be Constantinople, and is heavily Christian. But not like America," he said. "Here's a chart." He laid out a printed page for clarity, and brought up a file on an Army laptop he'd acquired.

"Okay," Kyle said, digesting the figures. "So ninety percent Orthodox, five percent Catholic, and the rest a mix, with only point oh oh three percent Muslim? Why is that such a problem? They can't all be troublemakers."

"Indigenous Muslims aren't a problem. These are Muslims from Bosnia and the Middle East. You'll recall that the Romanians arrested an al Qaeda member a while back who was using his cover name in the Iraqi embassy."

"I don't, actually," Kyle said. He hadn't known that, and he really needed to get up to speed. The government claimed WMDs and conspiracies and terrorists. Its detractors denied everything. The truth was likely somewhere in the middle, as usual. "They're coming from elsewhere?"

"Yes, it looks as if much of their explosive is former Eastern Bloc and sometimes former Yugoslav military munitions. They load up in the quiet parts of Romania then go elsewhere. And it's easily within range of the MidEast."

"Ain't it amazing how these scum are so devious? If they spent half this much effort on real work, there wouldn't be any trouble in the world."

"'A policeman's lot is not a happy one,'" Wade said. "Someone has to be babysitter and playground attendant."

"And trash collector."

"Yeah, it all sucks," Wade said with a nod. "So let's pull on the gloves."

Changing the subject, Kyle asked, "How are you doing on supplies?"

"Adequately," Wade replied. "Still waiting on the suppressor and ammo."

"Damn. We've only got a week left."

"Yeah, I keep a calendar." Wade winced. "Better than last time, but your pessimism is rubbing off on me."

"Pessimism?" Kyle asked. "I think positive. I'm positive the Army is going to screw up again."

"And on that note, I need a beer." He'd brought his own in a cooler again.

There was no friction between them over drinking. Kyle didn't think of himself as an alcoholic, just as someone who increasingly thought drinking was a bad idea for himself. Wade didn't drink to excess; this was the same twelve-pack he'd been working on for three weeks. He drank, Kyle didn't, and that was all there was to it. But Wade didn't seem to feel it was sociable to drink alone, so he always grabbed a soda for Kyle.

They dove back in to a history of Romania from the time of the Turkish occupation through Ceaușescu's butchery. "That was one seriously insane dude," Wade said.

"Yeah. Forced breeding program to outpopulate the West? And what were they going to eat in that little country?" Romania had less than 23 million inhabitants, and was no larger than a couple of Midwestern states. How he'd planned to increase to where the nation would even be noticed by most Westerners was a mystery.

"I think it was an attempt at individuality for him, seeing as how Moscow was threatening to march on him, and an ego trip against the modern world. If it's not that, I have no idea why he was such a twitch."

They kicked it and assorted maps and photos around until 11 P.M., when Wade said, "Time for me to get back to billeting. When and where tomorrow?"

"Call me at oh eight hundred," Kyle said. "I'll know then."

"Maintain a rigid state of flexibility?" Wade asked.

"You got it. Later." He showed Wade to the door.

The next morning at the school, a package was waiting on Kyle's desk. It was from post logistics, and contained multiple layers of cardboard and padding. He sliced the top with his Benchmade, and took enough of a glance to determine it contained round, black phosphated shapes: suppressors, magazines, and some assorted other parts. He left everything packed for privacy and to protect it.

Now what they needed was a place to practice. The choice was obvious but problematic. He grabbed the phone and speed-dialed Captain Schorlin, who was out on the range, prepping for the next class.

"Captain, I need to see about reserving some range time."

"Shouldn't be a problem. When?"

"Sir, we need to do some shooting inside to . . . well, we need to shoot inside." He needed to know it was going to be quiet enough before he tried it in the field.

"I assume these are weapons you really don't want seen in a civilian range?"

"Yes, sir," he said. They were somewhat distinctive. It was unlikely the word would leak out from here, but taking military automatic weapons with suppressors onto a civilian range was guaranteed to draw attention from someone, even if it could be legally arranged. "Rumors. This has to be on base somewhere."

"Kyle, there's some things I can't beat, and political correctness is one of them. You're going to need to call General Robash for that."

"Understood, sir," he said. "I just wanted to make sure I checked with you first."

"I appreciate it. If he'll help, I'll cover for you. But I'm only a captain. I can't buck the system that much by myself."

"Yeah, I don't blame you, sir. But thanks, and I'll make that call."

General Robash hesitated, too. "Son, I know what you need, and I know why you're doing that, but damn," he said. "There is absolutely no legal way."

"I was afraid you'd say that, sir," Kyle replied. "I'm just trying to figure out a discreet alternative."

"No, hold on a moment," the general said. "Just hold the line."

Kyle said, "Yes, sir," but the phone was already clicking. He waited, receiver to ear for fifteen minutes, fumbling with papers and his computer, until he wondered if he dare hang up on a general officer and await a return call.

Just as he was thinking that, Robash came back. "All right, Wade, call Sergeant Major Jack Parsons at this extension," he said and rattled off the digits. "He's expecting you to call now."

"Thank you, sir."

"For what? I didn't do anything. I don't know anything. I don't even know why I'm talking into this phone, since there's no one there." He hung up, but not before Kyle heard a snicker.

Kyle reset and dialed the number. It was answered on the first ring by a deep, gravelly voice. "Sergeant Major Parsons."

"Sergeant Major, I'm Sergeant Monroe."

"Right. General Robash told me you need some indoor time?"

"Yes I do, Sergeant Major. Quietly and without spectators."

"Right. Tomorrow at zero nine hundred suit you?" Parsons clearly wasn't one to waste time.

"That works for me," Kyle said. Parsons gave him a building number and a road. "We'll be there," Kyle agreed.

The next morning, he and Wade took their weapons from the Sniper School armory and loaded them into his truck. Military weapons were never supposed to be in private vehicles, but these weren't crated like military weapons, they didn't want anyone to think weapons were going into the building in question, and he figured the captain and the general could run interference if need be. Not that anyone should notice. The Ruger was in its metal case, and the AK was in a sleeve in a duffel bag.

"I didn't even know there was an indoor range here," Wade said.

"Neither did I. That was a certain amount of luck."

"Right," Wade said. "I'm still amazed you could pull this off."

"Actually, Robash called a sergeant major."

"Ah, sergeant majors," Wade said. "Is there anything they can't do? When God needs backup, he calls his sergeant major."

"About the truth," Kyle agreed.

The building was like many at Benning: brick, aged, and well maintained. But this one had a long forgotten secret: an indoor twenty-five-yard pistol range in the basement. Kyle was hoping the confines and closeness would give him a good idea of how the weapons would handle inside a city, with witnesses nearby, possibly even in adjoining rooms.

Simple enough on the face of it. But the reason the range was forgotten was because it had been closed before Kyle was born.

A very large, very black man in painted-on BDUs met them at the door. "Sergeants Monroe and Curtis? Good to meet you."

"Yes, we are, Sergeant Major Parsons. Thanks for meeting us." He winced slightly at a handshake that could crush pipe, and quickly passed the hand to Wade.

"I'm told it's for a worthy cause. If General Robash says so, I'm willing to bend the system. Once," Parsons cautioned. He motioned them in and turned to lead the way. He filled the doorway as he did, shoulders almost brushing the frame.

"So this was a common-use area once?" Kyle asked.

"Yeah, most posts and every National Guard armory used to have a twenty-five yard range in the basement. Lead complaints shut them all down," Parsons said as he led them through the building, now used for storage of desks, chairs, and crates, then down dim, dusty, echoing stairs. It was cool and musty, the air smelling of mildew.

"I can see that. Lead oxide," Wade said. As bullets were shot and impacted the backstop, they'd throw lead vapor into the air. It was toxic to breathe. Modern indoor ranges had filters and fans to handle it. Retrofitting old ranges was cost prohibitive.

"Yes. And that's why we aren't supposed to be here," Parsons said. "So do what you've got to, be done by lunch, and no one knows a thing."

"We'll be brief," Kyle promised. "And we won't shoot that much, anyway."

"Good. The lead risk is real. There's just times that's an acceptable risk militarily. But the EPA *doesn't* know that, so I've told the MPs to keep the area clear, and that some construction with nail guns is going on. Or rather, I told their first sergeant that, and he told them."

"That should do fine," Kyle said. If anyone could hear these weapons outside a concrete basement and on the street, they needed a new strategy anyway.

Parsons unlocked a thick, heavy door that had padding on the inside and a dirty, fogged window about four inches square set into it. The hinges protested slightly, but it swung easily enough. "Here you go," he said. "Call my cell phone when you're done and I'll come secure the building." He handed over his card.

"Thank you very much, Sergeant Major," Kyle said, and Wade chorused in.

"No problem, gentlemen. Whatever you're hunting, good luck." He smiled and left, boots thumping and echoing back up the stairs.

Wade closed the door. "Man, if I didn't know he was coming back, I'd hate being down here. It's like a forgotten dungeon." The building was so old it was lit by incandescent bulbs in metal cages. Floodlights illuminated the target area and backstop. Everything was old, covered in peeling white paint, and there were four lanes, each about three feet wide with motorized cables to run targets downrange. The area they stood in was perhaps five feet deep. The ceiling was seven feet high.

"Tell me about it," Kyle said. He felt creeped out, too. The echoes of his voice were tinny. "Anyway," he continued, "let's see what we have now."

He'd practiced with the .22, and had it assembled in short order as Wade watched. As claimed, G-Tech's suppressor slipped over the muzzle and pinned in place behind the sight. It was a can type, slender and about six inches long. He added the Harris bipod to the rail that had been fitted under the fore end.

That done, Wade screwed a larger suppressor onto the AK's muzzle brake. "We'll still get a crack, obviously," he said. "But the muzzle blast and flash should be minimal."

"Right," Kyle agreed. Nothing could be made silent. But if it didn't sound like a weapon to a witness, and if the flash and bang were reduced, the odds of being identified were greatly reduced. "And here's where the forty-five rules," he grinned. He'd never liked the 9mm.

"Yeah, the round is already subsonic, no crack," Wade said.

Kyle said nothing, he simply screwed another suppressor onto the specially prepared barrel Ed Brown had cut for him. It protruded a half inch beyond the slide and was threaded. He was glad to see it fit well. He'd assumed so; Brown was a very reputable maker. But they also had a hell of a waiting list at times, and had squeezed the job in among their other clients. All they'd been told was "urgent military contract," and they'd done it. It was nice to know patriotic support still existed among civilians.

There was nothing wrong with the workmanship. The barrel worked flawlessly; Kyle had already shot it in. The threads had been done perfectly, which was no big task, but accidents happened on some contracts. He was glad again to have insisted on first-rate work up front. The lowest bidder was often more expensive in the long run. And G-Tech's suppressors were functionally pretty, no-nonsense and sturdy.

"Oh, to reassure you on the lead," Wade said, "I bought us a box each of Winchester's fully jacketed stuff for the pistols. No exposed lead at the base." He indicated two boxes among the dozen he'd brought. They planned to try several rounds to find the best combination of weapon and cartridge.

"Good man," Kyle said. "I always wondered why they aren't more available."

"Production cost. They can't just pour the lead in."

"Oh." He felt stupid. That was a rather obvious problem.

"That still leaves lead twenty-two, and exposed lead on the AK."

"Gee, thanks."

"You know," Wade said conversationally, "the Romanians have the solution to that problem. Seven six two with wooden bullets."

"Wooden bullets?" Kyle asked.

"Yup. Specifically for indoor range practice. No lead, no ricochets, just holes in the paper."

"Wooden bullets. Romania . . ." Kyle muttered.

"Vampires and wooden stakes?"

"That's a hell of a coincidence," Kyle said. Weird irony.

"Yeah. Should we get some, just in case?"

"I really don't want to explain that to Wiesinger," he said with a frown.

"Yeah, better not. Still, it's funny."

With the suppressors on, no hearing protection was required. A faint *pop!* accompanied each shot of the Ruger, followed by the metallic *tink* of the empty brass hitting the side of the lane or the floor. The sound echoed on the block walls.

"Okay, we need a brass catcher. Twenty-five bucks and two screws to install," Kyle said as he finished a string.

"Sure. Meantime, this is one accurate little son of a bitch!" Wade marveled. He raised the weapon smoothly and quickly as he shuffled into stance, and commenced firing.

In ten seconds, he'd shot all ten rounds. He laid the weapon down, automatically extracted the magazine and observed the empty chamber through the locked bolt, and pressed the button to return the target.

As it swayed back toward them, rocking in the breeze created by its motion, one thing was clear: All ten rounds had hit in a circle no larger than a quarter inch, dead center on the forehead of the silhouette target.

"Nice," Kyle commented. "My turn."

The factory ten-round helical magazines functioned flawlessly.

The twenty-five-round aftermarket ones were quite reliable. But the thirties Kyle had picked up . . .

"These are just crap," Wade said in disgust the fourth time one misfed and jammed a round against the breech face.

"Yeah, we'll scrap those. I don't expect to shoot more than five shots at a target, anyway," Kyle said. "The larger ones are just backup."

"Okay, well I'm happy with that. Let's look at the support."

The modified AK104 was an ugly little gun. The barrel was barely twelve and a half inches, and the stock folded sideways.

"The bottom folder was longer, but caught on the magazine when deploying," Wade said. "This is from the AKSU Seventy-four and works much better. The muzzle brake," he pointed under the suppressor, "reduces felt recoil and flash, and maintains pressure for the gas piston, and the expansion chamber stops it from getting louder." That was a positive thing. It was common for a good brake to actually *increase* perceived sound. "It's threaded, and the suppressor fits right over it."

"Nice," Kyle commented. He'd shot AK-series weapons, but wasn't an aficionado of them. He could strip and clean and employ. That was all he needed to know.

"Bad news is that with this short barrel, accuracy with standard ball will suck. Suck bad. Way bad. So bad that . . . well, it won't be much good over one hundred meters with standard Eastern ammo. With the stuff I had loaded, it's accurate for about three hundred, but it's about like a pistol for power at that range. So any kill will have to be precision, not trauma."

"That fits our plans," Kyle said. He grasped what Wade was saying. Below certain critical velocities, wounding effect was greatly reduced. There would be a hole, but not a catastrophic energy dump into the target. Still, they intended to shoot accurately.

"I figured," Wade continued. "The rail attaches here and here, with pins. So it looks mostly standard issue like this, but can take the rail, scope, and suppressor in a few seconds. I actually thought about using Russian night vision and scopes, but while the quality is good, we aren't familiar with them, and it's not going to make that much difference if we're found."

"Right. We'll work with what we're used to as far as possible. And who'd question it, anyway? Either they know who we are, or we're mercs of some kind."

"Glad you approve," Wade said.

"Hell, Wade, either of us could run this, you know that. I'm nominally in charge due to rank and because someone has to be the place where the buck stops."

"Thanks," Wade said, seeming to mean it. He obviously felt complimented.

"No problem. Show me how to shoot it."

"It's going to be zeroed fifteen inches high, because it's got a twenty-seven-inch drop at three hundred and a flight time of point five zero seconds exactly. Ballistics tables are in my PDA, soon to be in the laptop, and we can study them as we go. I've found a couple of support points that give it a very stable position," Wade began. "First is in front of the magazine, fingers wrapped . . ."

Unfortunately, the rounds still had a supersonic crack. Both men reached for earmuffs in a hurry.

The .45 was fun, rocking lightly, its kick reduced to a slow shove, and the additional nose weight keeping it stable. The Ed Brown platform was one of the world's best, and Kyle proceeded to blow the middle from a target with dull thumps akin to a phone book being dropped on a concrete floor.

"I think we're in good shape," he said. "The twenty-two is near silent, the forty-five sounds nothing like a firearm, the AK is loud but much reduced and the nine millimeter has a crack when you're using standard loads, but is still not immediately recognizable. Let's try two rounds each of our combat loads and I'll stand upstairs to get a listen."

"Will do," Wade agreed, and started loading. Kyle shoved the heavy door open and jogged up into the clutter upstairs, leaving the door wide behind him. He'd been so busy shooting, he'd forgotten the aloneness the building exuded, and was used to it now.

Shortly, there came clicks, thumps, and clatters. Then Wade shouted, "Cease fire! That's it!"

"Roger!" he replied and headed back down. "Didn't sound like anything threatening to me. We're cool."

"Good. Call the sar-major and let's go get lunch."

With all preparations made, all gear—from rifles and GPS to pocketknives and a handful of paperbacks—packed and ready to either travel as luggage or meet them there, they started their final outprocessing. They checked their government credit cards to ensure they were active, compiled lists of phone numbers and email addresses, and gathered maps and flight schedules. Kyle called ahead to speak to the Regional Affairs officer at the embassy in Bucharest, Mr. Mick Cafferty.

"You realize it's . . . eight hours ahead here?" he asked. His voice was gravelly and tired.

"Damn. I'm sorry," Kyle said. It was damned near midnight there, and he'd woken the man they'd be working with.

"It's okay. Let's talk," Cafferty said. Behind him, a female voice was protesting. She didn't sound happy.

"Okay," Kyle said, "I need to know what we do when we arrive."

"There'll be a taxi waiting for you at the airport. It'll take you to the Marriott. You'll call me and I'll arrange for you to stop by the office."

"Understood." He was writing it down to add to his file.

Cafferty continued. "We have to be careful not to let people conclude you're more than glorified tourists. It's fine for you to stop by and 'ask questions,' but if you stay any length of time, the locals may become curious, and there are leaks."

"Yes, sir," he agreed. "Do we have visas?"

"Yes. They should arrive there in the next day or so. You're photographers for hire. Some group wants to do a book and video about Dracula again, and they sent you to get footage. You're spending their money and snickering at their foolishness—it adds to the cover story. I had to find some way to explain your presence."

"I guess that makes sense," Kyle said. He didn't want to contradict or complain, as it wasn't his arena. It did call for some acting, and he wished they'd had more notice. "Is there any question over us being such unknown videographers?"

Cafferty chuckled, a rasping, scary sound. "No. Thousands of nuts and researchers from hundreds of agencies with dozens of nations come through here all the time to see the Dracula sites. As long as their embassy or a producer vouches for them, no one bothers to check up. It's just not worth the work."

"Understood," Kyle said. "You'll have more intel for us when we get there?"

"Yes, we're still building a report. You're going to be here early in the operation."

"Better than being late. Anything else I need right now?"

"You won't come to the embassy. Some things the ambassador doesn't need to know, so he doesn't have to deny them, and so he can't refuse to assist. But that's my problem. It's only your problem if things go to hell,"—Kyle thought, when *things go to hell*—"and then you've got DoD and State to bat for you as well as me. You'll stay locally, I'll deliver your gear and intel. I'll email you if anything else crops up. How often do you check messages?"

"At least three times a day at the school," Kyle said. "Let me give you my home addy, too." He read it off phonetically.

"Got it."

"Good. I'll let you sleep. You have our cell numbers?"

"I do. Good night."

"Good night."

"Okay, not thrilling but better than last time," Kyle said to Wade. "We have someone in country who speaks our language and can run interference."

"Good. Hey, even the Army learns from its mistakes. Eventually."

"Right. Let's check off the list and call logistics. I'll make sure they load it all."

"Okay," Wade said and pulled out his PDA. "First item, AK-one oh four with AN/PVS dash ten scope and suppressor, two ten-round magazines and four thirty-round magazines, hardshell case and four hundred and eighty rounds of match ammunition."

"Check."

Their gear made quite a pile, Kyle thought, as it was taken to be shipped. Weapons, rucks, local and military clothes, body armor for out in the field, commo gear and computers, cameras and recording gear for "reporting," maps, charts, suitcases, a few personal items, and credit cards and cash. Some would fly as luggage, some would be flown to the embassy and meet them there, and some went with them as carryons. Wade was staying at billeting, he at his apartment, and they didn't need to wake up at ohmygodthirty this time. Which was good.

Kyle had never learned to sleep the night before a mission started.

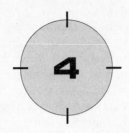

THEIR LAST MISSION HAD ENTAILED LONG HOURS trapped in commercial aircraft, pretending to be harmless civilians and getting shuffled around at airports.

This deployment was much the same, except the aircraft were military, or sort of.

"Sort of" meant after a civilian flight from Atlanta, the overseas Rotator flight from Baltimore to Rhein-Main Air Base, Germany, then to Aviano Air Base, Italy, where they'd debark before it continued on to Saudi Arabia. It was an old Lockheed Tristar, contracted to the Air Force from ATA, and all the passengers were military. Most were deploying unit elements on their way to Iraq, Kuwait, or Qatar, who'd transfer to military transport aircraft at some point. Kyle and Wade sat near the front, separated from others by a seat or so each way, and tried to get back into the tactical discussion.

"Pity it's not Pan Am like last time, with the free beer and that nice chicken," Kyle said. Though he recalled the chicken being Airline Standard Tasteless. And he didn't drink, even if there had been beer on this flight. But it was standard to complain. The military ran on complaints.

"True. But there's one really good thing about flying charter," Wade replied.

"Yeah," Kyle agreed. "We can talk about killing, and terrorists, and weapons, and not be dragged off by TSA." He met the eye of the passing flight attendant, who smiled thinly back at him. Clearly, she wasn't happy with the subject, but recognized it as something military and legitimate. It was a plus, but at the same time, they'd have to avoid slipping details that would place their mission to Romania. The other troops would tell tales, and those could become leaks. ComSec, it was called. Communications Security. Never say anything in the presence of those who didn't need to know.

Still, they could study background from books. Wade had a history of Romania he'd picked up online. He'd often expressed the theory that one could never have too much intelligence, and his schooling had been in sociology. He was engrossed in it when not dragged out to deal with mundane issues.

"Hey, Kyle, listen to this about Prince Vlad Dracula," he said, eyes wide as he leaned back and read aloud:

"'Some Italian ambassadors were sent to him. When they came to him they bowed and removed their hats and they kept on the berets beneath them. Then he asked them why they did not take their caps off, too. They said it was their custom, and they did not even remove them for the emperor. Dracula said, "I wish to reinforce this for you." He immediately had their caps nailed firmly on their heads so that their caps would not fall off and their custom would remain.'"

"Damn," Kyle said, "And I thought the drills in boot camp were harsh about hats under cover."

"And this one: 'He [the Sultan] marched on for about five kilometers, when he saw his men pale; the Sultan's army came across a field with stakes, about three kilometers long and one kilometer wide. And there were large stakes on which they could see the impaled bodies of men, women, and children, about twenty thousand of them, as they said. Quite a spectacle for the Turks and the Sultan himself! The Sultan, in wonder, kept saying that he could not conquer the country of a man who could do such terrible and unnatural things and put his power and his subjects to such use. He also used to say that this man who did such things would be worthy of more. And the other Turks, seeing so many people impaled, were scared out of their wits. There were babies clinging to their mothers on stakes, and birds had made nests in their breasts.'"

"He impaled his *own* people to scare off invaders?" Kyle asked, guts churning. Dear God.

"Sounds like. No wonder he got the reputation he did. But he's a folk hero to some of the locals, because he kept the Turks out."

"Yeah. Who'd want to invade? Damn."

"And we think the scum we're fighting are obscene. They've got nothing on this."

"I think we can be happy they haven't read history," Kyle said.

"They haven't learned from it, either," Wade said. "Which is why we're here. God bless job security and precision shooting."

"I think I'd rather be unemployed," Kyle said, somewhat darkly.

"Me, too. But in the meantime . . ."

"Nothing wrong with enjoying our work," Kyle finished for him.

"Bingo."

Both men napped for a while. It wasn't restful. It seemed all the troops heading for Iraq were nervous—understandably so—and wanted to party as hard as was possible without booze. They were loud and boisterous. The crew seemed used to it, and neither sniper was going to complain about fellow soldiers de-stressing, but it did leave them a bit wired by the time they landed at Rhein-Main, Germany. There was a three-hour layover, just long enough for the troops to find an open German bar in the airport and get soused.

On second thought, Kyle wasn't sure bars in Germany ever closed.

The leg to Italy was much quieter once they replaned, but the lavatories were somewhat worse for wear, with one hundred troops times six to eight beers. Still, there were worse things, Kyle thought. Getting shot at. Getting shot. Getting friends shot.

He fell asleep over Poland, and still didn't get any rest.

From Aviano, Italy, they took a plane to Rome, then boarded one for Bucharest. The constant changing of planes did mean a chance to stretch and unkink. But it also meant no sleep. They switched to civilian passports in Rome, and took a few minutes to wash and clean up. The sodas aboard had been useful as time wasters, and slightly refreshing, but Kyle wanted a bottle of water. He needed replenishment, and his military training insisted on water, not sugary snacks. Wade downed another ginger ale, and Kyle wondered how he did it. They'd both had four sodas before reaching Aviano, and that was Kyle's limit for the day and then some.

It was 8 P.M. local before they arrived in Bucharest, and they'd been awake more than twenty-four hours with all the movement. A few minutes of naps here and there hadn't done much for their metabolisms.

Otopeni airport was as modern as they'd been told, at least at first glance. It was also small. It wasn't what Kyle thought of as a hub. He'd seen regional airports Stateside that were bigger. Yet this was the main international center for the entire nation. The fixtures were older desks in metal; there were guards with submachine guns and, then there was the drab, rundown effect that followed the former Eastern Bloc like a bad smell and took years to fade.

Going through customs was straightforward; they showed passports and visas, and declared their cameras and gear. The agent they dealt with was a woman who might be attractive except for a severe uniform of white shirt and blue pants, hair tightly pulled back and square-rimmed glasses that made her face look humorless. She spoke good if accented English.

"What is the purpose of your visit?"

"We're doing a historical background segment for a documentary. Poenari, Bran, and then across into Turkey."

"Ah, the history of the Walachia?"

"Yes, at least this segment is."

"You'll be seeing at Tirgovişte?"

"I don't think so. All we have is a list of places, and our specialty is getting good photos. The actual analysis is left to the experts on Dracula." He grinned.

"Ah, I see. Well, if you have time, do enjoy yourselves also," she said as she stamped their passports.

"We'll try to," Wade said. "Lots of travel, not much free time."

"Yes. Let me see in your camera bags, please?"

They opened the bags, which contained only a small betacam, a professional digital video recorder, two digital still cameras and a digital audio recorder.

She gave them only a cursory glance. "Very good, gentlemen. Enjoy your visit."

"Thank you."

They headed for the restroom, which was modern but in need of cleaning, and took turns in a stall. A quick drain was called for, but the main reason was to dig deep into their personal checked luggage and get out necessary accessories—folding knives, flashlights, and Kyle's SOG Powerplier pocket tool. These were the very useful items one carried everywhere, in Kyle's opinion, but couldn't carry aboard planes anymore. They went in one at a time, Wade slipping in after Kyle was done. Kyle watched the bags while Wade gathered his Kershaw Boa knife and Gerber tool. They'd rather have firearms, but that was not yet an option. But with the basics in pocket and on belt, they were ready to face the world again.

Outside the doors, they sought a Romanian *taxia*.

"There's supposed to be one meeting us here," Kyle said, looking along the ranks of dull vehicles. They ranged from slightly worn to decrepit, as did their drivers. One nearby car started toward them. "'Otel?" he called firmly.

"Yes, hotel. Which one?" He wanted to make this man identify himself.

"Marriohtt," was the reply.

"Yup, that's it," he nodded to Wade. He motioned with his head and they started walking.

It was a worn but serviceable old Fiat, technically a four-seater but tiny by American standards. The driver tossed their bags casually into the trunk and they piled into the back, knees against seatback and heads brushing the liner. They clutched at the doorhandles—there were no seatbelts—as he took off and wove into traffic. There was no radio—the hole in the dash where it would go held a hastily mounted two-way for operations instead.

"You have cameras? Sightseeing?" the driver asked. He was about thirty, dark and swarthy with hollow cheeks, and not heavily built.

"Cameras, news," Wade said.

"Ah, very good," the driver grinned, nodding much. Perhaps he hoped for a quick image to make him famous. "Very good," he said.

He zipped through traffic quickly and agilely, shaking fists and shouting an occasional colorful curse at other drivers. The radio chattered, and he picked up a microphone and chattered back. He turned right and took them onto a long, straight street. They were quite some way from downtown, and it seemed there might be time for a nap.

Kyle leaned back and closed his eyes, trying to ignore the buzzing, rattling exhaust and occasional swerves. The radio chattered again and the driver replied.

It took a moment, but then Kyle opened his eyes. He tried not to move too fast, and eased forward again.

"Wade, I think I overhear something bad," he said.

"Yes?" Wade prompted, conversational and smiling.

"This stuff is almost like the other speech I speak, and I hear something about 'setup' and 'bring the cars' and 'they've got cameras, could be something . . . er . . . worthwhile.'"

Wade laughed as cover. "Oh, that's good. Got another one?"

"Yeah," Kyle said, grinning back. "An interception. They fumble, we recover. Pity it can't be at the forty-five yard line. Or the nine in your case," he said, hoping it would be cryptic for the driver. He might know some English, after all, and while it was technically a West Germanic language, there were enough words borrowed from Latin that the driver might recognize one word in five. Kyle chose his vocabulary carefully to avoid *language, valuable,* and any other word that would have a Romance language analog. *Never thought I'd want to thank Mrs. Howarth for those weeks of etymology in eighth grade*, he said to himself.

"Sure," Wade agreed. "That was a great game. Who's the referee?"

"I am. Unless you see the ball first."

"Got it," Wade said, nodding and grinning a broad mouthful of teeth. Kyle grinned also, though he didn't feel cheerful. Fights were never fun, and if it were to be a knife fight, he'd prefer his Ed Brown, which was tucked safely away, he hoped, in the embassy, awaiting their arrival.

But starting a firefight on the streets of Bucharest would be bad anyway. Ideally, they'd talk their way out of trouble, or intimidate or punch. Gunfire would not be discreet. And it wasn't an option, yet.

They were definitely not getting closer to downtown, and the traffic was getting lighter. "I think we were told about this in passing," Wade said.

"Seems to be. Oh, well."

Shortly, another car pulled in front of them. Then they turned onto a smaller, darker side street. It was rough and gravelly in spots. *Here comes the pitch*, Kyle thought. He kept a bored look on his face.

Then two more cars pulled in behind. Still he stayed reticent, and so did Wade, even though alarm bells were jangling in his mind.

The three cars were pulling in close. Kyle nodded, but played along so as not to lose the advantage of surprise the enemy thought they had. "What's happening, driver?" he asked. "They're too close!"

The driver said something noncommittal with a shrug attached, and slowed. It was a bit too rehearsed for Kyle's taste; they'd obviously done this before.

But not to two Army Rangers ready for it, you sons of bitches, he thought with a grin he kept concealed. It was time for a lesson in manners.

He and Wade locked eyes for just a moment and nodded readiness. They turned back to their individual sectors of fire, Kyle to the left, Wade to the right.

Then all the cars stopped and men were piling out. They were quiet, which wasn't a good sign. Quiet meant professional. Professional thugs rather than soldiers, granted, but not amateurs. They moved quickly, they and their shadows darting around the car, clothes and hands brushing against the glass and metal, making whispering sounds that would add to the fear a victim would feel.

Kyle and Wade weren't victims.

A hand clutched at the door next to him, and Kyle followed it back with his eyes. The man attached to it was skeletal, swarthy and had a broad moustache and long hair around deep eyes. His garb was drab, a jacket and pants with a dark shirt underneath. He held what looked like a tire iron in his other hand.

As the door started to open, Kyle kicked it as hard as he could with his left foot, then stuck both legs down to the ground as he twisted and braced the door with his shoulder. He didn't crave having it slammed against his shins. His antagonist staggered back as the door hinges crunched from being pushed beyond their limits. It was a light door, and he'd kicked hard. Next to him, he heard Wade grunt with exertion as he did something. There was no time to look, and Wade didn't sound too bothered, so Kyle kept his attention forward where it belonged. One can't do the other guy's job in combat. One has to assume the other guy will do his job properly, even if he's an idiot.

But Wade was no idiot, and Kyle was perfectly comfortable with him flanking, or backing up, or even leading. They'd meshed quickly as a team during the first mission, and that was carrying over.

Kyle was out the door and standing tall. Crouching would give him better cover, but he was several inches taller than these punks, and meant to use that imposing height as a psychological weapon. See the big American who doesn't back off? See the big American as he clutches your friend's tire iron and pulls him in close? See him punch your friend in the face?

It was a close, dirty brawl, and rules hadn't even been considered. That was fine with Kyle. He could play dirtier than these jerks. His hand hurt like hell, but his attacker, now his victim, went down with his face pulped and gushing dark blood from nostrils and lips. And Kyle had the tire iron.

He was in front of the door, and a younger man, teen really, from the rearguard car was closing from behind. So he kicked the door again, backward, to smack this new threat in the hip. The kid gasped, his eyes popping large above his scraggly beard as he stumbled.

He could hear sounds from the other side that indicated Wade was holding his own, and grinned. In a way, this was fun, a training exercise or warmup for a real fight. But another man was starting to swing the pipe in his hand, and Kyle found himself unable to move. The driver had leaned out the window and clutched him around the waist.

Snarling and trying to do two things at once, Kyle reached in two directions. He tried vainly to get hold of the driver's fingers and break one, but the man had clutched his hands together. No luck. And that club was raised and close. Ideally, Kyle should just shoot him with 230 grains of persuasion, but that was not an option. He realized he should have had his knife out and ready and gone to town earlier. Rules? What were rules? Except Kyle had been thinking traditionally. He needed to think like a coward and be vicious at once.

It was time for another kick. He raised his right leg and threw his weight behind it. It went straight, the incoming thug ran into it gut first, dropped his pipe, dropped to the ground, and spewed vomit onto the road. Kyle dropped a booted heel on the back of his head, then kicked sideways into his exposed face. That last one wasn't very effective, but it should leave scrapes and dings.

Meanwhile, he pulled at his left pocket until he got his Benchmade automatic clear, clicked it open and ran the razor sharp tanto blade along the driver's left arm, from knuckle to mid forearm. He used the sharp corner where the point met the blade edge, and it cut easily.

The driver howled and let go, flinging the black drops that beaded along the wound off to Kyle's left, the front of the car. That left one more man standing, considering his move.

Which was when Kyle threw the tire iron at him. It smacked into his head with a dull, ringing *thunk*, and down the guy went. A step to the side cleared Kyle from the driver's reach. The youth he'd caught with the door was trying to get into position for a rush, and Kyle rushed him instead.

Then the driver cursed and started to drive off.

Most of the thugs were scrambling backward, stumbling to their feet and beating a hasty retreat. Three other cars squealed away, but Kyle was only concerned about the one that held their luggage and very expensive cameras, which Wiesinger would try to make him pay for, no doubt. Also, that he and Wade would be in the ass end of Bucharest with nothing but cell phones and a long wait for backup, "long" being defined as "enough time to get killed."

He turned to see if Wade was okay, then ran to help when he saw what was happening.

Wade's legs stuck out from the passenger side of the taxi. He was obviously entangled with the driver and the steering wheel. The vehicle was rubbing against the broken curb. Then it was on the curb.

Then it bumped a building front, scraping metal and bouncing to a stop.

Kyle vaulted onto the trunk, then the roof, feeling the metal give under him. He reached carefully into the open window with a sharp knife and said, in Spanish, "*Llévenos reservado al hotel o le mataré. Muerte. Comprende?*" *Take us quietly to the hotel or I will kill you. Dead. Do you understand?* He added the basic verb because he wasn't sure *mataré* would translate. But *muerte* should be universal.

There was no argument as the driver replied, "*Da, domnule!*" in a squeak.

"I'm remembering that as 'Yes, sir,'" Kyle said. "'Da' like Russian and dominant something. If not, we'll deal with him. Let's go."

In moments, they were back inside, Kyle behind the driver with the point of his knife against his neck. Wade let his show in the mirror.

Wade looked like hell. His face had taken a beating, and still had a crease where it had been pressed against the steering wheel. He had some blood on him, but a quick check didn't show a wound. It was the driver's. Kyle had bruised knuckles and a sore shin, but was otherwise okay. He didn't remember banging his shin. The driver's arm wasn't critical, just superficial and running blood. "*Véndelo y conduzca.*" *Bandage it and drive.* The driver nodded agreement, grabbed a rag from the front passenger footwell, and stuffed it up his shirtsleeve. He gingerly took the wheel and started off again, carefully and as directed.

"Want to call our friend now?" Wade asked.

"No, let's get to the hotel first. I don't think our boy here is going to cause any more trouble." This was, after all, a military problem. Unless it became political, Kyle wanted them to handle it firsthand. Calling for help over minor issues would give the impression they couldn't handle the job. As long as they were in control, they'd stick to the existing plan.

"Fair enough," Wade agreed. "Are we giving him a tip?" He indicated the driver.

"Yeah. Don't fuck with the Rangers. That's a good tip for anyone."

The streets were getting better lit and better traveled. There were some gorgeous buildings, reminiscent of old Colonial architecture in America, and Turkish, and old Soviet. Bucharest was big, over two million people, and was old enough that the streets were a confusing maze. But the driver made no further attempts at subterfuge. He'd been totally cowed.

Thirty minutes later, they pulled up in front of the Marriott. It was new, white, stylish, and a very welcome sight. Kyle let out a breath he hadn't realized he'd been holding. Things could have gotten bad again.

The driver was sullen as they took their bags from the trunk and piled them on the curb. A bellman in Marriott uniform came to meet them. "Checking in, gentlemen?" he asked in English.

"Yes, reservation, Monroe," Kyle said.

"Yes, sir," he agreed. "You came in this?" he indicated the *taxia* with a concerned and curious wave. Then he stared at Wade's abused face.

"Eventually," Kyle said. He slammed the trunk and said to the driver, "*Tenga buena noche*, OK?" *You have a nice evening, okay?*

The driver muttered something under his breath and spun tires as he left.

The bellman looked quizzically at them, but led the way inside.

Twenty minutes later, they were upstairs and unloaded, sprawled on the beds and taking turns in the shower.

TV had nothing of real interest; it was all in rapid-fire Romanian that Kyle almost understood. He settled for a mindless game on the laptop until Wade came out, then went in to let hot water beat him senseless and ease some of the bruises from the fight. His hand hurt like hell and was going to be stiff for days. And it was his trigger hand, too. He'd have to be careful.

Within the hour, they were each crashed out asleep atop a bed. Neither one bothered with covers.

5

AFTER EIGHT HOURS, KYLE SIMPLY WOKE UP. HIS BODY just couldn't see sleeping longer than that, after years of training. They hadn't closed the curtains the night before, and it was sunny out. That took a moment to adapt to. He ran through a mental checklist and got started.

First, he fumbled for his cell phone and called the number provided.

"Cafferty," was the answer.

"Monroe. We're at the hotel."

"Fine, you need to get a *taxia* and come to the location where we can talk. I'll email you directions and address. Two hours, if that works?"

"Sure," he replied.

"Right. Bye."

"Bye," he said to a dead connection. It had been a really terse conversation.

"Come on, Wade, time to wake up."

"Yeah, I'm awake," Wade said, and dug fingers into his eyes, screwing up his face against the coming day.

They dressed and cleaned up, wearing slacks and shirts as a good compromise between business and tourist.

"I never realized how important wardrobe is," Kyle said. He had a full suitcase of clothes in different styles for this.

"Clothes make the man. Or make him something else," Wade said. "I could handle being a beach bum. Surfboard, chicks, piña coladas . . ."

"Doesn't take much clothing for that. It takes attitude."

"Damn."

"Let's get breakfast. Maybe our next mission will be somewhere with sunny beaches."

"More likely sons of bitches," Wade complained.

The nice thing about an expense account was that international chain hotel food was adequate. If you weren't paying for it, it was far easier and less adventurous than going out on the street. They had bacon, eggs, and some pastries, washed it down with Turkish orange juice, and were ready to tackle the day.

"We should be in the lobby waiting," Kyle said.

"Okay, let's go get the stuff," Wade said. In ten minutes they were heading back downstairs. He wasn't a bad photographer, so he carried a camera. Kyle was halting with the audio, but could do well enough to fake it.

A *taxia* pulled up outside and waited. The snipers rose from their seats and walked out casually, making sure not to hurry or look around. Kyle still felt as if they were obvious. He knew it was just nerves, and he'd dealt with them before, so he stuck it out, waiting for the feeling to pass.

The driver looked at a paper he carried and said, "Mon-ro?"

"Da," Kyle agreed. "Monroe."

They loaded luggage and climbed in. This vehicle, a VW van, had rates painted on the sides, a meter, and radio. The driver set the meter and off they went.

A fifteen-minute drive took them out of downtown, past a business district of older shops, into a residential area with small businesses to a *panzione*—a house with rented rooms. The driver pulled up in front and stopped, then helped them with their bags. He smiled and tipped his hat, accepted money from Kyle, then jumped in and sped off.

An elderly lady waited at the door. She was dark haired, slightly rounded, and short.

"Is this the place?" Kyle asked.

"Address matches, and she looks as if she expects us."

"Okay," Kyle sighed. At least she didn't look equipped to be a mugger.

At the door, she waved them into a cozy parlor and closed the door behind them. Two men were sitting waiting, both Westerners. Kyle and Wade both stiffened just slightly, in anticipation rather than because of a threat.

The closer man stood and approached. "Kyle and Wade? I'm Mick," he said.

Mick Cafferty was medium height, about fifty, slightly balding and barrel chested under his nondescript suit. Age was obviously catching up to him, but he wasn't giving in without a fight. They looked him over as he gave them a quick glance, then they shook hands all around. "And this is Sam," he said. Sam was barely shorter, pale and freckled and with reddish hair. He was dressed in common local clothes and his smile revealed slightly crooked teeth.

"Gentlemen." He nodded, then rose to shake hands. He sat back down again.

"You hear the news this morning?" Cafferty asked, giving them a deep gaze.

"No, what?" Kyle asked. Mission change?

"Bombs," Cafferty said. "Nine hundred pounds of TNT on a train in southern France, and four huge car bombs totaling another thousand in Bosnia. That's the stuff that's coming through here."

"Jesus," Kyle said. Wade was silent.

"Yeah, you got here just in time. Looks like close to twelve hundred dead or injured in a couple of hours. Statistically not that important, unless you're one of the statistics. But it's a tremendous issue politically and socially."

"I thought the French and Spanish were safe from attack, since they stayed out of the new round in Iraq?" Wade asked. The sarcasm was obvious.

"Yeah, that's what bin Laden is alleged to have said. Now we see what happens when you give a terrorist what he wants."

"More terror," Kyle said.

"Right. So we need something concrete fast—a kill, a bust of explosives, positive intel to avert something with lots of camera time. The good news is you've got more budget if you need it."

"Thanks," Kyle said. "Though I'm not sure what we need, besides a target and a place to shoot." Dammit, he wasn't a spy. He was a soldier. He watched the battlefield, broke things, and killed people. Tracking down political intel was for computer geeks or skulky sleuths.

"Well, let me know. I'm trying to get more of a free hand from State if I can," said Cafferty. "This working across agencies is a pain in the ass. Everyone has a form to stamp." He grabbed a mug of coffee, took a gulp. "I don't want to be seen too much, so you'll be talking to me by phone and dealing with Sam in the field when needed," he said as he put his cup down. "Let's show you around."

The house was owned and run by the CIA. It was small but modern enough, and they had a lockable room. The bathroom was shared, meals provided, and there was a phone line. "Dial-up modem only, to stay discreet. Make sure you use the local phone a few times to order *taxia* or food or whatever. Use the encrypted cells to talk to me."

"Understood," they both agreed. Kyle tapped the deep pocket where his phone was. It was a habit he had.

"You can stay here and at the hotel. Keep your special gear here," Cafferty said, which they understood to mean the weapons. He grabbed another mug of coffee from the kitchen as he led them through. The lady, the housekeeper, smiled at him and refilled the pot. He waved behind him as they walked back through the front, down the short hallway, and into the bedroom they'd use. "Only the government suspects this place that we know of, and they think it's strictly a waypoint for SEALs and such heading south and east. They shouldn't take much interest in you for a few days. Even after that, any investigation will take time."

"They'll make us eventually?" Wade asked, sitting on the bed. Kyle dropped down next to him. The mattress was a lot softer than he expected. Or maybe it hadn't been designed for two heavy soldiers to use as a chair.

"They make everyone eventually," Cafferty said. "As long as you get some shots or we have intel to share with the Romanians at the end, it'll be fine."

"That assumes we get either. For that we need you to get us in place," Kyle said, barely frowning. "We're just shooters. The spy bit is not something we know."

"No problem. We'll have you something soon. We're just waiting for one of our observers to find one of them again. It's never longer than a week, and it's been three days since the last sighting."

"Good, then."

"So how was your trip in?" he asked.

"Ah . . . exciting," Kyle said.

"Exciting, how so?"

Kyle and Wade looked at each other, then gave him a complete brief with observations and the plate number. "It didn't seem targeted at us specifically," Kyle said to Cafferty's wrinkled brow. "Are we wrong?"

"No, it was random," he reassured them. "They were fishing. Hotel is what tourists expect, and the Marriott is a common choice. But that's a bad sign, and I'll hint about it after you leave. The driver lucked out. Or didn't, this time."

"You seem to mean it's common. I'm surprised," Kyle said.

"Common enough. All part of the background here. You need to call the *taxia* service and ask for 'command,' which puts them on government notice and makes them honest. You got the low end. The middle end speak English until you're inside, then they don't speak it until you're twenty miles away. Twenty-five euros or a million lei and two hours later, you're where you wanted to be in the first place."

"Charming." Still, Kyle thought, it was better than Central Asia, where they shot at you or sold you out to another tribe or used you to settle local scores under the guise of fighting a war.

"It's been like this since the Wall came down?" Wade asked.

"Pretty much. Gypsies," Cafferty said. "Lots of them homeless and without family, from Ceauşescu's reign."

"How?" Wade asked.

"You read about all the orphans left from his forced breeding program?" The two snipers nodded. "Well, they grew up. Almost none have social skills, most aren't very bright—they never got any input as infants. Some can't talk. Most are illiterate. Almost all are unemployable. They sleep in the sewers, steal and rob to eat, and snort paint to pass out so they don't feel the cold and hunger. A worse nightmare than any stupid Dracula movie."

"Damn," Kyle said. "What can we do for them?"

"Nothing," Cafferty said, grimacing and sipping at his coffee. "There's not enough millions anywhere to deal with it. Some were adopted, the rest are abandoned, and there's still another few years' worth in orphanages who are kicked out as they turn eighteen."

"Shit."

"Yeah, and something we can't help with. Close your eyes, grit your teeth, do your job, and pray for them. That's all there is."

"Roger that," the snipers agreed together. It was the standard response to a situation one had to deal with, no matter how disgusting it was.

"As for you gentlemen, the *taxia* isn't the only thing to watch out for."

"Crime's bad?" Wade asked.

"Yes and no. Lots of scams you need to watch out for. Don't trust the hotel housekeepers—use a safe or keep your stuff with you. If you leave before cleaning time, leave the Do Not Disturb sign. Locked cases are probably safe, but any cash left out or in clothes or open luggage might wind up as a tip. Assume all teenagers and large kids are pickpockets, and keep cash split among pockets, ID up front and high. Don't eat anything unless prices and an actual menu of food are posted. Same for services—always assume they're screwing you and offer them one quarter what they ask. Settle for one half. Don't drink. The drinks are watered, overpriced, bad liquor that can give you a hell of a hangover, and they'll bring them until you say to stop. As soon as it hits the table, bang! you're charged for it.

"Watch out for fake cops. Real cops wear suits and carry badges. So do frauds. They'll whip out a badge, demand to inspect your currency to ensure you complied with the exchange law, then peel off a couple of big bills for themselves. So will the real cops sometimes."

"Goddam," Kyle muttered.

"Oh, it's worse than that," Cafferty said. "Drunk driving can be settled on the spot for a million lei. That's twenty-five bucks. If you've had a drink, you're drunk. Either pay up or go to jail. You don't want to go to jail."

"How bad are the jails?" Wade asked.

"You'll need SERE training to survive them," Cafferty said, not smiling. Survival Evasion Resistance Escape was not a fun course. It involved bugs, snakes, and being tortured by the "enemy."

"What?" Kyle burst out, surprised.

"We take MREs to the poor American bastards who get nailed over here, so they'll at least survive the ordeal. And God help a woman in jail. Not as bad as Turkey. But not good." He scowled deeply. "We've got one now State is trying to beg out. Her family is trying to come up with a bribe. I rather hope it's not taken, because she'll need that money for therapy afterwards."

"Fuck me," Kyle said.

"As bad as that," Cafferty confirmed. "Most people here *are* honest. But assume otherwise, because there isn't 'always one in every crowd' here. There's always a dozen. And you better be *very* discreet with your firearms."

"That's the plan," Wade said. "We shoot when and only when we have a target. Otherwise, cased."

"Good," Cafferty nodded. "The police will bust you in a second, and even diplomatic means here might not get you out. Might take DoD and State to do it."

Or a platoon of Rangers, blown off-course in a parachute drop, Kyle thought. But that would *really* create an incident. Even with Robash's assurance, Kyle's blood was running cold. The worst he'd faced in life was being shot and killed. He was starting to realize there were worse things, and that even with his combat experience, he was very naïve and vulnerable to cultural issues.

Coming back to the core of the mission, Kyle asked, "So you don't think they're going to be hard to find?"

"Actually, no. We have good intel. The problem is the local government leaks. We can fix them to a couple of regular places, but once away from the coast and the capital, no dice. We need to get on them and stay on them. That's why you're here."

"How do you mean?"

"Anything my people do is known. We need people who can shoot, aren't known, and don't drag a lot of paperwork with them. That's you. We don't want the Romanians knowing, we don't want them wondering why I'm breaking my routine tasks, and we don't want to try getting too close. Shootings happen. Up-close brawls with foreign officials don't."

"I'd hoped to have all this before we arrived," Kyle hinted.

"So did we," Cafferty nodded. "But as I said, we're still building the database. That's the key here—we're trying to get them before they do anything."

"Are you sure these are the right guys, then?" Wade asked. "I'd hate to wait for a bomb to go off, but we do want to nail the right people."

"Oh, it's them," Cafferty nodded. "They were involved in Chechnya, and some attacks in Georgia. That was more the Russians' problem, and they gave us some intel that is solidly corroborated. But it got too hot there, so they moved to the Middle East. With the current screwup there, they're moving this way. Have moved this way now. Gutless freaks won't ever stand and fight."

"That sounds like the right people, then," Wade said.

"Yeah, fits the pattern, doesn't it? Anyway, here's the dossiers so far," Cafferty said as he handed over five folders. Wade opened them, Kyle read over his shoulder, and Cafferty narrated.

"They'll have probably twelve to twenty lower people with them, to do hauling, security, and buying supplies so they aren't seen. If you get a chance to bag them, they're gravy, but don't hit a pawn and miss the bishops and kings. Underlings are only a symptom."

"Right," Kyle agreed. Though killing enough underlings would still cramp operations, there were enough suicidal idiots that it was only a temporary fix.

"So, from the bottom is Vahtang Logadze. He's Georgian. Not directly al Qaeda but a fellow traveler. He blends in locally, and we suspect he's their expert on shipping, which local officials to bribe, et cetera.

"Enis Altan is Turkish. He's facing death if he goes back there. He was 'helping' the Kurds, but somehow they kept getting ambushed. We figure he was helping Iraqi intelligence. On the other hand, the Kurds aren't popular in Turkey. He may have been working for a private group. But both the Kurdish movement and the Turkish government want him dead. If you kill him, we get some good bargaining points.

"Number Three, Anton Florescu is Romanian. He's helping get the stuff out of here into the rest of Europe, likely through the woods and north into Hungary or Slovakia. He's also seen a lot in the Carpathian Mountains and near Sighişoara. We're looking for a base there, but haven't pinned it down yet. But it's there, we're sure. So he's only a target of opportunity, and hold off if you think he might lead us to more. Like whoever orchestrated Bosnia and France." The snipers looked up from the binders and nodded.

"Number Two. Behrouz Jalali is Iranian, and a very bad boy. He's definitely part of al Qaeda, orchestrated several attacks on British troops in Nasiriya, and has now moved up here, figuring he just might get a lungful of cannon fire from a chopper there, but can kill babies at random in Europe, where no one is armed. He's come in twice, but we don't know where he is now. Shipped back out, gone to ground, hiding in Europe, who knows? Keep an eye out, and we'll snatch him if there's a chance. If not, just kill him on sight. There's nothing we want from him bad enough to risk letting him get away.

"And that just leaves our prime target, who you've heard of if you're following the news."

"Dammar al Asfan," Kyle said.

"Synagogues, Shia mosques, buses . . ." Wade recited.

"And a standing reward of fifty thousand dollars to the family of anyone who kills Americans or Israelis," Cafferty said. "Again, we'd like him alive, but if there's any doubt at all, shoot him. Shoot him twice. Run over him. Drag him down a gravel road. Stake him through the heart. Whatever it takes. You can even walk up to him in front of the police station in Bucharest and shoot him dead on the steps and we'll cover for you. The headlines alone would get you out. But discreet is better."

"Roger that," they replied.

"We don't expect you'll get all five," Cafferty said, answering the question before they asked it. "Just get one. If you find one, there might be another nearby. Get him, too, and then as many minions as you can."

"Terrorist Poker," Wade joked.

"Pair, three of a kind, four of a kind, full house?" Kyle smiled back. He turned to Cafferty and said, "We'll see what we can do. We'd rather find them in the woods, or some quiet little burg where we can disappear in a hurry. An urban kill that's not in a dedicated war zone . . . you really need a police sniper for that."

"I know," Cafferty said with a twist of his lips. "But we don't have one. So it's up to you to make the call. Don't create an incident if you don't think it's worth it. Except for al Asfan."

"What about military support?" Kyle asked. "Near the sea we've got Air Force and Navy, you say, and a possible exercise to cover for us. What about inland? Is there someone with a chopper or a truck who can come get us?"

"Truck. Sam. Me, if it comes down to it," was the reply. "Anything more than that is going to get us seen. And we can't trust the government at any level—city, county, or national. Too many leaks, too many moneygrubbers. They're worse than dedicated idealists, because they don't stay bought."

"Right," Kyle nodded. Behind him, Wade started singing, "It sucks to be meeeeee." Kyle ignored him. Wade sometimes went too far when he was stressed. He understood it, he just wasn't going to feed it.

"There's no way to get the Romanians involved?" He really preferred the idea of local backup.

"To do what? Unless one of them commits a provable crime here, any kind of local activity only serves as a warning to the bad guys that we know they're up to something. And to be honest, the Romanians wouldn't be able to round them all up. The local police are used to petty crooks and thugs, not international rings with cutouts and multiple IDs. Their military arm might manage it, and I'm still trying to get a hint through to the right people, but it has to be the right people or all I have is more leaks."

"I just wanted to check."

"Yeah, your ass is in the sling. I understand," Cafferty shrugged. He took another drink of coffee. He'd gone through three cups already. He wouldn't have a stomach left at this rate.

"Do you have our luggage?" Kyle asked.

"Oh, yes," Cafferty nodded vigorously and smiled. "It was still sealed. And nobody said I shouldn't look, so I hope you don't mind that I peeked but didn't touch. You gentlemen have unique tastes."

"Just what we need to get the job done," Kyle said.

"Wait here, I'll get the bags," Cafferty said and turned.

Before he left, the two snipers were conferring.

"Definitely the twenty-two in urban settings," Wade said.

"Yes, and pistols. If we get close, we might set one with a rifle to cover, and one with a pistol as bait or beater, and do it that way."

"We might," Wade agreed with what was almost a frown. "Though that's not something we've trained in. I don't worry about one of us shooting the other. I do worry about getting in the way and spoiling a shot, or taking a piece of it, or being ID'd."

"True," Kyle nodded. "We were hired to do it from a distance."

Cafferty came back with Sam, dropped three cases on the bed, then went for another load of bags. "All sealed when it arrived," he said. "It was transported in a lead-lined box, which we do all the time. No one has questioned us, and things are usually undisturbed. So we're copasetic unless you get seen."

"The weapons are safe here?" Kyle asked to confirm. Wade reached for the AK104 and started checking it over.

"Yes. The lady, Mrs. Cneajna"—whose name Kyle knew he'd never be able to pronounce—"works for us. This door locks. No one else comes in here. If the weapons are seized, there's nothing to tie them directly to you. Which doesn't mean someone won't try to rope you in."

"Right."

"It's up to you if you keep them with you at the hotel, keep them here and have to drive over and get them, or carry them on your persons. Try to avoid the latter, but I don't want to tell you how to do your jobs."

"Thanks," Kyle said. He wasn't sure if *he* knew how to do this job. "Are we going to have a car at our disposal? We can't carry these things on the subway or buses."

"Right. Get a rental car tomorrow. Go for something a couple of years old, not flashy, and that can take a bit of abuse. An Audi four wheel drive, maybe. SUVs are too obvious, and most of them are useless in this terrain." Most SUVs were built for looks only, as everyone who drove real military vehicles had figured out years ago.

"That means we'll have to actually use it a bit."

"Yes. I can recommend some restaurants that are worthwhile, there's the museum, and anything locked in the trunk should generally be safe. We've got to get you up into the mountains soon, though, because that's your cover, and that's where we expect some of the action. Small villages. You can shoot there?"

"We can shoot anywhere," Kyle said. "Open terrain is easier, woods make for better concealment, and in any urban setting witnesses and hard cover are problems. But with that," he pointed at the Ruger, "the AK and pistols, we can nail targets from five meters to four hundred."

"Good," Cafferty said. He sounded confident and reassured. "I'll get you the targets and try to get you in range, and run interference over anyone who might see you. Meantime, you can go. There's nothing to do but wait."

"Great," Kyle said. He hated hurry-up-and-wait.

"It shouldn't be so bad," Cafferty smiled. "You can be real tourists on tax dollars for a couple of days. You'll earn it."

In theory, they could play tourist. They had cell phones and could be reached anywhere. But they needed the weapons close at hand, didn't want to confuse a pursuit by having to get unlost from where they were before getting lost following anyone, and they were antsy about more of the local color. It hadn't taken much to convince the two snipers to stay at the hotel, no matter how boring.

The kicker had been lunch. They'd called the same *taxia* they'd used earlier. The driver was an elderly man who gave them a quick tour on the way to the car rental, which was a familiar Western chain.

In short order, they had a recent Audi Quattro in a tan color that was nondescript and, once dusty over its shine, would be invisible in almost any terrain. It hadn't taken much asking for the tan. Apparently, most customers wanted a brighter color.

The car was right-hand drive, and driving was on the left, so it was a mirror image of what they were used to. But the pedal layout was the same as they were used to. "You want to drive?" Kyle asked.

"Sure, I'll give it a whack. It's not far, anyway."

They were only about five miles from the hotel and they could see its silhouette from several blocks away. Just down the street from the Marriott was a Mexican restaurant. It was a little hole in the wall, looked clean, and had a bright awning in green.

"Worth a try?" Wade asked. It wasn't one Cafferty had mentioned.

"Why not?"

The restaurant had prices posted, they nodded agreement that it was honest and took seats outside, it being a modestly warm noontime. The menu was clear enough, and they ordered quesadillas and tacos. Ten minutes later, plates were set in front of them. Wade nodded and said, "Mulțumesc," and dug in.

His face told all. "Paprika?" he said, confused and shocked. "And something like sage? In *Mexican* food?"

Kyle agreed with his assessment. The stuff was greasy, over-cooked, weirdly seasoned, and of low-quality ingredients to start with. They forced it down and headed back for the hotel.

"Christ, that's worse than stringy goat and beans in Pakistan," Wade muttered on the way.

"Disgusting," Kyle agreed. "Let's stick to American staples or real local food, not their attempts to internationalize."

"Yeah. We got anything in the room to get the taste out with?"

"*I* have cookies and chips," Kyle said. "I can share, this once."

"You're my hero."

After expensive sodas from the hotel and some cookies, they felt better. "Damn, it burns me to pay that much for a drink," Kyle said.

"Uncle Sam is paying for it," Wade reminded him.

"Damn, it burns me to help people screw over my dishonest uncle, who nevertheless gives me a job and a roof and a chance to risk my ass over stupid things."

"Yeah, well. When in Romania . . ."

They tried to watch TV, took turns surfing the Web for games, news, trivia, maps, and anything of interest. It was a long, slow day, and they left early for dinner at the nearest restaurant Cafferty had recommended. It was walking distance.

"Local food, which hopefully they can manage to cook properly," Kyle said. He was still feeling a bit odd from lunch.

"You know, I see the international appeal of McDogfood's now."

"Yeah. You know exactly how bad it will be, and it's cheap."

They arrived at the restaurant and were shown in. They were seated shortly, in a smoky corner. Eastern European cigarettes, pipes, and cigars all clashed. There was a stale acridity to the green plastic curtains near them. The floor was linoleum and the tables were plastic and worn chrome. "Points for atmosphere," Kyle said.

"Hey, the food smells good," Wade replied.

It did. Aromas of real meat and potatoes, vegetables and fire combined to flush the queasiness from Kyle's stomach and make him hungry again.

The waitress was young, lacked curves and had the classic cheekbones and deep eyes of Slavic ancestry. Her English was very broken and accented, but the menu had some English and Kyle recalled his Spanish. She had a cute smile which she flashed when she understood him.

"*Salata de Creier*. Brains salad?" Wade read from the menu. He looked more than a bit bothered.

"No, thanks," Kyle replied. "Is that a vampire thing?"

"Veal brains," Wade said. "I'm not sure they've heard of Mad Cow. And it doesn't sound appetizing, anyway."

"Yeah, what else is there?"

"*Salata Primavara*. Lettuce, radishes, carrots, potatoes, green onions, sour cream."

"Okay. Anything weird in it?"

"A bit of sugar."

"I think I can deal with that," Kyle agreed. "And here's an entrée: *Biftec Rusesc*. That's Russian beefsteak. Sirloin with onions. That sounds good. Sprite or whatever to drink instead of alcohol, and *Prajitura cu Zmeura*, cake with raspberries."

"Just no brains."

"No. We should just not ask, let them serve us, and enjoy it." It was common advice for soldiers going to exotic locales.

"I'm not that brave anymore," Wade admitted.

The food started arriving at once, and they ate quickly, trying to enjoy the food for its cultural differences.

"Not bad," Kyle said. "Steak's a bit tough, but not bad."

"Needs more seasoning," Wade replied. "And the portions are a bit small."

"I think we're just pigs who eat too much."

"That could be it."

The crowd was building as evening grew later, and it was boisterous and cheerful. Drinking and talking, talking and drinking. Entire families were out together. It seemed weird. There were what appeared to be couples on dates, dragging parents and younger siblings.

"They seem happy at the decline of communism," Kyle said.

"Yup. No matter how bad things are now, they were worse fifteen years ago."

"That's depressing." Kyle had known that intellectually, but to actually see it was shocking.

They polished off dessert, paid, and left a tip, which neither of them was sure was considered appropriate. But they wanted to be remembered as dumb but friendly tourists if anything. The waitress smiled gleefully and waved as they departed.

It was a cool spring evening. It had drizzled while they ate, but then cleared slightly. They tucked their collars up as they headed for the car.

Wade turned his head slightly and asked, "So what do we think?"

"I think it's riskier than last time politically," Kyle said slowly, "and safer as far as military threats go. For some reason, that doesn't reassure me." Kyle didn't like military threats, but he understood military threats. This was new territory. They reached the car and he waited while Wade unlocked it.

"Yeah. Watch it," Wade said in warning, nodding very slightly. "I'm sure Robash is on our side. I'm equally sure other people would just throw us to the wolves and claim it wasn't their problem."

"Yeah, that's what I'm thinking. And we keep volunteering. I ask myself why."

"Why did we volunteer to get our asses kicked, frozen, drowned, abraded, and burned in Ranger School?"

"Same reason," Kyle admitted. "Because we can, and others can't, and the job needs doing."

"Yup." Wade started the engine and screeched into traffic. He'd picked up the local style quickly. Or maybe that was just how he drove.

"I dunno. I think if I'm second-guessing myself it means I'm getting too old."

"Well, you can retire at thirty-eight."

"You know, that seems old now. But I know it won't then." Kyle mused.

Back at the hotel, they took turns playing computer games and reading intel. There was a great time waster that involved computer representations of little plastic toy soldiers, complete with breaking them in pieces and melting them in puddles from the effects of weapons. The only problem was, every stage had an "objective." That was too much like work. Kyle just wanted to kill things for a while, mindlessly. The usual backpack-of-weapons-and-hundreds-of-mindless-ghouls-to-kill game was less fun without a network of participants, and was too simplistic. After two hours, Kyle figured out he wasn't going to enjoy anything.

"Look, I've got to take a walk or I'm going to go nuts. This is a Western hotel, it's like being down the street but with no TV. Once around the block should be safe. I can even hang out with the bellmen. But I need some more outdoor time."

"Let's both go," Wade said. "We'll keep it short." He grabbed a camera just to maintain appearances. Coats, knives only, though Kyle really wanted to carry his pistol, considering the trouble so far, and they took the elevator down. They were staying among crowds, and didn't want an incident, but Kyle still felt naked.

Downtown Bucharest was alive in a gritty, trashy way. There were surface trams and a subway, *taxia* vying for parking spaces and passengers, and lots of people. The people were dressed in every style from working-class pants and shirts with sturdy shoes to Euro-chic leather coats with Italian-made shoes and silk shirts. A few stood out even in that spectrum as unkempt bums.

"Like parts of Bosnia, only classier," Kyle said.

"They had less problems here. Which is still pretty frightening, when you think about it," Wade replied as they walked around the Central Market Square. "There's 'The Harp,'" he said. "Irish pub, owned by a real Irishman. Good place for food and intel, he said," referring to Cafferty.

"Right, we'll note it," Kyle agreed. "Food should be of at least British standards."

"Is that a good thing?" Wade asked.

"Compared to here? I . . . don't know. I'd say yes," Kyle said. He was joking, and tried very hard to keep a blasé expression.

"Smartass." Then they both chuckled and kept walking.

As they turned a corner, there were the signs of nightlife. Two or three late restaurants and a club or two lit the street. "I think we should avoid those," Kyle said.

"Yeah. If we get mugged in a taxi, I'd hate to see a bar brawl."

They let their eyes wander briefly. It didn't do to look like tourists, but they were obvious foreigners. They'd have to convey confidence, to hint that they weren't the kind to be messed with. If that failed, words or hands would have to get them out of trouble. Pistols were a last resort.

Kyle turned back around and almost bumped into a girl. She was almost as tall as his chin and was skinny. She also had worn jeans and an oversized shirt and lanky, unwashed hair. She was caressing his chest through his shirt and saying what could only be an offer of temporary romance for a few euros.

He wondered how she'd react to a counter offer of a shower, dinner, and a place to sleep? Or maybe that was part of the deal. He wasn't familiar with that aspect of the local customs and didn't want to be. But he knew what she was offering at her end, and said, "Nu," forcefully enough to make it clear he wasn't negotiating, hopefully not strongly enough to scare her.

She simply gave him a look of disgust and turned on her heel. She pulled up short to Wade's hand on her wrist. He twisted it and Kyle's ID folder appeared.

Kyle said, "*Buen intento, pequeñita.*" *Nice try, little girl.*

He saw what looked like a cop, decided he didn't need any kind of scene, and let her go.

She spat on his jacket and ran.

"Charming girl," Wade murmured.

"Yeah. I've had enough fresh air. Let's go be bored."

"Suits me."

A few minutes later, they crashed gratefully onto boring, hotel-standard beds. "You know, boredom means no excitement. No excitement means no danger. No danger means no compromise of the mission before we get a chance to screw it up the Army way. I think I can live with that," Kyle said. He breathed hard and sighed.

"I think I agree. We must be getting old. Or wise."

"Let's say it's wisdom," Kyle suggested.

"Wisdom it is."

6

DAMMAR AL ASFAN WAS TENSE. HE KNEW THERE was no reason for it. His cover was solid and he never handled shipments himself. Nevertheless, a ton of explosives was a sizeable amount, and there was a risk of discovery. Not everyone at the port was dishonest, not even most. All it would take would be for his pet inspector to be sick. He should call ahead if that happened, of course, but the type of men who needed and took bribes were the type of men one didn't want to depend on.

Still, there were several cutouts, and things should go well enough. The nervousness was predictable and familiar, so he concentrated on the task at hand and tried to avoid the worry.

He studied his list on the screen again. From here, the TNT had to be split for various destinations. There were the soldiers in Germany, fighting the American pollution. There was the new target of France, now that those filth had prohibited the proper wear of scarves among faithful women. The Balkans always needed some against NATO's intervention against the efforts to secure Muslim territory there. Then there was a need to ship some to Egypt for the African missions, and a sizeable amount for their brave Palestinian brothers, fighting the Zionist entity.

If it were up to him, some would also be sent to America to fight the Satan on its own soil. But he'd been ordered not to. The Americans were like a nest of hornets, angry when disturbed. That was true. But like hornets, they were a menace that had to be done away with, and one didn't deal with hornets by being nice. One dealt with them with fire and accepted a few stings. All the better to slaughter Americans now and bring on the jihad they so obviously craved. Let them attack the faithful. Every day they lost more soldiers in Iraq.

If every Muslim nation was thus attacked, the Americans would be too weak to defend any of the whole, and would have to accept peace on terms imposed by those Righteous in God.

But for now, those were not his orders. The Zionist pigs had to be punished, Europe had to be reminded that angry Muslims, denied their place under God's Will, were more important than the filthy money of American corporate and tourist whores.

After blood had washed the corruption from Europe, then the end war could begin. And al Asfan was patient and obedient, even as he looked forward to that day.

Kyle and Wade were still bored the next morning, and getting fidgety. After breakfast, they headed back to the room.

"You know, this whole vampire thing confuses me," Wade said.

"Oh? What specifically?" Kyle found it all confusing and amusing.

"A wooden stake kills vampires," Wade started.

"Yes."

"So what about other wooden items? I mean, wood-pulp paper can cause paper cuts . . . could you torture a vampire with a death of a thousand paper cuts?"

"Ah . . . I don't know," Kyle replied. Wade was really weird at times. Maybe it was the boredom.

"And then I got to thinking . . ." Wade said as Kyle muttered, "Uh-oh." "Diamonds and coal are fossilized trees. So if a woman smacks a vampire with her engagement ring . . ."

"I don't think myths are supposed to be logically followed through," Kyle said.

"Obviously. Those wooden bullets got me wondering . . . There's graphite lube we could use on our bullets. Would that work?"

"Can't hurt. Though we could use blanks and pencils."

"And then there's maple syrup."

"What?" Kyle asked.

"It's refined from tree sap."

"Ah." That was true. Was there a point? "Would it have to be injected? Or would just eating it be harmful? They don't have sugar maples here, so I doubt it ever came up."

"Right. We should try an experiment. On a U.S. Government grant, of course."

"Uh, Wade," Kyle interrupted. It had just hit him, and it was so totally ridiculous he couldn't avoid sharing.

"What?"

"*Latex* is also a tree sap."

For a moment there was silence, then both men roared with laughter.

"So assuming it's a *female* vampire . . ."

"Always wear your condoms. The life you save may be your own . . ."

"This is gonna hurt you a lot more than it hurts me . . ."

They laughed hysterically.

"Snipers shoot holes in myth. Film at eleven," Wade said.

The time they spent wasn't totally boring. They reviewed maps of downtown, the city as a whole, the region and of the nation and its routes elsewhere. Romania was poor, largely cluttered and chaotic, and had a large city and plenty of wilderness. Once in Romania, travel to the rest of Europe was easy and relatively paperwork free. It was ideal for what the terrorists wanted.

"If we're shooting in town, I recommend being inside somewhere," Wade said. "The field of fire is better from a rooftop, but there are helicopters. Sticky tar, rain, sun, and visibility are problems that seem to counteract any advantage we get."

"Yeah. If we can find old warehouses, of which there seem to be some. Or vacant apartments we can get access to," Kyle mused. "I'll call Cafferty."

Cafferty assured them there were buildings they could use. "I'll email you some addresses, you'll have to look them up on the local maps and place them. Got a printer?"

"No, but we have time to sketch. What about apartments?"

"Enough, vacant even, but that's another problem. You'll have to break in, and quietly enough no one comes looking. Then there's the homeless and orphans using some . . ."

"I get the picture," Kyle said. It sucked. They'd have to sneak everywhere. "We'll do what we can. But we're really better in the field."

"I'm trying to work on that," Cafferty agreed. "But you're likely to see Logadze within a few blocks of that area I marked, if you see him at all. Bye." The signal dropped.

Kyle clicked off and said to Wade, "Man, he hangs up in a hurry."

"Likely a CIA thing. Afraid of being traced from back when regular phones were used? Or maybe he's got some other missions going."

"That's possible. We may not be the stars of the show, just the stagehands."

After a moment, Wade said, "I want to get some video of the area. It helps our cover story, gets us familiar with things, and we can review it for good positions."

"In turns, or together?"

"That's a good question," Wade pondered. "What do you think?"

Kyle thought for a moment. "I'd say in turns right now. I'll stay here with the car, and can call you if I need to pick you up. You show me what you saw, and I'll go out later to confirm."

"Okay. Just hand me my trench coat and fedora . . ." It was only a half joke. Overcoats were common and practical when rain moved in. He grabbed the camera and gear and turned back to Kyle. "How do I look?"

"Like a geek with a camera," Kyle said.

"Perfect." He used the room phone to call and arrange for Cafferty's *taxia* to pick him up, drop him in the area in question and circle waiting for him. "Got my phone, I'll stick to main streets so I don't get mugged. I'll see you at dinnertime." He slipped out the door, camera on shoulder.

Kyle spent the afternoon downloading emailed maps and marking likely locations. It would be better to be together so they could cover and relieve each other, but that would depend on circumstances. They might need to split, with one observing and one shooting from different blinds.

To that end, they needed a radio code that anyone who happened on the same frequency wouldn't find suspicious. So he made a list of useful signals, then found easy and unsuspicious German words to use. He chose German because their accents would be less definable in it, as opposed to obviously American-accented Romanian spoken in short, innocuous phrases. Also, German was a bit less known here.

Kyle didn't realize how thoroughly he was engaged until a rattle at the door presaged Wade's return. He glanced at the clock to find four hours had passed. It had felt so good to be doing serious mission work.

"Whatcha get?" he asked.

"Lots of video, some still, and a wallet."

"A wallet?" Kyle asked, confused.

"A wallet. Some punk tried to lift mine and snatch the camera. That was his mistake. I didn't let go. Then I shoved him into the wall and demanded he turn everything over to me. That included someone else's wallet. So I asked the front desk to ensure it got returned, even though it's empty of cash. I figure the pictures, ID, and the wallet itself may have sentimental value."

"We are just magnets for scumbags," Kyle said, shaking his head. "Okay, you show me pictures, I'll show you the code I came up with."

"Okay."

Wade had useful shots down streets, showing the route he'd taken. Panned shots covered the crowds to give an idea of traffic and entrances to alleys and accesses. He'd also videotaped the fronts of several buildings to give an idea of their suitability, and taken images from corners nearby so as to help calculate fields of fire down to the street.

"Very nice," Kyle said. If anything, there was too much information here. "We'll cover this tomorrow when we're rested. It's amazing how tiring doing nothing is."

Wade snickered. "Sorry, you're right, it just sounds funny."

There were more emails waiting in the morning, from Cafferty and another user who referenced him. There were leads to several ships and two sightings. The note from Cafferty said, "Just to keep you updated. We'll get you something soon. Stand by."

"Soon" was not that day, however. They ate at The Harp and decided it was decent—meat pies and thick-cut fries. They forced themselves to watch local news so as to work on the language. It was easier to recognize patterns in context—weather, politics, and traffic. They both did a couple of hundred pushups in sets of fifty, just to keep fit and burn off calories. Kyle went out and found a couple of DVDs in US format at an only mildly extortionate price, which they could watch on the computer.

The movie version of *Starship Troopers* sucked, in his opinion. He'd read the book and found it gripping. This was just fluff, and the tactics were ludicrous.

"We didn't have coed showers when I was a recruit," Wade said. "I think we should petition."

"We have leaders who can recognize a threat when they see one. No matter how bad ours are, they're better than this."

"Yeah, but this is a movie."

They fell asleep around 1 A.M., after a hefty dissection of the film. It was the only action available. They'd enjoyed it far too much.

7

KYLE'S CELL PHONE RANG.
He twitched awake and grabbed it. "Monroe."

"We have Logadze," Cafferty said.

"Roger that. Where?" *Yes!*

"He's been seen in Constanta, and is heading here by car. We know where he usually hangs out. We'll want you to wait near there. I'll email to confirm, and here's the info I have . . . " He rattled off an address on the west side of town, named landmarks and suggested two buildings. "The first one is an old Communist-built office from the nineteen fifties, now vacant. It's abandoned and has plenty of windows. The second is an old apartment block, officially vacant and abandoned but likely full of two-legged homeless rats."

"We'll try your first suggestion, then." Kyle looked across the room. "Wade has the map up. I think I see where."

They hurried downstairs separately, Kyle by the stairs, Wade by elevator. They were dressed in casual office-type clothes reinforced with trench coats and civilian work boots, all of which they considered expendable and expected to trash. Wade had the digital cameras, a spotting scope and NVGs plus his pistol. Kyle had the Ruger in its briefcase and his Ed Brown and Colt in the pockets of his trench coat. Both carried small rucksacks of food and water, changes of clothes, PDAs with all the info downloaded, and accessories like eyepatches and gloves.

The car was running and ready by the time Kyle got downstairs, and Wade pulled out immediately.

"People drive like idiots here, anyway," Wade said, "so there's no need to take our time."

"No, just don't wreck." People *did* drive like idiots here. Not as bad as the DC Beltway or Chicago, but close. Nor were the Americans familiar with the social mores that went along with driving here.

Wade ignored him. Four minutes later he said, "There it is. Where do we park?"

"Dunno. Should I get out and you catch up? No, better not risk it. There must be a space along here." He indicated an angled line of cars.

They found a space. American civilians think in terms of parking within a block at most. They were used to walking, and thought in that regard more like Europeans. It was four blocks along before they found a space.

"We want the south side," Wade said as they got out, "so we're overlooking that square."

"Got it. Let's hope it's really vacant." The building was ugly, straight sided, and brick. The roof sagged in spots, and the gutters had pulled loose.

It was also barricaded, with heavy timbers over the doors and windows on the first floor. Some had steel bars. A few were bricked up. "Ain't that lovely?" Wade commented.

"We'll have to break in."

"Around back."

"Right."

A cobbled alley stinking of urine and trash led them past windows. Those, too, were boarded. They turned into a loading area inset into the back edifice, wide enough for two trucks and with loading docks. There were no openings not covered with wood, bars, or steel. "Damn," Kyle said.

"This one's a bit loose," Wade said. "And they're bolted in place. Why don't you shoot out a couple of those bolts?"

Kyle thought for a moment. The window started about five feet off the ground. "As long as I shoot obliquely in case of a ricochet, I don't see why not." It took only a few moments to slip his pistol and the suppressor inside his coat and assemble them. "Watch for brass," he ordered.

"Will do. It's clear." It was dingy and dark in the alcove, and the building behind had crazed and painted windows that looked abandoned, anyway.

The pistol thwapped twice, brass tinkled on the bricks underfoot. Wade bent down and scooped up the empty cases as Kyle stuffed the pistol away.

"That seemed to do it," he said. The bolt heads had been blown cleanly off, and the plywood sheet bent back as he pulled.

Then they were grunting and straining, because the plywood was three quarters of an inch thick and well secured. "Might have been easier," Wade panted, "to have brought a grappling hook and climbed up a couple of floors." He nodded up at the third floor, its windows protected by rusted bars and broken glass.

"Put it on the list," Kyle said through gritted teeth.

Then he twisted and was underneath the wood as Wade swore and pulled to stop him from getting squeezed. He stuck his hands in his pockets and fished out leather gloves, which he yanked on quickly before trying to tackle the broken sill and frame. He sought areas free from glass and heaved himself up, bracing his feet on Wade's knees for support.

He almost dislocated his spine as he bent backward inside. Then his hands touched dusty, filthy floor and he found it easiest to roll backward into a handstand, feeling like Olga Korbut.

As he collapsed in a heap, he decided old Olga had far more grace and control. But what the hell, he was inside.

It was also pitch black. He dug for his Maglight. That let him find a chunk of pipe, leftover from who knows what, which he slid down and out and pried with. His weight opened enough of a gap that Wade was able to easily toss in their rucksacks and clamber up himself.

With both flashlights out, they were able to look around.

"Time for night vision," Kyle said. Wade opened his bag and they both pulled on goggles. With the lights and occasional bright dots through knotholes or cracks, they could see well enough. The floor was concrete, pierced with mounting holes for long-removed machinery, and was very rough. It was littered with boxes, crates, lumber, metal, and assorted cobwebs, dead birds, and junk. "Fun place."

"That gray area over there," Wade pointed. Even though everything was monochromatic green, it was a habit to refer to something halfway between light and dark as "gray." "I think that's stairs with light above."

"Could be," Kyle said. "Let's check it out."

They were stairs. Once up a floor, the light from above was soft and diffused, everything showing as lurking shadows. After that it was easy, except for the mess and loose debris on the stairs. The metal clanged softly and swayed a little, but it seemed to be no more than the vibration one would expect.

"No one's been up here," Kyle said. "Probably too cold and drafty, and no place to get a fire going, so no homeless people."

"Whatever," Wade said. "Vacant is what we want."

They pushed on to the sixth floor, and stopped at the top of the stairs. Neither man had any intention of running across floors that might give way, or showing a silhouette at a window. They were cautious professionals. "Safe up here. But I think the third floor is high enough, gets us closer to the shot and leaves us a shorter escape route."

"Makes sense," Wade agreed. "Back down we go." They slipped quietly back along their steps and down.

"Okay, open windows on all sides," Wade said once they were there. "We're expecting him on the south, but he's coming from the east. Should we each take a side and wait?"

"Makes sense," Wade said. "I'll watch east with the spotting scope. You use the rifle scope. Switch every thirty minutes?"

"Okay," Kyle agreed.

Then it got down to waiting. Kyle found a rickety, splintered table he could reinforce with some old crates. He used his knife to peel off a few large splinters and used them to wedge the legs more tightly in place. That gave him a good platform for watching and shooting. He was back about ten feet from the window, which made him all but invisible but still afforded a good view. Behind him, he could see Wade, tucked back against a pillar, shoulders hunched and seeming willing to wait like a statue.

It wasn't especially cold. It was probably over fifty outside. But the building was effectively open up here, and they weren't moving at all. Chill leaked down the front of Kyle's coat, up his sleeves and in through his boot tips. Part of him noticed and grumbled. The other part kept watch.

There were couples, business people, ragged poor, and indeterminate others. The ages ranged from ten to ancient. With the bipod out and his hand on the grip, Kyle was professionally comfortable. He could—and had on occasion—stay like this for more than a day. He had his ruck open to his left, the food and water in easy reach and easily closed and removed with no evidence left behind. A color picture of Logadze was taped inside the open top to help in recognition.

Nothing happened for two hours. They stayed still and cold, eyes alert for their target, ears straining to catch any sounds from below that would indicate trouble. Lumps and bolt heads on the table were poking Kyle through his clothes, leaving indentations in the skin and to the bone in some places. His headset was irritating his ear.

Wade came over and slid down beside him, and he rolled off the table to take the spotting scope on the east. Standing let him work the kinks out, then it was time to sprawl on the table again.

Besides people, there were buses, trucks and cars, shifting shadows from clouds, and other movements. There were also the crazed and cracked windows. It helped that there was always something to look at. It hindered in that it distracted attention from the street. The eye patch over his left eye let him avoid squinting, and he panned slowly back and forth across the field of view the window offered.

Kyle picked out several missing panes he planned to shoot through when the time came. A silenced weapon did no good if one then broke out glass that would fall and clatter to give away one's position.

It was at 10:43 A.M. when Wade said, "I think I've got him." They were using their headsets to avoid shouting.

"Where?"

"East, one block, approaching on foot, north side of street. Now crossing to south side."

"Good." He wanted to keep the talk to a minimum, and no names would be used on air. He turned his face from the microphone and said, "Pretty good intel. And they can't just arrest this asshole?" Wade was moving closer, window to window, keeping Logadze in view.

"I get the impression they're like Colombian drug lords. Everyone knows about them, but no one wants to fuck with them."

"Yeah. How's progress?"

"Coming into your field of view any time. Navy trench coat, short, scruffy beard, gray slacks, and white shirt."

"I see him. That's our target?" He was suddenly large in Kyle's scope, disappearing momentarily as he shifted across window spars, to reappear again.

"I've got a positive match," Wade said. "That's our man."

"Got it," Kyle said without a movement. "I can't guarantee I'm going to get a shot."

"Okay."

"Because I am *not* shooting where I might hit a civilian, and I'm not shooting where it'll be obvious which direction the bullet came from, and I am not shooting outside of two hundred meters."

"Kyle, I'm on your side. Do what you have to," Wade told him.

"Right. Sorry." He resumed silence. It was easier to work that way, anyway. He could easily see Logadze in his scope. But there was no certainty he would get close enough. It was back to a waiting game.

But Kyle was patient, and trained to be more so. If this shot didn't work out, then perhaps the next one would. He rose carefully and moved to keep an open window pane between him and Logadze, skipping lightly sideways like a dancer, but a dancer poised with a rifle matched to his almost inhumanly accurate skill.

Logadze was obviously waiting for something. Of course, innocent people waited for things, too. Girlfriends, business partners, even to kill time between buses. But this man was waiting for the transfer of a case of explosives to take out more civilians with. Kyle just hoped that information was correct. It wasn't the remorse he'd feel over a bad shot, though that was real enough. It was the satisfaction of putting a cowardly, murderous terrorist asshole into the dirt.

Kyle Monroe really hated terrorists. If they wanted to kill people, he stood ready to receive them. But none of them dared meet men like him, because they knew they'd lose. Their targets were the small, the weak, and the helpless. And those were the people Kyle had sworn to protect.

So beyond the intellectual challenge of the shot, the tactical complexity of an urban environment with witnesses, and the political intrigue and risk, was a cruel but real thrill at the thought of making this scumbucket the guest of honor at a funeral. Or maybe "ghost" of honor, he thought with a tight smile.

He was there, across the circle, and easy to see. That wasn't the only consideration, however. At much beyond one hundred yards, the little .22 rounds would be inadequate. Certainly five or ten solid hits at two hundred yards would cause enough trauma to the heart or lungs to bring him down, but that took time, allowed easier tracking of the shots, and meant he might reach a hospital in time. He might easily catch AIDS from a dirty transfusion, but that would mean years to die. Their schedule called for it to happen somewhat sooner.

So there was nothing to do but wait, and hope. If they didn't catch him here, they could try again somewhere else.

"Watch concealment," Wade said. Kyle took a quick peek, nodded, and stepped back. He was getting too close to the window.

"I'm getting photos," Wade said. "Video and still. We'll have something they can update records with at least."

"Roger that."

Just then Logadze leaned back against the wall and pulled out a cigarette pack. He shook one loose as he fumbled for a match or lighter in his jacket pocket.

Got you, you son of a bitch, Kyle thought. All he needed now was a moment's break in the crowd. Even if the .22 exited the body, it would be so slow as to barely make a mark on the aged and weathered bricks. *One shot only, then duck.* It wouldn't do to have anyone try to trace the shot back. He leaned back, left arm braced against his body to minimize oscillations.

Logadze struck a match and raised it in cupped hands. Just as he reached his face, a break in the crowd left him clear and exposed. Kyle gritted his teeth for just a moment, then let icy calm flow back through him. He was waiting for . . .

Logadze cocked his head slightly as he breathed life into his cigarette.

. . . *that*, Kyle thought, and started to squeeze the trigger.

Then the crowd thickened again. Bodies came en masse from stores and entrances. Swearing, he let off the trigger and eased from his stance. He sagged back on his legs and drew the rifle carefully out of line.

"Son of a bitch!" he said.

"Eleven A.M.," Wade said from around his scope. "I think people are breaking for lunch." His squint was still in place and he was swiveling to keep the target in view. "And he's heading into that store," he said. "I'll wait."

"Do. But I'm betting he goes out the back."

"No bet," Wade said. "Still, we'll watch and see."

"Right," Kyle agreed. Blast. Just one more second! That's all he'd needed. "I *hate* peacetime urban settings," he said. "I've tried them for one day now, and I hate them. I'd rather risk gapping an officer at his desk with a regiment of armor around him than shoot in a crowded city."

"Yeah, I'm not pursuing the idea of being a police sniper after this," Wade said. "There are distinct advantages to heavy artillery as backup."

Kyle was already dialing on his phone. "Mick, no go. He went into a store," he said as soon as it answered.

"Damn. Are you watching?"

"Yes, but there's another exit, and he may have friends inside. Or hell, he may just bull his way through to the bathroom or something."

"Right. Call me when you have something. I'll try to get someone in there to follow up."

"Understood. Out." He punched off at once, the phone letting out a *beep*. It almost sounded like a protest against his rough thumb on the button.

Letting the frustration and anger subside, they resumed their patient watch. Every half hour, they switched off, letting their eyes rest for a few minutes, red and gritty and aching. It was chilly with no heat and no movement.

Lunch was cold MREs and local iron rations of nuts and fruit. The apples were okay, but small, bitter, and tough compared to American ones. Still, it was food, and it broke the monotony.

At 7:00 P.M., dusky and chilly, the Georgian had still not come from the store. It was long since closed and locked, and the foot traffic was dying rapidly.

"That's it, we're done," Wade said.

"Yeah, I concur," Kyle said. "Let's report in. Damn." He dug out the phone again. "Monroe here," he said when Cafferty answered. "No shot. Video and stills."

"It all helps. We know he's here and we'll get another chance. Don't sweat it."

"You weren't able to track him?" Kyle asked. He was a bit miffed that they'd been left here all day.

"No. Can't explain right now. I'll meet you at the panzione tomorrow, unless things change. Oh eight hundred."

"Eight A.M. at the panzione, got it."

Hadi Kadim logged into his favorite chatroom for the evening. Actually, it wasn't his favorite chatroom. He hated it. But if he might glean a few grains, it would be worthwhile. He'd come across it by accident one night, and had been about to leave when he caught a reference to a U.S. embassy. He'd stayed, curious, and found that one of the participants was married to an ambassador. She also liked to talk.

He'd mentioned this to his mullah, who'd asked for anyone with information about the American military to come forward. Embassies weren't exactly military, but he thought it might be useful.

The mullah had thought so. A week later, he had specific instructions on what to look for and listen for, and what to say.

JulianLee has entered the room.
6 people in chat.
BLKKTTY: Julian, good evening.
LEO155: Hi, Jule.

JULIANLEE: Greetings, all. I'll be lurking while I help my son
with his math.
LEO155: No prob. Crunch those numbers. Show no mercy. :-D

There was no son, and Kadim had no intention of lurking in the
chat sense. He watched every conversation that passed, and saved
the frame every evening. There were others who did similar things:
ModevalMac worked second shift and left chat running so he could
read and catch up afterward, then was actually present only on
weekends. But it was best that "JulianLee" not talk too much.
Watching was better. He couldn't see the private messages, but from
the ones he received he concluded there wasn't any substantial content to most of them.

Much went on that was neither interesting nor relevant. But he
cultivated favor by being quiet and friendly. Often, that was all that
was needed.

It was more than an hour before he started making notes. One of
his favorite people came online. Others found her to be an annoying chatterbox. He did, too, in fact, but she often said things of interest. She was the ambassador's wife.

Barbiemouse has entered the room.
FANCYDANCER: Barbie! Hugs.
BLKKTTY: Hi, Barbie.
BARBIEMOUSE: I am soooo frustrated and annoyed!
JAMESGUNN: Oh? What now?
*Private Message from JamesGunn to Blkktty: As if I don't
know already and want details.*
*Private Message from Blkktty to JamesGunn: She really is pre-
dictable. I wonder what we're doing wrong this time?*
BARBIEMOUSE: You wouldn't believe what's happening here
now.
JULIANLEE: Oh?
BARBIEMOUSE: My husband has just been informed that a cer-
tain intelligence agency is providing support to
an 'anti-terror' team here in country.
JAMESGUNN: And that's bad?
LEO155: SWEEEEEEEEEEEET! :-D
BARBIEMOUSE: Leo, you're too young to grasp how important
this is. This country is developing and still try-
ing to grasp capitalism and the modern world.
Treading all over their sovereignty won't let

them reach their potential. It's insulting and condescending to take such a smug, overbearing approach.

Private Message from JamesGunn to Leo155: Barbie, of course, would never be condescending to her poor, disadvantaged hosts who don't understand capitalism.

Private Message from Leo155 to JamesGunn: I'm sure she gives everyone she meets a shiny euro coin to show her respect for them.

BLKKTTY: You seem to be implying a problem beyond the diplomatic issues, Barbie.

Private Message from JamesGunn to Leo155: You'd think an ambassador would marry someone a bit brighter than Barbie. Doesn't thrill me about our State Department.

Private Message from JamesGunn to Blkktty: Oh, please don't get her started.

Private Message from Leo155 to JamesGunn: I'm not sure she is an ambassador's wife.

Private Message from Blkktty to JamesGunn: I'm amused at what we might hear.

Private Message from JamesGunn to Leo155: Oh, she is. Unfortunately. I've heard enough to confirm it.

LEO155: I'm told they're pretty good at capitalism. High prices. Screwing tourists. Cheap hookers. Hell, I might have to book a trip.

BARBIEMOUSE: Leo, that's exactly the attitude that causes problems here.

Private Message from JamesGunn to Leo155: hehehe. Dumbass. ;-)

BARBIEMOUSE: Anyway, there's a pair of Rambo types gallivanting about the countryside trying to take shots at terrorists.

JAMESGUNN: I'm still trying to find the problem with this.

Private Message from Blkktty to JamesGunn: Private Message from Barbiemouse to Blkktty: I'm ignoring Leo and James again.

Private Message from JamesGunn to Blkktty: I am so ashamed. ;-)

BLKKTTY: I don't think the intent is to annoy your hosts, Barb.

BARBIEMOUSE: Oh, I know. They have Good Intentions, of course. It just bothers me to see our hosts' hos-

pitality abused like this. Really, there's no reason it should be hidden from them.

JAMESGUNN: The less who know, the better. I didn't really need
to know. Are you sure you should be talking?

*Private Message from Blkktty to JamesGunn: she's clicked you
and can't see your posts.*

BARBIEMOUSE: They tried a shot downtown today and
couldn't do it. I'm not quite sure who they are,
but they're not impressive.

*Private Message from JamesGunn to Leo155: "Not impres-
sive"? I don't suppose Barb has ever done any shooting? Clandestinely? Against a probably moving target? If they'd taken
the shot, she'd whine about risk to civilians.*

*Private Message from Leo155 to JamesGunn: Hey, didn't you
tell me not to get bent out of shape? *grins**

BARBIEMOUSE: And they're obviously not very good, if they
can't make a 100 yard shot in daylight. Why,
when my first husband was in the 3rd Infantry
Division, there was a sniping competition at
800 yards.

BLKKTTY: It's likely a little different with innocent people
around the target.

BARBIEMOUSE: Yes, I suppose we should all be grateful they
didn't plug anyone on the street. But still, it's
only a matter of time before someone so insecure makes a serious error in judgment and it
all comes tumbling down. From what I gather,
they don't even speak the language. They're
just sort of floating around until told what to
do. Really, there should be a proper chain of
command. It just strikes me as so sloppy and
insulting to send two half-competent people
over when the Romanian SRI has very good
people of its own.

JAMESGUNN: So glad to hear an analysis from an expert in the
field. [sarcasm]

JULIANLEE: Now, James, Barbie is part of the diplomatic mission and is familiar with the area better than we
are.

*Private Message from JamesGunn to Leo155: Do me a favor
and don't mention this. It shouldn't be talked about.*

Private Message from Leo155 to JamesGunn: Not a problem.
Dumb bitch.
JAMESGUNN: I suppose so. Anyway, I have to log out. Later.
JamesGunn has exited the room.
BLKKTTY: Bye, James.
LEO155: Later, James . . . damn, that was quick.
JULIANLEE: I suppose I should bid you good evening, too.
There's chores to be done.
LEO155: Good night, Julian.
JULIANLEE: Good night, all.

Hadi resumed lurking and watching. He found chat rooms to be most unpleasant. It got very awkward when the Americans and the French got onto a kick with sexual innuendos; though rather than being offended as he used to be, Kadim was now largely bored. It seemed they had no depth, no sophistication, and made all their seductions crass and quick. No wonder they were so decadent, shallow, and lacking in respect.

But he was out again, and prayer would cleanse his soul. In that, he did respect two newcomers, Larry and Walt, who were devout Christians. He didn't believe in their savior, but they at least kept quiet when the conversations got perverse, and quietly chided the more obnoxious members. They seemed like halfway decent types, unlike JamesGunn, who was a typical anti-Islamic twit. His oft-repeated phrase of "No Palestinians, no Palestinian problem" had driven Kadim to a frenzied rage that only an hour of prayer had cooled the first time he heard it. Clearly, Allah was tasking him with patience and tolerance for such men.

For Allah's purpose, he could suffer such indignity. Allah had his own plan, and it would show its beauty and perfection when all was done.

For now, he needed to call the mullah and update him. There were shooters from somewhere in Romania under American orders. He wasn't sure of the significance, but he'd been told to report anything unusual from the dozen chats a day he monitored. Exhaling to clear his mind, he reached for the phone.

The next morning, Cafferty was waiting at the panzione. "Hi, guys," he said with a wave. "Let's talk. Problems." He stood at the back door, but inside and under cover. They hurried up the steps and through the canted kitchen door. Sam was present. He smiled and ducked into the front parlor.

Kyle bristled a little. He was afraid the problem was a perception of how they did their job.

"I hope the intel we have is okay," he said to try to probe gently. It was tight in the kitchen, and Ms. Cneajna smiled and offered them cups. He and Wade refused with thanks.

Cafferty took a cup and said, "Any pics we can clean up and use are good. The more we have on this guy, the better we can predict him. And anyone near him may turn out to be a coconspirator. If there's someone in your pics who was in others we have, that's a good lead."

"I got about thirty minutes of vid and twenty-three stills," Wade said as they walked the twenty feet through the house to the bedroom.

"Excellent! Glad to hear it." Cafferty opened the bedroom door and waved at them while sipping his coffee. Everyone sat back down, knees almost touching in the small space between bed and chair. He pulled a laptop and a bag of accessories from his briefcase, which was already by the chair.

"So what's the problem?" Wade asked casually, as they slipped in and closed it.

"Ambassador's wife," Cafferty said with a disgusted look. "She talks too much and to everyone. She's an annoying bitch. And he's too much of a wuss to get rid of her or ignore her. She doesn't run the embassy, but she sure as hell backseat drives a lot. And I *never* want to hear about her polyps again." He shuddered and winced. "At least we know he's honest."

"Oh?" Wade asked first.

"Yeah. It's got to be love, there's not that much money in the world. So he's not taking bribes."

Wade chuckled. "Or if he is, he spends it on a mistress."

Kyle grinned and asked, "And there's nothing we can do about her?"

"Kyle, if I could designate her as a target, I would. But it would be illegal, immoral, and cause more trouble than it solved. But, *God*, I hate that woman." His face was showing lines.

"What can happen? We're not up on State issues," Wade asked.

"As I said, the ambassador can bounce you out of here. He's first and last word. It's his job to take advice and act on it. But he listens to her far more than he should. She's much harder to keep control of. And she knows more than she should. She snoops, he talks, then she talks to others—I won't say friends. I don't think she has any friends. But there's a lot of people who pity her for some stupid reason." He gulped more coffee.

"That's why you don't want us at the embassy?" Kyle asked. "In addition to visibility, I mean?"

"Yup. She was whining and complaining about you 'missing' the shot. She overheard something and is making snide comments about the CIA's assassins."

"Dammit, I didn't take the shot because I didn't want to blow cover or kill a civilian," Kyle said. "Where the f—"

"Hey, don't sweat it," Cafferty said. "I know the realities. We'll get another chance. Absolute worst case, we tell the Romanians everything we have and see if they can nail a couple of them before word gets around. Without mentioning that we were trying to do it ourselves because we didn't trust them."

"You know," Wade said, "I rather think I prefer our job to yours a lot of ways."

"Yeah, I've got a coffee habit that would bankrupt most budgets, and if I come out of this without an ulcer, I'll call it a win."

"So what's next?"

"Well," Cafferty replied, scratching his forehead, "if it goes as before, Logadze here means Florescu will be setting up something regarding a shipment."

"And we'll get a shot at him?"

"If we see him, yes. And then we have to get you up into the tourist areas to get your photos of Dracula's digs. Otherwise people might start asking about you."

"Question, and I don't mean to be rude," Kyle said. This seemed like an opportune time.

"Sure." And another gulp of coffee.

"Why are you so terse on the phone?"

"Because I'm trying to pretend you don't exist," he said. "If I'm just liaison for a military mission, then I can shrug my shoulders and say it's not my fault. But if I talk to you too much, it becomes obvious my department is running the show."

"Fair enough," Kyle said. "I'm not sure I want to see the chain of command for this nightmare."

"Yeah, it's pretty confused," Cafferty said. "Anyway, if we don't get anything else in four days, we'll move you up into the mountains and see if you can offer any help to finding them up there."

"Fair enough," Kyle said. Good. Four more days of bad food and a decrepit city, and maybe they could do something worthwhile.

"Meantime, I'm trying to stop her from hearing anything. I don't know how the info gets out, but she's good at piecing tiny bits together and blowing them out of proportion. A great conspiracy theorist."

"She listens at doors?" Kyle asked.

"Dunno. But I do have to talk on the phone and to others, and I'm not the only person in country, or even in the embassy, who is involved. It only takes a comment at lunch to set her off. And some stuff that is public knowledge gets twisted when she gets hold of it. I'll have to see about getting her some really ridiculous info to discredit her and confuse them. That's more work for my people."

"Anyway," he continued, shaking his head, "let me see what you have, and give me a report," he laid down a microphone connected to the laptop, "and I'll get you more intel. Basic name so I can keep things straight, and talk."

Kyle nodded, grabbed the mic and said, "SFC Kyle Monroe. We departed the hotel at . . ."

Forty minutes later, with some leading questions from Cafferty, they were done. He'd split his attention to watch their video on screen, and to plug their camera into his own laptop. The photos were encrypted and emailed out, then the verbal report, then he pulled a chip from the side. He broke it in half with a heavy pair of sidecutters and held it up. He rummaged in a pocket, pulled out a lighter and scorched the broken edges until they melted. That done, he took it to a corner and pulled a very large magnet out of a drawer, then waved the two sections over it for more than a minute.

"Flash RAM?" Wade asked.

Cafferty said, "Yes. Much easier and cheaper than the old way, which was to either smash and slag a drive, or take fifteen minutes to overwrite and then reformat about two hundred times, I think. That's what the No Such Agency had set up for us. This way, it's done very quickly and for just a few dollars."

"What about security here?" Wade asked.

"Worst case, I try to smash the chip enough before anyone comes in, but this info isn't so critical. If they find it, we say he's a 'person of interest' and negotiate a swap of intel. I'm just being paranoid. Besides, there's Sam. He's the tripwire."

"Ah," Kyle said. It made sense. And likely the safe house changed from time to time.

"Okay, that's it for now. I'll work on this and try to get you another shot. And thanks. The intel is useful, potentially even more useful than a kill."

"No problem," Kyle said. He knew that. Every sniper did. But he wanted the kill because he hated terrorists, and to show the doubters that he could do it.

Then he mentally stepped back, because doing it to prove a point was dangerous. The goal here was to do a job only. Not to prove anything. Professionals didn't take revenge or show off. Professionals knew they were good. And looking back at his own record, Kyle had all the proof he needed that he was good.

They left first, out the back again, smiling at their reticent and almost invisible hostess. Kyle had to wonder what her stake was, but he trusted Cafferty, so he wasn't going to ask.

Turning to Wade, he said, "Now all we need is lunch."

"You know, there is a KFC here. It's real food and hopefully somewhat American."

"Good idea," Kyle agreed, smiling. "I haven't had chicken in a while. And it's bound to be better than their attempts at Mexican or Russian; there's corporate standards to maintain."

"We'll stop by on the way to the hotel. I think it's near there anyway."

An hour later, stuffed and sated, they sat back on their beds. They'd killed a twelve-piece drum of chicken, biscuits, mashed potatoes, gravy, and coleslaw.

"Yup, American fast food. Not healthy, not exotic, but very predictable, and damn, it was good!" Wade said.

"Shall we look at maps and dossiers again?" Kyle asked. "Or another bull session about hunting vampires?"

"Vampires. I'm thinking this whole crucifix to scare them off bit is inadequate. Who says there aren't Jewish vampires? So you also need a Star of David, a Buddhist Wheel, a Crescent, a Hindu Lion, a Pentacle, a—"

"I'll pull up a map and access an online poker game," Kyle said.

Wade chuckled and said, "Sure."

They took turns playing rounds of poker online, while looking at the city and national maps, just to be familiar with everything. They also had some tour guides and local publications. The newsstands and bookstores in the area had been very happy to take their money. As it wasn't their money, and the publications were a necessary expense, they'd been happy to spend it.

Dammar al Asfan checked his email and saw a flagged message.

Actually, it wasn't his email. It had been set up by someone who did nothing but set up free addresses for the cause, using a public machine in a café in France. But he had the username and password.

The message alerted him to another incoming message. That one was marked "spam," but he opened it anyway. It promised him generi(V!@gra at cheap prices with no prescription.

He copied the .jpg image the message was built on and pasted it into another window. From there, he saved it to a folder of a special program. That program stripped off the excess image and left a handful of letters that had been hidden underneath.

The message thus revealed made him snarl. The blasted Americans had two snipers in Romania, courtesy of the CIA. They were stalking his operation, allegedly, though they'd missed a shot at Logadze. As Logadze had not reported an attack, nor were there any news reports, he was skeptical for a moment. But this source was very reliable. He didn't know where they got the information, but the person in charge of intelligence assured him they were always correct, and so far, they had been. So he had to assume the assassination attempt had failed in the setup.

He sent a message requesting more information, then another alerting the relevant people to be especially alert. The next week was critical if they were not to suffer a setback of major proportions.

In the meantime, he'd inquire at the Serviciul Roman de Informatii through connections. Likely there was a record somewhere.

Engineman Third Class Daniel McLaren didn't actually work on engines very often. If a patrol boat or a Mk V Special Operations Boat had a problem on a mission, he'd get involved, and he was responsible for maintenance and tuning. He spent more time in the water than aboard, anyway. SEALs usually did.

His swim buddy for the current mission was a Turkish combat swimmer named Tuncer Akkurt. Tunj was bronzed, which was what his first name meant, ironically, and always had a cheerful smile. That smile wasn't visible at the moment, but it was definitely there. It always was.

The two of them were in the harbor of Constanta's port, keeping low and hidden from most of the shipping, and awaiting orders to observe or pursue the *Chernomertvetz* as she came in to port this evening. Pursuit might involve boarding with others to secure her (unlikely) or to plant surveillance equipment (more likely). For now, they were cold, wet, coated with Vaseline under their wetsuits, and burdened with weight belts, flotation jackets, and vests with pistols, knives, and other gear. They were mostly above the surface, their hoods decorated with odd-shaped bits of black fabric and their faces blackened with a waterproof grease. The sum effect was such that anyone looking at them from aboard a ship would think them mere debris of the kind that floats in every port, washed overboard from ships or kicked off piers, or, more commonly, thrown in carelessly or on purpose.

Two other swimmers, one American and one Turkish, were on the breakwater, where they could use night scopes and special filters to determine probable contents of various cargo. At a signal from them, McLaren and Akkurt would try to get near enough to use a chemical sniffer to verify the findings. Nothing could be 100 percent accurate, but the closer they could get to a conclusive answer, the better. From there, there were assets ashore who would take over. McLaren had no idea who those assets were, or if they were local, American, or some other ally. All he needed to know was that his part would help the whole mission. For a professional, that was enough. That he was in foreign waters without permission wasn't a consideration. That's what SEALs did.

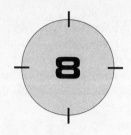

8

KYLE LOOKED UP FROM THE BOOK HE WAS READING and said, "Fascinating country. Pity Ceauşescu and his cronies looted it, or it could have had a lot more historical interest."

"It's getting there," Wade said.

"Yeah, I suppose twenty years or even fifty isn't that long. It just seems like a hell of a long time from personal perspective."

"That it does," Wade agreed. "Harp for dinner again?"

"I guess I can manage that," Kyle said. It would get boring eventually, but the place had a big enough menu to last several days without repeating.

Besides, it got them out of the hotel and killed some time.

After dinner, they went back to the hotel. Neither felt up to tackling the nightlife.

They were just sitting down to a mix of local and online news when Kyle's phone rang.

He stood and dug the phone out of his jacket pocket. "Monroe," he answered.

"Kyle, this is Mick."

"Yes, Mick?"

"I've got a lead for you guys. Right now."

Kyle snapped his fingers and pointed at Wade, who rolled off the bed and started grabbing gear.

"Shoot," Kyle prompted.

"There's a ship coming in tonight," Cafferty said. "Our marine mammal friends—" that would be the SEALs— "have got a probable ID on explosives from a sniff. We've decided to let this one through so you can follow it. It's big," he said, hesitating.

"How big?" Kyle asked.

"Might be a *ton* of conventional explosive, likely TNT. Not as sexy as Semtex or C Four, but plenty for a dozen small missions or one huge blast."

"What do you want us to do?" Kyle asked. This was a bit more than they'd planned on.

Across the room, Wade had the weapons bagged and was changing into local working-class clothes.

Cafferty said, "Go to the port in Constanta. The ship *Chernomertvetz* arrives in four hours. We can't imagine they'll let that stuff sit for long; it's standard to turn around fast. So they likely have an ally handy who'll clear them through customs, or a bribe or some evasion and they'll unload fast. Follow them wherever they go, report back, get photos of people and take further action if necessary."

"We're on it. Got a map and more data?"

"Yes, I just emailed your laptop. It's all there, including a phone contact for our friends. They'll give you regular updates on position and schedule."

"Will do. We're rolling now," Kyle said, nodding from habit even though it couldn't be seen.

Wade did see it and nodded back.

"Good luck," Cafferty said and clicked off.

Kyle shoved the phone into the pocket, snapped it closed, and went about getting dressed himself. He logged the laptop in with a touch and watched as it started downloading mail. A three-meg file. Lots of stuff.

"How did you know it was working-class clothes?" he asked Wade, in regard to his partner's dress.

"It's eight P.M. No way are we going out to a ball on short notice, if these guys even do balls."

"Right," he agreed, pulling on well-worn khakis. "Who's driving?"

"That depends," Wade said. "I grew up in central Illinois, flatland."

"It's hilly. I'm from southern Ohio. Better let me do it."

"Suits me. I'll navigate, take pictures, shoot if needed, and flirt with any chicks."

In ten minutes, they were stuffing gear into the backseat and scrambling into the front. "This time, we're actually using the laptop," Wade said. He was opening it to read routes and docking info. The Pakistan mission had resulted in much lost and damaged equipment, and other pieces that proved largely useless. So far this time, everything was working nominally.

So far.

"Hey, I'll take any advantage we can get," Kyle said. "What's our route?"

Wade navigated them out of the city very professionally. "Left at the third light," he'd say. "Two blocks, then right, immediate left." Bucharest was old. Even the new parts were built on ancient, twisting routes that hadn't been intended for modern vehicles.

"This is like old New England or the most cramped parts of Philly," Kyle said.

"Worse, I think. Left again up ahead. That's our route."

"Roger."

The highway was one designated as an "E," or European road. It was therefore in decent repair. They waited impatiently at traffic lights and stop signs, then powered away, swapping fuel efficiency for precious seconds.

It was quiet enough as they left town, but even this late at night, there were a few obstacles—chuckholes, horse- and mule-drawn carts and drivers in rattly old Yugos or medieval Fiats that could barely keep up—even an old diesel Volvo that smoked and sputtered as Kyle passed it. The road was a divided highway at first, a second pair of lanes obviously built alongside the older two-lane. There were quite a few intersections where "largest vehicle has right of way" was the unstated rule.

Wade got on the phone and called the number they'd been given. "Curtis here," he said. "How's it going? . . . Okay. Yes, two hours at least . . . Will you be meeting us? . . . Okay. Stand by." He started hooking the phone up to the laptop.

"What's up?" Kyle asked.

"Getting an image. We should be there in time. It takes a while for docking and clearance. Then they have to get cranes and ramps into position. But after that, they think it might be the first load off."

"What are we going to do?"

"We're going to observe from shore while they observe from sea. They'll let us know when they think it's the right load. I get the impression they were hoping to plant a tracer of some kind on it, and couldn't quite get close enough to the load."

"Damn. That would have made things much easier for everyone."

"Yeah. We'd just have to zoom in and shoot."

They passed through Dragalina, Fetesti, and several smaller, un-remarkable towns, each one a delay on what was a nominal hun-dred-and-twenty-mile trip. It was a two-hour trip if all went well, but it was near midnight when they rolled into Constanta.

"I'm not sure we want to get too close to the port," Kyle said. "We've got radios, would you feel safe making a recon on foot? I'll circle and recon by car and be ready to roll."

"Safe, no. But I'll do it," Wade agreed. "No weapons, I want de-niability, but if the radio isn't answering, you'll need to come get me." He sounded nervous.

"Take the Beretta," Kyle decided. "A magazine full of ammo might get them to duck long enough for you to get out, and I'll be ready with the AK. If they've got too many for us to tackle, just bow out early."

"Got it," Wade agreed. "But I'd rather not have a firefight here."

"Agreed," Kyle said.

Constanta was old, grimy, and broad. It had been named after Constantine, and had been a port before that. Parts had been built by the Turks, the Romanians, the Communists, Ceausescu's regime, and again by free Romanians. The architecture ran the gamut from Turkish to baroque and to modern, and the streets were as snarled and twisted as any others in this country. They came in on the Bule-vardul Tomis, past a sign for the Roman baths and then south toward the port.

The port wasn't quite what they'd expected it to be. It was bigger than they would have thought, and alternated between arc-lit oper-ations and dark industrial sections. There was a rail yard that went on for miles, and docks ashore and along a breakwater. Ships were moving in at a steady clip, and others departing. Shipping compa-nies hate port. If cargo isn't moving, money isn't being made. APM Terminals had a sign up, as did SC Socep. Workers, mostly men, were everywhere, loading, unloading, hauling, opening crates, back-ing vehicles.

Wade said, "It's the second pier from the south. The southern-most has petrochemical storage."

"You know what we're looking for?" Kyle asked. He'd been busy driving and had everything secondhand from Wade. He was having trouble visualizing things.

"Yes, it's a smaller, older ship. Diesel drive, no stacks, and is very low and curvy. I have the image they sent. It's grainy, but I think I can spot it."

"Good."

"It won't take long, I'm told. Ships don't like sitting in port, because they only make money when moving, kinda like truckers. So we can expect them to haul ass once they get docked."

The gate was guarded, but there was no fence. There were dark, shadowy areas, and it was toward one of those that Wade was angling in a crouch.

It took Wade only a few seconds to cut a slice in the fence and slip in. Kyle watched him disappear, his right foot catching for a moment, then gone. He had no idea what the inside of the facility looked like, other than it was full of containers and piles, rails and cranes. Wade would have to walk quite some distance without being identified, then walk back out unseen if he were to be able to ride with Kyle on the chase.

If not, he had cash and could arrange transport back by himself. On the other hand, with a silenced Beretta, cash, and communication gear, anyone finding him would suspect him of crime or terrorism.

And that was Wade's worry, Kyle reminded himself. His was out here, ready to chase. Wade had the inside watch.

Meanwhile, Kyle sat and waited. Every minute or two he revved the engine up to 1200 or so, just to stop it from fouling. It likely wasn't necessary in a modern fuel-injected car, but it was habit and ensured the engine was responsive. He used the heat to keep his feet warm, leaving the window open for Wade. But he ensured all the doors were locked and held firmly to his Ed Brown, suppressor in place, the whole assembly tucked under his left arm inside his coat.

"Arriving," Wade whispered hoarsely in his ears. Seconds later, his shape rose near the door, disturbing and macabre despite the fact that it was a perfectly reasonable act.

Calm down, Kyle reminded himself, taking a deep breath.

"This is a job for White Man!" Wade said softly. "Gypsies and Romanians all over the place. You'll blend in fine. I won't."

"Okay," Kyle agreed. "Let me see the maps and pics." He sighed. It wasn't Wade's fault, dammit, but anything that changed his plans was exasperating.

The ship looked easy to spot; it was very rounded at the ends. The bow and stern, he reminded himself. It had a large yellow crane at the rear third. The map told him where it was supposed to be docking.

"Okay, call our friends and make sure they have my number," Kyle said. "Call me to confirm, and I'll let you know what I find."

It was cool enough to justify wearing a polyester ski cap rolled down to hide his radio earpiece. With the microphone dangling inside his upturned collar, it should be invisible, and he should look like any common laborer.

He took the smaller of their two still cameras so he could try for images if needed, and climbed out, adjusting his collar as he did so.

From where the car was, it was easy to walk across the rail yard. There were several other people in sight, and no one seemed to care about the fact that it was unsafe and potentially threatening. Which in this case, Kyle reflected, was good. For him at least.

There was also a sea fog moving in. That worked both ways. It would hide him, but it would also mean he'd need to get close to the ship. Meanwhile, he had to maintain a lookout so he wouldn't have to interact with anyone. He could badly pretend to be Spanish, or hope to pass off as a Brit, or even just grunt a bit in passing. But if the conversation lasted more than two sentences, he'd be obvious.

A buzz surprised him. It was the phone in his pocket, set to vibrate to keep it discreet.

"Monroe," he answered.

"This is Kabongo, on the water." The voice was clear, but there was background noise, probably a boat engine.

"What have you got?"

"They're docking and tying up now. I've got someone watching from the water, but his angle is limited."

"I'll be there soon. How close do I need to be?" He was trying to keep his voice at a mutter but loud enough for audibility. It wouldn't do to be heard in English without a believable cover story.

"Five hundred meters should be close enough. We think the cargo you're looking for is a pallet of wooden crates. Should be one of the first loads off."

"I'll see what I can do. Let me know if anything else happens."

"Will do. Out."

"Out."

Once at the docks proper, there was plenty of cover. People were all over the place, but not in concentrations except where unloading a ship. Some sauntered, some loitered, some walked briskly. People were hanging off cranes, trucks, and ramps. Lots were smoking. It occurred to Kyle that cigarettes would help them blend in for tasks like this, and they should buy some. All he had to do was sit and hold one and he'd be presumed taking a break, whether authorized or not. He could also offer one and grunt to kill five seconds of interaction, then pretend not to speak the language. If he tossed a few broken words out and was happy to share his smokes, few would question him. In fact, he was getting the hang of this. Act as if you belong and people assume you do.

He saw *Chernomertvetz* quite far out, past a much larger cargo craft named *Yebar' Volgi*, a huge ocean freighter, and another huge ship he couldn't identify. The *Chernomertvetz* was small in comparison, only about two hundred feet long. Even from this far away in fog, she was worn and old, with rust running down her anchor ports.

Now to find a place to observe from. There were plenty of conex containers in rows, awaiting loading or removal. There were also stacks of crates and drums awaiting palletization. To skulk around anything would be to suggest an intent to steal. The best cover was just to stand out in front, shirking, leaning against the corner of a conex. It was wet with mist, but that was a minor issue. It didn't bother Kyle, and it didn't bother the men and few women who worked here, who were rough and burly and used to working in all weather.

Occasionally, Kyle nodded back at a passerby. Someone made a fingers to lips gesture for a cigarette, and he shrugged and shook his head. Apart from that, nothing to speak of happened for an hour. *Chernomertvetz* was tied up and the only action was the clattering of hatches and planks preparing for a massive offload. The sounds were discernible with effort and observation, because a bigger, closer ship was undergoing the same preparation. Then there were several powering in or out of the harbor.

It was quite practical for Kyle to look around, surreptitiously watching from the corners of his eyes while not actually staring directly. But after an hour of even that, he was gathering more curious looks than he thought was healthy, and moved a little closer and across the way. *Chernomertvetz* was well to his left, at nine o'clock to him. He had a good view of her entire side, as cranes started swinging into place and pulling loads from her holds.

He hadn't been told, but assumed there'd be other cargo, most of it legitimate. Either it would be done as cover, or the crew really might not know what was being carried, apart from one or two conspirators. So it was no surprise to see several large containers being withdrawn. He used the camera without flash to get several pictures, trying to time them for when no observers were looking in his direction. He was pointshooting rather than risk raising it to his face. It was entirely possible people snapped photos all the time, but probably not lone men leaning against boxes, with no apparent job waiting and using a US$1000 camera set for infrared as well as visible frequencies.

After five loads of the front crane, something came up that caught Kyle's interest.

That was definitely a pallet inside plastic. It looked like wooden crates, being too light in color for cardboard, and with corners too sharp. But was it the right package? The only way to tell would be to follow it, and there were a lot of trucks along here.

It was down behind an old Mercedes box van and being stripped to load individually. That was likely a good indication, he thought. It would be easier to load the whole pallet onto a larger vehicle, which would mean cheaper. To break this up here indicated a desire to conceal it shortly, and the small enclosed truck meant they didn't want it seen.

He made a quick note of the license plate on the blunt-nosed vehicle, noted the color—dark blue—and turned casually back the way he'd come.

Steady walk, he reminded himself. To run would attract attention. But he did need to walk briskly. He stretched out his pace, being careful of his footing and trying to find a good route. He wanted one that was reasonably direct, but wasn't an obvious beeline out.

He was a good halfway out, striding through the rail yard, when two men came toward him. He quivered alert, in case they were port guards or thugs from his quarry. But they waved casually for attention. He shook an arm back and kept walking.

One of them shouted, "*Ţigară?*" *Cigarette?*

"*Îmi pare rău*," he replied. *Sorry*. It might have been a simple attempt to mooch, but they kept getting closer.

Mugging in progress, he thought. Should he run, fight, or worse?

The decision wasn't an easy one, but there were matters at stake here. He had to get this info out and follow up on it. He couldn't be dragged in locally or he'd blow the whole mission. These men weren't his friends and did mean ill. He couldn't think of a way out that was particularly safe. So he'd have to do something obvious and hope to be gone before it was discovered. He scanned for witnesses, backup, anything that might change his decision. Then, sighing, he slipped his hand inside his coat for his pistol.

In a gully between tracks, about three feet deep, wet and muddy, he saw a section of slender pipe. Perhaps eighteen inches long, one inch diameter, and thick walled. That should help. He bent and scooped it as he dropped down into the rut, then stood back up with it in his left hand. He laid it casually over his shoulder and walked toward the two probable hostiles. Would it work?

They hesitated for just a moment as he raised the pipe. Then they resumed their approach, but at a slower pace.

Kyle increased his and plastered a smile on his face. Look at the man with the grin and the pipe. He's hoping for a good rumble to settle his late dinner. You can be his playmates. Come on, you bastards, *run*. Don't make me shoot you.

Because that was the only alternative he could think of—shoot them with a silenced .45 and hope no one noticed until he was gone. Unless a passerby interfered before the fight started by being awkwardly present, he would have to take them out. And he wasn't sure they didn't have clubs or knives or even guns of their own. Probably not guns, but he couldn't risk his mission over it.

In another moment, the two had made their own calculations, and decided Kyle was too eager to meet them. They angled sharply away to seek easier prey.

Smart move, Kyle thought. *For all of us.*

9

WADE WAS WAITING AND WATCHING. AS KYLE AP-proached, he slid over to the passenger side.

"It's a Mercedes box van, about ten years old. Last I saw, it was rolling down the access road, and should have come out there," he pointed to the second gate north. "Did you see it?"

"Yes, just a few minutes ago," Wade said.

"Carefully, then. We don't want to ride up on it." Kyle acknowledged and eased into gear. He left the headlights off, steering carefully by the lights glaring through gaps in the skyline. He coasted slowly out to where he could see the road.

"There," Wade said, and pointed. "That's them."

"I'll give them a bit," Kyle said. "Do we know what main route they have to take?"

"If they go straight, it's this one," Wade said, pointing at the map, then zooming in with a flick of fingers. "Toward Tulcea, Braila, or Bucharest."

"Four-lane?"

"To start with."

"Okay, call Cafferty, tell him. We're going to need backup."

Wade pulled out his phone. "Curtis here. We're following them onto the E Sixty. We'll need support . . . yes . . . understood . . . We'll do what we can. Yes, sir." He clicked off and said, "Fun."

"What?"

"He says they can pick up in either town, but don't have anyone nearby. We'll have to follow them ourselves for a while. And we're supposed to do that without being noticed?" Wade asked. "I think they overestimate our chances."

"No, we can do it," Kyle said. "In theory, we should have three to five vehicles. Anytime they turn, the first vehicle goes straight, then joins the back of the pack. If they go straight long enough to get suspicious of a tail, one car will turn off and then rejoin. By varying the passenger silhouette, we'd track them for hundreds of kilometers and not be noticed."

"Makes sense," Wade said. "And how do we do it with just two Americans, one black and one white, in a late model Audi?"

"Easy," Kyle said. "Warm up the NVGs and see how the landscape looks." They were onto the highway now, staying well back. It was an easy pursuit, for the moment.

"Ah, I catch your drift. We douse the lights and follow in the dark, and occasionally put them back on as we pass side roads." He fumbled in back for a moment, then sat up again with a pair of goggles. He snugged the straps on his head and adjusted them.

"That's it," Kyle said. "Though you may have to bail out and watch for clues if they stop somewhere."

"Sure. I could use more exercise." He removed the goggles and said, "They're good to go. Want them now?" There were still some streetlights along here, but it didn't seem they'd last long. The road was narrowing to two lanes again.

"No, keep them ready," Kyle said. "I may have only a second or two to kill the lights, you slip them on my head and I'll get them in place before running off the road."

"Before would be good," Wade agreed. "What do we do if they have sentries or night vision of their own?"

"Abort, shoot our way out or die."

"Great. The Truth. Now tell me some cheerful BS so I don't worry."

"We'll pretend we're lost tourists looking at exotic rabbits by starlight. Sort of like birdwatchers, but not as cool."

"There's people *less* cool than birdwatchers?"

"Politicians, reporters, and terrorists at the very least."

"Point made," Wade nodded.

The truck was moving at a good clip. Speed limits weren't enforced much, Kyle seemed to remember. Nor was there much need. The driver of the beat-up old Mercedes truck braked hard before bends and turns, then powered through them, the box back swaying dangerously over rippling, distorted tires. He didn't seem too worried about his cargo.

"Careless driver," he said.

"Maybe it's a decoy?"

"Could be," Kyle nodded. "But that's not something we can de-

cide en route. Maybe the guy's just an idiot with no imagination."
TNT and most other explosives were quite stable. The risk of explosion was almost nonexistent. But a crash and spill would blow any
cover available. "Maybe he has to be there on a stiff schedule.
Doesn't matter. We're here, we'll follow them. Hand me the goggles,
I'm going to shut off the lights around this bend." There was a small
but obvious side road that made a convenient excuse for them to
"turn off" and leave dark emptiness on the road.

Wade reached back, where he had laid out goggles, gear, and
weapons like surgical tools, ready at a moment's notice. It would
really screw them if they did get pulled over, of course. On the other
hand, if US$25 got one out of drunk driving, a couple of hundred
cash, name drops about the embassy and references to the DEA had
a decent chance of getting them left alone. If not . . . no one had
claimed the mission was without risk.

"Here you go," he said, as he slid the goggles into the space between Kyle's head and the roof.

Kyle grasped them and drew them down over his eyes. "There,"
he said. Wade grabbed them and started adjusting the head harness
into place, while Kyle flipped off the lights. He'd been blind for only
a second, and was still in control of the vehicle. As the curve
straightened out, their quarry became visible again, taillights ahead
of them.

"Going to do this for a while?" Wade asked.

"As long as we can get away with. If they don't have reason to
notice a vehicle behind them, they won't pay attention when we are
in sight. We should be fine."

"Until we get close and the shooting starts," Wade commented.

"Yes," Kyle agreed with a single nod.

They drove in silence for several minutes, Wade looking at maps
and watching the taillights, Kyle keeping his distance steady and
looking for the obvious dangers of people turning in front of them,
and for the edge of the road, which disappeared at times and even
the enhanced vision of the goggles didn't show.

Then the lights ahead slewed.

"They're turning off," Wade advised and grabbed the laptop
back from his knees.

"I see," Kyle said. "Where are they heading?"

"Inland. In toward the mountains."

"Isn't that where they keep disappearing?"

"I believe so."

"Tell Cafferty."

"Will do," Wade agreed, and reached for his phone. "Wade Curtis here. They're heading along Route Sixty toward Bucharest . . . Yes . . . will do." He clicked off. "He suspects they'll go past Bucharest to Braşov area, and will arrange to get someone there in the next day or so."

"The next day or so?" Kyle asked incredulously. "That's a long time."

"I gather he's shorthanded and we're about it."

"Uncle Sam certainly has faith in our ability. Too much, maybe." He drifted into the turn, watching for oncoming cars, whose drivers would have no idea he was there until they wound up in a torn sheet-metal embrace.

"So we do what we can," Wade said. His voice was calm, but there was a hint of strain, and Kyle smiled. He could see adequately. Wade still was using his Mod 1 eyeballs to scan with. This had to be a bit disturbing for him.

The PVS7-XR5 night vision enabled Kyle to see reasonably well by the stars and moon. Occasional oncoming vehicles' headlights caused the goggles to shift settings, which gave them some tense moments where he was driving by feel on a narrow road, with no shoulder and a foot drop into woods at the side. Add to that driving on the "wrong" side of the road, and it was exciting, and not in a good way. Some oncoming traffic appeared not to see them, but several drivers honked their horns.

"Sooner or later someone is going to hit us, report us, or figure out we're up to something," Kyle said.

"Yeah. 'Why isn't the CIA handling this?' he asks again."

"I get the impression most spooks are computer nerds, not tuxedo-clad, stone-cold killers," Kyle said. "I also get the impression that whether this works or not, we'll be referred to in whatever news does get out as 'CIA assassins,' and that the Agency will take the credit publicly." He eased the wheel to the right, trying to avoid getting too close to the edge. His American driving instincts were pushing him to the left, to avoid the "edge" on the right. It was going to take a lot more hours of driving to get used to doing it the "wrong" way, especially under stress.

"No bet," Wade said. "As long as the Army credits us as due. And maybe throws in a follow-up mission looking for terrorists at a bikini-judging contest in Aruba . . ."

"Miss Nude Bomber, maybe?"

"Hmm . . . we'd have to search them. Carefully."

"Of course," Kyle agreed. Jokes were necessary despite the mission. Or maybe because of it. Anything that relieved a little stress would help. Because of the goggles, he could only see the layered green world of night vision ahead and nothing to the sides. Wade's voice and the engine noise were his lifeline to reality. They'd tried the radio and given up. It was Italian pop and some obnoxious Russian stuff, neither of which they wanted to listen to.

The smaller, rougher road wove through small towns, where it would circle the town square or go through a roundabout. They paralleled the Ialomita River for some time, then turned roughly northwest.

"Near as I can tell," Wade said, "we're bypassing Bucharest to its north."

"That would make sense," Kyle agreed. "If they're headed for Sighișoara or the mountains."

"Not as fast, but less traffic and visibility, easier to find a tail—"

"Us," Kyle interrupted with a grin.

"Us," Wade agreed. "And it avoids accidents or stops where someone would see a lot of evidence. If they have trouble out here, they're less likely to be seen and can hide bodies."

"That's so reassuring," Kyle said. "Also consider that they may have a tail to look for tails."

"Joy," Wade replied and stopped talking.

Eventually, they rejoined the E60 and turned right, continuing northwest.

"Seems to agree with the Sighișoara theory," Kyle said. "If I recall the map."

"Right here," Wade said, angling the laptop. Kyle checked the road was straight, flipped up the goggles, looked at the route Wade traced with his finger, then turned quickly back to the road.

It was a long drive. At times they'd reach speeds of 150km/h or more. Then they'd hit hills or curves and drop down below 70. There were several tense instances where the truck would pass a slow-moving car right before a series of rises or bends that precluded visibility and passing. Twice, Wade leaned far out the window to try to see ahead for Kyle's benefit. They'd hit a section just long enough for bravery and urgency to overcome common sense and rip past whichever vehicle had hindered them, usually to shouts and honks about headlights.

Again they took a narrower local road, and again Wade reported it to Cafferty. "He says to be alert for sudden turns. They're likely to try to get on E Seventy," he relayed to Kyle.

"Understood." And it would be easy along here. It twisted and wove and the road was rising.

They did turn left onto another local road, and it was even rougher than the routes so far. The car crunched over loose and crumbled asphalt, occasionally skittering and skidding over gravel from underneath. There were potholes to dodge and cracks that let chunks of the road edges yawn dangerously away from the main bed.

The road narrowed and wound. Then up ahead there was an obstacle, and oncoming lights. Kyle braked hard and kept a good distance back from the slow-moving thing ahead, which resolved into a horse-drawn cart out way too late and with no reflectors or lights. It was far to the left, but there was still a considerable risk of someone smashing into it. The oncoming car whipped past and honked, whether at the cart driver or Kyle was impossible to tell. The cartman swore and shook his fist at the vehicle, then shouted something at Kyle as he powered around and back up to speed. He pulled into another curve and smiled. Everyone out driving tonight was an idiot, it seemed, himself included.

Another oncoming car flashed its lights at them as it approached. Then it was past, and its brake lights glowed brightly in the mirror as it slewed and turned. It was only a couple of hundred yards behind when it finished the maneuver. Then it started closing the gap, lights on high and a spotlight thrown in. Kyle flipped the mirror down to avoid the glare.

"Ah, hell," Kyle said. Worse profanity wasn't really needed. This had been almost inevitable.

"Police?" Wade asked.

"Dunno, but probably." The irony was perverse. Had they been using headlights, this would have been less likely. On the other hand, they might have been nailed that way, too. Sometimes, every answer was wrong.

Then the car's lights went out. Behind Kyle and Wade the back window exploded. Cold wind started roaring in.

"Shots fired!" Wade said needlessly. "I think they've got night vision, too."

"Not cops!" Kyle said, also needlessly.

"How? Scanner? Spooks at police headquarters heard a complaint? Looking for interference?"

"Who cares?" Kyle shouted.

"Right. Want me to shoot?" Wade asked, quickly over his surprise.

"If you'd be so kind," Kyle yelled, shifting down and nailing the gas. Wade fell against his seat as the acceleration caught him. He'd been reaching for the blankets covering the rifle in the footwell.

In seconds he had it, had clicked the scope on, and was drawing it up into shooting position. He fell flat and lowered the weapon but kept hold of it as two more shots crashed by. One took out more glass and starred the windshield. The other threw sparks from the side pillar, exiting with a scream.

"Shit!" he said, yanking the rifle back up.

The best thing to do when being shot at is to move quickly, keep moving, and not sit still and take it. But the shattered and open back window was a psychological hole that made things seem that much more vulnerable. Kyle's neck and back were itching madly, and his shoulder muscles twitched in fear. He steeled himself to keep driving and let Wade shoot, and pulled the mirror roughly back into place. At least he had an idea of what was going on behind.

The fuzzy monochrome and shadows inside the car made it hard to tell, but it seemed to contain three or four people, and rifles stuck up from at least two of them. Or maybe submachine guns with long barrels or suppressors. They seemed a bit short and thick for proper rifles. But whatever they were, they could definitely shoot right through the car, and through the Rangers.

"We need police-type body armor, thin and under the clothes. Put it on the list," Kyle said.

"Sure, when we get back," Wade said. "Wonder if the embassy can get us some."

"Have to hope so," Kyle said. "But we need it now."

He didn't want to close up on the truck and let them trap him, possibly with a vehicle in the other lane, either a conspirator or convenient civilian. But he didn't want to let their tail get up close where shooting was more accurate, or ramming became possible. It occurred to him also that they might have incendiary ammo and aim for the fuel tank.

Maybe he *could* get a bit closer to the truck, he thought. It was still a kilometer or more ahead, as he came over a rise in the road at better than 90 mph, almost 160 km/h. Then he had to turn hard, because the road had a reverse camber and they were floating, drifting off to the left, where very hard trees awaited them.

The road leveled back out and another round tore through and punched a hole in the left side of the windshield. Some scattered bits of fluffy padding came from Wade's seat. He didn't seem to notice, and sat up with the AK.

He had to shout to be heard over the roar of wind and engine. "We've got enough of a problem with the damage to this vehicle. If I shoot the driver or block, we'll have a major incident. I'm going to try for a tire."

"Makes sense," Kyle said. "Just don't take too long."

"Working on it," Wade replied, his nod unseen. "Easier with the back window gone. Get me a bend in the road so I have a better profile to shoot at. Moving," he announced, and shimmied between the seats, his thigh dangerously close to the gear shift. The passenger seat dropped as he yanked the recline lever, then he eased back a bit more.

Two more shots cracked through the vehicle, and Kyle grimaced, gripping the wheel until his knuckles turned white. Just because he'd been shot at before didn't mean he enjoyed it. But he was veteran enough to not flinch, and kept the car tightly controlled as they took a sharp bend to the right.

"Kick ass!" Wade said, and fired. The round popped through the suppressor, the bolt clacked as it cycled, and he immediately started squirming back into the front seat. "That'll teach the bastards to shoot at us!"

Though that did leave the minor matter of the Rangers' riddled ride. Front and rear glass were missing, and there was at least one small-caliber hole visible.

"We going to keep trailing?" Wade asked over the wind noise.

"Nothing else we can do," Kyle said. "That was a great shot."

"Thanks. They survived from pity," Wade said. "It's a pity I had to be discreet."

"Right. The question is, did our boys in the truck get the message, do they know we took care of their buddies, and will they do anything to us? Or just try to get away?" There were enough small side roads that anything was possible, and Kyle was not about to drive into a potential ambush. They might be Rangers and snipers, but they were only two men, and a squad of men with submachine guns could kill them handily in the woods.

"Dunno. But I assume they know we're here," Wade said. He kept the rifle on his lap, muzzle down at the footwell. He returned the seat upright.

"Yeah," Kyle said shortly. Things always went to hell, that was a given. So it wasn't really a surprise to be driving across Romania in a car shot to hell without approval of the local government, carrying unauthorized weapons.

Not surprising, but aggravating.

The truck's driver seemed to know he was being followed. He increased speed until the whole van shimmied and tilted on the curves. Perhaps he could catch a glimpse of reflected moon off the Audi. Or he may have had a spotter of his own with night vision. Whatever was involved, he was driving recklessly.

Kyle reflected on how a wreck would leave crates of TNT on the road, to be seized by the Romanians. If the driver and passengers were injured, they could just be left there to be dealt with locally.

On the other hand, he wasn't authorized to make that decision. "Call Cafferty," he said. "Ask him about wrecking them."

"Calling," Wade said. "Curtis here. Question. If we can harass the target into an accident, should we? . . . Yes, that's what we were wondering. Let me give you our current location while we're on air." He read off the road and approximate grid. "Yes, we'll try. We just had an encounter with a car of unfriendlies. They were encouraged to lose a tire . . . No, nothing traceable to us . . . Will do. Out." He turned to Kyle and said, "He says a wreck would be of immediate help if all else fails, but he'd prefer to know where they're going. So pursue if possible. If we can't maintain pursuit, we're authorized to shoot out a tire or otherwise cause a wreck, then find a hotel and hide while he cleans up the mess. I gather he really doesn't want us to do that."

"Roger that," Kyle said. So dammit, he'd stay on top of them and try not to spook them too much.

Every time they hit a town, he had to wonder if the truck was going to stop, turn off, meet up with additional forces or do something totally unpredictable. Fatigue was getting to him, his eyeballs gritty and hurting from the monochromatic vision the NVGs allowed. He drifted occasionally, and took two or three seconds to recover each time. Thought processes slowing, he realized. If he reached the hallucination stage, he'd have to make a quick stop and let Wade drive. Though Wade wasn't in much better shape.

"It just occurred to me that we have to lose this car when we do stop," Kyle said. The wind roaring throughout might have seemed an obvious hint, but they'd become used to it and were still running on endorphins from the battle.

"Shit, that's right," Wade said. "It's blatantly obvious what happened and will get questions asked."

"Questions we don't want to answer, even if it's, 'We were hijacked and drove fast.'"

"Yeah, not even that," Wade agreed. "What do we do?"

Kyle realized the battle had him hyped, and the untraditional battlefield had him confused. On top of fatigue, he was barely tracking. "You'll drive when we get close, drop me off to get a room. I'll walk in with a backpack. Not too uncommon. Then I'll call and tell you where, and you follow along."

"Sounds good. But it's damned late."

"Yeah, I know," Kyle said. "Nothing we can do about that."

"Town ahead. Damn, we've come a long way."

"Probably three hundred and fifty kilometers, two hundred and ten miles," Wade said. "It's five A.M., did you know that?"

"I didn't," Kyle said. "This would be a three- to four-hour drive back home. Here it's been six already."

"How are you holding up?"

"Groggy," Kyle admitted. "But not groggy enough to change drivers. We'll swap if they stop, if you're up to it."

"Not really, but I'm probably in better shape, since I haven't been driving. Curve up ahead."

"I see it," Kyle said. "Looks like they're turning again. I see brake lights."

"I think that's E Seventy they're turning on," Wade said. "South again. I'm really wondering if this is a decoy, except Cafferty seems to think this is part of their route."

"He knows more than we do. We trust him," Kyle said. "Not much point if we don't."

"True."

Every town was starting to look the same to Kyle, and all the kilometers of forest. He was relying on Wade to keep him informed. All his attention was on staying on the road.

"Heading into Bran," Wade said. "Tiny town, tourist attraction."

"What's here?"

"An old castle, allegedly used by Dracula during the war with the Turks. You should know this, Vampire Hunter."

"Yeah, vampires." He longed to say something witty, but his brain was fried.

Ahead, the road turned and the speed limit dropped. The truck braked hard as it hit the curve, then accelerated into town.

"That's a bit fast," Kyle said. "I'd say they do know we're after them. Maybe we can scare them into doing something stupid."

"Yeah," Wade said, "or into just driving on through the day, while everyone looks at the car with the windows missing."

"Right."

Then they were in town proper, the road a long curve ahead and to the left. The truck was three stops ahead of them. Then it turned off. Kyle had already braked for a sign and couldn't maneuver quickly.

"Got them," Wade said. "Left."

"Roger." He revved up and pulled ahead hard, tires squealing slightly. He ran through two signs as he flipped the lights back off and dropped the goggles down. They were close enough now that any sign of them would be a warning.

He came to the intersection, yanked the wheel left and took the turn . . .

Nothing.

"So where did they go?" he asked, hoping Wade had seen them.

"Dunno."

"Dammit! I don't want to say we lost them!"

"I'd guess another turn, then another. Their best bet would be to zigzag so we're always a street behind."

"Let's go six blocks fast and wait," he decided.

It wasn't as easy as that. The blocks weren't necessarily square or even. But he found another cross street that was fairly straight and sat there at the intersection, waiting.

After five minutes, it was fairly obvious the truck was either stopped somewhere in the area, or had evaded and left.

"Circle the area a few times," Wade suggested. "There's not much traffic out this morning."

"Good idea. Route?"

Wade read off directions and they drove around the village then crisscrossed it, looking for any sign of the truck or its lights. After that, they returned to where they'd lost sight and patrolled street by street.

"Nothing," Kyle said in disgust. "Do we wake Cafferty?"

"I'd say so. He needs to know."

"Yeah," Kyle agreed. "Dammit, I hate to fail."

"I got some photos. Maybe he can get something from that."

"We'll see. I'm going to stop here and call."

"Okay."

From a steep graveled roadside that wasn't really a shoulder, he punched his phone while Wade packed weapons away.

"Cafferty," was the sleepy reply. It was clear he hadn't actually gotten any sleep.

"Lost them," Kyle said. There was no point in wasting time.

"Shit. Where?"

"Here in Bran. They turned, they disappeared. We were about sixty seconds behind and slowed to maintain distance."

"Dammit," Cafferty groused. "This is my fault for not having more backup. There's only so much you can do with one vehicle."

"Well, we had them and lost them," Kyle said.

"Yeah, but this has happened before. Always in that area—Bran, Braşov, Codlea, they make turns in town and poof! Gone. Dammit." He really sounded disgusted.

"What should we do?" Kyle asked.

"Get a room and stay in the area. They may show up. Can you look around in daylight? I know it sounds stupid, but they can't hide the vehicle all the time, and even if they stole it or rented it, it'll give us more of a lead."

"Yeah, we can do that. Do you have the images we sent?" he asked.

"I do, but there's nothing I can get from them. I'm having them looked at by experts, but it will take time. Later will be better. And you guys will be rested."

"Roger that," Kyle said. He realized he was absolutely wiped out, now that they'd stopped the chase. "I'll ping you early."

"Only if you find something," Cafferty said. "I need sleep, too."

"Right, now what about the car?" he asked.

"What about it?" Cafferty asked.

"Shot up," Kyle reminded him.

"Oh, that. Dammit, I forgot." There was clear strain in his voice. "Abandon it, see if you can wreck it a bit against a pole or hillside. I'll take it from there. Hold on." There was mumbling off phone, then he said, "Call Sam when you get lodged and he will deliver another car to you. He'll be there in about four hours."

"Will do. Out."

Kyle wanted a good idea of who would have access to their room, and a certain amount of visibility made it harder for people to either sneak up or take gear out. He'd prefer a little strip motel.

It wasn't like America, though. This might be a tourist area, but it was also the absolute ass end of nowhere. Actually, it wasn't. The Afghan border was the absolute ass end of nowhere. Kyle had been there. But this was very sparsely populated and not the type of place with twenty-four-hour desk staff. The hotel they chose was small, old, and seemed to be based in a large house broken into suites. But there was parking outside, so there was a certain amount of clear space. He went in to register while Wade took the car to its grave.

It seemed unfair. The vehicle had seen them through a long chase and was to be tossed aside. Their first casualty, it felt like.

Still, better the car than the people they'd lost in the past.

Several minutes of knocking got someone to rise. A middle-aged woman came to the door in a robe, then put on her business smile. Kyle didn't even haggle over the rate. Better to be thought a dumb tourist. It wasn't his money, and she was quite helpful. He arranged for two nights for now, paid her in euros and asked about somewhere to do laundry before continuing the "hike" he and his partner were on, and did she know if they could get batteries for their cameras here? Yes, his partner was just behind, having stopped to get some early-morning shots of the castle.

Once he had the key, he went straight back to the room and flashed the lights through the open curtain. Wade arrived in moments and was let in. The obvious camera cases with the backpack meant no reason for anyone to question the padded "suitcase" that held the rifles.

"There's a tub, but no shower," Kyle told him. "Make it fast, I'm about to die from lack of sleep."

"Will do."

While Wade splashed in the old iron tub, Kyle called back.

"This is Sam."

"Sam, Kyle. I've got our hotel info."

"Go ahead." Sam was reticent but alert, and sounded competent. Kyle gave him the address and rough directions.

"Okay, I'll be there in four hours," Sam said.

Kyle bathed after Wade finished. Water cooled quickly in the metal tub, and it just wasn't efficient to get clean while sitting in water with soap and sweat in it. But it was what was available, and better than the last assignment. He scrubbed and got out. Shaving wasn't necessary, he could do that later. In fact, three days of beard made him look very unmilitary. He toweled off and headed for bed.

Wade looked up from the laptop. "Sleep until ten, then go looking?"

"What time is it now? Six? Yeah. That's when Sam gets here, anyway."

10

THEY WEREN'T WELL-RESTED AT TEN, BUT WERE FUNCtional. Kyle knew it was a false feeling of refreshment, but he could go another twenty-four hours at this point if he had to.

Sam was waiting in the car, and drove them to a nearby café. "Morning," he said. "Sorry things are screwed up. The boss is feeling guilty over it."

"Why him? We're the ones who lost track of the truck," Kyle said, disgust tingeing his voice.

"You followed them this far and fought off pursuit. I'm impressed," their host said.

Sam was short, shorter than Cafferty, and softly overweight rather than fat. He had freckles and reddish hair and might be thirty. What he was beyond a general factotum hadn't been said. But he sounded as if he knew what was happening.

"Still," Kyle said, "I'd like to succeed at least half the time when I'm given a location and target. Dunno about Wade."

"Oh, count me in on the frustrated side," Wade said. "I know I should be philosophical about it, but . . ."

"Yeah, we've been having that for years," Sam said with a grimace. "But we'll get there."

They ate brunch at the café, loading up on pastries and tea. Sam made a big show of pointing out sites on a map and suggesting "photo angles" for them. It was likely a meaningless cover, but it couldn't hurt. It wasn't so much the government they were worried about, sluggish juggernaut that it was, but that if someone saw three American men talking without a good explanation, they'd be suspicious to the terrorists, if they had observers around.

They split afterward, Sam heading for the bus stop that would take him back to Bucharest, and the snipers to the car, another Audi. They made another tour of the village, up and down streets, looking closely at garages or alleys that might hold a large truck. They found nothing.

"Place looks like it's frozen in the nineteen fifties," Wade said.

"Yeah. Let's go rest and think." Four hours' sleep after a grueling drive and shootout had not been enough.

They'd just entered the room when Kyle's phone buzzed.

"Monroe," he answered.

"Yeah, it's Cafferty. Got anything?"

"Replacement car. Nothing on the bad guys."

"Damn. I'm going to see about some satellite imagery. Probably a waste, but I've got to spend the money to be sure."

"Any word from our friends at sea?" Kyle asked.

"No. Or rather, nothing new. Near as we can tell, that truck was definitely the shipment."

"Damn," Kyle said. He was saying it a lot, but it fit.

They went back to the room and napped. While being cooped in a hotel had been a drain on them before, it was a chance to rest now. Once the action started, Kyle didn't have any trouble adapting to the local conditions. They'd been up all night, and now they needed rest. With years of military experience, all he had to do was lie down and shift against the pillow. He was out at once.

He woke two hours later, head spinning slightly but in far better shape than he had been. Once fed another meal, he should be back to himself again. Wade was stirring but still dazed, so Kyle left him alone to wake up gradually. Meanwhile, he grabbed the books they'd been using for reference and resumed reading. More intelligence was always a good idea; there wasn't much else to do and he liked reading. Some people thought he read too much.

As with their last mission, they had tour guides and phrase books. While not in-depth, they were excellent for getting an overview in simple terms and for hitting the high points. They had several different ones, from little pocket-size language summaries to atlas-size map and photo collections.

Kyle leaned back against the bed and flipped open one of the little pocket guides. It mentioned the castles in the area, here and at Braşov, then others elsewhere. There were crude, unscaled floor plans that were hard to read on a page three inches high, and rough historical and "Did you know?" sidebars to provide dinner conversation.

As he read through the section on Bran Castle, a phrase in the book caught his eye. Then another one. They connected, and an idea formed. It was insane, and he had to run through it twice with the same solution to decide it wasn't as crazy as it might seem. There was a lot of sense to it. Also a lot of insanity.

Wade yawned and stretched. "Think I'm done sleeping," he grumbled deeply. It was one of the few times Kyle could recall him being less than cheerful.

"Well, then get up, sleeping ugly."

"Right. I can't say you're my prime choice of roommates, either. You snore. Off key. Without any rhythm."

"I'm white," Kyle said.

"Ah, yes. You know how you can tell if a machinegunner's white?"

"No, how?" he asked. This should be good.

"He fires a burst of six. A burst of seven. A burst of five. A burst of six."

"That's obscure," he said. The joke had to do with white men and rhythm.

"Hey, it's hard to make fun of people who are that boring."

"No argument here," Kyle said.

He picked up his phone and called again. Cafferty answered, and Kyle asked, "Any word on the truck?"

"No, nothing."

"Okay, can you tell me where you've seen it?"

"Bran, Braşov, Codlea, Râşnov, Zărneşti, and Fundata, and then it disappears. Evasive turns and then gone."

"But always in this area?"

"Yes," Cafferty confirmed. "We've seen them up there, but we're not sure where. It has to be somewhere up in the mountains, because we've kept a good eye on the town."

"We'll stay here today," Kyle decided. "Tonight we'll look around."

"Got some ideas?" Cafferty asked, probing.

"A couple. Nothing concrete yet, and I don't want to get your hopes up." *And I don't want you thinking I'm a loon*, he thought to himself. "I'll give you an update when I have one."

"Thanks."

After they disconnected, he turned to Wade and said, "I need some supplies. Back soon."

"Oh? What are you going to—"

But Kyle was already out and didn't reply. A brief walk took him past three little shops.

It wasn't hard to find a more detailed map of the area, as well as a guide and another, larger floor plan of the castle. Everything was set up for tourists, so all the books were in Romanian, French, English, and German. Some were in Italian and Russian. But the ones with English content were all he was interested in. Of course, being tourist oriented, most of them lacked proper scales and details. But familiarity was necessary, even if it was incomplete. He paid in cash and hurried back.

"Whatcha got?" Wade asked as he charged in.

"Log on, please, and do a search for Castle Bran."

"Okay. I see you have more guidebooks," Wade said.

"Yes. I was thinking about secret passages underneath."

"Secret . . . Man, you've flipped."

"You think so?" Kyle asked with a grin. "Because according to Lonely Planet, there's a labyrinth of passages concealed by the fountain in the courtyard."

"Really?" Wade asked. He looked stunned.

"Really. Abandoned and not used. Not much more information than that, which means no one goes there."

"Search engine says . . . passageways." He clicked several links into other windows and explored for several minutes. "No maps. Lots of mentions. A couple of bad photographs from people who went in a few feet."

"Jackpot."

"You really think they're hiding in the castle?"

"I'd do it," Kyle said. "It's creepy, intimidating, and the local staff are predictable. That makes it easy to be discreet. Then there's those passages underneath, that are just closed off and ignored. The staff *never* goes there, or there'd be mention and maps. No one else can get down there, and anyone who does can be easily removed and hidden. Wouldn't be surprised to find a few bodies down there when we go in."

"*When* we go in? Man, you are nuts!" Wade said.

"If there's nothing there, we've got nothing to be afraid of," Kyle said, wishing he believed it. The whole thing was creepier than all hell. But it was logical, if he could accept the logic. "If there's something there, we need to observe at the very least, snatch someone, or make a kill."

"And if we wind up as more of those bodies? What then?"

"Then zey dreenk our bllluuud!" Kyle replied in a sonorous voice, hoping he could reassure himself.

"Right. Actually, if I *were* hiding down there, I think I'd deliberately drain a few bodies just to scare others away," Wade said.

"Yes, that's possible," Kyle pondered. "Anything that will scare the shit out of people and is so ridiculous no one else will believe it. So we want a camera, weapons and IR. There's no ambient light at all for starlight."

"And body armor and a neck guard and garlic . . ." Wade added.

"So, I need to call Cafferty and tell him."

"He's going to think you're nuts," Wade said.

"Probably."

"*I* think you're nuts."

"Hell, we're both nuts to be in this job."

"Yeah, but that's a good kind of nuts. Your way is just weird."

"Right," Kyle grinned as he punched the phone.

"Cafferty," was the answer.

"Mick, this is Kyle. What do you know about the passageways under Castle Bran?"

"Under . . . nothing other than that they're sealed off."

"Yeah, well apparently you can get in. There's a kid online with some pictures, and mention of them three or four places. Everyone knows they're there, but no one goes down there."

"And you think that's where they're hiding?"

"Who'd look there?" he asked, just as he'd asked Wade.

Cafferty paused for a long moment. "Damned good point. If there's rooms or caverns, they could have operations there, not be seen on satellite or by plane, not have much chemical leakage . . . I think you're on to something."

"We're going to check it out tonight," Kyle said, thrilled at the validation of his theory, and trying to cover up his nerves. "Unless you want us to wait?"

"That depends. Can you do it discreetly, without making an incident?"

"That's the plan. I'm not going to shoot any doors open or crack any walls. If we can't find anything without making a mess, we'll come back and let you know."

"Go ahead, then. I'll make a note of it right now. When will you check in?"

"Dunno. The phones won't work under there, I'm sure. Figure no more than twenty-four hours or there's a problem."

"Understood. Call me with anything whenever you can."

"Will do. Out."

Turning back to Wade, he said, "You know, one of the big problems is transport. We have to have a car to hide the weapons in, instead of taking them on trains or in taxis . . ."

"But we can't find parking spaces for cars like we can in America," Wade supplied.

"Right."

"We also can't add too many more men, or it becomes an obvious military operation," Wade said. "This really isn't an Army job."

"Yeah, I know," Kyle said, and was quiet again. Less screwed up than last time, but still a mess.

Wade interrupted with, "So how do we get into the castle? Try to get in on a tour and slip off somewhere?"

"That's possible," Kyle said. "I'm sure we could do it. But there's a lot of risk of being seen, or locked in. I think we should try from outside, through that entrance in the park. If we can get in, we should be able to get out, and it's outside, so we can make a little noise if needed."

"I have to wonder why that's there. I mean, it's too close and too obvious to be an escape route."

"Dunno. Maintenance for the well, maybe? Or . . ." he paused for a moment, ". . . set with traps to stop people who think they're smart. Or at least it is now if it wasn't before."

"That's a good bet," Wade said. "And if there are nasties down there, they're almost certain to have thought of that."

"So we'll take it under consideration."

"Tomorrow night, then?"

"No. Now. They could get more reinforcements. Let's get the weapons and move."

"Roger that."

They gathered up cameras, weapons, water, and snacks. They dressed and carried gloves to go with their boots, and darkened their faces slightly with paint. "Not real camo, just enough to dull our faces down, so we can wipe it off in a hurry and blend back in as civvies," Kyle said.

"Got it. Though I doubt many civvie backpackers are out this late with weapons," Wade said.

By 1 A.M., they were sneaking toward the entrance in the park, armed and ready.

"We don't want to spook the neighbors' dogs," Wade said. There were houses within a quarter mile of the castle.

"We'll just have to be slow and quiet." It occurred to him they should have asked for more backup for insertion. It was risky to walk all that way equipped as they were, but the car, as he'd noted, would be visible. The parking lot for the castle was a bit obvious. The roads lacked shoulders for even "emergency" parking.

"That's the plan," Wade agreed.

They were both wearing British combat smocks under their trench coats. BDUs would have been more familiar, but anything that might confuse others as to who they were was a plus. The rucks they wore were small, dark, civilian-style daypacks made of heavy ripstop nylon, and contained cameras and batteries, plus infrared light sources to be used once they were inside the tunnel. Kyle had his Ed Brown, with the Ruger slung under his arm inside his coat. Wade had his Beretta and the AK, stock folded, under his coat. The pistols were accessible on their belts; the rifles weren't easily deployable under the circumstances.

The forest was familiar terrain, being temperate deciduous second growth. Both men were well experienced with it. They flowed through the brush and widely spaced trees smoothly enough that had anyone seen them, they would have thought them wraiths. It was an irony they couldn't appreciate under the circumstances.

11

WITHIN AN HOUR, THEY WERE HUNCHED IN THE shadows near the stone-haloed door. Kyle gestured to Wade, who nodded back and eased closer, low to the ground and under the shadows created by the sickle crescent of moon. He nodded and disappeared into the dark entrance.

Then it was Kyle's turn, through the thin trees and mud and down into the culvertlike passage.

Wade had a tiny glowstick in hand, which lit the hole brightly to NVGs. His face was ghastly in green, his goggles bulbous in front of his eyes.

"Here," he hissed. Kyle slipped closer and looked where Wade was pointing.

There was a threshold. It appeared that someone had broken in in the past and removed the bottom panel of door to gain access. The damaged door had been blockaded as an expedient fix, but it looked fairly easy to climb over. Or at least it would have been without rucks and weapons.

Shortly they were up and inside, stepping on each other and pulling each other in. And inside was totally black ahead of them.

"Let's use the IR lights," Kyle said in what he thought was his softest whisper. It echoed in the confined space into something menacing and macabre-sounding.

Wade said nothing, but in moments they both had tiny lights with filters for IR frequencies clipped to their goggles, illuminating the way ahead without letting anyone not similarly equipped know of their presence. He slipped the glowstick into a pocket.

The passage ahead was carved from stone—narrow, low, and musty. It would be a slow walk at a crouch to get anywhere. Not only was it just wide enough for one person but not two, but the rock was cold and damp.

"You first," Kyle said. Wade's AK was a better weapon if they ran into trouble, being able to put out enough fire to let them retreat. That was Kyle's rationale. It wasn't fear. He told himself so again.

Wade eased forward in a duckwalk, then rose to a slight crouch. They were both going to have very sore spines and knees before this was over, Kyle decided.

Around them, the walls turned to bedrock rather than laid stone. They were well into the hillside. Ahead, the passage widened for what was probably the elevator shaft that had been built in the 1920s. A hasty, nervous glance behind showed the space over the door to be a tiny sliver just visible with night vision. Kyle wondered briefly what it would have been like first tunneling this, then moving through it by torch or lantern light, and shivered.

The shiver was due to the cold. He told himself that.

Shortly, they came to the dead end, which had an arch over a shallow recess. Or so it seemed until they got right up to it.

"Well shaft," Wade whispered, and again it echoed off into hisses and laughs. Kyle clamped down on his guts. Christ, this was creepy.

Without speaking, they squeezed side by side and looked up and down. Across from them there were elevator controls, which the books said had been installed by Queen Marie in the 1920s.

It took only a moment to determine there was nothing down lower. The shaft above went quite high, and nothing could be seen in the low light sources they had.

Wade leaned very close and whispered in Kyle's ear, "Do those controls look nineteen twenties to you?"

"No," Kyle replied, and felt ripples up his spine. "And that wiring is newer, too. Much newer." The wires were ripped out and it was obvious the elevator hadn't worked in some time. Leaning back, there was little to see ahead in the IR illumination. The light source was only good for about ten meters, and there was nothing in that range except elevator supports and rock. But beyond that, high up, was a faint glow that might be from a side passage. "See that?" he said.

"Yes," Wade answered.

He spoke again. "I dunno, Ceauşescu brought chicks here to screw? Had a secret torture chamber he inherited from Vlad? What do we do?" He hated to stop talking. The echoes were bothersome when he did.

"I suppose we go back and have Cafferty do a check," Wade

murmured almost inaudibly. The echoes were getting to him, too. Soft voices actually resounded less than the sibilance of whispers.

"Check for what? With what?" Kyle asked. All they'd found so far was a hole, which everyone already knew existed. There was light up above. That light hadn't been on for eighty, thirty, or even ten years.

"I hate to think what you're going to say next," Wade said.

"We ground our gear and climb," Kyle said. "Me first." Then he gulped, because he really didn't want to do it, but there didn't seem to be anything else to do.

"Thanks, buddy," Wade replied.

"Don't mention it," Kyle said. It wasn't what he wanted to do, but it made sense. They had to take a look, and there was nothing legitimate up there. Add in the disappearance of shipments in this area, and the mystique involved in "Dracula's Castle," and you had a great place to hide stuff where it wouldn't show at all. Even though it had been only an administrative center and may not even have been visited by Vlad, there was a fear associated with the place, and it was far more secure than any building in town.

With gloves and boots, the elevator rails and rock, it was quite practical to do a modified chimney ascent, legs splayed in front and behind and using hands to grip. It was a technique they'd both had to do before, and the dark helped in that it was hard to notice the drop below. But the creep factor was still very much there, seeing everything in monochromatic green and for only a few feet around.

Even with gear grounded, they were still loaded down. They needed their vests for cameras, pistols, batteries for night vision, and water. Under their arms they had slung their rifles, and another pocket held spare magazines for each. They'd considered leaving the rifles at the bottom, but there was no guarantee they'd return that way, and both wanted weapons with them even if it was awkward.

There definitely was light above. Kyle paused, swallowed and waited. Was that light from something in the courtyard far above? Or was it from a level between his current position and the top?

Very carefully, he drew a hand free from the rail and tilted his goggles back, smearing his cheek with dust and moss as he did so. Below him, Wade shifted slightly but waited without complaint.

It was a side passage, about another twenty feet up, and there was a dim glow as from under or around a door. It was on the far side of the shaft.

Taking a slow, deep, measured breath, he lowered his goggles and looked down at Wade, who nodded back. He'd seen it, too. And he looked downright scared.

There was nothing to do but resume climbing. Whatever was there had been built by people, and the worst threat was bullets or stupidity. The location was a mere coincidence, or chosen for fear factor, and it wouldn't do to let it overrule logic.

So he kept telling himself.

Two minutes later, he came almost level with the passage. Straining his neck, he tried to see.

Well, there was a door there, but the light coming in underneath it glared enough to make it hard to discern much else. There was no one waiting for them, of that Kyle was certain, and that helped a lot. Gingerly, he started crabbing sideways around the shaft, taking another two minutes or more to get directly below the opening. There was a tense moment when the rifle twisted under his coat and wouldn't unsnag. He couldn't move his arm, and didn't dare try to slide backward against his other arm, because he could feel his left foot slipping slightly.

Gritting his teeth, he rolled his body to free the rifle and coat, straining to hold himself in place with one foot, a weakly placed hand, and his butt. His Camelbak sloshed water and shifted on his shoulders. He hoped it didn't rupture and spill, though it was of very tough construction.

Then his arm came free, pulling the fabric with it and scraping the rifle across his ribs. But he could climb again.

He rose until he was level with the opening, then grasped the edge with his left arm and swung into the hole. There was just enough room for him to stand and leave a bare space for Wade.

Wade slid in, panting from exertion. The sweat evaporating from him could be felt as a fog. Kyle wondered why he wasn't as worn, then realized he was. He had sweated through to the coat and hadn't realized it. It was a cold, greasy sweat.

They were almost face to face, and had to be careful of each others' goggles. Wade whispered, "So what now?" Echoes sounded.

Kyle felt for a knob or handle. There was an old style latch, and the door was heavy timbers. It was rectangular but not neat, and had heavy iron rivets holding it together. The latch moved under his thumb, grinding and squeaking.

"We really need to look first," he said as he released it. "But I'm not sure how."

Wade looked around, the goggles poking like a pig's snout. "I'll bend sideways," he said. "You hold my legs and I'll look through one of those cracks at the bottom."

"Right," Kyle said, glad it was Wade's suggestion. He sure as hell didn't want to do that.

Kyle flattened against the door, legs wide. Wade bent over and braced a hand against the far side, then raised a leg. Kyle caught it and held it, with the sudden realization that a mistake would cause them both to drop somewhere around sixty feet. He leaned as hard as he could against the door.

Wade slowly straightened back up and stood. "Hallway, doors," he said. "No sign of people in hallway."

"So let's go in. There can't be anything honest in there. Assume enemies and shoot if needed. But only if needed."

"Roger that. Wish I'd brought wooden bullets."

"Yeah, me, too."

The latch was stiff and rusty, and so were the hinges. It was lucky, Kyle thought, that the door opened inward, or they would have had to swing around it over empty space to get in. But it moved at a push and groaned. Steeling himself, he eased it inch by grumbling inch so as to keep the racket minimized.

Inside was lit, but it was only due to the time they'd spent in total blackness using goggles that they could see at all. It was a bare glimmer from ahead.

Once there was room to squeeze between the wooden door and the rock, Kyle did so. Wade followed at once and they eased it back into place. It made a little less noise, and Wade placed a hand on one of the hinges to absorb the vibration. There was good news in that; it meant the wooden slab wasn't moved very often, so no one came through this way.

And that, Kyle thought, indicated another entrance elsewhere.

The passage they were in was another one tunneled into the rock and irregularly arched. Ahead a few feet, chambers were visible to both sides. Beyond that were alcoves and the doors Wade had seen. There had been lightbulbs here at one point, hung from the low ceiling in cages. The place seemed for all the world like a freezer, submarine, or execution chamber.

Communicating with signs and expressions, the two snipers unslung their weapons from inside their coats, reattached the quickdetach slings and moved noiselessly forward. They stayed on opposite walls, clearing the area ahead and across by eye, feet placed step by cautious step with a hand running along the wall for stability and tactile input. As they neared the two side passages, they slowed to a creep.

Wade gave Kyle a thumbs-up; his side was clear of anything threatening. So Kyle returned the gesture and stepped across the bare two feet of space to the other side and into the entrance. His IR light was still on, and he dropped down his goggles.

Weapon low and ready, he took careful, measured steps, raising his feet high enough to avoid catching on any protuberances. The walls were drier this high up, halfway to the castle, and were dusty but with little mold or moss.

The side passage opened into a pit, and Kyle recoiled mentally at once, trying not to do so physically. *OhmyGod* ran through his mind, and he gulped hard as his stomach flopped.

Bodies. Rotten ones.

A shiver shook him from toes to head, then his brain caught up with his visceral response. The top layer was two recently dead adult males, local-looking and scruffy, emaciated and pallid. One had had his throat cut, the other had been shot through the head. Someone had dumped them here to hide them. The smell was just starting to rise.

Below them, however, were older bodies reduced to mostly gristle and bone, and below that was a pit of bones, hacked and broken and still wearing moldered rags of fabric and leather. One skull had a diamond-shaped hole from a sword thrust through it. The bones were old and blackened. Even in night vision, the cut ends were dry and withered. They'd been dumped here decades, even centuries earlier.

Just what every home needs, he thought, *a pit to hide the bodies in.* He took a quick scan around to determine there was nothing else, just the bones in a chamber about ten feet across and quite some depth. That determined, he backed out slowly. He turned to keep both the pit and the main passage in sight, and skittered back to where Wade was. He nodded and waved Wade in the other direction.

Wade nodded back, his face a tight mask, lips and teeth clenched, and stepped into the other passage. He disappeared in a moment.

Kyle sweated. His eyes scanned the door, the rough-hewn corridor, and the dark shadow that led to the bone pit. It seemed to open wider and reach for him. He knew it was irrational, but he couldn't help it. He shuffled back against the heavy door and hunkered down.

Movement! He clutched at the rifle and swung it up toward the flicker he'd seen.

Then something tapped his shoulder.

Bats. It's got to be bats, he thought. Another motion flashed and he stared hard at it.

Water drops.

Right. Cave, water drops. Reasonable. He tried to let out the breath he was holding and couldn't. It wasn't the dark, or the rock, or the enclosure, or the bodies, or the mystique of the old castle and its sociopathic, larger-than-life former resident, or the fact that terrorists who wanted him dead had likely been here within the last few days and might be here now waiting to kill him.

It was all of that combined. He wasn't too macho to be afraid, and this was a jackpot of triggers. And Wade, his partner and what felt like the only human being in this world, was out of sight.

What was taking so long? Either there was something extensive back there, or Wade had run into trouble. He was shifting his feet, hesitating and wondering if he should follow, when the shadows shifted and Wade reappeared. He smiled, showed a thumb, and waved Kyle over.

They swapped places, shuffling around each other, and Kyle stepped into the tunnel.

It was only an alcove, about ten feet deep. Kyle scanned around and saw no signs of any opening. There was a slight depression at the end, about three to four inches deep at a guess, and it was wet.

Suddenly he was trying not to laugh hysterically. There was absolutely nothing here but a small depression, and Wade had taken a moment to relieve his probably considerable bladder pressure. It wasn't necessarily a great idea, as it did leave evidence. On the other hand, when a man's got to go, a man's got to go. And anyone familiar with the tunnels wouldn't bother coming down an obvious dead end that had never been put to any purpose.

Kyle had a gallon or so he needed to lose, too. He took the chance while he could, trusting Wade to guard his back.

Then he turned and walked back out, shoulders brushing the narrow walls. He grinned, Wade grinned back, and they resumed their search much more comfortably.

Farther along, the stone had a smoother, neater finish and the walls were wider, enough for two people to pass. The caged bulb sockets were still empty, but the light from ahead was getting brighter, and there were noises.

The first one made them freeze and drip cold sweat. They stood stock still, straining to hear anything else. An eternity later, there was another one. It was a soft, low sound. Kyle leaned far over to put his lips almost in Wade's ear to keep the echoes down. "Sacks being stacked."

Wade nodded. So there was someone here, and they'd want to get a look without being seen themselves.

Kyle realized it was getting quite late. It was near 5 A.M. now, and they were a solid thirty minutes from the entrance they'd used, even allowing for the fact that they knew the route and could travel much faster on the return. They were likely even farther from another potential exit. There was no way to use the cell phones or radios in here, and they had a deadline less than eighteen hours away, which sounded like plenty, but if they had to hide here . . .

The only good part of that was that eventually someone would be looking for them, and probably in force. Though Kyle would prefer to get out on his own feet, and soon.

Two doors to the left were barricaded. Kyle saw no reason to try to force them yet. Both were about four foot high, two foot broad, and made of heavy timbers. They had various initials and graffiti carved into them in Cyrillic, so someone had been down here since the Communists moved in. That was after World War II.

They crept forward, the passage twisting down and to the left. Wade stuck an arm out and Kyle stopped, waiting. He took a sniff and grimaced. He could smell a combination of sewer, chemicals, and mustiness. Something was down here.

Ahead, just visible around the curve, there was a sizeable cavern. It might be eight to ten feet high. It was lit from within, and that was the light that had filtered some hundred feet up and around to the entrance. Kyle had known that about caves but never experienced it: A little light went a long way when there was nothing to interfere with it.

He paused to consider the tactical situation for a moment. What they wanted to see was likely in that room, as was any potential exit. It was lit brightly by fluorescents, the hallway was not. So unless someone came into it they should be invisible in shadow.

He sank to his knees and then flattened his body for a crawl. He indicated for Wade to follow and get photos.

12

THEY GOT WITHIN FIFTEEN FEET OF THE OPENING AND waited there, watching. The room was nearly rectangular, about twenty feet deep by forty feet wide, and had a concrete floor painted gray. How and why someone had gone to the effort to do that was a puzzle, but Kyle chalked it up to the Soviet influence. What had been down here was a matter for speculation, but there were scars on the walls where equipment or possibly shackles had been attached. Perhaps being dragged down under one of Dracula's castles, shown a pit full of moldy bones and assured that screams could be as loud as one wished and unheard was a good way to break people's wills.

Actually, he reflected, it had done a good job on his own will, and he'd come here voluntarily. What poor bastards had come into these passageways, and why? Someone who slept with an apparatchik's wife? Someone who refused to let his wife sleep with an apparatchik? Or drug dealers and black marketeers? And had just enough echoes of screams made it into the courtyard above to maintain the legend and keep people away?

Or was it all in his mind, and this nothing but an ancient hideout like those in thousands of other castles, carved by some nutcase with too much money, and now in use by terrorists?

Movement! His field of view was limited to what was directly across from him, so it was only when people moved into that area that he could discern anything.

Six people came past, carrying crates. All were male, all likely from this area, as they were dark-haired and dressed in local style.

The digital camera Wade had didn't beep; it had been modified not to. It made no sound as he snapped a photo, then another. Assuming they got out of here without too much harm, they'd have a wealth of intel about the labyrinth and its occupants.

The men within were muttering and talking. Kyle could only half hear it, and recognized some of the vocabulary that was similar to Spanish.

One of them, tall and with long hair, was saying what translated to, "... glad ... load ... finished ..."

Behind him, a shorter, burly one replied, "... take it ... again ... distribute."

A third, carrying only one crate to the others' two each, said something along the lines of, "Shut up ... carry ... quick."

Wade crawled down next to Kyle and whispered, "Positive ID on Logadze and Florescu. Do we shoot?"

"Now's when I wish we had a grenade," Kyle hissed back. "We'll wait for a moment."

It was a tough call. They had a limited window, six targets and it was a lighted room at close quarters. They could come out shooting and trust to speed and surprise to avoid return fire, but the fact was that they didn't know what else was in the room. There might be nothing to hide behind. From here, they could shoot easily at anything in view and trust to their own skill to nail anyone who tried to get into line of fire to shoot back. Of course, one of the others might lob a grenade of their own down the tunnel. That would end things rather quickly.

We're snipers, Kyle decided. *We shoot calmly and methodically, not toe to toe, like a cop movie.* He indicated his intent to Wade with a hand, and snugged the weapon against his cheek. As soon as he got a decent shot with more than one target in the field, he'd take it.

There came the sound of scuffling sacks or crates, probably the crates they'd been carrying. The mutters continued, but more softly, and then the "squad," as he thought of them, trooped back past, heads down and intent on the job. Kyle shifted slightly and caught the first one in the scope's reticle.

The Ruger was theoretically almost silent. But in the tight confines of the passageway, the muzzle pop was a healthy crack that echoed.

"Oh, shit," he muttered, knowing what was to happen. "Back!" he hissed over his shoulder to Wade, bumping his head.

They shimmied back as fast as they could, while Kyle's target crumpled, the bullet having punched into his skull to pulp his brains. But the other five scattered and were obviously reaching for weapons, then shooting, and the passageway was a straight shot with no bends between the opening and the snipers.

Kyle realized that the best option still sucked, because it was to stand and shoot fast, hoping to disrupt their response.

He quickly raised the rifle again and started snapping off shots as fast as he could get targets. Wounds were more important than kills right now. Any hit would hopefully slow a man enough for a second shot to be effective. But any hesitation would leave Kyle and Wade exposed to full-bore military rounds that would go through both of them, or ricochet into them from the walls. They were in a bad position for any kind of defense. He hunkered down as low as he could, hugging the ground for what cover it provided.

"Over my shoulder," he said to Wade, hoping Wade would understand.

His third shot clipped an arm, and a yelp of pain sounded ahead.

Then an incoming hail of fire erupted from one of the figures, the muzzle flashes bright as he swung into view of the tunnel. The clatter of the bolt and the bangs of the rounds were concentrated by the close quarters into a deafening, echoing boom like that of a nearby thunderclap.

It took a moment for Kyle to react, and that moment was a good thing. There was nothing to do but stay low and return fire. He'd been in this position before. Sometimes, the doctrine of "keep moving" was not the best advice.

He realized that most of the rounds weren't that close. They were aimed at torso height, and that was a good two to three feet above him. Okay, so that was close, but he wasn't going to think about it even as he flinched. They hadn't hit him yet.

Nor, apparently, Wade, who took that moment to lay the barrel of the AK over Kyle's left shoulder and cap off three rounds.

After the shattering noise of the incoming fire, the suppressed bangs of the 7.62 rounds were inaudible, even though Kyle felt the suppressor dance against his collarbone. He wondered if any of the hearing damage he had was permanent, but only for a moment. That was something he had no control over, and there were more immediate concerns that required his attention.

Like that gunner, who was nicely within his field of view. He adjusted his aim slightly and commenced shooting. Four rounds ripped through throat and face, and with a gurgling scream audible between catastrophic crashes of fire, that man ceased being a threat and became a mere statistic.

The remaining four were not yet statistics. Even surprised and possibly wounded, they were returning more fire. One had what was most likely a Makarov pistol, bouncing easily in his hands as he fired toward the hole. Another was armed with what looked like a Czech Skorpion. Kyle couldn't be sure, because one of Wade's rounds shattered the weapon on its way to the shooter, and the following shot blew through his chest, leaving a bright streak and arcs of hot blood and tissue visible on the scope.

Another one turned to run, a mistake in combat and his last, as Kyle and Wade both adjusted their aim and squeezed. He was hit through the back left side of the thorax with 7.62 and right under the ear with .22. Which round was lethal first was academic; both were expertly placed shots with a bit of battle luck, and he dropped like a sack.

That left two who were reaching for weapons as Kyle rose and headed into the room. He didn't feel that staying in the obvious hole was secure anymore. The floor was slightly sunken, and he pushed off with his feet, took two lumbering, stumbling steps and rolled out, panning to the left, then right to make sure his flanks were safe. That momentarily put his back to his opponents, but dammit, someone had to clear the sides. He swung back as quickly as he could, and he was too late.

Because Wade had dropped both the remaining men with shots neatly above their blank-staring faces as they turned from a weapons rack.

Or maybe not so neatly. One had half his temple blown away by hydrostatic shock.

Kyle heaved a sigh he couldn't hear. His head was spinning and his ears ringing, his nose choked with dust and his throat itching from propellant, despite the suppressors. He was panting for breath and his heart hammered. But it wasn't time for the shakes yet. There could still be hostiles here.

Wade said something that didn't register for several seconds. He had to watch his partner's lips to grasp, "I'll cover the other tunnel. You look around." Kyle nodded and did so. First things first, he removed the ten-round magazine with its remaining single cartridge and clicked a full twenty-five-rounder in place. Keeping weapons loaded was a good habit for combat. Then he let it hang from the sling and drew his .45, which was a much better weapon for this. It was powerful and suppressed, and didn't take much room to maneuver.

He slid around the room in a sideways shuffle, looking for threats or exits. There was the entrance they'd used on one wall, the west, he thought, and the one Wade covered on the north, and nothing on the other sides except some indentations of a foot or so that might have held torches or racks at some point. But the remains of metal shackles on the walls and their positions made Kyle sure people had been tortured down here. It might have been under Ceauşescu, or Vlad, or the original owners before him. But it was ugly, and there was an atmosphere here that wasn't inspired by legend, because he'd felt it when he visited Auschwitz and that mass grave in Bosnia. Call it psychic, empathic, or just superstition, places that had this feel were places of evil that Kyle didn't like.

The six bodies were the only other occupants, and there were twelve crates, all like the ones that had just come in, as well as maps and documents on a cheap card table. There was a quickly made plywood rack that had held the weapons that were now lying with or near the corpses. There were a dozen chairs stacked in one corner and a small refrigerator, its cord dangling from a light fixture, hastily wired in and taped rather than plugged into an outlet. There was obviously no electrical code enforced here. One corner of the room had a sheet of plywood as a privacy screen and contained a large bucket and a box of sanitary wipes, its purpose being obvious. Which poor bastards had to carry *that* out when it was full?

Two radios sat next to the fridge. The antenna wire seemed to run up the ceiling. Was there an old wiring conduit? Or a passage to the surface? One unit looked to be 1980s Russian surplus, but likely had the range to reach the sea. The other was shortwave, and there was also a box with a connection for a cell phone, so there might be Web access down here. Kyle made a quick try at using the cell phone hookup, but it didn't match his Iridium.

The fridge contained detonators and timers for the explosives, stuffed behind stale sandwiches. That was a good way to store them, cool and dry. Several boxes of ammo were behind it.

He circled around again, eyeballing the ceiling of hewn rock and the floor of cracked concrete. Nothing to indicate other openings. Nodding to Wade, he angled over to the stack of boxes and examined the one by itself next to the stack.

The crates were the TNT. At a guess, there were five to six hundred pounds of it here. Unless capped with detonators, it was perfectly safe and stable even if struck by bullets, but Kyle thought about his earlier wishing for a grenade and shuddered. The shock wave would have killed their targets, certainly. It would also have painted Kyle and Wade as red ooze along the walls and likely brought the castle down. He decided he was very glad for the weapons they'd chosen for this mission. And he needed to remember that these freaks used explosives in quantity, and to not get careless.

"What do we do with it?" Wade asked, getting more photos. They'd need plenty of evidence. It was hard to make out the words. Kyle's ears were still ringing.

"Soak it in water like our fathers did with firecrackers?" Kyle replied, too loudly. He could hardly hear himself. The quip was the only idea he could think of. "Too loud to hear myself think" had always been just a phrase to him. He realized it was accurate at the moment.

Nevertheless, the joke was ironic. TNT *was* stable. There was little to be done to it without chemical action. "I suppose we can toss all the crates down the shaft. They'll shatter and make it much harder to use. Then we can send someone to get it. Alternatively, we just beat feet now and keep the place under surveillance until Cafferty can get a team here."

"Assuming he doesn't want us to deal with it alone," Wade said.

"Dunno. Do we want to risk that other exit? Or go back the way we came? Our other gear is there," he said in reminder.

"I don't think anyone's going to find that stuff," Wade said. "As far as we know, no one has been through there in years. And none of it can be traced to us."

"Yeah, and we don't want to come out in that park down there while tourists are around. I think we've got to take the other way out and hope it's farther away, then report in ASAP and get backup."

"Okay. Hey, we got two kills and four supplemental. That should make people happy. Except the terrorists."

"Well, let's not waste time. We'll take all the papers, then out we go. You first, shoot if needed." They had no idea if a driver waited below for them to return, or if there was another element carrying more crates. Likely not. The operation here didn't look as if it needed many people, and between bin Laden's reckless wasting of his own people on missions, the combined work of intelligence agencies, and the precision shooting of Kyle and Wade, al Qaeda had to be running short of competent people. But there were always more volunteers, with too much religion and too little compassion and stability.

"Roger that," Wade said. They stood and walked across the room, bypassing the six cooling corpses and the other crates. The explosives would have to stay where they were for now. They gathered up the maps, charts, printed spreadsheets, and the EUR 50,000 still in the bank bands revealed in the midst of it.

"Damn. Are we going to tell Cafferty about this twenty-five thousand euros?" Wade asked.

"Does he need to know about the ten thousand euros?" Kyle replied. They both knew they were joking. They'd turn it in. That might make them suckers, but it was evidence, contaminated by the scum who'd acquired it, and they wouldn't touch it.

Under the scattered pile was a fake leather briefcase, the flat, soft-sided kind that doesn't expand. They carefully folded everything in, eyes still alert for anything else that might come through those dark, staring holes in the walls.

The way out was just another passage carved into the bedrock. Beyond the room was nothing but crude steps, long and shallow, leading up the hill. There were no lights. The passage curved right and the steps got steeper, almost too narrow and steep. Then wide again. Whether it had been dictated of necessity by the geology, was intended as a trap to delay pursuit, or was simply the work of half-mad, half-blind or half-trained masons working in the depths of the mountain, it was hard to say. Along one section, the walls tilted far to the left, causing the men to lean against the side and their boots to brush the edge of stairs and rock. There was a hill east of the castle, so they were heading that way. Compass confirmed it.

This route was definitely much longer than the one that had brought them in. On the other hand, it didn't entail a climb up a greasy, moldy shaft for a hundred feet or more. It was straightforward enough, and in ten minutes they were out.

The great advantage of the infrared and night vision, Kyle thought, was that no one should suspect them of being there.

The bottom leveled out, and there were shallow puddles here and there, as if rain had leaked in. It was straight for about ten meters, then they were at an exit, the door metal and rusty, perhaps fifty years old. But the hinges had been recently oiled. There was a tiny peephole, perhaps three inches square, through which Wade peered. Satisfied, he unlatched the door and swung it inward.

The area beyond it was thickly overgrown with weeds as concealment. A sheet of plywood protected the growth from being worn down to an obvious path.

Wade cautiously crawled out, ignoring the wetness for discretion. He was low and slow, weapon behind him but ready to deploy if needed. Kyle kept watch up high and farther back, covering the oblique. "Clear," Wade said. "There's a pile of crates here, though."

"Those stupid bastards," Kyle said, following Wade out at a crawl just in case. "What do we do about those?" It was graying dawn and would be light soon. "Hold on, first things first." He grabbed his phone and punched for Cafferty.

"Yeah, what?" was the croaked answer to the third ring. Kyle could barely hear it, but there was ringing in his ears now. They should recover.

"I'd like to report two items accomplished, Numbers Five and Three, and a sizeable amount of contraband needing immediate disposal, plus documents."

"Holy shit!" Cafferty almost whooped, awake now and happy. "Where?"

"That's the problem. Under Bran, accessible only by tunnel on foot. And we've got gear under the Queen's elevator that needs recovering. We can stay and observe for now."

"Um, yeah, you better. I'm not sure what to do about that. How much contraband?"

"Eighteen crates, approximately twenty-five kilos each. The shipment."

"And these are under the castle?"

"Yes."

"Damn. That's bad—in several ways. I can't get anyone there for several hours, and that place will be crawling with tourists in a few hours. Then there was the inquiry about your vehicle, which has been towed."

"Ah, hell," Kyle replied, though it wasn't too surprising.

"Oh, hey, I'll deal with it. You've got two items off the list. I'm all smiles here. Stay and observe as long as you can, and I'll get back with you. How's your situation?"

"We're filthy," Kyle said. "And hungry and tired. Half deaf from a firefight. We really don't want to be seen in public. There's crates outside the door here, visible to backpackers, and looks as if they were brought in by ATV." There were flattened areas and one depression that showed broad tread marks. He looked around at the forest. It wasn't as thick as it could be, and there wasn't a lot of undergrowth. The slight meadow they were in looked to be one to attract picnickers or those craving a view.

"Damn. Amateurs," Cafferty groused. "Do what you can. I'll get you covered. Let me make calls."

"Roger. Out." He turned to Wade and realized he was still wearing his goggles; Wade had removed his, leaving deep creases on his forehead. He pulled his off as he spoke. "Okay, we need one of us at each entrance, keeping an eye on things. It could be several hours, he says. If nothing happens by nightfall, I say we go back in and bring the stuff out."

"Well, the problems with that are that someone is going to miss these assholes, as unpleasant as they are, and that door takes a key from this side. So if we close it, we can't get in that way. If we leave it unlocked, anyone snooping around the crates will find it and go inside."

"Damn," Kyle replied. "I'm too tired to think straight."

"That's why there's two of us, to poke holes in each other's theories," Wade reassured him.

"Right. Well, lock it. We know where the stuff is, the bad guys do, Cafferty and his people do. There's no reason for anyone else to."

"Assuming there's anyone not plugged into those networks."

"There is that. You want to watch here, I'll trot around front?" They were both having trouble hearing, and had to face each other and talk slowly.

"I suppose. Contact every fifteen minutes?"

"Sure. Or chatter if no one's around. We need to stay awake." It had been a long night, a short day of napping, another long night and no sleep today. They'd dealt with worse, but it was still a hindrance.

Quickly, they hefted and stuffed the remaining crates into the opening, along with the plywood. They'd be invisible from above and clearly in sight from the proper angle behind the bushes, but that couldn't be helped. Wade took the briefcase and slithered off into the sparse woods to find a spot from which he could watch the entrance and the distant road far down the mountain. There was probably a trail through the undergrowth or along one of the paths, but there was no time for that now; the sun was starting to reach fingers through the trees.

Kyle sought shadow and heavy growth to shield him as he made his way around the hill. He reslung the rifle as he did so. This was observation now, not fighting. There were noises above as the staff prepared for their battle with tourists who were interested, curious, smug, arrogant, or a combination thereof.

Kyle just had to hope Cafferty moved quickly. He didn't want to stay all day. He wasn't sure he could. Despite the trees, this was a well-traveled area. It was unlikely the terrorists would return during the day.

Still, they might have connections to the staff, and, face it: If Kyle

Monroe could sneak up and get into those passages in daylight, and he certainly could, then someone else could. Heck, a Boy Scout could.

In ten minutes, the sun shouldering the trees aside to throw light at the ground, he was where he could keep track of both the entrance they'd used and the area around it.

Ideally, he'd hide near dark undergrowth or leaves in a ghillie suit that would make him all but invisible. He hadn't brought his ghillie; it was inside the tunnel where they'd dropped their packs, because he hadn't figured to need it inside, and hadn't expected to come back out a different way.

But he was a U.S. Army *sniper*, and there was no one better at invisibility. There were enough native materials to hide him and he'd make use of them. Occasional twigs and weeds he plucked as he walked, long stems of grass, a handful of leaves. All this would serve to break up his outline and cover his skin. That done, unless someone got very close or stepped on him, he should be safe.

There was a nice spot, on a slope few would want to walk, near the base of a tree. Its bark was cracked into long hexagonal scales and there were protruding roots. He slid in against it, the ground wet and cold underneath, and wiggled his feet through the weeds around it. A quick shifting of the stalks destroyed his lower silhouette, and creative arranging of a dead branch with several forks in it and some scattered leaves disrupted his upper half, which was already mottled by the British DPM camouflage he wore. Some mud on his face and more leaves on his hat left him invisible, save his eyes. He arranged the phone wires and activated it before he tucked his hands in his sleeves.

"Wade, are you there?" he asked, remembering to speak much more softly than his tortured ears thought was proper.

"Yes, and hid. There's more activity. Seems to be all backpackers. We were lucky. They come through at all hours." Kyle adjusted the volume level up enough to hear it adequately.

"Quiet here," he said. "Let's hope Cafferty hurries."

"Roger that."

"Check back in a few," he ordered.

"Will do," was the reply, then it became quiet again. He could just hear birds, and couldn't hear the breeze soughing through the fluttering leaves overhead.

He knew he napped. He was dozing in and out, waking periodically as his body protested the cold or hunger, then fitfully dozing again, to awaken to some minor noise or touch of the twigs. In this prone position, he didn't shift much, and was still well-hidden. He didn't think anyone could sneak past his watch, but he couldn't be sure. He also couldn't find enough stimulation to keep him alert. The unpleasant conditions were inadequate; he'd trained in far worse. Poking himself with sharp pebbles didn't do it. Reciting song lyrics and Kipling poems would get him halfway through the verse before his brain fried out. He gritted his teeth and forced himself as hard as he could. Numb fingers needed massaging so they'd stay useful. And his entire front was wet and shivering cold.

Tourists started wandering by as soon as the sun was well up. They acted as one would expect—laughing, joking, making creepy gestures at one another. It was always fascinating to watch people, or at least it was for Kyle. The differences between people and chimps, he thought, were very few.

They came in gaggles and trickles until 10 A.M. with nothing substantial to note. Four times, people examined the tunnel entrance, saw it was barricaded and went away. One of them was a teenager who tried to climb over, but eventually his mother prevailed upon him to not be foolish. At least that's what he gathered from the few words of German he knew.

It was just after ten when a loose dog came trotting down the slope, tongue and tail wagging in happy doggie fashion. It came straight toward him, nose shifting from air to ground.

Hell, was the only thing Kyle could think. All he could do was hope the damned dog ignored him. But that wasn't likely. Dogs were smarter than people in many ways, very literal and hard to fool. This one was a mutt, but a handsome mix of shepherd, spaniel, and some kind of hound. It didn't bark or yip, but was certainly intent on finding the person it smelled. Or maybe it was the propellant or the stench of bodies it was attracted to.

Then the dog was sniffing at him. It didn't mean any harm, obviously loved people. Like him. He didn't dare hiss or shoo it away. He just had to hope it left soon. He'd even let it pee on him to maintain his cover, but he *wanted that dog to leave.*

No good. It was determined to sniff all around him. Naturally, eyes sought the dog. And just as naturally, those seeking eyes saw shape revealed where a casual glance would not have.

The dog belonged to a youth with a family group that included parents, grandparents, and possibly cousins. They were Romanian, neatly dressed and obviously reasonably well-to-do.

Even with an inadequate grasp of the language and ringing ears, Kyle heard the teen's statement clearly: "Hey, there's a man down there!" The pointing finger was an exclamation Kyle didn't need.

In moments, other eyes focused on his face, some shielded by hands to help refine the view. Then there were shouts and comments, mostly sounding curious.

But Kyle didn't dare be questioned. There was no point in hiding further, so he rose and sprinted, down and away.

It was ironic, he reflected, that tourists and locals by the dozens would now accomplish his task for him, preventing any terrorists from getting into the tunnel at this side. He just wondered if Wade was having any better luck.

The yells and occasional nervous laughs drifted away, as Kyle spoke into his phone's walkie talkie. "I'm busted," he said. "Got to find cover."

There was a vibration, he slapped the button, and said, "Yes?"

Sam said, "I'm pulling in, about ten minutes."

"Can you make it faster? I've just lost my cover and have locals looking for me."

"Ah, shit. Yes, stand by. Maybe seven minutes."

"Which direction are you coming from?" he asked. He'd started at the northwest, was now running east and past the hill where Wade was.

"From the east," Cafferty confirmed.

"Then it'll be six minutes, because I can run a mile in that time." And maybe more. As long as he was fast, most drivers wouldn't have time to notice him and the pursuit should probably forget him.

He didn't get much notice. A few passengers in cars pointed, but all in confusion, with insufficient time to decide what exactly they'd seen. Running men were unusual, but not very, so no one paid any real attention.

A one-mile sprint is not like a one-mile run. He bounded over rocks and low walls, tree roots and bushes, through hedgerows and up and down steep slopes where he slipped and scrambled. He was breathing raggedly when a blue Mercedes ahead flashed its lights and drew to the side. Then it stopped.

He piled into the back and slammed the door. "Thanks, what about Wade?" he asked.

"We'll have him in a few minutes. He's still covered."

"Good," Kyle replied. He panted and gasped, sweat pouring off him as Sam reached down into the footwell and grabbed a bottle of water.

"Here," Sam said as he passed it back.

"Thanks," was all he could choke out. Fatigue, the run across mixed terrain, and the gear he was still carrying added up to a hefty drain on his body. He shoved aside two raincoats on the seat and sat up.

"Just rest," Sam said. "We've got time."

Kyle was still heaving for breath and sipping water in between when Cafferty called on his phone, the car pulled over again and Wade climbed in the other side, clutching the briefcase as if it were the winning game ball.

"Yo," Wade said. "Good timing."

"Yeah, just," Kyle said.

"Call the boss and tell him," Sam said. Kyle did so.

"We're in the vehicle," he reported.

"Glad we got you," Cafferty said. "Sam will debrief you. And thanks again, that was a kick-ass discovery, plus two points." Kyle noted that Cafferty never said "kill" or used any other word that was obvious. It wouldn't stop professionals from divining his meaning, but it kept casual listeners from triggering.

"Good," Kyle said. "And thanks." He disconnected and said to Sam, "You're supposed to debrief us. Can we get lunch, too?"

"Yes, I can get some takeout. What do you want?"

"Anything dead," Wade said.

"Anything meat," Kyle added. The pounding pulse in his ears was dying down, leaving a faint ringing. His hearing was almost back to normal.

"Stew or sandwiches," Sam said. "They do some good beef sandwiches around here."

"And clean clothes."

"Will do. Kyle, I need your room key."

Kyle fished it out of his pocket and handed it over. Then he took stock of his surroundings.

The car was very quiet and smelled quite new. Sam was obviously familiar with the area and drove smoothly. Kyle was nodding in a doze when they got to a local safe house.

There was a back door, and they went in that way, Wade and Kyle wearing the raincoats. It was a bit warm for them, but less obvious than filthy, greasy, and torn camouflage, canvas pants, and work boots.

Heedless of company, both snipers stripped to underwear once they were in a closed room. As soon as Sam showed up with their bags, Kyle grabbed the shirt and pants he'd worn the day before—no, two days before—and Wade grabbed a pair of sweats. "Wish this place had a shower," Kyle grumbled. As with the hotel, it had a 1950s-style tub and no shower.

"Keep the drain open and splash the running water with a cup," Sam suggested.

"Good idea. So what have we got?" Kyle asked as he sat down.

"We found the truck. Abandoned. We're working on that. Let me see the cameras, Wade, and I'll run the images."

"Here," Wade said, pulling them out of his combat vest pockets. Sam pulled out a laptop and cables, along with spare flash chips.

"I'll start on these, then go get the food. Guys, you may as well clean up now, then we can get this done and let you rest."

"Roger that," the snipers replied.

Thirty minutes later, both were clean and munching on sandwiches. They were good, Kyle decided. The bread was nutty and crusty and fresh, the beef was tasty, if overcooked, and he was ravenous. He tried not to eat too fast, gulping water in between bites. It was easy to dehydrate in the cold and not notice it.

They called Cafferty again and were all connected as a conference call.

"Pictures look good," Cafferty said, his smile almost audible. "Very good. I'm calling that two targets down. It has to be approved, of course, but I call it good. Looks to be most of this load of explosives, but I don't see any of the last shipment we think they had, so either they hid more elsewhere or they moved it quickly, which is disturbing." He paused and there was the sound of sipping coffee. Kyle suspected if he ever collapsed, they'd need a coffee IV to resuscitate him.

"How are we getting it out of there?" Wade asked. Kyle was wondering about that, too.

"Not sure yet. I might have to send you guys in to secure it better. Could mean bringing it out, blowing the rear tunnel so it stays there, or something else. I'll have to think on that. We'll need a surveillance device planted there at once, so we can follow up on anyone who comes along."

"What type of device?" Kyle asked.

"Little camera, little phone, satellite relay stateside and someone watching it for movement. Actually, movement can be determined by computer."

"Where do we get something like that?"

Sam said, "I have something like that. Several."

"We can probably do that tonight," Wade suggested.

"Yeah, should be able to. But what if the door and the crates get discovered?"

"How many were outside? Six?"

"About that," Wade said.

"We'll have you grab those. As soon as possible. The car should carry them. Sam can come and get them from you."

"Could be trouble if we get found with that," Kyle said.

"Yeah, and I want them removed ASAP. If you get caught with weapons, I'm embarrassed. If you get caught with explosives, there's just no way to put a good spin on it. We really should involve host nation at this point, but we know there's leaks in SRI, and possibly in DGIPI, too."

Those were just alphabet soup to Kyle, but he assumed Cafferty knew what he was doing.

"Well, if nothing has happened yet, I'd say we wait until midnight to go up there."

"Reasonable," Cafferty said. "That's as quiet as it's going to get. Sam, can you show them a place to park and make sure they have something for traction? Two by fours, chicken wire?"

"Can do," Sam agreed. "I'll go get some now." He slipped out, still on the phone.

"If we do this right," Cafferty said, "you load up, bring the car back and Sam will swap in the morning for an identical model. I'll have someone come ashore to dispose of the stuff."

"Okay," Kyle agreed. "I've driven in mud before. I'll be careful. Worst case, I'll use Wade for traction."

"Hey!" Wade objected.

"By sitting on the back for weight," Kyle said, grinning.

A few minutes later, Sam returned. "Wire and boards," he said. The call fees on a four-way satellite conference hookup had to be outrageous to anyone except a government.

"Good," said Cafferty. "I've done what I can. The pics are uploaded where they need to go. And you guys need sleep. Call me around eight."

"Roger that," Wade said. Kyle just nodded.

Sam pulled out the third flash chip of the day and sheared it, then scorched it. He pocketed them for later disposal.

Kyle and Wade stood, grabbed their bagged dirty clothes and followed Sam to the car.

Twenty minutes later, Sam dropped them behind their hotel and they walked inside.

"First a shot-up car, now the boxes . . . What's next?" Wade said.

"We don't want to ask that," Kyle said.

They lay down at 1 P.M. and were unconscious immediately.

13

TWO HOURS LATER, KYLE'S PHONE BEEPED.

"Monroe," he answered, head dizzy from exhaustion.

"Forget tonight, leave town now. Find another hotel," Cafferty said.

"Roger. How soon is now?"

"Don't run, but walk fast," Cafferty advised.

"Got it. Wade, wake up."

Wade rolled and stood. "Ready," he said. "What?"

"Stand by," Kyle told him. "Go ahead," he said to Cafferty.

"There are Romanians digging through the castle now, and I mean "digging." Someone found the boxes, reported a suspicious individual in camouflage and they responded. So they're likely inside the mountain now, and you brought all the documents. They've got bodies, explosives and radios."

"Oh, shit," Kyle said.

"Very," Cafferty agreed. "We need observers and don't have any."

"We're observers," Kyle said. "We can get up there tonight."

"Kyle, they're all over that mountain," Cafferty said.

"Yes, and we're trained for exactly that mission," Kyle told him. It wasn't false confidence. Intel gathering near the enemy was exactly what they were trained for. "We can get within a hundred meters if we have to, but we can do plenty from farther back. Photos, descriptions, report."

"You're really sure?" Cafferty asked.

"Positive. My cover was fine in daylight, improvised, until that dog sniffed me. Wade stayed hidden. Nighttime with prep, no one will know we're there. We train against people who expect us and we still get through. This is our mission, Mick." Better than trying to play spies in town, he thought.

"Okay, I'll trust you," Cafferty agreed. Kyle respected people who didn't try to overrule experts in their own fields. Mick seemed like a decent guy. "But you better slip for now, hole up and come back later."

"Will do," Kyle said. "We're rolling." He clicked off.

"I only caught half of that," Wade said.

"We're hiding now. There's locals on-site who were tipped off. We're going back tonight to observe."

"Roger that. I'm packed, you need to grab your personal items, and I'll warm the car while you check us out."

"Got it."

"And as the token black man around these parts, there are so many reasons I'm glad it was you who got seen and not me. No offense."

"None taken," Kyle said. He'd have to dig through that to figure out which of several ways Wade meant it.

Meanwhile they were still groggy and tired. Braşov was the nearest major town, but was far too close for comfort. The best bet was to drive to Sighişoara and get a room there. It wasn't too great a distance, but should be safe enough. It was also a tourist trap, and had Vlad's house, now converted to a restaurant.

"Shish kebab for dinner?" Wade asked. It took Kyle a moment. Meat. Stick. Funny.

"Right," he replied. "Turkish style?"

"I'm sure they've heard it."

"Probably sometime in the last six hundred years."

The town was old, and looked it, but in a picturesque way. It had winding cobbled streets, old buildings in stone and stucco, brick and board, with shuttered windows, and a cemetery on a hill. The whole town was quiet and slow paced.

"Looks good, let's find a room," Kyle said.

Once again they let themselves be ripped off as tourists, not really caring to haggle over the rates and wanting to maintain the "dumb Drac hunters" image. Wade secured the room and Kyle found a small shop and bought bread, cheese, meat, and fruit for dinner later. He could feel the bags under his eyes swelling, trying to shut them. He pushed on to a shop that was like a miniature 1950s U.S. hardware store, and bought two brown canvas work shirts, two fishing-style hats and a roll of burlap. Another little place had sturdy thread and needles and shoe dye in brown, black, and tan. He didn't get gouged too badly, and the proprietors seemed happy to chat with someone who almost knew their language. He tried to be charming and bumbling, with talk of needing an extra shirt to look around in the mountains, burlap to pack his cameras, and did they know the best way to apply shoe dye, and did he need polish afterward? His shoes were a mess and he might be going out to dinner with friends.

Half an hour later, he was back in the room with tactical supplies and food.

"We're going to have trouble with the car again," Wade said when he entered.

"Yeah. Hold on." Kyle dug out his phone.

"This is Sam."

"Monroe, Sam. We're wondering about visibility and the car tonight. Any chance you can run us by?"

"If you tell me what you need, yes," Sam said.

"Okay, pick us up here at twenty one thirty. You'll have to wait several hours for us," he advised.

"I can get a room, and I have a book to read."

"Good. Thanks a bunch, and we'll see you then. Out." He turned back to Wade. "I really hope that's the end of the prep. Five hours of sleep is going to feel really good."

"Yeah. Check out this news report," Wade suggested. He'd brought up a news Web site for Romania in English.

"Let's see," Kyle said, swinging it around. Then he started reading. It was a rather sobering report.

An incident this morning has drawn attention to the historic castle in Bran, Romania. Tourists reported seeing "a man in camouflage clothing with his face painted" hiding in brush near a hidden entrance that is often called the escape tunnel. Meanwhile, backpackers found crates stacked in a hole dug on the mountain to the east, near the entrance to what might be another tunnel. The crates are reputed to contain explosives.

Often called "Dracula's Castle," Bran Castle was originally built in the 14th century and added to six times since then. The "escape tunnel" exits in a park at the foot of the castle, and was used as an alternate exit by Queen Marie in the 1920s. At one time, an elevator descended inside the mountain, but it had been reported as non-operational.

Authorities have secured the two locations and are investigating. Cameras, climbing equipment and generator-powered lights were seen earlier today, along with Army soldiers. The castle remains open for tours, although some of the grounds are inaccessible. There is also a guard mounted at the top of the elevator shaft, just off the central courtyard of the castle.

Reporters were chased away from the scene late this afternoon, but some witnesses say they saw what appeared to be "shroud-wrapped bodies" and more crates like those said to hold explosives being removed through the rear tunnel.

"Yeah, we can do it," Kyle said. They'd observed under tougher conditions. Still, he was having doubts. He'd hate to be fingered as a suspect in this. "I suppose we can check again after we sleep."

"So stop talking and start sewing," Wade suggested. They'd have to work fast to get any sleep.

The burlap tore into strips and left dust in the air. They placed them in three piles on the newspapers and started dyeing them.

"We'll have to wash the chemical smell out," Kyle said.

"Yeah, I have an idea," Wade replied.

In the meantime, they used the needles and thread along with scrap pieces of leather as thimbles to tack-stitch the strips to the hats and shirts. They stripped to T-shirts and underwear to do it, because the dye residue was rubbing off. They were both dirty and dusty in short order. But the process was familiar, and the ghillies began to take shape, or rather, lose it. When they were done, both outfits were formless piles of black, brown, and tan that should be ideal on forest floor.

"So what's your idea?" Kyle asked.

"We wash them in the tub with several handfuls of dirt," Wade said. "Should kill the smell."

"Good," Kyle agreed. He dressed quickly and stepped out to grab a bagful of earth, carefully scraping it from a flowerbed near the quiet back entrance to the building. When he returned, Wade had the tub filling and the ghillies soaking, excess dye bleeding out and running off. When the colors stabilized, they added the dirt and agitated it, rinsed, then laboriously separated the tangled strips. They looked old and smelled musty when done.

"Got to get them dry, or at least mostly so," Kyle mumbled. "Think there's a dryer here?"

"Dunno."

The hotel did not have a dryer. There was likely a laundromat nearby, but that brought up visibility of both them and what experts would recognize as camouflage. They settled for squeezing the suits, shaking them and hanging them up on the open closet door to air dry.

"Damn near dinnertime," Wade said when they were done. "Or nap time for us."

"Yeah." Kyle pulled his jacket up over his shoulders like a blanket and lay down. It was a way he'd found of taking a nap that was comfortable and easy. Wade rolled under the covers still in his clothes. Shortly after that, they were unconscious.

Waking at 9 P.M., much refreshed, Kyle called Cafferty.

"Anything new?" he asked.

"I'm looking," Cafferty said. "They've got tech crews there. They've confirmed identity on the bodies, and so have our people. So it's official now: Nice job."

"Thank you, sir."

"You deserve it," he continued. "As you suggested, it appears they took it up there with an ATV. Several trips. Must have had it stashed in the area."

"That makes sense. Whoever had the ATV took off, and they figured it would be quiet enough at night in the mountains."

"Right. If they'd made one more trip you could have nailed them safely and been done, but you couldn't know and I'm not complaining about these freaks being taken apart by Romanian coroners and then disposed of as trash. We also found some stuff in the documents."

"Oh?" Kyle had expected they would, but he was curious.

"Not much for you yet, but we found a schedule on three more shipments on their way. Our people will deal with them at sea if possible. If not, the Romanians will be waiting for them now. I told you you'd gain us a hell of an edge if you did this."

"Okay," Kyle said.

"Which means 'thankyouthankyouthankyou.' *Mulţumesc. Gracias. Danke. Taki. Merci. Tessekur—*"

"I get the idea, and you're welcome." Kyle was smiling, though. They really had done a good job under nightmarish conditions.

"Hey, this is good news. And tell Wade, too, please."

"I will. Wade, he says 'thanks' in five languages. Confirmed targets, ATVs, and documents with leads."

Wade flashed thumbs-up and a tired smile.

"So are we still on for tonight?" Kyle asked.

"If you want to," Cafferty said. "Sam is almost up there. It's your call on doing it. We're happy with what we have so far, but will of course take more."

"So we'll get you more."

"Much appreciated. Out."

"Out."

That taken care of, the snipers plotted out their return to Bran.

"I hate to say it after all that work, I'm wondering about the camo this time," Kyle said. "Dumb tourists is how we play it. I'd rather not have the weapons at all, but we need to stash them somewhere. Maybe Sam can meet us and haul stuff."

"That's a good idea," Wade agreed. "I think we should take cameras with us. Phones yes, but don't use the radios. There's no need to put out anything they can readily ID."

"Okay. You'll have the camcorder and an IR source, I can bring another flashlight. We'll each have night vision and scopes. If we get caught, we play up the vampire legend bit, and why shouldn't we be curious about men around the castle at night? That should get us thrown in jail then out of the country in short order, as rude, snoopy American tourist idiots."

"Better that than the truth," Wade said. "Rude, snoopy American sniper idiots."

"Do you hear me arguing?" Kyle replied.

"But no camo or ghillies?"

"I'm still thinking about that," Kyle said. "If we get caught in them, we're rather obviously more than camera geeks. On the other hand, if we ditch them before getting caught, they'll be almost impossible to find. On the other hand—"

"The idea is not to be seen at all," Wade supplied.

"Exactly. Take the ghillies," he decided.

They were both ready when Sam called and said, "Outside, waiting."

"Roger, open the trunk," Kyle said.

In two minutes they were in the back seat, bulky packs between them. "Weapons are in the trunk. We'll need them again. I didn't want them left in a hotel," Kyle said.

"Reasonable. I've got them taken care of," Sam said. "We'll meet back up in the car or I'll swing by wherever you check in next."

"Okay. We need to be dropped along the north side," Kyle said.

"Sounds good. You'll bail out moving?"

"Yes, but not too fast," Kyle said. "We want to be discreet, not put our dicks in the dirt."

Sam laughed. "I was Airborne, I know what you mean."

The road curved all the way around the castle and the hill. There was one oncoming car, so Sam slowed. They wanted it past and no witnesses when they departed.

The car whipped past, he eased off the accelerator to avoid bright brake lights, and said, "Go!"

Wade was on the left and shoved the door open. He stepped out, holding onto the door and went to a full sprint before letting go. As soon as he was clear, Kyle kicked out the rucks and hopped over himself, then jumped out running.

It worked fine until his foot caught a hole and he stumbled. He bruised and abraded his knee and shin, jammed dirt into the heels of his hands and jarred his whole body, completing it with a bang to the left shoulder and head on a downed branch.

Wade was alongside at once. "You okay?"

"Superficial, hurts, help me get hidden," he said, teeth gritted. Damn, it was painful.

Wade helped him limp up behind growth so he wouldn't be seen from the road, then walked back to get the rucks. While he was doing that, Kyle's phone vibrated.

"Monroe," he answered.

"Sam here. Looked like you fell. Are you okay? I can turn around if need be."

"Minor, I can make it. Thanks for checking."

"Not a problem. Still looking at oh five hundred for a pickup?"

"Not much after that, so yes," Kyle said for clarification. "Night is safer than daytime."

"Good enough. Call if you need anything."

He pulled up his pants leg to examine the wounds. A bare flash of his light showed cut and torn skin and oozing blood, but it could manage without a dressing tonight. It would just be stiff and ugly tomorrow.

Wade came back and stacked the rucks, then added a few weeds to break up the silhouette. "Rest a few?"

"Nah, I'm ready," Kyle said, shaking off the effects. His ankle and knee ached, his shin, knee, and hands burned and stung, but he was ready to go.

They made sure no oncoming lights were visible, then darted across the road, Kyle favoring his left leg and dragging a little. In seconds they were concealed on the other side and working their way through the trees.

It was just after midnight when they reached their insertion point, far up the hill. From there, they planned to hike down and move more slowly and cautiously as they approached the castle. Eventually they'd sneak into positions and hole up, watching, taking notes, and recording. They'd exfiltrate around 0500 the same way and be picked up. Sam would take the memory sticks, tapes, and their notes, and they'd go catch more sleep, unless leads indicated a change of location.

It went as planned at first. They hunkered down in some brush and donned their ghillies. On their faces, ears, and hands they smeared camouflage grease from a compact. After checking each other over, they flowed down the hill, shadow to bush to depression to tree, always in the dark and hidden. Kyle was slightly ahead, the shape of his face broken by a black "branch" of camo paint and several brown splotches. The small ruck on his back contained his supplies for the operation, and his garb under the ghillie was drab brown, sturdy working clothes Sam had picked up for them.

Behind and to the right, Wade had a more traditional makeup of "dark on the high areas of the face, light on the low." The layman often thinks that dark-skinned people don't need camouflage, but skin is skin and it shines in light, from oil and sweat. Wade had the additional burden of the camcorder, which had a duct-taped adaptor to fit the day/night scope. The IR capability was good for only a few meters, and they needed to be much farther away than that. The hope was that the enhanced monochromatic image, thrown through the lens gap and focused by the camera would still be good enough to be subject to analysis by experts. If not, their observations and memories would have to do.

The trees were largely evergreen, with budding deciduous scattered throughout. It smelled fresh and earthy, unlike the dank, musty smell in the tunnels. Woods were scary to a lot of people, but Kyle and Wade lived a good part of the year in them. There was no artillery or armor here, the risk of being shot at was small, and they'd had a brief chance to familiarize themselves with the area the night before. All told, Kyle was quite confident despite his aching leg and figured Wade was, too.

But these woods were rather sparse, and the undergrowth wasn't much. They'd have to be careful on the approach and keep concealment in mind for the exfiltration. If they had to depart in a hurry, it was better behind brush than sprinting across open ground.

Kyle sank carefully to his knees, to avoid exacerbating his injury further or making any noise. Wade dropped down next to him and watched the other way. They took turns pulling their ghillies out of their rucks and donning them. While coats in front, the backs were bulky and thick with fabric. But that tangle of dark and earth tones was what would hide them from almost any observation.

They stayed on their knees and crawled downhill. The castle was visible now and then through the trees. They crawled through spiky dead needles on the forest floor, around branches dropped by bushes, and through damp spots in depressions, methodically and quietly. Every few trees, Kyle or Wade would rise carefully, easing around it to judge their approach.

They could hear and see quite a bit of activity. There were four pickups and two cars, and a bank of lights attached to a generator illuminating the hole. There were people present, but no numbers were certain.

About a quarter mile back, they dropped to a low crawl, slithering along like lizards. They moved in uneven zigzags, never leaving a straight line toward the site. Straight furrows were a dead giveaway, with an emphasis on *dead*. Both men were far too experienced to make that mistake.

Kyle gingerly wiggled around a dead branch, not wanting to disturb it and make any noise. It wasn't just the humans below who were a concern, who were behind noisy equipment and wouldn't find them easily; any spooked animals might rip straight past an observer and alert him to the fact that something was out of place. Terrain involved more than just ground and plants.

Once around the branch, Kyle crept up on a slight rise. If he had figured correctly, it would give him a good view.

It did. As his eyes broke the crest, he could see the vehicles again, and easily observe the people among them. Wade wasn't visible, but should be several meters away and on a different lay of land, so discovery of one wouldn't reveal the other in close proximity. He had been to Kyle's left, and a careful search showed his hand, left out for Kyle's benefit. Kyle made a very slow wave back, and both pulled in under their ghillies, becoming effectively invisible.

Kyle had the still camera, and took an initial photo from under his ghillie, through the hanging tendrils of burlap. The shot would give a good overview to try to place later closeups against. The field of view was good, but the acuity wasn't great at this distance, in mixed light. Still, the experts could dig a lot from a picture by analysis.

He withdrew a small notepad from a pocket. The pages were waterproof plastic, not paper, and would survive fairly harsh weather. He kept a tally of the personnel and made notes for descriptions for most of an hour, alternating with picture taking. Meanwhile, he was alert for any sounds, motions, or other threats around him.

The military standard report is based on the acronym SALUTE: Size, Activity, Location, Unit, Time, Equipment. He noted each section as he acquired the information. In addition to the six vehicles, there were eleven people, nine males and two females. Two were in coveralls and handling human remains. The rest were in police-type fatigues with filter masks and gloves. Two were using laptops, one inside a car and the other across a hood. Three were photographing and examining items brought from inside the mountain. Three more were seen intermittently, bringing items from inside. There might be more in there, as a cable led from the generator through the door. Location was obvious, but he wrote it down for record as "east tunnel entrance, Castle Bran, 0123 hours" and the date.

The bushes around the opening had been dug out, as had the tunnel entrance. It had obviously been buried after being originally built and left as an emergency escape route. That combined with the hideout underneath and the secret staircase inside, plus who knew what else, made this a place needing a lot of investigation for historical purposes. But science wasn't why Kyle was here. He made notes as to how the entrance had been partially cleared by the terrorists, and how it had been opened up since.

A careful look through the telephoto lens at the personnel didn't help much. There were unit badges on the uniforms, but not clear enough for him to determine. Perhaps Wade was having better luck with the spotting scope.

No one inside the circle of lights should be able to see them, and that left only the two working at laptops and one of the photographers who'd chosen to stay out of the actinic glare. He noted their positions in a sketch. Soft fog was falling into the low areas, and it hindered his observations.

The crates of explosives were not in sight, so at least the six outside had been removed. Photographers were taking pictures of one of the communication devices on the ground, set against a meterstick for scale. It wasn't a radio, and was probably some kind of encryptor or antenna booster for the cell phone, because he'd seen it attached to that cable inside. The report said the bodies had been removed, but examiners were going over several small items with gloved hands, indicating possible blood. It could also just be a precaution against bacteria, however. One woman was making notes and checking an item with a magnifying glass, turning it different ways. Kyle took a photo of that, and of each other item he could see brought out.

He had four memory sticks, so he could get 200 photos. Also, the digital camera allowed him to delete unwanted images when he acquired better, clearer ones of the same items. It kept him busy comparing and shooting. It lacked the Hollywood glamour of their last operation, but was likely as useful long term and much safer. On the whole, Kyle liked a challenge but preferred not to get shot at. It was part of the job, but not one to embrace. Soldiers who got off on that didn't live long.

Two workers came out carrying what appeared to be a body. Kyle zoomed in closer and tried to see.

It wasn't quite a body. It was body parts. He didn't recognize the specific bones in question, but the blackened skull and sheared long bones, along with cracked and dusty ribs with desiccated flakes of skin still attached had almost certainly come from the pit he'd discovered. In the available light and through the camera eye, even despite the mist, he could tell this was decades old at least, more likely centuries. Which poor, forgotten bastard had that been, and who had taken a dislike to him? Likely that would never be known.

The only good part for Kyle was that above ground, outside, he had no fear of corpses. He'd seen more than his share.

A sharp sound made him freeze, even though he hadn't been moving at the time. He went into a trained, reflexive brace and replayed what he'd heard. It had been a crack and a swish, as of someone walking through the woods. Then it came again. *Patrol*, he thought.

The only thing to do was stay motionless and trust his camo. The only real risk was that his boot soles might be visible. They were a paler tan and might glisten in the now condensing dew.

One of the keys to good concealment was attitude. It wasn't a psychic power, or at least not to Kyle. He'd heard some who thought of it that way. To him it was an attitude, a sense. Being too alert caused one to quiver and stand out to an observer even if it was only at the unconscious level. To blend in, one had to be part of the scenery. So Kyle closed his eyes for a moment and tried to think like a pile of leaves.

The footsteps were clearer now, even over the hum of the generator. He thought he heard voices, soft and low under it. They were quite close, likely within twenty meters. But there was no urgency or caution to them, as there reasonably would be if Kyle or Wade had been ID'd. The worst thing to do would be to anticipate trouble and move. That would not only reveal them, but might be perceived as a threat and earn them incoming fire . . . and not only was neither man armed, that was exactly the type of engagement they wanted to avoid. Facing nothing worse than arrest and damage to their professional pride, he knew Wade was doing exactly what he was: holding and waiting.

Movement to his left alerted him, and again he didn't react. Boots came into view and moved down the hill. In a few seconds he could see legs, four, then torsos, two in Romanian mottled camouflage. It was the older type and likely passed down from military to police. Two men carrying shortened AKs strode down the hill, talking back and forth. They turned to Kyle's right, the north, and kept walking. They were obviously trying to keep spectators out of the area.

Kyle heaved a slow, quiet sigh. They'd been within four meters of him and not seen him or Wade. Score 2 for the snipers. And keep them in mind during the exfiltration. He was able to get photos of the Romanians from behind and to the side. They probably weren't relevant to the operation below as far as useful data went, but he had the opportunity and took it. Too much data could be sorted. Too little was a problem.

The guards came by about every half hour, it seemed, taking the same route. They were obviously there to chase off tourists and weren't taking a serious look for anything. Still, it didn't hurt to be prepared. Kyle improved his camouflage by covering his boots with a few twigs. He used enough to break up the outline, not enough to make it obvious something was covered. And he tensed up every time they came by. Wade fixed his own camo, and flashed a smile as he did so, barely visible under his ghillie.

They took more photos, made notes, waited for the guards on each circuit, and ignored the cold, dampness, prodding twigs and needles, and crawling insects. It was 0347 when Kyle checked his watch. They'd like at least an hour to exfiltrate and be rolling at 0500, to be clear of any daylight or early traffic. He eased out his cell phone and punched for Wade.

It was odd to be calling someone only a few meters away, but it was safer than trying to get his attention now. He kept sight of his partner, who looked back when he felt the vibration. A quick flash of thumb acknowledged receipt, and then they were crawling back, progress measured in mere centimeters per minute.

Kyle got his NVGs back on and scanned the terrain ahead. It was clear, and they were out of line of site of the work party. A thick, spreading bush ahead of him offered good concealment. He angled cautiously around it, pausing every few movements. Even detected movement could easily be overlooked if it didn't continue for long.

He judged the distance to be far enough and rose to a high crawl. Wade moved closer, and they took long, plodding "steps," knees and hands lifted high to avoid disturbing growth. Another couple of hundred meters and Kyle decided it was safe to bunch up.

In moments they peeled off the ghillies, wrapped them as padding around the cameras, and stuffed them in their rucks. Securing the straps, they shouldered them and began to walk, bent low still, meandering through the trees and across contours. Kyle fished out his phone and punched for Sam. "We're almost to our point," he said.

"Roger," Sam replied.

Then they were heading down toward the road, still alert for the patrol or others they hadn't seen yet. They ducked and darted under the canopy and over the deadwood.

They were only a hundred meters or so from the road when Kyle saw movement and froze. Wade keyed off his act and likewise stopped. Slowly, they both sank down where they were, to minimize profile.

The movement was a person. Then a second one came into view. Young men, dark clothes, civilians. They were trying to be discreet as only untrained, overeager, self-absorbed teenagers could. Kyle cursed silently. His mind ran through options.

If the kids, who were obviously going up to spy for themselves, went past the snipers without seeing them, no problem. The patrol could handle them. If they saw either of the Americans, then they'd have to decide how to respond. They could act authoritative and try to bully the kids into submission, and Kyle liked that option, except he was clearly a foreigner. The kids might just bellow for help or try to fight. That wasn't discreet.

He could try to disable them gently, say by wrapping them around a tree, or knocking them cold, or wrestling them down, gagging and lashing them. But that would make a certain amount of noise and would definitely be considered a hostile act by anyone responding.

That left one of two options, which would likely be effective but were not very military.

The boys were heading straight for Kyle, would likely pass within two or three meters of him, so the odds of them seeing him approached certainty.

One of them spoke in surprise and Kyle was able to extract, "There's a man up there!" from it. It had been a slightly louder than conversational voice, because the teen had been nervy and working at caution, so overcompensated when jarred.

Right. Stand and walk. "Stay there, partner," he whispered, not using Wade's name where anyone might hear it. Word of foreigners at the castle wouldn't be that unique. A black man accompanying a white man, however, would be rather easy to find after word made the news.

As Kyle stepped forward, the other boy said something like, "Who are you?" and moved aside. That left a clear gap between them. Kyle intended to walk through, smile, and look triumphantly guilty at getting a glimpse of the castle before these kids had, and just keep walking. If he did it right, they'd stop, stare, and either walk away or get jealous and rush in to prove they were as good.

He was just between them when the second one, to his right, said something involving "camouflage face." That was one of the key-words from the news report. Both of them tried to close and grasp at him.

In a perfectly conversational tone but with his arms thrown out and waving wildly, Kyle said, "Boogaboogabooga!"

They stepped back for just a second, gasping, and Kyle took off in a sprint.

Noise behind him was Wade, who said something like, "I veel dreenk yoor bluhd!" as he also dug in and raced. They turned parallel to the road and headed east. Kyle unpocketed his phone once more and said, "Sam, we're blown. Pick us up on the roll," as soon as it was answered.

"Three minutes and closing," Sam said. "Windows are down for gear. I'll make a pass each way, about two minutes apart."

"Roger that," Kyle said. "Stay on air." He clutched the phone and resumed dodging as a dog nearby started to bark. There were houses here and there, with perhaps three dim lights showing through the curtains of early risers. He really didn't want any more witnesses.

Behind him, he heard the youths shout in confusion, and behind them came shouts that had to be from the patrol.

Actually, Kyle thought, it might work out well. The two guards would catch the kids, and be unlikely to split forces over allegations of two men already leaving. They'd prefer to believe they were competent and that no one had gotten past them, that their captives were trying to be clever, and that all was well. They'd congratulate themselves over a simple collar and never suspect their perimeter had been broached going in and coming out.

He saw the illumination of lights ahead on the road. There was a car behind coming up the hill, and he raised the phone. "Is that you?" he asked.

"I think so," Sam said, sounding tense and amused. "Slowing."

"Roger."

Wade bounded in alongside, then they were both running straight at the road then parallel along it in a rough gully. Kyle was cautious for his feet. His right leg was hurting like hell now.

"Cross over," Sam said.

"Wade, go," he pointed. Wade was on the other side in two seconds, and as Sam rolled past, he tossed his ruck through the rear window and dived in behind it. The car picked up speed and moved far ahead of Kyle, then over a ridge.

Kyle kept going at a run. He was doing a lot of running on this mission. He figured it would be another five hundred meters before Sam turned. Two minutes. That would put him well away from the castle grounds.

He dodged obstacles of rock, timber, clumpy grass, and holes. There were pieces of the edge of the road missing, that had tumbled off the side and into the ditch he was running through. He grimaced as his ankle twisted slightly on uneven ground and sent shocks up his shin.

But then there were lights ahead. He raised the phone and said, "Ready."

"Wade's in front, you take the back," Sam advised him.

"Roger." He turned and began running back the way he'd spent so much effort coming from, so he'd be pacing the car.

It came alongside and he shoved his ruck through. Hands clutched at it and took it, then he was diving headfirst through, hands on the ledge, then the seats, then tumbling in, his wounded leg scraping and stinging. But he was in.

"Stay low," Sam said and gradually sped up. They rolled right past where they'd had their little dustup and kept going. Kyle took deep, slow breaths as the sweat poured off him, trying to calm his nerves and twitching muscles, aching leg and itching skin.

"Okay," Sam said, letting out a breath of his own. "I see two men around twenty years old and two Romanian police. Is that a good thing?"

"That's a good thing so far," Kyle said. He explained what had happened.

Sam nodded and said, "Likely they won't go looking. Okay, there's baby wipes to clean up with and your spare clothes are in the bag in the footwell. Get neatened up and I'll drop you at the hotel. Sounds like you did great until the punks showed up."

"Yeah," Kyle said. "I think I may take up drinking again."

"Romania does that to people," Sam said.

14

TWO HOURS LATER, THEY WERE ENSCONCED IN THEIR
room and cleaned up. Once again, everyone was on their phones
in a conference call. Wade and Kyle both gave verbal debriefings,
reading their notes verbatim, then giving detailed interpretations.
Wade proceeded to shred the coated pages into tiny pieces they'd
scatter among various trash cans and outside. Sam had taken the
memory sticks and they were being processed already.

"So how did we do?" Kyle asked. He hoped the information had
proven useful. It had been a rough task to acquire it.

"Well, there's good and bad news," Cafferty said.

"Yes?"

"The good news is, the photo interpretation people confirm your
kills from yesterday. The less than good news is the Romanians discovered your packs. They've got the bodies, the explosives, the
other bodies, and the commo gear. That's not necessarily bad, as
long as they don't tie it to us."

"What's the bad news?" Wade asked.

"Someone got a photo of you, Kyle, in profile as you ran that first
day."

"Ah, shit."

"Not your fault," Cafferty insisted. But he obviously wasn't
happy about it. "They haven't ID'd it yet, but it does mean if you
get spotted somewhere else it might bite us in the ass."

"Damn!" Kyle said. He was seething. That damned dog! He was
totally invisible and had been sniffed out by a mutt. And a friendly
mutt. He liked dogs, he couldn't be mad at it for being a dog, so he
was mad at the situation.

"The real bad news is really not your fault," Cafferty said, bracing him.

"Right. Hit me, then." What had Murphy done now?

"Ambassador's wife heard some of the news, and some of my report, and a few other things, and is on the warpath."

"Oh, fun." Kyle couldn't think of any profanity that fit.

"My problem, not yours," Cafferty assured him. "But it's a bitch, and so is she. More relevant is that the bad guys know we're after them. On the other hand, they know we can dig them out. I'm still trying to assess this."

"What next, then?" Wade asked.

"Stay hidden. I have a deportation order for my two snipers, from the ambassador. Luckily, you aren't my snipers." He sounded sarcastically gleeful at that.

"How much trouble is this going to cause for you?" Kyle asked. The internal politics of this were a nightmare he couldn't begin to grasp.

"He won't ship me out yet. I'm too useful. And your bosses and my bosses pulled favors higher up. He's not happy, though."

"I can understand his position, a little," Kyle said. He wouldn't like some chairwarmer like Wiesinger running operations without his clearance. And the ambassador did have other issues to deal with. From that perspective, Kyle was a really small fish with annoying habits.

"A little? I grasp it perfectly," Cafferty said. "But I have to do my job, you've got to do yours, and he has to deal with it. At some point, he'd be replaced if he got in the way too much. So rather than do that, he just makes my life a living hell."

"You know, I think I prefer my job," Kyle said.

They waded through the pictures, Kyle and Wade adding notes from memory to go with some of the less intuitively obvious ones. The mental wringer added to the physical stress had them almost hallucinating by the time 9 A.M. rolled around. Kyle thought of that old Army ad campaign and winced. "We do more before 9 A.M. . . ." Yeah, as if that was a selling point.

Still, it had been a very productive couple of days. He couldn't complain about the accolades they were getting. Cafferty, and presumably others, were very happy.

Kyle would be happy to get a good day's sleep. So it thrilled him no end when Cafferty said, "I think we're done for now. You should be secure where you are. Keep the phone handy, and Sam will stay in touch. Now get some sleep. I'm going to need you again and I want you functional."

"Yes, sir," he said, with Wade in parallel. They grinned at each other and crashed back on their beds.

Kadim woke to the alarm and rose. It was far too early, before even morning prayers, but this put him on the same schedule as the Americans, some of whom seemed to keep chaotically odd and later hours.

He had almost missed vital data, he realized shortly after he logged in. The chatroom was busy and moving quickly.

JulianLee has entered the room.
7 people in room.
FANCYDANCER: Hi, Julian
LEO155: hi
AUSSIEWALT: Julian, long time no see
JULIANLEE: Yes, it has been a while, Walt. Peace.
AUSSIEWALT: Peace to you. Did you know this is Lent for me? Or is that just a greeting?
JULIANLEE: I hadn't known. What did you give up?
AUSSIEWALT: Caffeine
JAMESGUNN: I gave up self-restraint for Lent. For six weeks I'm denying myself nothing.
FANCYDANCER: *LOL@James*
BLKKTTY: -)
LEO155: I gave up sobriety one year.
AUSSIEWALT: Leo, if you stayed drunk for 42 days, you'd get the punishment you deserved from the act it-self. :-)
Barbiemouse has entered the room.
BARBIEMOUSE: STEAMING MAD!
BLKKTTY: Hi, Barbie
FANCYDANCER: What's wrong, Barbie?
JULIANLEE: ??
Private Message from Leo155 to JamesGunn: Right, nutcase in, old artillery puke out. ciao.
Leo155 has left the room.
JAMESGUNN: Good luck, Walt. I live on caffeine.
AUSSIEWALT: I only have a little, but I enjoy Coke and coffee. Thanks.

Private Message from Blkktty to FancyDancer: do we really want to know?

BARBIEMOUSE: You wouldn't believe what those IDIOTS have done now!

Private Message from FancyDancer to Blkktty: She needs help. Letting her talk in here can't hurt and might let her feel better.

Private Message from Blkktty to FancyDancer: bites tongue* Yes, I suppose that's true. I'll try to be nice.

JAMESGUNN: Barbie, please do me a favor and do *not* discuss foreign service operations in chat.

AUSSIEWALT: What are we talking about?

JULIANLEE: Barbie has some issues with government policy, I understand.

BARBIEMOUSE: No, it's not the policy. Well, yes it is. But those two CIA hired goons almost blew up a historical site yesterday. I can't say which one, but if you do a Web search you might find it. And they left several people dead and blew their cover, and it's going to turn into a diplomatic *mess* that my poor husband has to help deal with.

JamesGunn has left the room.

FANCYDANCER: he works for State dept, right?

BARBIEMOUSE: in some capacity. And this is in his lap.

Private Message from Blkktty to FancyDancer: he's the ambassador.

FANCYDANCER: the ambassador???

Private Message from FancyDancer to Blkktty: OOPS! I didn't mean to blurt that out!:-[

AUSSIEWALT: here's a link to the story

JULIANLEE: Thanks, Walt. Barbie, is it that bad?

BARBIEMOUSE: Maybe not. If we can get them to stop or at least talk more before running in shooting, it would be a good mission. But as it is, it's verging on criminal.

BLKKTTY: maybe you should report it to the host nation.

BARBIEMOUSE: Maybe I should.

Private Message from Blkktty to FancyDancer: I was being sarcastic. Now it's my turn to be embarrassed. :-/

AUSSIEWALT: Castle Bran? That's one of Prince Dracula's HQs.

FANCYDANCER: I've got a performance early tomorrow. Got to go.

Private Message from FancyDancer to Blkktty: I know you won't, but please do NOT tell Barbie I'm a stripper. It'd be all over the net. Tryout at a nice new club tomorrow. Better music, less smoke, richer clients.
Private Message from Blkktty to FancyDancer: good luck. Hugs. I won't say a word.
Private Message from FancyDancer to Blkktty: Thanks! :-) Hugs back, gone.
FancyDancer has left the room.

AUSSIEWALT: Good luck at your . . . shoot, missed her.

BARBIEMOUSE: Yes, it's a Dracula site, but it's also a very important historical building otherwise. And it's being used by terrorists and Rambo military types as a battlefield. They both need to think about their priorities. Or at least the military does. I sometimes wonder which group is worse?

AUSSIEWALT: I have to get to church and help them set up for the evening service. Good luck.

JULIANLEE: be well, Walt.

BARBIEMOUSE: Take care. Hugs.

AussieWalt has left the room.

BLKKTTY: Got to chase my kids back to bed. Back later.

BARBIEMOUSE: sigh. And I really need to talk.

JULIANLEE: I don't know much about things like that, Barb, but I can be a friendly ear.

BARBIEMOUSE: Oh, there's not a lot to say. I really don't know that much.

JULIANLEE: Well, I'm staying in chat for now. You just ping if you need me, okay?

BARBIEMOUSE: Thanks, Julian

BARBIEMOUSE: I suppose I really should call the host nation.

JULIANLEE: Will that improve things? If these men mess up, wouldn't it be better to deny them?

BARBIEMOUSE: . . . that might be true. I don't know.

BARBIEMOUSE: I suppose I should get it out of my system. But I can't name names or places, okay?

JULIANLEE: Okay.

Yes, it was just fine with Kadim if she said anything at all. He'd send the saved chat in its entirety to the mullah, and then it could go where it was needed. Perhaps a sufficient incident would get the political resolution that was needed. If not, it was better that soldiers get killed rather than children or civilians. If the military wanted a solution, they'd find one. Civilians really didn't have any power, and the politicians didn't care.

Kadim was proud to do this small part for his people and the world. There was definitely good to be seen in the outcome.

Two hours of chat and instant message yielded a lot of talk from a woman who was obviously stressed. Her husband would do well to take her home. Or at least keep her out of such troublesome affairs, which she wasn't equipped to handle. On the other hand, she was the source of the information. It was a moral quandary for Kadim, but he would pray to Allah to calm her soul and to resolve it in His way.

BRAN, Romania: Investigations continue in this historic little village today. Two days ago, a "man in camouflage clothing" was seen hiding near an abandoned entrance to Bran Castle. At another, previously unknown entrance to the east, investigators found several crates alleged to contain explosives.

The Romanian government still has not made any comments, but witnesses claim to have seen several shrouded bodies removed, possibly as many as twenty, along with other crates similar to those found to the east. The area is being patrolled, and investigators are at work around the clock.

Bran Castle, a 14th-century fortress, may have been used by Prince Dracula in his war against the Turks. There are rumors that the bodies being removed are remains of some of his victims. While he is often attached to the vampire legends, Dracula is not known to have drunk blood. He did, however, impale prisoners on stakes and torture them at length.

Other reports, from sources close to the operation, say that the bodies are those of dissidents and the crates were explosives to be used to create terror in this still developing nation.

Al Asfan pored over the new report with interest. So there were definitely two CIA operatives specifically tasked with harassing his operation. They'd taken out the chase car for the delivery, then apparently killed—because they hadn't reported in—Florescu and Logadze. That angered him until he broke out in a sweat and gritted his teeth. Worse yet, most of the new load of explosives was now in Romanian government possession, and they'd lost some very expensive communication gear. On top of that, the most secure operating location anyone could have ever dreamed of had been exposed.

He'd told those idiots that driving directly into Bran was stupid. One never headed straight for a safehouse, but detoured around the long way. Instead, they'd drawn an arrow straight in, and either been seen or deduced.

It was time to close up here and move on. There was a good place on the French Riviera where he could stay quiet for a while.

In the meantime, he should see if those CIA infidels could be taught a lesson. There were local assets who might trace them. The ideal result would be to leave them dead, publicly and creatively. Barring that, enough attention would perhaps make the Romanians stick them in jail. So far, there were questions about the men who'd abandoned a car in Bran. A few more questions should suffice to get them taken in.

With a mean grin, he reached for the phone.

15

KYLE'S PHONE BUZZED. HE WAS FINALLY GETTING used to that and not suffering what was known as "beep-ilepsy"—reacting with a jerk when it vibrated.

"Monroe," he answered.

"Kyle, it's Mick. You need to get hidden in a hurry. The police are looking for two Americans, one black and one white, wanted for questioning regarding the incident at Bran."

"Shit," Kyle replied. He couldn't think of much else to say.

"Indeed. I'm going to try to shift notice away from you. We still don't want to come out if we don't have to." Kyle translated that as, "At a certain level, you're expendable to maintain security." It should by rights piss him off, but he understood it. He believed Cafferty would dig them out if they got caught. He also believed that the man would milk it as much as possible for favors and position first.

"What do you want us to do, then?" he asked for clarification.

"Move again, you rent a room, Wade needs to stay out of sight. There are enough young American males here that you won't immediately attract suspicion."

"Will do. We'll check in when we can."

"Good luck, and I'll try to distract them. We'll get you another target yet." Kyle doubted that, but they did have two so far.

They waited nervously until well after dark. Then Kyle settled at the desk and headed for the car with most of the luggage. He returned for the rest and cleared the route ahead of Wade, who kept his hat on and collar up to reduce visibility. They encountered no one on their way out the back, and were shortly on the road, Wade sprawled in back with his face mostly covered.

"I could nap like this," he said.

"Sure, then you can handle the next early call alone."

Kyle drove out of Braşov and onto E574 toward Sfîntu Gheorghe. That was another small town that should have enough tourists and hotels to help them stay hidden. After that, he wasn't sure what to do. Likely, Cafferty would try to draw attention away from them and onto some other suspect. Then they'd be able to depart. He wasn't sure they'd get much more done on this mission. Still, a ton of explosives and two terrorists was a good tally. But it irked him to let the bigger brains go.

Ten minutes into the trip, Kyle was sure they were being followed. "I've got the same Dacia sedan behind us as two blocks after we left," he said to Wade.

"Cops?" Wade asked.

"I doubt it," Kyle said, trying to see past the headlights in the mirror. He'd caught the vehicle once or twice at stops, but couldn't get much more at present. It had stayed a car or two back so he wasn't sure how it was manned, but was now following within a few lengths. It was obviously intended to be intimidating.

"We don't have weapons in the car, do we?" A ripple of adrenalin went through him. They'd wanted to be prepared for a police stop, and shooting it out with the police wasn't anywhere on their agenda. It wouldn't have helped any situation.

"All in the trunk that I know of," Wade said.

"Shit."

Kyle had done quite a bit of off-road driving, both stateside and in Bosnia. He'd done plenty of miles on road. He'd even done the usual teenage "stunt driving." But this was combat driving against a possibly armed enemy. He was fairly sure he could find a way to get lost if they got to another town. But that wouldn't solve the problem, and would leave an enemy loose, which he hated to do. The ideal solution was to turn the pursuit around.

He just wasn't sure he had the driving skills for that. The ideal outcome was to disable the pursuing vehicle and stun the driver for capture and interrogation, then follow up against enemy infrastructure. That meant no more than a smashed bumper for Kyle and Wade's car. Any major damage or disabling of their car would bring the government in. That was a far less desirable outcome, because it would mean a capture of a mere flunky who might get away, and their capture and the resultant incident.

The only thing that came to mind was to try to cause a crash for the pursuer, quickly get control of them and get information. Kyle didn't think of it as torture, because he intended a simple punching and beating of someone who helped terrorists blow up innocent people. After that, they could be left for the police or Cafferty. The other option was to see if they had a radio or cell phone and threaten them into contacting their leadership, so Cafferty or Kyle could trace them.

Frankly, he had no idea what he was really doing, but couldn't think of anything good. So he jockeyed for favorable position for the crash. After that, he had only guidelines.

First was to get them close enough and fast enough that he could cause a minor accident. Kyle didn't know college physics, but he did know some ballistics. Faster velocities greatly increased energy, and in this case would also reduce response time. So he needed to accelerate and act fearful until they caught up, make sure the road was quiet, then lock up the brakes.

He started with some gentle acceleration. He wanted to appear to "discover" the possible threat and run away. Let the enemy, who likely didn't know exactly who they were, get overcautious.

It worked. Within a couple of kilometers, the tail had matched his speed and closed distance. They had him right where he wanted them. He edged the speed up a bit more and looked for a good spot.

Actually, it was hard not to edge the speed up as they got closer. He didn't like tailgaters, and this was not the place for it, with the road bumpy and uneven and occasionally pulling the car toward the edge. He used that, since it was going to happen anyway. Let them think he was scared and fleeing.

Right then, he found exactly what he was looking for. The road curved to the right, leaving them on the outside. It wasn't banked, and there was no other traffic visible at the moment. "Impact," he warned Wade, and stood on the brakes as he left the turn.

It appeared the pursuit wasn't in the mood for a wreck. The driver braked hard himself. But he was in the curve, and started to skid. The lights bounced as the car shuddered and slid on the loose pavement. Then it angled off the road, still at a good clip, and plowed through the weeds. It had almost turned on its side when it slammed into some trees.

At once, Kyle pulled half off the road, there being no shoulder, and put the emergency flashers on.

"Get weapons, cover them, stand clear of the car," he ordered as he popped the trunk release. Wade rolled out the door and reached for the rear. In a moment, he was down into the growth and Kyle threw the car into reverse. He wanted to conceal the other vehicle from anyone coming the same way they had. Anyone traveling the other direction should see nothing, if all went well.

Wade was good. Kyle had known that, but the man continued to demonstrate it. They needed to keep control of the situation, and Wade did it through the expedient of shooting the headlights out of the vehicle with the AK. The occupants had a good look at him, then it went dark. He had his little xenon flashlight out, which they'd not needed yet, and used it to blind the occupants. They knew he was armed with a suppressed and highly illegal weapon, was aggressive, and had backup. That was an excellent start to an engagement.

Kyle slammed into park so fast the transmission made the ratcheting sound that says it's been abused. He twisted out, seat belt clattering against the rear door, and reached into the trunk for his Ed Brown. It was right under his ruck, and the suppressor was in the same case. By the time he'd bounded down the slope to the Dacia, he had it mounted. That put him right at the driver's window with the gaping hole pointed through the frame—the window was down.

"Get out and lie down!" he snapped in English, thrusting the big pistol forward.

"Okay!" the driver said, eyes huge and nodding agreement.

Score 1. The enemy had admitted to knowing English. That made it much easier.

"Wade, get on the phone," Kyle said. He wanted to ask questions and move quickly. Wade pulled out his phone and Kyle turned to his prisoners. There were three, all locals, males in their 20s. They were facedown and clearly not prepared for a military engagement.

A shot went right past Kyle's head and scared the hell out of him. He dropped, rolled, and prepared to return fire. Then the driver was on him and wrestling for the .45. He could hear Wade shooting, the suppressed fire in contrast to the appalling reports from someone's pistol.

Then he ignored all that. The driver was trying very hard to cripple and kill him. Kyle was underneath, his attacker astride a leg, and they both went for the obvious knee to the balls at the same time. The attacker got the better of it, because he could let gravity do some of the work, and Kyle had to clench against the incoming blow. His own strike was weak. The hand that ripped at his Adam's apple had ragged, long nails, and he coughed and choked. He managed a nice clip against the driver's forehead with the butt of his pistol, which stunned his opponent just enough for Kyle to break his grip. But then they were both tangled up again.

He didn't know what this guy ate, but he probably didn't own a toothbrush. His breath reeked. He tried desperately to roll over, but they were against the car and couldn't. Up and down, trying to get position and control, they struggled for several seconds. In a fight, that's a long time.

The muzzle of the AK appeared, and Kyle was glad for the support. But the driver grunted and heaved, twisting them both into a ball again. Wade backed out.

"Alive!" Kyle said, hoping it was neither too soft nor a shout. The others weren't helping, so he presumed in the back of his mind that Wade had killed them. But they needed at least one alive, and that was a problem, because the driver didn't need one of *them* alive.

They were both getting banged about by the car, fists, the pistol, and several broken, rotten but still sharp sticks underneath. Kyle was aching and sore all over. Finally, though, he got a foot against something and pushed. That turned them both over, and he was able to butt his head down against the man's large, angular nose. That momentary stun let Kyle wrench his hands free, and he delivered a hefty smack across the eyebrows with the pistol. The eyes under him crossed and rolled up.

Wade was moving in muzzle first, and Kyle rolled back to rest. His shins had been kicked, his groin kneed, his ribs punched. His throat and head had taken a lot of damage, and he was abraded all over from sticks and grass, as well as muddy and filthy. He rasped for breath, and took a full minute to cough and clear his throat of phlegm and dust.

"The other two are dead," Wade told him while he recovered. "One had an old Tokarev, the other a cruddy old Czech revolver he never got to use."

Kyle just nodded. He couldn't believe he'd been so overconfident. Even idiot punks were dangerous when cornered. After all, they had no reason to expect to live, so they'd fought accordingly. They would have done so sooner had the wreck not stunned them.

"Let's talk to the driver," he said. "And quickly." He wiped his lip and his hand came away bloody. He'd bitten the inside of his cheek and banged his lips and teeth. Nothing loose, but shredded and cut.

Wade tapped the man on the forehead with the muzzle of the AK, and he recovered with a wince and a jerk.

"You talk and you don't die," Kyle said. Part of him was glad for the fight. It now meant he had zero qualms about smacking this asshole around for intel. Chasing them had been one thing, but these guys had been armed, so they'd been sent to kill.

"I don't know anything!" the man said at once. It was too quick to suit Kyle. He swung the suppressor right between the man's legs and blew a round into the dirt.

"I think you do," he said. "Shall we bet?"

"I got only a telephone call," the man said. He was wide-eyed under his welted and bleeding brow and matted shaggy black hair.

"Cell? Mobile phone?"

"Da, yes," he agreed, nodding and wincing.

"Where?"

"Here," he said, and reached for his pocket. He stopped when Wade raised his chin with the suppressor.

Carefully, Kyle reached into the pocket. There was only the phone in there. He flipped it open. "Standard phone," he said. "Maybe Ca . . . our friends can trace it."

"Maybe," Wade said. "Yes, I'm still here. We had a mixup. In control now. Send backup. Stand by." Kyle had forgotten that Wade had had his phone live. "Can you trace a call on a standard cell? Or the number? Roger." Wade looked over and said, "He says to find the number first."

Kyle turned the phone around and said, "Which number do you call?"

"Number five on list," the man said. "Is who sends us orders."

"And the others?" He looked over the list.

They were all family members or friends, it appeared. Number Five was labeled with a little factory icon for workplace.

"Such nice people you work for," Kyle muttered. He read the number off for Wade.

"He says it's another cell number, but not far from here. He's seeing if he has a way to check it."

Kyle realized their prisoner shouldn't be hearing this, and that they were exposed if anyone happened by and wanted to help the people with the flashing lights and open trunk, or had heard the fight. They were in a very bad position if discovered.

"Into the car," he said. "We'll talk while we drive."

It took another few minutes to go through all the pockets and the car. There had to be stuff they were missing, but two cars whizzed by while they were doing so, and Kyle was frantic to get away. Getting caught now would ruin a lot of plans.

It was rather obvious, Kyle thought as they dragged the man up the bank. The car had been crashed, shot, left with two bodies and a third one dragged away. They couldn't very well stick him in the trunk; modern trunks were easy to open from inside and all their gear was in it. So he'd have to ride in back with Wade. They didn't have cuffs, he might try to attract attention, and there was the risk of a fight.

The mission had officially gone to hell, Kyle decided. It had taken five days this time? Not a record, but only because there were some missions in hell from the word go.

He did most of the handling, because Wade was still talking on the phone. "Yes. Got it. Okay, we're about to roll, we'll need Sam to meet us. Roger, staying live." Wade lowered the phone and said, "He can get the call traced, but he needs time to set things in motion first."

"Okay," Kyle said. He shoved the punk in back, Wade piled in and jammed the suppressor into his belly, and Kyle slammed the trunk before getting back in front with his pistol. It felt good to sit.

Wade said, "He has to call someone else to get the serial number on the phone and set up to trace it. Once that's done, we call the number and they can ID it within a local area."

"Right. What do we say on air?"

"Dunno. I leave that to you."

"Right." Kyle built speed back up and resumed driving, though with no destination now. Driving was just a cover. "Find out what more he knows."

"Right. So," Wade said, turning and prodding with the AK. "Who is this boss?"

"I don't know."

"And how did you meet him?"

"Sorin introduced him by telephone. I never met him."

"And you take money from a man you've never met to drive around, cause wrecks, and shoot at people? You must be a loser." Wade called up to Kyle, "Should I smack him around?"

"I think he's too stupid and cowardly to know," Kyle said. "Too much of an idiot to know what he's doing. Bet he drinks most of his income. I'm surprised he's literate."

The ploy didn't work. The man kept silent, lips tight.

"Well, when we do find out, I can just shoot him and roll him out the door," Wade said. "Or just roll him out the door and hold his foot, let him drag to death. Should be fun. I've never seen that one done."

"That's true," Kyle said, getting into it. "We grenaded that one asshole across a cliff face. We dropped that other guy out of a helicopter. We crushed one under a tank. Fed one to sharks. That was kinda neat. Then there's the one we drowned in the toilet. Think his head will bounce and concuss him to death? Or just grind away until his brains smear?"

"Dunno." There was silence for a few minutes, and it was obvious the man was bothered. He kept pulling his eyes away from the door, but soon they'd dart back again. "Fuck it," Wade said, shifting quickly. "He won't talk, let's give it a try."

"Sure, how fast?"

"Oh, hundred K should do fine," Wade said. "Better than a good belt sander."

"He's in Tirgovişte," the man said, believing they meant it. "But I don't know where."

"Pity," Wade said with a snarl. "That means you just gave us information for free and we'll still grind your head off. Ready, boss?"

"Ready. As soon as we hit this straight."

"I DON'T KNOW!" was the insistent response. "I know they smuggle drugs, but I never was told names. I wasn't supposed to."

"Drugs, yes," Kyle said quickly. "And the DEA sent us to deal with it." Better to use that story than to let anything slip. On the other hand, this cretin was even more of a mercenary. There was no cause for him, no end goal. He'd kill someone for a few lei just because that was his job. Kyle's teeth clenched as he gripped the wheel. It was morally right to smear this scumbag. But it wasn't his job to deliver that justice. When they found a terrorist organizer, however . . .

The phone buzzed and Kyle stole a glance at it. "It's Sa . . . another element," he said. He clicked the button and raised it. "I'm here."

"Where is 'here'?" Sam asked.

"On E Five Seven Four, now heading back to Braşov and then to Tirgovişte. We're going to try to scare out this punk and nail him."

"Okay, it might work, though we can only get a rough estimate on the phone's location."

"Yes, but we have a prisoner who's deathly afraid of having his face ground off as we drive. You don't mind if we waste him? The government's okay with it? Right. We'll hide the body so no one has to ask any questions." Most of that was pure bull, but Sam should figure out what he was doing and ignore the extra chatter.

"Clever," Sam snickered. "If you've killed a couple already, it really doesn't matter actually. Though we don't endorse it and officially forbid it. I'll head in that direction. If time permits, I'll take your prisoner and we'll see if he'll tell us more. Though as we can't use force, it might take a while. Meanwhile, please do keep him alive."

"Thirty minutes and dump him in a river. Understood. We'll meet you there," Kyle said. He clicked off. Over his shoulder to Wade he said, "We don't need him. If he won't talk, grind his face so it's not recognizable and we'll chop off his fingers before we dump the corpse. The local cops won't know and the government just doesn't want anything that can be traced."

"Got it."

The prisoner spoke. "Domnule, sir, I have a family," he said weakly.

"Good, your widow can marry a man, then." Kyle was trying to sound as callous and casual as possible.

"I really don't know any more," he insisted. He was quivering and squeaking in fear.

Then Wade wrestled him face down on the seat. The man might be 140 pounds and Wade was in much better shape. It took only a few seconds.

"Say when," Wade said.

"Straight road, no witnesses, any time."

And Wade pulled the door handle.

The man screamed and flinched hard enough to make Wade jerk as air rushed past.

Almost, Kyle thought. "Just so you know," he said. "This isn't about drugs. The man you work for blows up children on buses in Israel. He's also killed people in Egypt, Spain, and France, and some of my buddies. You picked the wrong people to play with, and you're going to die very slowly because of that."

Wade was good. He gave about five seconds for that to sink in, then knelt and thrust the man's head out the door. He started leaning forward, weight on the man's neck.

"I KNOW AN ADDRESS!" came the shriek. Wade yanked him back up into the car.

Kyle exhaled as quietly as he could. He was sure Wade did, too. Because no matter how much they hated these assholes, they couldn't really torture someone like that. And this poor bastard was just a flunky who likely didn't endorse terrorism.

"So tell us," Kyle said.

"I . . . I," the man stuttered, forgetting his English.

"Wade, grind his face off, I'm sick of this crap."

"I'll have to show you!" he insisted. "I don't know the name, but I visited there once."

"Man, this is getting good," Kyle said with mock glee. "First you know nothing, then you know a phone number, now an address, I wonder what else you know?"

"That's all! I swear!" he insisted.

"Likely true," Wade said. "This little coward just pissed his pants all over our back seat."

"One more reason to get rid of him. But let's see if he knows where this place is. And you better not be lying," he said. "If we don't find him in Tirgovişte, we'll find an even more painful method."

16

THE MAN WAS QUIET AND WHIMPERED OCCASIONALLY all the way to Tirgovişte. Wade took no chances and kept the AK's suppressed muzzle in his guts. It was about 120 kilometers, near a two-hour drive with the local road conditions, and at that rate, Kyle was abusing their bodies and the car with road vibration.

"Okay, we're entering Tirgovişte, where to?" he asked.

"North and east corner," their prisoner said quickly. Kyle used one hand to pull up a map and kept the wheel steady with the other and his knees. The town was about 90,000 population, not huge, and the roads were sized accordingly—several large arteries and lots of small ones that didn't matter.

The phone buzzed and Kyle answered. "Yes?"

"Sam here. I'm entering Tirgovişte. Where are you?"

"Stand by," Kyle said, and found the name of the nearest large street. It was a "Strada" named after somebody "escu," like so many others. He picked an intersection nearby.

"I'll be there in ten minutes. Want to transfer your prisoner?"

"Sure," Kyle said. "See you." He disconnected. "Man, that's a bitch," he said.

"Oh?" Wade asked.

"Yeah, Sam is coming to get him."

"Sam?" Wade asked, playing straight and sounding scared.

"Yeah. That's rough. Tough shit, kid. You're all Sam's now."

"Sam?" he asked, unsure and sounding bothered.

"Yeah. I would do exactly what you're told if I were you. Sam will kill you if you try anything."

He had no idea what Sam actually planned, but cowing the man into submission couldn't hurt, and might make him more pliable.

Shortly, they saw a car flash its headlights. A wave indicated Sam, and they pulled in behind him. He was heading toward the river.

Then they were along the river on a quiet street, and side by side. Sam leaped out, opened the rear doors of both cars and helped Wade shove the frightened lump of a prisoner into his vehicle. Heavyweight cable ties appeared, and they lashed him at ankles, knees, and wrists. He was dumped unceremoniously into the footwell and mostly covered with a thick blanket. Wade said, "Good luck, kid. Do what he says and you might survive."

Kyle almost burst out laughing.

They departed a few minutes apart, giving Sam the lead. He rolled into a housing area and down several streets. Periodically, he'd pause, then drive on. Kyle took a moment to look around. The houses were small, mostly with tiled roofs. There were little flowerbeds and fences. Nice Old World neighborhood, straight out of a book. Who'd think to look for a bomber here?

The phone buzzed and Kyle was waiting. "Yes?"

"He's not sure which street it was, and I think he's telling the truth. It's somewhere around here, he says, but he's not certain."

"Terrific. What next?"

"Let's try that trace. Stand by and I'll call the boss."

"Roger, then call Wade." Kyle left the phone live. "You still awake back there?" he asked.

"Sure am. Are we on it?"

"Going to try the trace and see what it scares up."

Sam came back. "Okay, he's ready. Call him and we'll see what happens. Switching to Wade now."

"Got it," Kyle said. This was nerve-wracking. He had no idea what technical tricks were needed to pull this off, and he still felt as if he were responsible. He urged calm on himself and grabbed the prisoner's phone. How many phones and radios did he have here? Cameras? Weapons? This was nothing like the movies.

It was a bad idea to do all this talking on a phone while driving. But that was pretty far down Kyle's list of worries right now. He dialed the number next to the work icon and waited to see what would happen.

"Da?" was the answer, in a voice that was male, adult and not much else.

"I work with your employee, and we have problems," he said. "We've been ambushed!"

"Who is this?" So, the man spoke English with a Middle Eastern accent. Even better.

"This is Frankie," he said. "From the ship."

"You are most unwise, Frankie," came the reply, just as Wade said, "They've got it, Tirgovişte as he said."

"No, you're unwise," Kyle said, deciding to apply some psych warfare. The guy had to know there were problems. Kyle wanted to see if he could scare him up. "We're coming to Tirgovişte to splatter your terrorist fucking brains on the bricks. We call it Excedrin Headache Number Seven Six Two. Adios, Motherfucker." He disconnected at once. No need to let the man get any response in. Act tough, in control and most people would believe it.

"Got it localized pretty closely," Wade said. "Within a couple of blocks . . . half kilometer south of us."

"Right. Now to see how fast we can get there."

"You'll have to nav," Wade said. "I'm busy."

"No problem." A few blocks wasn't great, but perhaps they'd catch him on the way out of somewhere. They were closing in, and Kyle would be scared if he knew people were shooting his henchmen, stealing his explosives and tracking his phone calls.

And Kyle found it amusing how many allegedly brilliant people assumed cell phones were secure because there was no wire. This was the second time. And last time had been a satellite phone that hadn't been able to tell them much other than within a few miles. This time, they had it down to mere blocks.

Al Asfan tried not to panic. He forced calm into his mind and told himself it was all Allah's will. Allah would not let him fail. The road might be rough, but it was all part of a plan, and he was one of the slaves of Allah.

Still, it was a frightening course of events. He'd have to leave at once. While he'd like to call back and insist he wasn't afraid and challenge this arrogant American to meet him, he really didn't know who the man was, how many he had with him, or what the stakes were anymore. He was losing assets and people and needed to withdraw. Only a fool refused to retreat. He was no fool. Leave at once, head for France where the Arabic community would protect him, and regroup. This all would come back in its time.

He needed to hold things where they were until he could get to his other hideaway. From there he could arrange travel and call in favors to slow pursuit. But it was time to leave now. Rafiq bin Qasim, Allah bless him, had tried to hold out in Pakistan and had died because of it, when the Americans had slipped agents into the area. Al Asfan would not make that same mistake.

If he'd known the same shooters who got bin Qasim were the ones after him, he might have been even less confident. As it was, he grabbed an already packed bag and headed for the car. He left the cell phone behind. It was obviously betraying him, and he had another.

The Americans spread out two blocks apart, though "block" here was slippery. The roads wound and crisscrossed. But they were in approximately the right area. Now they had to wait and see what happened. Kyle had a picture of al Asfan onscreen, and assumed Sam did, too. Of course, in the early light, and with considerable time since the pictures were taken, it wasn't going to be that easy to identify the target.

"I may have something," Sam said. As before, they were using satellite phones with headsets, and stayed live. The cost per minute was horrendous to Kyle's budget, but not even a blip on the chart to Uncle Sam.

"What?" he queried back.

"Male of approximately right age and description with a large overnight bag. Looking around, may be nervous. Getting into a Mercedes model echo five zero zero, dark brown. He is facing east. Starting car. Driving."

"Where should we intercept?"

"Identify target first," Sam said. "Then we'll follow if we can," he warned. "Let me find a good cross street. I can follow him a few blocks."

"Intel first, then shoot, roger," Kyle said, as both acknowledgment and for Wade's benefit. "Camera ready." He caught Wade's nod and turned back to the map window on the laptop. The scale was small and the language a bit awkward, but he found the street Sam named. "Yes, I can get there. Rolling," he said, and gave the engine gas.

Wade had the camcorder ready, as it had the best resolution for night, and any frame of its video could be enhanced. It was effectively an autowinding still camera the way they intended to use it.

The question was, did they have the right target, or was it just a similar-looking businessman on his way to the office early? That could lose them the whole lead. Kyle began to see why espionage could be addictive. It wasn't as heady a thrill as shooting, but it was plenty exciting, and the high went on for hours. This wasn't even his part of the gig, and it was a rush.

He reached the intersection and said so as he shut off the lights. Sam replied, "About twenty seconds, start filming."

"Roger, start filming. Wade?"

"Filming to the west, waiting for target," Wade said. All the talk and confirmation might not be necessary, but it was better, in Kyle's opinion, to be redundant. Any errors could thus be caught.

A car came from the west, and the driver was a single male. Kyle ducked so Wade could get a good pan, even if windows did interfere with visibility. "Got image," he said. "Comparing," and he reached for the laptop as he scrolled back to a good shot. Sam rolled past the same intersection.

"Want us to wait?" Kyle said, worried that it might be the wrong man and they need to do another search.

"ID him if you can. Follow me if not."

"Roger." He looked expectantly at Wade, who was squinting at the image on the viewfinder and looking hard at the laptop.

"Probably him," Wade said. "Ninety percent certain, and I don't think I can do better without daylight."

"Probably him!" Kyle repeated. "We're following."

"Roger that," Sam said. "I will turn off when you join the tail, and take up position behind you. He shouldn't have seen me as more than headlights yet."

"We're still just tailing?"

"As long as we can," Sam said. "If he IDs us, go for a shot. Can you do that while moving?"

"Can, but it depends on the environment. Even if you aren't worried about witnesses, bystanders complicate shooting."

"Roger. We'll do what we can."

"How's your passenger?" Kyle asked.

"Oh, him? Quiet. Apologetic. Apparently, he's not thrilled to find he was helping terrorists. And he seems scared of us."

"Good." Kyle was just as happy. If the man had ethics and morals, it would be nice to get him back to his family. Though likely the Romanians would want to deal with him first.

"How are you doing on fuel?" Sam asked. "I can get another couple hundred kilometers."

"Ah. Not good," Kyle admitted after a glance at the gauge. "Maybe half that."

"Right, when you get close, you fuel up, I'll take the lead. But that means when we swap back he'll know he's probably being followed by you. And I'll be getting low. So if he's not where he wants to be by then, you shoot."

"Right. Can you clarify the rules of engagement again? Just for my benefit."

"No problem," Sam said. Then his voice took on a dark tone. "If we can't trace this guy, you're to kill him, by shooting, wrecking, whatever you can do. Avoid collateral casualties as much as possible. We want the body identifiable, and we don't care if there's witnesses. Just wipe this rat-fuck son of a bitch off the face of the Earth, and we'll handle cleanup and publicity."

"Understood," Kyle said. That was encouraging and scary. Encouraging in that they'd nail this dirtbag. Scary in that Kyle and Wade could very likely wind up as pawns for politics thereby. But hell, no one had claimed the job was safe when they took it.

They were on open road again, and heading back toward Braşov. They had a good distance between vehicles, though that had worked against them last time.

"Wade, be ready to shoot," Kyle said.

"Ten rounds of match grade in each pocket," Wade acknowledged. "I can be out either side window in five seconds, or shoot out the front or back glass faster."

They were again climbing the Transylvanian Alps. Despite the dark connotations attached to the name, *Transylvania* meant "across the forest." It really was pretty terrain. With the sun rising to the east and burning out pockets of mist and dew, the first blush of spring on the trees and the road a crumbled charcoal line, Kyle decided it really would be a nice place to visit. The mountains were high enough to be fun, not so high as to be work. They reached around 2500 meters.

And even here, there were bomb-throwing scumbuckets. There was nowhere on Earth, from the most productive, most desolate, to most idyllic these trash didn't pollute. Kyle had met troops from several dozen nations, including Iraq, the former Soviet Union, China, and Vietnam. Some of them were officially threats or enemies, and yet in every case, they could look at each other soldier to soldier and recognize patriotism and the willingness to serve. They could all sit down to a drink together and be comradely, even if they might have to shoot at each other later. Business was business. And despite everything different about their cultures, soldiers all hated terrorists. They were undisciplined, unprofessional, and cowardly thugs.

And Kyle was really hoping to catch this one.

As they cleared one rise, he saw a small village ahead. It was after 8 A.M., and business was in swing. He grabbed the phone and said, "Sam, I'm gassing up. Shift it in gear."

"Stand by," came the response. Behind him, he could see Sam's car accelerate. Ahead, al Asfan was starting to pull into the village traffic. This was where it was risky. He could turn, go straight, catch them in traffic and lose them. But so far it had gone well. Kyle eased over to the side so Sam could blow past him. "I've got him," Sam acknowledged. "But do hurry."

"Roger."

But Wade had to stay hidden when around Kyle. Black man and white man together. That's what people were looking for. Wade tucked down with a blanket as Kyle pulled neatly into the gas station and popped the fuel door. The attendant was right there as Kyle waved a wad of lei at him. "*Umpleți repede, vă rog,*" he said. *Fill quickly, please.* The man grinned and complied, and pumped away.

Gas, or petrol, was hideously expensive here. It also wasn't of the highest quality. But it wasn't Kyle's car or money, and he was in a hurry. He handed over the cash and waited impatiently for change, because it would be suspicious to leave without it. He wasn't going to waste time haggling, however. He nodded, said, "*Mulțumesc,*" and started rolling. The attendant gave him a quick, quizzical stare and a glance in the back, but Wade was hidden. He might think someone was asleep, but he didn't seem overly suspicious.

"Stay down for now," Kyle advised. "No need to be seen."

"Roger," Wade said, muffled under his cover. It had to be stuffy down there.

"Sam, I'm rolling."

"Straight through town and keep going," Sam said. "We're just leaving now. He's starting to look at me in the mirror, so hurry."

"Shortly," Kyle said. He didn't want to run anyone over or otherwise attract attention. There were goats in the village, and school children, and dogs. He passed a small school, some houses, and then saw fields pocked amongst the trees again with another stop sign ahead. Far in the distance were several cars and one of the ubiquitous horse-drawn conveyances so many farmers still used. The sun was well up and bright now, and visibility was excellent barring a faint haze that was still burning off.

"You can get up now," Kyle told Wade as he floored it, and drove like the maniac he'd been at sixteen. He piled up behind a little Dacia, waited for a break in oncoming traffic, and rocketed around, revs at five grand and foot to the floor, on the wrong side from his American perspective. Then he jerked back in and braked hard to pace the next vehicle. Over another rise, he saw clear road and stomped it again, running up to 160 km and beyond, the car bouncing and careening on the rough pavement. Then he had to whip back in behind another vehicle, a truck this time.

He slammed against the seat belt as he braked behind the cartful of something, whatever one hauled with horses this time of year, then dodged quickly around. Sam was clearing another rise and the target was ahead of that.

"Arriving," he announced, blasting up the hill with his foot through the firewall, heedless of the gravel flying. It was quite enjoyable.

"I see you," Sam said. "I'm turning as soon as you see him."

Kyle cleared the crest and saw their target down below, heading toward Braşov for certain. "Got him," he said.

"I see a road to the right. I'm pulling off and will follow about two minutes behind. Good hunting."

"Will do," Kyle said.

Hopefully, al Asfan was much more comfortable now that the car following him had pulled off. They'd find out soon.

The downside was that Kyle had to keep him in clear sight, which meant creative dodging and weaving. Everyone drove like that here anyway, but it did stand out the third time he got honked at for almost going nose to nose. Sooner or later, al Asfan was going to catch on.

It was on the edge of Braşov that he finally twigged. He stared steadily into the mirror for several seconds, then nailed the gas from his formerly quick pace to a breakneck one. Kyle was about two blocks behind, just close enough to see the reaction.

"He's seen us, we're going to shoot," he announced.

"Understood, good luck," Sam said. It was only a friendly comment, of course. Luck didn't enter into it. Wade was a professional shooter, and if they got a field of fire, they'd take it. But they would have to get in close and be quick.

Traffic built up in a hurry. This was another decently sized town, with a few main routes and a lot of convoluted smaller streets. Kyle was hoping to get close before al Asfan turned off. So far, however, he seemed to want to stay in public, possibly thinking that would protect him.

He would be disabused of that notion very shortly.

"Wade get ready. I'm about a block back."

"You got it."

A few moments later Kyle saw him in the mirror as he sat up in the rear, legs across the seat and into the passenger side footwell. The rifle was along his body, held close where it would be less visible, the suppressor near his face. That wasn't the safest way to hold a rifle, but there wasn't much safe about what they were trying to do.

Meanwhile, al Asfan had definitely figured out he was being pursued. He drove faster and even more recklessly than was the norm here, and ducked between two other cars.

"I'm not sure if he's trying to lose us or keep someone between us as cover," Kyle said.

"I'm watching," Wade said. "If I think I have a shot, I'll yell and take it unless you say not to."

"I trust you. Take the shot," Kyle said. Wade wouldn't risk hitting a civilian, and he had already proven he could take shots at moving cars.

"Will do," Wade said. "If we can get a drive-by afterwards, I'll make sure we finish it."

"If our cover's blown, yes," Kyle said, as he braked hard and slewed through the tail end of a light and cars stopping for it. He was momentarily on the right and it felt both normal and weird, with his American background and his experience here. "If we're still covered, we'll risk letting him survive. They can always find him in hospital. No offense to our planners, but I'd rather walk out of here." He gunned the engine, yanked back into traffic and ignored the honks and shouts.

"Got it," Wade agreed.

Al Asfan couldn't mistake their intent. If they were observing, there should be another car or a stationed spotter. That they came through traffic indicated their purpose was to stop him physically. He seemed to lack the fortitude for that engagement, because he tried to cut farther into the flow.

Cursing, Kyle accelerated again, then braked, slipped into a space that was barely big enough, then back out. But if he could prod him into a wreck, they could cruise by and ping him through a window, with no one the wiser. Conversely, if they got in a wreck, they'd lose him.

It was hard to decide who had the advantage of traffic. Al Asfan was having to break trail, but he had a largely unsuspecting crowd around him who didn't react until after he wove. Kyle had to deal with traffic that, while slow or stopped or recovering, was already scared and chaotic. But sooner or later, one of them was going to make a mistake, and if he played it right, Wade would get a shot.

Al Asfan still didn't seem to realize he had snipers on his tail rather than spies or cops. He stayed four cars ahead and looked happy there. On the other hand, four cars was a respectable distance, and far enough to get them stuck at a light. Kyle needed to get closer.

Only he couldn't. Traffic was snarled and tangled, cars halfway between lanes. He eased between two other cars, ignoring their honks as he rode the white line. There might be four lanes here, but there were no turn lanes to speak of, and he didn't want to be stuck in the right hand lane when someone decided to turn. The light ahead was turning amber, and he needed to get across quickly. He revved up, honked and pushed forward.

It worked. The cars on either side assumed him crazy and shifted over a few inches. That's all it took, and he was through as it turned red, ignoring louder honks from the cross traffic.

Their quarry was already through the intersection, and a car behind him was trying to back into a parking space. Kyle cursed and shifted over, forcing another car almost into traffic to avoid hitting him. At this point, he was willing to swap a few fender benders. Three car lengths and closing. If he could offset the car to some degree, Wade would have an oblique shot.

"A few more feet and I have him," Wade said. He was hunched over the rifle, one leg braced on the seat, one in the floorboards, one elbow over the back of Kyle's seat. That left the suppressor right alongside Kyle's face.

For just a moment, there was space ahead, even though the car beyond that was braking hard. If they wrecked, Wade would likely lose the weapon and smash into Kyle, the airbag tossing them both at the roof. But screw it, Wade needed a shot. Kyle maintained steady speed and said, "Shoot!"

A pop like a balloon on steroids blew past his ear. The driver's window on al Asfan's car exploded, and he swerved.

"Nice!" Kyle shouted, louder than he expected. He couldn't help grinning, either. That had been a sweet, sweet shot, and they had their score.

"Not nice," Wade said, snarling. "I fucking missed."

"Dammit," Kyle said, elation turning to depression. That was twice they'd missed now. The two they'd gotten had been sitting ducks. So far, their intel gathering was far outweighing their shooting and stealth. And some of that was luck.

Worse yet, now that he was being shot at, al Asfan was ignoring all traffic laws. He blatantly drove on the wrong side, cars ahead screeching and swerving to miss him. Kyle was momentarily blocked by another car, and that driver, a middle-aged man, looked over in shock.

Then he pulled out a cell phone.

"Dammit, diversion!" he yelled, hoping Wade had an idea. Wade seemed to. He pointed the muzzle in the general direction of the man, who braked hard. That let Kyle slip over into oncoming traffic.

Oncoming traffic was heavy, honking and swerving. Kyle fought for control of the car and himself. Wade leaned out and fired again. He'd been trying for a tire, but missed it by a hair and threw asphalt from the road. Kyle couldn't fault him. Shooting between two moving cars was rough, and he'd made the last tire shot handily. But that driver hadn't known he was being shot at. This one did, was evading and in front, and Kyle was avoiding wrecks and trying to catch up. On the whole, it was a god-awful situation.

The terrorist seized a break in traffic and dove across to the left, then down a side street.

"Not again!" Kyle shouted and dodged back into their lane, clipping a car which didn't brake hard enough and missing the turn because of a truck.

"No way to stop or slow down," he said. "I'm going to zigzag out of the area and we'll get clear."

"Roger," Wade said, tucking the rifle back under the blankets. "I don't see anything behind us," he reported.

"Got it," Kyle acknowledged. He changed lanes, steadied out, and prepared to turn left.

He didn't get the chance. Two police cars screamed across and blocked him. Two more were behind, lights flashing, sirens silent. Then police were tumbling out with weapons.

17

"**D**AMN. CALL CAFFERTY," HE SAID. "SAM, WE'RE busted," he said into his own phone.

"Dialing," Wade said.

He didn't need to speak Romanian to understand the shouts as, "Get out of the car slowly with your hands in sight!"

"Do it," he said, just as Wade spoke into the phone, "We're pinned by police, help."

Wade continued, "I'll leave the phone connected until they take it away. Kyle, I'm complying, phone in hand."

"Then reach the phone out first and slowly," Kyle said. He'd seen weapons from this side before, several times. But there was no cover and no way to shoot back now, and he'd heard that Romanian police were very eager to shoot sometimes. There were also hi-tech guns disguised as cell phones. The combination was bad. He felt a hard knot in his stomach as he reached and opened the door using the outside handle. "Be very helpful," he told Wade. "Might get us a bit better treatment." Though Cafferty's warning about the police hereabouts was bright in his mind, and he wondered if they were to get an obligatory thrashing before being tossed into a cell. Could even State get them out of this? He extended his own phone, still live for Sam to listen in.

He continued his progress as his brain whirled. Wade was stepping out, one foot at a time, phone held high so it was obviously not a weapon. Kyle waited for him to finish, then followed, hands open and clear.

The car's hood was hot but not painful as he was slammed down onto it. The cuffs, however, hurt moderately. Hands were plucking at his clothes and voices were shouting at him. He caught glimpses of batons, pistols, and tear gas, and wondered which they planned to use.

"*Sînt American*," he said clearly. "*Sînt armuri în automobilul.*" *I am American. I have weapons in the car.* They were going to search, anyway, so he may as well admit it and be helpful. Police, like soldiers, liked to have control of a situation. And unless one's goal was to fight them, it was safer to let them have it.

"Are you carrying any weapons?" he heard behind him in heavily accented English.

"There are none on my person. Oh, a knife in my pocket," he added hastily. He'd forgotten that the knife he carried as a "tool" could be perceived as a weapon by others.

His pockets were emptied onto the hood, he was felt down for anything hidden, then placed on his knees. Wade was already in that position, he saw, but then they were turned in opposite directions to prevent communication.

The police found all the weapons. It took only a few minutes before the .22, the AK, both pistols, the suppressors, cases, ammunition and their knives, flashlights, pocket tools, and cameras were all laid on the ground. A crowd had started to gather, but was chased away with a few curt words. It gradually built up again until it reached a level the police considered unacceptable, then was chased away again.

"Who are you and what is this?" A man in a gray suit, presumably a detective, asked him.

"I am Kyle Monroe. I am an American. I would like to talk to my embassy before I say anything else, domnule," he replied. He wasn't sure what if any rights he had here, but there was no need to talk unnecessarily. At the same time, he didn't want to be rude or evasive. They might have the legal right to smack him around for answers. And they did need to talk to the embassy.

"Why did you shoot? Who are you working for?" the man asked. He was neat-looking and appeared confident and calm despite the agitation around him, but clearly wanted answers.

"If you call my embassy and ask for Mister Mick Cafferty, he can explain everything," Kyle said. *I hope.* They'd been told they wouldn't be abandoned, but the government was notorious for changing the rules partway through.

"Spell that name," the detective asked curtly. Kyle did so, grateful that they seemed to want answers more than to bust heads.

"We will discuss this at the station and there you will answer my questions. You are under arrest and in much trouble."

"Da, domnule," Kyle said. He could hear Wade being questioned and harassed further over. Perhaps they'd heard stories of American street gangs and drug dealers. There was a drug trade here, after all. Heroin.

A van pulled up and the doors were thrown open. They were shoved rudely but not viciously into it. It drove away at once, swaying them off the plain metal benches they sat on. There was a single dome light for dim, shadowy illumination, and not much else. It was a steel box.

"I hope he doesn't brake hard," Kyle said. He could see them being slammed around like bugs in a box.

"Know how to get cuffs around front?" Wade asked.

"No."

"Like this," Wade said, rolling on the metal floor and forcing his wrists past his hips, then tucking his feet through the cuffs one at a time. "Gives leverage in case there's an 'accident,' and lets you scratch your nose."

"Thanks," Kyle said, dropping and rolling and yanking until he, too, had his hands in front. It had hurt a bit, the cuffs cutting in, but he did feel better with them in front. He was restrained still, but not helpless. "And how often have you had to do this?"

"Let's not go there at this time," Wade said.

"Fair enough." He spent time examining the cuffs. They were well-worn but solidly built, and there was nothing to be gained by unfastening them, anyway. All it would do was annoy their captors, if shifting them to the front wouldn't have done so already.

Shortly, the van stopped and someone opened the doors. Figures waved them out into a dark, dank basement and through a steel-barred gate into a concrete receiving area. The staff were all male, mostly smaller than the snipers but with attitude and control to back them up. They may not even have known why these two were here.

Again Kyle and Wade were searched, fingerprinted, photographed, shoved around like sides of beef, then dragged down a passage and tossed into a small cell with a sink and toilet, both slimy gray with mold. They were separate from any other prisoners, but the noise indicated there were quite a few in the building.

"Well, we're not hurt yet," Kyle said. He was still worried about abuse and torture. Enemies he could face bravely enough. Being cooped up was a different threat entirely. The room was a concrete box with a barred door. There were two concrete benches, shelves really, to sleep on. Both were filthy and dusty.

"So we sit and relax and wait," Wade suggested. "We both need sleep."

"I suppose."

It seemed Kyle's responses had put off any further questioning for now. They were left in the cell. They swapped jokes and war stories. Kyle started to wonder about food and water. Then he stopped wondering, because they obviously weren't to get either anytime soon.

He untensed enough to use the toilet. He hadn't gone in hours, and was puckered and wound up tight. Between the arrest and political incident, and not getting their target prior to that, he was very worried. If there was a dead terrorist to ID, they were in a much better position than if not. There were two others they could claim as kills, but that might not improve things. Results aside, few nations approved of operations in their territory without their oversight. After all, the people being disposed of had their own home countries which would be disturbed.

There was just no way this was going to end well, he thought.

He sat on one of the benches and leaned back. It was cold, smelly, drafty, and dank in there. The lightbulb above in its cage, glaring into his eyes, reminded him of the non-functional ones in the castle. He had a quick flashback to the burial pit and shivered. They certainly knew how to hide people in this country.

He really hoped Cafferty could do something. He was their only link, and if he decided to deny them, it would fall on Robash, who would have to deal through State, which wasn't happy with them.

He looked across at Wade, who was pretending to be calm and not succeeding. There was an uncharacteristic twitch to his left knee.

"Scared?" he asked.

"Trying to sleep," Wade said. He didn't deny the inference and didn't crack a joke. He was scared, too.

Sleep was the only thing that would pass the time, and they'd need to be alert when questioned. Hopefully, they'd have a representative with them when questioned. He thought that was considered normal procedure in most of the world, and hoped it held true here.

He twitched awake, gasping in pain. He was still sitting up, and his head had flopped sideways. Added to the tight muscles, it caused him an excruciating cramp. He rubbed it, then his gritty eyes. Then he muttered to himself and lay down. If he could sleep, he should. Wade was already out, breathing evenly but tossing fitfully.

Kyle had never felt hopelessness in this measure. There was nothing to give him any hope at the moment. He wasn't religious, his only friend in this hemisphere was next to him, and he had no idea what the government would do. As he drifted back into a disturbed doze, that colored his dreams.

It was some time later, hours at least, when noise came down the hall.

"Someone's here," Wade said. They were both awake but lying, staring at nothing.

One of the guards was clanking keys in the lock. "*Veniti*," he said. *Come.*

"Better something than sitting here. Maybe we'll see a phone or a judge," Kyle said.

"*Linişte. Văplimbaţi*," the guard said curtly. *Silence. Walk.* Kyle picked up his gist.

They preceded the guard down the hall, not cuffed, and wondering what was next. The passage was scrubbed but ugly cinder block, and would have been foreboding had not Kyle seen the holes under Bran already. On the other hand, there were definitely people with guns here, and he was definitely at their mercy. Movies aside, trying to break out of a police station, with no map, no communications, and no idea of where they were was suicide. It made him feel even more helpless, and he didn't like it. He glanced at Wade, who was silent and had a firm set to his jaw. He was scared, too.

They waited while the guard clanked open another heavy door. He waved them silently through into what was a normal office hallway. They blinked at the much brighter and more modern lights, and stood waiting. The guard motioned them forward and pointed at a door.

They entered and were in an office. A Romanian in a suit awaited them, along with two men in Romanian leaf-pattern camouflage, similar to U.S. Woodland pattern but splotchier. The ranking one didn't come across as a cop but as a government authority figure of some kind.

"Captain Monroe, and Lieutenant Curtis," he said with a nod. His English was accented but clear.

"Uh, yes," Kyle agreed. The ranks were wrong, but he wasn't going to object just yet. The names were right and this man was obviously from the government. He knew who they were and was going to want answers.

"Mister Cafferty spoke with me. I am a little annoyed that the U.S. chooses to run operations in my country without consulting."

"I can understand that completely, sir," Kyle said. He felt relieved, though. Cafferty knew they were here, and they were speaking to an official, not a local cop. And being out of the cell and in an office, not an interrogation room, was a good sign.

"So you will finish this in cooperation with DGIPI." It was a statement, verging on an order.

"Ah, yes, sir," he said. Then he said the thing he was afraid would get them back in jail. "But I must consult with my government first." He also wanted to know who exactly the DGIPI were, but that could wait a few minutes.

The man, who had not yet identified himself, stared coolly at him for a second that seemed endless. "With yours, and not with mine. You forget which country you are in." The obvious threat was left unsaid.

"But," he continued, "you are obviously disciplined and professional, judging from your accomplishments so far. We shall all discuss this. Then, we shall hunt terrorists. You will come with me." His face betrayed nothing.

With that, he turned and headed out, two of the men nearby picking up the case that held the Ruger, a rifle case that apparently held Wade's AK, and a box that sounded like it held pistols, from the clattering. That left a cardboard carton full of clothing and other gear. The police stood aside and pretended not to see what was going on.

"That's a hint, I think," Wade said, nodding after the mysterious spook.

"Yup. Forward," Kyle said.

Out the door, down the steps. It felt partly like freedom, and partly like a step toward a firing squad. Outside was dusky again. They'd been in jail all day and not fed.

They were led to a car with an open rear door. It was a large, black BMW sedan, and they climbed in without urging. It was away from the station, and the official had told them they were involved in the operation. Given that, their property accompanying them, and Cafferty's name mentioned, it should be safe. But the specter of the cell followed them and would for a while. They sat silently.

In a few minutes that seemed oddly compressed, the car stopped and the door opened. In the growing dark, they went where directed, up steps into another office. It seemed the Romanians liked steps. Their chaperone and his soldiers flanked them. Others waited inside.

Then they saw Mick Cafferty, sitting in a chair. He looked grim, until Kyle realized it was fatigue. The man was gulping a cup of coffee, and it probably wasn't his first. He smiled when he saw them, and it was an ugly smile on that lined and worn face.

"Glad to see you gentlemen," he said.

"Likewise, sir," Wade said, while Kyle was still shifting mental gears.

"How are things?" Kyle asked.

" 'How are things?' " Cafferty repeated, eyebrows raised. "We've annoyed our hosts, killed people on their soil, chased terrorists through their streets, allowed a shipment of explosives we knew about to come in without warning them, admitted to espionage and deceit . . ."

"That bad?" Kyle asked. Maybe they were all to be back in jail soon. Or just deported on the next plane.

"That bad. But you got two who were confirmed and scared up another, plus the explosives, which were secured. If we didn't have that to show, it would be bad. As it is, you impressed several bureau chiefs, including Dvidiu Pavenic." He pointed at their escort.

"Really?" Wade asked. Both snipers were still in shock.

"Really," Cafferty nodded. "There's new respect for our ability. We got you in, you tracked these bastards right under everyone's noses, and pulled them out."

"And the secrecy wasn't embarrassing?" Kyle asked.

"Not publicly. If you'd made a scene at any point and the press had caught on, that would have been embarrassing. But as long as it's quiet and our hosts get the credit," he hinted, "we can finish this."

"Hell, we knew we'd never be allowed to boast, anyway," Kyle said. "And I don't care about credit. General Robash knows what we're doing, and I don't crave to have hit squads bent on revenge. Anyone who wants the credit can take it."

From behind him, Pavenic said, "That is a very professional attitude, Captain. I like how you think, and I like how you shoot."

Kyle turned to face him. "And I like your honesty," he said. "With Mister Cafferty to approve, we're at your disposal." He wasn't quite sure he felt that way, but he knew they were under local command now. Still, that meant backup for any operation, and no need to worry about local issues. They could just shoot as they were told and let someone else take the blame. As much as Kyle liked independence and the trust placed in Wade and him, he could use a break.

"Yes. It's a pity Mister Cafferty didn't know to come to us first. But of course, he couldn't have known."

"Sir?" Kyle asked.

"Like yourself, we are a counterterror unit," he said, though Kyle had never thought of himself as a "unit." He was a soldier who took the shots and gathered the intel he was told to. Target acquisition was largely not his problem.

Pavenic continued. "We are a small platoon within DGIPI. And we all know our people, so we know there are no leaks here." That might not be entirely true at all times, but it likely was in regard to terror. No one competent wanted to shame themselves in front of their buddies, or get them killed through carelessness.

"And there was no way to know that," Cafferty agreed, "But I am very glad it turned out this way."

"So are we," Kyle said. It had likely made it much easier to get out of incarceration with the equivalent of the FBI interested.

"Then we are all happy, and happier still when these filth are shot, eh? Every nation that shoots a few makes it that much harder for the rest to operate and find homes. We shall get your property, and discuss what we are to do. I will return." He left, as did his henchmen, though Kyle was quite sure there was one posted outside the door.

As soon as the door closed, he took a glance around and asked Cafferty, "How bad is it?"

"Well, it could be better," Cafferty admitted. "We're on probation, and if we don't have something else to show, it's not going to be good."

"So you still need us to pull off a shot?" Wade asked.

"That would make things better," he admitted, drinking more coffee. "There are other ways, but that's cheapest and simplest."

"No pressure," Wade said, but he was grinning.

"None," Cafferty smiled back. "We told him you were officers. It made a better appearance that we required that status for a mission, rather than 'mere' NCOs."

Kyle nodded. "I thought that might be it. Understood, sir."

"Is there a temporary pay raise with that?" Wade joked.

"Sure is," Cafferty said. He leaned back, fished a European five-cent coin from his pocket, and dropped it on the table. They all chuckled.

"You're lucky," he added. "High profile prisoners are harder to have accidents with."

"Yeah, I was worried about that," Kyle said. Hell, there were

American cops who would have shot first or applied a club. He didn't imagine it was any better or worse here. Police were charged with the peace, but were also human beings, subject to prejudice and attitude.

"It was very tense," Cafferty agreed. "But I made calls, the ambassador made calls at the behest of State and DoD. We got someone over there. I hope you're both okay?"

"Hungry, thirsty, tired. And not thrilled about working with the locals." It was true, he had to say it.

"Well," Cafferty observed, eyebrows raised slightly, "it *is* their country. And I'd rather work at this level with Mister Pavenic than let the word leak out. DGIPI is known for their . . . vigorous attention and forthright approach."

Kyle looked at Wade, who nodded back. They both understood the implication. The government as a whole wouldn't hear of this, except as statistics. And there'd be no due process. DGIPI would bury the bodies deep and erase the records.

"Then we'll do it their way," Kyle acceded. There was nothing else to say.

The Romanian counterterror chief returned a few moments later. He was smiling faintly, and the smile became a grin when he saw the nods from the Americans. "Excellent," he said. He spoke a quick, fluid sentence to the captain with him, and the weapon cases were placed on the table. "Your tools, gentlemen," he said.

"Thank you, sir," Kyle said. He and Wade both dived in to assess the weapons.

They had been well dusted for fingerprints by the police, and some powder still drifted from ports and wells. But someone, likely with the DGIPI, had wiped them down with oil. They spent a few minutes stripping and cleaning with long-practiced fingers while they discussed strategy. The Romanians drank tea and Cafferty chugged coffee. What he really needed, Kyle thought, was a caffeine IV. He looked up from his work as a tray of sandwiches on dark bread arrived. He was grateful for that. His hunger was severe. It was decent roast beef with butter, salt, and mayonnaise. It would go a long way toward reviving him.

"We have posted guards at the borders, airports, and the port. While that doesn't prevent him from leaving, it does make his task harder. We were hoping to drive him underground," Pavenic said.

"That's where we found him last time," Kyle said.

"Perhaps not literally this time," spook said. "Nevertheless, with his photograph on television, he seems nervous. We are hoping to shortly get reports on his whereabouts."

"Assuming he comes out and is seen," Kyle said.

"Yes, there is that. However, we were able to trace his car to its owner. The owner also had a satellite cell-phone relay station, and several maps and charts. While not conclusive evidence, it was enough for us to question him further. He was hesitant at first"— Pavenic sounded rather pleased with that, and smiled a very cold smile. Kyle had an American's belief in due process, but a soldier's hatred of terrorists. The latter ruled and he wasn't very bothered by the probable torture that the accessory had suffered—"but he eventually told us what we wanted to know. It appears there was some kind of contact missed, because al Asfan was not in his hotel when we arrived. But we know where he is, approximately."

"Oh?" The question was asked simultaneously by Kyle, Wade, and Cafferty.

"Yes. He had another hideout in the Carpathians and tried to get there. He apparently figured out it was occupied and is now trapped. The road in that area is blocked, and we have the area monitored. But that still leaves a lot of mountain and forest to search. He could slip out at night, and we do have to let other vehicles through from time to time. We need to find him quickly. We will have the Army search, but he may be dug in quite well. As you have taken two of them so far, it seemed polite to invite you along. Besides, it allows me to keep an eye on you both without worrying over your whereabouts." He smiled again, with some humor.

"Oh, I'm in," Kyle agreed. "We both are." He looked over at Wade, who nodded slowly with a big grin. "There may not be enough left of this asshole to bury after everyone gets a shot," he said.

"There is a problem here?" Pavenic asked with a cold, feral grin.

"No problem," Kyle said. "Should I leave him alive for the rest of you?" he joked.

"That's rude," Wade chided. "I just may get the first shot."

They all chuckled together. Kyle asked, "Do we get to meet our counterparts?"

"As we have time," Pavenic said. "I shall be leading. Our sniper is Sergeant Tibor Dobrogeanu." He pointed. The man stepped forward and nodded.

It was pretty obvious who he was. He held a ROMAK-3 rifle, well cared for and customized to fit him. It had been customized the professional way, with duct tape, files, and spray paint. Only amateurs prettified their weapons. Experts went for function. Dobrogeanu was tall, blond and very lean, and looked very confident. He'd make a good, lanky Southern farm boy, and Kyle knew without asking that he could shoot. He was reaching out a hand, and Wade shook it, then Kyle. His grip was firm but without any attempt to prove how strong he was.

At once, the rest of the team was running through, gathering gear and piling it around. They nodded or shook hands at a run. Pavenic yelled orders, grinning and gesturing flamboyantly. Periodically, the team would respond with "*Da, domnule!*" in shouted unison.

Cafferty came over, sucking coffee, and said something to Pavenic. The CIA man looked like hell, Kyle thought. His eyes were sunken, his skin waxy. Whatever stress the snipers were under, this man looked as if he were fighting a war by himself. Or perhaps avoiding a war.

The two exchanged nods, then Cafferty came toward Kyle and Wade. He nodded with a faint frown and directed them to a corner for a bit of privacy.

Once there, he asked, "How are you feeling about this?"

"At least it's like being soldiers again—outside and shooting," Kyle said. "Woods, hills, support. I like it. It's much more our mission than the espionage stuff."

"Kyle, you got two so far. Another has been arrested and we're working on a fourth. Stop beating yourself up."

"Yeah, I know," Kyle said, frowning. "Still, we got found."

"Everyone gets found. That's why we have State, and why I've got a bank of favors I can draw on. Hell, it'd be a miracle if you hadn't been caught during this. We warned you at the beginning."

"I suppose," Kyle said. He did recall the emphasis. He just hated to be less than perfect.

"I trust Pavenic, but keep in mind he's very aggressive. You're on your own as far as orders go. I have no authority and you're volunteering to work with him. If there's any roughing up and it gets reported to the UN . . ." he tapered off.

"War crimes charges?" Wade asked.

"Could be," Cafferty said. "So you make the calls. I've got to slide out of here. But good luck, thanks for everything so far, and we'll talk again in a day or two."

"Right," Kyle said. "I just wish I knew more about this."

"So do I."

He turned with a half grimace, half smirk, and trudged out.

Meanwhile, Pavenic came over and asked, "Is there any equipment you need?"

"Yeah," Kyle said. "Our boots, some clothes, weather gear of some kind. Whatever radios you're using, or we'll use ours." He paused to think.

"Preferably our own stuff, if it can be gotten in time," Wade said. "We had all we needed at the hotel."

"I will see to it," Pavenic said. "That should only take an hour or so."

While they waited, Pavenic briefed them. It wasn't as bad as Kyle had anticipated. Pavenic laid a large map out across a conference table and used a wooden pointer. He waved it like a rapier, jabbing it when excited.

"Al Asfan was seen here as he left Braşov. Our informants tell us he has a facility of some kind in the mountains here." He jabbed the map over the Carpathians, near Comănesti. "We have a helicopter observing, and there is something there. So we will investigate."

"Flying in?" Kyle asked.

"We are flying nearby. I do not care to land on top of explosives," Pavenic said. "I am crazy, and vicious, it is said and is true." His men snickered. He smiled. "But I am no fool. We will approach a few kilometers on foot, quietly. The helicopters will maintain watching, and I have called Army units to patrol the lower elevations. They will stop and inquire of anyone, and shoot anyone who does not stop. The police are likewise blocking the road."

"But this is a large area," he continued, "and if al Asfan thinks we follow, he may leave on foot or by vehicle and manage to escape. So we will leave at once. I would like him by daytime." His expression said it would be by daytime or else.

Loud but cheerful voices came from the outer office, and in a few seconds, one of the operatives clumped in. He was dressed in urban casual; raincoat, jacket, shirt but no tie and sturdy shoes, and was carrying all their luggage. He looked like a cartoon gunbearer for a safari.

"We don't really need the cameras," Kyle said as he smiled. He reached out and helped the young man untangle from his burden. "Those were mostly for cover, anyway." Wade stepped in to grab other bags.

"This way you don't have to fish for them later," the man said.

That was true. "It's appreciated," Kyle said. "But we'll have to do a check for anything we left." He was thinking of notes or possible small items forgotten behind furniture.

"There is nothing left in the room that is not the hotel's," the man assured him with a grin.

"I'll take your word on that," Kyle agreed. The man was a professional at this; he'd likely gotten everything.

"Captain Monroe," Pavenic called, and Kyle turned, still holding the betacam. "Here is your new rifle." He came over with it extended at port.

Kyle took it. It was another ROMAK-3. The ROMAK looked a bit like a Dragunov, but had been built up from the AK action. It wasn't impressive, because Eastern Bloc theory was for the sniper to support the infantry squad, not be a force multiplier by gathering intelligence and disrupting operations by shooting important targets. It was what Kyle would call a designated marksman's rifle, not a sniper's rifle.

But this one, like Dobrogeanu's, had a Dragunov stock fitted to it, proper windage drums on the iron sights and a decent-looking long scope with tritium reticle. It was also, he discovered when he checked the ammunition, chambered in 7.62 NATO, not 7.62 × 54R Russian.

"Not bad," he commented softly. This might shoot well after all.

"It will shoot as well or better than you," Pavenic said.

"Want to bet?" Kyle asked with a challenging smile.

"I will trust you, Monroe. But if we get al Asfan first, you will buy the dinner."

"Deal," he agreed. It was a win/win proposition. Either he or Wade bagged another bad guy, or they assisted. If it all failed, there were a lot of people higher up to take the blame, and both nations would pass it off on each other. It was much more like the military he was familiar with, and would be a more comfortable shooting environment. And if he had to buy dinner, he had cash for the purpose. Uncle Sam's cash.

18

WITHIN ANOTHER TWENTY MINUTES, HE AND WADE had gotten dressed, equipped, and armed. They were in British DPM smocks, canvas pants, and boots. They wore their tactical load-bearing vests with Camelbaks, knives, holsters, and ammunition, plus compasses and radios. They carried their ghillies rolled up, and each had their weapons. Wade had the AK104 and his Beretta, Kyle had the ROMAK3, the Ruger, and his Ed Brown. He still liked something for quiet shots, and there was nothing quieter than the Ruger, but the ROMAK allowed him heavier shots if called for.

They were issued headset radios. They weren't too dissimilar from the kind they'd used before, but Kyle decided they'd take their cell phones, too. "We can avoid interception with those," he said.

"True, and it can't be a bad thing."

Then they were in vehicles and driving for the local airport. Kyle and Wade were in a Mercedes SUV with Pavenic, who had ditched his suit for a camouflage coverall and an AK. It seemed he wanted to keep an eye on them after the car stopped. He hoped it would clear some before it was time to shoot. Kyle couldn't really blame him. It wasn't a long trip, but visibility was poor from the back seats, and the driver was as aggressive as any local, plus had government authority to flout the laws even more. It was a nauseating drive, made worse as the amphetamines kicked in. Kyle didn't approve of drugs, but he'd heard pilots took these to stay alert on long flights, and they'd had little sleep the last week. After being stuffed with sandwiches and water, he'd felt better, but sleepy. Now he was awake and things were spinning. Things kept spinning even after the car stopped.

They flew out by helicopter. This was something Kyle had heard about but never done. He had flown in helicopters often. What he'd never done was fly in a French Puma built under contract by Romanians using their own engines. The design was older than Kyle, and this craft wasn't the newest of the fleet. Still, his hosts were offering it, and the pilot had to be good enough to fly it, and so, hopefully, was good enough to land it. There was no need to create a fuss and it wouldn't matter. Kyle climbed aboard and took the outside seat. Wade was directly across, Pavenic next to Kyle with Dobrogeanu next to him. The others filled in and stuffed their gear.

"How many on this mission?" Kyle asked just before the engines started. He'd seen a number of personnel running through the headquarters, but wasn't sure who was support, operations, pilots, or just home station staff.

Pavenic indicated a helmet and headset. Kyle squeezed it over his head. It was a tight fit. As soon as he had it secure, Pavenic said, "Sixteen of us. I want to limit the number in the area to avoid bumping into each other. Between mobile phones and radios, we should easily be able to call the Army for assistance if needed."

"Okay," Kyle said. He preferred more lead time, and he didn't think it was possible to have too many troops. But it wasn't his operation anymore, if it ever had been. He was just the guy who made the shots.

Across from him, Wade gave him a nod and a thumbs-up. They'd be fine.

The chopper was in decent repair. They rose quickly through fairly smooth air and headed toward the mountains. Helicopters always shift a bit through air currents, the density affecting lift. Every time it buffeted or dropped, Kyle had an image of them being taken out by a missile. It wasn't as if Stingers or their equivalent were unknown among terrorists.

He realized a lot of it was nerves, and much of it caused by ghosts from the past. He'd not thought about Jeremy or Nasima for some time. He'd been too busy out here to dwell on them. That was likely good, but they were still present in his unconscious. He thought for a moment about Jeremy, young and eager and funny in a refreshing way, different from Wade's cynicism. Then Nasima, who'd been a civilian guide, but very bright and with a dry wit.

Just thinking about them calmed him down. That was a first. Perhaps he was coming to terms with things at last. God knew it had been long enough, and one couldn't live in the past forever. But pain was part of life, and he needed to deal with it. He just wondered why it was always coming to him on his way into action. Was it fear for himself? Concern for Wade? Or just caution for mission safety digging a bit too deep? Analyzing the emotions kept him busy and did lower his stress level, even if it made him morose. He took the harness offered him and strapped it on without much conscious thought.

The pilot took his time. If they'd known where their target was, faster would have been better. As they didn't, there was no reason to hurry. He felt out the buffeting winds and settled over the trees, then gradually lowered. They were no more than twenty-five meters up when the signal came.

It was a respectable rappel, and the trees were an obstacle. The snipers had done rappelling, and did refreshers often. Wade was far more current than Kyle. Adding the height and dark to the fatigue and nausea, Kyle almost lost dinner. He gulped back and clamped down on his stomach. It was a standard descent, and he snapped the carabiners around the rope, checked it, and leaned out the side.

The rotor wash was rough, but he slid below it and things steadied out. With cool, fresh air to help, he was soon much more comfortable. The dizziness was gone, the nausea retreated a bit, and he was himself. He looked around and realized he'd been hanging for several seconds. It was time to catch up.

They slowed as they reached the tall pines, feet spread to kick away from limbs and trunks. This was when it was dangerous, with limbs to stab and blind, tangle and catch. Kyle wove and twisted his way through the timber until he could see the ground a few feet below him. He dropped the last few feet gratefully, then unsnapped from the rope and unfastened the harness. He jogged over with his stuffed ruck to form up with the others. Pavenic was waiting, smiling.

The helicopter powered away to drop another squad of six elsewhere, and a four-man element at a third point. They'd advance in three different directions, hoping to catch al Asfan at one of several likely spots. This group was heading straight for the "facility," which looked on photos to be a small barn or large shed.

Pavenic spoke quietly, everyone in a huddle with one man on watch.

"We will split into pairs, one leading, one behind and to the side for support. Minimize radio talk. The target of this sweep is three thousand, one hundred meters that way," he pointed up the mountain they were on, then checked his compass—"at ninety-one degrees." He double-checked by GPS. "We shall start at a slow walk, then crawl upon suspicion of threat. Understood?" He repeated it in Romanian, even though most of the team did grasp English. The snipers nodded, his own people whispered, "*Da, domnule!*" quietly but firmly, and they were on patrol at once.

These had to be the darkest, dankest, creepiest woods Kyle had ever been in. The hanging limbs and shadows were spiderlike and black against the sooty gray sky behind them. Midnight was near, and that's when al Asfan was likely to make a break for it. Anytime from midnight to five was the best guess.

Of course, that assumed the man was competent and trained in this environment. One had to always assume the enemy was both genius and fool, and allow for both possibilities at the same time. And no enemy ever reacted to plan, no matter how many plans one made. One followed the plan until things went to hell, then discarded it to fight by one's wits. Abandoning the plan too soon or too late was what caused one to lose.

"Going to take a lot of luck," Kyle said as he looked around. "Well, we know we've gotten two and the explosives."

"Hey, looks good so far," Wade said. "We'll find him."

"Not sure about that," Kyle said. "But if anyone does, it'll be us. Pride is at stake."

"Good enough," Wade said.

They advanced up the large hill, amplified eyes alert for anything unnatural. Night vision does take considerable practice to use, but an experienced professional can find many things that would escape a newer soldier. Various materials will reflect differently and show outlines even behind camouflage that would be effective in daylight.

It was a hill by American standards. Not like the Rockies, but perhaps like the Appalachians. Still, it was cool, becoming chill, and damp with the spring weather. Nice weather for hiking for fun, not nice for crawling in weeds. But then, there were no nice conditions for crawling in weeds, except Arabia, where there were no weeds. And there was the sand.

They spread apart to allow different angles for shooting or observing. This time, there was no risk of the government finding them; it already had. This time, they had backup. It made Kyle much more confident, and he reminded himself not to get cocky. Amateurs could still be good observers, and just because much of the enemy's operation was amateurish didn't mean there wasn't a vet or two among them. They hadn't created as much havoc as they had by being unintelligent, just by being prejudiced and stupid. So Kyle made a conscious effort to avoid rushing.

Nothing happened for the first kilometer. They came to a dirt trail that they'd seen in the photos, which was one of their landmarks. It came from the left, north, and curved to the east. The plan was to secure the area and then advance up both sides. So they examined the area for any fresh traces, smells, any sign of human activity. The DGIPI pilot would call down his observations. Until then, there was nothing to do but wait and be alert.

Pavenic called through and asked, "Report?"

"Nothing," Kyle said. "Clean, undisturbed."

"Good. We continue." The phrasing was simple and obvious to them, not so to anyone listening. It was well to assume the target had radio gear.

They had the easy part, continuing as they had. The Romanians had to cross the rutted path. That would take a few minutes, but there was no reason not to advance. They couldn't get far ahead at a crawl.

Another five hundred meters of tangled weeds and uneven ground passed, trees reaching down to caress them. Kyle was used to it. He'd spent much of his life in the wild. But it might be making their quarry nervous, as he was not from terrain like this. It was dark and foreboding, and a shot might come at any time. Combat didn't start when the enemy shot. Combat started when one hit the ground.

"As discussed, down," Pavenic ordered. Kyle dropped slowly to his knees and into a crawl, the nerves in his hands reaching out for warnings. He wore thin Nomex flying gloves, which kept off bugs and allowed good movement. He could feel feathery touches of leaves through them, and the ground. It was safer and less visible down here, but also slower, and it hindered their own views of their surroundings.

Forward and up they crawled around trees and shrubs, every movement careful. Neck back so as to see, with the NVGs dragging the head down and straining muscles. Hands and knees soaking up moisture and cold. Sweat beading under the arms. It reassured Kyle, because it was familiar.

"Possible sentry," Wade hissed through the phone.

Moving very carefully, he reached to his own phone body and pressed to transmit. "Where?" he asked.

"Appears to be a hasty position, under a bush. Do you see me?"

Kyle squinted to the last position he'd seen Wade in, then scanned forward. "Barely, but yes." There was a shape there, and a part of a boot. It wouldn't be visible to anyone ahead, but from here it was just discernible.

"Twenty-five meters ahead, left of the large gnarly tree, I think it's an oak. Spreading bush."

Kyle examined the area. One side of the bush did have a bit more hollow underneath it, where the natural debris and fallen leaves had been removed. He changed his angle slightly to the right and took a good look. There was something there that was probably human. Under the branches and leaves it stood out at the correct angle.

It looked as if the person revealed had used starch and/or an iron on their shirt. That flattened the nap of the fabric and created a reflective surface. To their night vision, it may as well have been aluminum foil. The guess was confirmed when the person shifted restlessly into a new position.

"Question is, who is that?" Kyle asked.

"Dunno. We have to check on whether or not it's one of ours," Wade said. It shouldn't be, on this side, but one didn't fire unless one was sure. Unless the target shot first.

"Calling." It took some time to move his hand to the radio controls, and Wade waited patiently while he did so. "Monroe here," he whispered inside his coat, eyes still watching. "We have a potential, IFF." He hoped that was clear. Identify Friend or Foe.

"I understand you. Where is the target?"

Kyle gave approximate grid coordinates. "Up slope from us. If anyone is on a slope, have them wave down and report."

"Wait . . . Do you see response?"

"Nothing here," Kyle said.

"Then you are clear to go."

"Understood. Out." It took another full minute to shift his hands and contact Wade again. "We're clear to fire," he said.

"Roger."

That wasn't all there was to it, however. There could be other enemy, presuming this *was* an enemy, within range. So it was necessary to secure the area first, then try to arrange a silent kill.

"I will traverse left and set up for shot," Kyle said. "Secure and observe."

"You will traverse and shoot, I will secure and observe," Wade repeated.

"Moving," Kyle said.

"Moving, roger."

It took nearly twenty minutes to shift to a spot with good visibility of the enemy's face. Kyle didn't recognize it, but he was armed and he wasn't in uniform, so he was a target. And the AK he held was ready. The first shot had to disable at the very least, to let them stay alive. That wasn't a problem. It would be better, however, to get a kill, so there would be no incoming fire to create a problem. The only reasonable way to do that was with a silenced, subsonic weapon. The 10 22 wasn't powerful enough for a reliable, instant kill. But fifty meters was a long range for any pistol, even an Ed Brown.

Just then, Pavenic spoke in his ear, "We are prepared to attack a perimeter position." He was speaking in clear, so he anticipated starting at once.

Kyle shifted as quickly as he dared. If they could get inside silently and set up, then they could have easy targets at the backs of their enemies as the DGIPI attacked frontally. That would roll all these guys up.

It took twenty seconds to shift the radio, while he cursed and sweated, expecting them to open fire any second. What was needed here, he decided, was some kind of radio that could handle internal squad communications, communications up a level, and a frequency for command. All of those should be selectable by voice.

But he did reach the control and brought his attention back to the task as he said, "Hold, hold. Do not fire."

"Holding fire, understood," was the response.

"Curtis and I can get inside, then we can roll up the entire perimeter," he said.

"How long do you need?"

"Another twenty minutes," he said. He could bag this guy now, and then they'd get past him.

"Hurry if you can," Pavenic urged him.

"Roger."

He continued his lateral movement and picked a log as his shooting position. Logs often crumbled when stepped on, but all he intended was to rest his arms on it. He elbowed along, dragging the rest of his body as silently as possible, the ROMAK dragging behind him from a sling over his shoulder in case he needed it.

He felt movement, and froze. It was just a small nocturnal animal of some kind skittering past, but he paused to ensure it hadn't attracted attention. A measured minute later, he resumed his creep and eased up against the dead limb. It was starting to rot and was slimy with fungus, mold and moss, but that wasn't something he worried about. It was cold to his forearms as he gingerly checked its stability. It didn't shift, and he was satisfied. A quick mental check of his condition and surroundings assured him he was well-masked and still unseen. Now to set up and shoot.

Slowly, he drew the pistol up under his body and secured the suppressor. In five minutes, it had grown in front of him like a metal log, lying atop the limb and pointing forward. He hunched and shifted, twisted his head and hands until it was where he wanted it. The only practical way to sight it while wearing NVGs was to extend it at arm's length, dead center. It was odd to see a single sight picture with both eyes, but that was the nature of the goggles, which focused one incoming image for both eyes.

There were the guard's eyes. He wanted to put this round right between them. For ease of function and consistency, he had stock 230 grain ball ammo. With his sight settings, it should be only two inches of drop at fifty meters. And the sight pattern barely cleared the suppressor's body. So he would lean way down, hold there, and place the front sight blade halfway between the bushy eyebrows and the combed hairline. The wind was negligible, and the heavy projectile wouldn't need any windage adjustment.

Right there, and as long as the man was holding still, squeeeeze.

With a thump that might be mistaken for an animal against a log, the .45 bullet erupted from the suppressor. Kyle could just see the flash with night vision. Anyone else could, too, and he tensed in case of fire. But the only response was for the enemy guard to jerk his head back, then slump forward. The shot had been dead center on the bridge of the nose.

"Go, Wade," Kyle muttered into the phone. He eased back from his brace, letting his eyes scan over the pistol for any potential targets. He relaxed his grip and prepared to shift for any new threats.

"Roger," Wade replied. Kyle saw movement from the corner of his eye as a "bush" rose to its knees and crawled forward. Wade was moving unnaturally but slowly. Several minutes later, he stopped just to one side of the corpse, his Beretta out and ready. He shifted in until the suppressor nearly touched the skull of the body, and fired an insurance shot that popped softly. It never hurt to make sure a corpse was really dead.

"AK, radio," he muttered back. "Cell phone. We need to hurry in case he's expected to check in."

"Got it. Is the other side of the road manned?" While Wade dealt with that question, he radioed Pavenic and said, "We have removed one sentry. Stand by and we'll clear the road. I think you can advance on our side safely."

Wade reported back right then. "I see what's likely a position, well dug in. I identify a rifle barrel. I cannot take a shot from here. I can spot for their sniper."

"Roger," Kyle said, then switched channels again. "Wade says he can perform terminal guidance."

"Please do," Pavenic replied. He sounded quite pleased. A few moments later, Dobrogeanu came on air.

"I am ready," he said.

What they were about to try would be dangerous against professionals. Against these amateurs, it was a different story. The big threat was that the enemy would not react predictably. An expert, upon being alerted, would call that fact in, then commence suppressive fire until reinforcements arrived. A frightened neophyte might shoot wildly, alerting everyone, call on the radio, or panic and do something really stupid. Either way, the other sentry had to be removed. It was just a case of how responsive he'd be.

Wade came on air and relayed his observations. "Fifteen meters left of the road. On a line horizontally, just above the water-filled ruts near the large pine with roots extending into the roadway."

Dobrogeanu replied back, "I see a pile of brush with ten centimeter limb running sideways from a pine tree. There is a light color boulder about two meters downhill."

"I see it," Wade said. "From that boulder, target is one boulder width higher, one meter left of the tree, just under the limb."

"I sight something in that location. It appears to be dull fabric." Dobrogeanu sounded confident and eager.

"Confirm target," Wade said.

"Confirm. Target acquired."

Pavenic came back on air. "At my order, Dobrogeanu will fire. All others will hold fire. Ready. Fire."

The ROMAK pop-cracked, and the animal noises stopped suddenly, leaving things silent. Hopefully, nothing else would happen and they could now advance.

From uphill there was a loud whisper. Someone was looking for the perimeter guards.

"Damn," Kyle said.

"I have a target," Wade said urgently.

"Shoot," Pavenic said.

The suppressed AK104 was no louder than a rock thudding on a tree. A third enemy dropped dead. But again, the local noises stopped.

"Well, we're known now, I think," Kyle said.

"Yes, but we have position."

Kyle didn't answer. It was true. They were military against amateurs, and even a defended position wasn't going to help the amateurs. But that didn't mean the professionals wouldn't take casualties.

The six of them progressed up the hill. Kyle really wished for more backup in the form of the Army. He knew there were disciplinary problems and potential leaks, but he still didn't like the low numbers. It was simply a matter of the number of people needed to cover the area.

On the other hand, there was no way a common Army unit could move that quietly en masse. They'd need an elite unit, anyway, and that would take time. As it was, the perimeter could be secured by any conscripts available until better forces came along. But it still left them as sixteen men spread across a large chunk of countryside, and only six on the advance.

Sure enough, there was response. It was a trained response, too. They might not have the experience of the snipers or DGIPI, but they knew how to move and were doing so in a coordinated fashion. Several figures were moving, low to the ground and hard to discern; they sounded heavy, which indicated equipment.

"They have night vision," Kyle heard from Pavenic. Someone had observed one of the enemy.

"Roger." So hold very still and try for a shot.

For long minutes, bare shuffles could be heard. The high ground was the tactically better, and these men had it. Also, they had hard cover in their positions, and possibly body armor, too. They'd be hard to dig out.

But waiting was something Kyle was used to. All they needed was to wait for daylight, then saturate the area. That it came down to a standoff at night was a good sign.

Nothing. For half an hour they lay and waited and watched. No obvious targets revealed themselves. Kyle asked Wade and Pavenic, who inquired back the other way. They shifted around to get different perspectives, aware of the fact that they were known this time, and that their targets were also adept at cover. If these troops had the mindset of many Muslims, one would expose himself to fire, and his buddies would return it in force against the attacking position. While that was always a risk, it wasn't one to be taken without support.

And it was too late now to retreat, or try a drop directly on the facility. They had to be sure their target was actually here, or risk pouring force here while he escaped elsewhere. With men this dangerous, "probably dead" in an explosion was not sufficient. A body or at least photos were needed. If the building was booby trapped, they'd have only estimates as to al Asfan's presence or lack thereof. That wasn't good enough.

Which meant that someone, very likely Kyle Monroe, was going to have to fight through or around these troops, and try to get a visual on al Asfan.

They knew there were sentries ahead. The sentries knew there were attackers. It was a standoff, and it favored the attackers, but it wasn't the best scenario. With that many people on the hill, al Asfan could more easily slip out, even with IR or night vision scans. He was willing to waste his troops to escape, and they were willing to be wasted, most likely. But that also meant a substantial hole in his network when this was done.

If nothing else, that was a nice consolation prize. But Kyle wanted this bastard's blood. So he sat and waited patiently for a signal.

The tableau was broken when Pavenic said, "Monroe, we have contact with Target Primul."

"Where and how?" he asked at once, quivering and even more alert, nerves bristling. Had they been seen?

"Through the captured mobile phone."

That made sense. If the man wanted to get hold of them, that was the logical way.

"What does he say?"

"He says he wants to talk to one of you directly. He thinks there's six snipers, for some reason."

"Disinformation from Cafferty," Kyle said.

"Ah, yes. You have your own leaks, despite your mistrust of us." Pavenic sounded a bit put upon.

"Not my department," Kyle said. Nor was now the time for a debate over the merits of one nation over another, the reliability of personnel and the relative risk of known and unknown leaks. Now was the time for shooting. "Give him this number."

A few moments later, Pavenic replied, "I have done so. Please do keep me aware of your discussion."

"I'll try to connect through the radio," Kyle agreed. He could hold it up and let it transmit from the earpiece. It might be audible. Or . . . was there a way to connect them directly?

No, he decided, after a few seconds of study. With a few cables, it would be possible. But not with materials on hand. His pondering was interrupted by the phone buzzing.

"Yes?" he answered.

"Sergeant Kyle Monroe," al Asfan said, barely above a whisper.

Sergeant. Not "Captain." So this guy did have some decent intel. Kyle wasn't that surprised. It wasn't all that unlikely, with the leaks they'd had, that someone would get his correct rank. It was a bit odd that the terrorist would make an issue of it. One never gave away intel advantages, unless it was part of a psy-war ploy. So this character didn't know as much as he wanted to, and was trying to impress them with the little bit he did. Still . . .

"Yes, may I help you?" He neither acknowledged nor denied the name or rank. Hopefully, he didn't sound surprised, either. In truth, this stage of an incident like this called for a professional negotiator. But they didn't have that option, time was short, and there was a real risk this asshole could blow something up. Best to keep him busy here, if he really was here. He wouldn't make the mistake of using a traceable phone again, so was either using a satellite cell, or had some way to spoof his signal. Actually, they knew he'd done the latter.

"I intend to see you dead."

"Of course you do," Kyle said. "Actually, seeing it shouldn't be hard. Just wait until I die from old age and come to the funeral home."

"Don't play stupid. You know I control this situation. I could make some other phone calls and have some bombs set off."

Hell, you might have arranged that already, in case you die. But I sure as hell won't say so. Kyle had little idea what to do at this point, except he was sure the things shown on TV were wrong. Meanwhile, he'd managed to get the headset mic next to the cell's speaker, and hoped it was being heard.

"What is there to talk about?" Kyle asked. "Or are you just trying to postpone the time when I blow your head off?"

"I just wanted to tell you that there's explosive in the building. Attacking it will cause it to blow up. Also, several other bombs will be triggered if I don't send orders not to."

"Okay, you have bombs. We knew that. You want to kill kids. We knew that. Is there anything important?" He wanted to goad this man into talking more, so they could glean intel.

"I am explaining to you why I control the situation. Don't be a fool, or much blood will be on your hands."

"The only blood on my hands," Kyle said, "is going to be yours. Sorry, jackass, but 'Waah! Waah! Look what you made me do!' doesn't impress me. If anyone else dies, it's your fault, and it might get you to live a bit longer. That way I can watch the expression on your face while you bleed to death." He intended no such thing. Revenge was dangerous, and Kyle could create such thoughts himself, if he really wanted to. The fact was, he hated killing, despised having to shoot people like this, but there was no way anyone had found to reach them otherwise. And given the choice between killing them or letting them hurt others, Kyle knew which he preferred.

"I have just sent an order," al Asfan said tightly. "People are going to die because of your arrogance."

"Hell, if my word can cause death, I've got every right to be arrogant." He figured that would shake things up. He also *did* feel guilt over any pending deaths. If they'd gotten this guy earlier . . .

No, that wasn't true. Kill one, and the next idiot stepped into his place. "The War on Terror" might be a good political name, but the reality was there were always people wanting to tear civilization down, and there had and would always be a need for men like Kyle to deal with it. Bin Laden was in hiding or dead, and the bombings continued. Bin Qasim was dead, and the bombings still went on. But if they kept taking out the brains of the operation, and the demented whiz kids who built the bombs, eventually they'd trim it to a manageable level.

Until next time.

"I had hoped to reach you and talk like a man," al Asfan said. "I see I was mistaken. Another bomb has been ordered."

"I do hope it's France," Kyle said. "Everyone hates the French." He was taking a guess there, but playing on current politics. He really had to convince this nutcase that he didn't care about bodies, that he, too, was a sociopath. That would mean al Asfan would have to find another way to antagonize him.

There was silence. That might mean it was working. Of course, the guy could also be ordering several dozen bombs around the world as a "fuck you" gesture.

Likely not. If he had all those bombs, he would have been setting them off. That he'd ordered all that explosive meant he intended to. But most of it had been captured.

So tweak him again, Kyle thought. "Why don't you come here?" he prodded. "Afraid?"

"Afraid of being shot by cowards who hide in shadows? Why, yes, I am. Are you afraid to meet me like a man?"

"Not at all. I'll give you my map coordinates and you can come meet me."

Best case, he'd get in, bag this trash, and nothing else would happen. That seemed unlikely, but he had come here to deal with this, so he might as well. But he didn't want to sound eager. Nor could he sound impressed by the threats toward civilians, or they'd never stop.

"You and DGIPI and your five other gutless snipers. No doubt you'd wet your pants upon my appearance, but then you'd attack me, like so many rats. I prefer a better way."

"So do I," Kyle said. "I advised them to just bomb the shit out of you from the air, but they want to be reasonable."

"Of course you will not bomb me, because the retribution would be horrible," al Asfan said smugly. "We know you are a nation of cowards."

"Yeah, whatever," Kyle said. "Is there anything important to discuss, or should I get back to hunting you? I even have a terrorist hunting call here. *Allahu akbar!*"

"One more mindless insult and you shall cause another bomb to go off. Many more people will die for your ego." He was shaking now, audible through the phone. It was dangerous to tread on religious ground with lunatics, and not something Kyle would ever do with decent Muslims around . . . but there weren't any here and it was helping to infuriate his enemy. Al Asfan's threats were very repetitive. That was a good sign. It meant he had no other refuge.

Always the way with terrorists. They built the bomb, placed the bomb, chose the victims and the reason, but someone else "made" it happen. It was appropriate for five-year-olds. But from terrorists, wife beaters, or rapists, it drove Kyle into a frenzied rage. Which is why he was here.

"Right. You set off your bombs. I've got work to do." He deliberately held the phone down underneath and cycled the bolt on the Ruger. Then he disconnected.

Because there was no more intel to be had from this source at present, the enemy obviously feared snipers, and cutting al Asfan off denied him control of the conversation. He should be well stewed by now.

"Did you catch all that?" he asked Pavenic and Wade.

"*Da.*"

"Yup. Guy's nuttier than a box of granola."

Pavenic continued, "I recommend we press on. He made no threats against us, and we can secure this area. I suspect he is here, or he wouldn't be trying to distract us."

"I concur," Kyle said. "Fast or slow?"

"As dictated," Pavenic said. "After all, we would prefer not to take casualties to filth like this. We shall continue slowly and go to the fast attack if circumstance changes."

"Roger. I recommend we pick a probable target and saturate it. That will split their attention among all of us, and we'll have Wade and Dobrogeanu spot for additional targets."

"That should work," Pavenic said. "Do you have a target?"

"Wade does. Wade?"

"Target, individual with rifle. Reference, large pine to one o'clock, just above a ridge of rock . . ." Wade read them in until everyone had acknowledged some kind of target, either the man, or the spot where Wade said there was a man. The volume of fire should be sufficient to ensure success. Of course, there were quite a few others in these woods, and God knew how they'd react.

Still, battles were like that. It was time to bring it on.

"On your order," Pavenic acknowledged.

"Roger. Stand by on my order. All elements take aim. Commence . . . fire!"

The sound wasn't that of shots. It was one disciplined, controlled roar that shook the hill. Through his goggles, Kyle could see a rifle slump down into the dirt below the position. *Scratch another asshole.*

It also had an effect on the other enemy. They opened fire, just as wanted. Kyle hadn't left any traceable signature with a suppressed .22, but the larger rifles did have muzzle flash. Flash suppressors attenuate the blast somewhat, and more important, divert it from the sight plane of the shooter. But large-caliber rounds always have a nimbus of fire.

The return shots were chaotic and ragged, but there were a lot of them. Then there was the glare and bang of a grenade. Wade was shouting another target reference, but Kyle couldn't make it out clearly in the din. So it came down, as it usually did, to two groups of people shooting it out, each hoping for the other group to make more mistakes.

Kyle was about to deliberately make a mistake. They needed to get through this line and find their real target. There wasn't time to discuss it, and the mass confusion offered a chance. He wasn't about to let al Asfan slip away yet again, so he took immediate action on his own authority. His headset spoke, someone reporting himself wounded. So the enemy weren't totally incompetent. Or else they'd been very lucky. Other shouts came, both directly and through the radio. Most were Romanian. A few were fractured English, from

Pavenic. Some sounded as if they might be Arabic, and one was probably Russian.

He unfastened his ghillie by ripping the buttons. He wasn't going to be hiding, and it would slow him down with what he had planned. He wrapped it around the ROMAK and dropped it. It wasn't as safe as pulling the firing pin, but he was in a hurry, and as tangled as it was, it would take time for anyone to get it, even if they found it.

That done, he stood to a crouch and ran forward, dodging from tree to tree. Taking cover and concealment was not something he needed to think about; he'd had fifteen years of practice. At each position he scanned ahead for threats, then rose to dart forward another few meters. He kept a close eye out for the perimeter guards, and saw one, cuddling the ground and trying to look invisible. That was probably the smartest thing he could do, but it wasn't going to help here. Kyle swung the Ruger and tapped two shots past the helmet and deep into the collar. The man convulsed and probably yelled—Kyle wasn't sure. But as the man arched up, another bullet through his throat made it academic. There were major blood vessels in both locations, and even if he didn't die at once, the battle was over for him.

Kyle was panting up the mountain. Even though he'd practiced the method, uneven movement took more energy than a straight run, and it was uphill. Adrenaline coursed through him, making him warm. It would also make his shots a bit less accurate. He kept scanning ahead for other threats, but it seemed to be clear along this line. Then he saw one far to his left, focused on something farther downhill.

He knelt, raised the Ruger and got a sight picture just as his elbow met his knee for stability. A squeeze and it was over, the round catching his target right below his helmet line, almost through the ear. The man dropped and spasmed as he died, and that was it.

Except for the grenade he'd been holding, which detonated a few moments later, blowing him and large chunks of landscape around. Still, that meant no more grenades—at least not from that source. Another banged farther away.

It sounded as if the fire below was slacking off. That was either an indication of success or of lines stabilizing again. But that wasn't his concern. If he'd moved properly and the reports were correct, the facility in question should be a bit farther up the hill.

He slowed slightly, both to reduce the rasping tear of cold air through his throat and to keep better track of his surroundings.

Ahead, the terrain appeared to level out, with mist starting to fall. That was probably where he wanted to go.

Wade spoke in his ears, "Where are you, buddy?" It was the cell phone.

"I'm closing on where I think the cabin is. Get them to encircle closer if you can."

"Will do. I'll be along in a few."

"Roger."

He topped a slight rise and entered a meadow. Ahead, he could see a rude lodge built of clapboards and blocks. It was of good size, perhaps ten meters by six. But that didn't mean that was all there was to it, and even that space was enough for plenty of people or explosives. He kept walking, slowing his pace slightly and making sure he kicked brush and weeds. It wouldn't do to surprise a man who was a raving paranoid and liked blowing up children. If he was here, Kyle wanted to let al Asfan feel he had total control of the situation. Then Kyle, or possibly the others, would exploit that imagined superiority.

Closer still, he could see signs of light within. A few slight gaps around the door glowed with a dull yellow, as of a flashlight or low-power bulb. That also was a good thing for Kyle and his people. Any target would be illuminated.

But that meant he had to go in and check. Al Asfan might already be heading out. And Kyle was damned if he would get away again. It might let the man feel competent and worthwhile. Or be taken as a sign from Allah. You could never tell how a nutcase would interpret things.

Worst case, al Asfan wasn't there, a flunky shot Kyle or blew him up, al Qaeda set off a bunch of other bombs and went public. Tough for the CIA, the army, the president, Romania, the United States, and whichever poor bastards were within bombing range.

And, tough for Kyle, who would be dead with nothing to show for it.

He really didn't want to do this, but the opportunity had come around, and he was going to take it. And when he got back, he'd have a polite discussion with General Robash, who'd hopefully have a less than polite discussion with others, to the effect that snipers weren't Delta, and weren't spies. They watched and shot.

Kyle moved back to his knees and crawled through the wet grass. In seconds, he was sodden from dew. But the dense air, mist and tall growth should reduce his visibility and sound. A few burrs, jabs from sticks and thorns, and the wet chill were minor things to trade for tactical advantage.

He kept a good scan going. Nothing threatening was apparent, and he reported that to Wade. "I'm about fifty meters out," he said. "I won't speak again until I know what's there." He didn't want to be given away by the sibilance of a whisper.

"Roger that. Good luck," Wade said.

"Roger and out."

He wove through the grass, lower and more cautiously. But he didn't want to take too long. There were no positions visible, a careful scan across the woods showed nothing in the way of people, though there was a fox or something similar trotting at some distance. The building had no windows.

Controlling the buzz in his head, his throbbing pulse and cold sweats, he stood and stepped straight toward the door, through knee-high weeds and boulders. He hesitated for just a moment at the door, studying the weathered, grainy planks.

19

THE HANDLE WAS ON THE RIGHT SIDE. IT TURNED EAS-
ily enough, and he pushed, half afraid of a blast or shot. The
door had swelled from weather and stuck slightly at the top, but
gave to a bit more force. The dim light within was still far brighter
than that outside, and he blinked against it. His glance took in
crates, dust on a badly cracked floor and cobwebs. He held the rifle
in close and eased through the opening.

To the left was al Asfan. He was standing, smiling, and held a device in his hand, with wires running to a backpack. Kyle took that
as a warning, and made no sudden moves. Adrenaline should have
been ripping through his body, but he'd exhausted all he had already.

"Please sit, so I can keep an eye on you," al Asfan said. His smile
wasn't there anymore, just a smirk. "I have no reason to trust you."

Kyle sat on the floor and said nothing. He ignored the chunks of
concrete poking him and waited. He wasn't sure what to do under
the circumstances, so he would wait until something happened he
could deal with, then react accordingly. Al Asfan was wearing that
pack, the thing in his hand could be a detonator, and Kyle wanted
to know a lot more about the situation before he tried to shoot. It
might be a switch that triggered on release. He had no reason to
trust, either.

"Remove the headset slowly," al Asfan said. Kyle sighed very
softly. He'd hoped he might get a word out. Still, his silence would
be a broad hint to Wade. Eventually. "Now lower the rifle slowly."

Which assumed Wade could get up here in time. So he'd stall and
hope. In the meantime, he'd keep an eye out for exploitable mistakes, and curse himself for being rash. He lowered the rifle muzzle

first. Caution and stealth. And they shouldn't have split up. An Army of One, he thought to himself.

Bad idea.

"This is a mercury switch," the terrorist said. "Attack me, tilt it just a little, and it will connect. I use them to avoid having people handle my bombs." He smiled a little.

"How special for you." No fear. At least not visible. He looked the man over. Work jacket, pants, boots. A bit muddy. He'd been outside. A Browning Hi-Power tucked into his belt. The backpack. The wires. The switch.

"It is special," al Asfan said. "Few can do it well. I've counted five bomb-disposal experts among my score."

"Not bad. I'm up over thirty terrorists and their buddies," Kyle replied. He wasn't going to accede anything to this jerk.

"You should watch your words." That while shaking the switch in his hand. Kyle cringed inside and felt his anus pucker. He forced his eyes away from the stubby tube and back to his opponent's eyes.

Was that a real switch? he thought. It wasn't smart to shake it, if so. But then, this man was insane and stupid, and he'd only stirred it around in the air, keeping it vertical. So assume it was real, for now.

"Hey, I call it like I see it," Kyle said. "You wanted to compare body counts, so I gave you mine."

Again the twitch of the switch. Again Kyle kept his face clear, though inside his guts were ice, his stomach flopping and acidic. He might get an ulcer from this, if he survived.

"I will not kill you yet," al Asfan said. "Perhaps I will not kill you at all. But I do require your silence and stillness while we deal with your assistants. Then we shall leave this place. Would a ransom be paid for your survival, hmm?"

It was very unlikely the current administration would back its troops that way, he thought. It was always bad policy to pay a ransom. They might send a team from Delta, if it was deemed worthwhile—assuming this jackass intended for him to stay alive. The best way to help that was to play along.

"Very likely," he said conversationally. He wanted to be loud enough for Wade to hear, but not obvious. "We're not the easiest people for the CIA to replace."

"Isn't it interesting how often the CIA makes such critical mistakes?"

"Yes, but we also get a lot of things right. Those don't get heard about. Like your buddy bin Qasim."

"He was shot by Delta Force in Pakistan," al Asfan said. "I watched. And that is why I moved to Europe, where such cowardly tactics are harder. Witnesses might see such skulking and object. That is the weakness of your world."

"I killed him," Kyle said, pushing. "Through the head and chest with a three oh three Brit. And if I'd known you were there, I would have hung around to get you, too."

That got a reaction. The man snarled, his face in an ugly, screwed-up mask. "Then I am glad to meet you, so I may send you to hell!"

"No problem. I'll be waiting when you get there and spend eternity blowing your ass away," Kyle replied.

A growl and clenching of his other fist was the only immediate response. This man didn't like being outmaneuvered, out-talked, or out-flanked. He really wasn't very bright. But he was dangerous.

Kyle stared at the mercury switch for a fraction of a second. He thought about a shot at that hand, hoping the energy imparted would destroy the switch. But from what he recalled of the subject, it wouldn't take much of a connection to cause it to trigger. If he managed a head shot, it would be dropped and trigger. A center of mass shot wouldn't kill fast enough, and the switch would be dropped and trigger. Frankly, he couldn't think of anything to do that would not cause the switch to trigger. He wasn't sure of the power of TNT, but he was sure that there was enough present to paste him throughout the bunker, even if it didn't detonate hard enough to take the rest of the cache with it, because a surreptitious glance revealed as many crates as he'd seen under Bran. There were also radios here, Russian surplus and shortwave. That meant messages could be sent, to either start or stop bombings. But which? If they hadn't been ordered yet, all he had to do was kill this jerk, which was easy. Grabbing him and shaking him would do it.

Which would also kill Kyle.

It wasn't that Kyle was against dying for his mission. This way would be relatively painless, in fact. But he wasn't eager for the process if he could think his way out of it.

He must have telegraphed just a bit of his intent. The smirk was back as al Asfan said, "That is the difference between us. I don't fear death."

"I don't fear it, either. I just like to make mine count for something," Kyle said. "I'm not sure killing you is worth the effort." He was going to harass this asshole until something happened. The worst that could happen was death, and that meant a qualified kill of a terrorist. "I mean, you're going to stand before God and tell him you helped blow away innocent children? Won't he be so proud?"

"I am changing the course of nations," was the response. But he wasn't quite so firm or assured.

"Right, you're scaring people into changing so you don't kill their kids. Big, brave man. Even here, you strap on explosives, because you know with any weapon or bare hands, I'd rip your fucking head off."

"And which of us is known? Whose name makes people shake in fear?"

"Mine does, to shitballs like you," Kyle said, growing more confident. "You heard about me in Pakistan. And I don't need to flaunt my name to know what I am. I'm the best fucking shooter in the world, and you know it, I know it, the people I work for know it, and I don't give a damn what anyone else thinks. I don't get a kick out of scaring kids. Matter of fact, I love kids. I'm not afraid to admit it, either. Die to save a kid? Yeah, I'll die to save a kid. That's what a *man* does. It takes a special kind of person to kill a kid and be proud of it. And do you know what we call that kind of person in the civilized world? Usually something along the lines of 'pussy.' " He was leaning forward now, and had his hand nearly in his jacket.

He was going to die, he decided. He was terrified of the event, and not afraid to admit it to himself. But as soon as he could reach that pistol, he was going to try a shot for that switch. Worst case, he died. Best case, he disabled the switch and made a followup shot. Either way, he accomplished his mission and this freak died.

"So says a man who can't die!" al Asfan challenged. "Death is not to be feared. Allah chooses his own and brings them to paradise. Infidels afraid of how they will be judged fear death."

"Yeah? Well I'll be happy to look your God in the face, tell him I splattered four baby-killing, woman-scaring, scumbag terrorist assholes personally, along with three dozen junior-grade assholes who worked for them, and let him judge me on that. I've got no problem at all, pal. Go ahead, tilt the switch!" Kyle had known reverse psychology to work sometimes. Perhaps this would be one of them. Because he had his hand inside his coat and brushing the Ed Brown. That was his confidence. Not a bomb to blow up everything and make a mess, but a surgical tool to eliminate this cancer, if he could get hold of it.

"You're bluffing." Al Asfan grinned and shook the switch, seeing if Kyle would react. Just a bare jiggle, but how much would be needed to set it off?

"TILT THE FUCKING SWITCH, YOU COWARD!" Kyle shouted, snarling to hide the sheer terror he felt. He gripped the .45 and started to draw, knowing it to be the last thing he would do.

The terrorist grinned hugely, and the mindless hatred shone through his eyes. He shifted his hand and turned it sideways, a loud popping sound disturbing the air.

That's an odd last sound to hear, Kyle thought, the pistol clearing his coat and coming up, up into sight plane. Al Asfan was staring stupidly at the switch, because it hadn't worked, and Kyle raised his aim, letting it drift up, up over that confused, wrinkled forehead. He snapped the trigger.

The first round smashed through al Asfan's forehead and the confused glint in those eyes disappeared into death. Kyle let the pistol rock back and down, snapped the trigger, and a second round went through the middle of the face, just left of the nose. Recoil, drop, and shoot, and a third round punched through the chin, making a shambles of the jaw and shattering the spine behind it.

The man was a corpse. Three 230 grain bullets at barely subsonic speed had shattered his head with nearly 1700 foot pounds of energy, like a half dozen full-strength swings of a ball bat, only much quicker. What was left was reddish-gray slop with shattered bone fragments in a rawhide bag that could only charitably be called a scalp.

Kyle was panting, sweating, shaking. He sat for nearly a minute, unable to move. Every sense was overwhelmed by the event, and by the sheer stress. He didn't know what had happened, but he knew he'd never been closer to death. His pulse had to be 240 beats a minute and was just starting to slow. His ears heard something else, but he wasn't sure what it was yet. They were still ringing from the shots.

"Yo," he heard it again, above the headache and aftereffects of shooting in an enclosed space. It was Wade.

"Yo," he said back, unable to find words of his own. He looked around to see his partner entering the doorway, AK in hand.

"Not bad," Wade said. "Three shots off under that kind of stress. You really are a sniping God."

"Thanks," Kyle said, flushed and feverish, sweating and shivering. "I don't know what happened. But it didn't go off."

Wade walked past him, carefully, and bent down next to the body. He pulled a piece of string loose and studied it.

No, not string . . . it was the wire from the mercury switch, neatly cut. Kyle stared dumbly at it for just a second. Then he knew. There was 7.62 millimeters of wire missing, that had to be embedded in that little crater in the wall he hadn't seen until he followed Wade's eyes to it. He drew a line back from the wall and figured the shot had gone over his shoulder, within a handsbreadth of his head.

That had been the popping sound he heard.

"Holy shit," was all he could say.

"Hey, no problem," Wade said.

"No problem my ass." With the situation explained, his brain came mostly back online. The inexplicable was terrifying. The rational, no matter how unlikely, was just impressive. "How far was that shot?"

"Seventy-five meters," Wade said. "From that tree." He pointed. It was a broad, spreading oak at the edge of the meadow, skeletal in the spring night. Kyle had to lean out the door to see it clearly.

Seventy-five meters, and at a target the diameter of the bullet, seeing as the bullet was larger than the wire. On the range, quite doable. From a tree, through a door, over a friendly shoulder, through a wire connected to a backpack of explosives. With wind and at night. That was one bastard of a shot.

Kyle dredged up the phrase he used at the school to students who impressed him. "Way to go, Sniper. You rock."

And had saved his life, with perhaps a half second to spare.

"I owe you one," he added. Al Asfan had been going to blow them both away. And though that was a sacrifice Kyle now knew he could make, he was just as happy he didn't have to. There were far better things to die for than that asshole.

In fact, there were far better things to *live* for.

"Hell, after Pakistan and the castle, I think we both owe each other a few," Wade said. "Let's not keep score or it'll get messy."

"Done," Kyle said.

Wade bent back down and pulled the Browning from the corpse's belt. He cleared it and handed it to Kyle. "Souvenir."

"Thanks." It was a needed distraction, and he examined it. Older, worn, but matching numbers and Belgian production. "*Fabrique National de Armes de Guerres. Herstal, Belgique.*" There were other symbols from whoever had issued it originally.

He looked back up at Wade and started to get to his feet at last.

Wade twitched at a sound in his ears and grabbed his phone. "Yes, it's safe. Come on in."

"On second thought," he continued to Kyle, "I'm calling in a favor. *You* do the paperwork on this."

"Ah, hell, just shoot me and be done with it," Kyle said.

Then they were both laughing hysterically. They were stressed as much as they'd ever been, and needed to lose it somehow. Kyle reached out a hand, and Wade grabbed it. Then they were shaking hands, hugging, and whooping.

Shouts from outside interrupted them, and they leaned back, panting. "We're here!" Wade shouted. Kyle was still too shocky to do much.

Then Pavenic was at the door, a pistol in hand, two troops behind him with rifles. Seeing the two snipers alive, they relaxed slightly and moved inside.

"I assume that is him?" Pavenic asked, looking at the corpse. There wasn't enough face to identify. Likely dental records would be insufficient, if indeed there were any. Fingerprints might do it.

"It was," Kyle said. "It came right down to the wire."

Then he realized what he's said and roared with laughter again.

Noticing the expression on the Romanian's face, he said, "Wade, you explain. I've got to go take a whiz." He really did, very badly. He was amazed he hadn't wet himself over the incident. It wasn't every day you sat on the floor in front of a loon with half a ton of explosives in the room and his finger on the button.

He brushed past for the door as Wade said, "Ah, well, look here, because you won't believe me if I tell you."

Dobrogeanu was outside standing guard against threats, and there were two wounded who were watching each other. Kyle made it quick, draining against the side of the building, then turned back in. Pavenic was examining the wire, and his expression was priceless. But there were more important things.

"It's secure here," Kyle said. "Should we call the Army and get your casualties out?"

"We await the helicopter," Pavenic agreed. "I just called. And I have something for you," he said, turning. He took two steps forward and grabbed Kyle in a huge embrace, European style, then again for Wade.

Then he started whooping, before switching to an obscene Romanian folk song.

20

IT WAS THIRTY HOURS LATER, MIDMORNING, WHEN
they met to gather loose ends. Kyle had told his story, sketched
everything he could, shared photos with their new hosts, looked at
their reports and images and spent the entire day doing paperwork
and loving it. No matter how bad it was, it was infinitely better than
watching a madman wave a mercury switch around. He'd remember that.

Which didn't mean his current love affair with paperwork was
more than a fling.

And there were no friendly deaths this time. Their wounded allies
were recovering, Sam and Cafferty were unhurt, Wade was unhurt,
Kyle was shaky but would be fine in a few days. The mission had
been pulled off and no one had died. That alone was cause for another celebration.

He'd add that to the tally for tonight. Apparently, many toasts
and drinks were planned at the DGIPI headquarters, in the section
used by the counterterror platoon. For now, they were all eating
catered food while they wrapped up. And it was *good* food, local,
without pretension or gimmicks, just ethnic and hot and delicious.
Almost dying had nothing to do with it.

They all sat back for a moment, pausing between one round of
forms and another. Something that had occurred to Kyle a while
back came to mind.

"Mister Pavenic, Mister Cafferty, I need to ask one favor," he
said.

"Yes?" Mick prompted. Pavenic just looked at him and waited.

"The Ruger and the Browning. Could Romania officially
confiscate these?"

"We can," Pavenic said. "But why? I'd thought for you to keep them as well-deserved trophies."

"That's just it," Kyle said. "The Ruger is Army property. If I try to take the Browning back, likewise. The best that can happen is they'll be stuck on display at the school. The worst is that . . . a certain person in my chain of command"—he didn't mention Wiesinger by name—"will have them disposed of. That means cut up and destroyed. No military weapons can be let into civilian hands, thanks to Bill Clinton. But if they're seized by your agency, and turned over to a dealer, I can then arrange to buy them and import them. They're perfectly legal weapons if they aren't military property." He couldn't have the suppressor for the Ruger, of course. But otherwise it was just a very nice little rifle.

"A rimfire rifle and a basic pistol are illegal for soldiers to take to a country where they can buy almost anything?" Pavenic asked. "I will never understand bureaucrats. But yes, I'll do it."

"I'll call about the import," Cafferty said. "And have the papers to you before you depart. What about you, Wade?"

"The AK has a short barrel, and automatic fire. Somehow, I don't think they'll let me have it," Wade replied. "So let the school have it for braggin' rights and I'll shoot it when I'm there. But I wouldn't mind a real tour of Bran Castle before we leave. The top parts."

"Yes, me, too," Kyle said. "Heck, it can't be nearly as scary."

"You haven't met the tour guides," Pavenic said with a chuckle. "But yes, you shall have a tour, and dinner, and we shall toast success."

"It was a good mission," Kyle said. "And I think I deserve one beer."

Author's Note

THERE REALLY ARE TUNNELS UNDER CASTLE BRAN.
Publicly known are the elevator shaft and the tunnel attached to
it. Frankly, I don't believe that the only purpose of those was for
Queen Marie to reach the garden at the bottom, and it's too close
to the building to be an escape route. The elevator does have a
1960s or later control panel, in the photos I've seen. So there's
something down there. It might be burial catacombs or a "real" escape tunnel to the mountain. It might be merely a hidden study or a
cache for valuables in case of attack. Considering the recently discovered secret stairs on the east side of the Castle, that ascend three
floors to the study, it's hard to guess. The staff of the Castle and all
the sources I've seen are remarkably reticent. There's probably
something there, almost no one knows about it, and it seems as if
many people want it forgotten. If it is victims of some old regime,
or private graves, that might be best. On the other hand, even a
video tour of collapsed crawlspaces taken with a remote camera
would be a fascinating little addendum to the history of the castle
and the area. Perhaps someday they'll arrange it.

My thanks to members of www.thehighroad.org for support. My
continued thanks to the U.S. Army Sniper School for research. As
always, any errors in shooting or tools are mine, and likely inten-
tional for dramatic effect.

CONFIRMED KILL

To Morgen Kirby,
for bad puns, worse jokes,
and a disgustingly delightful acronym

1

SERGEANT FIRST CLASS KYLE MONROE TRIED TO THINK about other things than an impending parachute jump.

It wasn't that he didn't like jumping. He did—though he preferred "admin jumps" to maintain proficiency, or an occasional civilian free fall, to a combat jump over hostile territory. At least he assumed so. He'd made over a hundred jumps. He'd been in more than enough combat, too, but this was the first time he'd jumped in to meet it. It was also the first time he'd done a free fall military jump outside of the High Altitude, Low Opening course he'd been rushed through in a few days. HALO was supposed to be a four-week school. He'd done it in nine days. Officially, that was impossible.

That was the Army. There was never time to do it right. But there was always time to do it again after screwing it up the first time . . . if they could replace him.

Of course, they'd also have to replace his buddy and spotter, recently promoted Sergeant First Class Wade Curtis, sitting next to him. Replacing the third member of their team, Colonel Joseph Melville Wiesinger, who was sitting across from them, wouldn't be hard and would be a very good idea, Kyle thought. He had no idea why the man was along, except to grandstand and try to hog glory. That was typical of this type of officer, and likely the only reason he had come. It wasn't as if Wiesinger had a lot of depth to him.

The C-141 wasn't the most comfortable craft to ride in, though there were a lot worse. Still, the inside was all metal and harsh. The steel frame had an aluminum skin, with tracks and padeyes for pallets on the deck. Harnesses and webbing hung here and there. The latrine was much like a Porta Potti, tucked under the cockpit. They were pressurized for now, but it was still cold. The USAF jumpmaster and flight engineer wandered through periodically to check the craft, and they were happy to share the huge cauldron of coffee they had with the three soldiers.

The problem was that Kyle and Wade tried to avoid caffeine because it affected their nerves. As snipers, they needed to be and wanted to be as steady as possible. While the coffee would warm them, it was contraindicated.

Wiesinger was theoretically a sniper, too. He was drinking coffee by the gallon. Kyle studied him again. The man looked very unmilitary, as did Kyle and Wade. The two NCOs had learned to do that as camouflage, to blend in. It was often useful to look like grubby bums rather than soldiers. In Wiesinger's case, he was simply a slob, in uniform or out—overweight, shaggy-haired, and with little regard for his uniform or civilian clothes. Kyle grimaced. Amazing how fast things went to hell every time.

As usual, it had started out with a good idea . . .

Kyle had previously been an instructor at the U.S. Army Sniper School. He'd been pulled out for two temporary duty missions to stalk and kill terrorists, first in Pakistan, then in Romania. Following that, it had been decided—and he concurred—to reassign him to avoid damaging the class schedule again and again. Wade Curtis had changed units twice in that time, from 10th Mountain Division to 3rd Infantry Division, and he'd also been given orders. The two of them were now assigned to an innocuous numbered detachment at Fort Meade that sounded like an administrative position. That put them closer to their boss General Robash, made deployments a lot easier, and let them use the range at Aberdeen Proving Ground for practice, as well as get some face-to-face practice time with the outrageously highly paid professionals from Blackwater Security, whom State Department hired to guard foreign leaders against terrorists and rebels.

Those worthies had even tried to recruit him. He'd been offered $300,000 a year plus expenses, based on his experience. He'd thought long and hard before turning that down. Perhaps when he was ready to retire in a few years . . .

Though honestly, it was more likely he'd be forced out with High Year of Tenure than voluntarily retire. He couldn't say why, except that the Army was his life and he was a patriot. Why else would he let them send him to exotic, distant lands to meet exciting, unusual people and kill them?

Unless he was a masochist?

He'd come into his office one cool, crisp morning, feeling very comfortable and confident, and found Wade and General Robash already talking. The general nodded and indicated a chair. Kyle would have stood otherwise, out of respect, even though he knew the general was casual about such things.

"We have another one?" he asked, sitting easily in his Army standard swivel chair.

"Indonesia," Wade said. "All-expense-paid tropical vacation. Gorgeous Balinese dancers, equatorial sunshine, fine crafts and artifacts . . ."

"Kraits, saltwater crocodiles, and Jemaah Islamiyah terrorists," Robash had finished. Even when he sprawled, he looked professional.

"Endangered species." Wade grinned. It was a cheerful grin, but not one to reassure potential enemies. Wade was a hair over six feet, a coffee-skinned black man with rock-solid, lean muscles and the quiet confidence of a man who didn't need to prove how good he was.

"Not endangered enough," Robash said, his expression half smile, half grimace. The general was broad and bulky with a gravelly, resonant voice that rarely needed a microphone. He'd aged a bit over the last two years, directing the two snipers and possibly other units—they didn't need to know—to hunt down, dig out and exterminate terrorist leaders and bombers. The massive activity in the Middle East was proof it was working. The enemy was getting desperate as real professionals closed off avenue after avenue, closing inexorably in on what would be a bloody finale.

Then it would have to start all over again. Old enemies changed and evolved; new ones were created. But as long as there'd been civilization, there'd been those who hated it and wanted to tear it down. It was job security for those who defended it. A security many of them would be happy to do without.

"Good," Kyle said. He took professional pride in his part. He and Wade would never be known in any history book, but the results were their trophy.

"Good," Robash agreed. Not that there had been any doubt the two snipers would take the mission. Kyle was vaguely aware that he could refuse if he didn't like the op, and either other arrangements would be made, the op would be changed to suit him, or, if the general or others didn't like his reasons, he could be replaced. But so far, as rough and violent as things had been, he and Wade had come

454 | ONE SHOT, THREE KILLS

out okay, and the terrorists had become usually nameless statistics in unmarked graves.

Dead, along with two close friends of Kyle's. Old news now, but still a cold part of his soul. Jeremy, his spotter in Bosnia, before all this, and Nasima, their local guide in Pakistan, a stunning and brilliant young Pashtun who'd been their translator before things went to hell and she got shot during their escape.

Kyle wouldn't turn down a mission lightly. His friends were worth a hundred terrorists each, easily. The score wasn't even close, though revenge didn't enter into it other than as a faint glimmer in back. As he'd told his last target right before shooting him, any scumbag can hate things and blow them up. It takes a real man to leave others alone. Kyle had nothing against Muslims, he'd met too many good ones. And that made him despise the bad ones even more, for tarnishing the image of his friends and allies.

"So, what's the mission?" he asked, making it official.

"Aceh."

"Ahchay?" He had to look at the map Robash was fingering on the table. A province of Indonesia at the far west end of Sumatra.

"Aceh. It damned near floats on oil, and could be the next Brunei. The sultan of Brunei was the richest man on Earth until Bill Gates came along, so you can imagine the political stakes. Most of the nations on Earth aren't even in the same universe as that kind of money, and Indonesia doesn't want to let it go. Jemaah Islamiyah is linked to al Qaeda, of course. They blew up the nightclub in Bali, have attacked other targets including hotels, and are now moving after Indonesian and corporate interests. They figure the civil war in Aceh and the antigovernment insurgents are good support for them. This group, the 'Fist of God,' are sadistic sons of bitches who like to be more discriminating. They choose very visible targets on an individual basis."

He continued, "There have been more ambushes, which are symptomatic and not really our problem. There have been a handful of hostages taken, and all killed in that gruesome hack-through-the-neck-with-a-rusty-saw method these pigfuckers have taken up. Those are our problem. Last month a ship was intercepted on the way in, with a large amount of explosives. Read: 'several tons.' Intel and traffic indicates they're planning something big. It might be in Jakarta, it might be in Singapore just to play hell with things, or it might move up into India or Pakistan or across to the Gulf. There are a lot of routes out of there.

"Much like Pakistan, we have a decently friendly government

which is full of leaks. They have some decent intel and forces, but they can't get in close without being exposed. So we made our offer, and with the recommendations of Pakistan and Romania, they agreed. You gentlemen are getting quite the reputation." He flashed a thin, cruel smile.

"What's the target?" Kyle asked.

"We have no names, but we're working on them. We want you to take out the so-called brains behind either the explosives smuggling or the executions. There's an excellent chance they're one and the same. The first means you stop the source of those explosives you were dealing with in Romania. The second means you save civilian lives."

"Sounds good," Kyle said. "What's our terrain?"

"Jungle, mountain scrub, and some smaller urban areas," Robash said, indicating on the map. It was large enough to show crude features but not details.

"SR twenty-fives and M fours, at an initial guess," he said.

"Makes sense," Wade said. "That gives us range and concealment and some grenades for support."

The Knight's Armament SR25 was an updated version of the Armalite AR10—the predecessor to the M16 and AR15. It was in 7.62 × 51mm caliber, the Winchester .308 that was the standard for Western snipers and many deer hunters. It had been in production for decades, but had only recently been accepted into the military.

It had come about during operations in Afghanistan, where, for the first time since World War II, there was sufficient range to justify a larger caliber round. The M16's 5.56mm cartridge was great up to 300 meters—far better than many shooters gave it credit for. But at long ranges, size does matter. Old M14s from the 1950s had been hurriedly pressed into service, and they served well. But it was a sixty-year-old platform lacking a lot of modern modular features. The SR25 shared a trigger group and operating mechanism with the M16 and M4; could accept different upper assemblies and barrels, and different stocks, grips, sights, scopes, and bipods; and was inhumanly accurate—as accurate as the men who used it, for precise killshots on enemy leaders, support personnel . . . or terrorists.

The SR25s would mate well with M4 carbines that the two were so familiar with. Those had short barrels, collapsible stocks for ease of carry and for adjusting length of pull to match clothing and armor. They could and would be fitted with 40mm grenade launchers to provide additional firepower and some combination of night vision scopes or EOTech's holographic sights for quick targeting. An

Aimpoint model was the standard issue, but both men preferred the EOTech.

They were given some leeway on their missions, because General Robash understood the need for a certain amount of individuality, and trusted their judgment. Unlike movie snipers, the two men were highly technical professionals, able to gather intelligence silently, select a target, determine the range and trajectory, and take it out, whether "it" was a generator, a facility to be illuminated with incendiaries for a passing Air Force jet to demolish, or a terrorist surrounded by sentries and sure of his immortality. They didn't boast, didn't show off, and when they parted ways with the manual it was for a good reason.

"The first thing is to get you gentlemen to HALO School," Robash said. "It's remote enough the easiest insertion is just to drop you in to our allies. Saves security issues at airports and we don't need to smuggle the weapons and gear in, like last time." For their mission in Romania, they'd flown commercial, met with CIA and State Department personnel, and transferred weapons around clandestinely. It was certainly doable, but there was no need to expend the political effort and money if they could just slip in, or in this case, drop in.

"Has to be HALO?" Wade asked. It wasn't asked out of fear, just out of curiosity.

"Yup," Robash nodded. "We've got scheduled flights going through that airspace from the Philippines. You just bail out as they fly over. No one will even know."

"I like that part of it," Wade agreed.

"And we can just carry all the gear with us this time," Kyle said. "Why does that sound too easy?"

"Oh, don't worry about it," Wade said. "I'm sure something else will screw up, just to keep us feeling at home."

"That's what I like about you, Wade," Kyle said. "You're so optimistic."

"Yeah, something will get FUBAR'd," Robash said. Fucked Up Beyond All Recognition. "But we're going to try to stall it as long as possible. And I've got messages at my office and State ready to drop, if something happens. Unlike Pakistan, you'll be within range of a whole battalion of Indonesian special forces—the Kopassus. They hate terrorists, and the only reason they're not doing this now is because there's one or two leaks no one can track down. But the unit as a whole is clean."

"Nice to have backup," Kyle said. "Though frankly, I'm tired of getting into situations where we need to be bailed out." It had nothing to do with sharing credit. Kyle was fine with that, and certainly didn't mind letting other soldiers play when it came to shooting bad guys. But when things got to that level, it always sucked to be him. His wounds had been minor, so far. But he'd lost two friends and come within three tenths of an inch and a hundredth of a second of dying last time, being saved by a perfectly placed shot from Wade. If you bet your life, sooner or later you lost.

"Hey, practice makes perfect. Third time's a charm. Proper Planning Prevents Previous Piss-Poor Performance. I've got all the clichés we need to get through this," Wade said.

They all chuckled.

"Okay, so we HALO in, ruck our gear, we're meeting an ally?"

"Yes," Robash said. "And most of them speak at least some English. Reduces the burden."

"Oh, this is too good so far. Please give me some bad news."

"Very well, ninety percent of the people you'll meet will as soon kill you as look at you."

"See?" Wade said. "Don't you feel better now?"

"Right." Kyle nodded to Wade. "Why is that, sir?" he asked, turning back.

"Aceh is riddled with anti-Indonesian sentiment. They're all Muslims of one type or another. Some few in charge support the government because they're siphoning enough money. The rest feel put upon. Some are rebels, some are allies with the terrorists, some are having tribal feuds. And now you're going to give them a reason to hate Americans directly, not just intellectually."

"Got it. So, discreet, make nice, don't offend any sensibilities, don't hit on the local women, be model advisors?" he guessed.

"Pretty much."

"And then drop some tangos quick and wave politely as we leave. How are we leaving if not with a battalion of Kopassus?"

"We're figuring you walk to the beach, call by cell and transponder, and the SEALs pick you up in a boat."

"And then we puke all the way home," Wade said. "Sorry, but my skin looks horrible when I turn green."

Kyle looked over his spotter's coffee-colored skin and said, "I'd figure it'd just add to the camouflage."

"Yeah. Oh, I'll do it. But I *do* get seasick in a hurry."

"Sorry about that," Robash said. "But you'll only be aboard ship a few hours to Singapore, then you'll just fly back on another Air Force jet. No need to entrust your gear to anyone."

"Yeah, that's not bad, really," Wade agreed. "Kyle?"

"Sure. I assume you have a detailed plan for us, sir?"

"I've got a rough itinerary and outline. You take care of the rest of it, and Colonel Wiesinger will handle the logistics."

"Yes, sir," Kyle said, frowning slightly at that. Wiesinger was very by the book, and had been a royal pain a time or two.

"But the first thing on the schedule is to get you gentlemen to HALO School, fast. Can you leave Wednesday?"

"Two days? Yeah, I guess. Good thing we're both unattached. Mostly." He had a semi-regular girlfriend, but he didn't need to worry about plans for departure. They had their own homes and accounts and just got together for fun.

"The Army greatly appreciates your dedication to the cause of freedom by not getting married." Robash smiled.

"Hell," Wade said, " 'marriage' and 'freedom' are kinda mutually exclusive, anyway."

"Tell me about it," Robash said, flashing the ring on his finger. "Sometimes I think it's on my testicles. But you gentlemen pack, I'll work on the fragorder and arrange for the movement orders for all of this. See you soon, and good luck."

"Roger that, sir," they both said automatically.

2

WHEN THE PHONE RANG AT O6OO, KYLE WAS JUST getting ready for the duty day. He was out of the shower, toweling his longish-by-Army-standards hair, and naked.

"Monroe," he answered.

"Sergeant Monroe, Colonel Wiesinger. The general is in hospital."

"What? Sir?" It was a shock he wasn't ready for, this early in the day.

"We're not sure," the colonel said. He sounded worried. But there was an undertone of . . . eagerness? "Likely a heart attack is my guess. He's been transported. I don't have any other intel yet."

"Roger that, sir. If there's anything I can do to help, do let me know."

"Will do, soldier. Carry on."

"Yes, sir." Kyle hung up slowly, thinking that was an odd phrase to use. It was too cliché. Almost as if Wiesinger hadn't had enough practice dealing with troops.

Just what was his background anyway?

The phone rang again. It was Wade.

"You hear?" he asked.

"Just now. Shit, pal, that sucks personally and professionally."

"Yeah, tell me."

"Listen, what do we know about Wiesinger?"

"Nothing, really. Want me to dig?"

"If you would."

"No problem. See you at the shop in an hour?"

"Right." Sighing, Kyle turned to get dressed.

• • •

Wade was very good with intel. Kyle was better at politics, though at times like this he realized he was a rank amateur compared to the men, mostly officers, who spent their careers at desks figuring out where the bodies were filed. The proper innocuous paperwork could kill a career or make it. He had a battlefield grasp that matched his knowledge of first aid, but he was not a surgeon.

Of course, Wiesinger might be more butcher than surgeon. But he undoubtedly had friends to have gotten as far as he had. It was a game Kyle didn't want to play. He drove mindlessly, parked, and got out. He unlocked the office, which was in an old but clean WWII building that was drafty in winter and had humid spots in summer. But it was discreet and private and theirs alone. He sat down and started on paperwork.

Wade had his cell phone to his ear as he strode in only a few minutes later. "I appreciate it, Sergeant Major. Yes, I will do so. You've been more than helpful . . . Sure, if he wants some range time, send him down, that's what we're here for. Thanks. Bye." He clicked it closed. "Are we secure?" he asked.

"I don't think we're bugged and he's not here," Kyle said.

"Good. Well, I found out an amazing amount, my friend."

"Yes?" Kyle prompted, figuring he wasn't going to like this.

"Colonel Joseph Melville Wiesinger is the son of Brigadier General Joe Wiesinger, retired."

"Never heard of him," Kyle admitted, brow furrowed.

"Exactly. He was an administrative general in the Pentagon."

"So he was nobody." One-star generals were a dime a dozen at the Pentagon.

"Right. But he had enough pull to get his boy in through ROTC. He's not Academy."

"Didn't think so. Academy grads can be assholes, but they typically know what they're talking about even if they do quote the book. He just has the book."

"Yup. He was a staff officer from Day One. Logistics mostly."

"Hell, nothing wrong with logistics," Kyle said. "You can't fight a war without them."

"Right," Wade agreed. "But he wasn't an issuing officer. He was a procedure-and-documentation wonk."

"Ah, I see."

"Right," Wade said. "He's done nothing but sort papers, except for a year each, commanding an infantry platoon and company."

"One year?"

"One year, just to fill the box. And his year as CO was nineteen eighty-nine. He wasn't in Panama or Kuwait. Nothing close to combat. But he had to be a commander to make major in time. And as a major and light colonel at the Pentagon he was obviously a staff officer. And now he's a colonel detached from the Pentagon with half intel and half operations designators. So he's had a career full of nothing but pretty uniforms and neat stacks of papers."

The phone rang and Kyle snagged it. The normal Army greeting rolled off his tongue. "Sergeant First Class Monroe, this is not a secure line, how may I help you, sir or ma'am?"

"Sergeant Monroe, Colonel Wiesinger."

"Ah, yes, sir?" he said, switching mental gears.

"Nothing new on the general, but he's in critical care and is breathing and does have a heartbeat. I don't know more about it than that."

"Good to know, sir."

"Agreed. He's got a hell of a job here and I've got some pretty big shoes to fill. It occurs to me I don't know as much about this operation as I need to, in case of ongoing problems."

"Well, anything we can do to help, we're at your disposal, sir," Kyle said. It was good when officers admitted they didn't know everything.

"Glad to hear it. Please calculate me into your travel arrangements. I'm coming along to get a firsthand look at how this is done."

"Ah," Kyle said, and then followed it with the only possible answer. "Yes, sir. I'm on it."

"Good. See you tomorrow for the flight to Bragg."

"Roger that, sir."

After they hung up, he turned to Wade. "He's coming along."

Wade got his first joke off quick. "He sleeps with you." He didn't even look up from his desk.

"Oh, fuck me, how do we stop this?" Kyle ran his hands through his hair and rubbed his eyes. Suddenly he was tired again.

"I'm not sure anything you say will change his mind," Wade said. Considering, he added, "You might try just loading him down with details and stuff that's intimidating."

"I could," Kyle agreed. "But no, I think we've just got to bite this one." He sighed again. "He is a sniper, right?"

"On paper . . . but he went through the course during the Clinton Years."

"Oh." For a long time, the sniper school had been audit only. Once selected by his home unit, an existing infantryman attended the course for credit and then returned. It wasn't until later that the course became pass/fail.

Before that, candidates had been required to have both small-arms expert qualification and a maximum score on the Army Physical Fitness Test. Most commanders were good about selecting only those soldiers they felt could handle the job intellectually and morally. Then there was selection within the sniper teams for those who could handle the realities of it in the face-to-not-face conditions of battle.

But there were ways to pencil-whip qualifications and call favors to get any school slot. It didn't take much of a stretch of imagination to think Wiesinger was one of those. He certainly didn't have the physique to suggest great fitness, and his quick temper alone would contraindicate letting him handle any task requiring patience.

"And he wants to come along," Kyle said.

"Hey, it's good that he realizes he's behind the curve," Wade said.

"Yeah, though realizing it ten years ago would have been better."

"No doubt. Still. It can't be all bad."

"You are so cheerful, my friend," Kyle said. "No, it's not all bad. But the bad it can be is still plenty bad."

"Hey, we're in the Army to be screwed over. It's the Army's job to provide the screwing."

"Yeah. But just once I'd like Vaseline." He sighed and stretched. "Dammit, I've got to make lists and calls. There's only one good part to this," he said.

"Oh?"

"We're so short on time he'll pretty well have to approve what I call."

HALO School was at least fun. "Fun," of course, assumed the attendee liked waking up early, PTing a few miles, loading up with a ruck and parachute, then jumping into free space.

"How can you jump out of a perfectly good aircraft?" was the standard question from those who would never consider it to be fun. The stock answers were, "Two perfectly good parachutes on my back" and "It's not a perfectly good aircraft, it's a U.S. Air Force aircraft."

Physicals were necessary, as well as dental X-rays, presumably because the lack of pressure at altitude might loosen fillings. The two reported to Fort Bragg and were weighed, as always, to ensure fitness. While some soldiers always pushed their weight limit, Kyle and Wade had 20 pounds of leeway each and muscle tone that made it a mere formality. They were close enough in size to be buddied together and were assigned an instructor, a man ironically named Sergeant Storm. He was intense, and both blocky and short at five foot eight.

In a couple of days, they were rammed through the physics of ram-air parachutes, repacking and emergency procedures, and were hung in training harnesses to practice. It was a fairly simple procedure for them, just strenuous and intense enough to not be boring without being a strain. Wiesinger was slightly taller and a bit heavier. They didn't see him much except in the evenings. The reports on Robash were that he was in hospital, critical but stable, and would be out of the picture for several weeks at least.

Then they moved to the Vertical Wind Tunnel, and practiced the rudiments of steering in free fall. It was easy enough for Kyle. He'd made a number of civilian skydives and knew the mechanics. It wasn't appreciably harder for Wade. He followed the guidelines and picked up on proper arch, bending to steer, recovering from a tumble and other moves. It was fun all around as students from all services watched the fan-generated wind blow each others' faces out of shape and billow up the loose, training jumpsuits that caught the 150 mph air to keep them aloft against gravity. Wiesinger had one advantage: he fell like a brick. Even cranked up, the buffeting winds couldn't tumble him.

Their fourth evening, Wiesinger looked them up. "News, gentlemen," he said.

"Yes, sir?"

"General Robash is in Walter Reed. It was a heart attack, but they think there may also have been a minor stroke. They're looking at angioplasty."

"Thank you, sir," Wade said. "Damn, I hope he's okay."

"Yeah, he's a fine officer and a good man to serve under. Anything we can do for his family?" Kyle asked. He was anxious. Losing Robash would mean a new commander, new ways of doing things . . . and Wiesinger might be the one to assume that post.

"Nothing yet," Wiesinger said. To his credit, the inevitable excitement and thrill he was getting from being in charge for the time being wasn't shining through. He really was concerned about his boss. "I'll let you know."

Kyle was worried, and it wasn't just having to deal with Wiesinger. It was that he really respected Robash as a good officer and a friend, as much as one could be friends with a general. And professionally, the good working relationship they'd built would change drastically if anyone else took over. Stability wasn't a realistic expectation in the military, but catastrophic changes were rough.

From Benning they transferred to Yuma Proving Ground, Arizona, and jumped daily. Ten thousand feet with no gear under a 370-square-foot MC-4 canopy was even easier than a civilian jump. But the altitude increased each time, and more gear was added. The rig's mass limit was 360 pounds of jumper and equipment. The three of them were going to not only bend but torture that limit on their insertion. They worked up to altitudes that required oxygen, and even higher. Twenty-five thousand feet was the standard maximum altitude, but they did a jump at 30K and another at 35K, the weather outside the plane being positively arctic. Tears could freeze, skin could get frostbitten. Insulated jumpsuits were necessary, to be discarded after landing.

The word came down that Robash was recovering slowly and would require surgery, but would most likely survive. His military career was still very much up in the air.

"Frankly," Kyle said, "if Wiesinger takes over, I'm going to have to slip out to another assignment. I just don't know if I can work with him."

"Yeah, I know what you mean," Wade nodded. "The slot calls for a general, though. They'll have to assign someone to it."

"Unless they promote Wiesinger into it."

"I was avoiding that possibility."

The school was a good one. It was a no-bullshit, all-fact-and-practice session that both snipers appreciated. They were confident of their ability to perform the jumps in question when they were done, and didn't feel any time had been wasted. They thanked Sergeant Storm profusely.

"Glad to hear I'm doing my job well," he said. "If you have any suggestions, by all means give appropriate feedback on the end-of-course questionnaire."

Because of the speed they'd rushed through the course, there was no graduation party. Their class was only the three of them. They outprocessed quickly and departed.

By the time they returned to Washington, there was more information. Wiesinger had his cell phone out as soon as they hit the terminal. "Angioplasty didn't work," he told them. "He's got two fully blocked arteries. Surgery on Wednesday."

"Damn. Prognosis, sir?"

"Oh, he should be fine," the colonel said. "He was doing his morning four-mile run when he collapsed. So as long as nothing happens during surgery, he's plenty healthy enough to recover, I understand. Meantime, I've got to run this."

"Yes, sir," Kyle said. There wasn't much he could say, and he wasn't going to make a scene over the issue.

Instead, he got to work on prepping for the mission.

Wiesinger basically left that to him, which was good and bad. Autonomy wasn't a bad thing for a professional, but it did help to have feedback from one's teammates.

"Who carries which rifle?" he asked Wade.

"Take two of each? SR25s for shooting, M4s for support. Means one spare rifle we have to lug, but allows us the option of one shooter and two support, or two shooters and one support."

"Good enough. I hate carrying extra weight, but flexible firepower is a good thing. Any idea what our local guides will have?"

"No," Wade said, shuffling through a printout stack. "That's not mentioned. Not much about them at all."

"Yeah, we keep getting that. I'd really like to know more about these people when we can."

"Indonesia uses a variation on the FNC. Insurgents may have that, or AKs, or M sixteens, or some Singaporean clone with no license fees paid."

"Okay, I'll keep that in mind," Kyle said. Wade had all kinds of information stuffed into his mind. "Is there an FNC we can examine for familiarization?"

"Not officially, no. But Sergeant Major Lewis has a troop who owns a civvy semi-auto version imported in the nineteen eighties we can shoot and take apart on the range. Different trigger group, but same teardown and characteristics."

"God Bless the Second Amendment," Kyle said. "Though it's a hell of a world when the Army has to call civvies for intel on weapons."

"C'est la guerre."

Beyond the technical information was the political situation. Kyle picked up another stack and looked at what background they had.

The Bali club attack on 12 October, 2002, had been blamed on the Al-Qaeda-linked Jemaah Islamiyah network that operated throughout Southeast Asia. The network's commander, Riduan Isamuddin Hambali, had been captured in Thailand and handed over to U.S. custody. But someone else had taken over. As with all the linked groups, they were getting desperate. Propaganda said they were surviving and coming out in revenge. Many Americans even believed that. But the fact was that Kyle, Wade, other operations, and world opinion were hurting them badly. And as the smarter leaders were killed, the less experienced and less stable often moved into positions of authority. It was the vortices at the tail of a large storm. But such vortices often produced tornadoes.

"I'm just amazed at the extent of these operations of theirs," Kyle said.

"Well, hell, look at their backing," Wade said. "Bin Laden has or had two hundred and fifty million dollars, four wives, fifteen children, several large chunks of stock in major corporations, insurance on projects at the World Trade Center that *made* him money when the planes crashed. He's loaded, and so are his buddies."

"Yeah," Kyle said, "Two hundred and fifty mil, four wives, fifteen children, a private resort and he calls Americans 'excessive.' Sure wish I could be as modest as him." He kept reading.

One of the problems they faced was that the United States and Indonesia were treading delicately toward improved relations, after Indonesian Army atrocities in East Timor in 1999. And if they were discovered, it would be a slap in the face. Once again, shooting a terrorist was only one small part of the mission.

"This just sucks, buddy," Kyle said. "We'll be teaming up with insurgents against another group of insurgents, both of whom are fighting a government we want to be friendly with who is officially on our side. All are filled with snakes, and all are fighting other factions at the same time. You're black, I'm white, it's half industrialized and half jungle, full of billions of American dollars, millions of terrorist rupiah, millions of black market yen, dong, dollars, pounds, and whatever."

"Yes, and there are Dutch personnel with the oil companies, and mixed Malay and Chinese Indonesians who are Muslim, Christian, and Hindu."

"And a population way too high to make sneaking in the woods safe for any length of time," Kyle added. Alarm bells were sounding in his head, and part of him really wanted to bail on this one. But he couldn't. Not only would Wiesinger be an asshole over it, he owed it to Robash to finish what they'd started.

And he owed it to himself and Wade to maintain their reputation. Not to mention the civilians who were being abducted, tortured, killed, and possibly raped.

"So it's a challenge," he said. "We could ask Delta Force to handle it."

Wade snickered. "They're trying to remain unseen. And they were likely smart enough to not accept this one. Or else they're using us to see how not to do it."

"You are so reassuring," Kyle said with a shake of his head. "But hell, if we quit when it looked ugly, we wouldn't be here."

"Yeah, and I wouldn't be hearing the stories about you in the bar two weeks ago."

"Ah, hell, what now?" Kyle asked. "And never you mind the stories."

"Heh . . . I'll assume she's a lady. Will she be waiting when you get back?"

"That's a question I haven't even looked at yet."

Nor was he sure how. "Janie, I'm going to fly halfway around the world to skulk in the jungle and kill some asshole who likes to hack people's heads off and blow up wage slaves and schoolkids. Will you miss me?"

Somehow, that didn't work, even if he could discuss it.

"The Army is sending me halfway around the world. I can't tell you where or why, and I may come back with holes in me again, or not at all."

No, that wasn't much better.

"Good luck with it," Wade said.

"Thanks," Kyle said.

Sighing, he leaned back over his desk to other issues.

It was up to Kyle to inventory every damned thing they would take. It called for computer and book searches for National Stock Numbers, prices for items not on hand, weighing everything to ensure it would all fit under the 360-pound total mass allowance for these parachutes.

"Man, I've got a problem here," Kyle said.

"Yes?" Wade looked up from his console, where he was sifting reports on Indonesia.

"Wiesinger is seventy-two inches tall. Allowed one hundred ninety-five pounds. He claims two hundred ten and to make tape for body fat index."

"Okay."

"There is no way that bastard is under two twenty."

Wade looked thoughtful. "I'd say you're right."

"Well, he insists he's two ten. I can pack him a hundred and fifty pounds of gear. But if he's two thirty, that'll be twenty over. He goes splat. I've never seen the paperwork to do for a dead colonel. Pretty sure I don't want to. If I leave that twenty out of the calculations, it could be twenty pounds of ammo we need and don't have."

"Sucks to be you, pal. Split the difference? Pack him at two twenty? Ten pounds shouldn't break the chute. Actually, I'd assume the engineers put fifty pounds of leeway in there. He'll descend faster, but likely not fast enough to rip fabric or go in."

"Hmmm . . ." Kyle considered. "I might want to call Para-Flite and ask them to give me a no BS max."

"Then figure that for Wiesinger at two thirty and us at our weight minus three pounds for safety? Still means a risk, but a calculable one."

"Yeah. Thanks. I appreciate it."

"No problem. Glad to help keep us alive."

Kyle was still gritting his teeth at the thought of Wiesinger coming along. Wade and he worked well as a team. Adding in a third who hadn't trained with them was a bad idea no matter how you looked at it.

But he didn't get a vote. And he was the one who had to deal with Wiesinger the next day. That conversation wasn't fun.

Wiesinger called in and said, "I've been looking over your list, Sergeant Monroe. Hell of a long list you've got here."

"Sometimes, sir, yes." Kyle was tense. There were things on that list he didn't mind one way or the other. There were some he would argue to keep. There were some he'd consider a court martial over.

"I'll authorize you to take your forty-five," Wiesinger said, "since it's a military pattern and caliber. But you will carry ball ammunition only, none of that custom stuff. I don't want to see any silencers or other doodads, and Uncle Sam sure as hell isn't paying if you lose it."

"That's fine, sir, thank you," Kyle agreed. He hadn't expected even that much cooperation. Maybe Wiesinger was just a bit stodgy and wouldn't be in the way, rather than turning out to be the tin-plated asshole he'd come across as in the past.

"You can take the knives. I don't have a problem with that, though why you want to carry all that crap is beyond me. But as long as you have your issue gear, have at it."

"Yes, sir," he said. Two for two so far. And he carried "all that crap" because it had saved his life more than once.

"SR25s, suppressors, and all related gear, that's fine. I haven't shot that one yet, but I'm told it's good and you'd know."

"It is, sir. Thanks." That meant he'd have to get Wiesinger out on the range for some practice time.

"Aimpoints if you want them. That's the standard, and the EOTech has not been tested as thoroughly."

"Got it, sir." He and Wade had their own EOTech sights anyway. They'd take them as civilian luggage. And there were rave reviews coming out of Iraq. Part of him realized there wasn't *that* much difference, and he was doing it just because he'd been told not to. His independent streak got him in trouble at times.

"Please put together an appropriate list for me. Basic gear, an M4 and a standard M9 bayonet. I'll work on our travel arrangements and finances."

"Got it, sir. It'll be ready."

"Good. Don't worry about any pre-mission briefings. We'll deal with that in theater."

"We're not consulting our usual experts, sir?" he asked, confused.

"No, we're going to dispense with that and work through local assets and phrase books this time," Wiesinger said.

"Sir? Why not learn some basics? It's been very helpful in the past," Wade asked.

"According to your after-action reviews, it hasn't mattered squat," Wiesinger snapped. "Either you had translation books with you or a native. I don't see any need to risk OPSEC by dealing with civilians."

Kyle was aghast. He wasn't sure what clearance Mr. Gober, the ethnologist who advised them on languages had, but he knew the man was utterly reliable, never knew their actual destination, and was no threat at all to OPerational SE-Curity. To not utilize a resource seemed to invite trouble later. It was impossible to have too much intel.

"What about a cultural brief?" he asked.

"That's what the Internet is for. It's not as if we're trying to blend in and assimilate like Special Forces. We're just going in to take a shot and get back out."

Wade seemed composed. Kyle was ready to throttle this idiot. The problems they'd had on the two previous missions all came down to a *lack* of intel on their part, and Wiesinger proposed to jump in blind.

But the basis of the military was order and discipline. There was nothing they could do. Any appeal would stop at Wiesinger, unless it went farther up to a command level. The answer from there Kyle didn't need to hear—it would be to follow orders from the officer leading the mission, unless they could prove his doctrine was unsound . . . which would take longer than the time available and likely be fruitless.

"Understood, sir," Kyle said. "We'll do it the way you suggest." *Officially, anyway, you fat clown,* he added to himself. He hung up and sighed. It was sometimes harder to fight the chain of command than the enemy. You could at least shoot at the enemy.

That afternoon, they drove to Aberdeen Proving Ground to shoot. While Meade had a 600-meter known distance range, it was on land controlled by the Department of the Interior, and standard ball ammo was not allowed—only special environmentally safe rounds. As they needed to train with the ammunition they'd use, another facility was desirable.

The time they spent at the range was useful, but quiet. They adjusted sights, practiced correcting for wind, and made slow, methodical shots. They were quite capable of longer distances, but the range they had was sufficient to maintain proficiency and technique.

It was seventy rounds each into it before Kyle said, "I'm happy. Let's go to the office and talk."

"Okay. And clean weapons?"

"Yes. It's meditative."

"So it is. But only for a select few."

The vehicle assigned for their use didn't get much of a workout. They drove it to and from the range, because military weapons couldn't be transported in civilian vehicles, officially, and they used it for occasional supply runs. Otherwise, they found their own vehicles much more comfortable. Kyle was silent for the drive, and Wade followed his lead.

Once inside the office, papers spread on the floor, weapons cleared and stripped—a process that took them less than a minute apiece—Wade finally raised the specter.

"Kyle, you're really not in your happy place regarding all this, are you?" He managed the sarcasm without sounding goofy. Quite a trick.

"No, but I'm working on some ways to improve that."

"Oh?" Wade prodded.

"We can't consult Mister Gober regarding a mission. However, I've developed an interest in Indonesia. It has a fascinating history, a varied culture and could be strategically important in the future. As far as language goes, Mister Gober is the best man I can think of to talk to. Let's look him up."

"It does sound like a fascinating place, and I think we should. Perhaps we'll even vacation there, too." Wade was grinning.

"And luckily for us, he's based out of the D.C. area. I gather he does a lot of consulting on this type of thing, and I heard him mention a paper for Georgetown."

"Meet where?"

Kyle considered. While public would be less likely to be connected to any activity, that was in part because communications security sucked in the open, where any casual passerby or anyone with a parabolic mike could hear them.

"My place," he said. "Shouldn't arouse suspicion to do it once."

3

BILL GOBER WAS A LITTLE THINNER THAN LAST TIME they'd met him. He was still portly and cheerful, but seemed to be more lively. His shirt and slacks were as casual as always, and the case and backpack he carried were stuffed with a laptop, disks, and books. He studied languages, and seemed to have a stack of references on the most obscure ones—Dari and Pashto for Pakistan, and no doubt something for here. Last time, he'd briefed them on Romanian.

"Good morning," he said.

"Morning, Mister Gober," Kyle replied. "Coffee?"

"Please," he agreed. "Some cream, some sugar. Languages?"

"That will be fine," Wade agreed. "Some familiar, some gobbledygook."

"That should be easy enough," he agreed as he sat. Kyle had moved his coffee table closer to one chair. It wasn't as if he ever used it for anything other than piles of reference material anyway.

"So, you mentioned Indonesia, and you specified Aceh. That's a rather contentious area."

"So we've heard," Kyle agreed.

"Well, the national language is Bahasa, and most people will speak it. However, Aceh also has the language of Aceh or Atjeh, with eight dialects. Officially, it's Austronesian, Malayo-Polynesian, Western Malayo-Polynesian, Sundic, Malayic, Achinese-Chamic, Achinese. It's actually distantly related to the languages of Madagascar and Hawaii. It's fascinating to track the development of languages across such a large area.

"Anyway, about three million people speak that. Actually, a

phrase book should suffice, and some basic Bahasa, and some Dutch, as a lot of people still speak some Dutch."

"Dutch?" Kyle asked. He knew they were involved in the oil industry.

"Yeah," Wade said, "that was the Dutch East Indies until some bright boy decided to make it all one nation."

"Correct," Gober said. "There are fifty-two languages in Sumatra alone, and a total of seven hundred and thirty-one for the whole nation, of which five are extinct or nearly so. It's a very mixed area with a lot of cultural clashes."

"Sounds like," Kyle said. Seven hundred languages. Damn. "Do you have phrase books for Achinese and Bahasa?"

"No, but I can acquire some. Many military and technical words are actually English."

"Well, this isn't a military mission," Kyle said.

"Yes, but I assume you will be talking shop?"

Gober was obviously curious as to why they were pretending not to be running a mission. But he didn't ask, and was simply offering the information he thought they could use. Kyle had to respect that, and was disgusted at the situation. The man was no security threat at all, and yet they were ordered to treat him as such.

"We might talk shop with some Indonesian military people, yes. Actually, we might talk about oil, too. There's a lot of jobs opening up out there." That left the hint that he was looking for security or mercenary work after his enlistment was up. That should be all the misdirection needed.

Not, he thought, that Wiesinger would give a crap. He'd be pissed about them "breaching security" and "going outside the approved sources."

Not that Kyle gave a crap what Wiesinger thought. Which, he reflected, was one hell of a way to start a mission.

"Very well, I'll put together some common phrases for military and industry. I can send you online links to recommended phrase books you can buy. Will email work?"

"Yeah, it's not as if it's a military secret or anything, we just don't want any unfriendlies learning that U.S. personnel are coming, even off duty. My email should be fine." He hoped that explanation would cover any potential allegations that Gober had been informed about the mission. As far as Kyle knew, Gober had never been informed about any mission, only that "troops are deploying to somewhere and need a brief on languages."

"Okay, then here's what I have on Bahasa," Gober said, pulling out a couple of burned CDs and a thick book. "Face price on the book. I can let you have the CDs for free; they're public-domain sources. They're dictionaries and basic grammar, the book is a proper style manual. And these," he said as he pulled out four more slim, bright books.

"Those are children's books," Wade observed.

"Yes, with simple words and bright pictures that are easy to remember. An excellent way to learn some rudimentary vocabulary. And this is a CD of a speech, which is transcribed in Bahasa and phonetic English to display with the audio. It will help with aural recognition and inflection and accent."

"That's incredibly helpful. Thank you," Kyle said. They were loaded for bear, if they could find the time to review it.

"You're very welcome. I appreciate the business, and let me know how things go if you can."

"Once we return, we will."

"Good. And if you ever have a mission in Indonesia, you'll be prepared."

Was that a hint that he suspected more than he was being told? Kyle didn't let anything show. But he was amused at the potential irony.

"Well, anything's possible with all the training we do. I don't think we're sharing tips with Indonesia yet, but things are improving."

"Excellent. Keep me informed on General Robash's progress if you can. He's a good man."

"Will do, and thank you, sir." They all rose. Gober hefted his backpack and they escorted him to the door.

Once the ethnologist left, Wade said, "Look through the stuff now?"

"Sure, why not?" Kyle agreed. "At least a quick overview."

Wade brought out his laptop and plugged in. A quick connection with a LAN cable and they were ready to share data. They started downloading from the CDs.

"Wow, this is weird," Kyle said.

"What?"

"The number of words that are straight English. I see 'white paper,' 'telkom,' 'konstruksi,' 'elektronika,' 'transportasi.'"

"Lots of those could be from Dutch," Wade said. "But yes, that does help. Quite a few tech words."

They continued reading. Several minutes later, Kyle did a double take.

"Wait a minute," he said.

"Yeah, I saw that," Wade replied. "So it's not just me?"

"I don't think so," Kyle said.

The phrase on the screen in front of him was, "Prajurit itu tidak kompeten." *That officer is not very competent.*

Below that was, "Kolonel itu telah berbuat salah." *The colonel made a mistake.*

Beyond that were comments about engineering or artillery errors. But those two phrases together seemed to be telling.

"Gober knows," Kyle said.

"So it seems," Wade agreed. He was smiling a tight-lipped smile. "Which explains why he came over on less than twenty-four hours' notice, without needing to prep. He was ready."

"Doesn't help much," Kyle said. "But it's nice to have the support."

"I wonder if Robash had already contacted him and Wiesinger cancelled?"

"Could be. But why? It seems like he's trying to cover all bases himself."

"I think that's exactly it. Cut the budget, keep the cards real close to the chest, keep all the credit within the unit, and proclaim his genius."

"Great. A glory seeker." Kyle had several decorations and a couple of wounds from his missions. He'd never made the papers or even the military press. He didn't care. They were all on the same team, and as long as the mission was accomplished, everyone knew who'd done what.

"Let's break for lunch." He needed to unwind his brain for a few minutes.

"Suits."

After that, they needed to research the area. There was far too much wealth of information online, and as usual, half of it was dated, unsupported opinion, or flat-out worthless crap. Confirming data from at least two primary sources was more work than finding the intel.

Aceh certainly had a colorful history and present.

Aceh was as rich in oil as they'd been told: 1.5 million barrels per day. Natural gas production was 38 percent of the world's total. Other products of Aceh included iron, gold, platinum, molybdenum, tin, rubber, coffee, tea, and tropical timber. The locals were unhappy because all the income was taken away to Jakarta and they were left at the bottom end of the economic scale. Typical government thievery.

There were several factions for independence—GAM, Gerakan Acheh Merdeka, also known as the Acheh Sumatra National Liberation Front (ASNLF). "Acheh" as opposed to "Aceh." Apparently, the spelling difference was a point for them, which said something. Kyle wasn't sure what, but if they couldn't agree on a spelling in English, it wasn't likely they could agree on much else. GAM/ASNLF was split into at least two factions, one of which was negotiating with the government, the other which decried that and called them traitors.

There was also Hizb ut-Tahrir (HUT), the Islamic Party of Liberation, which claimed to not support terrorism but wanted a return to the Caliphate and hated the Saud family. However, there were indications that their condemnation of terrorism ended with the press release.

"I need a dance card for this," Kyle said.

"Yeah, tell me about it. Who's on first?"

"I dunno."

"Third base."

"I don't give a damn," Kyle replied, grinning. "Okay, actually, I do. You taking notes?"

"Yeah. Can we get a degree in international relations in lieu of attending class, just on the research we're doing?"

"It would seem fair. But I doubt they'll do it."

"Right. We probably have the wrong political viewpoint for college, too," Wade observed.

"Because we think that the way to solve this is to identify the trash and take it out?"

"Got it in one." It served as a mini break and to help them remember the dry data they'd just digested. Both men did it without conscious effort, and resumed silence again at once.

There were a number of prominent women figures in Aceh's military history. There had been an Admiral Keumalahajati in the late 16th century. There had been four queens who successively ruled the latter half of the 17th. Guerilla commanders in the Dutch Colonial War era included Cut Nya' Dhien, Cut Meutia, Pocut Baren, and Pocut Mirah Inteun. During the 1945–49 fighting, the women of the "Revolution of 45" in Aceh not only served as service staff and medics (the Pasukan Bulan Sabit), but also involved themselves actively in fighting in groups such as Pocut Baren Regimen.

Women as troops and leaders certainly didn't sound very Muslim to Kyle. He said so.

"I dunno," Wade said. "This is all new territory to me."

GAM had had members trained in Libya. "I notice an ongoing pattern in all this," Kyle said.

"Oh, you do?" Wade asked sarcastically. It seemed as if every problem surrounding Muslim terrorism came back to Syria, Iraq, Libya, rural Pakistan, or extreme factions in Saudi Arabia. "I think if we took out about a hundred people worldwide, the whole problem would go away."

"Yeah, but they'll never let us do it, we wouldn't be able to find a lot of them, and it'd be suicide to go through their suicide squads to get to them."

"Yeah, why don't so-called suicide squads just kill themselves? I'll send the ammo."

"Heard it before," Kyle said. He did smile, though. "Wish it worked that way."

"So they have Muslim extremist women soldiers toting AKs and trained in Pentjak Silat and other lethal hand-to-hand techniques," Wade said. "Just what I want for a date on Saturday night."

"Reading this, I see why they're upset, actually," Kyle said. "They beat the Dutch six times over eighty years, costing the Dutch one hundred *thousand* troops. And then here: 'On twenty-seven December, nineteen forty-nine, seven years after withdrawing from Acheh, the Dutch signed a treaty with the newly fabricated "Republic of Indonesia" on the island of Java to transfer their "sovereignty" of Acheh to Indonesia, without referendum of the people, and against all the UN principles of decolonization.'"

"And the fight with Indonesia was on." Wade nodded.

"Yeah. They transferred title of an area they didn't control and only owned on paper to someone else. Damn. Why did the Achinese have to side with the goddamn tangos? I could support these people."

"The point is they have," Wade said. It was an unneeded reminder.

"Yup. So we get to do the dirty work."

"So, the Free Acheh Movement has wide support from the local population. The Indonesian government sent the special forces, called Kopassus, to hunt down members of the movement. Aceh was declared as a Military Operational Area. There are allegations of atrocities that rank pretty high on the filthometer. The Achinese estimate twenty-five thousand casualties in custody and in 'secret concentration camps,' which is one I really wonder about, but they believe it, so it fuels the fire."

"What do we know about our allies?" Wade asked.

"They're a separatist faction, but they're one that is trying to negotiate with the government. Of course, that means the nutcases want them dead, too, for betraying their vision of independence, conquering Java and imposing a New Muslim Order."

"What? Most of them can't think like that." Wade had studied a lot of sociology. He didn't believe stereotypes easily.

"No, most of them just want to be left alone and get the money going to Jakarta. But a few percent are just nuts." And if it weren't for the nuts, Kyle and Wade would be out of their current job.

"Forward that link to me. I've got to read up."

"Will do . . . sent."

"Got it, thanks." It was odd, Kyle reflected, to keep swapping messages with a person a few feet away.

The two pored over the language, maps, cultural pages with things such as recipes and holidays. The more familiar one was with an area intellectually, the more easily and quickly one could acclimate. That was a huge plus when trying to be discreet.

They were closing up the office at 1600 hours when Wade said, "We really should go visit the general before we leave."

"I agree," Kyle said. He felt guilty about not having done so, even with duty interfering, and he did feel friendly toward the boss who gave him such excellent support. "What are visitation hours?"

"Until nineteen hundred, I believe."

"Hit him now, dinner en route?"

"Works for me. Be good to see how he's doing."

Robash had been transferred to Walter Reed. It took a few minutes to find his location, an hour to drive through traffic, munching fast food on the way, and twenty minutes to get through security levels. Fortunately, senior NCOs visiting general officers was a very common and reasonable occurrence, and they were let through without too much hassle.

Robash looked comfortable, but tired and in pain. He also looked a little less bulky than he had. He hadn't been fat, he'd been *big*, but now he was just another patient in a bed, with a few wires and tubes.

"Good evening, sir," they said.

"Gentlemen. It's good to see you." His voice was even more gravelly than usual, with a croak to it.

"How are you feeling, sir?" Kyle asked.

"Like I lost both canopies and hit the ground."

"Sounds like fun. You look okay."

"Bullshit. I look like hell," he said. "But I'll live." His voice was definite when he said it.

"That's what we want to hear."

"Good. I didn't die on you. You're not allowed to die on me. How goes the prep?"

Kyle said, "HALO trained, lists made, orders on hand. Getting there."

"Good. How's Colonel Wiesinger doing?"

"Fine, sir," Kyle said. "We'll be ready on schedule."

"Don't bullshit me, son," Robash said, sounding stronger. "What's your opinion as an SFC?"

So much for not stressing him. Kyle met Wade's eyes, then looked back.

"We are managing, sir. He's more of a micromanager than I like, but I won't let him push me where it's not safe, and I won't argue with him otherwise." He blushed, because he was doing exactly that.

"Yeah, listen, move in close for a moment, will you?" His voice was strong but quiet.

They leaned in and listened.

"Look guys, BS aside, I know you don't warm to Colonel Wiesinger much," he whispered. "But he's the officer we've got. He can administrate, he understands the subject, and he knows where to get resources. Work with him, don't just pretend, and try not to let him rub you the wrong way. He's abrasive, but he's not bad."

"Roger that, sir," Wade said. Kyle was a moment behind. He suspected from what he'd encountered that Wiesinger's competence was all behind a desk. Yes, one needed that, depended on that to get the job done, but it went better when the officer had a grasp of how things operated in the field. The book existed for a reason. At the same time, the book was a guideline that didn't cover all situations and didn't apply to some situations it did cover.

"Anyway, I need to rest now. Good luck and good hunting. Rangers Lead the Way."

"Will do, sir," Kyle said.

They stood and left, shaking hands as they did. Robash's grip was weak, but Kyle could still feel the strength under it. That by itself reassured him the general would recover.

Kyle showered quickly and threw on a shirt and slacks. He was already late. Janie would probably understand him visiting the general, but he'd also been wrapped up in work and busy with HALO. It wasn't as if he could ignore her and expect her to hang around. They'd been dating for just over a month. And she was a nice girl. He wouldn't mind having her around for a while.

He drove fast, and was at her apartment by eight. She came walking briskly down off the steps, denying him the opportunity to knock on the door. He still got out and held the truck door for her, though. It might be old-fashioned, but the rules of etiquette and gentlemanly conduct had been drilled into him from an early age, and the Army encouraged polite behavior. It was a big plus for him in the social arena. He ushered her in, careful of her long satin skirt. He worried about lint. The truck wasn't as clean as it could be; he'd been on the range. Black satin fabric would show a lot. Her blouse was opened enough to show some cleavage, so he figured she wasn't too mad at him. If she wasn't happy, she had no problem letting him know.

"Where have you been?" she asked as she got in. She was upset and worried rather than angry. And he had called ahead.

"I'm sorry, Janie," he said, meaning it. Damn, she looked good, and it was great having someone to talk to about things other than shop. "General Robash is still in hospital. I had to go visit."

"He's your commander?" she asked.

"Well . . ." How to explain it? "He's in charge of our operations. I respect him a lot. I'm worried about how things will change if he can't recover. Can I leave it at that? I don't want to talk shop."

She softened. "Sure. I guess I thought you were ignoring me. Let's eat?" she hinted.

"I'll have to eat light, Wade and I grabbed a bite between the shop and the hospital." He pulled onto I-295. He was relieved. He didn't want her mad two days before he left.

"Good," she said. "Then I won't feel jealous of you plowing through enough food for three of me. You must work out a hell of a lot to eat like that."

"Sometimes," he said. "In the field I might hit six thousand calories a day. And you look fine, really. Eat what you want." Women were exasperating with their obsessions about diet and weight. She looked good and he didn't understand her worry.

She smiled. "Kyle, I plan on making love to you before you take off again. You don't have to sweet talk me." Then she gave him a sidelong glance.

"You know I'm leaving?" he asked, suspicious and worried at the same time.

"I assume if the Army sent you to a parachuting school and you're spending long hours with checklists and research that you're about to leave. Right?" She smiled again. It was coy, indulgent, mischievous, and exasperated all at the same time.

"Uh, yes. I just try not to let people know, as professional paranoia, and I don't like questions about it, because I can't answer them."

"You teach sniping, right?"

"Yes," he admitted. It had come up in conversation.

"So I assume you're teaching either our people or someone allied, out in the field. You're going to Iraq? Afghanistan?"

"Janie, I can't say. I'm sorry."

"Dammit . . ." She looked frustrated. "Okay, I guess I understand that. It must be hard on families. Is that why you got divorced?"

"Part of it. A big part," he admitted. Yes, it was hard to have a social life, with people worried that you might not return. Some spouses could adapt to that. Others couldn't. He was also very wrapped up in his work and not as sociable as some other men.

"Tell me when you'll be back, at least," she begged. She leaned far back and stretched, and he could see her curves. She was in good shape herself. He'd met her at a gym.

"If I knew . . . but I don't. At least three weeks. Hopefully not much more than that. I've left instructions for them to tell you if there's a problem."

"If you're dead or crippled, you mean," she said. "Sorry, that was harsh. I appreciate you thinking of me. But, Kyle, there's something I want." She leaned over and whispered something in his ear that made him flush in anticipation. "And again when you come back. So come back? Please?"

"Hon, I want to come back anyway. But I'll be really careful." He reached over and took her hand.

"Good," she said gripping back. "I've seen your dress uniform. Don't get another Purple Heart. And I'll have a steak tonight. Hot and naked. Then you the same way." She smiled again and it was anything but coy. It looked like the smile of a wolf.

In the office the next morning, still tired and elated from a long night in bed with Janie, Kyle printed out a checklist and started packing rucks. He had three, with duplicate items for each and personalized gear. Both Wiesinger and Wade had brought in spare uniforms and toiletries tightly rolled in plastic bags. He started with "personal items" and checked them off the list. After that, it was ammunition, MREs in case local food wasn't available immediately, water, maps, and compasses, all the essential military gear that is rarely thought of by civilians but must be carried. Batteries for radios, phones, sights, and accessories were on the list aplenty. Interceptor body armor was quite heavy, so Kyle had substituted police-weight vests that wouldn't stop a rifle bullet but should slow it enough to reduce the wound. They'd stop most fragments and pistol calibers, and likely knives as well. But he'd taken enough fire to want something over his vital organs.

Beyond those he had his and Wade's pistols. Wade still took an issue M9 Beretta. Kyle had his gorgeous but slightly dinged Ed Brown that was as exotic as one could get. But it had saved his life at least twice by being available and flawlessly reliable. He'd thought of taking his Colt Mustang, too. It was pocket sized and had saved his life in Bosnia and Pakistan. He hadn't carried it since. It didn't weigh much, but they were on a tight chart. Besides, they weren't likely to be in town much and in the field he'd just as soon have a few extra magazines of .45.

They had knives, Wiesinger had an M9 bayonet, Wade a Ka-Bar, Kyle his high-end Gerber. Pocket tools. Flashlights with infrared and red filters, both little Mini Maglites and the blindingly bright Sure-Fires, which could be used to stun people.

As he reached the end of that list, he dragged over a duffel bag and another, handwritten list.

"So what's in the bag?"

"All the stuff Wiesinger told me not to take."

"Oh?"

"And ammo. Standard seven point six two NATO ball."

"Don't we have enough of that?" Wade asked.

"We have US issue, that incredibly solid stuff that just bores holes. I have old 'West German' issue that will shatter at the cannelure when it tumbles. But it is NATO spec, so no one can nail us for war crimes."

"You're a sick and twisted individual. I'm proud to call you 'friend.'"

"Yeah. Funny story about this stuff. The Germans and Swedes complained about the fragmentation effects of five point five six in Vietnam. Accused the U.S. of 'atrocities.' So Natick Lab demonstrated that their ammo fragmented worse. They shut up."

"Heh. I like it. How much do you have?"

"Two battle packs of two hundred rounds."

"How are you transporting it?"

"Since it's all going in our rucks and dropping with us, it's going in there. I'll mark off the issue stuff and load this instead. It's NATO, he may not even notice it's not U.S."

"And he can't do anything if he does."

"Right."

"This was a whole lot easier with Robash signing blank orders and handing us cash."

"We need to ask about cash," Kyle said, frowning. "I assume he'll want to carry it personally, but we better have some."

"That's your department. I don't even want to try to negotiate with him."

"Yeah, I know." The frown turned into a grimace.

All four rifles were laid out ready. All had threaded can type suppressors. It increased the length slightly, but reducing muzzle blast by 36 dB and all but eliminating the flash made shooting much more secure. There were four 100-round Beta C-mags for the M4s, which "could be loaded on Monday and shot all week." One of the SR25s had light olive green furniture.

"What did you do to the weapon?"

"Aftermarket furniture from Cavalry Arms. I've bought a bunch of AR components from them, they have a rough, sanitized idea of what I do, and they mentioned prototypes last time I spoke to them. So they agreed to send me some."

"Looks good, but why add the green plastic if all it will really do is piss off Wiesinger?"

"That by itself is enough."

"Gotcha."

"But it's also very stable and has better ergonomics." He showed the sculpted, adjustable ErgoGrip and the stock, which let the rear swivel be mounted sideways as well as underneath. The front freefloat tube had rails on four sides for mounting accessories. Those rails were now green. "The color will help disrupt the outline of the weapon even before taping and camo. I'd endorse them if we could make endorsements."

"Yeah, I can see that. 'I'm Sergeant First Class Kyle Monroe, a U.S. Army Sniper. I shoot terrorist assholes. When I'm out dropping them like used rubbers, I always swear by Cavalry Arms for furniture for my rifles.' I'm sure that phrase would sell a thousand sets."

"Wade, you have to see it," Kyle said, "they do the desert tan everyone's getting in the Middle East, they do black, green, brown.

Yellow and orange if you're trying to be found in the Arctic or at sea, and blue, purple, and frigging *pink* for style."

"I'll bet that would go well with your pumps." Wade was not going to let this go.

"Yeah, whatever. Anyway, if it helps me hide and pisses off Wiesinger, I'll do it." He really was enthusiastic about the plastic, though. Shooting was his life, and he tried to have the best of everything related to it, and he wasn't ashamed to extol the virtues of good hardware to others. "I've also got Bowflage tape to hide things."

"Fair enough. I've got a bit more on Indonesian culture."

"Good."

"Mostly secular. Prayers are announced every day, but most people don't bother. They do smoke. They do drink and it's accepted. The national philosophy of Pancacila stresses religious tolerance among other things. They really don't approve of religious curses of any kind, so keep the 'Goddamns' to a minimum."

"Useful, and good. I don't object to prayer, but watching it five times a day creeps me out. I guess I'm too Western." Kyle frowned. He didn't like being uncomfortable with other people's beliefs, but he also didn't care for those beliefs.

"So, we're dealing with a modern but different culture, not people stuck in the Stone Age."

"That's nice for a change."

"Don't get used to it," Wade said.

"No worries." Kyle wasn't a pessimist. But after fifteen years, he had a certain pragmatic realism.

Kyle got everything packed in rucks and harnesses and palletized for the flight to the Philippines. As he'd expected, Wiesinger didn't even look at his before it shipped, just asked Kyle if everything was accounted for and signed off. As everything he'd asked for was to the letter, it shouldn't be a problem. Wade's and his were different, but that fact would only come out if, or rather when, things went to hell. By then it would be too late, and hopefully he'd approve or at least ignore it. Kyle was going to do what he thought was right no matter what happened. The tricks he'd learned were the tricks that had kept him alive.

They briefed Wiesinger with everything they'd studied, except for the bits they'd gotten from Gober. Wiesinger had his own data, some of it woefully dated, some new to Kyle and Wade. But it would have worked better had he not been so remote throughout this.

There were times when a unit needed to dispense with formality, sit around and bullshit and work the edges off. This was one of those. But Wiesinger had to do it the Army way, which worked fine for stand-up battles. This, however, was COIN—COunter INsurgency. It was almost always messy and in the dirt, and the rules were different. Kyle had a lot of reservations, but did his damnedest to impart what he could. He wasn't going to short the man on intel just because of personal issues.

"One important thing, sir," he said. "Terms of address."

"Meaning?"

"It's a bad idea in these circumstances, where we might be overheard, to be formal. 'Sergeant' or 'sir' or 'colonel' can twig a listener that we're military. We want to come across as journalists or common thugs or even mercs. If they think we're actually soldiers, it could escalate badly. So we need to use first names."

"I guess that makes sense. I go by Mel."

"Got it, Mel. We may use a 'sir' now and then, but generally, we need to start practicing now."

"Roger that . . . Kyle. I can't say I'm happy with the concept of missions that require that kind of skulking. In the future, we may need to address that."

Kyle didn't think there was any way to address that. "We can see, sir," he said. He was eager to end this processing and get on with the mission.

The next day, they boarded an Air Mobility Command C-141 toward California and Hawaii, there to transfer to Guam and the Philippines. After more than twenty hours in transit, the best Kyle could say was that Wiesinger had been mostly silent. The plane hadn't been silent, and his ears ached from hearing protection and pressure changes.

Then it was into another C-141 for the final leg, with their gear pallet with them, and the inevitable nerves.

4

KYLE TOOK ANOTHER TUG AT HIS LEG STRAPS. HE'D once made a jump with straps insufficiently snug, and the shock of the opening canopy had almost crushed his testicles. It wasn't a lesson he would forget. He always double-checked his straps and triple-checked the legs and laterals, which held the bottom of the container firm against his back. They'd just donned the rigs now, and it hurt where the straps dug in. Wade had his adjusted and didn't move. He looked very relaxed. *Good act*, Kyle thought. Kyle was tense, sweating in the jumpsuit, even with it zipped open at the throat and the temperature in the plane down below fifty.

Wiesinger was fumbling back out of his container harness. Right. He needed to drain excess coffee in a hurry. Idiot. That was another reason not to drink coffee on the way in; it was a diuretic. There was no way to go around the gear, with the ruck hung in front. Kyle laughed silently.

It was a quiet half hour later before anything else happened. Kyle was reading a novel, his usual pulp SF with an exploding spaceship on the cover. He figured to leave the book for someone on the crew, assuming he didn't have to file it to prevent problems. He asked and was told someone would be happy to take it. He nodded and sat back down, leaning against the cargo webbing behind him.

They got the signal from the jumpmaster to go on oxygen. The signals were Army standard, even though the jumpmaster was Air Force. He was a Special Operations Weather Parachutist, who jumped before assaults and put out the data the pilots needed. He jumped along with a Combat Control team who provided landing, flight control, and terminal guidance for munitions. It made sense, but Kyle had never even known that job existed. There weren't many of them. Up here, in lieu of his gray beret, the man wore an insulated flight suit, parka, and oxygen mask, as well as a harness on a line to keep him inside the aircraft. Kyle secured his mask and plugged into the plane's bottle, then had to pop his ears as the pressure dropped. It got much cooler, too. For that, he was welcome. He'd been sweating his ass off inside his suit. The ramp cracked open, and a sliver of light appeared. It was a dark sky, light only in comparison. The air currents changed and roared and the temperature became decidedly chill. The sliver became a band became a hole into space, with a faint rumbling Kyle could feel. He'd done this only a few days before in training. It was different now. No recovery crew, and an international nightmare if they were found on landing—though from this altitude, any errors were likely to be in the first few seconds and fatal. He took a deep draft of oxygen to reassure himself, and stepped up.

The jumpmaster crawled to the corner of the ramp and the fuselage and stuck his head out enough to view conditions. It wasn't as if he could actually see the landing zone from here. That would require a lot of work on the soldiers' part to reach. He could check for storms, bad cloud cover, and confirm the approximate location just as a double check. That done, he stood carefully and held a thumb up. The jump light turned green, indicating they were over the drop point.

Kyle nodded. He shuffled forward, the ruck between his legs causing him to waddle. He checked behind and got a response from Wade, who was just behind him. Wiesinger was following, and gave him a nod that seemed to imply he should hurry the hell up.

Hampered by the ruck, Kyle took long, loping steps down the ramp and leaped into blackness.

The wind snatched at him, slapping him across the front as he fell head down, then tumbled. He stiffened his body in a hard arch—arms and legs spread-eagled and drawn back behind the plane of his torso. It worked as it was supposed to; he became stable and face to Earth.

For just a moment, all was still, silent, and weightless. Add the blackness before the few dim light sources beneath penetrated his vision, and it was as close to perfect solitude as one could get. For that moment, Kyle was alone with nothing but his thoughts.

Then gravity started to return as friction with the air braked his acceleration. His weight built back up as the sibilant breeze increased to a buffeting roar. Icy daggers of wind stabbed through the edges of his goggles, chilling his eyes. It was like a motorcycle ride in deep winter, the rarefied air at 35,000 feet well below 0°F.

The jump was a cross between HALO—High Altitude, Low Opening, which was designed to keep troops invisible from observers until the last moment, and HAHO—High Altitude, High Opening, which allowed lots of time under the canopy to literally glide to a target some distance away. They'd left the plane during its normal flight path, and would fall to 25,000 feet, where they'd deploy their canopies and fly several miles to their designated landing zone.

The altimeter strapped to his wrist had a luminescent tritium dial. He glanced at it and read 32,000 and some feet. He didn't worry about the dividing ticks between numbers. All he was waiting for was the needle to hit the 25. Total free fall time should be about thirty seconds, as thin as the air was. Lower down it was seven seconds per thousand feet, roughly, but at this altitude the friction was lower and terminal velocity higher.

Below, the ground was dark, with bare, shadowy shapes of mountains. Off to the sides were lighted areas. Those were small towns, oil and gas operations, and far to the north, Lhokseumawe. First things first: Determine direction. That was north and down.

Kyle fell through wisps of clouds, the denser, wet air changing the sound of the wind to a rumble. Clouds could be very dangerous. At 120 mph, even raindrops could cause injury. Hail could be lethal. But these were just tendrils of high cumulus in an otherwise clear night. A dark shape falling to his right was Wiesinger. Everything was equally affected by gravity, but Wiesinger had more mass in the same area, so he had less wind drag. Kyle and Wade were close enough to barely matter. He bent and spun, seeing Wade behind and slightly above. Using the lights to orient himself, he turned back around. So far, so good.

The altimeter swept past 25 as his goggles started to fog. He brought in his arms, the left on his helmet, the right reaching and snatching for the release.

The pilot chute snapped into the air, trailing the bagged canopy and its banded shroud lines. It stretched the lines taut, popped the fasteners on the nylon bag and began to unfurl into an inflated wing. All Kyle felt was a firm tug at his crotch and chest straps. The sound was that of a flag flapping in a strong breeze. Then he was half sitting, half hanging in the harness and facing the horizon instead of the ground. A quick glance let him reach for the brakes and tug them loose from their Velcro, and he was able to steer.

Working quickly, he drew his Night Vision Goggles from a pouch on his front and slipped them over his helmet. In a few seconds, he could see things much more clearly. He immediately looked up to see if his officially overloaded canopy had any tears. It seemed fine for now. He let out a breath in relief and looked below.

In the clear monochrome of the enhanced image, his trained eyes resolved dark areas as woods, lighter areas as fields, and found roads and industrial areas off to the horizon. Below was a hillside field, likely around 2000 feet, with a beacon flashing straight up. It should be exactly 2112 feet. That was their LZ. The "beacon" was a tiny pocket flashlight set to strobe, mounted in a can. It would be hard to see from the sides, but was plenty visible from above with image intensifiers.

Now it was time for a long, hopefully boring, ride. Another check didn't show any problems with the canopy, but he *was* coming down fast. That was to be expected with an additional forty pounds of weight on the harness.

He drew the left brake in tight and made a tight circle, moving his head rapidly to scan the sky with the narrow aperture of the goggles. There was Wade, above and behind, and Wiesinger below and behind. He'd fallen faster, being denser. He chuckled at the alternate meaning of that term as he completed the turn and resumed "flight."

The wind shifted as he fell through different levels of atmospheric movement. It required adjustment every few seconds to keep oriented. That was also due to the fact that no canopy was ever perfect once deployed. A single line tauter than the others would affect the steering.

He had been told the wind should be from the west, so he angled that way, wanting to stay upwind so he could be blown onto the LZ if there were problems. The ride took a long time, sitting in a harness much like a ski lift, only going down instead of up. He paid attention to his oxygen bottle. It should have plenty for the time involved, but if it ran out, his only option was to take a deep breath of whatever dregs he could and pull one brake in to spiral down as fast as possible below 14K feet.

The altimeter swept slowly, steadily down into the 14,000s, then past. He should be fine with ambient air now, but he'd stay on oxygen anyway. There wasn't any need to ditch it yet. He'd wait until 12K to be sure.

It was actually a nice night, though still cold. The stars were brilliantly bright. Below, they were matched by the glow of lights, warm and mellow from sodium in residential villages and the edges of towns, stark bluish where mercury vapor lights were in use.

They'd been dropped very close to the mark, and Kyle found he had plenty of altitude to spare. He was west of the LZ and still at 9000 feet and some. That wasn't a bad thing. He yanked down on the left brake and the end cells fluttered, lift lost. The right continued on at speed, throwing him into a counterclockwise turn that got tighter until he was almost facing down as he spun. After a few seconds, he eased off, steadied out and spiraled the other way to avoid dizziness. He checked the altimeter. Six thousand. Altitude for the beacon was supposed to be 2112 feet, which he couldn't rely on, and his altimeter was accurate to perhaps 50 feet anyway. Still, it was time to get into a landing pattern.

He zigzagged back and forth, losing altitude while remaining over essentially the same spot, as he turned upwind each time. Over the trees were rising thermals that held him aloft, so he steered over the meadow and the lower growth higher up. He dropped smoothly and steadily. In the last thousand feet, he turned downwind, past the beacon.

Then he turned upwind to reduce his forward velocity before landing, and removed his goggles. They offered no peripheral vision at all. He had done it right so far and was just where he needed to be. It was, in theory, a straightforward task, but in the dark, over unfamiliar terrain and with no immediate weather conditions, it was still a job to be proud of. He sailed into the clearing and watched nervously for terrain features, all of which were hidden by scrub that might be eight inches or eight feet high. The ground below was rough, bumpy and uneven. Tendrils of mist wove lazily among the growth tops. But it was either land there, or land lower down in jungle. Landing in jungle was not an appetizing option.

He'd seen Wade as he turned; he was just behind Kyle and turning himself now. Wiesinger was nowhere to be seen. He'd been below, and should be down already. But either he wasn't in the area, or he was very adept at hiding.

Kyle didn't think he was that good at concealment. Still, the only thing to do at this time was get down and hidden, then deal with other issues. He slipped the ruck and let it drop on its cord, which would give him much more maneuverability for landing, as well as lightening the mass to be supported by the canopy once it hit.

The ruck touched down with a thump and suddenly his descent was much more gentle. He'd made it, overloaded and without ripping the canopy and plunging to his death. Sighing in relief, he checked the steering brakes he'd use to land now. He was near ground, five meters, and preparing to flare, when gunfire erupted lower down, at the edge of a patch of stunted trees.

IT WAS ONLY A FEW SHOTS, BUT HE WAS ABOUT AS EX-
posed as one could be without being naked. He didn't like it.

Kyle kept his stance and didn't panic. When it seemed he'd hit at
any moment, he pulled both brakes smoothly in until his hands
reached his crotch. The back of the canopy's cells closed, slowing it
and causing air to billow up. After a few seconds, it would stall,
drop and reinflate. But he should be on the ground before then.

As soon as his boots touched, he rolled out in a parachute landing fall. It wasn't always necessary, especially with the square
canopies, but it never hurt, and when taking fire, it was the fastest
way to get on the ground. He yanked at the left brake, gathering the
line in his fist until the canopy came horizontal and folded to the
ground like a fan.

He wasn't watching that event. He was unbuckling the thigh and
chest straps and grabbing the only weapon he could reach in a
hurry: his Ed Brown .45. It cleared the holster inside his jumpsuit,
and then he scurried backward into some growth, dragging his ruck
with him. Once concealed, he pulled the night vision back on. Waiting for muzzle flashes as a means of identifying potential threats
wasn't the best way of operating. He wanted to see.

A fluttering shadow would be Wade landing. Beyond that were
occasional, deliberate shots. Deliberate was bad. Afghans would
have been spraying the landscape with no hope of hitting anything.
Slow, careful shooting was the mark of a professional. Several professionals. He marked several faint muzzle flashes for later reference.

Wade had seen where he landed, and rolled and crawled toward
where he was now hidden. Once under cover himself, Kyle slithered

over to meet up. He came face to muzzle with Wade's Beretta, which bothered him for only a moment. He knew his partner's skill and nerves, and trusted him to identify a target. It looked eerie in the monochromatic green of the night vision.

"We're here. Where's Mel?" Wade asked, lowering the pistol, sinking back down and all but disappearing into the ground. There was a ring of apparently clear air around them, a trick of the eye, but beyond that was a tarp of mist over everything, stirring lazily. Kyle made note to use that movement to watch for threats, who'd disturb the air as they approached.

"Dunno," he replied. "We need to figure out who we're making contact with, too." Great. A twerp of an officer, and he was missing, too. But it was reassuring in a way. A certain amount of trouble was inevitable. If it was going wrong already, they could hope for steady, minor screw-ups rather than a precarious balance until it crashed totally. And goddamn, it was hot down here. Insulated suit over BDUs, helmet, and warm, humid, tropical air.

"Well, the fire is coming from out there in at least two directions, and outgoing fire from the beacon area suggests our friends." He pointed downhill to the eastern edge of the clearing. "If the beacon was captured, I'd hope our allies would attack in a more vigorous fashion, especially as we're on the ground. Either that, or yell for us."

"Logical, assuming professionals. These are the rebels, however." Professionals were predictable. Amateurs were fuzed explosives, just waiting for the hammer to fall. "But it's either that, or wait until it's over and hope the good guys win."

"So what do we do? Seeing as our fearless leader isn't here?"

"That way," Kyle pointed, "and we'll try to get attention. Any reason not to use flares to backlight the trouble?"

Wade considered this as he drew his M4 from his harness and snapped the stock open. He had loaded it aboard the plane in violation of Air Force regs, and the crew hadn't even suggested he stop. They knew what troops on the ground faced, and they supported them. He clicked a shell into the M203 grenade launcher mounted under the little carbine and slid the breech closed.

"Can't think of any," he said. "Anyone with ears knows there's a fight here. If it's big, they'll be here before it's over. If it's small, we'll be gone before they get here. I count three to five enemies over there, about fifty meters by ear," he pointed.

"I agree," Kyle said. He was pulling the upper and lower halves of the SR25 from his ruck, and slapping the pins tight to assemble the receivers. He grabbed a twenty-round magazine and slid it in. At times like this, it didn't hurt to "ride the bolt" forward until it was almost locked, then tap the forward assist to finish closing it quietly. But the SR25 didn't have a forward assist. He let the bolt fly to close with the reassuring ratcheting clack of the locking breech. Then he removed his night vision again. It was bulky, eyes had advantages, and he had the scope if he needed it. He hesitated for just a second before unzipping his jumpsuit and squirming out.

"Sorry," he said, "but I'm about to cook."

"No problem," Wade said. He had shed his already. He leaned back with the stock low on his shoulder, sighted for distance, and then "aimed by ear" at the apex of the firing. He squeezed the trigger on the grenade launcher.

Whoomp!

"Let's move," he said, and shimmied out of the tangled brush into the open space between trees. They hid again before the illumination shell burst under its parachute. Both kept their eyes averted out of habit, to avoid affecting the night vision goggles, though the gear they had could compensate for the glare. The firefight paused for a moment, then rose to a brief, furious level. Most of the fire was generally outgoing from the snipers' area, which was a good sign, assuming those were the allies they were to meet. Then it got dark again as the illumination burned out.

They crawled forward, Kyle holding his weapon in his left hand. That meant they each had an arc of fire. If they'd had Wiesinger, he'd cover the rear and they'd be protected all around.

Wade would shift a few feet, knees splayed and spine flexing like a lizard. He'd take cover and pause. Kyle would choose his next position from wherever he was and move to it. The growth was thick enough to provide good concealment and cover, and the air was humid and dense even though it wasn't too warm. That meant noise would damp out faster.

They'd covered perhaps thirty meters when Wade signaled Kyle forward.

Kyle slithered up alongside. He said nothing, simply waited for Wade, who pointed. Ahead of them was an Indonesian with a Pindad Senapan Serbu 1, the Indonesian-licensed version of the Belgian FNC carbine. He was slowly approaching the parachutes they'd just left.

The trick now was to get his attention, without getting shot by him or letting anyone else locate them.

Wade reached a long arm out and shook a branch on a bush. It wiggled, and the Indonesian froze, weapon held ready. Wade shook it again, twice. Then three times.

"*Keluar*," the man said softly. Come out.

"Americans," Wade replied. "Coming out." He led the way, after a moment's glance to see if Kyle approved. The man simply faced him in a squat, ignoring another shot that was some meters away. Who or what the target was was impossible to tell in the dark, dank growth. Kyle slipped out and joined Wade.

"You are?" the man asked in English, looking cautious rather than suspicious.

"Kyle and Wade," Kyle said. They were just "Kyle and Wade"; no last names, nothing to indicate military rank or an employer.

"I'm Bakri. Pleased to meet you." He was very slim, about five foot seven, and had a scraggly beard. It didn't really suit him. Nor did the smile that revealed crooked teeth. But the name was right for their contact and he wasn't shooting at them. Incoming fire seemed to indicate his loyalties were with them. Good news, after a fashion.

"And you," Kyle said.

"We're under fire?" Wade asked, prodding for intel. The chat seemed out of place, under the circumstances.

"Just a skirmish, you say? We have met a different rebel patrol, I think."

"You think?"

"It's hard to say in the dark," he admitted. "Where is your other man?"

"That's what we're trying to figure out."

Just then, a round crack-snapped through the leaves above them. They all ducked.

"Wonderful," Kyle said. "Do you mind if we return some fire?"

Bakri grinned a mouthful of teeth. "Feel free."

Kyle and Wade had the best weapons in the area and were undoubtedly the best shooters. A quick glimpse through the AN/PVS-10 scope showed Kyle the shine of clothes that had been excessively pressed or starched. Someone was trying to look "professional" in their uniform, and was instead standing out like aluminum foil. He sunk lower for stability, aimed, and fired.

There was a thrashing motion and then nothing. One down. Wade had pegged someone else, and the locals had hit another. It was eerie to be in a battle, yet to have everything be so clean. After another handful of shots, the enemy faded away. It had barely been rougher than a field exercise, other than the fact that a dozen bullets had passed overhead.

"What now?" Kyle asked, as they finally shook hands.

Bakri whistled and his troop scurried in. There were four of them. They were introduced as Rizal, Fahmi, Hassan, and Syarief. Kyle nodded, but in the dark they all looked the same; skinny, grinning Malays in camouflage with rifles.

"What is your status?" Bakri asked.

"We're down, someone knows that men with parachutes are down, and we're missing a man," Kyle said.

"And this surprises you?" Wade asked.

"No, not really," Kyle admitted. He was lying. He was endlessly amazed by all the myriad ways things could drop into the toilet. "Bakri," he said, "We need to look for our other man. Any ideas?"

"Where was he when you last saw him?"

"About two hundred meters below us and two hundred downwind." The fat bastard had dropped like a stone, squeezed into his jumpsuit.

Bakri looked around, considering things. "That way," he indicated, pointing uphill and into the scrub. Then he turned and rattled off something in Achinese. Two of the others went off to check on the enemy and gather loot.

"You lead, please?" Kyle asked. "I'll navigate and Wade covers rear."

"Got it," Wade agreed. Bakri nodded and slipped forward, twisting so as to minimize disturbance of the growth. It was a casual movement for him. The snipers were trained professionals with lots of experience in many terrains, but Bakri had grown up here. The leaves and stalks made barely a whisper as he passed by. His men spread out to patrol for threats. Kyle was reassured. They were quite professional, unlike the eager and brave but unschooled allies they'd had in Pakistan.

It was a bit nervy, with the growth at the edge of the treeline thinning quickly in just a few steps. They all slunk down to the ground. Bakri had an old, crude night vision monocular Kyle didn't recognize. He and Wade had state of the art American ones that were far more effective, but they were unfamiliar with the terrain. It was a toss-up who'd see Wiesinger first, if he was alive and in the area.

Shortly, Wade spoke. "I see a figure up ahead. Large, armed with an M four. Likely him."

"I hope so. If there's anyone else here meeting that description . . ."

"Yeah, one of him is enough," Wade agreed jovially.

Wiesinger had actually done the smart thing. Once down, he'd buried his canopy and container. He was sitting, back to a tree, scanning with his night vision. Kyle swallowed hard and stood slowly, arms out and weapon slung. He wanted Wiesinger to see him. He also didn't want the man, whose capabilities were in question, to panic and take a shot. At the least, it would attract attention. At the best, or rather worst . . .

"Halt, who goes there?" Wiesinger asked in a whisper.

"Kyle, Wade, and local allies. Good to see you, Mel," he said. Although it was only good in the sense of not having to fill out the paperwork for a lost colonel.

"Ser . . . Kyle. What's our status?" Wiesinger had almost forgotten to use names instead of ranks. Easy-enough mistake, but they'd practiced to avoid that. Kyle wasn't sure if he was just that military minded, or that in love with his rank. But he'd need to avoid it.

Kyle decided to keep patient. The man had been out of the loop. "We're down, uninjured, ready to travel, with our local contact and have repulsed a minor skirmish. We count two kills."

"Good start to the mission, then?" The colonel nodded as he rose and gathered his gear.

"Sort of. We're ahead." The fact that a couple of easy kills made the man think things were "good" spoke volumes. "Good" came from not engaging until necessary, and not being seen.

In two minutes they were all together. Kyle had an unvoiced theory that Wiesinger's stealth had been predicated by fear, not strategy. Still, they were all down, had their allies and guides, and were ready to commence their operation. Kyle wasn't enthusiastic.

If fourteen years of service had taught him anything, it was that that meant things were about to drop deeper into the toilet.

"Okay," Bakri said. "We walk. About six kilometers. Downhill."

"I like that last part."

Bakri grinned, and chattered softly in Achinese. His troops spread out two ahead and two behind, with the Americans and him in the middle.

It wasn't a rough march, but it was no walk in the park, either. Each of them was carrying close to 200 pounds of gear, between ruck, harness, and weapons. Kyle and Wade tired but carried on quietly. Wiesinger was puffing in short order. Obviously, his PT had been pencil-whipped, too. But he did keep up.

"Permission to sling helmets, sir?" Wade asked.

"Yeah, it's rough enough as is."

Kyle didn't like that. Certainly, he liked removing his helmet in these conditions, and would have made that call. But officially, they should wear them anywhere it was potentially hostile. That Wiesinger, who loved the rules, would change them when the whim suited him was a bad sign. On the other hand, it did mean he could see reason, as long as it was poking him in the chest. Perhaps some field time would be good for him.

It took three hours for six kilometers. The terrain was rutted and steep in spots, heavily grown and with tangled roots. Downhill was both blessing and hindrance as it meant watching one's balance carefully. Despite the cool dampness, they were all sweating in short order. The Indonesians drank from canteens. The Americans sucked it from their Camelbaks. Kyle worshipped the man who'd invented the backpack-style water bladder with its drinking tube. He'd tried several times to build one when younger, based on mention of the idea in a Robert Heinlein novel from the 1950s. Some things just took a while to germinate, it seemed.

Eventually, near dawn, they arrived at a well-maintained and well worn Toyota Land Cruiser being guarded by a sole female soldier, who appeared out of the scenery when Bakri whistled.

"Haswananda," Bakri said. "She is very good at stalking."

"Hello," Kyle said.

"Hello," she answered with a nod. She was probably pretty under the sweat and grime, and had muscles like a runner showing on her arms. She was long in the limb and about as tall as Bakri. "I am called Anda."

"Anda it is," Wade agreed. Wiesinger said nothing, but shook hands briefly.

Rucks in back, weapons on laps, Anda and another troop sprawled over the gear, and two more soldiers on the roof rack, they started jouncing down a track that came to a road a few meters along. But the growth was thick enough it wouldn't have been found without major effort.

"Any updates?" Kyle asked Bakri, as Wiesinger dialed his cell phone to report them down.

"We have another group involved, I think," Bakri said as he drove. "Whoever was shooting at us. They seem to know where we were to be, and that makes me unhappy."

"Yeah, a leak somewhere," Kyle agreed.

Wiesinger asked, "Is there any way to split your group further? To avoid leaks?"

"I have done so, Mel," Bakri said. "That is why we are only six. But if I have men in their groups, they have men in mine. Some are hostile, some are seeking wealth or politic advantage, and some just talk much."

There was silence for a few minutes. The question and answer had both been obvious, and Kyle was embarrassed. Certainly, one should ask the obvious, but there were more diplomatic ways than suggesting one's hosts had missed something so simple.

"How far?" Wade asked, breaking the awkwardness.

"About an hour. It's only fifty kilometers."

Kyle nodded invisibly. He was glad for a helmet, and donned it again. The rutted road caused them to bump heads from time to time. Bakri was shorter and safe, but Wiesinger was even taller, and could be heard cursing quietly. At least it was quiet. The guys on the roof had to be taking a beating, especially when one considered the trees overhead. Then there were roots they banged over . . .

The good news was there was a camp at the end of it. Rather more than a camp. It was a village with buildings. They were concrete and block, Spartan but weatherproof, and the three of them were bedded down on mattresses in short order. They weren't much as mattresses went, but were better than torn car seats, truck beds of trash, airplane seats or cargo racks, muddy pits, dank caves, or any of a number of other things Kyle had slept on. And there was cold rice and fruit for snacking. They used flashlights sparingly in the growing half light.

"We rise at nine and get back to it," Bakri said. "Normal we travel by night. But we need to get start soon."

"Understood," Wiesinger said. "Post watch, gentlemen. I'll take third rotation."

"Yes, sir," Kyle said. It was a perfectly reasonable order and a fair privilege of rank to be last so as to get uninterrupted sleep. But it bugged Kyle anyway. He realized it was an overreaction on his part that he'd have to get over.

Wade said, "You first, I'll take middle. Works out to fifty minutes each."

"Thanks, buddy," Kyle said.

"No problem. You owe me."

"I always owe you."

Wiesinger snapped, "Keep it down!"

"Sorry, sir." Kyle sighed and sat back, weapon in hand and alert.

A few minutes later, he knew he'd have trouble sleeping. Wiesinger snored like a B52 on takeoff.

6

KYLE WOKE TO WIESINGER SLAPPING HIS BOOT. HE rolled up silently, hand on weapon. It was a trained reflex.

"Get ready, we're moving," Wiesinger said in a taciturn voice.

"Roger that," he said.

Wade was already stretching and reaching into his ruck for a toothbrush. Health care is important, especially in the field. One can avoid soap so as to blend in with the brush, but hand washing, with at least water, and tooth care are vital. They tidied up in a few moments and were ready when Bakri stuck his head back in.

"Good!" he said. "We take trucks to a meeting point." He turned and left with just a wave of his hand. The Americans followed him out. Three trucks were in the village, two Land Cruisers and an ancient Land Rover. There were troops to fill them, including one with an RPK light machine gun and another with an RPG, a rocket loaded and a spare sticking out of his pack.

As they gathered around the vehicles, Wiesinger asked, "What is the plan, Bakri?"

"Meet up with rest of unit. Then travel to where we can observe the target. We have avoid it so far to keep cover, as requested."

Wiesinger faced Kyle and Wade. "The target at this point is the village of Khayalan. Our brief says explosives are going through there. This intel is secondhand from several sources. So we're going to confirm on the ground. If we confirm, we'll take appropriate action. If we do not confirm, we'll have to determine where the target is and reevaluate."

" 'Appropriate action' means shoot the guilty parties, or call in fire?" Kyle asked. He hated euphemisms. Sometimes, they were just politeness to avoid scaring the more delicate personalities. Sometimes, euphemisms meant the mission was officially disapproved and the operator would get hung out to dry.

"Probably the former," Wiesinger said, which was reassuring. "If we can take out the brains, it hinders the operation."

"Yes, Mel." Kyle knew the doctrine; he'd been doing this for a decade. Likely, Wiesinger was used to briefing non-snipers. This was one of those things you let slide, Kyle decided.

Wiesinger turned to Bakri. "Is there enough room inside, or do we need to shuffle stuff around?"

"We'll fit," Bakri said. "We just need to put it all in."

"Sounds good. We're at your disposal to help load."

"We load now." Bakri grinned. "Climb in." They all boarded the first Toyota, Wiesinger in front, Kyle behind, and Wade behind the driver. Wade and Wiesinger had their M4s convenient to the windows. Kyle's longer SR25 would be a bit harder to get into play. The other one was still broken down and cased in Wade's ruck. The rucks were all in back.

For a first, their allies had hot food in paper cups. It was a chicken-and-rice mixture with what might be mangoes and spices. Sweet and hot, it was quite refreshing, and Kyle enjoyed it. So did the others.

"Native food adds so much to a mission," Wiesinger commented.

"When it's good, yes," Wade said. "I can't recommend Romanian style Mexican, or Pakistani dried goat and beans, though."

"Mnnph," the colonel replied around a mouthful of rice. "I'll take your word on it. But this stuff is good."

"Yeah, I'm partial to it. All in all, I'm not going to jinx things by asking what could go wrong."

"It'll happen soon enough," Kyle said, feeling pessimistically realistic.

With the other vehicles loaded with six troops each, the little platoon rolled off with cheerful waves. In this area, they could operate fairly openly, weapons ready in case of skirmish with government troops or another faction. But there were large sections of the country where weapons would get them shot on sight by overwhelming force. Kyle and Wade had both been under such circumstances before.

"How long is the trip?" Kyle asked Bakri, who was driving. Anda and another, even slighter, woman, Irta, were stuffed in back atop the gear. They were small enough not to be too inconvenienced, but they couldn't deploy until Kyle and Wade cleared the back, unless they shot out a window and risked cuts.

"About four hours," Bakri said. "One hundred kilometers."

Fifteen miles an hour. Yes, that wasn't a bad rate. American civilians were spoiled by superhighways and well-laid streets in good repair. Most of the world still had dirt tracks with the occasional two-lane road. Speed above 35 mph was very respectable. And under the circumstances, there was nothing to complain about. The vehicle was in decent repair, ran well, and didn't shake.

It was even possible to doze, until Wiesinger snapped, "Kyle, wake up and pay attention."

"Yes, Mel," he said. He grumbled slightly. It wasn't as if they could do anything as far as a fight. If fire came in, he'd wake at once. If not, he couldn't help navigate. But if that's how the commander wanted to do it, he could will himself awake.

The best way to do that was food and drink. He sipped a mouthful of water from his Camelbak and reached over his shoulder to dig a granola bar from an outer pocket of his ruck.

The key to staying awake was to nibble just a little every time one started to zone. He got an hour from the bar and a few sips of water and was thinking about a second one. It wasn't as if he couldn't use the calories anyway. Wade was reaching back to grab something from his own gear, likely the jerky.

A burst of machine-gun fire ripped across the convoy, stirring the thick air.

"Awas!" Bakri shouted. *Take cover.* The order wasn't needed. The troops were already diving for cover. Wade kicked the door on his side and rolled out, and Kyle was only an instant behind him. The drivers were backing up rapidly, but the rearmost vehicle took a hit and stopped. The driver convulsed and gurgled, then died.

As long as we don't land on a preset mine or a coordinated attack, Kyle thought as he rolled into the weeds. But staying in the vehicles would be suicide.

Another burst blew past, along with aimed shots from rifles. He heard the distinct snap of a bullet through the growth.

"Kopassus!" someone yelled.

"Oh, fucking shit goddamit no!" Kyle shouted. It didn't mean much, he was just pissed. Of all the things that could go wrong, a firefight with government troops from an elite unit was about as bad as things could get.

"We need to attack!" Wiesinger said.

"Negative, Mel. Cover and low." He scrunched lower into the ground. He was in a faint hollow between the roots of a tree.

"The proper response to an ambush is to attack, seizing initiative. Get them to attack!" the colonel shouted.

"Mel, you attack these badasses, you will *die*," Kyle said. "And they're friendly to the US. We stay low and attempt to disengage. Bakri, how many and where?"

The wiry little Indonesian was alongside in a crouch, and obviously scared but not panicking.

"Probably two squads," he said. "One with machine guns and grenade launcher. One rifles."

"Explosives?" Kyle asked.

"I assume yes."

"And that's why we don't charge, Mel," Kyle said. "Claymores, if this was a planned attack." He ducked as a round snapped past. "Dammit, they're along a long front. Suggestions?"

"Machine gun and grenade launchers," Wade said. "Puts us as close to par as we get. Then you and I pick targets." Kyle noticed he didn't mention Wiesinger.

"Roger. Bakri, you know how to use this?" Kyle offered the M4 with its underslung grenade launcher. He unfastened the pouch of grenades from his harness.

"I do." The man nodded, appearing deadly serious while grinning widely.

"Fine, get your men to drive them out, we'll shoot." He slid the weapon and grenades through the soft, damp dirt. He could clean them later.

"I understand."

"Wade, spot and backup?"

"Can do," he agreed. He slid the two halves of the SR25 over to Kyle, with one magazine. Kyle could bless him for remembering to grab an extra weapon.

"Mel, can you pick targets with the M four? Or should we swap?" He fitted the two halves together and pressed in the pins.

"I'll manage, *Kyle*," the colonel said. "I do know how to shoot."

"No such thing as a stupid question in battle, sir." He let the honorific in to try to defuse things slightly. "Stand by for targets."

Another burst was followed by a scream.

"Goddamit, they're good," Kyle said. "I don't want to fight them if we don't have to. For one thing, we're supposed to be allies."

"For another, they're pretty goddamned good," Wade admitted.

"Yeah. Bakri, flush them," Kyle said.

Bakri spoke a few words, and his troops and he opened up with the RPK and the grenade launcher. With both support weapons and eight riflemen shooting at one area, it took only a moment for the troops there to pop smoke grenades.

"There they go," Kyle muttered to himself. Behind concealment of smoke, they'd hopefully not advance.

"Reference twisted tree, target, running, two five meters." Wade called it off in a rapid singsong.

"Sighted," Kyle said, seeing the movement. As Wade spoke, it resolved from shifting leaves to a camouflaged something into a running man. He led, squeezed, and the man dropped, clutching at a thigh. The German 7.62mm should have well nigh shattered the femur and mangled the muscle. He might not be dead, but he wasn't combat effective.

So, as Kyle realized he should have expected, Wiesinger wasted five seconds and a round putting the man out of his misery. No, it wasn't a bad thing to do. But at this juncture of a battle, the idea was to inflict as many casualties as possible. If the enemy thought the count too high, they'd retreat. And they were theoretically allies, dammit. The goal was to *not* kill them.

"Mel, we want them alive," he hissed.

"Right." The colonel nodded. He seemed overly excited. That was better than fear for the first real firefight he'd ever been in, but goddammit, Kyle didn't need to babysit anyone.

"Got 'im," Wade said laconically as he snapshot another. There hadn't been time to call the shot, and there was no need to pass it along. "I also see movement at five zero meters, clumpy bush that looks like oversized grass."

"Roger. Pick anything that moves and nick it. Just nick it."

"Understood," Wade said. Wiesinger was silent.

"Bakri, can you see there?"

"I see," he said. "I should shoot?"

"Just in front of it. If that doesn't work, go into it."

"I understand." The little man squinted along the sights and fired. The shot was wide to the left. He cursed in Achinese in a way Kyle didn't understand, but sounded very earnest. He clicked the breech and started to reload.

A shot threw splinters off the tree right over his head, the shards stinging Kyle in the face. He flinched, but Bakri didn't, continuing with the motion to load and close the breech. Only then did he roll around the tree to a different position. That convinced Kyle that the man was *very* experienced.

The second grenade landed barely under the tendrils in front of the bush, blowing half of it away. The leaves were thick and stalky and absorbed much of the fragmentation, as did the soft dirt the grenade had landed in. Still, lots of growth was removed, and parts of what could be two figures started to bug out. Kyle slammed a round through someone's upper arm, causing a rough thrashing motion. Wade hit something else and screams became audible over the fire.

Then it got quiet.

"They have retreated," Bakri said. "They will move some hundred meters or so and regroup, then depart to treat wounded."

"What about the seriously wounded and bodies?"

"What of them?" he asked with a grin and pointed.

Kyle looked out to where the first target had been, the one he'd shot in the leg and Wiesinger had finished off. There was nothing but a rut in the grass where the corpse had been dragged off.

The hairs on his neck stood straight up.

"Holy shit, that's a good trick."

"Never a body. They, we, both the same game," Bakri said.

"You little bastards are the best skilled allies I've ever worked with," Kyle said reverently. The Bosnians were competent but not imaginative. The Afghans were eager but unskilled. The Iraqis were constantly fearful of turncoats. But the Indonesians were competent, cool, and devious.

"We were lucky," Bakri said. "They could have caught us from behind as well. Three more men made the difference."

"I'm glad it was a small patrol," Kyle said. "Back to traveling?"

"Yes, but we will be tracked. Kopassus always tracks."

"Wonderful. There goes our cover. What do we do now?"

"Leave the area," Bakri said. "They want stronger targets, is that how you say it?"

"Hard targets?" Wade asked.

"Yes. Operations. Not patrols they want. We were just a chance."

"Makes sense," Wiesinger said. "Where?"

"This way," Bakri said, gesturing.

Wiesinger stood up and started walking. Stifling a curse, Kyle tackled him.

"What the fuck are you *doing*?" Wiesinger snarled, his face hardening.

"Mel, there are still hostiles in the area."

He bit off the second part of his statement. *So stay concealed, you fucking idiot* wouldn't sit well. Wiesinger's act was that of a man who was used to exercises that were called clear at the end, with no ongoing threat.

"Right," the colonel said, looking sheepish. He stayed down.

They advanced in three elements, covering all arcs with additional weapons forward, slipping along a few meters from the road. Wiesinger wasn't bad at concealment, Kyle thought. Nor was he good. He clearly had studied all the right books. But he had little practice.

It's like having an older, fatter second lieutenant along, he thought. He sighed. It was uncharitable, but the thought he had was that at least the man was large enough to stop a few bullets.

They finished an advance and wiggled into the dirt, to cover the next element. With eyes shifting around, Wiesinger spoke softly.

"Sergeant Monroe, U.S. weapons are supposed to stay in U.S. hands."

"Yes, sir, they are. And when the shit hits the fan, I want backup and I don't care who it is."

"We have no positive confirmation of their loyalties." Wiesinger really wasn't getting it, Kyle thought.

"Then it's a bad idea to have them behind us with rifles, yes?" he said reasonably.

Wiesinger jerked. It clearly hadn't occurred to him that there were armed men and women behind him with M16s, FNCs, AK47s, a Jagawana Forest Guard Gun that looked like a Sten and fired 9 × 21mm, and large knives.

"Mel," Kyle said, "things are never the way we'd like them to be on these types of ops. Our allies are usually poorly trained; we're lucky this time. The food can suck or be nonexistent. Plans change, people screw us over, others help us. It's all a guessing game. I'm guessing we can trust Bakri, because we have to. He could kill us in our sleep. Or turn us in."

Wiesinger said nothing, but nodded perhaps a half inch.

Two more advances brought them to the vehicles. One had a hole through the radiator tank, but one of the men was at work with a propane torch and solder. Another had the windows well shot out. There was one lethal casualty, a man they'd only nodded to, never been introduced, and two wounds and an injury—sprained wrist from a fall. With some grunting of pain, the three were bandaged as best could be and they all gathered around to discuss plans, their hosts speaking Bahasa for ease.

"So where do we go?" Wiesinger asked. The man had no patience. Bakri looked at him, then resumed talking.

Kyle and Wade sat silently, alert, while the Indonesians jabbered quietly around a map spread out on the lead Toyota's hood. It was

Kyle's experience that after the locals had hashed things out, then they'd talk to the Americans and finalize things. But they needed time. Especially as no one liked to feel the foreigners were trying to run the show. There was a diplomacy issue here that Wiesinger's lack of self-confidence couldn't help.

"Here, Khayalan," Bakri said, just as it looked as if Wiesinger would butt in. "But to get there we must go this way." He indicated a circuitous route along the hills. "To avoid attention."

"How long a drive?" Wade asked.

"Eight to ten hours."

"Oh, that's not bad," Kyle said. Likely less than three hundred kilometers then. Narrow roads and convoy security would make a long trip even slower. "What's there?"

"Just people we can supply with," he said. "Then we go to Khayalan for the target."

"Got it."

It wasn't a pleasant trip, cooped up in a small, cramped vehicle, sweaty and worried about attack. But Kyle and Wade had been through worse. Well-trained troops were a confidence builder, and they were literate and experienced. There was food along, more fruit and some cold chicken and rice. Kyle wasn't a rice fan, but it was a staple for most of the world. The Indonesian spices varied from scorching to sweet, so at least it was interesting. This was a far richer area, resource wise, than the ass end of Central Asia.

Wiesinger was mostly reticent, which was a good thing. The man was just naturally abrasive. On the other hand, no matter how poorly one got along with teammates, knowing something about them was important for cohesion. But it just wasn't the thing Kyle wanted to mention, so they stayed each with their own thoughts.

They sank down low in the seats as they passed through towns that were five or six blocks long. One had a divided main road with a central canal. Whether it was for water runoff or transport, Kyle couldn't tell and didn't ask. He was busy being not noticed. That road was asphalted, but others were cobbled. There was a motorcycle with a rickshaw sidecar he found really amusing. People wore native garb, Western clothes and American or Chinese hats. The ramshackle houses had steep roofs of tile or tin against monsoon rains, and were different but not dissimilar from the colonial styles in Asia. Dutch rather than French, but with obvious cultural roots.

There were militia fighters on patrol, and Bakri waved to one group but detoured around rice paddies to avoid another.

"They would collect toll," he said. "Cost us time, money, and risk for you."

"Appreciated," Kyle said. "We're not in a hurry."

"Yes we are," Wiesinger muttered.

"Not to die, Mel," Kyle snapped back.

He did find the schoolgirls cute, on old-style bicycles in skirts and with traditional head coverings. They smiled and waved and were absolute dolls. He hoped they weren't targets for anyone.

Then they were back out into the wilds again, occasional single and multiple dwelling settlements carved out of the forest. It was a constant fight as the humans tried to go one way and the jungle resisted, even grew back.

Shortly, they pulled into an open field that was terraced down a slope like stacked plates. It was the brightest green Kyle had ever seen, thick with rice and palms of some kind. The buildings were low wood.

They stopped and obtained ammunition and food, and swapped troops around. It was done quickly, and the Americans stayed in the vehicles.

"People are needed for the crops, and they will notice if we are gone for long. We can only patrol a few days at a time when the Army is here in force," Bakri said. Though obviously that "in force" was still a fairly token presence.

"What is important is that you not be associated with groups like ours, who want to negotiate," Bakri said. "Very risky. We must get you into area where rebels are common. Your target is there anyway."

"We appreciate the risk," Kyle said. "Good people all over the world are taking risks on this. We've been in other countries doing the same thing."

"What is it like?"

Wade said, "Rough, dangerous, but rewarding. There's no headlines over it. But you know you've done right."

"Yes, the same with us. I do this for my children," Bakri said. "They should not live poor, but they should not have to fight. If we can meet Jakarta partway, then ask for more, it is better. But if not, we'll have to fight more."

"Our government is trying," Wiesinger said. "But paperwork takes a long time. This is the first time I've been away from it in years."

Kyle felt a flash of empathy. He despised paperwork. Was

Wiesinger pushed into it because of his father's legacy? The perfect staff officer, even if he hated it?

"Yes," Bakri said. "We were all happy when Timor-Leste became free. But the fighting was fierce. We would like that, too. And we could negotiate on oil and gas better than Jakarta. We are closer, so have less entangles."

"I agree," Kyle said. "But we can't make that decision. Seems like every real soldier I've met, even among Bosnians, Iraqis, and Russians, was a decent guy I could drink a beer with and get along with. We all hate terrorists."

"Yes, because they are cowards." Bakri nodded vigorously. "We and the Kopassus and Army and Marines are all men, and fight like men. It's frightening and dangerous, but that is the price." He shrugged his shoulders. "Attacking journalists, drivers, women, children . . ." He spat forcefully out the window. "I would like a hut in the jungle and a week with each of them. Perhaps ten days." His clenching jaw bespoke a far less cheerful and angrier side that Kyle hoped not to experience. "If you can, will you let one live for me?"

Kyle was silent a moment.

"We've discussed that before," Wade said into the pause. "As enjoyable as that would be, there's the risk of escape."

"Ah, yes. Better not to. But some deserve more suffering than life offers. There is Allah offering judgment."

"I pray for that, too," Kyle said politely. He wasn't very religious. But he did hope for justice as it was deserved.

"We turn onto a road now. Keep guns out of sight."

"Okay," they agreed, and slid the weapons lower. They were all wearing camouflage of various kinds; still, people were more likely to twig on weapons than clothes. They came out into brighter light and onto a two-lane blacktop in good repair. Kyle removed his brimmed boonie hat and the others followed suit. That and keeping arms inside the windows should help reduce visibility. There were fields on either side, flat and a brighter green than any American growth. The forest stood back around them, tall and riotous.

Then they turned back off the road. They'd been on it only a kilometer or two and had passed one car going the other way at high speed. The three vehicles, spread widely and packed, could easily be mistaken for work trucks.

This trail was much rougher, but that was due to use. It was a dirt road and well worn. Sleeping was impossible, with heads bobbing around like toys as the suspension squeaked in protest. The light flickered occasionally as a fluke of nature left an opening in the thin rain forest. It wasn't as thick as South America or Southeast Asia, but it was thicker than all but the heaviest, tangled second growth Stateside, and much taller.

Bakri waved and pointed, and the second vehicle pulled off in a very narrow shoulder area to keep watch. The trailing vehicle squeezed through the gap and took second place. Kyle approved silently. Far better than others he'd worked with, for certain.

These were roads under here, Kyle decided. About like access roads on an Army training range. Some were graveled in sections, old and scattered and pressed into the mud. Some were grown with low grasses from little use, and some were plain mud.

It rained one day in three here. The daytime temperature was steady near 30°C, 86°F. At night it dropped to a balmy 72°. The humidity did the same, from 90 percent down to 70 percent, day after year after century. They were so close to the equator that weather, apart from monsoons, didn't really exist—only climate. It was hot and would stay that way, barring a few days here and there. The remaining escort pulled off onto a narrow path and disappeared.

Shortly, they were driving along a track so little used it was barely visible as a trace, the growth on either side brushing against the sides of the vehicle, scratching and scraping. The windows were still open, and everyone drew back to avoid getting jabbed.

Wade said, "I remember doing this once in Macedonia, along a trail."

"Yes?" Kyle prompted.

"Well, the next time someone tells you that something is better than a poke in the eye with a sharp stick, you believe them."

Everyone, including Bakri, chuckled. Everyone except Wiesinger, who seemed lost in his own thoughts. But he was examining the terrain and the woods, so Kyle figured it was just concentration on his part.

"We stop just ahead," Bakri said. "We are above and east of the target."

"Understood. What then?"

"Can you get closer on foot to observe?"

"We can do that," Kyle agreed. "Show me the map."

They were 1705 meters from the target, by Kyle's reckoning. He entered coordinates into his PDA, GPS, and on a paper notepad for backup. He planned to advance on foot the first kilometer, then on knees and at a crawl, and set up an OP—Observation Post—where they could see what was going on. Keep records of comings and goings, identify important persons and equipment, and then exfiltrate and determine proper action.

He explained what he intended, and consciously added an, "Is that okay, Mel? Or do you suggest something else?"

"No, Kyle, I concur," he said. Whether he actually did, or really had no idea and was letting an NCO lead, Kyle didn't know. But neither was really bad.

"Tell me about the area," Kyle asked.

"Khayalan is a small village. We avoided the road through it, which is unpaved. We are at right angles to it. The houses are block and sheet steel, and there is a small administration building. Occupants are one hundred twenty-three according to the last census, taken in two thousand. They have a large number of young males, and I believe they have considerable small weapons. Vehicle traffic is approximately four cars per hour, including a patrol by the police every three to four days and vehicles transporting workers to the oil facilities at six and twenty hours daily. There is a small general shop, a bar, and a mosque. Two side roads lead into the woods for rubbish disposal." He pulled out a sheet of paper with blocks drawn on it. Each block contained a routine Bahasa phrase so as to look like a shopping list. But with a few strokes of a pen and some words added, it became a passable map of the target area. Good operational and communications security.

Kyle was agog. He'd never had a local ally provide such a thorough pre-mission briefing. "That's a very impressive report," he said.

"Thank you. We've gathered what information we can."

"But you don't know if our target is there?"

"No. I was not told who that is. They said it was a sensitive matter." He looked both amused and put upon.

Wiesinger must have felt everyone looking at him. "That was through CIA," he said. "Pursuant to new rules of intelligence release after September eleventh."

"Heck, sounds like we might have saved a trip," Wade said, a bare tinge of disgust in his voice.

"Well, shall we head in, Mel?" Kyle asked. "Get an OP set up and see what happens?"

"Yes. You lead, serg . . . Kyle. Wade can guard the rear. I can offer support if needed. I'll take this," he indicated the M4. "Will you be using the SR25s?"

"That's likely best," Kyle agreed. "Range and intel gathering.

We'll talk through phones, make sure they're set on vibrate. Bakri, how will we meet up?"

"I will drive by, or you can call my telephone."

"Sounds good. Assume twenty-four hours. If you don't hear from us, be very cautious, and report it back. Do you have a number for that?"

"I do, to someone in Jakarta who speaks American English."

Probably CIA. That wasn't as desirable as the Army. CIA might take weeks or months to deal with it, based on their own assessment of how valuable the three men were. Army would go balls out to get them. But you worked with what you had.

"Shall we give them one of our numbers, Mel?" Kyle asked.

"I'd like to, but negative. Maintain security."

"Understood," Kyle agreed. He didn't like it, but it made sense. The phone number could be tracked. If it was to an intelligence service, that might be expected. But if it was traced to a foreign military, that was another thing entirely. "Bakri, you have it?"

"Tomorrow at the same time, carefully if I haven't heard from you and report it back. This is my telephone number." He showed it to them on the lit screen.

"Got it," Kyle said, as they all programmed it into their own phones. Goddam, this was almost like operating in the modern world, Kyle thought. He tried not to get too optimistic.

That done, Bakri got into the vehicle and quietly pulled away. Kyle led the way off the "road" and into brush. More concealment was desired.

"So, what is our probable target?" Kyle asked.

"Mosque," Wiesinger said. "The current assumption is that if the presence isn't obvious, it's in a mosque. They've been doing that a lot lately."

"Right. And we're looking for explosives?"

"Explosives, weapons, anything we can report as activity."

"Got it," Kyle agreed. Wade glanced over and thumbed up. He was busy digging the soft-cased rifle from its straps on his ruck. He took the one Kyle held, and handed over the modified one.

Kyle actually had it assembled before Wiesinger twigged on the green-colored stock and the rail covers over the hand guard. "That's not paint on that weapon, is it?"

"No, it's aftermarket furniture," he said, and braced for the storm.

"From where?" The colonel was clouding up.

"An outfit called Cavalry Arms." Kyle pretended not to understand.

"Acquired how?"

"Personal expense, Mel. Didn't want Uncle to have to pay for it."

"I wasn't aware Uncle authorized it, and I know I wasn't asked."

"Sorry, sir," Kyle said, slipping the honorific in again. "This was an experiment we'd already arranged, and I forgot to inform you."

"Are there any other surprises I'm not aware of?"

"I don't think so, Mel," he said. Heh heh. He'd pulled it off. It was only one little victory in an ongoing bureaucratic battle, but it improved his morale.

"Good. Let's get to it." He accepted the ghillie Wade handed over, and started pulling it on. "But don't try to cowboy this operation, Kyle. I will take you down."

There was nothing to say but, "Yes, sir." Goddam, the man got bent out of shape over piddly crap.

At least there was nothing the man could criticize about Kyle's ghillie. In addition to strips of shredded burlap, he'd used sections of camouflage netting to improve it. It was a coat made shapeless with tans and greens, more of the former, that being the predominant color in woods, and certainly on the ground. It was disruptive enough in shape to make him near invisible at a matter of feet.

Each of them grabbed food and technical gear, then stowed their rucks in a hollow. Everything inside that could be damaged by water was sealed in freezer bags. They didn't need the three hundred pounds of gear represented for recon. It would simply bulk up their profiles. Careful positioning under growth should hide it from any view. Kyle noted a tree and cut a blaze in the bark very low down, peeling it back with his Gerber. He noted the position on his GPS. That should be enough to let them recover it later. In a worst-case scenario, nothing inside had any names or official U.S. identifiers. It was just military gear.

The three were ready in a very few moments. Kyle stepped slowly forward, his weapon in a drag bag over his shoulder. With his face painted and dirtied, the ghillie tumbled over him and the growth around him, he looked like a shambling tree.

Behind, Wiesinger was a little noisier. It wasn't anything most civilians would notice, but Kyle did. If he did, another professional might. He gritted his teeth. Hopefully, the man would steady out in a few minutes. If not, Kyle was at least leading, so he could set the pace. After years of instructing, he was afraid Wiesinger would be a rabbit, hopping eagerly forward and drawing attention.

The first seven hundred meters were largely uneventful. They shifted through the branches, careful not to shake them, watching for clumps of brush that might get crushed, soft spots that would hold boot prints and roots that could trip them, not to mention boobytraps or sensors. They didn't anticipate any, but one doesn't until it's too late.

Once or twice they froze and sank into the growth because of noises. But none was threatening, and actual human noise was scarce at this distance. Trees and humidity damped a lot of vibrations. Still, the situation demanded caution. Hours of infiltration and weeks of intel were riding on this. A minor screwup could kill a lot of people and waste a lot of time and money.

The GPS Kyle held said they were a kilometer away. It was time to get romantic with the dirt. Slowly, he eased to his knees and down, gently laying the drag bag behind him. Gingerly, he put his hands down—he wore thin Nomex aviator gloves to avoid scratches, plant toxins, and insect bites. Behind him, he heard the very faint sounds of Wiesinger and Wade following suit.

It was hot. Under the ghillies, it was stifling. He sipped at his water, glad he had filled the Camelbak to overfull. He'd had 105 ounces forced into it, and had drank a good half quart before gearing up. He thought of water in quarts. This temp required a quart an hour when active. He sucked a couple of ounces when he paused again, and would bring the container to normal capacity in a few minutes. Bursting it would be bad.

At five hundred meters, he went from hands and knees to a belly crawl. It was essential to avoid a profile. From a secure position, he'd identify a new location, ensure the route was clear of debris or growth that would leave an obvious trail, free of wet or low spots, of which there were plenty, and not open to observation. That confirmed, he'd slink forward like a lizard after a fly, pulling with hands as much as pushing with feet and knees, to avoid leaving divots. Once he felt secure behind the mark, a tree with shrubbery at the base, he fished the phone out of his front pocket.

"Wade, Kyle. How do things look?" he asked when his partner answered.

"Clear, good. Did you know you rolled a limb as you crawled over it?"

Kyle felt a ripple of shock. That was an amateur's mistake. "I didn't even feel a limb," he admitted. Was he tired? Or was it just one of those mistakes that happen? Either way, he had to avoid that.

"Yeah. Eyes open, buddy."

"Will do. Please relay to Mel. Call me if you need me."

"Roger that." Here they were, on profile for a mission, halfway around the world. They were perhaps ten meters apart, and they were communicating through thousands of miles of space by Iridium phones. Were Iridium satellites, or the satellites they used, low orbit? Geosynchronous, high enough to orbit over one location? That was 23,000 miles and some, he recalled. But beyond that, he was hazy. Those details were out of his control, so he hadn't dwelled on them much, but he was curious now and would check.

He resumed a slow advance from concealment to concealment. That was something he had control over, and was expert at.

A half hour later, he had the edges of the village in view. He figured their distance as 330 meters. And Bakri was almost certainly competent enough to have done this. Instead, they'd come halfway around the world.

Oh, it made some sense, he thought, as he slithered under a vine that drooped between a bush and a tree. They could ascertain the target and make the call, and confirm the kill. A local could claim anyone as the target, as had happened in Pakistan. That had set off a tribal war that almost got out of hand. The CIA's after-action review had been very stern about confirming reliability of allies. And if the locals were paid money or favors for killing a target, it was hard to know if they actually had. It was hard to drag bodies in for confirmation, and claims of body counts were always inflated.

But that still made it annoying to see first-rate troops kept in the dark and used as taxi drivers for a mission they were actually better qualified to handle.

At 275 meters, he decided the view was good. That distance was based on the road and the approximate center of town, and assuming Bakri's hand-written grid coordinates were correct. Somehow, he knew Bakri could handle a compass.

He dialed Wade. "We'll set up OP here. Spread out and we'll take shifts. Two on, one asleep, switching off every hour on watch, four hours to sleep."

"Roger that."

He relayed the same information to Wiesinger. "Does that work, Mel?"

"It does. Do you want to sleep first?"

"I could do that, yes, Mel," he agreed. He wasn't keen on trusting Wiesinger, but Wade would keep a good eye on him. One hour on, one off actually meant both were on, but one was responsible for notes and keeping an eye glued to a scope in case a shot presented itself. The "off" partner would still be observing while also watching for encroaching threats and other issues.

Issues such as weather. Kyle could hear rain beating on the leaves far above. He shrugged mentally, confirmed that Wade had the same info as the colonel, and hunkered down to sleep. It was hot and itchy under the ghillie, soon to be hot, damp, and itchy. That was the nature of the job. He placed his phone back in his chest pocket, where it was somewhat uncomfortable, but where he would certainly feel the buzz if he was called.

He folded his arms in front, laid his head down, and focused on a blade of grass. Things went fuzzy and he was asleep.

It was a restless sleep, as rain and sweat mingled and soaked his clothes, grass and dirt shifted and brushed him, and bugs ran over him. There were other animals in these woods—wild boars, orangutans, assorted rodents. None came near, but the small ones were annoying enough.

He felt the buzz of the phone, and woke at once. Years of practice kept him from jerking. He simply snapped awake and shifted a fraction of an inch. He reached gingerly for the phone with his right hand, keeping eyes and ears alert for a threat.

"Yes," he whispered softly. He had it close enough to his lips that he should be heard. A move that combined head and hand brought his ear to the other end, smoothly enough that it shouldn't show as movement, and quickly enough to catch anything that might be said. He also started flexing his muscles, to get circulation going and prepare for anything from a crawl to a charge.

"Wade here. Wakeup call."

"Roger that. You're next?"

"I am. You and Mel have it until twenty hundred."

"When is sunset and EMNT?" He realized it was getting dark. End Mean Nautical Twilight. Sun twelve degrees below horizon and eyes no longer adequate.

"One eight one six hours, another one seven minutes for sunset. Nominal four eight minutes for EMNT, but I'd guess three zero minutes with those hills."

"Roger that. Go sleep."

"Out," Wade agreed.

Kyle dialed Wiesinger.

"I'm on watch, sir, you're off, Wade asleep."

"Understood. We tracked a vehicle and personnel. Approximately two zero men arrived by bus at one seven four three hours."

"Understood, noted," Kyle said. Most of what they'd observe

was routine or meaningless. Only if they saw one of the three targets or suspicious activity would they follow up. Whatever was here might not arrive for days, or might have moved on, or might never have been here. But with Bakri's initial recon, the odds were good there'd be trouble. Then they'd troubleshoot, to use a pun. Kyle smiled very slightly. Jokes like that and random thoughts kept him alert and sane hour after hour on missions like this.

He reached back into the drag and drew his rifle and scope. Assembling them, he now had a sturdy, bipod-mounted scope he could use in near total darkness, with a weapon to support it and to provide fire if need be.

Nothing had happened by 1900, other than dinner that he could smell from here, with fresh fruits, hot peppers, and rice. His slow sweeps of the scope had acquired nothing of military note, though he noted vehicles, and a mosque service. It was sparsely attended that he could tell, perhaps thirty or forty people, mostly male. Though others might be worshipping in their homes, within earshot of the imam's prayers.

He buzzed Wiesinger and ended the call before he answered. A buzz in response indicated acknowledgement. Gratefully, Kyle came off the scope, blinking his eye. It had been sweaty against the rubber guard. He allowed himself two minutes to zone while he dug for an MRE. He'd chew it slowly, component by component for the rest of the shift. The remains would be stuffed into the outer envelope, which he'd keep in his shirt so as not to leave any evidence. Shortly, he'd have to relocate slightly and dig a small hole to piss in. He'd been holding it since they left the vehicle and geared up.

It was incredible, Kyle thought, that with technology so crude and in an area so remote, a terrorist group could pull off the attacks it did. Not for the first time, he was disgusted that such effort wasn't put to productive ends. Or that brave and eager young men could meet real military recruiters rather than terrorists. He recalled the story of a Foreign Legion veteran who'd gone on to become a billionaire. And very many senior politicians and executives were veterans. Aggression was a very human trait. But it didn't have to be destructive.

Christ, it was hot, even in the "cool" evening at less than 80°F and 75 percent humidity. Sweat was not just running off him, it was running out of him as if he were a squeezed sponge. That would cause problems. While the book said to keep water in your body, in a case like this, one might as well pour it out. Instead, he decided to wait until he just barely felt heat effects, and his sweat thinned, before drinking. His water supply would last slightly longer, and that was important.

And perhaps it would rain again and he could suck absorbed water from a rag. But it was going to be a rough night. He blinked his eyes as liquid ran. At least the salt content was low, as much as he was leaking. His eyes didn't sting, but certainly were uncomfortable.

He kept ears alert for anything that might approach. Certainly Bakri had patrols in the area, but it made sense to be wary. Then there was the road. That had to be watched while Wiesinger watched the village.

At 1948, there was action. A group of men slipped out of the mosque, each with a backpack, and boarded motorcycles. Kyle made note of time and activity as they slipped away. He thought there were nine. He'd confirm with Wiesinger in twelve minutes.

Wiesinger didn't call at 2000. Kyle gave it five minutes, then called himself. He had a creepy feeling he knew what had happened.

It took three rings, which made sense if Wiesinger was expecting a single only to alert him. Or unless it meant . . .

"Mel," was the answer, sounding very sleepy and confused.

"Oh, Jesus H. Fucking Christ on a crutch in a tutu!" Kyle swore in a whisper with his hand over the mic. Asleep, on watch. Something no soldier should *ever* do. Something inexcusable. And the man had in theory been to Ranger school, so he should know how to force consciousness when needed, even for days at a time.

"Did you get a count on that motorcycle activity, Mel?" he asked, knowing what the answer would be.

There was a long pause. "I didn't. Do you have it?"

"I have an estimate only, Mel. I was covering security." And it was taking every ounce of strength he had not to shout, scream, call the man an incompetent, reckless, derelict fucking idiot.

"Understood. I'll take next watch."

Kyle wanted to tell him not to bother. Instead, he decided to bull through the remaining two hours and cover both security and observation. Wade needed his sleep.

"Understood," he said, hating himself for lying. There was just no good going to come of this. He dug out a small camera that would take photos through the scope. Had he had any inkling Wiesinger would dope off, he would have had it all along.

It was a relief to wake Wade at 2200 and the two of them to go on together, even if Wiesinger should by rights take another hour. He'd worked with Wade and trusted him. They'd saved each other's lives several times, and Wade had pulled him out of deep depressions over dead friends. He synopsized the situation.

"Well," Wade said, "he's obviously lacking in field experience. So we need to cover him and us. Consider it a tradeoff with the better allies, who are really good, my friend."

"Yes they are, and I know we can't get a perfect mission," Kyle said, watching a caterpillar of some kind worm along a long leaf. "We'll manage. Wanted you to know. Here's the activity I've got—" He read off his log.

"Roger that," Wade agreed. "I'd say nine or ten men on motorcycles with backpacks leaving a mosque simultaneously is unusual. But I'm not sure what it means."

"Neither am I."

The forest was loud even at night, with bugs, birds, and larger forms all chittering, whooping, and cackling. It scared many people, but Kyle had spent so much time outdoors he only noticed when it stopped. Around here, he'd learned that such things presaged a vehicle arriving. So he was unconsciously leaning over his scope without realizing why when the truck arrived.

The truck pulled into the village using only parking lights and was ground guided by a man with a flashlight. It stopped quietly in front of the mosque. At once, a dozen men formed a line to unload it.

Boxes. The labels weren't English and weren't Bahasa, but were some Asian language. Kyle thought it might be Korean. It wasn't Japanese—it could be Chinese or something else. Kyle snapped a dozen pictures.

Boxes at night, lights out at a mosque, prearranged and being offloaded in a hurry by a small group of young men might not mean anything to a peace-love-dope dove who wanted to believe in the good of mankind, but it did to Kyle. He wanted to believe in the good of mankind, too. But years of experience had taught him that those boxes were probably explosive.

Should they exfil now with the intel they had? He had sketched the markings as best he could, and would track down a translation somewhere. Meantime, more might happen.

There was activity at the mosque until dawn, after 0500. As the sun rose, things went back to normal village-in-the-boonies mode, with a few men catching a bus to the oil fields and a small patch of agriculture.

With a few thumb strokes he called Bakri.

"*Pagi*." That was *selemat pagi*, or "Good morning."

"Bakri, Kyle. We need to catch that ride now." His satellite cell was about as secure as one could get. But Bakri's went through an Indonesian telecom. It might be monitored.

"Okay, I'll send a boy over," Bakri said conversationally. "As soon as he gets off work."

"No hurry. We're outside waiting. Goodbye."

"Goodbye."

Then he dialed Wade. "That's enough. Wake the lump and let's start moving."

"Understood."

Wiesinger had other ideas, though. "The plan was to do twenty-four hours of surveillance," he said.

"Yes, Mel, but nothing is happening daytime. All the activity is now over."

"You don't know that." The voice was stubborn.

Kyle gritted his teeth for a moment. "Mel, I've already called to exfil. I apologize for not waking you, but it didn't seem the kind of detail a colonel needed to be bothered with. I believe we have what we need, and while we might get a little more, it's important to act on this quickly."

After a pause, Wiesinger said, "Very well. But remember who's in charge here, sergeant."

"Yes, sir," he agreed as he disconnected.

Kyle should be in charge. He'd worked at this, studied it, done it. Wiesinger was a staff puke, and an egotistical one.

But he had a bird on his shoulder, even if it sat atop a chip. So it was necessary to follow orders a lot, humor him a little, and just pray the man wised up. The only other options were all capital crimes, and not the sort of thing Kyle Monroe would ever entertain. He was too professional, too dedicated to violate the Army regs.

But he might beat the hell out of them on this mission.

7

IN LHOKSEUMAWE, ANOTHER ELEMENT OF THE OPERA-tion was quite pleased. Agung received the current shipment of incoming explosives and had it quietly stowed in the warehouse.

It was certainly an impressive sight, Agung thought. Part of him had a craving to take a photograph for the Movement's archives, and so he could remember this and smile. But that would be a risk. Evidence like that would get him shot in the spine by the Allah-cursed Kopassus, or executed publicly. It could get others killed or jailed, and there was the risk of rape and torture for the women. So he would settle for fond memories.

Instead, he would cause tears for others. He had 850 kilograms of explosives in five packages. One would kill the lackeys of Pertamina, who sold out to the Americans' Mobil Oil for money. One would attack an Army administrative office in Lhokseumawe. That one was pleasure, for what they'd done to his cousin, though it was business, too, as it would spread fear.

Two of the remaining were shipping overseas, through the Philippines and Pakistan. Whether or not those were the final destinations, he neither knew nor needed to. They'd go aboard ships, and as of then, his responsibility for them was ended.

That left one package of fifty kilograms of PETN-based breaching charge. That had a very special purpose. The thought of that one made him smile even wider. It would light a conflagration Allah himself would be able to see. The satellites in orbit should have a great view, and the images would certainly make worldwide news.

And a few thousand crisped corpses, plus the panic in the market, should drive the cost of doing business so high that the West would have to make the Javanese bastards come to terms.

• • •

Faisal was not smiling. He had never killed a man before.

Of course, he wasn't going to kill a man now, technically speaking. Decapitating a man would be like decapitating a goat. Or so he was told, never having done so. He was a city dweller from Medan. A decapitation death would cause blood to gush everywhere.

So instead, the man would be stripped and shot. Then, as the camera was turned on the dressed and set corpse, it would be knocked over. Then Faisal would hack off the head with a large knife, in this case, a pedang—an Indonesian tribal knife.

The video would be sent out to the press to prove the act. Faisal's face wouldn't be visible, but his eyes would, beaming in triumph.

Except he wasn't sure they would be. There was little honor in killing a helpless, handcuffed man. There was little pride in butchering a corpse. It might be necessary, he believed action was called for, but was very distraught over it.

What Agung said was true: the West, particularly America, needed to know that its imperial ventures weren't popular with the typical Muslim, only with the elitists in power, who had sold out faith for money. It was true that the hostages they were taking were part of the military or industrial operations against Islam and could be considered combatants. It was true that they were infidels and nonbelievers, and thus by their own beliefs not harmed by being decapitated or dismembered. It was true they were taking Achinese oil and leaving the people bereft, then abusing them.

But it was also true that the Quran taught not to violate bodies, to allow them to be buried quickly, and, even if oil industry workers were helping the military indirectly, they were merchants and exempt from attack.

The different interpretations of the same scripture troubled him. He prayed as he should, hoping for guidance. So far, none had come.

Back at Bakri's village, tactics were discussed. First was to identify the boxes Kyle and Wade had seen.

"I don't recognize the language," Bakri admitted.

"No problem, we know someone who does," Kyle said.

"If you're thinking of your civilian, forget it," Wiesinger put in. "He doesn't know we're here, and to tell him now would create all kinds of hassle."

"Mel," Kyle said, "he's an ethnologist. He's the best chance to recognize a bad photograph from a scope image, and be at least able to guess the language."

"And if that picture says 'TNT' or 'Pentolite' and he knows we're in Indonesia, it tells him a lot more than that. Compare to images online."

That would be totally fruitless, but, "Yes, Mel," Kyle agreed.

An hour later, even Wiesinger was convinced. Without knowing what language, one couldn't even guess the meaning.

So Wade file transferred and painted it up in an art program, a copy of a copy of a photo taken through the image intensifier of a scope looking through humid air late at night. They attached it to an email and politely asked Gober if he could identify it. Oh, and by the way, could he hurry, they were in Time Zone-7. Please forget any reference to Indonesia you may have heard implied. Kyle phoned Robash's office, where a polite sergeant took note to call Mr. Gober and let him know there was a message waiting.

Lunch was brought in as the conference continued. Bowls of rice with aromatic seasonings, chicken, and more mangoes. It was good, Kyle reflected, that he liked tropical fruits. There were a lot of them in these dishes. And one of the bowls could legally pass as an incendiary. He'd had Pakistani curries, Tex-Mex chili and genuine Thai cuisine. But this stuff was flaming gasoline by comparison. He nibbled at it in between bites of the sweet stuff, which was a combo he'd have to remember. It was quite interesting.

"We never saw a truck with crates before," Bakri admitted around a mouthful of the fire-bomb. "And it sounds as if it was sent away quickly. Also the men on motorbikes are curious."

"We'll need to follow up on that," Wiesinger said. From his tone, Kyle guessed he wasn't sure how.

"I was surprised at the low attendance at the mosque," Kyle said.

"Oh?" Bakri asked.

"It couldn't have been more than a third."

There was silence for a few moments. Then Bakri spoke. "One third is quite high. High enough to be of note. I would expect that for a holy day, not for a normal workday."

"Oh," Kyle said. He'd assumed near 100 percent attendance, as in Pakistan and Iraq. "They were mostly young males."

"Then that is certainly a sign of one of the more militant factions," Bakri said.

"Damn." He hadn't realized how secular people were here. Actually, he'd only heard Allah mentioned once in a day and a half, now that he thought about it.

"We need a better look, then," Wiesinger said, "to figure out what's there."

"You stand out," Bakri said. "Better if one of my men goes in."

"How do we do that?" Wade asked.

"Watch." The grin on his face was inscrutable.

Wade was as antsy as Kyle, and had been checking mail constantly. "Response from Gober," he said.

"What do we have?" Kyle shifted attention at once.

" 'Gentlemen: As near as I can tell, that pictogram is a logo that closely resembles the Thai word for "explosive." Hope this helps. Signed: E.' "

"Well, we had guessed that," Kyle said.

"Is there any legitimate reason they might have explosives there?" Wiesinger asked.

"Not without government people bonding and delivering it. Foreign marks are a sign of smuggling," Bakri said.

"Definitely the right track then." Wiesinger smiled in satisfaction.

Kyle wondered why. It wasn't a difficult conclusion. It didn't bring them a target or any way to stop whatever events were happening. It was only a report.

But, he realized, the colonel lived for reports. To him, this was a major event. He sighed. There were two types of soldiers in the Army. Wiesinger would never understand Kyle's type, and he would never understand Wiesinger's.

After a nap, they were back out on the road, on a slightly different route. There was still a Kopassus unit south and east that might come looking for them, and anyone tromping around in the woods from the village might see traces. They circled wide and came down from the hills south of the town, moving through thicker brush as they did so.

Kyle was again impressed. Snuggled under weeds and a ghillie, sweating a little less than the day before now that he'd had some time to acclimate, he watched two of Bakri's men, Rizal and Fahmi, slip to the edge of the village. They were young, and eager, and grinned a lot, but had shrewd looks when faced with problems. Both were very mature and wise for their ages.

He wasn't sure, but he thought both were about fifteen.

The buildings on this side were older. Trash didn't seem to get dragged into the woods as often, but rather was left carelessly against the back walls or just tossed a few feet. Disgusting. Even animals knew to shove waste out of the nest. The professional in Kyle, who had studied camp security from day one, was appalled.

There was another truck tonight. It was smaller, a decrepit old stake-bed with canvas covering something in the back. In front of the mosque, two figures peeled the cover back. With a faint whistle, the line of men materialized to unload it.

And Rizal and Fahmi stood up and walked into town.

It took serious balls to do that. But it would probably work, Kyle figured. If you acted as if you belonged, people generally didn't question you—though there was the risk that everyone in the group knew everyone else. Still, it was dark.

They joined the line and passed crates for about three minutes. As the last few were being dragged along the splintered wooden bed, Fahmi took the box in his hands and walked straight into the mosque. Less than a minute later, as the last crate came down, he appeared outside the back door. He gingerly picked his steps through rotten timber and packing boxes for mundane stuff, and headed into the woods at an oblique angle, quickly but with caution. Rizal appeared around the side, dropping into the undergrowth and starting to crawl. In seconds, he was lost to Kyle, who was a trained professional with a night vision scope. No amateur should find him, certainly not ones who had no reason to suspect him.

Two hours of crawling and sweating later, they were back in the vehicles and heading for safety, the crate in the back unopened as of yet.

8

CAPTAIN HARI SUTRISNO DIDN'T LIKE FILING REPORTS that would lead to greater interference from Jakarta. Still, certain events required a report, and this was one of them. Nor was it the first such, and that angered him. Indonesia was quite modern, a producer of electronics and raw materials, but the damned Europeans and their lackeys seemed to think it was a backwater like Iraq or Yemen.

He started the page with date, rank, name, and unit, then noted the incident by date and time from his records.

"While on patrol for operations or training missions by GAM elements, encountered three technical vehicles with suspected insurgents.

"Upon sighting weapons, improvised ambush and attacked. One vehicle was disabled.

"Unit consisted of rifles and RPGs with one known machine gun and a 40mm grenade launcher. Estimated force of 15–20.

"During the engagement, private Edi Sudradjat was killed, two wounded. Estimated enemy casualties four wounded.

"Faced with strong opposition, I withdrew my forces and planned for pursuit and observation. Enemy disengaged in a fast, professional fashion and took casualties and all equipment.

"For note: estimate two Caucasian males in unit. Possible Australian or European. Concern is potential mercenary forces assisting rebels. Recommend all units be alert for other incidents of this type.

"For note: force was quite highly trained, far better than typical for GAM. Consider possibility that Caucasians are military advisors. No purpose comes to mind other than to foment insurrection and separate Aceh, thus leading to negotiations for resources."

He listed routine operations, requests for supplies, and wrote, by hand—for he was formal about such things—a letter to Private Sudradjat's family, praising his service.

The email report went out at once, and should be looked at by 0900. The handwritten letter would take days, but it was best, he thought, to have a personal memento to go with the harsh truth.

While a competent enemy was a challenge, it also was a threat. And who were these foreign troops? Could someone be trying to split Aceh? Cash in on arms sales? Create trouble with Mobil and put pressure on Jakarta?

He didn't have enough intel to guess. Nor was that his problem. But he would find and if possible capture these strangers.

The crate contained blocks of TNT. Forty-eight of them, half a kilogram each. That was a standard size for most of the world.

"How many crates were on those trucks?" Kyle asked.

"More than twenty last night, ten more tonight," Wade said.

"At least twelve hundred and twenty-four pounds of HE. Someone is planning a party." Kyle had seen lots of HE—high explosive—military and civilian. He was fine with it as a military materiel. The thought of sociopathic freaks with it gave him the creeps.

"Could be more than that," Wade reminded them.

"I am most unhappy," Bakri said.

"Why, specifically?" Kyle asked.

"Because if this is used against Mobil or the government, it will make our struggle that much harder. If someone has this kind of resource, they should be sharing their skills and helping us. This can't help. And if it's being sent elsewhere, it will make my people look like terrorists." He was quivering in anger.

"We'll report back what we can," Kyle said. "We are usually listened to as a source of intel." But inside, he knew if State wanted a scapegoat and couldn't ID the real culprit, they'd use Bakri's men to take the fall, to improve relations with the Indonesian government.

Wade offered a more useful comment. "And if we ID these bastards positively, we'll dispose of them."

"Good," Bakri said, nodding vigorously. "But we must find where this is going, or at least where some of it is going."

"Do you have any ideas?" Wiesinger asked.

"I am guessing some of it will head for other groups. I can inquire carefully. But I don't know where else they might be using it." Bakri looked rueful.

"Well, what do we know, Mel?" Kyle asked. "Any specifics as to groups?"

"We really aren't supposed to discuss that outside of our own channels," the colonel said. He looked at the glares he was getting from those around him. Disgust from Kyle and Wade, offense from the Indonesians. "But I think we should," he added, almost too quickly.

"The group in question, the Fist of God, is a fringe group of Jemaah Islamiyah." His pronunciation wasn't the best. Obviously, he'd read but not talked about it much. "They've been conducting attacks on U.S. personnel near Lhokseumawe. So far, there are two hostages unaccounted for, just disappeared and presumed dead, and a third was decapitated two months ago. We have another hostage at present. They—Fist of God—are believed to be one of the sources for the explosive that you . . . tracked on your last operation," he said, referring to Kyle and Wade's mission in Romania, intercepting explosives as they came across the Black Sea into Europe.

"And we now have that explosive to compare," Kyle said. "And it looks much like the TNT we intercepted, only in different crates."

"It also looks like the stuff they're finding in Iraq and Pakistan," Wiesinger confirmed.

"I know of that group," Bakri said, and they faced him. "Very dangerous. They are threatening to attack the oil."

"Why?" Wade asked. "Isn't the oil necessary to Achinese independence?"

"Yes," Bakri agreed. "But they have come beyond independence to jihad. They want an imaginary paradise according to the oldest form of the Quran. They want to kill all Hindus and Christians, split away from the modern government in Jakarta, and live as wanderers, nomads. It won't work."

"So they'll attack a refinery? A well? A terminal?"

"Perhaps all of them," Bakri said. "But we'll need to find out. I may actually have to talk to the government and tell them of this." The expression on his face was at once amused, perturbed, and amazed.

"No," Wiesinger said, shaking his head. "They don't know we're here, and the repercussions would affect U.S. interests."

"What about my interests? And those of my family?" Bakri asked.

Wiesinger froze. Obviously, this had gone from an office plan to a real world fight in his mind. He now had no idea what to do.

"First we find who and where," Kyle said firmly. "Then we sit down and discuss who's affected how. Then we decide what to do. We may need silence, backup from your government or ours, or a quick raid and vanish. It's too early to make calls. But Khayalan isn't the root source, merely a way stop, right, Mel?"

"Yes, so it seems."

"I would have said so, if I had been asked," Bakri said. He was smiling, but obviously exasperated underneath.

"Sometimes State and the CIA really piss me off," Kyle said. "I'm sure they meant well, but they didn't cross-check well enough, and now we have a dead end."

Wiesinger said nothing. He had his phone out, and wandered away for privacy. Kyle let him. Hopefully, he'd get some guidance from somewhere. As it stood at present, the mission was a wash. Oh, they could still shoot a player in this and hinder the operation, and that was better than nothing. The brains behind the program were still at large, however. Depending on where, he or they were probably unreachable.

If it came to an urban engagement, Kyle intended to refuse. That had worked in Romania with lots of CIA backup on scene and favors from the host nation, and it had still resulted in several international incidents. Then it had taken a crack anti-terror squad as well. There was just no way to set all that up here, he figured.

The colonel came back. "Okay," he said, "that took a three-way with our people, State and Intelligence. They want us to acquire more intel at Khayalan and determine the source if we can, or follow further up the chain. Then they'll tell us whether we shoot or pull out." He looked quite unhappy.

Kyle knew the look. Wiesinger felt the mission was a wash, and he'd just become a cog for a possible future one, rather than a commander. Kyle had felt that way several times early in his career. It was the nature of the business. And no mission was ever a waste: Just ruling out bad intel was useful, though it could be hard to be so objective halfway around the world.

"We know which way they traveled," Bakri said. "We can travel that route and observe. Also, we can set up posts to see what else comes along there."

"How many men do you have for that?" Wiesinger asked.

"Enough," Bakri said. "But I'm not sure I should discuss such matters." His grin was cruel.

Thankfully, Wiesinger didn't take the bait. He didn't manage to hide his anger and distress, though. The man wanted control, and wasn't getting it.

Bakri had two cell phones for his group. The Americans had three. That suggested five groups with a total of nineteen people. Fahmi would lead one group, Bakri another, and each American one. Each group would take a different part of the route and watch for traffic in and out of Khayalan.

Kyle wasn't keen on letting Wiesinger operate without Wade or himself along. But it was just observation, and the man was steady enough under fire and could move adequately. Sighing, he realized he was running the show while maintaining the pretense of a subordinate. And everyone knew it. If Wiesinger could just come out and say he was an observer and advisor and let Kyle run things with the locals, it would be easy. But the ego the colonel carried would never let that happen.

And maybe he'd fall asleep again, leaving the work to soldiers. No, it wasn't a kind thought.

By nightfall, they were distributed in five groups along two roads that diverged from the track through Khayalan. A third route was, as Bakri put it, "An easy way to meet the Kopassus." It was unlikely the explosives had gone that way.

Kyle was sure enough of his element, four of Bakri's men including Rizal, who spoke some basic English. Combined with Kyle's very rudimentary Bahasa and the commonality of many technical words, they were able to communicate adequately.

His phone buzzed and he grabbed it. "Kyle."

"This is Mel. First item, truck, one one three zero hours. Same vehicle as last night. Eight items same as last night. Over."

"Roger."

"Item Two. Six motorcycles departed zero zero one five hours. Backpacks medium. Likely capacity three zero pounds each. Over."

"Roger." So they might see stuff their way soon.

"Item Three. American Mobil employee Frank Keller reported killed, decapitated according to video released by Fist of God. State Department and Indonesian ministries following up. Over."

"Roger. Shit." Someone else dead, just as a childish gesture. Kyle gritted his teeth.

"Any chance of recovering one biker and contents of ruck interrogative. Over."

"Yes, Mel. If I see any, we'll get one silently. Shall I relay to Wade interrogative. Over."

"Have done so. Plan to intercept one rider. Over."

"Roger. Out."

"Out." The exchange wasn't entirely by the book. He suspected Wiesinger was shaky on radio operations. Besides, these were cell phones. One could be conversational.

Kyle looked carefully around, then relocated by several feet. He wanted to be well away from the road in case of observation or attack, or some geek hopping out to take a leak on the side of the road. He also wanted to be where he had a good field of fire. If the opportunity presented itself, he intended to take out the last rider in line. The goal was to make it appear an accident or have it be beyond sight of the leaders. That would give them time to get the road swept clear and neatened.

He found a nice spot, a slight depression still damp from the rain the night before. There was a ridge next to it, likely caused by some near-surface root. It was shielded from the road by some thick, leafy scrub that would make him effectively invisible. The mound would provide cover, and he had a great long oblique view along and across the road. Two trees marked the right and left limits of his weapon. So it would be like skeet shooting through a window.

A couple of soft whistles brought Rizal and the other three over. He explained what he was going to do. He used a lot of gestures and simple words.

"I understand," Rizal said. "You will shoot, we will catch."

Then it was back to waiting. It could be twenty minutes or more, assuming the bikes were even coming this way. Two lonely trucks had passed all evening. This was about as far into the boonies as one could get.

Far in the distance, Kyle heard the sound of engines whining. He quivered alert. The sound faded out, then came closer. So they were probably heading this way, but that could mean business for Wade, too. Or both of them if the group split up.

Then the whine rose and came up the slope of the road.

How many? At least three were present, but were all six? It was critical to hit the last bike and not one in the middle. No matter how good a shot Kyle was, and he was perhaps the best anywhere, a target that fast was hard to hit. If the bikers thought it was an attack, it was probable the rest would just ride on. He snuggled into the rifle and checked his scope.

Then they came into view.

The riders were in a perfect bell curve distribution. One machine was out ahead, then another, two side by side right behind that with the fifth close in and the sixth a good twenty meters back. Kyle could take a shot, but there was no margin for error.

The first cycles flashed through the field of view, and Kyle assessed the lead at an unconscious level. He stretched his left hand far forward on the handguard. This would be like shotgunning a clay pigeon on a sharp left launch. He grumbled to himself for not taking the other side of the road.

But then the last one was in front and he swung, using a technique he'd learned from Peter Capstick, an outdoor writer long dead but whose books had fascinated Kyle. With his left hand out and the rifle pulled tight into his shoulder, he waited as the image of the speeding rider in the blur of trees passed through the swinging scope. The reticle aligned with the rear wheel's upper arc and he snapped the trigger, letting the rifle finish its swing.

The suppressor caught most of the gases and muzzle blast, but still left the supersonic crack of a boattail match bullet. But that wasn't obvious as a weapon sound to people not trained to recognize it. Indeed, the other riders didn't seem to have heard it above the banshee howls of their engines. They disappeared in a whirlwind of leaves.

Meanwhile, the last rider skidded on the edge of control. The bike slewed and went down. He'd held it just long enough for the others to be over a slight rise. So unless the rider ahead was very nervous or well trained, it could be minutes before he noticed his buddy missing.

"Go!" Kyle whispered hoarsely, and Rizal nodded.

The driver had laid the bike down well, and was just standing to dust himself off as he was swept off his feet by a torrent of small figures. He was beaten senseless and carried off. Rizal righted the bike and began rolling it as the other two scuffed over the tire marks with branches. Unless the other riders dismounted and made a good search, they should have trouble seeing any signs.

Kyle was already on the phone. "One target recovered. Stand by." He left it at that as his small squad sought deeper cover. Sooner or later, the riders would notice. They might return, press on or call for someone else to investigate. It wouldn't do to be around.

A kilometer later he was badly out of breath. It wasn't the distance, it was the encumbrance of the ghillie, the mass of his ruck, the weapon and the very uneven terrain that required a loose-jointed, shifting run. The distance should give them plenty of time to respond to happenings on the road.

Twenty minutes later, the other bikers hadn't returned. That meant either they were calling for other forces, or more likely, had no idea where the incident had actually happened. They might have no idea it had happened at all, depending on how observant they were.

The bike had been pushed a good two hundred meters back the other way and dumped on the other side as misdirection, in a small rivulet. Kyle's shot had taken it through frame, rim, and tire. He figured the odds of a perfectly aimed shot at the wheel having about a one in three chance. Sometimes, luck did matter.

Rizal had the captive trussed with parachute cord and duct tape. He hadn't taken any liberties, but he hadn't been gentle about it, either.

Back on the phone, Kyle called Wade. He gave his coordinates. "Relay and we'll meet here. I'd like extra firepower just in case, and I don't want to try to drag a prisoner too far."

"Understood."

While they waited, Rizal left the man gagged but started softening him up. His methods were direct and brutal. By the time Wade showed up, the victim was wincing and crying, snorting for air through his nose because of the gag. Rizal handled that by gripping the man's nose shut with pliers.

The snorts turned to whimpers and moans. Wade arrived, then Bakri and his other man, Syarief, with Anda covering the rear. Wiesinger was last and following GPS. He still held a compass but wasn't using it. Kyle said nothing, but he and Wade exchanged glances. GPS could be spoofed, batteries could die. If you couldn't find your way with a compass, you didn't belong in a task like this.

Wiesinger was smart enough or scared enough not to mention the battered and bleeding body in the middle of the group. He simply remained nearby in a squat, as most of the troops spread out for a perimeter. Kyle decided to tweak him. He pulled out an MRE and started slurping cold spaghetti and meatballs. The colonel faced away.

There was trouble when Bakri stepped over and peeled off the gag. The man started to scream, either curses or cries for help. A boot to the teeth shut him back up, but it was clear answers wouldn't be forthcoming.

That was, until Anda snapped off the man's belt and tugged at his trousers. Rizal clacked the pliers suggestively and the response was nodding so hard it might cause a sprain.

Kyle didn't approve of torture, and officially should have stopped it. But this wasn't his country, or his troops. They weren't even legally troops. And this scumbag was helping kill people anyway. Innocent people. Kyle didn't approve. But he wasn't about to stop it.

"Ruck contains fifteen half-kilo blocks," Wade reported. "He claims a destination of . . . where was that?"

"The oil terminal," Bakri said. "They are planning to attack that, as well as civilians."

Kyle frowned. There were literally billions of gallons of petroleum at the terminal. A properly staged attack would destroy it beyond any hope of salvage, and kill hundreds, perhaps thousands of people.

Those were headlines that would cause corporations to pull out. Add the death toll to that, and it could be considered a victory for the terrorists.

Or would they pull out? There were trillions of dollars at stake here. Perhaps Indonesia would respond with more military force. If so, that escalation could be as bad. Thirteen hundred islands, 200 million people held together by a government bureaucracy, not any common heritage. What was the term he'd heard? *Disintegrasi*. Not something that was considered funny here. Indonesians were either very protective of their nation or wanted out. There was none of the humor that accompanied the comments of say, Massachusetts or California seceding from the United States. National disintegration was something most feared.

Some more cuffing and kicking yielded very little more information. The "man" was about fourteen and scared. He knew little more than hearsay. But he had the explosives and an address to deliver them to. When it was clear he wouldn't be of more use, Rizal drew a large, leaf-bladed knife, bent over and made two brutal chops. The first split the skull like a bloody melon. The second severed the head.

Wiesinger looked rather green. Obviously, he hadn't seen many, if any, deaths before. Kyle couldn't say he was enthused by the activity. But there wasn't much he could do, and they did need the information. He had to deal with his conscience on the grounds that he had neither suggested, encouraged, nor endorsed the activity. But a lot of things in this job were disgusting.

"What shall we do?" Bakri asked. "I am reluctant to start a local war against other Achinese. It could only spread."

"Yeah, I see that," Wade said. "Their friends, your friends, and the government all on you."

"Is there any way to share that intel with the government?" Kyle asked. "Without admitting we're here?" he added for Wiesinger's benefit.

"There are sympathizers in the Army," Bakri said. "But the Army would claim in propaganda that we were all involved. They'd send more forces after us to thank us."

To which Kyle said, "Oh." Of course. He knew that and had been briefed on that. Were it mentioned to the government, the operation would disappear overnight and crop up somewhere else. The Army would attack what rebels it could find to show it was doing something. That would make things worse for their friends and do little about the real threats—a hostage and an imminent attack on the oil terminal.

"We need a more informed captive," Wiesinger said. "Can we arrange that?"

Bakri considered. "I'm sure we can, given time. But who would know? The lorry driver is not likely to know. These message boys," he pointed at the corpse, "don't know."

"What about the imam at the mosque?"

"He would make a good target," Bakri agreed, "if we could get him to come out."

"He always greets the truck, right?" Wiesinger offered.

"He did twice," Wade agreed. "It's a pattern."

"Hijack the truck?" Kyle asked.

"If there's a way." Wiesinger wasn't stupid, Kyle realized. Just bad-tempered, inexperienced, insecure, and conceited.

"But will he talk?" Bakri asked. "The imams are quite agitating in the news. Very stubborn."

"Bakri, it's my experience that such men talk a lot, and are happy to send young men to die, but have no balls for a real fight." Kyle had seen such press releases. Men who vowed to "fight to the last drop of blood" when the blood wasn't theirs.

"You may be correct. Certainly I've not heard of their exploits."

"Camp out here today?"

"I think we must. And at nightfall we must move quickly." Bakri looked around at the growing dawn. "And we should travel some more distance now for safety."

"Let's move, then," Wiesinger said, sounding as if he was in charge. Kyle wouldn't mind that if the man actually did take charge and do it well. He seemed to want the glamour but not the work.

They compromised on moving south, toward the hills. The ground rose only a few meters overall in the five kilometers they traveled. Rain started to fall, large drops splatting through the trees, and they were well soaked in short order.

They traveled a narrow path that might be for game or people. Such paths were often dangerous, but it was fast and they carried substantial firepower. Several wild boars trotted by, but upon seeing a large armed party, snorted and gave them a wide berth.

They passed a troop of orangutans who squeaked, which made Kyle nervous. Certainly there were other reasons for them to sound off, but he was still worried about the attention. And the squeaking was almost creepy. He'd expected bellows or shouts from orangutans, not the high-pitched sound.

It could be worse, he thought. Various parts of this archipelago had saltwater crocodiles, kraits, and komodo dragons. There were tigers around here, too. Life seemed so much more interesting away from home. But it didn't interest Kyle that much. Each was a challenge and a curiosity, but he preferred to go home afterward.

The sun began pattering through the trees after the rain lifted, and they sought shelter. Various downed giant timber, broad, leafy bushes, and hollows served as such. They posted watches and tried to sleep in the oppressive heat and humidity. Kyle was down to just a T-shirt, over Wiesinger's complaints about camouflage and insects. But if he couldn't sleep, he'd be no use, and the bugs weren't deterred by thin fabric. Wade followed suit. Wiesinger didn't, no doubt to lead by example. Kyle saw him sleeping while on watch. He tossed and twitched, sweat running off him in rivulets rather than beads. Kyle was merely beaded and his shirt stuck. That was enough for him. He shook his head at the mentality of his officer and turned his attention back to potential threats.

9

FAISAL RIPPLED WITH EXCITEMENT AS HE STOOD BE-
fore the camera. An hour earlier, the man beside him had been
tied down and shot through the heart. After a few seconds of
thrashing and screaming that echoed over the gunfire still ringing in
Faisal's ears, he'd stared and stiffened and died. A couple of large
bandages and a change of clothes, and the stiffening corpse "sat" on
a chair, propped from behind by well-directed hands.

"Everyone look at the camera," Erwin said. "Good. We'll add the
audio in a moment, so get ready . . . and . . . now!"

Screaming "God is great!" Bambang and Wismo wrestled the
chair and body over, fighting each other as much as it. Wismo was
a monster of a man, almost six feet and near two hundred pounds.
The head struck the floor with a thunk, and that was a good pretense for unconsciousness. Faisal took his cue and jumped astride
the dead man's chest.

He was dizzy and remote as he worked. It almost felt as if another were using his hands. The long, slim pedang grated off bone
and gristle, slicing and sawing and hacking. The lime and arsenic
etched blade left streaks of black oxide in the flesh as blood smeared
the knife. Erwin moved in close with the camera, to get a nice shot
of the opening gap. Bambang got close to the body and the microphone and gurgled a scream that sounded horrible. This really
would come across as a killing.

Then it was done. Faisal took the head by the hair and held it up
so Erwin could get a close shot. Then, in carefully rehearsed Arabic,
he said, "Thus to all infidels who oppose the will of Allah."

Then the camera was off and they were all singing, shouting, and dancing. "God is great! God is great! Now you are a man!" and clapping him on the shoulders.

He smiled, but wasn't sure he felt it. How much of a man did it take to butcher a corpse? How honorable? It wasn't something he felt like boasting of. His brother had shot men, soldiers in battle. This couldn't possibly compare.

But he did smile, and took the accolades. This could be a start to greater triumphs.

The video would receive attention in the press, though it wouldn't have the effect the Fist of God desired. In America and to a lesser extent in Europe, the TV-watching public had seen enough beheaded corpses to not be shocked. Every week or so, another headless corpse. Every day, another twenty Iraqis, Palestinians, Afghans, or some other people dead. Every month, a few Israelis. It was a status quo that they didn't really have any hope of changing.

Beneath that, however, was a growing undertone of disgust. Some knew that the killings were a violation of the Quran's teachings. Many others didn't care, and simply wanted revenge. The military and intelligence services were frustrated and angered at the inability to respond because of the political and diplomatic hogties they wore. In short, the problem was growing, neither side willing to back down, and one far more powerful than the other, even if it was showing restraint so far. But sooner or later, something would snap.

Then the terrorists would get the rivers of blood they prayed for. But much of that blood would be theirs, and those of the people they spoke for, whether those people supported them or not.

Kyle heard the shot through his sleep. He wasn't sure if it was incoming or outgoing as he rolled over. Trained reflexes kept him on the ground as he snicked the safety off his rifle and got ready to rock. Someone had discovered them and was deemed hostile. But Kyle needed to know who and why before shooting. Fratricide was bad. He twisted to his belly but stayed under the leaves.

Wiesinger woke, too. "Report!" he snapped, loudly enough to be heard but not give away position.

"Unknown, Mel, I'm standing by."

Wade dove in nearby and said, "Hostiles, small arms. South and closing." He was close enough to talk and spot, not close enough to be caught by the same area effect weapon.

"Roger that," Kyle said. "Outgoing!" and hunched down for a target.

Except it was very tough to see in this terrain. Nor did he want to stick his head up. Bakri was shouting something, and the machine gun opened up with a two second burst. Another fired back, shredding leaves a dozen meters away.

In the pause before more rifle fire, other voices were yelling.

"Was that English?" Wade asked.

Kyle had heard it, too. "I think so."

"Hold fire," Wiesinger said quietly. "What's the phrase?"

"*Jangan tembak*," Wade supplied. There was no need for it; Bakri spoke English.

Bakri looked at them quizzically from his position, but relayed the order. The outgoing din died down, and everyone hunkered behind cover. A few seconds later, their opponents also slacked off. Into a momentary lull, Kyle yelled, "Do you speak English?"

"Bloody right. Who wants to know?" The English was clear, but there was an accent. Whoever spoke it was well educated.

Wiesinger shouted, "U.S. Army. Who are you?"

"Australia." Nothing happened for several more seconds, until the other party said, "Want to call truce and parley?"

"That's probably a good idea," Kyle said. "Weapons down, everyone." He turned to Wiesinger and quietly said, "Is that okay, Mel?"

"Do it," the colonel said.

Cautiously, Kyle stood, his right side behind a tree and ready to dive for cover. Ahead, a man dressed in Indonesian camouflage, but clearly Caucasian, also stood. He was carrying an M4A1 with an M203 grenade launcher and an Advanced Combat Optical Gunsight, pointed at the ground.

Kyle cautiously hefted the SR25 into a low port and stepped forward. The other did likewise. In the thick growth, they were only about twenty meters apart, but had been well hidden from each other until they stood. It was a wonder they'd met up at all. They could have skulked within meters and not known.

Wiesinger had been way too incautious by adding the "Army" to "U.S.," in Kyle's opinion. "We're Americans" would have been enough to start the negotiations. There'd been no reason to announce their identity to an unidentified force, which still could contain hostile elements.

They stopped about ten feet apart. The other man was skinny, about five foot eight, and had a rugged moustache. They looked each other over, then looked around surreptitiously for any observers or other presence. They'd been doing that as they walked, of

course. The obvious act was just part of a meeting between two soldiers unsure of each other.

"Kyle Monroe," he identified himself softly.

"Jack Stephens," the other said. "U.S. Army?"

"Ranger, Sniper, sergeant first class." He nodded.

"Staff sergeant, Special Air Service. This is Akbar." He gestured
at his local guide, who was shorter but stockier than Bakri. "What
the bloody hell are you doing here?" His trained speaking voice
slipped for a moment, to a Western Australian accent.

"I could ask the same thing," Kyle said reasonably. He eyed Akbar. Presumably he was loyal, but he was still only vouched for by
a probable ally. Akbar nodded back with a surly but not unfriendly
expression.

"Right," Stephens agreed. "Should we both guess, or admit we're
hunting Jemmies?"

"Jemmies. I like that." Kyle grinned. It was hard to find an obvious but rude term for Jemaah Islamiyah.

"Yeah, what do you call 'em, mate?" Stephens asked.

"Dead, whenever possible. Scum when not."

"Good man." He returned the grin.

"Do we need to get together and talk?" Kyle asked. "All of us?"

"I reckon that's an idea," Stephens agreed with a curt nod. He
turned and whistled a sibilant note.

Slowly, his unit stood. There were two other Aussies and six Indonesians.

Kyle nodded to Wade, who turned to both Wiesinger and Bakri,
and their force rose and moved forward. Shortly, all twenty-five of
them were in a loose huddle, a circle of squatting and lounging men
and women in the trees, with three of each team, including one
Aussie and Wade, facing out on watch. It was quiet now, except for
dripping condensation. As his hearing recovered, Kyle could hear
the fainter sounds of animals and shifting growth.

"Wiesinger, colonel, U.S. Army. I'm in charge of our op." Kyle
could see he'd started already, insecure and making sure everyone
knew it, while imagining he was coming across as confident.

"H'lo, sir," Stephens nodded, then turned his attention back to
Kyle. Kyle forced himself not to grin. That the colonel was a REMF
was obvious to an operator like the Aussie. "So what shall we talk
about?"

The negotiation would be as delicate as seducing a virgin, Kyle
realized. They both knew what the other was doing, but neither
wanted to be the first to say so. They likely had a lot of intel in com-

mon, and some peculiar to their respective services that could prove useful, or horribly wrong or worthless. The trick was to not give away bad intel, or swap good intel too cheap, or wind up offending erstwhile allies, or letting anything slip to locals of untested loyalties, or . . .

Kyle grimaced to himself. He wasn't a diplomat. He was a shooter. He *should* pass this off to Wiesinger, except the man clearly had no clue.

"Yes, we're hunting Jemmies," Kyle admitted quietly, but in a rush. "Specifically, ones interfering with our personnel and interests, though we're open to others if they're in the way."

Stephens was partially hidden under a broad leaf, shadow disrupting his silhouette. It was an unconscious move that marked him as a true professional.

"Makes sense," he said. "We've been handling PNG, and there's ties to Timor-Leste, Sulawesi, Borneo, and here." He pronounced them correctly, rather than in Aussie Strine.

"You probably have far better intel than we do," Kyle admitted ruefully. The Aussies had been in and out of Papua New Guinea for decades. He knew of it vaguely, had read a brief on East Timor, and knew of attacks on the others. That was it, done for intel.

"Well, if you're not adverse to lending a hand, I don't mind swapping some for what you need. Tea?" Stephens asked, his smile broken by camouflage paint as he held up a small cooking pot, a "billy."

"Sure, why not?" Kyle agreed.

Wiesenger proved again to not be as bad as he came across. He'd been quiet so far. When he spoke again, he said, "I assume the ties you're referring to are Laskar Jihad from Sulawesi, and Organisasi Papua Merdek from Papua?"

"Indeed," Stephens agreed as he unfolded a small trioxane stove, pulled open a previously used and tightly folded fuel package with his teeth and broke another third of a bar of fuel off. He slipped it in place, flicked a butane lighter, and pointed at his back. One of the reticent locals pressed on his Camelbak, squeezing water up through the plastic straw and into the pot.

"But they're all linked, about like we are," he continued. "They scratch each other's backs and share intel on targets and techniques. Better than we do, a lot of the time. They really care less about the credit than they do about killing Americans and 'your lapdogs.'"

"You, the Brits, the Saudi government, the Poles, the Filipinos, the Japanese . . ." Wiesinger offered.

"And Bali and India for daring to be Hindu. Then there's Singapore across the water."

"Singapore is involved?" Wiesinger asked, surprised now. So was Kyle.

"Yeah, they have a team around here somewhere, too, because of Kumpulan Mujahedeen Malaysia. The Kiwis don't yet, but likely will if they ever catch some fire or think they will. The Filips do. The Brits have had teams in these parts since Malaysia in the sixties."

"Pity we can't all team up," Kyle said.

"Yeah, that'd be nice. Of course, Indonesia wouldn't like that, and the Kopassus is running a lot of ops, too. Some of which get out of hand."

"Yeah, we know," Kyle said. He didn't admit to having a shootout with them. "Christ, what a mess."

"Yeah, a big one. Even if we settle out the Middle East, we'll still be fighting this one in twenty fifty."

"So who are you after?" Wiesinger asked.

"Straight to the point, eh?" Stephens asked. "We're looking for Ibrahim Beureueh, who we think was the thug behind that second Bali bombing. But he's with the GAM and they're slippery—not all of them are bad, and we're not opposed to GAM in principle."

"Yeah," Kyle admitted. "I've got to say these are some of the most respectable indigenous forces I've ever worked with." He nodded to Bakri, who returned it.

"Indeed. We don't want to help the Indo government, but we don't want to step on their toes. It's ripe for being used as someone's bitch to settle a score."

"Heh. Been there, done that, somewhere else," Kyle said, recalling being used to fight a tribal war in Pakistan. He sat back on a damp log. It didn't matter. He was soaked with sweat and humidity anyway. He reached into his gear for a canteen cup.

"Sorry to hear that, mate," Stephens said. The water was boiling and he fished the pot off the stove with his hooked finger through the bail. He dumped in a handful of tea leaves and set it down to steep. Then he blew the stove fuel out before leaning back again.

"So we're creeping around until we find this bugger."

"We'll add him to our list, but we're mostly west of here," Wiesinger said.

"Right. So what about you?"

Kyle glanced at Wiesinger, who nodded at him.

"We're looking for incoming explosives, and whoever's been snagging hostages," he said.

"We heard about the hostages. Fucking animals. But what about explosives?" Stephens asked. He looked interested.

"Whole pallets full. Wade and I stopped some last year on—" he glanced again at Wiesinger—"the Black Sea. Coming out of Russia, most likely, through the 'stans, then into Europe and now down here. Literal tons. Mostly just commercial HE. But enough to blow craters."

"Kee-rist. That's something I should report," he hinted.

"Go ahead," Wiesinger agreed.

"Thank you," Stephens said, waving at one of his troops, who'd been professionally silent. The man handed him one of two phones. Stephens was going to report it anyway. Doing so now meant they all agreed to it, and the Australian military would have more lead time on what it was doing. Meanwhile, Wiesinger whipped out his cell phone.

Wiesinger said, "Wiesinger here. We've met an Aussie SAS patrol seeking Ibrahim Beureueh, I spell, Bravo Echo Uniform?" He looked at Stephens and relayed the rest of it, "Romeo Echo Uniform Echo Hotel. Have agreed to swap intel on my authority. Discussed deliveries being made to this location. Recommend our assets communicate with theirs. Mission on profile otherwise. No additional intel . . ." There was a long pause. "Yes, that is good to hear. Thanks. Relay our support. Wiesinger out." He closed the phone and said to Kyle, "Robash is out of the hospital, recovering at home on convalescent leave. His heart looks good, his cognitive function is back and he should be back on duty in a few weeks."

"Kick ass," Kyle said. That was cheering news.

Stephens finished his own call to some Royal Australian Naval vessel, and then poured tea into the Americans' cups, just a few mouthfuls each, then some for Bakri, his own men and his local liaison. The billy was refilled and put back to brew another batch. It wasn't that a hot drink was needed; it was more of a social issue. They were agreeing to sit, talk, and share a supply, no matter how small. Kyle recalled with bemusement the serious issues around such in Pakistan, where you weren't fed until they decided they weren't going to kill you.

"So where did you meet the Singaporean unit?" Kyle asked. He wouldn't have expected that one. The others he could deduce.

"Tiny island called Sulawan in the Karimata Strait. Friendly natives, lovely beaches, and a gorgeous crater lake. Oh, and kraits, saltwater crocodiles, roving pirates, and typhoons."

"Sounds like a charming place."

"Actually, I could retire there. I just might. One of the girls . . . anyway. They were staging from there to Borneo for some Irian Jaya mixup."

"We really should pass that to State to follow up with, don't you think, Mel?" Kyle asked Wiesinger.

"Yes, but let's hear more." Wiesinger was attentive as Kyle had never seen him. The man thrived on details and reports. He was probably great in the Pentagon. Better than he was out here.

Stephens nodded. "The Filipinos are operating in Sulawesi Utara, of course. Stuff comes from there up into Mindanao, which makes it their problem. The Brits and Malaysians and Singaporeans are worried about stuff flowing up the Malay Peninsula, and of course from Irian Jaya, and through India to Pakistan. That tells you how effective we're all getting at stopping their shipping."

"That's odd," Kyle said. "We just found explosives coming *in* from Thailand."

"Not really," Wiesinger said. "They sanitize it by doing that, and draw attention from it going the other way. Also, it wouldn't surprise me if it's being stolen or is pirated. These routes are never efficient. That's the one major advantage we have."

It was amusing to hear the government bureaucracy referred to as "efficient," but under the circumstances it was probably accurate in this context.

"So this is becoming a major point?" Kyle asked.

"Yes," Bakri said. "Some of my brothers will take any ally, no matter the reputation. And they have taken these. For transporting the explosives, they get a portion. They get training in it. They get to cause trouble for the government. But there is trouble the government will negotiate over, and that which they won't. The terrorism . . ." he tapered off.

"Right. And we can't tell said government," Wade said.

"Wish I could help you," Stephens said. "But we can't do anything that might wind up jeopardizing us. I'll give you support, but I can't get directly involved."

"Fair enough," Wiesinger said. "Likewise, I can share certain data, but I can't get into your op without clearing it through our government. That would take some time." That was an understatement, Kyle thought. That would take years.

"Right. So what more should we talk about, and should we head somewhere with better shelter? I think I feel a storm coming."

"We're heading south and east," Kyle said.

"We're south. If we hurry." He looked at the patches of cloud through the canopy.

They rucked up and started slogging. With a combined unit this size, there was little to worry about. They made good time.

"What's with pirates?" Kyle asked. He'd heard of that, but not in detail.

"Various," Stephens said. "Sometimes they grapple a pleasure boat or small tramp. Steal the valuables, kill the men, gang-rape the women to death, and abandon it."

"Oh, charming."

"Worse sometimes," one of the other SAS men said. "Rod Iverson, sorry. Good to meet you. Anyway, they've been known to fake lights or logos and pretend to be customs inspectors for some nation. Same story. And some of the customs inspectors are pirates, or as close as you find—milking the job for sex and cash bribes. Wouldn't surprise me if that's where some of the explosives are coming from."

"Always a way to make money," Wade said.

"Yeah, pretty much. Also some people buy scrap vessels and register them with valid names, then hunt down an appropriate matching ship in good shape and take it and all cargo, minus crew of course. They sell the cargo, and sometimes sell the fucking boat for a few million, then skip. By the time insurance for the real owners and a government catch up, they've got a small fortune."

"Devious," Kyle said. It pissed him off. With his skills, he could be rich if he didn't have a conscience. A highly trained soldier who could kill at two thousand yards? He could charge a hundred grand a hit anywhere in the world and get it.

Two hours of forced march and eight kilometers later, they were in a clearing with very crude huts—timber and woven boughs with leaves, some with tin roofs. The rain started beating the upper canopy as they slid into a large hut that belonged to a local headman.

Whatever language he spoke was quite different from Bahasa. Kyle could barely recognize one word in twenty as being close to something he'd heard. He settled for listening to Stephens and his guide-interpreter, Akbar, jabber away, while he studied their host.

The man was Malay, with a slight paunch. He looked sixty but might be forty. He was adequately fed and had all his teeth, save one up front. He wore Adidas shorts acquired from some Western source and was armed with a kris, a spear, and a revolver. It appeared to be an ancient Webley .455, and held only three cartridges.

The canvas holster was worn in front, somewhat like a codpiece. The kris was buried in its wooden scabbard and looked to be rather old. Clearly, these were more ceremonial than functional. Several of his advisors, guards, hunters, whatever they were, were gathered around with light bows and spears and blowguns.

All smiles, the chief, whose name Kyle wouldn't even try to pronounce, came over and clapped him on both shoulders. Glancing at Stephens and getting a nod, he returned it. Then Wade and Wiesinger did, too, and Bakri. It appeared there were status issues. The other Indonesians were ignored.

The rain was reaching a torrent, though not as much as it would during monsoon season. Quickly, they were broken into groups and ushered into other huts. Kyle and Wade wound up alone in one, the occupants apparently hunting or gathering.

Outside, the rain poured down, splashing craters in the mud and the puddles already growing. It was dark, almost twilight, as the pools merged into a lake, then a sea, with stalks of greenery fighting to float above it and twist in the current. The tin roof shed water well, but the sound was a cross between being inside a snare drum and standing under a waterfall. Conversation was near impossible for several minutes.

Kyle stood, watching the water rise until it lapped at the lip of the floor, then slowly oozed in in a growing arc, then spread out to cover the worn, smooth gray planks. Through the frame of the door, the forest was a dark green-and-gray world, still in stark contrast to the flatter, artificial color of the walls.

With no one else nearby and Wiesinger gone, it was safe to actually talk about him. Still, Kyle looked surreptitiously around before speaking, and kept his voice low.

"You know, it's not that he's wrong so often, or shits a screaming worm about it . . ." he offered.

"It's that he never comes out and says, 'I was wrong' or 'I'm sorry,'" Wade supplied.

"Right."

"He can't be the first officer like that you've met."

"No, not at all. I just don't understand why they stick around so long."

"In his case, he's a daddy's boy."

"Yeah, I sorta noticed."

"Right. He wants a star so bad you can *see* the hard-on in his eyes. Just to prove he's as good as Daddy. And he's insecure enough to be a micromanaging ass."

"How did he wind up under Robash? They're nothing alike."

"Dunno," Wade said. "I'd guess he pulled strings but . . . how often do we have to deal with him?"

"Briefly on logistics last time," Kyle said, thinking, "and I had the general slap him down on some stupidity. We're dealing with him now. Other than that, maybe a dozen unpleasant phone calls."

"Right. He doesn't like the job. He doesn't like any job. He just wants to be a general like Daddy."

"Perfect problem for the Pentagon wienies; they can shuffle him off. Not so good for out here."

"You have a gift for understatement I envy, my friend," Wade said, smiling. It wasn't a happy smile.

"And he's not stupid. He's studied a great deal. But it's all book knowledge. Like that sleeping in full uniform in the middle of a jungle. It'll kill him from dehydration."

"Yeah. I've heard about officers like that in Vietnam. Damn near or did get their men killed."

"Well, time to kill. Euchre?" Kyle grabbed a barely used deck of cards from a pocket on his ruck. They were sealed in a plastic bag.

"If we must."

The hut had two chunks of carved log to sit on, a table of bamboo and split wood, and a window with a shutter. It was rustic but well built, and apart from the wet floor, quite tight and dry. There were two pallets at one side, presumably for adults and children, and a hearthplace. With the oppressive humidity inside and the hissing rain outside, it was quite soothing. Kyle felt lulled.

He kept busy and awake by sorting through his ruck. No matter how careful one was, trash built up, and that was weight one didn't need to carry. He stuffed all the odds and ends into an empty MRE packet, and placed it in the top compartment where he could easily reach it for disposal at a convenient time—fire by preference, buried if not, civilian trash if need be. There was nothing that specifically linked him, but there was no need to advertise anything American.

Wade beat him three rounds in a row. "Damn, I'm tired," he said.

"That's what they all say. Want to take a nap? I'll cover."

"Yeah, if we can get fifteen minutes each or so, we should. Thanks."

He leaned against a timber and barely heard Wade's, "No problem."

10

THEY WERE REFRESHED BY LATE AFTERNOON, AND IN-
vited for roast boar. Kyle ditched his trash in the fire, and the local children were delighted at the chemical colors of the flames. The
Malay were an attractive people. He could see why Stephens had
found a girlfriend on whatever island it was. Even the few overweight ones had nice skin tones and features. A couple of the
women were absolute babes, and knew it—they batted eyelashes
and the works. He thought of Janie and wondered how this mission
would end up. He was only a little dinged so far—scratches, aches,
bruises. It would be nice to avoid major wounds or stress that
would hospitalize him. This time.

The families stayed mostly in their huts, though it was from politeness. The children played around the edges, in awe but not afraid
of the strangers. The boar, roasted in thin strips rubbed with local
herbs, was quite tasty. "Good grub," Stephens said. "We encountered the village by accident, and occasional gifts keep them quiet.
Pocketknives, flashlights, lightsticks. They're too savvy for trinkets,
but are in a rather remote location."

Actually, they weren't more than thirty miles from a huge industrial operation. But in this jungle, that was a considerable distance.
There was little road other than the coastal highway and in the
cities.

But they were nice people, and between game and fruit didn't
seem to have to work much. One of the few tropical paradises left,
and assholes were trying to tear it apart.

"Where do we go from here?" Kyle asked the group.

"South and East," Bakri said. "We should come up on the road
and then set our ambush."

"Ambush?" Stephens asked. Wiesinger looked unhappy. There was just no way to keep track of the information here. It would be better if he just shared everything, Kyle thought. They were all on the same side and the enemy would know soon enough.

"We're going to capture what we hope is a leader and get more intel," Kyle said, watching Wiesinger to see if he objected to sharing the information.

"Right. Leave us out of that, then," Stephens said. "Intel sharing, fine. An attack on anything concrete that will get headlines, even if we're not in them, fine. In between is a whole range of items that don't fall under 'winning the war' or 'staying discreet.'"

"Any way to get back together afterwards?"

"As long as there are no embarrassing bodies to talk about, certainly. Call my mobile. I'd kiss the arse of the man who invented those. Before that, it was pay phone, weeks with no reports, or lug a radio with all that entails and the risk of discovery."

Wiesinger accepted the number, and Kyle made note of it. That earned him a look of disgust from the colonel.

"Always good to have a duplicate, sir," he said. He wrote it as a simple series of digits with no breaks. It shouldn't be readily identifiable if found.

"Right," Wiesinger agreed. That was from the book. And it was something Kyle used because it made sense. An error or a casualty could leave them without contact information. "We'll call in a day or two. Good luck to you."

"And you." In seconds, Stephens's unit had disappeared into the brush.

"Our turn," Kyle said. "And we need to hump fast."

Bakri had a map out. "Here's where I recommend. It's where the trucks have been coming through."

"So we seize a truck and roll into the village?" Wiesinger asked.

"That is what I suggest. If they notice the driver is different, we can delay them a few seconds and apply force. Most of them don't carry weapons at hand."

"Could get nasty up close."

"Yes, but we should win. We have enough soldiers, and surprise."

Kyle was willing to risk it. Enough fire fast would make most people duck for cover. It wasn't sniping, but it should be over quickly. Wiesinger took a few moments to assess the risk, and agreed.

They headed out at a fast walk, two locals leading, two trailing, and the others switching off two on each flank. After an athletic hour of sweating and gasping for air, they reached a road.

"Not the safest way to travel," Wiesinger hinted.

"No," Kyle said, "but the traffic is light and we have a scout well ahead in case of trouble. As long as it doesn't get too mushy, we won't leave much sign."

"Very well," the colonel conceded. He did seem to be coming around, albeit slowly.

It was one of those marches where one quickly zoned and didn't notice the passage of time or distance. Kyle had done this for years, all over the world. He had good-fitting boots, a well-designed MOLLE ruck with contents suited to him personally, and a weapon he was comfortable with. There was nothing to do but pick up the feet, put them down, and pace off the distance. They were covering about three kilometers, two miles an hour, and would do so for a solid eight hours. That would put them where they needed to be for the ambush, hopefully with time to set it up. If not, they'd camp a day and try again. If that didn't work, they might need to actually assault the village and kill a few.

Kyle wasn't opposed to that on moral grounds. Most of them had to know what was going on. The darkness was merely a cover. But there were undoubtedly children, women, and a few men who really weren't in the loop. Besides, taking out towns was sloppy and attracted attention. That's why he'd opted for the surgical task of sniping. He'd changed entire battles with less than five bullets.

They were in darkness again before 1900. It was perhaps the darkest night Kyle had ever experienced. There was no light pollution from cities, the moon was invisible behind clouds and canopy, and no one was using any lights. Even Kyle's night vision goggles showed little detail. All was fuzzy and indistinct. But he could see ruts and worn ground well enough, and kept moving, occasionally feeling with his foot or shifting when he found a dark spot. "Dark" on NVG meant a hollow, but whether three inches or three feet deep was much harder to tell.

They took no breaks, eating and drinking on the march, no smoking, stopping with a buddy on guard to take a leak and then catching up quickly. Wiesinger seemed very bothered when the two women stepped off the track and squatted. But hell, they had to drain too. The act wasn't of any interest to Kyle other than as an intellectual observation that they were adequately hydrated if they needed to go. The process was familiar. That it was a little more awkward for women than men in these circumstances was a minor note, but if they didn't complain he saw no reason to. Wiesinger really needed to relax.

It was hard to tell how many of them there were, and Kyle was within the group. The noise discipline and movement skills of these people were excellent. That was of far more interest. On the whole, it had been a lot smoother so far than it could have been, and that was with sporadic firefights.

"Twenty-three hundred," Wade said as they stopped. He was panting. "Should give us an hour. We're about five kilometers east of Khayalan, I think." He pulled out his GPS to confirm.

"What's your suggestion?" Wiesinger asked.

"Well, Mel, they seem to have a driver, shotgun, and someone in the back. Two good shots will deal with the shotgun and cargo guy, but someone will have to tackle the driver of a moving vehicle. Ideas?"

Bakri said, "I think Syarief can do that. Syarief?" he switched to rapid fire Achinese. The man smiled and nodded. "Sya is a master of pentjak silat. I think he can silence the driver and keep the vehicle on the road."

"Good. Both shots from the left?" Kyle asked. He knew silat was an Indonesian martial art. He wasn't aware of any details.

It was agreed that on a blank signal from Wade, spotting, Kyle and Wiesinger would shoot the passengers. Syarief would swarm up the side of the truck and subdue the driver, who would be kept alive if possible. Then they'd see about securing the imam.

There wasn't time to waste, as the truck could be along anytime. The forward scout was only two kilometers away, which would be only a few minutes of warning. Syarief darted across the road. Wade cuddled up to a tree and laid his scope over a low branch. Wiesinger stood by another bole, and Kyle ascended a few feet with the help of two men. He wanted to have his sight plane a good ten feet up to ensure plenty of window for the man riding shotgun.

He stood on two men's backs, scrabbled up over a branch, and wrapped himself around the trunk. It wasn't a largish tree, but it was thick enough to hide him. And, he discovered, thick enough to make shooting awkward.

Then it was time to wait. This was the approximate time the vehicle had been observed on previous nights, but there was a variation of nearly an hour. Nor did it come every night. But it did seem they were moving a lot of stuff at present.

His phone buzzed. It was Bakri announcing the truck. "Two kilometers, forty kilometers an hour. About three minutes."

"Understood."

Kyle found a position with his rifle steady, both feet twisted and placed for something approaching stability, and the truck came over a slight rise.

Wade fired the empty cartridge from his pistol, the primer explosion a loud snap like a firecracker, and the slaughter was on. A thrown coat spread across the windshield, surprising the driver and causing him to let off the accelerator. Kyle's bullet blew through the skull of the passenger and out in front of the driver. Wiesinger caught his target in the shoulder with the first round and finished him off with the second, though a solid scream escaped. The man's weapon tumbled over the side. Syarief clambered up the cab in a move Kyle would like to have seen, since the truck was still going at a respectable sprint, and grabbed the driver, who was busy staring in horror at his passenger. With a quick twist of Syarief's hands, the driver was thrashing and choking, panic evident on his face as his breath was cut off. Syarief wrestled his victim away from the pedals and the truck slowed.

In a matter of moments, the corpses had been carried far back from the road and left, guts slashed, for the scavengers. Both rifles held by the truck's security detail were in the hands of Bakri's men, who engaged in a quick shuffle down the pecking order. Lesser weapons were handed down to those in need, kept as trophies, or stripped for needed parts as called for. The remains wound up in someone's backpack. The corpses' possessions were looted, as were the driver's: cash, web gear, boots. The clothes were stripped and dumped elsewhere. Likely, there'd be nothing in a day or two.

That done, Wiesinger and Wade boarded the back and stashed themselves between crates. There were not only explosives here, but there also were three AK47s and a box of clothing and gear, as well as two other large cartons of produce and dry goods. Kyle now swapped for the M4. He left the SR25 behind with one of Bakri's men, whom he cautioned not to use it. Wiesinger still looked shocked at letting non-U.S. troops handle the equipment, but it wasn't possible to carry a ruck and a spare rifle for this. Kyle was worried, too; he didn't want the weapon jarred or the sight played with.

Bakri slipped in alongside the driver. From what Kyle had overheard, the driver had the muzzle of a pistol against his testicles and was being told that cooperation would save them, trouble would get them shot off.

Still, Kyle was nervous. Was there some sort of signal to be given as the truck arrived? Had they already been sighted? A firefight with him on a raised platform in the middle didn't appeal. Worse, he'd not donned even the light body armor he'd brought. He hadn't had time. It was still in his ruck, being watched by one of the Indonesians. He had grabbed his helmet and wished he hadn't. It had an obvious profile and made it harder to squeeze in.

But there was nothing to do but soldier on. In six minutes, more or less, they'd know. He checked the chambering on the carbine, hefted it again, and got ready. He and Wade would try to subdue the imam and load him into the track. If need be, Kyle wasn't opposed to a leg shot to make the bastard easier to carry.

One other thing bothered him. The passenger had been a woman. She'd held a rifle and was definitely a combatant, and a probable supporter of terrorism. Still, he'd never shot a woman before, and hadn't been expecting to. It bothered a chivalrous part of him. It didn't reassure him much to realize she would have done likewise. There were Anda with her Pindad SS1 carbine and Irta with her AK47 on this side, both of them fair targets for any opposition. People armed and ready to shoot were combatants.

Then he stopped worrying, because they were slowing and there were voices. Bakri had said he'd face the driver, so as not to be seen himself. But would the driver cause problems?

That was answered when Bakri fired. The driver screamed. Kyle cursed and came up.

Luckily, the men unloading the truck were not armed. He dropped off the bed and grabbed the imam by the shoulder.

The cleric was skinny, bearded, and wearing a black cap. He spun and started to shake Kyle off before realizing Kyle was considerably stronger. Then Wade caressed him with the stock of his M4, leaving a butt imprint in the fabric of his cap, and probably in his skull as well. The man staggered and fell.

Kyle heaved the limp form straight up and Wiesinger caught him. Then someone behind Kyle grabbed for the carbine.

He shoved, punched, and pulled away. He really didn't want to fire a burst. Their stealth was obviously blown, but bodies would make things worse.

Then the truck was rolling backward as Bakri reversed them out of the area, and Wiesinger was pulling at the back of Kyle's shirt. It cut into his throat momentarily, until he got an arm on the bed and heaved. His left leg caught on the wheel and was pushed up, causing him to swing.

Suddenly, he was up, Wade pulling on his arm. He wasn't sure how Wade had beat him to the bed, but he didn't care. They were moving.

As they picked up speed, there came a shot, and the sound of revving motorcycles.

"Well, at least they're all combatants," Wade said. Bakri was driving now, the old driver having been unceremoniously dumped out. The truck careened into one of the turnarounds, then spewed dirt as it accelerated. Kyle scrabbled around, unchoked himself and got a good grip on his weapon. The cycles came in pursuit, and he started firing.

It wasn't sniping. It did take calm nerves and precision, but it wasn't sniping. They were all moving, the terrain shifted and there was nothing to call a baseline. He rapped out bursts and kept them low. With a hundred rounds in the double drum C-mag, he could get thirty-three such bursts.

Overhead, Wiesinger *was* trying to snipe. The bullets snapped over Kyle's head. They didn't hit anything. Moving platform to moving target was a tough shot. It was something Kyle wouldn't attempt, and he had had a hell of a lot more practice than Wiesinger.

He and Wade had each fired a half dozen bursts before the first bike went down. Two others collided with it and the rest gave up in a slewing, swerving tangle.

"Well, that was royally screwed up from the word 'go,'" Wade said.

"That's because we're playing this like cowboys and not soldiers," Wiesinger said. "Dammit, from now on I will be the voice of reason."

"Oh, can it, Mel," Kyle said, anger welling over. "We're all unhurt and we have the objective. We've got good intel from allies and locals. We're in a better position to follow up on our primary objective. All that despite you falling asleep on watch."

Silence reigned. He wasn't going to look at the glare on Wiesinger's face; he could feel it. Wiesinger wasn't going to discuss his mistimed nap. Wade wasn't going to get in the middle. Absolute silence and stillness reigned for several minutes. Wade took the time to check the imam for injuries and lash him into a pretzel. Kyle watched the rear. He didn't give a rat's ass what Wiesinger did.

They were well ahead of pursuit for now, but there were no turns on this road. Additionally, radios or phones could have a roadblock waiting for them. It would only take a log or a few seconds of rifle fire to stop the vehicle. They had to ditch the truck soon.

"Here!" Bakri announced. The road angled downhill. Everyone

dismounted, two of them carrying the bound and gagged imam. Bakri slipped the vehicle into neutral and bailed out.

The truck spent most of a kilometer oscillating in greater sways until it caught enough brush to stop. That should help confuse the issue. There was a solid 1500 meters on both sides they might have taken. So the crucial thing was to take the opportunity now and maximize that cover. There would definitely be more forces coming.

Meantime, an entire shipment of the explosives was in Bakri's hands. His troops each carried a few pounds stuffed into their bulky, shapeless packs. They slipped into the woods along a broad front, shifting past protruding branches so as not to leave any obvious sign.

"I hate to destroy it," Bakri said, indicating his pack. "But I can't use most of it."

"Then don't hate destroying it. You took it away from the terrorists. And we'll take some, too." Kyle wasn't proficient with explosives, but he could insert a detonator without blowing a finger off. And it gave them more power. "And the Aussies might want some too."

"Ah, I see value in this commodity. Perhaps I should broker." His sense of humor appealed to Kyle.

"Then we'll have to come back and hurt you," Kyle said, deadpan.

"But don't worry," Wade said. "It's not personal, just business." He smiled. Bakri returned it, not quite sure if it was a joke.

Wiesinger had his phone in hand. "I'm not sure why I'm doing this," he muttered loudly enough to be heard. He punched it, raised it, and spoke. "Stephens. Wiesinger. Shipment acquired. Employee acquired. Where do we meet you? Understood. Out." He turned back to the others. "We're going to head south and up into the hills to meet."

"Where?" Bakri asked.

Wiesinger fumbled with a map. "Here, as near as I can tell."

"Ah . . . no, here, I think," Bakri said. "I know the place."

Chagrined, Wiesinger nodded. Kyle wondered how shaky he was on other things. His shooting was good but not sniper quality. His navigation was good but not Ranger quality. On so many things, the man was "good" rather than "exceptional." Which meant an office was the right place for him, as Kyle was tired of thinking.

"Twelve kilometers uphill," Bakri said. "Can you handle it?"

"Certainly," Kyle said, feeling as if he would die from the heat.

But if two skinny little Indonesian teenagers could lug a struggling prisoner, he could manage himself and his ruck.

He was glad of the MREs, but they couldn't last much longer. The locals were eating cold rice from their packs, and fruit in plastic bags.

Cold rice. He shuddered. Rice was something he tolerated, as long as it was spiced or sauced somehow. The thought of a diet based on the stuff didn't appeal to him. Whether or not his American diet was healthy, it was what he was used to and very tasty.

They reached a clearing, almost a meadow at 1500 feet, and Bakri called a halt. They'd traveled a thousand feet vertically and several kilometers horizontally, and Kyle realized he was mixing measurements. It was amusing. Quarts for water, feet for elevation, meters for shooting, and of course everyone here used metric. Grains for bullet weight, inches for drop. He had to be tired if he was starting to laugh at the technicalities of the job.

He didn't realize how tired until he sat down harder than he expected and had trouble when he tried to get up. That let him lean back against his ruck, however. That little rest felt good. Sleep was a luxury on this mission, rations were on the low side and would get lower, and energy expenditure was outrageous, with all the walking. It wasn't the distance. It was the terrain. Between rough surfaces that took a toll on the ankles and detours around growth to avoid leaving signs, actual distance was more than double the map distance. Any break was a good thing. The others seemed to think so, too. They all packed in and set up a bivouac.

Twenty minutes later, as everyone was settling in, Stephens arrived.

"So that's him," Stephens said, indicating the trussed body.

"Yes. He hasn't said anything yet," Kyle replied. God, it was good to sit down. He'd never admit to fatigue when his hosts were so stoic, but he was drained.

"We haven't asked anything yet," Bakri said. He nodded to his henchmen.

The interrogation was ugly enough to push Kyle away. The imam kept invoking Allah, and vowing to do vile things to the children of his captors. Unfortunately, they needed his mouth intact to tell what he knew. The diatribe and invective continued. Even though it was in Bahasa and Achinese, Kyle could hear the viciousness. He wasn't going to be an easy man to break.

While they pretended not to know what was going on behind a cluster of trees, Wiesinger broached the subject.

"Kyle, we're on very shaky legal and moral ground back home if anyone hears of this."

"I don't endorse it, Mel," he said. "Officially, I asked that it not be done."

"Yeah, and that'll get you what? We could see Leavenworth for this."

"Mel . . . sir, it often happens out here that the realities go beyond the theory. There's every chance of doing one's job right, and getting courted or dying anyway. It's one of those things that just doesn't offer any good answers."

Wiesinger hesitated, his round face squinting and working. "I want it to stop. Can you tell me how?"

"The only way I can think of is for you to ask. Bakri might listen. He might move it farther away so you don't have to know about it. He might tell you to go screw. At best, you'll delay our acquisition of intel. At worst, you'll piss off our host and blow the mission. And as best as we can tell, this bastard helps blow up vacationing families and children of blue-collar workers. I detest the necessity. I can't say I'm morally bothered by the suffering. It's something I have to struggle with all the time. I don't know what the answer is."

Wiesinger was silent again.

Kyle fell asleep. If he was needed, they could wake him.

He woke refreshed. He'd slept deeply. So deeply he didn't recall hearing any more torture. He blinked and stretched.

Wiesinger was asleep next to him. He'd stripped to his T-shirt this time. Wade was on watch, talking to one of the other Aussies and two Indonesians. Two M4 carbines and two Senapan Serbu rifles pointed in different directions. That seemed safe.

Wade saw Kyle move and came over. "Wiesinger was asleep. I suggested not waking him."

"Okay. Now what?"

"Bakri suggested letting everyone rest. We've got intel."

"I'm awake. Tell me."

"We've got a story of a facility nearby that produces product for income, and configures explosives. From there, it moves to the coast. Some is shipped, some is kept for insurgency. He couldn't or wouldn't specify what, where, or how much."

"Probably didn't know," Kyle guessed. "Was it bad, the interrogation?"

"If we might get captured, I want you to shoot me," Wade said. He didn't reveal much emotion, which was a hint, also.

"Damn," Kyle said. When younger, he would have paid money to see terrorists tortured to death. Or thought he would have. Then the realities of it had disgusted him. Now, listening to it was just a job.

He wasn't sure what to think about that, either. But second-guessing himself out here was a bad idea. That could wait for return stateside. The only thing to worry about now was the impending risks to himself and civilians.

By late afternoon, everyone was awake. Stephens boiled tea. Several of the Indonesians cooked up a pot of rice with local fruits, leaves, and a couple of chickens someone had managed to swipe during the raid on Khayalan. It wasn't much, but it was hot and refreshing. The Americans passed around some MREs and a hoarded tub of Kyle's shoestring potato snacks. There was dried meat from a previous expedition. As a feast it wasn't much, especially with all the walking they were doing. But Bakri had called for his trucks again—they were needed at farms but could be broken loose for a day here or there—and said he was having them bring food, too.

Food, fuel, batteries, water, and ammo. Everything else was secondary. It took a lot of supplies to keep even a short platoon going more than a day. They had no real logistics tail to support them. That greatly impeded their operation. In Pakistan, they'd had the same problem. In Romania, they'd had cash, credit cards, and were in a modern environment. They had cash here . . . and nowhere to spend it.

"I have another report," Bakri said, and everyone moved in except the sentries. "We have a location on an explosives site. It is here." He pulled out a map. "A village once called Impian. It was abandoned after a flood in November two thousand two. Our enemy is said to be there."

"Advance as two squads, overwatch?" Stephens offered. "Encircle, observe, gives us a good position for attack or retreat? I'm happy to help if there's a big payoff in intel or damage."

"We'll get there first," Wiesinger said. "I'll do a commander's reconnaissance, then we'll see. We want to nail the people behind it, primarily. Destroying it is secondary. Further intel is an ongoing issue."

The colonel was standing far enough away not to hear what Kyle heard, which was Stephens muttering, "That presumes you're in charge, lardbum." He didn't snicker. He understood exactly how the man felt.

Stephens was lucky. He could refuse to listen to Wiesinger. Sergeant First Class Kyle Monroe didn't have that option.

No one argued about it. Really, there wasn't much to do until they did get a look at the area. Stephens was too bright to get in a pissing contest with a foreign officer. Wiesinger assumed he was in charge. Bakri of course had his own ideas.

An hour later, the trucks arrived, four of them. It was incredibly tight with all three Americans crammed in the backseat, their gear in the rear, and an Indonesian with his gear up front. The Aussies filled a second one with another local. That left nine more shoved into the other two vehicles.

It was a ride like any other, though Kyle prayed they would not get attacked. There simply wasn't any room to swing a weapon into play. Still, between riding uncomfortably or marching forty miles, he'd take the painful ride. Wade and he kept elbowing each other in the ribs accidentally, and gouging their knees on the receivers of their rifles.

Then it was late afternoon and they arrived. With the need for stealth, Kyle was used to operating at night. The near twelve-hour days this close to the equator gave lots of dark. So he'd spend most of the time as a nocturnal hunter. Still, he was pushing the envelope this time.

"Arrived," of course, meant a solid ten kilometers away, for safety. They'd do the rest on foot, with Anda and Corporal Rod Iverson out front. They were both reputed to be the best trackers anywhere. Hopefully, their skill would be reinforced by competitive nature and they'd catch any hint of a perimeter before it knew it was being attacked.

Wiesinger was still too loud when he moved, but better at it than he had been. He might eventually shape up. In the meantime, Kyle stayed close enough to let the man follow his lead. Usually the colonel would.

Stephens crawled up close. "According to Iverson, Anda, and GPS, it's fifteen hundred meters that way." He pointed. "What now?"

"I'll do a recon and determine where we stand. Kyle, you have a notebook? I'd like it, please."

Kyle knew better than to argue. He peeled off the pages he'd used and secured them in a chest pocket, just as a security measure. He handed the book to Wiesinger, along with a pen.

"You're going in there?" Stephens asked, brow wrinkled through his camo.

"I've got to know what we're facing before planning the assault," Wiesinger said, his voice half reasonable, half condescending.

Of course, Kyle had never heard of anyone doing a "commander's reconnaissance" in that fashion after they graduated Ranger school. It was an easy way to die, as one lieutenant had learned in Grenada. He'd go along with Wiesinger and pray he wasn't going to wind up a statistic.

"It's seventeen twenty," Wiesinger announced as he looked at his watch. "I will be back by nineteen hundred. Monroe, you're with me, Curtis, take charge of U.S. material."

"Yes, Mel," they echoed. Wade didn't look unhappy. His expression was carefully neutral. Kyle looked at him just as neutrally. He wasn't sure that, if they'd been able to, they'd grin, sigh, or look disgusted. So with nothing further to say, he turned and followed his officer.

Iverson squatted nearby. He looked somewhat miffed at his recon being second-guessed by Wiesinger. Or maybe "somewhat miffed" was too mild. The man was lean, but muscled like a wrestler, and had a very dark, clenched-jaw expression. Kyle gave him a shrug and a shake of the head as he passed. *Not my decision, pal.*

HALF AN HOUR LATER, KYLE RECONSIDERED. *MAYBE*
I'm getting too cynical in my old age, he thought. Wiesinger directed him where to go and let him take the lead.

"You've got more time in the field, so I'll tell you what I want and
you get it done," Wiesinger had said. Which was one part of doctrine that had been wise advice for thousands of years. Tell the NCO
what you want and he'll do it for you.

So Kyle led in a crawl, fast enough to be worthwhile, slow
enough for silence, around a substantial arc of the village. It had
block and tin buildings, a road that dead-ended into it and electricity from what Kyle reasoned was a propane generator. On second
thought, it had to be liquefied natural gas. There was enough of it
here.

And the place was silent.

Khayalan had been quiet. This was dead. A few cautious looks
through night vision confirmed it. There was evidence of a fight, including bullet spalling on walls. Add in scavengers trotting through,
and the smell . . .

"This is supposed to be an operations center, and I see nothing.
But it's not been down for long."

"I'd say a day, tops, or we'd see more scavengers," Kyle agreed.

"So who took them out, and why?"

"Unknown. Government, other rebels are all that comes to
mind."

"Okay, let's call the others," Wiesinger said. He looked scared,
badly. Kyle didn't blame him, though. His own fear was more inter-
nalized, but just as real. The growing twilight didn't help.

The rest of the ersatz unit moved in quickly. The evident lack of a perimeter, the darkness, and thick air let them approach upright at a skulk instead of down at a crawl. Within an hour, they were all present.

"Talk to me," Stephens said as he came up.

"Let's wait for Bakri," Kyle suggested.

"Righto." They huddled under broad leaves and inhaled the dank air, redolent with rot and chlorophyll.

When Bakri arrived, Kyle said, "Mel and I have covered the perimeter from here to there." He pointed. "No signs of action or habitation. Spalling and other light-arms damage, including fractures suggestive of grenades, are present. It appears no one is home. Obviously, we'd like to test that theory carefully."

Wiesinger nodded. "Suggestions?"

"If you want mine," Stephens said with faint sarcasm, "I'd pull us into thirds, split around the perimeter and then have one element approach with crossed lanes of fire in case they need support. Assuming we all trust our marksmanship."

"The cover is good, the men are all adequately trained from what I can see," Kyle said. "Sounds good. Bakri?"

"I will be happy to cover fire," he said. "I would not want to tell my men to stand in the middle of the fire."

"Right," Wiesinger agreed. "We'll go in with three volunteers. You each take your teams around one hundred to one hundred twenty degrees, then we'll call for the advance."

Syarief, Rizal, Iverson, and an Aussie named Fuller, their demolitions expert, joined them. The locals were armed with AKs and were excellent in the jungle. Iverson and Fuller each had an M4 that was almost a clone of the U.S. issue. They knew how to handle their weapons. Still, Kyle wanted the locals flanking, not behind him. Eagerness got people shot. Iverson and Fuller he was comfortable with. The SAS had a first class reputation.

Kyle had to agree with Stephens on the utility of satellite cell phones. No bulky radios for this, no codes, no worries about transmitters being located, no battery issues. Radios were often necessary, though, especially with air support. That they had no radios also meant no air and no arty. These operations were quite lonely. Even more so when fire came in.

They waited while Bakri's forces moved closer to the road, and Stephens's around a good chunk of the circle. It was twenty minutes later when Wiesinger grabbed his phone. "Roger that. We're ready." He punched it off. "Let's move." It was dark. Very dark.

They slipped in closer, weaving through the boles and vines, bushes and leaves. The silence was foreboding. Kyle's nerves stuck out like naked wires. There was something here, he was sure. He didn't believe in supernatural inputs. Fifteen years of instinct told him so. He didn't know what, but he felt the threat. He took another glance at the M4 he carried. Chambered, safety off, finger poised. He had a canister round—basically a 40mm shotgun cartridge—loaded in the grenade launcher in case he needed more oomph. It should be plenty. Wade also had a canister; Iverson and Fuller, the Aussies, had HE loads in theirs; and two of Bakri's men had RPGs. Add two machine guns, and it was actually an effective infantry platoon.

Except they were four units, really, and hadn't done more than a couple of marches together. There was plenty that could go wrong in the dark, should something spook someone.

They reached the cleared area, the ground beyond grassy and even. This place had been burned out of the jungle a long time ago. And it was empty, but had certainly been occupied since 2002. The trash and debris lying around was proof of that.

Kyle stepped out first in a low crouch, weapon shouldered and ready. Wiesinger moved in front and went prone with the SR25. Wade took one side and the Indonesians the other. They waited several seconds, ears cocked for anything beyond the cacophony of animal life.

Wade made the phone call. "Seems clear. Close in." He tucked the instrument away and resumed his guard.

Jack Stephens and two of his natives swarmed in the other side so quickly and silently they seemed to be wraiths. *Damn, but there were good troops around here*, Kyle thought. Which meant that if—when—this got nasty, Kyle would be in the midst of a battle of professionals, not a brawl of amateurs.

Well, he had wanted a challenge. Here it was. Be careful what you wish for . . .

Bakri came in from across and to the right, along the road edge. They were all through the village now. That meant they were targets from the buildings, but to hit them up close would expose the attackers to multiple shots and no backstop. That was the best they could manage.

Wiesinger said, "We need to control that large building near the center. I assume that's an administrative center."

"Sort of," Bakri said. "Official meetings would take place there, yes."

"I want to go in fast and hard, just in case."

"Of course."

The elements recombined into two large squads, front and back. Kyle felt his phone buzz, and he checked his watch as he raised his fist. When the second hand hit 12, they'd storm this building. He coiled himself like a spring, ready to explode. He took a quick glance around that showed everyone ready, fingers twitching near but not yet on triggers.

Then it was time. As one they rose. Kyle was prepared to blow the hinges off the door, but it hung askew. Wiesinger, the largest by far, kicked the door as two of Bakri's men went in low. Kyle went in high, expecting to take some kind of defensive fire.

Nothing.

No, not nothing.

Dear God!

There were bodies galore, bloated and rotting, but that wasn't what caught his attention. He'd expected bodies. It was the apparatus and the wall decorations. For they weren't maps or charts. They'd all been desecrated, torn down or ripped, but it didn't take much to see them for what they were.

Wade came in the rear.

"Child porn studio?" he said, voice tight, disgusted, as if he might vomit at any moment. Kyle felt the same way.

"Yeah. And the terrorists . . . killed them." He looked at one of the bodies. Even before the flies and scavengers, it had been ugly.

"I never thought I'd say this, but I agree with and support the terrorists." Wade sounded a cross between revolted and amazed.

"Here," Wiesinger said, pulling a grubby sheet of paper from the wreckage. It was a color printout of . . .

"Yeah, why don't you take this, sir," Kyle said, fishing a lighter from his pocket.

"Thank you, sergeant. Much appreciated." Wiesinger struck the paper alight, dropped it, and vigorously wiped his fingers in the dirt on the floor, then on his pants.

"Man, it never ceases to amaze me how far some people can sink," Wade said. They all stared as the picture disappeared into ash, ghostly outlines still hinting at the scene on the photographic paper. The colonel stomped it with his boot and ground it to nothing.

"At least there's some places the terrorists won't go," Wiesinger said. It wasn't much comfort. It simply pointed out how far they did go, if this extreme was what they wouldn't do.

"Any evidence we can use?" Stephens asked. "Sources, ID of any kind?" He looked rather perturbed himself.

"Not without substantial digging, I'd say," Wade answered. "I'm hoping we don't have the time."

"We probably have the time," Wiesinger said. "But we're not going to take it. Let's call this a map marker and move on. If it wouldn't blow cover, I'd torch the place."

"Roger that, Mel," Kyle agreed firmly.

Stephens jogged out to go to the adjoining building where his team was. Kyle turned and ducked for the door.

It was then that a torrent of fire shattered the frame, tossing splinters of block into his face.

He dropped at once, eyes closed, and crawled back. His eyes were stinging from chips, not burning from dust. He'd have to get them clear enough to fight with, and hope the injuries didn't require more sophisticated treatment. But he was inside the door and covered, he hoped, as several crashes echoed. Outgoing fire was good. He blinked his eyes carefully, not wanting to gouge them with any sharp fragments. Then he pulled at the lids to let tears flush the dust. They still ached and itched, but he could see, even if his vision was a little blurry.

Alert again, he listened before sticking his head out. There was a lot of fire out there. Whatever the force was, they were large. Small arms. Few automatic weapons. No grenades so far. Wiesinger and Stephens were shouting back and forth between buildings.

"Force to the rear is about a squad. One RPK machine gun. Mostly AKs," Stephens called.

"In front is two support weapons," Wiesinger replied. "One RPK, one RPG not in use." That was potentially disturbing. A rocket-propelled grenade would kill everyone in the building.

"Mel, do you want any targets?" Kyle asked in a lull as his ears rang. If not, he could just shoot. But he was a precision shooter first.

"Wade, Kyle, find that RPG. Then the machine gunner."

Wade said, "Roger, Kyle, far left, second block building, rear corner, under bush."

"Sighted," Kyle said. He aimed and squeezed, but the pain and the sudden shock of rounds in an enclosed space had him shaking. His first round missed, high.

"He's relocating," Wade said. "Look for him two buildings south, same position."

"Sighted," Kyle said. The first shot winged his target, possibly a shoulder. That shook him up enough that Kyle's second shot was center of mass, just before the missileer could move. Just to make sure, he followed the body down and carefully put another sideways through the ribcage.

He shook his head. The concussion of rounds fired wasn't helping his vision or his hearing. Still, three shots wasn't bad for a valuable threat. "Where's the gunner?" he asked.

"Stand by!" Wade said. "He's gone!"

"Shit, that's bad!" Kyle said. Gone where? Behind another building? The next notice they got could be large amounts of autofire.

Wiesinger was shouting orders. "Bakri, have your RPG gunners take out those two buildings there."

"It will take a moment," Bakri yelled back. They were split up now, with part of the force inside Kyle's building, and most of the rest scattered for cover.

Wiesinger yelled into his phone, "Stephens, consolidate to the west and hold against that element. We will secure here. As soon as we are in control of our own territory, we will combine reserves to attack them . . . Yes, that sounds good. Out."

Kyle flinched momentarily as Bakri's RPG team demolished two buildings. The explosion slapped at them even here, a visible wave front tossing dirt and leaves ahead of it. It inflicted several casualties on the enemy, including one body tossed like a rag doll. But Kyle still didn't see that machine gun, and there were other support weapons out there, among troops who knew how to use them.

To highlight that point, a roar washed over him from behind. Screams and shouts, some of surprise, some of injury followed it, faint and hard to discern under the pain that meant he had hearing damage. He wasn't sure what had come in, but it was dangerous.

It was a good time to relocate. Kyle shifted over to a crack under the window he could just see through, flopped across a chair cushion and got ready.

No, it wasn't a cushion. It was a gas-bloated corpse on the splintered wreckage of a folding chair. He grimaced in distaste. But the bastard was dead, and nothing was leaking from the body, and he'd seen worse. Screw it. He'd take his shots and then move.

"There!" Wade called. "Reference: Building to left of the one we just blew. Window on right side. Target: machine gun crew. Range five five meters."

"Sighted," Kyle agreed. There wasn't much of them visible; they were being cagey. Or maybe they were as afraid of getting blown away as he was.

They were more afraid in a moment. He fired and missed, but

took splinters out of the frame. He'd been trying to peel off the top of one man's head, but he'd ducked. Still, they were both staying down for now, which meant they weren't shooting. It wasn't a win, but it didn't hurt anything.

"Roger that," Wiesinger said into his phone. "No dice. They're covered, we're covered, this could go on a long time. Might consider regrouping and retrograding under fire." He didn't sound happy.

"I advise it, Mel," Kyle said. "We're not here for a protracted battle. We're here to find a target." He gratefully hopped off the body and found another loophole to shoot through.

"Roger. We can move into the jungle in squads and cover as we go." He flipped open his phone. "Stephens . . . Yeah, that's where we're thinking. Roger that. You, us, locals. Out." He spoke again. "The Aussies are first, we're second, providing cover for Bakri."

"I am not happy being last," Bakri said. It was the first open admission that he wasn't entirely sure of his allies.

"No one would be," Kyle said. He was pretty sure it came about because Wiesinger didn't trust the locals. And, while they were better than any others he'd worked with, they still weren't a professional force, and other than Bakri, he couldn't be sure of their loyalties. So he reluctantly agreed. Besides, he had to back up his commander. That was his duty.

"Very well," Bakri said, twitching. "Be sure we get lots of support fire."

"Count on it," Wade promised him, pulling out his other C-mag. The first was likely more than half full. But the fresh one meant one hundred rounds. That was support fire. Kyle copied the gesture. He also checked for a canister load in the grenade launcher. Anything in front was the enemy, as far as he was concerned, and he'd light it the hell up at every opportunity.

Wiesinger cut into his thoughts. "Stephens is ready, our turn."

"Roger. Good luck, Bakri. See you in two minutes."

"Yes," the man said with a simple nod. He sounded a lot surer of Kyle than of the colonel.

Kyle rose and slipped back, panning across an arc in case of threats up close. It wasn't likely, but it never hurt to be sure. A grenade tossed in would end the party real quick. But if he shot the thrower beforehand, it was just more fireworks outside. He did wish he could do something about the bursts of machine-gun fire alternately beating at the blocks and slapping through the door. At least, being dark inside, the shadow would help protect him even from night vision.

Wade turned, assessed the move and followed, while Kyle took the cue and slipped out the back. That meant scrambling through a hole that had been a window and still had broken frame and glass. He tore his pants but avoided anything worse than a stinging scratch. Wiesinger was outside, squatting, back against the wall. He seemed very glad of backup. Kyle nodded and took the other side. Then Wade dropped between them.

"We're clear, fire around either side," Wiesinger said into his phone. He dialed again. "Bakri, move." Closing that, he said, "Gentlemen, that way," and pointed into the woods.

The incoming fire was much stronger. Poor Bakri was taking a beating from a substantially larger force. The Aussies and their allies dumped a few hundred angry lead hornets between the buildings, and the incoming fire slackened for several seconds. But once the enemy realized they were retreating and shooting largely blind, it picked up again.

"Dammit," Kyle said. He dodged trees and headed into the jungle, seeking cover, concealment and a good, clear field of fire. One out of three would suffice. Two would thrill him.

Wiesinger cursed. He had his phone again. "Bakri's got five men in a building with no rear exit. They'll have to come out the side into fire."

"Grenade," Kyle said at once. "One of ours." RPG rounds were too powerful.

"You can't be serious. That's—"

"Which building, and tell them to duck," Wade said. He was already closing the breech on his launcher, having swapped canister for high explosive.

"That one there," Wiesinger pointed. "But you can't really mean to—"

Wade cut him off with a *Whump!* followed by a loud bang, as a flash cracked the wall. The resulting hole was about eighteen inches at best. But it was enough for skinny, dazed Indonesians to wiggle through, after peering to be sure they were safe from further fire. The third man beat at the opening with his rifle butt to enlarge it. Bakri and his others were slipping into the dark woods. It had gone well enough, it seemed.

There was a roar overhead that turned into a thumping, angry drone.

"Oh, shit," Kyle said as he looked up. Choppers. That meant military. Fast meant Special Forces, the Kopassus.

"Who the fuck called them?" Wiesinger asked angrily.

"Not a bad ploy," Wade shouted. "Use a porn shop to generate income. Use it as a cover. If the government captures anyone, you blow the cover, destroy it to show your good graces, then call the government and claim the kill. Icing on the cake to catch your enemies right there."

"It may be more chance than that," Bakri said. "But I do not wish association here. It is beyond sin."

"Son of a *bitch*!" Kyle said. "Fucking move, sir." The helicopters were hovering over the village. He assumed ropes and troops would follow. Wiesinger took the hint and started dodging.

The three squads broke into a ragged retreat, occasionally returning fire to threats. Kyle hoped, *hoped* the Kopassus would stick to the immediate area and not pursue further. But if they had backup on the ground or another assault, they could encircle. There was no good answer then. He was an American, an ally, but siding with rebels who were not, without diplomatic clearance. Best case, they offered a bunch of intel and got freed, while blowing the entire mission. Worst case, an Indonesian jail. And Bakri would likely wind up there either way. Indonesia jailed people for ten years for just flying the Free Aceh flag. Actually bearing arms . . .

And that assumed the Indo troops didn't just shoot them as mercs without asking any questions, which seemed the most logical and likely response.

The pursuit wasn't immediate, but Kyle wanted to put a few kilometers between them quickly. He didn't crave the headlines that might come: US CIA SNIPERS, INDONESIAN REBELS ASSOCIATED WITH AL QAEDA, and CHILD PORN STUDIO. Nor did he crave to get shot. Distance and dark were friends.

A long, loping time later, through tangled skeins of brush, he hunkered down and camouflaged himself. He scurried over and through a patch of thick weeds, then under them. He was far enough removed from the edge of the glade to not be visible at a glance. The spreading leaves would help deflect any heat signature, which he had to be putting out, as hard as he was breathing. He forced that breath to a slow, measured heave and listened. The rotors were steady, hovering, which meant they didn't anticipate any anti-aircraft fire from below. Under that droning, hypnotic beat . . .

Shooting and shouting, sparser now than they had been. A couple of final shots, and then the beating of rotor blades rose to a thrum. One helicopter swept overhead, shaking the air and trees and then dopplering away.

His phone buzzed a few minutes later as he was pondering his actions. He slid it out slowly and carefully. Departure of the aircraft didn't mean all patrols were off the ground. It was a possible ploy that would easily catch the eager or untrained.

"Kyle," he whispered.

"Mel. We're going to approach and recon."

"I advise against that, Mel," he said. Dammit, no.

"Bakri is missing five men. They were in a building with no rear exit and no commo. Another building, not the one we blew."

"Shit. Understood." That was a potential disaster. He listened to Wiesinger's orders. They were pretty much from the book, and in this case, were good enough. He saw no need to quibble.

Twenty minutes later, a marathon approach by the standards involved, they were at the edge of the clearing. It didn't take much effort to count the five stripped, decapitated bodies in the middle, nor the pile of five heads, each shot through from the back.

Bakri quivered, tears in his eyes. "I suppose this is better," he said. "They could have been tortured, exposed, jailed. But they are thought part of this . . ." He waved his hands around at the smoking remains of the operation. "They are shamed."

"We know, Bakri," Kyle said. "It doesn't matter otherwise. And I think their names are safe."

The sadism of the act was that they were dead . . . That meant that any guilty parties, or any party worried about guilt by association, would be relieved at the killing of their own people. Subtle. Kyle respected that in a way. It also made him want people dead.

A quick recon revealed other bodies. Their opponents had likewise been stripped, clothes and weapons taken. It was thorough and impersonal, a revealed contempt for the capabilities of the locals.

There just weren't any good guys here, Kyle decided. Respect and compassion took energy these people used to either stay alive or kill with.

"Where to, then?" Kyle asked diffidently.

"We bury them. Then home," Bakri said. "We must think on the threats." He stared for a moment, then turned determinedly and trudged into the clearing. Kyle followed, and looked around for something to use as a shovel. The others followed.

FAISAL LOOKED AT THE TWO NEW HOSTAGES. THE OTHers saw them as a prize. He didn't. A Chinese woman and her half-American daughter were hardly people to boast of capturing and killing.

They'd been taking hostages and killing them, cutting off their heads, since early 2004 in Iraq. It hadn't accomplished anything. The theory, he'd been told, was that the Westerners, especially Americans, were terrified of death and of dismemberment. Their culture demanded clean bodies, even to burying them in vaults, preserved against time. A few dead as object lessons was more humane than a battle involving hundreds of casualties. And besides, they were infidel deaths, not Muslim deaths.

Only, the fear hadn't come. Outrage and disgust had come, with harsh words and threats. But as usual, those faded. If anything, it seemed the Western world didn't care if a few people, or a few hundred, were decapitated. The headlines disappeared within days. Political and military impropriety stayed in the headlines for weeks, but the death of a hostage was hardly mentioned at all, and only briefly, before attention turned back to sports, scantily clad women, and pointless pastimes. Imam Ayi and the planners said the problem was that they were not being terrifying enough, grisly enough. Sufficient violence would provoke a reaction.

It didn't seem so to Faisal. And if it did, what reaction would it elicit after so much lethargy? A minor protest? Or would the enemy come awake like a krait poked with a stick?

And why was a culture so disinterested in its own casualties an enemy? Money was the key to all dealings with Americans. In that regard, he could agree with the attack on the oil terminal. That, they'd have to pay attention to. But again, might it be in a rage that would kill millions of Muslims in retribution?

He would just as soon have these hostages released. He already knew he wasn't going to accept the "honor" of beheading them. A relationship to an executive in Mobil's employ didn't matter to him. The Chinese woman was a civilian, apolitical and absolutely not worthy of note in this battle. It couldn't be right to use her so. And certainly not her little girl.

But how to get the leaders to listen to him?

Agung was furious. Whole shipments of explosives had disappeared. Billions of rupia in bribes, finder's fees, and simple operating costs had come to nothing. More than two thousand kilograms, enough for two hundred small bombs or ten really big ones, had been intercepted by the Australian and Singapore navies, and by some damned team in the jungle. He wasn't sure if that was the Kopassus, the Australians he'd heard skulking around, or, as rumored, an American hit team. He knew of them. Several of his group's best and most powerful men had been executed by assassins, either at long range or in close engagements. He'd heard names of several of them, but the names did no good without corroboration. Some new group was operating, that wasn't SEALs and wasn't Delta, but might be U.S. Army or Marines or CIA hired thugs. Whoever they were, they managed to sneak in right under the noses of government officials. He'd never admit it in public, but it terrified him. He could get a bureaucracy to do anything, from issuing building permits to sharing classified documents. But any inquiries about this came up blank. The government didn't know. The criminal networks didn't know. These men were shadows.

So the alternative was to create a trap for them, whereby they'd be taken care of by their own putative allies. Numbers were the strength of the enemy. But the Fist of God had a strength too. That strength was *purity*.

In the meantime, the explosives they did have should be delivered without delay. The fire and tears would cleanse at least one city, and perhaps the headlines would be enough, this time.

If not, a few true innocents would cause as much, if not more anguish. If the oil companies couldn't find employees willing to risk the wrath of Allah, then the problem would solve itself. And there was another factor . . .

Captain Hari Sutrisno looked at the reports. There was something more here than was immediately apparent. When a group of rebels was dropped into his lap with a phone call, he took the opportunity, and this source had proved reliable repeatedly.

At the same time, he didn't like being played for a fool or used as a toy in someone else's game. It was obvious in retrospect that he'd been meant to find the faction at the porn facility. Clearly, they were outsiders or mere guards, not participants. The firefight he'd interrupted had also been a side issue. So who had been running the vile operation? Who stopped it? Who found it? Who had called him in right on top of them? He had answers to none of these questions at present. But he would. No mistake about that, he would have an answer.

In the meantime, GAM was increasingly factional. That boded well for crushing it at last and maintaining a unified Indonesia. Any part he could do for his homeland he was honored to do. If promotion came with it, he wouldn't turn it down. But that wasn't his motivation. Duty was his motivation.

It was a good day for terrorism.

Pakistan was a safe place to hide, but operations there were not viable. Any disruption caused massive government response. Saudi Arabia was the same way, with Iraq becoming so. There was little to strike in Afghanistan or elsewhere in Asia. Europe had battened down tight. The current U.S. leadership had indicated a willingness to retaliate, and unless elections put in a more "sensitive" president, threats were all that could be offered, not any practical attack. Iran was Shia, not Sunni, but had a certain popularity for its hard-line leadership, even despite doctrinal differences. Turkey already had its own factions, and the Balkans were too close to Europe and had received major setbacks recently, in part due to Kyle and Wade and the CIA operations there. The African Muslim states were staunch allies of the terror networks, even if they didn't say so. That left a handful of places where attacks could be made with impunity and effect.

So it was that small bombs were detonated in Kuala Lumpur in Malaysia, Quezon City in the Philippines, and Surabaya and Medan in Indonesia. Another in Lhokseumawe ripped through a pipeline, spilling thousands of barrels of oil before cutoffs worked to staunch the flow. Flames roared as the crude petroleum wicked through the growth and vaporized. Panic ensued as it neared an Arun gas line, but it was brought under control with a lot of effort and resources, and not a few casualties.

The Fist of God claimed credit, and vowed a much larger blast in three days, plus other unspecified actions, if several GAM prisoners were not released and money from petroleum production not directed toward Aceh.

Early the next morning, Kyle was blinking sleep from his eyes as he sat on a dirt floor. He'd been woken in a hurry.

"We've got a major fucking situation here, gentlemen," Wiesinger said. He had them in a hut, as if it were a briefing room. Stephens and his men were along, too. Still, it felt like a stateside lecture rather than a field strategy discussion. The news of the attacks and capture had come in overnight.

"Indonesia is making the correct response, which is to pour another ten thousand troops in here and shoot anything that is a threat. Unfortunately, their assessment of threats includes our allies. It's a 'if you're not with us you're against us' gesture. So we can't stick around with our allies.

"At the same time, I'm reluctant to abandon our local help, because operating without them will be a considerable handicap."

Yeah, Kyle thought. *And utterly inhuman, crass, and rude. But don't let that bother you, sir.* At least it was a good reason to be woken up. The shit had hit the turbine.

"At least two groups are actively trying to get us nailed. Ideally, we let the government handle them while we pursue the threats to U.S. interests. But we can't get the intel we need to do that, and after the fiasco last time we tried an urban encounter"—he fixed Kyle and Wade with his glare—"it's not advisable. This has escalated beyond what we're set to handle. But if we withdraw, we admit defeat, which is something I'm not prepared to do."

No, Kyle thought. *No medals that way, sir. Got to put on a brave front. Even if we should have shared intel first and called for backup earlier.* And the urban screwup last time had still got the mission accomplished.

To be fair, much of the trouble the snipers faced was from higher up and from outside Department of Defense. But the snipers were on the spot.

Wiesinger continued, "And there's hostages. Fist of God has captured the wife and daughter of a U.S. executive. The bitch is, his wife is a Hong Kong native, meaning Chinese now. That seems to have been planned. If we wind up with dead Chinese nationals as well as American nationals, we'll have knots that will take months to deal with. The fear is that China will make incursions like ours, or even more overtly. They might deploy naval forces in these waters, for example, which is near India as well. They don't get along well, and Indonesia can't defend against a force like that and may just kill everything moving in Aceh to show they're dealing with the problem.

"So we're facing an international incident that could create a dozen wars, and has already got troops out in Indonesia and the P.I. There's a lot of diplo crap flying between China and everyone else. No one wants them here, but everyone agrees they have the right to. We're being asked for intel and action. I am open to suggestions."

"Vaseline," Stephens said. He wasn't in this chain of command and could feel free to kibitz. "Apart from that, I'm for calling my government and bailing. We've got an amnesty offer for my group and families, if we can extract them. With our casualties of the last month and a half, I can take four more people from your allies, if you can't get Washington to make the same deal."

It was sensible and fair, Kyle thought. This was a full-scale war, even if shadowy at the present. Two fireteams with local insurgents had no business trying to do more than radio out troop movements and enemy targets. And that was a job the SEALs or Air Force Combat Control or Marine Recon were much better equipped to handle than two Rangers and a desk officer. Not that it mattered worth a damn. There wasn't much to stop this. The government wouldn't be able to make a decision fast enough to matter, and Kyle didn't like the idea of abandoning civilians.

"Do the Chinese actually care about a civilian?" Australian Kevin Fuller asked. "I wouldn't imagine they care about an expat."

"Probably they don't," Wade said. "But it's a convenient excuse to bring ships down here and rattle sabers. They might also grab some more islands in the South China Sea on their way, as forward operating locations."

"Can't accuse them of being stupid," Iverson said. "Scheming, conniving, soulless, but not stupid."

"I guarantee both we and India will respond to Chinese vessels in the Straits of Malacca," Stephens said. "Wouldn't surprise me if you, the Brits, and the Japs came in, too."

Kyle said nothing about that. He agreed with what he heard and saw no reason to comment. Instead . . .

"Can we find the hostages, at least?" he asked. "If the bomb threats are urban, to hell with them, that's not our gig. I agree with you on that, Mel." *Did I just say that?* he thought. "But if we can find the hostages, we can at least report that. If they're in one of these little villes, we may be able to do something. That will take the Chinese pressure off, if we can accomplish that."

Wiesinger considered. "Good. I like it. Where do we look?"

"That's what the locals are for," Kyle admitted. "But they must be able to find something. Even if we can just localize it, it helps a rescue force."

"I'm not sure how much we should share," Wiesinger said. "Our objectives are different from theirs."

"Hell, Mel, should we put our feet in buckets of concrete? Washington isn't on the spot, they don't have the information we do. Decisions have to be made here." Wade sounded closer to an outburst than he ever had.

Wiesinger stared at him, looking as if he was about to start shouting. Obvious rage was boiling up. Stephens interrupted with, "I concur. I can call and tell my chain that I need to stay. I have that much autonomy. Stick with our locals. I'll trust yours if you trust mine. Any intel helps. I don't want to read about two dead civvies in the news."

Wiesinger closed his mouth. The comment about a mere sergeant having autonomy to make that decision obviously stuck in his craw. He'd been content so far to relay the orders from above and report back. He wasn't stupid, but he was lacking in imagination. The idea of handling the mission was obviously new to him.

"I agree," Kyle said. "I'd rather be recognized as a savior than a killer. This might do it." It wasn't much of a statement, but it might get the colonel to see the promotion potential of acting without orders. Of course, that might get him started on a path of throwing the book away. Which wasn't what Kyle and Wade did. They knew the book, they used it when applicable, and strayed only when the situation called for it. Soldiers, not grandstanders.

Wiesinger agreed to the inevitable. He was clearly struggling with authority and autonomy. He nodded acquiescence and called in Bakri and Akbar, who'd been outside and clearly weren't happy about being barred. Akbar especially had been second fiddle all the way along, with only his five men versus Bakri's nineteen, now fourteen, and the foreigners. He was older, and twitched in annoyance at the insult to his status.

The gruffness was very visible. Kyle watched as Wade tried another dose of battlefield diplomacy.

"Our government doesn't trust anyone, even us," he said. "It's not like running a unit in the field, the way it was in World War

Two. Now, everything has to be passed up and certified. But we're still expected to be responsible. It's the world we live in."

The locals were slightly mollified, and more so when Wiesinger relayed the suggestion that they find intel. It wasn't his idea, but there wasn't any point in fighting about it. Let him have the credit if it got done.

Bakri nodded and grabbed his phone. "But I can only do this once," he said. "If I'm overheard, I'll be called a conspirator."

"Understood," Stephens said, twitching his moustache. "We'll back you and evac you if needed." It was probable that a phone tap existed somewhere in the chain.

Nodding again, Bakri dialed. The conversation was fast and jabberish, and switched between Bahasa, Achinese, and some other language. The Americans looked askance at Stephens and Akbar, who motioned them to retreat away.

Once in the far corner of the room in a huddle, nostrils full of mildew and sour sweat, the Australian and Akbar began translating for the others.

"He's asking about the Chinese bitch, way to strike a blow for Malays everywhere, show those Javanese bastards how things will be. But he's asking them not to blow up the oil, because it's money. It fits what his position is, and he's not a friend of the government, so no one should twig. Doesn't mean they'll tell him anything, though."

The local and the Aussie conferred, and Stephens continued, "He's really playing the 'Chink bitch' angle, because the Chinese minority runs most of the country. It's a good act. I'd believe him if I didn't know better. He's asking for a piece, asking about more hostages, and can he get some taped footage, but again, we need the oil, don't blow it up. He's offering more hostages, government officials, says he's heard of some Americans and Brits and will try to get them, wouldn't mind a few car bombs on those American assholes. Okay, he's done, more some other time, how's the wife and kids."

Kyle almost choked to avoid laughing. It couldn't have ended quite like that, but still.

Bakri closed his phone, pulled the battery, dropped the phone to the ground, and smashed it flat with his rifle butt.

"And now the government thinks I am part of those scum," he said, his mouth tight. "Between phone calls and abandoning my crops for weeks at a time. But I know who to talk to. Of course, he may only know someone else . . ."

"Good man," Kyle said. "We'll back you up. And if we gap these assholes, you're clean anyway." Though that wasn't a guarantee, and nothing Kyle had any control over.

"Where to, then?" Stephens asked over tea. He brewed every time they might have fifteen minutes. It was good tea, too, the times Kyle had tried it.

"Almost to Lhokseumawe," Bakri said. "Long drive. Then I must ask more questions."

"So let's roll," Wade said.

It sounded to Kyle a lot like their first mission in Pakistan, where Nasima had guided them around, gaining intel by asking at places a well-bred lady should avoid. Then they'd gone there anyway. Then she'd died, shot. He didn't feel the same way about Bakri, obviously, but he still didn't want to see the man die.

Anyway, they were all soldiers this time.

"Less than a hundred kilometers?" he asked.

"Yes. We do not wish to go into the city. We seek Fiktif, south of there and inland."

Another hamlet in the jungle. "What do you know about it?" Wiesinger asked.

"I suspect it," Bakri said. "It was site to a certain situation. The army protects the government-claimed oil fields. There was rebellion and threat against surveying for more gas and oil. So they killed a number of rebels. U.S. Mobil lend bulldozers to bury the dead in a mass grave."

Kyle had seen mass graves in Bosnia. He didn't imagine they were any prettier in fetid jungle humidity. "U.S. Mobil did that?" Besides the moral considerations, that sounded diplomatically foolish.

Bakri shrugged. "I didn't see it. But it's not the first story. And bulldozers were used. Perhaps some manager allowed them to be borrowed and didn't complain. But that's why people want Mobil gone. The money doesn't help us and the Army attacks us. I'm thought crazy or criminal to want to keep it and work with Jakarta. But we could use the money here. Better that than poverty worse than we have now. The money that is supposed to be used for development is used for 'security issues,' meaning more soldiers."

"Anyway," Kyle said, uncomfortable with the situation, "you suspect the town is still involved?"

"I suspect it is largely empty, due to an attack by the Army. But it would be another good, empty place to stage from."

"So let's roll," Stephens said.

13

ONE HUNDRED KILOMETERS—SIXTY MILES—WAS A
trip of about four hours. That was due in part to the narrow,
rutted back roads they took for security purposes. Not only were
they in rough shape, but they lengthened the trip by about 30 percent. Still, despite rain, the roof worked and the weather was warm.
Itchy and sweaty warm, in fact. But Kyle Monroe wasn't one to be
bothered by weather, after almost sixteen years of service. Wade and
the Aussies were equally reticent. Wiesinger shifted uncomfortably
and swore quietly, but had the grace to not complain any more
loudly than that.

They were quite close when Kyle's musing was interrupted by a
horrific explosion.

Someone screamed. It might have been him. He snatched at the
door handle, which wasn't working. It flopped loosely in his grip.
He shoved with his shoulder and the door flew open, letting him
tumble into wet, friendly dirt. It hurt his shoulder, then his ear stung
as he rolled across the butt of his M4. But he was alive and concealed. A quick self-assessment came up with minor burns that
stung, a couple of scratches and a hellaciously aching foot as his injuries. At that he was lucky. A glance indicated a low-quality RPG
round had torn the front off the truck, disabling the engine. It could
just as easily have killed him and others. He didn't see any bodies
immediately at hand, but that was just a glance. He had no idea
what the tactical situation was, other than that they'd been attacked.

There was sporadic shooting. He listened for a few seconds to
place the sources. There was both outgoing and incoming fire, so
they'd tripped something. Likely, Fiktif was being used and there

were outer sentries. Either they didn't know or like Bakri, or they'd suspected he was a threat. But that wasn't important now. What was important was coordinating with his allies and defeating or retreating from the threat. Shaking off the daze, he got to work.

Cell phones. He used a phone more than he used a rifle anymore. But it made sense. "Mel, Kyle. No reportable injuries, alone, ready to respond," he said once Wiesinger answered.

"Understood. We are grouping in two elements, five zero meters outboard from the vehicles. If you find it hot, withdraw rearward. We suspect a perimeter."

At least they were all on the same page. "Roger. Line open. Transiting." He slipped the phone into a pocket and got ready to move. At several dollars a minute, he guessed, the phone was a dirt-cheap way to keep him alive. And he better not see Wiesinger's smartass criticism of phone charges this time.

No obvious threats nearby, sources of fire some meters ahead. Giving himself the okay, Kyle picked covered locations he would use for the movement. The place in question was about thirty meters away, but he couldn't see a damned thing through this growth.

Sensing movement, he froze and tensed on the trigger. An Indonesian was ahead. Then he saw an Aussie with the man. Dammit, who the hell was who? This was getting bad in a hurry. When it was just you and the bad guys, it was easy. In uniform with professionals, it was doable. Now was a goatfuck in the woods with everyone in part uniform and part civvies. The only uniformed forces were officially allies to them and threats to their actual allies. He didn't dare hold his fire against a possible threat, and didn't dare shoot an ally.

Nor would he be distracted again.

Oh, shit, that hurt! He'd run into a limb that poked him in the cheek, right under the eye. He dropped and cringed, blinking as his eye teared up. Dammit, Kyle, get control, stop flopping like a fucking chicken! He'd twisted his left ankle slightly, too. Remember: Bad guys, good guys, and shooting. Methodical and professional.

Somehow, he made it another few meters, and was seen by someone who recognized him. They approached cautiously, leery of both pursuit and his trigger. Then he was being dragged into a hollow with a long, rotten trunk as cover. It was Haswananda, with one of the men helping her, as Kyle was near twice her weight, more with gear.

"I'm fine," he motioned. "Saya tidik apa-apa."

"Yo, buddy," Wade said softly from a few feet away. "Ready?"

"Yeah," he said. "A poke in the eye with a sharp stick."

"Ouch," Wade said without any real emotion. It was an acknowledgment rather than a commiseration. "Mel figures the village is defended."

"You don't say." It didn't take a lot of intel for that.

"Estimating the force about equal to ours. He wants to push in and capture if possible."

Kyle grabbed his phone. He wanted to hear this straight even if it was going to be the same as Wade told him. Passing orders down the line could result in "Capture France" becoming "Invade Russia in the winter."

"Mel, Kyle here, mostly functional and fully mobile. You say we're to capture?"

"Correct. If we can acquire a prisoner we'll get intel some way. Or else we overrun the position and look for what we need. If they're making this much noise, they're a target."

"Understood. Where do you want me?"

Wiesinger's basic plan wasn't too bad. An initial counterattack heavy on the ammo and light on the movement. The Aussies were to encircle one side, the north, and their locals the south. Bakri's remaining force—he'd taken another casualty—was to set a forward perimeter. Kyle and Wade were to attack designated targets. If they could get a good reversal, it was likely the enemy would rout. They didn't have highly trained Western special operations troops and Army Rangers as backup. Skulk and retreat was likely what they did anyway.

And if the village was willing to make that much noise defending against a casual intruder, they had something to hide, that was certain. Serendipitous intel, if they could handle the situation.

Bakri's men and women moved forward, slipping from tree to shrub to undergrowth. Kyle and Wade followed behind, SR25s out, with Wiesinger behind them holding both M4s. Bakri's RPG gunner had two rockets left. The RPK machine gun had one drum of seventy-five rounds. They couldn't spend ammo at U.S. rates for this.

The village was barely visible as shapes. There were figures, but no clear targets yet. And they weren't shooting. It wasn't likely they thought the threat gone, so they had to be doing something else. Kyle paused, forcing his breath into long, slow, silent heaves, and watched for clues.

Then he pulled his phone out.

Dammit, Wiesinger had closed off. Likely to save batteries or money, neither of which Kyle gave a damn about right now. Both were assets to be expended. He redialed in a hurry, and waited through three rings. While waiting, he donned the headset. Better to have it directly in his ears than trying to fumble it and a rifle.

"Mel." Wiesinger finally answered.

"Explosives. I see possible crates and someone who may be capping something."

"Shit. Understood." Wiesinger clicked hold and apparently made other calls. He was back in less than a minute. "You and Wade will take targets designated by Stephens and Fuller."

"Understood and standing by. Out."

Kyle had dealt with explosives far too often to be reckless. These sideshow freaks were perfectly capable of screaming, "*Allahu akbar!*" and blowing themselves to smithereens, taking any bystanders with them. That was bad enough when the amount was in kilograms. When it was in tons . . .

He'd been there once, facing a nutcase with a suicide switch and tons of explosives in the same room as he. He wasn't eager to do so again, to put it mildly. His stomach flopped and felt acidic.

When his phone vibrated again, he clicked it as fast as a video game button. "Kyle."

"Kevin Fuller here."

"Go." He slipped the headset on, so he could keep hands free. He didn't like the wire hanging, but he could deal with it when not moving.

"Reference: central building. North side. Two men. Both targets."

"Roger, but going to take a few minutes to get into position."

"Better bloody hurry, mate. They've got what looks like a twenty-four-kilo crate."

"Understood. Tell Wade, too. He may be better placed."

"Roger."

Kyle shifted laterally a few meters, to find a thin spot in the foliage. Yes, there were two men, who appeared to be fitting detonators to blocks of TNT as they looked around furtively. And fifty pounds wasn't so much, really. If he could get it to detonate, it would solve several problems. But was it TNT, and was TNT sensitive enough to detonate if shot? Or could he hit the detonator?

Better try for the crate. If they ran, it averted the problem temporarily. If he scored a bang, it was gone, they were gone, and a message would be sent. The blast radius shouldn't be great, the effect would dissipate in the open quickly, and the jungle would buffer it. It was worth a shot.

The range was about one hundred meters. The fire had slowed to an occasional pot shot, as the attackers strove to coordinate their efforts while the defenders were hesitant to move on the offense for fear of being flanked or running into an entrenched force. Standoff.

Luckily, the new injury had been his left eye. He winced as he closed it to aim. Add in the dust damage from earlier, and his eyes felt like hardboiled eggs.

Through the scope, Kyle could see one of them place a block end-down on the crate and start twisting a detonator into it, with a fuse of some kind, probably Detcord, trailing. He took careful aim and dropped a round right through the block.

TNT *would* detonate if shot, or else he'd hit the cap. The flash caused his scope image to stutter. The bang shook the ground. His scope image returned at once and he could see lumpy red paint splashed across a wall. That was one of the two men. The crate became splinters in the air, falling, twisting lazily. The other shattered body fell several meters away, and wisps of steam arose from a hole in the loam. A few moments later, a stiff breeze swept past him in the woods. It was hot, chemical, and gusted in his ears.

All hell broke loose. He'd accomplished something, alright. He'd kicked a nest of hornets. The fire wasn't accurate, but there was a lot of it.

Fuller read off another target. "Some arsehole just came out of the darker gray hut. RPG. Tracking . . . he's moving left." Weapons fire interrupted the conversation.

"Skulking behind a pile of rubbish and a Toyota?" Kyle asked between bangs. There was movement there.

"That's him. I'll tell Wade, too."

"Got it."

This was getting hot. There was something going down here.

The enemy grouped into two elements, with hard cover of the buildings and several prepared fighting positions. That gave them a significant advantage for defense. At the same time, they probably didn't know what size force the Americans and allies were, or where the elements were. This was where snipers, serving as designated marksmen, could be the force multiplier that would break the engagement.

Only . . . Wiesinger wasn't giving any orders, even for a frontal assault.

Kyle dialed again. "Mel, Kyle here, I recommend we take targets of opportunity, with just enough supporting fire to convince them we're still here. Press the advantage with accurate fire and we can inflict substantial casualties."

"Uh, yeah, sounds good. Not quite what I had in mind, but I approve. Stand by."

Not quite what he'd had in mind probably meant he'd frozen. The fights were getting stiffer each time. Which should give him time to adapt, but didn't seem to. And now he was de facto commander of a platoon, which he'd never done in wartime and barely done in peacetime.

So that explained the knot in Kyle's guts. Usually at this point in a fight, he was icy calm and detached, coming back to reality and shakes afterward. His unconscious knew there was a problem this time, and he was nervous. Troops needed effective orders. If not, they needed ineffective orders so they had something to do and something to bitch about while they got shot to hell. No orders meant a goatfuck.

There was a slight increase in the rate of fire. Wiesinger had apparently ordered everyone to shoot accurately, which wasn't a bad modification. If a handful of rounds came close and one hit, the psychological effect would be considerable.

Kyle sought what appeared to be an RPK machine-gun muzzle, and waited patiently. A head rose just slightly after a while, and he was able to punch a hole through the top inch. The resulting thrashing and waving of limbs indicated debilitating pain at least, maiming or death possibly. Either way, there was no more shooting.

The enemy was figuring out that they were outmatched. They fell back in a coordinated withdrawal, with suppressing fire at likely threats—a few bursts were within meters of Kyle, but far overhead. Then the fire tapered off. Kyle had no targets, and shortly, no one did. Silence reigned, part of it hearing damage from lots of shooting.

Wiesinger called through Kyle's headset. "Kyle, we're going in. Follow Stephens and cover the left, south."

"Roger that."

Kyle rose slowly and crawled forward. The silence could be a ruse or there could be a few suicidal types behind. He waited until he saw the Aussies spread on the ground at the edge of the cut growth, which was in the process of growing over the abandoned village. It was amazing how fast things grew here.

Then Kyle was easing out onto the grass, which was still eight inches deep and enough to hide him in part. Wade was a few meters over. Wiesinger wasn't in view. Either he was slightly behind or was waiting to see what happened. Under the circumstances, if he really was acting as commander, that was reasonable. Kyle couldn't help but feel it was an excuse.

But that assumed the man wasn't just behind his field of view. And that wasn't something to fret over with threats in front.

Bakri's men moved in, and shortly, it was clear the village was vacant. There might be a few wiggling wounded or someone cowering behind, and those could be threats. But the main force had retreated in the face of their fire.

Which seemed too easy to Kyle. If he had a defended position with hard cover against small arms, he'd have held it until the attackers ran low on ammo, which on foot in the jungle shouldn't take long.

But then, these groups were experienced, smart and trained, but not to the level of Rangers or the SAS. And they couldn't afford casualties. Besides losing force, they'd lose manpower for working and income.

The force regrouped in the middle, still low and covered by buildings in case of a counterattack. They put sentries in an outer perimeter, and swapped ammo around to even things out. It was getting pretty tight on ammo. Wiesinger had shot a lot. The Aussies had been frugal, but had borne the brunt of the advances thus far. Kyle and Wade wound up with fifty rounds in each drum and four thirty-round magazines apiece. It was heartbreaking to destroy the extra drum, but it wasn't realistic to expect enough ammo or time to reload a hundred rounds. Kyle stripped his empty Beta and scattered the parts. He bent up the feed lips and cracked the drum as best he could. No one would be using it now.

There wasn't time to do much cleaning, but he did open the receiver of his M4, wipe the bolt carrier down, and add some more oil. The SR25 hadn't been fired that much. He gave it a few drops of Cleaner Lubricant Preservative and grabbed an MRE to munch on. It was the last complete one he had.

The good news, he supposed, was that with ammo and food gone he had much less mass to haul.

It took less than five minutes to quarter the area, and everyone was ready to proceed.

"Time to search in detail," Wiesinger said. Bakri nodded and sent a team of five men on a patrol.

"Considering the reception, we might not want to eat anything here," Wade said.

"Good advice," Stephens agreed. "Could be anything from worm-infested dog feces to strychnine waiting for us."

A bang shook the ground. Kyle dove for cover with everyone else.

"Booby trap," Stephens reported. "Some wounded arsehole had a grenade."

"Right, let's cover this slowly," Wiesinger said.

"Not yet, Mel," Kyle cautioned.

"Why?"

"How many bodies do you see?"

Wiesinger looked around. "Four . . . five."

"We have two. We were attacking a defended position. If they have five casualties, where's the rest of them? Could be fifty, a hundred of them."

Wiesinger looked stunned. He hadn't even thought of that.

"I'll take perimeter," Stephens said. "Akbar," he called, than rattled off some local language. Kyle didn't need to catch the few words he did to grasp, *Expect a counterattack and look for bigger booby traps.*

"Mel, there could be entire buildings full of tons of explosive here." The hair on his neck was standing up as he recalled a low building in the Carpathian mountains that was on the receiving end of this logistical chain. There'd been a ton there. How much could be here near the source?

"Yes, but we need intel."

"I agree, but don't open anything without a lot of peeking."

"Understood, Kyle." Wiesinger appeared to get it about 5 percent. Hopefully, that was enough.

If not, what happened next was. There was an outhouse behind one building, on the edge of a clearing that had once been a field. It was a modern composting type with a "turd gobbler." One of the locals approached it and eased the door open. A flash, a bang, and the whole thing caved in, taking his body with it.

As the shouting died and the current bizarre state of normalcy returned, Kyle vowed to squat behind a tree if he needed to go.

But Wiesinger seemed to get it now.

"No one go into a building. Watch for wires. Scan windows first."

The search was rather brief. It wasn't that there were traps there: There weren't any buildings not trapped or mined. The personnel had departed into the jungle on foot, leaving a mess that they hoped would nail anyone who found it.

Kevin Fuller was tasked with setting charges to detonate the whole mess. He moved cautiously but quickly. He did a recon and stared through a few windows before starting. He returned muttering curses.

"Whole bloody thing's wired together," he said as he took a crate and started fixing detonators. "Looks like about a thirty-second delay. We, or whoever, was supposed to discover one, start on it, and the whole shebang goes off, taking anyone in the radius with them. Looks to be about six tons total."

"Doesn't that defeat the purpose of having it stored to send elsewhere?" Wade asked.

"No, it's not an efficient setup. Instead of fusing every charge, they've fused one crate per building. The rest will follow as at least a low order blast. There's a wired remote, a radio, and the trips and timer. Moderately competent. Anyway, we put this there and run," he said, pointing at a building that had been rather stuffed, including crates under beds. "Denies them this load, and will draw a lot of attention they don't want."

"Attention we don't want either," Wade noted.

"Right," Wiesinger said. "But we've got to take it out or wind up facing it."

"No argument, Mel. It just sucks to be us."

"Gentlemen, I've learned in the last few days that there's a lot not covered in the manuals."

"Yes," Kyle agreed. Just yes. Was the man getting a clue at long last?

Ten minutes later, they moved out in column, slowly and with lots of advance and flank. The Indonesian Army would be after them, as would the terrorists and any other groups who may have been told by either side that Bakri was a betrayer. The first time Kyle had done this in Pakistan, the risk was of a firefight with hicks. The second time, it was of arrest by non-friendly Romanian government agents with a reputation for brutality or a confrontation with a mad bomber. This time, it was pretty much three different well-trained armies who might hunt him.

No pressure.

Nor had they acquired much intel. Anything sensitive had either been taken along by their enemy or was protected by bombs. It was frustrating and creepy.

Still, they'd been accomplishing the secondary objective. A *lot* of explosives weren't going to be used for terror. Seven or more tons so far, which had to represent a big investment on someone's part. But they didn't have the key figures behind it yet, so it wasn't a solid win.

Their first two missions had been completed, even if as bloody messes. Not every mission could be perfect, but dammit, Kyle wanted to get the people, not the tools. The people were the real threat.

A tremendous roar announced a mass detonation behind them. That felt good. Several tons of explosive would not be used to attack civilians. But it was all a matter of shoveling back the ocean with a pitchfork. More would be forthcoming if they couldn't hit the people behind it.

So they had to work on that.

Stephens and his locals were making phone calls, trying to get a few more hints. With active cooperation four ways, they might find a lead. Who had heard of the new hostages? Wasn't it great? Did they need more? Who would know? Is there a number? Yes, please leave a message. It's regarding some further supplies I may have for him. Yes, we both know what we're talking about. Allah Akbar.

It wasn't too suspicious. The rumor mill was in full swing. One source credited Bakri with taking the hostages. Another claimed Bakri had set up the last ambush by the Kopassus. Bakri took it in good humor, suggesting a few other rumors to be put out about himself. It was brave of him. He was effectively a marked man no matter who found them. Anda scowled. It was rather obvious her interest in Bakri was more than professional, and she didn't want to see him dead.

Rumors they got aplenty. Facts were far fewer, and most were items they already knew.

Kyle noticed everyone bunching up. They were looking at something, and he headed that way, alert for any threats others might not notice. There was a break in the trees, which probably indicated a human feature. In this case, it was a road for lumber operations, well rutted, muddy and red. With tire tracks.

Fresh tire tracks. They'd either called or had vehicles waiting.

Bakri said, "I'll send a team back for vehicles."

"Yes," Wiesinger said. "We'll wait." They melted back several meters, so they could just see traffic, but should be invisible themselves as long as everyone was still and low.

"We'll take a gander a klick up or so," Stephens said. "Try to find out how many and where."

"Roger that."

Kyle and Wade covered each other while doing a better cleaning of weapons. In this humid, warm environment it was necessary. Kyle had been amazed to find mildew on the nylon strap he used to carry the M4, but it was that soggy here.

Anda and a man he didn't recall came by with fruit they'd gathered and some dried beef. The fruit was warm, obviously, but sweet even if there were some insect bites. The beef was tough and not very flavorful apart from a hint of salt. A couple of stringy bits stuck between Kyle's teeth. He knew they'd be there a day or more before he could floss or pick them out. He'd had that problem before. Still, it was fresh fruit and more protein. He was grateful.

Stephens and his scouts returned. They infiltrated their own lines with barely a word or sound. Once alongside the Americans, he reported.

"Looks like a dozen vehicles. Heavily laden. Some signs of either a struggle or casualties with limps being loaded. All have new tires. Heading north and west, farther into rebel territory."

"So we follow and ask as we go," Wiesinger said.

"Bakri, can you pull off being a lost member of the party trying to catch up?" Kyle asked.

Bakri paused a moment. The idiom likely threw him off. "I can do so. Whether they believe I can't say."

"Do what you can," Wiesinger said. "We've got to be close."

They didn't have to be, Kyle thought, but likely were. Which also had its dangers when dealing with men who knew they'd die and believed in a cause.

Bakri led one squad of his troops along the edge of the road. The rest stayed in the trees with Kyle and the others. They were several meters in, where they could hide easily from vehicles and still be close enough to provide fire. Sooner or later—hopefully sooner—a vehicle would come along. Anyone using these remote roads was likely to have at least rumors.

Of course, they might also not want to stop for a group of armed men, or they might be hostile.

Kyle crawled over and under brush, thick and green and rich with rot and fungus. The jungle was an organism that sometimes seemed to move visibly as it fought to reconquer the holes people scraped in it. Down below, Bakri and his friends walked through thick, yellow mud rutted by trucks and rain. Roots and grasses were already attempting to move back into those wet depressions. It was easier, not to mention safer, to be where Kyle was.

That explained the difficulty of tracking anyone here. A single sentry with a wired phone or cell could give an innocuous signal to shut down any threatening operation, once he sighted a threat on the road. Coming through the jungle limited one to carried gear only, and posed risks of terrain and traps. Helicopters were very viable, but one had to have a suspect before using them, and could expect to take fire on approach. It would take elite troops to handle an insertion fast enough to matter. This whole area was riddled with small villages scraping out a living in crops, which was quite easy with the climate and rainfall, or providing labor for oil and timber operations. It was a wonder there wasn't more violence.

It was near dusk when a vehicle came along. Twelve hours of driving, fighting, and rucking. Kyle was as drained as his Camelbak. The only good news was that there were enough trickles and streams that they were able to filter water and refill the Camelbaks after a fashion. It took some time to pump the little filter, and twice in three days they'd had to scrape the element clean of mildew and sediment, but they did have fresh water. Far better than the cold desert of northern Pakistan. Not as nice as the hotels of Europe. Same assholes trying to kill people, including Kyle Monroe.

The incoming truck was a thirty-year-old Mercedes diesel stake-bed carrying timbers. Kyle and the others slunk into the growth so they wouldn't be seen. The temptation was always to stand and stare, but the necessity was to stay out of view. Especially when the party might be nervous.

Kyle heard voices, including Bakri's. They were loud but not antagonistic. Kyle felt his phone, wondering if Syarief with the remaining phone would call for backup, but nothing happened. Shortly, the gears clashed as the engine revved, and the truck drove on. A few minutes later, Bakri called, "Come out!"

He was past the treeline himself, barely visible in the grayness. "I think I know where," he said. "We'll need lorries. The fuel cost is starting to hurt me, too."

Wiesinger took that as a hint. As they closed up, still squatting, he drew out a thousand dollars worth of rupees. "I can issue more if need arises."

"You are gracious and I thank you," Bakri said. Unlike the Pashtun, who would only take money as a carefully offered gift because of their pride, the Achinese were far more practical. This operation was costing them in people and money, and they saw no reason not to make the U.S. help defray costs. Kyle found that a lot easier to deal with. Which was good, because Wiesinger obviously wouldn't have been able to handle Pakistan.

"Where, then?" Wiesinger asked.

"Closer to Lhokseumawe. That makes sense. They didn't take the hostages far."

"Is your source reliable?" Stephens asked.

"Yes, because they're not a source." Bakri grinned. "I just chatted, said we were patrolling for trouble, how were things? And they said they were fine, but had been ordered by members of the Movement to stay away from Impian, and we should, too. They expected a government fight soon. I can't think why else they would order that."

No, there wasn't a reason. If they suspected trouble, they'd simply be silent. Telling people to stay away indicated a fear. It also wasn't that smart to offer that information, as they had no idea of Bakri's loyalties.

Which made sense. They were simple local workers and the exact type of intel source one looked for. The captors had to know their cover would be blown eventually, so were just stalling with the warnings to stay away. Tactically, they were better off in a village they controlled than the people who'd tried similar approaches in Iraq, where the neighborhoods were all shifting alliances and no one controlled an area.

They moved deeper into the growth and set up shop, with one third on, two thirds sleeping, and got a few hours rest. It was near midnight before the transportation arrived. Kyle awoke bleary-eyed but ready to move when Wade nudged him, and started down the slope. The trucks of their local transport element were getting to be pretty messed up. He made note to suggest to Wiesinger that any balance of cash be donated to the cause. These people had put out a lot of effort and resources at great personal risk already.

Once aboard the vehicle, they were served packs of rice and chicken with fruit and peppers. It was cold but filling and tasty and welcome. Rations had been very scarce for most of a day. A solid cupful of food with a good drink of water filled his belly and helped revive Kyle, but he was still groggy. He went back to a fugue state between wakefulness and dreaming. It was too rough a trip to sleep, but he was too fatigued to stay conscious. He'd passed days at a time in such states, reacting and responding as needed without actually recalling events until afterwards. Add in a tight position and slumped posture, and he was all aches within minutes. He knew it wasn't going to be fun.

Thirty kilometers, less than twenty miles. They scattered the four trucks with drivers along a couple of kilometers of road, and left a couple of cell phones. Two trucks were hidden well enough to not be a problem. The other two were noticeable, and ripe for questions or robbery.

Back into the woods. They hunkered down again, well hidden under brush and deadfalls with ponchos for cover. They operated in darkness, using red-lensed flashlights sparingly, and set sentries. Anda and Iverson slipped off to recon the target. It was a wonder, Kyle thought, with all the skulking around, that they hadn't run into one of the other national patrols. But it was a long archipelago and the numbers involved were small. He wondered why they were having so much success at recon, but that was because all the factions were theoretically allies. They didn't fight each other. Except now they were.

He reflected now was a good time for this mission. In six months it was going to be ugly, with GAM possibly fratriciding and no one trusting anyone. The end result of this operation was going to make it much easier for the government to crack down on the rebels, because all cooperation would end. They'd be picked apart and defeated in detail.

Which wasn't his concern. His concern was U.S. interests. The Indonesians needed to fix their own country. He couldn't and wasn't allowed to, and was smart enough not to get involved, even if it hurt like hell to see it coming apart. Anda, Bakri, Akbar, all the others could be dead before the winter.

He drifted into a restless sleep, not helped by the knotty root poking him in the back.

14

THE NEWS WASN'T GOOD THE NEXT MORNING.
Iverson and Anda came in, wrung out, near delirious, and barely
coherent. They couldn't confirm hostages, but did confirm a large
armed force.

"At least one fifty, likely two hundred, bare chance of a few
more," Iverson said. He accepted a cup of tea and sat back under a
canopy. He was blond somewhere under the dirt, and perhaps
twenty-two. But he had a maturity years beyond that. His wrestler's
physique was suffering from the ordeal, but he swallowed water at
a prodigious rate. He'd recover.

Anda simply curled up to sleep, her head on her pack, clutching
her rifle like a teddy bear, and looking disgustingly cute. It was a
natural camouflage. She was one deadly little lady, and a better
infiltrator than Kyle. He respected and was amazed by her talent.
And she could walk him into the ground. These people lived on
foot. Cars were a tool or luxury, not something taken for granted.
Thus they had a lot of early training he wished he, and especially
younger recruits, had.

Kyle looked around. "We've got twenty-four now?" The odds
weren't promising. No matter how good the training and the troops,
numbers did matter. He leaned back against a tree and stretched.

"I can get another ten men in less than a day," Bakri said.

"We need to approach this slowly," Kyle insisted, "but I don't
think we have a lot of time."

"No. The Indos are about to start shooting 'terrorists' by the
thousands in retaliation for the hostages. Morally I concur, but
they'll include our friends. Politically . . ." Wade tapered off.

"Yeah," Kyle agreed. There was nothing else to say. It was certain that the Indonesian military would wipe out most of the insurgents. It was certain that whatever word did leak out would be greeted largely with support, and it was certain the ringleaders and brains would use it as an excuse to escalate. With oil fields at stake here and elsewhere, and a goodly supply of suicidal fanatics, the situation would get a lot worse before it got better.

"The thing is," Wade said, "most people *will* agree with Indonesia, and if they don't do something, China and India will start operations.

Long term, I'm not sure the U.S. or Europe is going to like the direction that will take. We've got to get this fucker fast."

"I agree," Wiesinger said. "We'll have to sacrifice some stealth and supply intel to the Indonesians."

"The problem, Mel, is that the terrorists have sympathizers in the Indonesian military. This is the ongoing problem we face on these missions. Most of our allies are firmly behind us, but a handful are antagonistic or have simply been paid off."

"Yes, so we'll be picky about who we talk to," Wiesinger said with a smug look. "I'm not stupid, sergeant."

"Not implying you are, Mel," Kyle said, shaking his head. *Hell no. I'm on record as stating so.*

"So you gentlemen put together a briefing. I'll review our options regarding who to talk to."

Paperwork, Kyle thought. Yes, that's the way to win a war. Paperwork. Against an enemy, with no defined force or mission, that evaporates into the jungle at a moment's notice. Just bury them in red tape and international cooperation. You go, Colonel.

"Yes, Mel."

Wiesinger walked toward their personal lodging while hefting his laptop. He seemed incapable of handling a decision without an office, even if that office was a couple of ponchos over rucks with a square of bark as a door.

Kyle and Wade simply swapped looks of disbelief. Kyle wondered if Wade had the same churning in his stomach that Kyle did.

Stephens had been silent. "What's his story, then?" he asked now.

They gave their ally a brief rundown. It didn't appear to surprise Stephens much. "That's dealable with. As long as we know what he's like." The sergeant was cheerful enough, and had likely seen similar things.

"Actually, I think he's correct on one count," Wade said.

"Huh?" Kyle asked.

"We aren't set to try to find a ton of explosives in an industrial area, nor do we blend in. The Indonesian military has to handle it. Besides, the hostages are more our department, and we've already cost the terrorists a few tons of hardware. Really, more cooperation at the beginning, with Bakri and Jack, had we known about him," Wade nodded at their counterpart, "would have made a lot of this unnecessary."

"We might find the charges," Bakri protested.

"And if you're around when it goes off? Who will get blamed?"

Bakri chewed his lip. "Yes, that's true. But I can't contact the government. If they find out what I have done, they're not likely to respond well."

"So it's up to Wiesinger," Kyle said. "But I bet State won't listen to his theories. If he starts calling on his own authority, we can bet on a leak blowing any chance of interception. There goes our credibility, there goes the U.S. image over here, there go we, out of the country if we're lucky, jail if not, and then a week later the thing blows up anyway."

They sat for several minutes, no real ideas developing. The desired result was clear, but the path wasn't.

Wiesinger came back. "Well, that was pointless," he said. He sounded angry.

"No dice with State?" Kyle asked.

"I got treated like a beggar with his hat in hand," the colonel said.

"Mel, we concur on telling the Indonesians. We're just not set to handle this."

"That option was just taken away from me. I may be the officer on the spot, but some bureaucrat with no experience in the field gets to ride over my operation."

Kyle almost had to laugh. Wiesinger really was starting to get it. If he'd just see his own role in this, he'd snap into place and have it. Somehow, though, he didn't think that was going to happen.

"So," Wiesinger said, a thoughtful look on his face. Kyle wasn't sure he'd ever seen such concentration. Rather than quoting the book, the man was actually going to make a judgment call. "If we don't tell the government, but they find out anyway, we can deny any involvement. All we need is an incident like the last one, with the government showing up. Only we arrange it with the right people at the right time, so they nail the terrorists instead of us."

"Dangerous, Mel," Kyle said. "But I agree, for what it's worth."

Wiesinger nodded slowly. "Bakri, we need the best evidence you can find on where they're hiding or traveling. Then we arrange a brief, loud mixup and some frightened phone calls. The trick is to leave just as the cavalry arrives and not too soon or too late."

"My job is finding them." Bakri grinned. "I do not envy you yours."

Another patrol went out. Wade insisted he'd cover it. Kyle tried to argue with him.

Wade said, "Dude, you're ragged as hell. You've had less sleep than either of us, you've been handling a lot of the thinking, and you need more rest. Take it." Wiesinger wasn't in earshot. He was sleeping.

"Okay," Kyle agreed. Yeah, he was exhausted, fatigued, tired, hungry, and feeling chill in the 70-degree night. The dings and bruises didn't help. The offer was too good to pass up, and he fell back against his ruck to sleep, covered from the sky by a poncho slung over branches.

When Kyle awoke, it was to Wiesinger batting his foot. "Kyle," he snapped. "We've got too much to do to spend the day in bed."

Kyle didn't shoot him. He just rose and grabbed his toothbrush, then snuck out to a bush to drain. He calmed down enough to deal with the prick by the time he returned.

Wade was back, too. He was out of water and grabbed the first offered canteen. It took him three gulps.

"I was impressed," Akbar said. As Stephens's local guide, he'd gone along. "It was dangerous, getting so close."

"How close?" Kyle asked.

"Thirty meters or so. I don't see any signs of them there. No food taken in, no guards. It's an armed camp and a staging area, but it's not where they're holding hostages."

"That's too close, Wade. Don't do that again," Wiesinger said.

Wade gasped. It appeared to be from the exertion of the march back, but it was probably to cover his annoyance.

"It was dark, they weren't inclined to go past the tree line, the ghillie covered me very well, and I didn't see any night vision in use. Should I write a report for you?"

He was half joking, from his tone, but didn't flinch when Wiesinger said, "Yes," and brought out his laptop. Kyle groaned silently. What a way to run a war. In fact, he had half expected and half hoped it would have failed by now. Jungle humidity and muck was rough on equipment.

Wade made no complaint. He sat down with the computer in his lap and sipped more water while he ripped out a report. He typed fast. Kyle was okay, but Wade could throw text at probably eighty words per minute. In less than ten minutes, he had a substantial statement of what he'd seen at the village, detailing persons, weapons and other equipment, supplies, and events. It was almost certainly a rebel training and operations site. There didn't appear to be anything that would suggest hostages. Dead end.

They all gathered for a strategy session.

"Okay, let's look at the map," Kyle said. "They were captured here, and were taken south. We have rumors of them here . . ."

"And here," Bakri said. He pointed.

"So what people are offering definitely places them within a few miles of us," Stephens said.

"Drive and do it again?" Bakri asked.

"Slow, but I don't see a better way. Where else does this particular group operate?" Kyle frowned.

"Tolol. But they . . . might be there," Bakri said. Obviously, he had thought of something.

"Oh?"

"It's a setup near an oil field. Not an actual village, but people shelter there. There was a killing there of an employee protest." He paused over the awkward phrase. "They shot the protestors. It might appeal to their odd sense of justice to do the same thing back."

"I'd say you're right." Hell, yes. That was very likely it.

"Why?" Wiesinger asked.

"Just how they think, sir. Revenge. Blood for blood. Lots of these groups. It's certainly worth looking at. And we might just find our head asshole there. And pull off the original plan, too."

"It's here," Bakri said.

"Not far."

"No, ten kilometers. Walk?"

"Better drive," Kyle said, grimacing. "How close is safe?"

"Three kilometers."

"Doable. How?"

"Access road here, along the edge of the oil field."

Kyle looked at the map. It wasn't much of a "field." It was more clearings in jungle and brush. Roads were typical industrial access, graveled.

"Won't they notice us?"

"If we're seen as a group, yes. Weapons hidden, and in one vehicle at a time. Luckily, you won't be remarkable as Americans."

"Good."

Kyle and Wade had traveled in all kinds of disreputable vehicles. The Land Cruiser was actually one of the choicer ones. It even had working air conditioning. So of course, Murphy had to compensate with a spine-grinding ride over a "road" that was rutted, rooted, and full of sinkholes in the soft loam. Kyle was glad to be in front. Wade was stuffed in with Wiesinger's bulk and two rucks, and Anda and another were squeezed in the back. The "gravel" road was not in great shape. But that seemed to mean it wasn't used much. There were few signs of even temporary repairs. If this was an important path, it would have been paved.

It didn't take long to reach the location they'd set for their staging area. Bakri slowed and drew over to the roadside. Kyle eased the door open and slid his feet out, then sank slowly into the mud. The door creaked slightly as he pressed it gently closed. Wade was behind him, and a splash indicated Wiesinger stepping in a puddle. Kyle swore under his breath. It probably wasn't loud enough to attract attention, and no one was around, but dammit, the man was an increasing liability.

Shortly, their squad was hunkered together in the woods beside the road. The humidity was palpable, but that would help damp out sound, too. Small advantages added up to victory, and Kyle would take them.

"Which way from here?" Wiesinger asked.

"Three kilometers that way," Bakri said.

"How long?"

"An hour if we move well."

"What's our plan?" Kyle asked.

"We need an evac route first," Wiesinger said. "Stand by." He wandered off a few feet and messed with his phone.

"I would truly like to be kept in the loop on these discussions with HQ," Kyle muttered to Wade.

"But that would compromise secrecy."

"Maybe. Or else he's just a self-centered asshole who doesn't think enlisted people matter."

They stopped, not wanting to drag their allies into the discussion. Stephens had expressed his position, and Bakri said volumes with his silence on the matter.

Wiesinger came back. "Okay, we have extraction in process. It will take a few hours. So we should use that time to patrol. Not too closely, but I recommend three recons. Two on this side, one on the far side of the road."

"Growth is thinner over there," Bakri said.

"Right. Who do you recommend?"

"Anda of course."

The slight woman smiled and nodded, then grabbed another by his arm and slipped away in just her clothes, no ruck. A single look back let Kyle focus on her calm eyes, pouty lips, and clear skin. She really wasn't bad-looking at all, even out here. Cleaned up, she was probably very pretty. He wasn't sure if she'd ever attended a dance or dinner. Probably not.

"Kyle, you and I should make one patrol. Mister Stephens, will you go with us?"

"Right," Stephens agreed with a nod. "Send Wade and Kevin? Iverson can cover here."

"Okay. Bakri, we'll be back in . . ." Wiesinger stopped to think.

Kyle did the math in his head instantly. Three kilometers of rough terrain each way, an additional hour for margin, two hours of recon. Nine hours in this growth, you moron. You've read the books.

"Eight to nine hours," the colonel finally concluded. It must have been thirty seconds.

"Permission to leave rifles with Mister Iverson, Mel?"

"Why?"

"We're recon, don't need to carry weapons. If it gets to that we'll want to run more than fight. That's what sidearms are for." He slapped his Ed Brown, which was in the standard issue holster on his right hip, where it had been since just after they landed. He would even have bathed with it on, if they'd been able to bathe. A few minutes of rain dancing had been the limit of external hygiene, plus a few diaper wipes to sanitize hands. They were all pretty rank.

"I'll take an M four," Wiesinger said. "If you wish to take just a sidearm, I'll allow the choice. Wade?"

"Just the Beretta, Mel. Rifles can stay here."

"Right. Let's decide who goes where."

As they each chose a direction to approach the facility from, Kyle reflected on the irony that the officer whose standard-duty weapon was a sidearm wanted a rifle, while the two rifle-toting grunts wanted to travel light.

Kyle didn't need much for this. He had his water, his pistol, and four extra eight-round magazines and his tactical load-bearing harness. He removed the rifle magazines from it and filled the pouches with a few spare MRE packages, mostly fruit and crackers, with GPS and cell phone. He took the ghillie, rolled up, to don when needed. Fresh camo paint, brown, just to darken his skin against notice. Most people used way too much green. Nature was brown, when it came down to it.

Stephens was waiting, wearing a dun T-shirt and carrying a little day pack. His web gear was hung with full pouches. He had a Browning Hi-Power in a thigh rig. His equivalent to the ghillie was a camouflage nylon fishnet with burlap braided in. It was a cover rather than a garment, but should work fine. All were wearing nearly identical "boonie" hats, broad brimmed and soft.

Wade and Fuller were already out of sight. "Time to walk," Stephens said, looking plucky and cheerful. Kyle fell in behind him, with Wiesinger bringing up the rear.

The first kilometer was easy, at a relaxed crouch, simply alert for anything obvious. There were no signs of human passage and the animal noises were typical. It took about twenty minutes to cover the distance, or the speed of a slow stroll. They ducked from tree to bush to hollow, avoiding standing tall or crashing through brush. The key, even when in safe terrain, was to not draw attention.

The second kilometer was slower. They dropped to low crouches alternating with hands and knees. They dispersed across a front a hundred meters wide and ten deep, each taking his own route. Discovery of one should not mean discovery of the rest. That allowed at least a chance for the other two to escape discovery or exfiltrate, while the one who was sighted would be very loud and aggressive once escape was impossible. If the enemy was busy, they might not notice non-threats, like two other troops departing.

It took about an hour to cover that kilometer, which left almost two in their timetable, plus a spare, to cover the last few hundred meters before commencing recon proper.

Kyle stopped about two hundred meters back, in mid-afternoon light. He found a nice elevated spot with a thick tangle of greenery, which he hoped wasn't poisonous in some fashion, and got ready to work.

His first task was to draw a map of the facility, using GPS, a parallax range finder, and a terrain map. From there, he scaled his own sketch on grid paper with a protractor and scale.

There was a pipeline running through about 100 meters beyond the buildings, and off in the distance, across a field that had been burned clear and was partly regrown with scrub, was an oil well capped with a boom-type pump. He estimated it at 525 meters.

There were four buildings, low, block with metal roofs. One had windows on the back side, which faced them. The others did not.

One had a small vent window on the side. He kept making notes and drawing. They'd compare all three later.

While scanning with the M49 spotting scope, he kept watch for Anda. Nothing indicated her presence, and he knew she was there. Nothing. Excellent.

He did see sentries. Three of them, carrying rifles. They were squatting in shade and watching the road, totally bored. That made sense. There was no real threat. But why sentries? Obviously they feared something.

His phone buzzed and he clicked it to answer while digging for his headset. "Kyle."

"Jack here. Stand by." There was a click.

"Mel here."

"Good, we're conferenced," Stephens said. "And should be clear of any interference."

"I've got a map. Windows on the second building from the left, south, are facing us. They raise. Can't see inside well. There's stuff in there, but the shadows make it hard to discern."

"Understood. Assume the sentries are trained well," Stephens said. Kyle nodded. He'd been suspicious anyway, but now he saw the threat.

"Oh?" Wiesinger asked.

"That's a soldier, an Army deserter, I would guess."

"Oh?" Again.

"He has most of a uniform, a fairly military bearing, and an SS carbine," Stephens patiently explained, saving Kyle more aggravation.

"Agreed," Wiesinger said. Kyle tried not to groan. It had been fairly obvious to him what they were looking at. Likely, all Indonesians looked the same to Wiesinger. He really wasn't that observant. They swapped intel for ten minutes, or more accurately, Kyle and Stephens did. Wiesinger did at least confirm a lot of what they saw, but offered little additional insight. He even complained about the cost of a conference call by satellite. Kyle clicked off and then sighed.

Two hours of observation gave good, refined maps and not much else. There wasn't much activity. What there was was hard to pin down. Kyle positively identified a dozen people in addition to the three guards. But there were signs of habitation elsewhere—clothes hanging out a window to dry, fresh trash, other indications. There could be a large force here.

Kyle's phone buzzed again. It was Wiesinger. "I'm calling this done. Let's head back."

"Roger."

It was important to make the exfiltration as smooth and silent as the infiltration. Being done didn't mean the threat level changed. Kyle was half afraid Wiesinger would stand up and walk out, as he had a few days earlier. But he showed decent aptitude. Though Kyle did spot him from fifty meters away when they were a good kilometer out. He almost tripped over Stephens, who was within ten meters when he whistled and stood.

The three headed back in the same skulking crouch they'd used on the way in. Kyle felt . . . odd. Sometimes he felt lighter afterward, threat diminished. Sometimes he felt more burdened from fatigue. This time, he didn't feel much of anything, which was bothersome. He was either too fatigued or too mentally strained to care. That was dangerous.

Anda had different intel when she returned. "I saw through the door. Looked like a child."

"Child," Kyle muttered.

"How sure are you?" Wiesinger asked.

"Quite sure. Small height. Long hair. White socks and short skirt or trousers."

Kyle said, "Probably. I can't think why else we'd find someone of that description."

"I count twenty-three men." She gave descriptions and locations.

"Hell, I counted five more, allowing for the ones that positively compare," Kyle said. Wade counted two others, and Stephens another. There were almost certainly more than that, asleep, on patrol, or out running chores.

"What's our approach then, gentlemen?" Wiesinger asked.

"Backup," Stephens said. "Tell the Kopassus where it is. Let Indonesia take the bite. They're competent, they'll have troops trained for hostage rescue specifically, and can overwhelm this group."

"I agree," Wade said, after swapping a glance with Kyle.

"I am not happy with the government," Bakri said. "But if I am not associated with this group, my position is better. I agree it should be done."

Wiesinger looked anguished. He was being advised to throw the book away and violate policy, procedure and State Department regs. But this was Defense, not State, and Kyle frankly didn't care what some suit with a theory thought. It took several seconds, but the man came to a decision.

"I'll call," he said. "Who do I call?"

Everyone looked askance.

"I'll search online," Wade said. Once connected, it took ten minutes for him to find an Indonesian government Web site with links to the Aceh province. A bit more digging turned up a phone number to the regional police office.

Wiesinger dialed the number. "Do you speak English?" he said. "Yes. I know the location of the two hostages, the woman and her daughter. Yes. My name is . . . Robert Richardson." He hadn't paused much. Kyle grudgingly gave him credit. "Yes, they are in the facility at Tolol. There are more than twenty men armed with rifles. I saw others to the west—" They were actually to the east—"but they seemed to be a different group. When I spoke to them, they said they were scouting timber. That is all I can tell you, but they are definitely there right now." He clicked off.

"So we wait," Stephens said.

"Shall we back away, boss?" Kevin Fuller asked.

"We might want to. Assume they'll use the road or aircraft."

"Why stay at all?" Wiesinger asked.

"Because someone will escape, no doubt, and we want to get that person for more intel. Meantime, we're surveillance."

Another night in the dark, but they did have food that had been brought by the now departed trucks. There was no reason to have anything within several kilometers that could be seen by infrared or visually from the air.

It wasn't very satisfying, Kyle thought, to travel halfway around the world and do recon the locals were capable of doing, just so Uncle Sam could have an official report, and then hand the task off locally. But really, this was a bigger event than they were trained or equipped for. The second round of hostages and the second bomb were too sensitive. But they'd intercepted several tons of explosive and tracked a source, as well as taking out one sizeable cell. It might seem like nothing but days of hiking in rain forest and watching state-built villages, but it had been worthwhile. The action of the last two missions had spoiled him.

"That's what it's like, mate," Iverson had said, while Fuller and Stephens nodded. "We spend weeks or months creeping around in the crud, calling back reports, and they tell us we did a fine job. Half the time we don't know why."

Kyle couldn't see them in the dark. They were just vague shadows. It was really dark when the moon was down, with canopy above them and growth all around. That did mean they should be well hidden from anything passing by.

They ate cold rice with water buffalo, veggies, and peppers. It was a bit slimy here and there where fat had congealed, but it beat the Chicken with Noodles MRE all to hell. The Chicken with Noodles was flat, tasteless, bland slop. With that at the bottom end, and some very tedious unseasoned rice in other parts of the world, the local cuisine was quite respectable.

Everything was in their rucks, and they sat back wearing them. They might have to move on a second's notice. Besides the risk of losing gear was the risk of leaving evidence. Even if it didn't trace back to the troops, it left suspicion, and it was sloppy. So they all sat geared up and ready to move. The Americans had their helmets back on, in case of fire. It was easier to wear them than carry them. Kyle's had been in his ruck since they landed, the soft headgear preferable for what they'd been doing. But if they were to move fast or take possible fire, he was going to wear it. He and Wade also had thin, police body armor that would stop many pistol rounds or slow rifle bullets. It couldn't hurt and might help, especially against fragments.

There wasn't a safe way to play cards without risking losing some of them. Talking was contraindicated. Dozing wasn't approved of, but was hard to avoid. At least the weather was clear and warm, and it was easy and comfortable to drift off. Kyle did so, trusting the active sentries and enough of the rest to be alert. It wouldn't take much of a hint to wake him, anyway.

Some hours passed. The military could respond within minutes by helicopter, as they had done many times before. They could respond on the ground within an hour or so. It might take time to confirm the story or marshal troops, but the response itself should be quick.

Or it could be that they were infiltrating already. It was near midnight. The infiltration might be silent, but once the shooting started, everyone should know. Still, the delay was frustrating.

"Where the hell are the government troops?" Wiesinger called in a harsh whisper. He was obviously agitated.

"I doubt they're operating on our schedule, sir," Kyle replied. Every time you added a variable, things got more screwed up. Relying on any government to be there when you needed it was foolish.

Now it was possible the target would bail out again. Enough well-placed attacks and they'd figure out, if they hadn't already, that someone was closing in. In which case, they'd either disappear, go on the offensive against the much smaller unit, or pull some kind of fuck-you gesture that would kill a lot of people.

Really, this mission had been badly set up, and it was probably no one's fault. State didn't want foreign troops with U.S. intel, neither did CIA or NSA. There wasn't any way to field a large enough U.S. force. The choice of troops was wrong. Just like operations that required stealth, where the first reaction of the President or Congress was to toss in the Marines, who were first class shock troops, but not the kind for a subtle approach. Here, snipers for intel and precision shooting were being used as deep roving scouts and in a position that really required a suit with connections. Last time they'd had that, they'd just provided the shooting. This time . . .

The whole point of using snipers was to avoid a face to face. In Pakistan, even when things went to hell, the al Qaeda target had had no idea what was happening until Kyle put two bullets through him. A face to face here was inevitable.

"Right," Wiesinger said, "I'm going to make a close patrol to get better intel. Bakri, I need one good man to go with me. Kyle, Wade, you provide overwatch from here. Stephens, can two men follow for backup against patrols, in case I need to exfil?"

"Yes, Mel," he agreed. "Though I recommend extreme caution. Any discovery at this point could be bad." He was trying to hint that the idea was insane. If the military showed up on the ground while he was patrolling, Wiesinger would be a target himself.

"I concur, Mel," Kyle said. "I advise against it. Very strongly. But I'll give you all the backup I can if you go ahead."

"I am," Wiesinger said. He didn't get the hints. He didn't sound scared, either. Either he was a lot braver than Kyle had figured him for, or he really had no clue what he was doing. The first was bad—it indicated recklessness. The second was potentially lethal.

"I will go," Anda said. She looked scared but determined, which Kyle thought was a good combination.

"Ah . . . why you?" Wiesinger asked, and the question was obviously posed because she was female.

"I know the area and are small enough to hide. Scout is what I do," she said.

Bakri just nodded. "Hati hati," he said. *Be careful.*

"Okay," Wiesinger agreed, looking unsure. "How long do you need to get ready?"

She checked her weapon, unslung her pack, downed most of a canteen in a few gulps, and said, "Ready." She had the SS1 she'd acquired as booty from some battle across her chest and extra magazines filling her pockets and disrupting her slim figure.

It was almost amusing to see big, bulky Colonel Wiesinger confused and unable to handle a woman half his age and size.

"I'll call with reports," he said. "Expect us back in six hours." He shouldered his patrol pack and ported the M4 he held.

"Mel, if you can't talk for stealth reasons, blow Morse Code into the mouthpiece," Wade said.

"Uh . . . I don't know Morse," he admitted.

"Well then, blow SOS if you're in trouble, wait five minutes and fire a burst if needed. We'll find you," Stephens said reasonably.

"Right." He stood for a moment, nodded at Anda, turned and walked off.

Everyone held the tableau until he was safely distant. Stephens snickered tightly. While his advice was workable, the intent had clearly been to shake the man up.

"I think he missed the whole point of being a sniper," Kyle muttered.

"Actually, Wiesinger's almost like a sniper," Wade said. "Except that he does it up close, without a lot of thinking, and doesn't aim much."

"Funny. I notice you tell more jokes when you get scared. How funny are you feeling right now?"

"Like Robin Williams, only darker and younger," Wade replied, glibly and without pause.

"Shit."

15

FAISAL WAS DISTRAUGHT. AT SOME POINT, THEY'D crossed a line into sin. He didn't know where that line was, but he was quite sure they were past it.

Killing infidels and using them as object lessons for others was something he'd learned to accept.

However, the current events struck him as very wrong. Imam Ayi said that they were not to rape or torture the new hostages, and expected that to satisfy Faisal's reservations. The group would hold them safely until the West succumbed to logic and faith and removed itself from Islamic affairs. Or, as seemed likely with the recalcitrant dogs, the hostages would be quickly and mercifully killed to reinforce the demand. Their bodies would hang for all to see.

Except, no matter the scripture and Ayi's interpretation, Faisal couldn't accept the killing of a little girl and a woman as justified. At every prayer he begged Allah to intercede and to show him what was right. By Muslim law, these were innocents. By Western law, both were merely family members and not active participants. No matter the shock value that would be gained, some things were unacceptable to God and man.

Only, God was silent.

He needed the advice of the imam, but couldn't admit why. That was disturbing in itself. But if he asked gently, wisdom might reveal itself bit by bit. He rose and left the hut, grabbing his rifle on the way. The walk would help him phrase his questions.

The foremost question was why he could get no answers. That was innocuous enough. He had that ready to ask when he reached the long, low building that served as the mosque, and also as Agung's headquarters.

The imam had tea steeping, and invited him in. Faisal studied him. His eyes seemed to be both at peace and driven. An intensity of peace. Faisal longed for that feeling himself, rather than shadows of doubt. He wouldn't mind a beard, either, rather than the scraggly growth he wore.

He accepted a cup of tea, and inhaled the aroma. It was sweet and fresh and fragrant. By itself, it cleared the mind. A sip teased his taste buds, adding another sensation added to all that he felt.

"You are troubled," Imam Ayi said. "Tell me and I will see what I can offer."

Faisal hesitated, then blurted out, "What does it mean when God is silent?"

"God is never silent. One simply has to look for Him and His message. What is your question?" he probed.

"I am not sure, Pak Hajji." Pak Hajji, father of the Haj, the pilgrimage to Mecca. Would Faisal be able to make that trip someday? "There are issues of rightness in my thoughts that I must find answers for. Issues I can't properly put into words." He was leery of discussing his qualms. They might get him removed from the cause, his loyalty questioned. He was totally loyal and wished to serve, so he saw no point in suggesting otherwise. He held the cup tightly, not realizing it.

"Then pray as you do. Sooner or later, when Allah sees fit, He will show you your questions and answer them. You will know."

"Thank you, Pak Hajji." The wisdom was beyond his comprehension. He'd have to think it over for a while.

"In the meantime, drink tea and think. I find it clears the mind."

Faisal hoped something would.

Kyle was woken from a restless sleep at dawn. "What?" he asked, snapping awake and raising his rifle.

"Easy," Wade said. "Wiesinger got captured."

"Oh, fuck me." No, it wasn't a nightmare. It was all too real.

"Yeah. Anda came back, said they got close and he insisted on going in closer. Someone saw him and they gave chase. Firefight, which Stephens heard an hour ago, and they seemed to want him alive."

"Right." Something occurred to him, and he asked very softly, "How sure are we of Anda?" Ripples were running up his spine. She had suggested going, was trying to charm Bakri, and he might not be catching hints of . . .

"She is in tears, sobbing and hyperventilating. Poor girl thinks she's created an international incident by 'losing' the American colonel."

"Good. I mean, not good but . . ."

"I understand you."

"Right," Kyle said. He was still waking up, eyes gritty even without the abuse of previous battles. Damn, they were taking serious fire this time. Worse than Bosnia. He was starting to get a grasp of what an earlier generation had dealt with in Vietnam. They had his increasing respect and sympathy. This crap sucked.

"So we need to figure out what to do," Wade hinted.

Kyle woke up the rest of the way. He was the ranking American. Non-Americans couldn't decide on this mission, so he had the job.

His buzzing phone saved him from an immediate answer.

He fumbled it out of his pocket. "Kyle," he answered.

"Kyle, Gilpin here. You heard about the colonel?" Mister Gilpin was the civilian executive for General Robash. He had a hellacious GS something pay grade and was retired military himself.

"Yes, sir. Working on it now. I'm guessing you got a call from the enemy?"

"Yes. What the hell happened?" The man might be a civilian, but he had the decision-making authority that General Robash did. This was no time for bullshit, and Kyle wasn't the party on the spot—the colonel had made the decision himself.

"He was on a patrol and got captured. The other element returned and told us."

"Right. Well, they want a million dollars into an account, they want Indonesia to release a number of prisoners, and they're adding him to the bargaining over the 'imperialistic venture between American corporate whores and the Javanese occupiers known as Pertamina.'"

"Sounds about right. What time frame?"

"Twenty hours from now. Frankly, we won't miss a colonel, or even you guys. No offense, it's just the situation."

"I understand perfectly, sir. That's why we're here. But you need those civilians."

"At the very least. And any leads on the explosives for the oil terminal. We concur on that threat, and that's now the priority."

"That one's a bitch, sir. Could be a truck, a plane, lots of people with crates. Really nothing we can do about it. Which is why I concurred with the colonel's decision to tell Jakarta." He was sticking his neck out here.

"Yes, so did I," Gilpin said. "And State are a bunch of assholes

who can't make a decision without a formal meal and a five-star hotel. General Robash is trying to take over again, and I'm insisting he
rest, so if you can offer any good news, it'll help him, too."

"Best reason of all, sir. How is he?"

"On his feet most of the time, sitting some, a bit short of breath,
some pain, bitching about not being able to smoke cigars again, and
threatening to kick someone's ass if he's not given a sitrep."

"Damn! That's good news." He smiled. "But we'll do everything
we can, especially if it'll keep the general calm."

"Good man. I know you can't give me nightly briefings to tuck
me in the way Wiesinger does—" it was the first Kyle had heard of
that, but hardly surprising—"but do keep me in the loop."

"Will do, sir. What do we do about exfiltration?"

"From where you are, we're going to get you to the north coast.
Any advance notice appreciated. You'll be met by mammals."

Mammals. SEALs. It wasn't a code per se, it was just a way to
avoid using a word that would excite anyone overhearing it at either
end. "Understood. Can you get a satellite map of this facility . . ."
He grabbed a map and read off coordinates. "Those are as close as I
can get."

"I downloaded those to Wiesinger's laptop earlier."

"Dammit, he didn't tell me or make a backup."

"I'll send them again. Which account?"

Kyle spelled out his address and said, "So let's get it done."

"Good luck."

Kyle clicked off. "The general's bitching up a storm about not being in charge," he said.

"Hot damn, he's going to make it," Wade said with a grin.

"Yeah. And we're in danger of losing a colonel."

"Good news all around," Stephens joked as he came up behind.
Kyle and Wade might think that, but would never say so out loud
except in very secure quarters between themselves.

"But we've got twenty hours, and those two civilians are at stake,
too. Suggestions?"

"Only one," Stephens said. "But I don't think you'll like it."

"What?"

"You get into the building where they are, off any threats, and
shoot anything that moves."

"If we can get in there, I'm all in favor," Kyle said. "If the government shows up then, we're in a much better bargaining position,
even if we have to relay by phone. They don't dare risk the

hostages." He got the laptop plugged into the phone and dialed the server. A large file was waiting for him.

"I dunno," Wade said. "Jakarta knows that. Does their local commander know that?"

"Well, a frontal assault is out," Kyle said. "I'd want ten times the force we have to consider it."

"How about a frontal diversion?" Stephens asked. "Make a lot of noise, draw them out, subject them to fire from as many directions as possible while another group goes in to get the hostages? We are trained for that."

"Good, but are the three of you enough?" Kyle asked.

"Dunno. There aren't really any good options here."

"Or else we try to nail them through windows. Then the distraction, then the assault."

"Problem is," Kyle said, "we need more troops trained on sniping and hostages than we have, plus a good infantry commander as well. I hate to say it, but we could really use Mel here."

"That just tells me how much things suck," Wade said.

"Yeah, well, we knew that. Let's talk to Anda."

The woman arrived at once. "Yes?" she asked as she slipped into their shelter.

"Tell us everything you can." Kyle laid out the map he'd sketched and the satellite map. The latter was more accurate, the former probably easier for an amateur to read.

Nodding, she began. "We approach, low and slow. Then we crawl. We come in this way here," she indicated on Kyle's sketched map. "There is large tree with big roots. Good to hide, but causes trips. Then we move over here. We see backs of buildings like you did, but not more. We walk all the way south around to here, where I was earlier. Mel say he want to get closer. I tell him two hundred meter! Two hundred meter safe, closer are plants cut. He point to high area of ground, say he stay behind it and look. I move back by pipe, keep small. He crawl out, low. Did good, but patrol come between us. They see and move in. He try to shoot, get one, only wound. They circle him. He try to move back, but they move in closer. He did kill one, but rifle snatched and he beaten to ground. I wanted to help, but would have meant catched."

"Yes it would. You did the right thing by coming back," Kyle said. Son of a bitch. The asshole had been too eager on low ground, hadn't waited to ascertain patrols, and probably wanted to show up the local girl, if not Wade, by moving closer to prove something. Moron.

And they'd taken him without shooting him. So they might want intel, too. Would they kill him for publicity, or keep him and torture him? The deadline was much more important now.

"Sorry. I want to help," Anda said.

"Anda, you did a good job, really. This isn't your fault. Mel should know better. But you say he was alive?"

"Yes, beaten down, dragged along, then marched on feet. They took his things."

"Well, boys and girls," Kyle said, "that gives us an additional complication, seeing as we're bound to rescue Mel."

Jack gave a wry chuckle and said, "Better you than me, mate. Better you than me."

"And they know he's American, since they called our contact. That makes him much more valuable to them as someone to threaten. At least as they see it."

"Well, we can't leave him behind," Wade said. He didn't need to add *much as I'd like to.* "So we'll take him into the calculations. And the gear he lost."

"Right. Which included some grenades. Wonderful."

Faisal stared at the American. The man was *huge*, bigger than Wismo, and most of it wasn't fat. Certainly he was overweight a little, but he was not far from two meters tall, possibly a hundred and ninety centimeters. He had to break one hundred kilos. His shoulders were almost twice as broad as Faisal's.

And his gear was all military—rifle with grenade launcher, ammunition, knife, water bladder. It was nice gear, too. Faisal lusted after it, and they'd said he could have his choice of an item after they beheaded him or if he was ransomed. The men who'd caught him had already demanded the rifle and backpack. Faisal thought that back-mounted canteen a marvelous creation. Or the GPS unit.

He tried not to be nervous as he eyed the new bargaining chip. The man was blindfolded and tied to a chair. He should look terrified, but didn't. That was a disturbing sign.

Or was that a tremor? Yes, it was. He was scared, and that was reassuring. Faisal caught his courage again. Yes, the man should be afraid. He was helpless.

"Untie me and fight me like a man," the American said. Faisal spoke English and understood him. The tone was arrogant and demanding. Even tied, there was no submission.

"Guess you don't speak English," his soon-to-be victim said. "But if you're expecting me to beg, fuck you."

Faisal didn't catch the obscenity exactly. He'd heard it around the oil crews and knew it was rude. Still, this man was not acknowledging his position and didn't seem remorseful over the political situation. He was conceited, smug. It made Faisal furious.

At another level, he wondered what killing this man would accomplish. He left, silently, as he'd been told. Silence was intimidating. Actions, not words. He glanced at the Chinese woman, stoic and silent in her terror, and the little girl, wrung of all emotion. She was too young to grasp what was actually going to happen. All she knew was, she was scared. Days of tears were gone. All she did now was sit.

He really wasn't sure where this was to go. Part of him wanted revenge for his brother, dead because of a fight at the oil refinery. But the actual killing had been by government troops. The Americans were mostly making a living, like the Indonesians they hired. A damned good living, especially the executives, but they weren't hateful. This was a soldier sent to fight their war, so he was a fair target. But he was also a soldier like Faisal, and he could see himself in a similar position. The Quran spoke of mercy, but was that mercy misplaced on enemies who'd show none? And what of a man's wife and daughter? Yes, it would pain that man, but was it really necessary for innocents to die?

It was a quandary he'd needed to consider for some time. Except . . . he hadn't discussed his quandary with Imam Ayi. He'd been afraid to mention the real issue. Why was that?

It was because he knew what reaction that would get: He would be disgraced and driven away, mistrusted and sneered at. Just for questioning. Yet did not the Quran tell them to test their faith? It shouldn't be a sin to ask for guidance.

Unless the matter at hand was a sin, in which case none would speak of it.

Faisal opened his eyes and sat back. A sudden surge flowed through him. Despite their differences, Ayi had been correct. He had spoken the truth. Through an object of sin, a message had come regarding rightness.

It was time, and Allah had made his wishes known. God is great, all praise be to God.

And now he knew what he had to do. It might mean death or disgrace, but it was Allah's wish. I am but a slave of Allah, he thought as he stood. There was no fear within him, despite the dangers to his body and reputation. There was no fear, because his soul was ready to do Allah's bidding and await His justice.

• • •

The tiny platoon slipped closer. Kyle was quite impressed. This group knew the jungle, knew patience and stealth. They didn't move without orders, and didn't stop without them. A few weeks of professional polish and they'd be a first-class infantry unit. If there was any way to get the Indonesian government . . .

No, politics wasn't his venue. Stick to the military side. Though he didn't crave to read about Bakri, Anda, and the others in some newspaper.

They'd spent all day approaching from two different directions. It was afternoon again. Kyle was starting to hope for some kind of ending. He hadn't dared take his boots off in the last three days, and his feet were itching, stinking, and hurting. He worried about athlete's foot or other fungoids, rot or rash or infected blisters. People died from foot problems. While that wasn't likely, he didn't crave long hospitalization or surgery, either.

With this many people, twenty-three without the colonel, they were creeping. They were paired or in threes, watching each other, watching behind, watching ahead, trying to close in on a facility that had to know of their presence. It was a wonder everything hadn't been loaded into vehicles and taken away, but there were no vehicles on-site—probably due to the risk of discovery. The captors apparently didn't crave to walk out on foot with two distinctive hostages who might be seen by aircraft. That actually was a slim risk. Visibility from altitude while moving wouldn't be clear. But without troops experienced in aviation, they probably didn't know that. Clearly, they were reluctant to enter the jungle where other forces might be.

So the good news was that the bad guys were bottled up for now. The bad news was that they were cowardly, sociopathic little fucks to start with, and might panic. Kyle had heard this called "Murphy's Law of Thermodynamics." Things got worse under pressure.

He ate scraps as they moved. Leftover apple jelly from the MREs, some hard candy, cracker sections. Likely they'd see no more food until this was over.

It was near dark, and he was losing track of days and time. It was never really light down there. But in twelve hours at most, the hostages would be killed. It didn't get much darker than that. The Straits of Malacca and the surrounding waters would be full of Chinese, Indian, Singaporean, American, and Indonesian vessels, and everyone would want a piece of GAM and any other rebels. The low-intensity civil war would turn into a slaughter. It could even become major.

Kyle was still musing, awaiting a report from the advance scouts. They were within a few hundred meters of their target, just over a kilometer, choosing every meter before moving, relaying messages by crawling and delivering them in whispers, or by hand signs.

A hiss ahead alerted him to an approach. He looked up to see Anda, Syarief, and someone who seemed to be their prisoner.

"We bring him to you," Anda said. "As my commander order. I would kill him."

"Well, let's see what he says," Kyle said, looking him over. Skinny, young, dressed in cheap clothes. Anda might really want him dead, or just be playing bad cop. He'd see where it went.

"My name is Faisal and I know where the hostages are, and also an American soldier."

"Shit. This is either Lady Luck rolling a seven, or painting us with a huge target," Wade said as he shimmied up.

Kyle nodded. "Fairy Godmother or Practical Joke Department. Guess it's my call."

"He says. I don't trust him," Anda said.

"What can you tell us?" Kyle asked.

"Will you give me your word you will not harm me? Or let the government?"

"Son, I can't speak for the Indonesian government. I won't harm you. I can ask our State Department to help you if you help us. But I won't promise something I can't deliver." He noticed the boy—man—didn't ask for protection from the locals. Either he thought that fruitless, or he was willing to take his chances. That meant something. But what?

"That is fair," the boy agreed. He was in turmoil over something. "I must tell you something bad."

"I'm sure we've heard worse," Wade said.

"It is I who cut the head off Keller. I know now it was wrong and not Allah's way." The words were out in a rush.

"Jeeeezus," Kyle burst out. Rage gripped him, and he gripped his rifle. But he didn't raise it. Anda swore quietly but brightly in Achinese and reached for a knife. Wade waved her down.

"I was to do it again tonight, to the woman and child. But I cannot. It cannot be right, it cannot be just. So I disobeyed and came here." He seemed very small and helpless, terrified of dying on the spot. But he stood and waited, eyes wide.

"Son, in this, your God and mine agree. You've done the right thing, and we'll do anything we can to help you." Kyle forced his hand to unclench. The kid had fucked up on a global scale, and in a way that Kyle was morally and legally bound to kill him for. But he'd admitted his mistake and wanted to make amends.

If he could help them bring down this gang of scum, that just might do it. Especially since he was facing death from his own people at this point.

"Can you draw a map and give us names and numbers?" he asked.

"I can."

Kyle wasn't inclined to trust the boy. He could still be a ruse. He wasn't saying anything yet, but there was no way this boy was leaving before Kyle was sure of his loyalties. Otherwise . . . well, he wasn't going to say anything. But shooting a spy was legally and morally safe, and far less bothersome than things Kyle had witnessed on this and other missions. He clutched at his knife briefly, because he didn't have a suppressor for the pistol, and would need a quiet kill.

Once provided a pen and paper, the boy began to draw. The map fit what they had on download and from recon, and the layout described was reasonable. So far, so good. The kid almost certainly didn't know there was a satellite providing data. Nor was he likely to know the limits of its resolution, so he could be challenged with the magic power of the satellite if need be, "magic" defined as "technology the boy couldn't explain and didn't understand." As to their own patrols, he could probably guess. He seemed to realize things were about to explode.

"How many people?"

"I'm not sure. It changes. More than one hundred today, I think. Many came in from an attack on the place where bombs are built. Kopassus, they said."

Kyle avoided grinning. That his group was being mistaken for the feared Indonesian elite was good for PR. Wait until the word got out that it was six Westerners and a handful of locals.

"We heard about that attack," he said. "You're sure this is where the hostages are?"

"Yes. A Chinese woman and her child and a large American man who speaks rudely."

"That would be him. Windows and doors on that building?"

"Windows are glass, but usually raised. Doors are wood."

That was useful. "Okay, we'll talk this over. Anda, don't kill him. Just keep him here."

"I understand." She switched to local dialect and said what had to be "Come here, boy."

Kyle liked her. She took no shit. She shot well. She was quiet and soldierly. There were some women like that in the U.S. military, but not nearly enough. Political Correctness had devalued soldiering in favor of a sensitive image. That called for cute uniforms, makeup, and press releases, and no harsh language. Anda probably didn't own makeup or heels and swore like any other soldier, in a very crude, personal fashion. She was all business.

As the locals left, he turned to Wade. "Right, so what do we do?" Kyle asked. He was running out of ideas.

"First thing is to get around to where Mel is," Wade said. "And then we need a large force to raid. In addition to a large diversion while we snatch him."

"Or," Kyle said, "what they *think* is a large raiding force. How much ammo do we have?"

"Close to a thousand rounds for all three weapons."

"That should be enough."

"What do you think?"

"I think we have the locals go in the front, led by Stephens. They stop short of actually entering. They fire the place up loud. We're in place to shoot through the windows at anyone we see. Requires us to be spread slightly, and we'll need our phones open. Thank God Wiesinger let us all bring phones. One phone would be as useless as tits on a boar."

"Right," Wade said. "Call the Aussies and Bakri? And we need to get a bit more on our informant. He showed up too soon."

"Have him call Jakarta and report it just before we attack?"

"Good. Very good," Wade agreed, grinning a yard of teeth.

Kyle called Stephens in and explained the situation. Stephens agreed.

"Sure, I can make noise. I also have no authority to throw my command away. Much as I want to help, noise is it, then we have to skedaddle. If I wind up dead, command will kill me. If I don't wind up dead and create an incident, command will kill me. I was advised today in no uncertain terms that unless I have a reasonable prospect of acquiring more intel, I'm to sever ties and continue my mission, which is recon and intel for my government."

"Understood, and I'm sorry for taking you for granted," Kyle said. He realized he had been. The Aussies were not part of his command.

"Hey, glad to help. Wish I could stick around. Sounds like a bit of a bash."

"That's the idea. Anyway, you lead the locals, get a good amount of attention and fire, and we'll shoot from the back. If we can break loose or secure our objective early, count on us to drop quite a few." Kyle figured they could each drop a man every five seconds if they weren't seen. That was conservative. If no one tracked their fire, one minute would be twenty-four out of the hundred dead. But that assumed they secured their objective. Likely, they'd be extracting under fire. Which was going to suck.

"Now, who's carrying the hostages?"

"I'll carry the adult," Wade said. "You lead. If Wiesinger's healthy, he can carry her. That leaves you or I to take the child."

"And if Wiesinger's injured, we toss him a weapon and bid him good day."

"Nice thought, isn't it?" Stephens smiled under his moustache.

"Oh, I'm serious," Kyle said. "Our mission is the civilians first. Wiesinger's expendable, and I was told so on the phone. If he can't walk, I toss him a spare weapon—" other than his Ed Brown, which he wasn't parting with—"and he can cover the rear until backup arrives, either Indonesian or American. But I can't and won't jeopardize the mission for a commander who got himself captured."

"You sound so upset by that," Wade said.

"Maybe. I do hope we all come out. It's a pride and professionalism thing." He'd lost two people on these ops. He didn't want to lose a third. Disliking the man made it harder, if anything. Kyle didn't like being a judge of worth. Too much like playing God.

"Right. Let's get the details down further. We know they'll get fucked up anyway," Stephens said.

"Explosives," Wade said. "Bakri has that TNT."

"We use it?" Bakri asked.

"Some of it," Wade said.

"Good. We need detonators," Kyle said.

"I can spare some," Stephens said. "Fuller has a few. I can get resupplied."

"It also detonates when shot," Kyle said.

"Frequently," Stephens agreed. "But you can't bet on that. Use detonators. We should have some fuse you can light with a flame. We usually use a firing device, though."

"God, I'd hope so. Wish there was some way to put timers on them."

"I can do that," Fuller said as he arrived to Stephens's wave. "I have some. Usually they're for minutes or hours, but they'll dial down to seconds."

"How hard to activate?"

"How much risk can you face? If they're preset for time and mounted to the charge, press the button. But there's no safety."

The skin on the back of Kyle's neck crawled. A backpack full of HE and await a button to get pressed on something.

"Okay, with an M four, an SR25 and a spare for use on arrival, plus grenades, extra explosives and shock factor, we should be able to make a good entrance. I want small charges I can toss outside to keep threats at bay once we're in. I want something small enough to toss inside as a flashbang, even if it might cause minor injury. And I want a couple of large ones, a couple of pounds, that we can toss as ersatz artillery."

"Doable. Boss?" Fuller asked.

"Go ahead. I'll account for the fuses and detonators."

"Understood. Give me a few minutes." He nodded and slipped away.

"So," Stephens said, "we make a lot of noise, kill as many as we can?"

"By all means," Kyle said with a mock bow.

"Thank you, Sergeant. Most appreciated."

"My pleasure."

"Mine, actually. But lots of noise and body counts. You use the distraction to rescue the damsels and the ogre. Let me know as soon as you've done that, because I need to didi mao like no one has ever maoed before."

"Yeah, it would be embarrassing if you got caught."

"It would bugger all. You yanks have a huge government, a corporate interest here and a lot of firepower. No one will fuck with you much. We live in these parts and have to deal with Indonesian refugees and smugglers, pirates and politicians. We dare not get caught."

"I understand," Kyle said. "I'll see that it's mentioned in the appropriate places that you not be thanked for the risks you aren't about to take since you aren't here."

"Good, as long as we all understand that."

"Okay, that's the rough plan. Now, for finer details . . ."

16

FAISAL MADE THE CALL AS REQUESTED. KYLE GOT THE number from Gilpin, after a brief debate. Wiesinger probably could have had more authority if he'd just demanded it as necessary, rather than being a toady. Kyle called directly to the local military district this time—though "directly" was subjective. He had it patched through the military to a civilian line and back to Indonesia through some other cutout so it couldn't be traced.

After two rings, a male answered, "Malam." *Good evening.* Kyle handed the phone over to Faisal as soon as he confirmed contact.

"My name is Faisal Rachmat. I am reporting the location of the Chinese hostages, and an additional hostage who works for the oil company," he said. They'd decided not to admit to American military presence just yet. Stephens and Akbar were listening to his prepared speech, ensuring he followed the plan. So far, Akbar was nervous but agreeable. Like Bakri, he hated the government, but knew there wasn't much choice in this case.

"Yes, a woman named Lei Ling Park, now Madden, and her daughter Suzanne Kii Madden. The American I don't know the name of. The head of the camp is Agung, and Imam Ayi is advising them. The explosives for the oil terminal are to go off at noon. They left here aboard a lorry, gray, thirty-five-hundred-kilogram capacity, Mercedes . . ." He rattled off all he knew. It shouldn't take more than a few minutes for a military operator to realize this was real intel, not a hoax. It might be a setup, but it wasn't a fraud.

"I am doing it because I know it is wrong to kill women and children. The Achinese do not need this kind of reputation. Please stop the terrorists, they are enemies of us both." A moment later he handed the phone over to Stephens.

Stephens spoke briefly. "That's what we have. Hope the information is useful, mate. We're departing now. Goodbye." He handed the phone over to Kyle. The Aussie's voice would confuse the government further as to who and what was involved.

Kyle stared at the phone as he clicked it off. "Well, that's that. Well done, son. You've just become a good guy."

"What must I do now?" He looked nervous, excited, and a bit bothered.

"You stay with us," Kyle said. "We may need more information." He also wanted the kid where he could watch him, and might need to shoot him. It was a cold thought. Meantime, he'd have to deal with fighting with one foot in a bucket.

The platoon split for the last time. "Don't forget to call," Stephens said, grinning and batting his eyelashes. Kyle snickered. With that, the locals and the Aussies disappeared like ghosts. The local contingent was already on its way to the staging area. The Americans' gear was with Bakri, who had detoured away to provide vehicles for exfiltration.

Kyle felt very alone then. It was hard to find a more hostile area. At this point, anyone they met was an enemy. And some were putatively on the same side, which meant shooting at them was undesirable.

Kyle sucked down water. He was going to be expending a lot of energy shortly. It was hot already. He'd be soaked in sweat, and wanted extra liquid on hand. Other than that, he had weapons, ammo, body armor, and technical gear totaling fifty pounds or so. There was nothing light about infantry work. He would feel much more secure in the armor and helmet. It was familiar, so it was psychologically protective, too. But he couldn't wear the helmet and reach the scope properly. Given a choice between better defense and better offense, he chose offense. It was what he did, after all. But there was no point in lugging the helmet for later, so Bakri had it. Kyle would just have to be exposed for the duration.

"Okay," he said, and pointed. Wade slipped forward as point man. He walked carefully, lest his ghillie tangle in the brush.

They slipped into a position from which they could cover the building where the hostages were supposed to be. The "supposed" was key. They might have been moved, if anyone noticed Faisal gone. They might have been killed. Or they might be there with a battalion around them. But doing nothing definitely meant they'd die.

At a nod, Faisal moved out between them. He was painted with camo and covered in burlap rags that hung loosely. It wasn't as good as a ghillie, but it was easier to move in, had been fabricated in a few minutes and still broke up his silhouette. Kyle had the suppressor on the SR25 and was prepared to dump a match round through his brain if there was any sign of dissemblance. The kid might be remorseful, but he'd also sawed somebody's fucking head off. That wasn't easy to forgive.

Kyle followed along. He took tall steps to avoid kicking low growth, watching and feeling for his foot placement. He used no night vision equipment at present, relying on his natural sight. Once close enough to shoot, he had the night capabilities of the AN/PVS-10 scope.

Ahead, Wade sunk back down into the growth. Faisal moved in behind and to his left. Kyle liked that position, and sat back a couple of meters, where he had a clear right-handed shot at the boy without risking Wade.

"Lie down flat," he told Faisal. That would put him in a position where a few seconds reaction time would be available, and he couldn't reach both soldiers in that time, though he might reach one.

"How's the view?"

"I've got a window, and an armed man," Wade said. "Nothing else yet. Let me relocate a few meters." He squirmed across the ground like a sidewinder, disturbing very little foliage.

Once settled in, he took another look. Through the phone he said, "Chair, legs. Hold on." One more move and he said, "Mel. Got him."

Faisal said, "The woman is to left, and the girl left of her."

"He's right so far," Wade said when Kyle relayed that.

Kyle said nothing. It was reassuring, though. The boy had ratted out the scumbags, had given correct data and was doing as he was told. It seemed he was what he said.

Kyle appreciated that. Given the choice between an unrepentant coward he'd have to kill and a kid who had a conscience and the guts to stand up when he knew things were wrong, the latter was a much better companion. No one said doing the right thing was easy. But it was often the judge of character.

"We need to get closer," Kyle said.

"We've got about ten hours," Wade said. "How close do you want to cut it?"

"I want at least two hours leeway, in case they get eager or spooked. Sooner is better. Exfiltrating in daylight would suck rocks.

Then there's the government, who may just get out of bed and show up."

"I think I can get within one hundred meters in this growth. The problem is finding a good, clear field of fire I can move from in a hurry. Trees are handy, but these monsters are hard to climb and I'd be limited on field of view."

"Right. Any high ground? How much elevation do you need?"

"Three meters would do it. I see a rise over to our right. Might work. There's a downed tree with a root ball, too. If the angle is good . . ."

"Right, do it."

It took an hour of maneuvering to get good positions. Wade was standing, leaning through a root bulb and prepared to do so for hours if need be. He was effectively invisible from any direction, from more than a few meters away. Faisal was lying down where he wasn't visible and couldn't move fast. That was the lot of turn-coats—no one ever trusted them completely. He seemed mature enough to know this and didn't complain. Kyle was on the rise, in a bush, carefully picking leaves off to clear his field of view slightly without letting the bare patch show.

Kyle phoned Stephens and gave him an update. "We're in position, we're checking objectives. Information is correct so far, say again, correct. We have visual contact."

"Roger. Say when. We're standing by, close and ready."

"Roger, out." He clicked back on to Wade, ten meters away on land and 48,000 miles away by phone, to avoid talking above a whisper. "Any time we decide, we're on."

"Roger. What are we looking for?"

"Fewest threats in the building. You have the door?"

"I can see the door. Anything coming through dies."

"Roger. I can cover right front approach. That leaves a blind left."

"So we've got at least a fifty-percent reduction in threat."

"Yeah, but we need one hundred."

"I know."

They really needed an entry team as well. They also needed satellite TV, couches, and hot dogs. They weren't getting those, either. The rule was to use the resources at hand.

"I don't think the conditions are going to get better," he said. "So let's wait and see if the traffic level drops."

"Roger. Right now there's six people in there. They're setting up the video and making sure the victims know."

"Cocksuckers. Just fucking cocksuckers." Kyle trembled with rage. He wasn't sure words existed for his state of mind.

Faisal started crawling. Kyle waved him over.

"Yes?" he asked.

"They will set up camera and lights, then count down the time, praying for Allah's help. They will shoot through the heart and then dress in clean clothes to hide blood. Then they cut heads with large knife."

"Understood. Tell Wade," he said. He handed over the headset. He was nauseous. This was worse than the corpses under Castle Bran, almost as bad as watching Nasima get shot in Pakistan.

Faisal spoke through the phone to Wade, then nodded. "He knows."

"Good. Wait some more. We do a lot of waiting in this business."

"I understand. I hope you can save them."

"We'll do everything we can." Though he wasn't sure what that could be.

"It's not going to get better that I can see," Wade said. "They come and go. Averaging six assholes in the latrine."

"Another distraction would be nice. A quiet one. Sports? A bar fight?"

"I can distract them," Faisal said.

"What?"

"I can distract them? Draw attention?"

"Oh, I heard you," Kyle said. "Are you sure?" He realized he'd let the boy get right up behind him. Then he realized he wasn't concerned.

"I can walk down and distract them. They know me."

"They're going to be very suspicious about you leaving and showing up."

"If I can get any outside, you have less inside. If I'm in the way . . . just shoot me, too. Save the girl."

"Son," Kyle said, "I can pick a fly off a cup. You'll be fine. You get them out, I'll nail them. Do it."

"Then I go now."

"Clean up first." Kyle soaked a bandage in water and handed it over. Faisal scrubbed his face, and dumped the ersatz ghillie. He was still dirty and grubby, but might pass.

"Clean enough?"

"Your face is, yes."

Faisal nodded faintly and stepped forward, an aura of calm around him.

"Allah be with you, son," Kyle said to his back.

"Thank you." He nodded again and slipped away.

"Brave kid," Kyle said into his phone.

"Yeah, I heard your side of it. I hope he can do it. A few seconds will make the difference."

"Yup."

Kyle watched as the boy picked his way through the growth. Kyle mostly trusted him. At the same time, the kid might, just might turn his coat again, now that everyone was brought in. It wouldn't make sense to blow cover like this . . . but at the same time, these weren't sensible people. And if they knew they were going to get nailed, they might decide to hold ready on the hostages and invite a firefight. If they could kill a bunch of troops and the hostages and pin the blame on "overeager soldiers" they just might. It was the kind of complex plan that appealed to amateurs, and did sometimes work.

But Kyle didn't believe it. The boy—man— seemed honest, and had given far too much intel for something like that.

But there was still a chance of fear taking him, once he was face to face again. Impressionable age.

Kyle was willing to take the risk. Even if the kid did waffle back like a second-rate politician, he'd still be a momentary distraction, and Kyle had trained for years to exploit those. That would be all the time he needed to start blowing away any threats inside.

Faisal reached the edge of the clearing, far back from the road, and stepped onto the ground. He wasn't seen at once.

"He's down," Kyle reported to Wade. Then he called Stephens.

There was a tension in the air. It was eagerness, fear and alertness, seasoned with a little bit of hate and cynicism. *No matter what happens, you gutless fucks aren't getting out alive*, Kyle thought.

"So let's do it. Ready?"

"Ready."

"Ready," Kyle lied, and called Stephens. "Commence in exactly three minutes. One eight zero seconds from . . . mark!"

"Three minutes, one eight zero seconds, understood. Six, seven, eight . . ."

"Confirmed. Out." He redialed. "Wade, in one six five seconds, one six four, one six three . . ."

"Roger. I will commence fire two seconds prior. Two seconds."

"Two seconds roger. Rangers' Bullets Lead The Way."

"Amen to that."

They stopped talking and got ready to shoot. Kyle wanted to peer inside, but Wade had that. He'd chosen to cover any approaching targets from outside. That meant faster but less-precise shots, so Wade would have fewer incoming threats. They had to hope for some slight confusion inside to keep the hostages alive for a few seconds. Once threats were minimized, they were storming the building and shooting everything except the hostages, with the explosives as distraction to give the impression of overwhelming force.

Wade's first shot was a muffled bang from back where Kyle had paused earlier. Kyle thought he heard a second one, but it was lost in a cacophonous roar from the front of the compound, diagonally from both sides of the road. It was nicely done, and four figures dropped.

"Three down," Wade reported. "Two more not in range."

"Damn. Get them." Kyle rose and moved. Wade was hidden and wouldn't be traced. So Kyle was now acting as a decoy for him, should anyone follow the shots back. He was also getting closer so he could pour out some fire.

"I think they're ready to do it," Wade said. "Oh, sonofabitch. We've got a roomful of scum and three hostages. That frontal assault has convinced them to do it now as a fuck-you gesture."

"Plan fast," Kyle said. "Save the girl first, mother second, Wiesinger third. I wish I could say it was personal, but he is a soldier on a mission. He's last." Dammit, they'd come from off to the left. He'd had no shots.

"Roger," Wade said from behind his scope. "I count eight targets. Cameraman should be last. The new knifeman is wearing khakis and a ball cap.

"Yeah, got it. Can we get closer?" He took a careful look through his own scope as he snuggled up to a tree for cover and support.

"I don't think so. Better angle here, unless we get right up close or inside. If you shift a few meters left, I think we can create a fire zone around the hostages and just shoot anything that steps into view."

"Roger that. Anyone with a firearm has to be first. Once we have them down, we need to leapfrog in." He started moving in a crouch, quickly but stealthily.

"Yeah. Going to be rough."

"Faisal is out front," Wade added a few moments later. "I damned near bagged him by accident. He was talking to one of them."

"Dammit, why did he have to wait until now to choose the right side?" Kyle asked softly while he waited. He didn't realize it was aloud until Wade answered.

"Young, idealistic. The problem is there's no challenge and no army for kids like that. They imprint on the first powerful figure they meet, and in much of the world, it's a self-serving asshole. Get them to a recruiter and they turn into something else."

"Me," Kyle said. He recalled having the exact same thought a few days before.

"And me."

"Roger," Kyle said. "Get forward." Wade was a few meters closer. But Kyle couldn't move from his position until he knew there were no threats to his charges, or until Wade had a good, clear field of fire from a different angle. The lights went out in the building, which was a good sign. He clicked the scope to night vision and let his eye adapt to the monochrome.

Once they'd killed the lights, it took a few seconds to get reoriented. People were scrabbling about on hands and knees, slowly rising. Kyle chose one and put a bullet straight through the top of his head.

I know what the last thing to enter your mind was, asshole, he thought with a grin. He scanned for another and settled on an exposed hand that was just visible at the edge of the window. His shot shattered metacarpals and blew through the wrist. Now if he could find another wrist and the ankles, he'd crucify this motherfucker twenty-first century style.

I've got to calm down, he realized. He was taking too much pleasure. One should enjoy one's work, but not to this level under these conditions.

Maybe some of it was just relief over being able to shoot at last. He hoped so.

"I'm good," Wade said. "Move."

"Roger." He came off the scope and slipped forward again. He couldn't see Wade, which was good.

The noise up front continued. Rifle fire in two calibers was joined by machine-gun bursts and the occasional slam of explosives. He picked out an RPG round and what was probably an Australian grenade. Then there was the sound of TNT in small charges. Good. They should think the entire Indonesian Army was down on them.

"If you see a threat on the hostages, shoot ASAP," Kyle said. "And if I think you can get one of them through Faisal, I'll do it. I hate like hell to say it."

"He knows the risk."

"Yeah. So did Nasima. Doesn't mean I like it." Though Faisal had his own crimes that Nasima hadn't. Still, he was taking a big risk to do the right thing, and it always sucked to watch good people die.

"I know."

"We've got to advance. Cover them. I'm moving twenty meters. You follow."

"Roger."

Kyle stood and rushed.

It was a very unsniperlike tactic, but it was an infantry tactic. He took distance off with meter-long strides and slipped up behind a tree, leaning as high and far forward as he could to get some kind of field of view.

He really should ask about police work, executive protection, or Secret Service when he retired, he decided. This was exactly the type of work they did. The muzzle of his rifle was describing little circles. But the little circles here equaled large circles at one hundred meters, circles that encompassed the hostages. A figure stepped into the path of the circle, and Kyle didn't jerk or twitch. He simply let the muzzle drift around on its orbit, not forcing it, and snapped the trigger as it passed the appropriate part of the arc. He'd led just enough, and the bullet smashed through the back and shoulderblade of the threat.

There. Movement, and it wasn't female or Caucasian. He snapped off a shot and watched to make sure he'd hit. "Go, Wade!" he said.

Moments later, a bush with a rifle sprinted past. Wade took up position lower and closer. But they were losing angle while they gained proximity. A mucky depression behind the buildings was for runoff or sewage and would make advance and shooting awkward.

Kyle started his next run and caught a glimpse of movement just as he lowered the weapon and began to sprint.

There was no time to try to recover. He had the headset on and said, "Shoot now!" in a whisper.

Wade took the shot. Kyle didn't know how it worked, but he was momentarily in his next position, barely forty meters away. Wade would take another twenty on his next advance, probably to that corner there. Then they'd go around.

And he could just see a man with a raised pistol, chambering a round. His intent was obvious.

He shifted imperceptibly, bringing the reticle over the man's head. A squeeze of the finger and the window imploded in an instant before the man's brains blew out, scrambled by a 180-grain boattail match .308 bullet. The report clapped Kyle's ears, followed at once by another report from Wade's weapon as he came past at a run. The muzzle blast was contained, but these were still supersonic bullets with a healthy crack. It wasn't deafening, but there was enough noise to be obvious.

Kyle sought another target, saw only a shadow against the wall thrown by stray illumination. There was no time for a good shot— the man was moving fast—but he put a bullet into the wall hopefully only a few inches away. If he could get someone to flinch, that gained seconds. Wade fired again. Kyle sprinted past and came right up to the tree line.

No one else had rushed the hostages as he lost sight of them. Wiesinger should have tried to throw himself on the civilians to give them cover with his ample bulk. He hadn't, that Kyle had seen. Kyle would give him the benefit of the doubt that he was either surprised or holding still to avoid spoiling a shot, rather than being paralyzed with fear. He was blindfolded, too. And holding still did make targeting easier. Wade should be in a much better position now.

In front and to the sides, he'd seen a huge mob forming. Everyone was bent on killing those hostages. Brave men. Big, strong, powerful men. There were three Aussies and a dozen Indonesians out front, and they'd show the world their manhood by killing a little girl, a woman, and a man tied to a chair.

Kyle wanted to puke.

Still, a mob of cowards might be easier to handle when he went charging in among them. He'd drop the SR25 and unsling the M4 banging against his ass. That would give him one hundred rounds and a 40mm canister, which in his line of work they jokingly called a nice helping of Have a Shitty Day. He was two buildings away and on flat ground. One hundred meters and a bit. Easy range for him.

Faisal slipped back into camp. He'd been gone eight hours, which wasn't too suspicious, unless someone had gone looking for him. In that case, he was about to die. Allah be praised. He'd trust Allah to show him where he must go.

"Faisal! There you are!" Wismo called. "Where have you been? You're a mess!"

"Sleeping. And toilet. Then I took a walk and fell." He showed a muddy streak on his trousers. "I had to wash and, and then it was time to pray. Breakfast. It's been a really busy night. Are we ready?"

"Ready, yes. You're late! Ayi is looking for you. They're going to start the killing soon, and film before dawn."

"I'm sorry. I'll hurry right over. They didn't agree to our terms, then."

"No," Wismo sounded disappointed. "But you wait! The Chinese are sending warships, and the Americans, and the bloody Hindu Indians. It's a sea full of impotent infidels, trembling at our word!"

"Very nice." He didn't think so anymore. Would the Chinese use nuclear weapons? American cruise missiles? The Army send a million troops to burn the jungle clean? Would the entire Asian sphere invade? This wasn't a game to be played at this level. "Have you a few moments? We can talk."

"I suppose. You didn't get the news when you woke up?"

"No, I was praying on what I am to do. Allah is favoring us. That many nations and ships brings hope for a war of scriptural size. Isn't it grand?"

"Indeed."

It was reasonable that he head toward the hostages. He just couldn't appear too eager or too reluctant. That, of course, put him closer to the fight. He realized now he wasn't in a hurry to die. If need be, yes, but not as an assumed course.

It was troubling, all the changes he was feeling. He'd been secure in his place. Now he wasn't.

The trick now was to get close to the building, but not yet inside. He was needed out here, to distract people. To kill them. He'd killed before, or helped, and it had been heady and exciting. This was harder.

Harder . . . because they'd fight back. But he couldn't admit that. That was a sign of cowardice. Allah had given him this test. Could he kill when there was threat to his own life? That is what he had to face. He was loitering in front, speaking softly so Ayi didn't look for him at once. There was a rack right outside with rifles. He couldn't pick one up yet, because there was no reason to.

"Hey, Faisal, where's your pedang?" Wismo asked. He'd noticed at last. The knife had been taken when he surrendered.

"Oh, I'll have to get it. Thanks for reminding me." Where were those shots? It had to be time.

He was saved from further stalling by the bullets he was hoping for and dreading. As the shooting commenced, with two simultaneous bangs, Faisal said, "It's an attack! Give me a weapon!"

Wismo had been frozen. He nodded stupidly and grabbed an AK from the rack.

"Come! Let's get them!" Faisal shouted, waving his arm and running for the door and the rack. He paused and turned, making sure Wismo followed him. "God is great! We fight!"

With that he jogged a few yards back from the door.

"Kyle, Faisal has an AK. I'm still worried about trusting him."

"Kill him if you have to. I hate to say it, but we can't risk it."

"Yeah. He's not an immediate threat yet."

"Roger," Kyle said. The man could be trying to play the act, or provide cover, or just defend himself. He could also be a threat. It was hard to know where his loyalty lay at this juncture. Dammit, he'd been an enemy, a turncoat, an ally and now was a threat again.

Kyle sprinted up the side of the adjoining building in a sideways crab that kept his back to the wall. A few more seconds . . .

All Faisal could do now was what he felt to be right. Allah would guide his hand. If he was to live or die, he would know soon enough. He'd been prepared to give his life to kill others. He felt a sudden thrill that his life might save others. He didn't know Kyle Monroe's musings on the subject, but at that moment he understood the principle exactly. This was what a man died for.

No. This was what a man *lived* for.

Yet the irony was that he would have to kill so others might live. There was so much in this world to consider, so many things he'd never had time for. His emotions were cascading through him, thoughts flashing. He realized his devotion had been to blindness. The leaders didn't want him to see the world outside of a narrow scope. There were so many ways to look at events, depending on viewpoint, so many things that one could never hope to learn them all. *That* was the greatness of Allah—that he could create a universe so grand it was beyond comprehension.

That, too, was worth living for.

In a euphoric haze of revelation, adrenaline, and fear, he spun. Bambang was out the door, the others bunched up just inside. He waited as they staggered and shoved, firing one shot high into the jungle to make it look as if he was doing something. A deceit, yet for right. He'd decided that wasn't possible. Now he was doing it again. So gray, this world. How to decide right and wrong?

The AK kicked into his shoulder as he fired. Half the magazine, about a second and a half burst, went into the group coming out of the doorway. He was amazed at his own accuracy. He'd started low on purpose, knowing it would kick high and right. But it was the best burst he'd ever fired.

A crowd was gathering, some coming out, some in, some rushing in to see what the problem was. Releasing the trigger, he swung toward Wismo. Wismo had already deduced what was happening and had his own weapon raised, a murderous, hateful glare on his face. He fired first.

Faisal felt the freezing burn of bullets entering his body and tried to gasp. Then he felt a horrific pain in his face.

"HE'S DEAD," WADE SAID. "DAMN," KYLE MUTTERED.
He tried not to let it affect him, to take it in stride. Hell, the
man had sawed Keller's head off! But he'd figured out it was wrong,
come around at considerable risk to himself, and died. Kyle felt
more anguish over losing him than he would have over Wiesinger,
who had theoretically always been an ally.

But Wiesinger was still alive, along with two civilians, and it was
his duty to see them free. He put the matter behind him and resumed shooting.

"Ready," Wade said, and Kyle slapped his left hand down to help
push off the ground. He drew the SR25 closer to his side, like a football, and came up at forty-five degrees, like a sprinter off the blocks.
He heard Wade fire at some threat or other as he crabbed sideways,
ran two long steps, shifted past the corner of the building, and could
see the building front at last. He'd have to shoot off hand now,
standing. But the range was eighty meters and that was very easy
shooting for him. He could see a side window that had dim backlight from the moon and operations up front. So he could provide
more cover. They might pull this off yet.

He brought the rifle up to his shoulder, snugged into the sling
with his left elbow on his harness, tight behind the pocket on his
vest, and took one deep, measured breath to slow his pulse.

"Ready," he announced.

Movement! It was inside, but just under the window where he
couldn't see or shoot. All he saw was the top of someone in a
crouch.

The problem with suicidal nuts, he reflected, was that they didn't
care if you killed them. When their purpose was to kill hostages,

there was nothing you could offer or threaten them with. Only now one was about to kill Wiesinger or a little girl. He hoped it was Wiesinger, and it really wasn't personal.

His mind, experienced in dozens of firefights, honed by years of study and practice, whipped through an intuitive calculation no computer could ever match.

Those walls won't stop 7.62, he thought to himself.

All he had to do now was figure out where the crawling body was. Or at least, where the child was not. It wasn't efficient to simply fill the space with bullets, but it might be the only option.

Then Wiesinger appeared in his sights, apparently kicking out at something.

Kyle dropped his aim and fired three rounds, rapid.

Ba-ba-bang! It was almost fast enough for automatic fire, and his skill, the improved grip, and the weapon's mass allowed him to put all three in a very tight group. Dust blew up inside and out from the block shattering. Yes, hard-ball 7.62 ammo would punch through block. There was a substantial fan of gray in front and a hole through. If anyone had been behind that, he wasn't going to move soon enough to be a problem.

There was a definite gaggle of people outside the door. The rest were all tied up with the assault up front. But they'd have to sneak out or do some massive damage to disperse the enemy. This wasn't over yet. But first, they had to get to the hostages.

"I'm down," Wade said.

"Down how?" In the area, covered, wounded? The statement wasn't clear.

"Ready to roll."

"Understood. Fifty meters and closing."

"Roger. Give me five seconds."

A loud explosion was a bomb landing in front of the building. Wade's throwing arm was as good as his shooting. There were no friendlies there now, Kyle recalled. Damned shame. "Dying like a man" wasn't a bad thing, but living was far better. He'd say a prayer for Faisal's soul when he had time.

He was seen now, and badly aimed fire came his way. He couldn't plan on that to last; these people had proven competent. He was at extreme range for a canister load, but he needed something fast. He slung the SR25, letting it bang against his legs, and replaced it with the M4. He reached forward, aimed coarsely and triggered the canister load in the grenade launcher, the recoil thumping his wrist. He followed it at once by raising the carbine to his shoulder and rapping off quick shots into the mass. He dropped to one knee, then the other, then to his left elbow, getting low so he could pour out more accurate fire with a lower profile. Also, Wade would be on the other side, doing likewise. They could shoot over each other.

Between grenade, canister, and bullets the locals were disrupted. They scattered for cover. Now was when it got dangerous.

In a moment, Kyle was on his feet, calling into the phone, "Running!" as he did. It wouldn't do to have Wade shoot him.

"Likewise!" was the reply.

Weapons low, they sprinted toward the building. Kyle would twitch his arm now and then, to pan the muzzle across someone on the ground. Alive, wounded, dead, it didn't matter. He was paying insurance with bullets. He wanted them all down before he made it in, so he wouldn't have to face them on the way out.

He saw Wade skipping and crabbing for the door. "I've got the right," he said. He was better left handed than Wade was. They'd cross over as they entered. Kyle reached into a pouch and pulled out a three-ounce piece of TNT with a jury-rigged timed detonator built from a stopwatch. The timer was set for three seconds. The start button was protected by a thick piece of tape. He peeled that back, cautious of where his thumb went.

"Roger."

"On three. One, two, threeee," he grunted as he piled on the power. Two seconds later, they crashed into the thin door, Kyle having a flashback to a hut in the Carpathian mountains, where he'd done that and come face to face with a ton of explosives and a loon with a suicide switch. He lobbed the improv flashbang and stepped aside. A moment later, it exploded and shook leaves off the roof.

He spun through the doorframe and swung right, Wade swung left a half step behind him. Three bodies were on the floor, and he paid the insurance with three bullets, the sound echoing loudly and hollowly despite the suppressor. A rifle with 36 dB of reduction was still louder than a shouted conversation.

"Clear!" Wade announced.

"Clear!" Kyle agreed. "Glad to see you alive, sir," he added.

Wade went back to the door, got low, and resumed shooting. That left it to Kyle to get the hostages unbound. The dimness was occasionally lit by explosions from outside. Kyle needed some light, and had his Mini Maglite ready. With an amber lens it wasn't quite as obvious, but gave enough light to work by. There was another faint source behind him. A laptop.

Both Wiesinger and Suzanne, the child, had wet themselves. It might have been fear, stress, or simply the long wait. It wasn't something Kyle would hold against the man, except it was so representative of the mission so far.

They hadn't blindfolded the girl, and she stared at him with huge eyes. Her head swiveled like an owl's as he stepped deliberately behind the chair she was lashed to. She didn't cry or utter a sound, but when he cut the bonds and the pressure slipped off her wrists, she stumbled out of the chair and ran for the corner, curling up in a ball, back to the wall and arms over her face. Then she started bawling with huge, wracking sobs.

"Good," he said, to no one in particular. "She needs to get the stress out."

Lei Ling, her mother, was apparently conscious of being rescued, but still stiff and frightened behind her blindfold. Her daughter's distress didn't help. Kyle realized he probably should have freed her first. He'd been sentimental.

He pulled the hood off her head, and she blinked, head darting around to see what was happening. She recognized them as Western and soldiers, deduced they weren't terrorists, and that she was safe. Her eyes teared up from both the light Kyle was shining, and from relief. Kyle cut her hands free, then reached down for her feet, laying the rifle within inches of his hand as he did. He wanted it close by just in case of another altercation.

As he pulled the shredded rope away and stood, she pointed at her daughter. "Please?" she asked. He nodded, and she gave an almost smile as she staggered, stumbled, and finally crawled over that way. Her legs were likely numb from hours or days of inaction. But she gathered her daughter up in her arms and cuddled her, leaning back against the wall. The expression on her face might be grateful, under the sunken eyes that had seen too much fear.

Kyle wondered if he'd looked like that last time, as he'd faced down a lunatic with a backpack full of explosive and a trigger in his hand.

"Gentlemen," Wiesinger said, panting slightly. It was hard to blame him. "That was some very, very fine shooting." He appeared about to say something else, but just sat while Kyle cut the ropes and removed his hood.

"Thank you, sir," he said. "As long as it's a happy ending, who cares if it's by the book?" He shoved another grenade—canister again, into the launcher.

"There is something to that, Sergeant Monroe."

Wade had gotten his cell phone out. "Contact made with Mel. All elements intact and movement capable. Last two referenced persons accounted for, alive and able to travel with transport. Need transport to Point X-ray . . . waiting."

Wiesinger was rubbing his wrists to restore circulation. They were badly abraded. Presumably, he'd been fighting the rope. He twisted his ankles and stomped his feet a few times.

"I think I'm able to move. Are my boots around?"

"Don't think so, sir," Kyle said, taking in the rubble in a sweep of his eyes. And the corpses. Some rail-thin little imam in a hat and prayer shawl. That had been who Kyle had hit through the block wall. He'd been disabled but hadn't died fast with that gutshot. Pity. Not. That was the freak who'd told Faisal it was holy to chop the heads off people. Even second hand, that information made Kyle quiver in disgust. One of the other bodies had a shattered wrist.

"You might have to barefoot it a bit," he said to Wiesinger.

"If I have to, I have to. Is there any reason to stick around?"

"Not that I can think of," Kyle said. "This way." He indicated the door.

Wiesinger accepted the SR25 and checked the load, limping badly. The battle was mostly at the front still, long bursts, short ones, individual shots, occasional explosions. With both sides dug in, it could last hours. Kyle only wanted it to last a few more minutes while he got everyone into the brush. After that, they should be fine.

Kyle stopped for just a moment. The cameras, two of them, were feeding into a laptop. They had been recording. They were still recording. They looked to be modern models that might shoot infrared, or be able to be processed to show dim features.

That was not only prime intelligence either way—of who the snipers were and how they accomplished the recovery, and of who the terrorists were—it was potentially a propaganda bomb that would scare many more of these assholes into quitting the game.

Kyle checked the screen. They were still filming.

"Wade, light the bodies!" he said. He pointed as he swung a camera across. Wade shone his Surefire in blinding momentary bursts while kicking the faces toward the lens.

"Thanks." Kyle pressed STOP, typed a new filename of KYLE and saved and closed. He shut the laptop down, pulled the cord and reached behind to cram it into his patrol pack. Some things were too convenient to let go.

Lei Ling carried her daughter. The girl wouldn't let anyone else near her, and clutched tightly. Wade took point, Kyle took rear, with his better-rate-of-fire weapon, and Wiesinger stumbled along in the middle with the spare SR25, feet hurting from poor circulation and lack of shoes. He'd been bound tighter. Apparently, they'd perceived him as a threat. He seemed to be recovering somewhat, and increased his pace.

The obvious problem was that any notice they got would make them a major target. At this point, there was no reason for the enemy not to kill the hostages. Kyle was dripping sweat, more than the water he'd drunk earlier. If things just held off another minute . . .

Someone shouted and a bullet snapped past. Lei Ling howled and ran faster, which was probably the best reaction to have.

More fire came, and Kyle spun. He fired two sustained bursts and the canister, then reached back and grabbed a hand grenade, heaving it in a long lob. He wasn't sure of a particular target, he just wanted lots of noise to keep heads down. Once in the woods, he'd have the advantage against any reasonable number of opponents.

The weapon was hot and jammed on the next round. He cleared it instinctively and latched the bolt back. A few seconds of cool air couldn't hurt. Meantime, he grabbed his Ed Brown. It would make noise, and anyone close would find out just how hard 230 grains of lead hit, like that guy running to intercept and raising a fucking shotgun. Kyle clicked the safety, squeezed, rode the recoil, and squeezed again. The two heavy bullets crashed into the man, who stumbled and staggered. He might or might not die, but he was no longer a threat.

Then they were heading into the trees, Wiesinger cursing loudly as he winced and danced, feet getting poked and toes getting jammed.

Kyle speed-dialed. "Stephens, we're clear, and thanks, buddy. 'Go SAS!' or whatever you say."

"We've been gone. They've been shooting at each other for five minutes, mate, with an occasional encouragement from our allies. 'Who Dares, Wins.'"

"Damn, sweet. And nice phrase. I've got to run. Later."

"Ciao."

"Bakri," Kyle said, as the next number answered. "We're in the woods at the south, you say there's a road?"

"Four kilometers ahead. You should hurry."

"Dammit, that's a long hike. You can meet us?"

"We can. Talk more as you close."

"Roger." He was panting hard, putting distance between him and possible pursuit. There was a lesser deadline now—making sure everyone knew the hostages were alive. He dialed Gilpin. "We have them, we're on foot, we're departing. Awaiting local transport."

"Outstanding. Bring it on home and I'll put the word out." The civilian exec sounded thrilled.

"We're not clear yet. Possible pursuit, possible government risks. An hour to transport, another to the coast, then we have to get clear."

"That leg will be waiting. You just put distance on." Kyle could hear Gilpin talking into another line, a landline. The word was going out.

"Yes, sir."

They stopped for about a minute, Wade pulling spare pants from his ruck and ripping them to strips that Wiesinger could wear on his feet. Kyle dropped the bolt on the M4 again, and reholstered his pistol. Lei Ling was gasping and dry heaving, but showed no intention of stopping if she didn't have to. "Three more kilometers," Kyle said slowly, not knowing her grasp of English.

"I can make it," she said. Her voice was a raspy contralto with an obvious accent. "I won't stop until we're away from those sick fucks." Apparently, she spoke English well enough.

Kyle shared water all around. Suzanne wouldn't drink, shaking her head and tucking into her mother's shoulder. Wiesinger and Wade each gulped enough for Kyle to feel the load lighten. Then they were moving again, Wiesinger managing a slightly better pace in his improvised slippers.

"We're out," Wiesinger muttered.

Kyle wasn't sure. It would be quite obvious to the enemy that they'd head for the city or the coast. Bakri's cover was blown for certain. Putting that together, pursuit wouldn't be far away. These people weren't rational, were bent on killing, and they weren't going to let their sacrifices escape easily. Random death in the street was one thing, but this was a picked target. They were determined to get Lei Ling and her daughter, and getting the Americans was gravy—it would prove they were a force to be taken seriously. As the U.S. couldn't operate openly in Indonesia, and not on a large-enough scale clandestinely—probably not at all after this—it would be a net win.

The whole solution, Kyle reflected morbidly, was best solved with large bombs.

That was post-battle depression hitting him. He was shaky, jittery, and scared. He always was. It was part of doing the job. Then would come euphoria, and a desire to get drunk and screw. He didn't drink anymore, and Janie was half a world away. He'd deliberately not been thinking about her, because he didn't need anything holding him back or distracting him.

He kept on, ducking leaves, dodging trunks, ignoring the birds and ground animals. None of the larger forms were present, which was good, as spooked herds could be a giveaway. He had to assume their enemy was smart, cunning, and right behind. He made periodic pauses and watched for signs of pursuit before hurrying to catch up. The dark didn't scare him. The dark was his friend.

"We're about there," Wade said. "Perhaps two zero zero meters."

"Roger. Stand by." He dialed Bakri. "We're there."

"There will be a car along shortly. Lights will blink twice."

"Better yet, blink them some other number and I'll confirm."

"Very well, I think I understand."

It was an old trick. While Kyle didn't think any faction could have a tap on the cell phones, it was possible the government did. If they knew any signs or passwords . . .

Shortly, they all pulled up into a ditch. It was wet and cool and wonderful, even with slimy rotten things pooling in it. A car was far to the north, several minutes away. It was traveling perhaps thirty-five miles per hour.

The lights flashed three times.

"I see three flashes," Kyle said.

"Yes," Bakri said.

"Everyone up," Kyle hissed.

It was the worn, ugly Land Cruiser, and Kyle was delighted to see it. Fatigue was hitting him hard now. It stopped, and four of Bakri's men debarked and spread out, acting as a rearguard. That was awfully nice of him, Kyle thought.

Lei Ling and her daughter were ushered gently into the cargo compartment of the Toyota, the little girl hiding her face from the men with guns. It was understandable. To her, virtually any armed man, and certainly any Indonesian, was a threat. They were cramped because the rest of the Americans' gear was back there. Amazing. They were going to exfil with all their gear except what they'd expended. That might be a first.

Wade stood to at the rear, weapon raised and ready. Kyle ran to the front. After the civilians were bundled in, Wiesinger climbed in the back. Wade ducked around and leaped feetfirst in next to him. Kyle swung around and took shotgun, as the four troops jumped onto the bumpers and fenders and Bakri revved up and popped the clutch. They juggled weapons around and he got an SR25 while

Wade got the M4. He wasn't going to worry about it. He checked the magazine and then reached a hand back. Wade dropped two more magazines into it. Easier to swap them than the rifles.

Kyle didn't remember much of the trip. Fatigue and stress had finally overwhelmed him. He knew he was conscious, and once shot at a threat that turned out to be merely shifting shadows of leaves looking like a human outline. But he recalled neither the twenty kilometers of road nor how he acquired the dozens of bruises and scrapes that came from the rough track they drove on. There had to be several generous samples of his DNA in the truck, though.

Then they jounced hard and slewed left out of the woods to race along a shore road that was in good repair. It had to be an oil-company access.

Whatever had happened to cause Kyle to zone in the woods was over. He was alert enough to continue, even if ragged and worn as hell. But he'd been there before; he'd trained for that for fourteen of his sixteen years of service.

Captain Sutrisno watched silently. Next to him, Murizal, his exec, growled.

"Easy, soldier," he cautioned. "There are rebels and there are rebels. If they kill these filth, let us not complain. At the same time, if any of them die in the process, that is Allah's will. Bakri is smart and honest. We'll watch him more closely. But there is no need to shoot him or arrest him yet."

Indeed. It was Napoleon who had cautioned never to interrupt an enemy when he was making a mistake. If the factions could kill each other, then the ones who survived would either be more reasonable or less of a threat. Though there was still the issue of Americans and Australians operating in Indonesia without permission. That made Sutrisno far angrier than any dispute between GAM groups and Jemaah Islamiyah. The presumption and arrogance was insufferable, no matter the motives. Sutrisno's people were quite capable of handling these missions. That his unit, and apparently their own government, had been kept in the dark was a grievous insult. But that was for the politicians.

He forced calm upon himself, and let it radiate out to the others. Nothing should be done yet. The Americans had run away, Bakri's men had departed, the Aussies had long since ducked, showing a canniness he had to respect. They were men not afraid to retreat, and who made a game of it.

The faction here had suffered a huge loss. They'd taken perhaps twenty-five casualties in the fight, and some survivors were scattered widely. Others were pursuing the Americans. They'd be dealt with shortly. For now, the stillness returned. It was a patient twenty-minute wait before movement picked up again.

First came two rebels, lightly wounded and terrified. They stared in despair at the wreckage and corpses. Sutrisno grudgingly admitted the foreigners were good troops. It was an impressive ratio of damage. These two simply huddled in shock, ignoring the occasional moan from a dying comrade. A dozen more wandered back from the road, confused at the disappearance of their attackers. Then someone figured out the hostages were gone. There were shouts and accusations.

An hour later, an advance party of three arrived, scared and suddenly in a standoff with two of their wounded allies. That was most amusing, but no shots were fired. An hour after that, a larger force came in at the prompting of the scouts: sixty-seven GAM rebels, skinny and underfed and bearded, indicating strict Muslim beliefs. All had weapons. All wore fatigues of some kind. The combination marked them as a threat to the nation, and with the hostages gone, there was no reason to show any mercy, except for some few who might provide intelligence if motivated. The rest could be an object lesson.

Sutrisno checked his kit. The flag was ready. It was a large, new Indonesian flag, which these people hated to see. Sometimes the Kopassus would attack with miniature flags hanging from their rifles. Today, they'd leave no survivors, but they would leave a full-size flag as a slap. This was Indonesia. It would stay Indonesia unless and until the government decided otherwise, and rebels, especially terrorists, were not going to change that schedule.

Sutrisno whistled, and his company of Kopassus rose from the growth to bloom into a swath of death.

18

THE TRIP OUT SHOULD HAVE BEEN A CHANCE TO relax, but they weren't free yet. Not until they were on the deck of a U.S. ship, and even then, they needed to get into friendly waters. Kyle was a Ranger. He could go a long time under stress, underfed, and without sleep. But he was groggy after moving so far, so fast in this climate.

He was still hyperaware, too, and that took a toll. He listened to the chorus of insects as they drove, shifting with the greenery. The road noise and engine sounds changed. Occasional other noises were natural enough. Then . . .

"Coming car, everyone down and weapons hidden," Bakri said.

The headlights grew and illuminated the inside of the roof as Kyle scrunched into the footwell. He drew the SR25 in tight, the muzzle past his ear. The lights swept across as what sounded like a truck roared past. He counted two and started to shimmy back up.

Bakri swore in Achinese. "They are turning around. Coming in pursuit. It's a security vehicle."

"Wade, make it go away," Kyle said. He was having flashbacks to Romania and one of their too many car chases.

"Roger," Wade said. He leaned out the window, bracing a leg across Wiesinger's lap, ignoring his momentary protest. He raised the M4, clicked the safety and squeezed. Four shots rang out, four empty cases *tinged* as they ricocheted inside, and then the lights swerved.

"Tire and three radiator shots. That should slow them down."

"Yeah," Kyle said. He already had his cell phone out.

It answered. He'd known it would, but ever since the snatch, he'd been nervous. "Gilpin."

"Yeah, Monroe here. Is our transport ready?"

"They're hidden. Do you need backup?"

"Not at this moment. We may any minute. I'll keep the line open."

"Don't. I'll have them call you directly."

"Roger that, Monroe out." He clicked off.

Thirty seconds later, the phone vibrated in his hand.

"Monroe," he answered.

"McLaren. We didn't meet on the Black Sea, I'm told." It was an American voice, and it was coming from very nearby. That helped Kyle steady out.

"Good to not meet you again, McLaren." He kept looking over his shoulder anyway. Nothing else at present.

"Well, we'll meet in about three minutes, according to my math. Unless I dropped a decimal and you're actually in San Jose."

"I wish."

"Okay, you'll come to a bend to the left in the road," McLaren said.

"Bend to the left, roger," he spoke aloud for Bakri's benefit.

"Continue straight ahead on foot."

"Straight ahead on foot, roger." They'd have to carry gear and the girl.

"Distance is two zero zero meters."

"Two zero zero meters, roger."

"I'll find you."

"You'll find us. Roger." He hoped so. Fumbling in the dark on the coast would suck.

"I'll be wearing a black trenchcoat and fedora."

"Black trenchcoat and fedora you say." He had to grin at that.

"Would you settle for black camo over a wetsuit and boonie hat?"

"McLaren, I'll settle for you wearing a pink fucking tutu, as long as you get us out of here." Hot damn, they were going to make it.

"Tutu not an option. I'll note choice for next task. I see headlights," McLaren said, serious again. "Flash them."

Kyle cupped the phone low and said, "Flash headlights twice."

"I count two flashes," McLaren said a moment later.

"Confirm two flashes. That's us."

The road curved sharply just ahead. Bakri leaned into the brakes steadily, and they stopped right at the curve. The civilians necessitated a full stop, or Kyle would have risked bailing out on a roll. There was no additional pursuit from either oil-terminal security or terrorists yet, and hopefully there wouldn't be. But the sooner they were gone, the better.

Kyle rolled out to his feet, facing rearward. Wade sprang out and sprinted around back. He threw open the hatch and motioned for Lei Ling to pass her daughter up. Kyle was past and scanning for potential threats.

Then Suzanne started screaming.

There was no way she was going to let a soldier take her again. Wade returned Kyle's inquisitive glance with a shrug and a look of helplessness.

They were both saved when Lei Ling jumped out, staggering slightly, and let her daughter clutch her around the neck. "I do it," she said.

"Run," Kyle said, pointing, with his rifle held ready in the other hand. Wade grabbed his ruck in one hand and Lei Ling's arm in the other. They bounded forward, off the road, and down a rocky beach that turned sandy, dark from occasional oil spills.

Wiesinger, already out, followed along, grunting in pain in his bare feet. The man lumbered and had an obvious silhouette, Kyle groused to himself after a moment's glance back. But at least he wasn't complaining anymore. And he was making respectable time on feet that had to resemble hamburger. The man wasn't entirely a coward. He was more a self-centered ass.

Then it was Kyle's turn. He ran past the driver's side. Bakri had his arm out and was looking as casual as one could under the circumstances. "For all of us, Bakri, thanks. This has been our smoothest mission so far."

"If that's so, you are a brave man. Good luck, and *salemat jalan*." Good travel.

"And you." He shook the offered hand.

That was as much as there was time for. Bakri coaxed the truck forward as Kyle picked up two rucks. They had been packed in a hurry and were quite bulky, even with food and water depleted. They tangled on his back as he slung one on each shoulder, but it wasn't a long trip; he could manage. He picked his way down the beach at a run.

As the Toyota pulled around the curve, Kyle tripped. He threw the butt of the SR25 out and broke his fall. But he caught his right boot toe between two rocks, banged his knee, and skinned an elbow.

Wincing, he stood and resumed his path, limping. It felt as if he'd torn the boot open, though a quick glance didn't show any obvious rips in the leather. His foot was squelching, but that could be sweat as much as blood. But it burned like hell, and was sharply painful. His right knee had either loose skin or sharp pebbles embedded in the skin, and stung with every movement. His elbow lit up with every shift of fabric or breath of air over the open wound.

He saw the boat, and a young American in an odd camo pattern with a flattop haircut and some godawful variant of an M4 Kyle wasn't familiar with, with rails all over the receiver and barrel, a bulky suppressor, some kind of night vision, and other gadgets. But it helped prove he was an American, and was likely devastatingly effective.

"Monroe?"

"Yeah, injured, rocks," he said through clenched teeth. "Teach *me* to hurry."

"McLaren. Here." The SEAL reached out a hand and heaved, taking the weight off Kyle's injured foot. Kyle dropped the rucks and then they were swinging their legs over the gunwale of a rigid inflatable boat. McLaren stepped back and grabbed a ruck in each hand, barely straining.

"Anything fragile?"

"No," Kyle said, as the two packs sailed over the inflated tube. He chuckled. The question had been an irrelevant formality.

The boat had a cockpit of sorts, enough for two crewmen to stand in. One stood there now. Another man crouched forward at a Browning M2HB .50 caliber machine gun. Kyle's foot sent streaks of pain up his leg as McLaren piled in.

"Go," the SEAL said. It wasn't much above a whisper, but it was enough.

Then they were moving, slowly, as the heavily muffled diesels rumbled.

McLaren was speaking into an encrypted radio. "Got all three items, and two supplemental. Both female. Request female medical support who look as nonthreatening as possible, over . . ."

Kyle sank back and let the gunwale take his weight. Damn, that felt good. He was on a friendly vessel and didn't have to worry about his command or about taking charge himself.

"You realize I *am* going to puke," Wade said. He sounded cheerful about it, though.

"Red, white, and blue?"

"Or Army green. Something patriotic. Goddam, my man, we did it again. Busted up, worn out, but we saved a little girl. Dunno about you, but I feel pretty goddamned good!"

"Yeah," Kyle said noncommittally. He really did feel good, but the exhaustion and tension were fighting inside him. He could feel a thrill of victory later. Right now, it was the agony of the feet.

But he did have to smile at the pun.

19

KYLE WAS LEANING BACK, LIMP, WHEN THEY HIT DEEP water minutes later. Whether it was wave pattern, or shelter from formations, Kyle didn't know. But the motion changed from a light rocking to a heavy tilting. He understood why Wade got sick. He felt none too good himself. Though only part of it was the ocean. It was his medical state. He wasn't sure how bad his foot was, but it was screaming at him. Surgery for certain, though he thought he had it all there. But hell, that meant they couldn't use him for a couple of months. He snickered to himself.

"So, we meet at last, Sergeant Monroe," McLaren said. He cleared all three rifles and stowed them in an open crate. Made sense. Random holes in the tubes would be a bad thing. The boat was metal hulled, but required the inflated gunwales to support it.

"I think we're meeting at first," Kyle replied. Dammit, Wade's humor was catching.

"Right. Anyway, what I've heard impresses me. Both you and Wade."

"Thanks," Kyle said. Wow. Yes, they were all on the same team and all good at what they did, but the SEALs were about as overall best as you got. For one of them to say he was impressed was praise indeed.

"What's the camo?" Kyle asked. He looked his host over again. Young, bulky but lean, no nonsense about him.

"Standard BDU pattern in gray and blue. Civilian purchase, but great for beaches at night. Or nightclubs."

"Good. I wonder if the Army would approve them."

"Not likely, Monroe," Wiesinger said.

It was annoying. He'd been making a joke and chatting to unwind, while being friendly with a man who was saving their lives, and the asshole had to prove he had no sense of humor.

"Ah, shit," McLaren said, cutting off further conversation. Kyle shifted and looked astern, following the SEAL's gaze. He couldn't see much from this low level.

"What is it?"

"Some kind of small craft. But bigger and better armed than this one." He stared a bit longer. "Looks like a fifteen to twenty meter patrol craft. Same kind that's involved in quite a bit of piracy."

"Define 'better armed'?" Wade asked. He looked a bit queasy, but it wasn't the enemy. He'd looked like that the whole way out.

"Oh, probably a twenty-three millimeter Russian. Enough to blow the hell out of us before we do more than love taps with the fifty." He turned to the bow and shouted, "Mike, bring the fifty!" Turning back, he said for no one's benefit, though they all heard him, "But we'll damned sure try."

Kabongo had been largely invisible up front. He was a massive black man, with shoulders that looked to be carved rock. The defined shape of them could be seen right through his wetsuit. He carried the dismounted .50 Browning at port arms as he came sure-footedly astern.

In moments, the two SEALs had it mounted to a rear pintle that had obviously been retrofitted. The welds on it were crude but sturdy. Apparently, it was intended that the heavy firepower be used forward. That was a limitation they obviously didn't approve of.

"Piracy?" Kyle asked.

"I dunno. Fifty attacks in this area this year. That were reported. Plus tramps who went missing in unknown conditions that might not be storms. Or it could be contracted to the companies. Or it could be your friends. They might have seen us come in and then waited for us to leave. I don't think they're government."

Kyle's phone buzzed. He started in surprise, and grabbed it.

"Kyle."

"Bakri here."

"Yes, Bakri?"

"I was just called and threatened with death."

"Damn. There's nothing we can do at this point."

"That is not why I called. Our friends had observers. They said they would hunt you down at sea."

"That explains the boat behind us." He stared at the dot on the waves.

"I'm sorry."

"No, thanks much. You protect yourself." Damn.

"I will do so. It is to get violent here. Very."

"Good luck. I'll call with my home number if I get a chance."

"I hope to be here. I may change phones."

"If that happens, I won't try to find you. Not safe."

"I agree. Good luck and God be with you."

"And also with you."

He clicked off and turned to the others, painfully. "That explains that. Assholes aren't willing to let go."

"Didn't we do that a couple of shows back?" Wade asked. They'd been chased from Pakistan into Afghanistan.

"That group wanted revenge," Kyle said. "This group is still trying to bag the target and win points. They kill the Maddens, they get a war started."

"Well, maybe they'll turn away," Kabongo mused. "It's not as if they've got good odds."

"We've dealt with these assholes before," Kyle said. "They won't turn away. A bloody nose won't do it. You have to knock teeth out before they get the hint. And some of them never do."

"Well, we're not that easy to hit," McLaren said. "We're small, moving fast, have a very low radar profile, and a head start. That might be enough. On the other hand, we're not going to make thirty knots in these seas with all this extra gear."

"Should we jettison?" Wiesinger asked, coming from the front. He'd been talking to the civilians, or at least trying to.

"Don't think it'll make that much difference, sir," McLaren said. "And truthfully, the mass is holding us deep enough for better propulsion. I don't want to start tossing stuff around. Especially as we may need ammo. Call me a miser, but I hate to throw away even government property if I can avoid it."

"Same here. Thought I'd offer."

"I appreciate it."

"What about the Indonesian coast guard?"

"They're a long way away, might not believe us and would be royally pissed. We'd all be in jail and on the news. Your call, it's your mission."

"Sir?" Kyle asked.

Wiesinger shook his head. "Let's outrun them. I really don't want that kind of attention drawn to us."

Or to your next promotion, Kyle thought.

"Right. Do you want to call Gilpin or should I?"

"I will," Wiesinger insisted. Kyle handed over his phone at once.

The colonel dialed. "Wiesinger here. Yes, sir, injured but recovered . . . Thank you, sir . . . We're aboard the boat and being pursued, last-ditch effort to get a kill, we think."

Lei Ling cringed. Kyle thought, *Nice going, asshole. Scare the civvies*. But he should have been expecting it.

"Yes, sir," Wiesinger said. "Understood. We are at sea, hope to call with better news soon. Out."

"Oh, shit, they're firing!" Kabongo said.

The blob on the horizon flashed occasionally from reflected moonlight. That was a silver light. This was redder, uglier. And it had a tempo that only comes from mechanical equipment.

The first burst was nowhere near the U.S. boat; Kyle didn't see any splashes or hear anything. But it would be used to range them. By halving the difference every time, it would take less than five bursts to get the distance. After that, it was simply a case of pouring enough fire out to get lucky as the boat tossed on the waves.

The second burst was a lot closer. It splashed behind them.

"Can't you stop them with the fifty?" Wiesinger asked before the next burst. He'd missed the earlier conversation.

"Not that easy," McLaren said with a shake. "We can blow it full of holes, but it won't sink at once. If they've got the pilothouse armored, they can keep closing. And they must have backup to recover them if they do sink. Closer than ours."

"Time to call a chopper?"

"No, sir. Not while we're in Indonesian waters. The twelve-mile limit is the minimum. We're at an oblique course to clear various underwater obstacles. So it'll be a half hour or so, and I'm saving the chopper. Would suck to have them show up, then leave because of fuel issues. We may need them a lot. Besides, we're forty-five minutes from the *Juneau*, the Amphibious Transport Dock ship picking us up," he elucidated.

"Will some precision fire help?" Wade asked.

"Hell, if you think you can tag something, go for it." McLaren shrugged. "Far be it from me to stop an ally from killing a bad guy. And fire downrange never hurts."

Wade grabbed both of the long rifles from the locker and made sure he grabbed magazines of match grade. He tossed one to Kyle. Both snipers loaded and shouldered the SR25s and sat down, Kyle wincing in pain.

He hunkered low to rest the handguard over the tubular gunwale. This was going to be tough shooting. It wasn't helped by the odd angle he had to keep to stop his foot from being squeezed, and hence sending sharp pain shooting up to his testicles.

McLaren started popping off bursts every time the shifting waves brought the two boats into line. The .50 BMG is a big cartridge, verging on being a light cannon shell, but half inch holes in a boat with good pumps aren't an immediate threat. And he'd have to hit it first. But a single 23mm hit on the smaller craft could cripple it. The engines were exposed to incoming fire, and there was no protection for the occupants. Nor could the multiple compartments of the tube take too many hits from explosive or even solid projectiles before the boat would founder. Both craft had low radar signatures and manually aimed weapons, making it a game of visual chase and shoot in the growing dawn.

Kyle winced as he shifted his seat. Cold seawater swirled around his ass and testicles. His stance had his foot braced against the gunwale and it hurt. Whenever another slop of water rushed over the boot, it would sting again, coldly, then slowly warm back up. While he wasn't getting seasick, the shifting waves were disorienting him. Every swell caused the boat to sway, and the gray horizon blended into the black sky and gray mist. And it was dawn again, dammit. He needed some serious sleep once the threats were diminished.

A snapping, ripping, popping sound was a 23mm projectile through the air nearby. That got Kyle's undivided attention, until he forced himself into his shooting trance. Nothing he could do would stop the incoming fire, except to hit it at the source. No panic, no shakes, just take the fire and make the shot count. A swell slopped over and soaked his sleeve, burning the raw patch on his elbow. He squinted for just a moment and got it under control.

He brought the rifle into plane and caught the pursuit in the scope. Now he had to find a worthwhile target, and he wasn't that familiar with even U.S. military boats, much less foreign ones. He could see a lit pilothouse, a gun mount up front with two men crewing it, and some assorted spidery equipment of no real interest. The best targets were the gun and the gunners.

This would work out to simply be a shot at a moving target, he figured. Or not "simply," as the target was moving, he was moving, and the platform under him was subject to sudden direction changes.

"Range?" he asked Wade.

"I'd say one four hundred meters," Wade replied.

"Long ass shot. But okay. Guns and gunner."

"Roger tha—" Wade replied, drowned out by another burst from

McLaren and a wave breaking over them. They were now soaked through, eyes stinging from the salt and chilling quickly.

Kyle put that out of his mind. The shot was what mattered. He closed his eyes for a second to clear salt and let his mind refocus, then opened them again.

The swells were fairly steady, and the boat was moving with *that* motion. The other boat was moving with *that* motion, so he should lead about *there*. And how high to compensate for range? Could he recall the chart? He was zeroed for five hundred meters, and velocity at that range was about 1548 feet per second, figure the additional range and . . . He relaxed and steadied the rifle. It didn't do any good to fight motion, in fact it made things worse. He'd have to squeeze the trigger quickly, losing some small accuracy in exchange for meeting the window he had.

There . . . and there . . . and *BANG!*

Wade's shot was a bare fraction of a second after his, and an empty case smacked Kyle in the head. It stung for just a second, but didn't burn through the sheath of cold water.

By scope, both shots had missed, because nothing happened. But Kyle had caught a glimpse of what might have been a ricochet. It was the only evidence to work from, so lead *there* and . . . BANG! as another burst crashed overhead.

Miss, but it was the best he could do. So shoot again. Breathe, relax, squeeze . . . BANG! Another of Wade's ejected cases caught him. He should move, but it was a minor annoyance and he had work to do.

One of the gun crew spun and tumbled. Good. It might have been his shot or Wade's. It didn't matter. Kyle knew how good he was, and how good Wade was, and they didn't need to compete. That was the right lead, and he fired again as it came by, and again. The remaining man tugged frantically at the gun. Perhaps one of the shots had damaged it? Or it could have just jammed. And shoot. And shoot.

Then the gunner staggered back, ducking a round. He seemed to crash against the pilothouse and fall over as the boat swayed. He scrabbled to his knees and disappeared inside. At this range by starlight it was a tough call, even with a night scope.

"Score two," Wade said.

"Yup. More targets." They were in good shooting position, comfortable enough and able to stay here for hours, with range and windage for the target. There was no hurry to move.

"Looking," Wade said. "Nothing. Want to try for the pilot-house?"

"I have an idea. Get the scope," Kyle said. An idea that was goofy, except that it might work.

"Stand by," Wade agreed. He fumbled with the rucks until he found his, then inside until he found the spotting scope.

"Mr. McLaren, I have an idea," he said. McLaren looked at him. "I need to borrow your shoulder."

"Show me," McLaren said, looking quizzical.

Kyle cleared the SR25 and laid it down, rose and took the grips on the .50. "You stand in front, facing me, gripping the mount. I'm going to steady over your shoulder. You're a strong man?"

"Strong enough. I got ya. How the hell are you going to aim, though?" he asked as he squatted and wrapped himself around the mount.

"I'm not. Wade is. Wade?"

"Ready!" Wade agreed.

Wiesinger said, "Monroe, you're a fucking nut. But good luck." He was wincing from saltwater on his feet.

"Thanks," he replied shortly, as he lowered the gun back down over McLaren's shoulder. The SEAL reached up and wrapped an arm around the heat shield. "Perfect," Kyle agreed.

He fell back into trance, closing his eyes, opening them, judging the combined motions, picking a lead. "Shooting!" he announced, and gave the paddle a press.

The .50 fired and slammed. A single round banged out. McLaren shouted, "OW!" from the noise so close to him and the recoil. The empty case whipped out and over the side, a flash of slightly heat-crazed brass.

"Need me to stop?" Kyle asked.

"High and right, several meters," Wade called.

"Your ass! Keep shooting!" McLaren said. "I'll deal!"

Kyle nodded and shifted just slightly. McLaren was inhumanly strong; even with a good part of the 85 pounds of the .50 balanced against his shoulder, it took effort for Kyle to move him. Which was good. He chose his new point of aim and settled back in. With no scope, the boat was just a toy on the horizon.

"Shooting!" The .50 crashed, McLaren shouted, Wade called, "Roof, left, one point five meters."

"Dammit, it's not steady enough. Going to take a lot of luck."

"More mass!" McLaren shouted. "Kabongo, time to make your swim buddy smile!"

"Will do, Dan. Stand by." Kabongo had been gently offering water to the civilians and Wiesinger. He came running over like a boulder with legs. He got behind McLaren, reached around him and grabbed two of the three struts on the pintle mount. He strained until his arms bulged and hugged tight. Then he straightened up.

The end result was two shoulders under the receiver, braced with four feet and the metal structure.

"I'll need to move it," Kyle cautioned.

"You move, we'll move. Shoot, damn you!" McLaren said.

"Roger. Targeting. Shooting!" Another round of crashing and yelling. He was off the mark from the shifting, but that couldn't be helped.

The 23mm mount was working again. Several hornets on steroids and rocket fuel ripped through the air. Three voices yelled, "Shit!" simultaneously. Then they had to not laugh, because it *was* hysterical.

"High, right, about three meters," Wade called. He was able to track the rounds by heat trace and by disruption of the dense, humid air.

"Roger," Kyle agreed, and depressed ever so slightly. Both SEALs were bleeding from the side of the head. At least he hoped it was scalp and that he hadn't blown their eardrums out. They were about three feet from the muzzle and facing the other way, but it couldn't be pleasant.

Hell, he wasn't enjoying the swells, the spray, or the incoming fire. These guys were just nuts. But a good kind of nuts.

A burst came in, and the pilot, who hadn't been introduced, swore in a shout. Kyle glanced back. A round had blown through one of his instruments. One of the tubes had been hit, too, but in an oblique crease along the top. If they didn't ship too much water, they should stay afloat. But there was no way to bail.

There was nothing to do about that. Kyle came back to his weapon and reacquired his position from muscle memory.

And fire. "Shit!" McLaren shouted.

"Glass gone!" Wade shouted triumphantly. "Nail him again!"

"Shooting!" Kyle said, and waited for the waves to match up again.

BANG! "OW, goddammit!" "Son of a *bitch*!" "Hit inside the pilothouse. They're turning!"

McLaren slumped. "Holy shit, that was a workout. Wish I could have seen the shooting!" He turned to observe. "And they are leaving. Nice." He heaved a deep breath. "My ears thank you for finishing." He was greased with blood on the right side of his face.

"Kick ass, brother," Kabongo said with a nod as he dropped to the other gunwale. "Call me officially impressed." His face was abraded along the jaw line and under the ear. That was what the bleeding was. But he still might have suffered hearing loss.

"Yeah," was all Kyle could say. It had been an athletic workout for him, too, and a mental drain. But he'd made the shot. Several shots.

Even Wiesinger said, "Monroe, I retract any doubts I had about your shooting ability. That was fucking amazing."

"Thank you, sir." Yeah, the man wasn't a total waste. Another couple of field ops and he might turn into a respectable officer. The problem, Kyle realized, was that he had a second lieutenant's manners, experience, and ego, and a colonel's service time. No one had done him any favors by keeping him in administrative slots.

Far off were the lights of another boat. A bigger one. Presumably official from somebody.

"Is it time to call the chopper yet, Mister McLaren?" Kyle asked, his voice high and tight.

"It's time!" McLaren agreed. "By the time it gets here, we'll be in good water."

"Use your left ear," Kabongo said. "We can bandage each other while you call."

The chopper flew escort in the graying dawn. It would have been a faster trip aboard the aircraft, but would mean two winching operations. Kyle was happy enough to wait the extra two hours. The helo also flew interference when the Indonesian patrol boat came to inquire. It landed on the tail of the boat and someone debarked. After a few minutes of face to face, he reboarded. It was impossible to tell through the scope what the details were, but Kyle gathered another "training exercise" was being stretched until it could be seen through. But that wasn't Kyle's problem, and the intel could be freely shared, now. A few extra kills for the local forces always sweetened relations. The overhead cover was also welcome as the boat started listing. Water was slowly but steadily filling the compartments of the starboard tube.

It took a subjectively long time to reach the *Juneau*. Kyle wasn't up to date on ships. He knew an Amphibious Transport was designed for Marines and helicopters, and was a moderately large craft, but seeing it was substantially different.

"How big is that?" he asked.

"The Mighty J, LPD Ten, displaces seventeen thousand, five hundred tons full load, is five hundred sixty-nine feet long. She carries eight hundred thirty-five Marines full load, plus a crew of about four hundred, plus flag crew for amphibious landing operations." McLaren rattled off the specs. That helped Kyle see it for what it was.

"That's the size of a small aircraft carrier," Kyle said.

"Pretty much. The Wasp class are carriers, for practical purposes, with Harriers as well as helos. But *Juneau* is plenty big enough for this."

"How do we get aboard?" Wiesinger asked.

"We steer right into the well deck at the stern. Slip this sausage right up her . . . ah," he looked around at the two huddled civilians, who were wrapped in a blanket, wide-eyed and silent. "Well, in the stern. Nice and safe."

"You've all saved our lives," Lei Ling said. "Go ahead and swear. It can't be worse than engineers."

"Thank you, ma'am, but we should learn to use proper punctuation anyway," McLaren replied.

The helo made another pass and Kabongo waved them off. It was past dawn now, and the ship was filling the northeast view. Kyle had never dealt with ships, though he had seen a bunch in port here and there, including the Black Sea. Being in this position to a major warship was a new experience.

The flight deck of the *Juneau* was crowded with running people as they approached. Then the crowd shifted as the chopper landed.

It really wasn't long, according to his watch, but it seemed to take forever to approach the dark cave of the well deck. *Juneau* was sunk at the stern so they could guide the craft right in. A rail on the left, port side, was crowded with people, and cranes and winches stood ready. The pilot of the boat, a Petty Officer Murphy, was busy with controls and wheels. He hadn't said much for the trip, but had stuck to the cabin area. Navigating a tiny boat in deep water had to be a difficult task, Kyle thought. Every time he ran into other military careers, he was amazed at how much was involved. There weren't any dumb grunts, as certain frothing web posters and "reporters" implied. These people were all technical professionals.

Then they were inside, the bright morning light doused and replaced with the yellow-tinged glow of large spotlights. The smell of the sea mingled with machine oil and metal. The noise was a steady hum with mechanical clatters and bangs interspersed. They drew up to the rail and Kyle felt like a bug as people stared down. He was too tired to care, and these were all friendlies. It was damned good to see nothing but U.S. uniforms.

Two female medics, as McLaren had specified, wearing very feminine-looking makeup, and civilian clothes with no insignia other than ID packs on their arms, came to escort Lei Ling and her daughter. They were smiling and cheerful to reassure the little girl, and whisked them up the ladder and away to sick bay for observation. Suzanne looked suspicious but didn't complain. There were running Marines in MARPAT camo with rifles, maintenance crews in color-coded uniforms, crewmen in dungarees, and the SEALs and their support staff in wetsuits.

"Who're they?" someone asked, pointing at the shaggy, filthy soldiers, as three sets of hands helped Kyle scramble one-footed up a ladder. Kyle had to wonder just how bad he looked. Death warmed over? Or totally roasted?

"Army Delta or something. Rescued hostages, my man! U.S.A! U.S.A!"

There was no need to correct the error, and Kyle was too damned tired. He assumed Wiesinger would say something, but even he was quiet.

A medic came over and knelt down next to Kyle. "What's wrong?"

"Superficials on knee and elbow," he said. "My foot may be worse."

"No problem. Sit here and lie back." The man nodded as he inspected the injuries, and had a relaxed confidence that came only from knowing he could handle the situation. Even though the injuries couldn't possibly be critical, and Kyle had seen, experienced, and inflicted worse, it still helped him relax. He lay back as they gurneyed him to sick bay through echoey metal corridors. Passageways? Companionways? Whatever the Navy called them. He was in a daze and didn't even notice when he arrived.

He came alert again because his foot twinged as they cut the boot away. He risked a look down as they snipped and peeled the sock.

At first it was hard to recognize it as a foot. It was gray and wrinkled from days in the jungle and the water, curled and cramped from the cold. But it resolved to its proper shape, and the swelling and discoloration at the toes wasn't bad. A slight encrustation of blood was under the nail of his big toe.

"Don't even think it's broken," the medic said. Kyle could see the three stripes of a petty officer first class printed on his sleeve. "Got to hurt like hell, but we can drain the hematoma and you should be fine. We'll X-ray anyway, of course."

"Bring it on," Kyle agreed. "I'm not going to complain. But I would like something warm to drink and eat if you can."

"Not supposed to until after treatment. But you're hungry?"

"Yeah, and cold. I'll even eat Navy food," he joked with a smile and a wink.

"Then I'll have them bring you some Navy food, and you can tell the cooks what you think personally." The medic grinned back.

"Done deal."

He was unconscious before it arrived.

Four hours later, bandaged up, showered, fed excellent food, and wearing borrowed USMC utilities, Kyle felt human again. Dammit, it had been a good mission, even with that pusillanimous Wiesinger along. And they were heading for Singapore and ready to fly home. He dozed again, and the painkillers had nothing to do with it.

The next morning he rose early. He was having trouble getting back to a diurnal schedule, and Wiesinger's order that he be up and about pissed him off. The allegation of "malingering"—while he tried to eat and drink enough to cover the ten pounds he'd lost in a week, plus the painkillers keeping him from screaming when he put weight on his foot—didn't sit well. But he said, "Yes, sir," and got up. He shaved and trimmed his hair back to Army specs, cleaned up and met the others on deck.

The three soldiers were finally back together, watching the sun rise somewhere over the Philippines as they stood at the starboard forward railing. The monstrous port of Singapore was ahead and around them. Ships and docks stretched literally for miles—everything from wooden sailing boats to supertankers and freighters. There were islands all around. A large percentage of the world's ocean traffic came through here. It was the nautical equivalent of Chicago's O'Hare Airport. The lanes were crowded in every direction.

Wiesinger said, "Good news: the Indonesian military stormed the site, finally. They found enough evidence to convince them, I assume, because they did raid Lhokseumawe. They shot the hell out of a bunch of people, but they did intercept a truck with bombs disguised as welding tanks and toolboxes. The target was one of the main tanks at the terminal. Could have taken the whole damned place up."

"Yeah, good, sir," Kyle agreed. "They don't have security around that place?"

"Apparently it has holes. But the Australians have offered an intel brief about sources for explosives. Pisses me off that State won't do it."

"Yeah, that always sucks," Kyle said diplomatically. Frankly, he preferred anonymity, and Robash was the man who could bump his career. What the rest of the world thought wasn't that critical. "One more thing to deal with."

"I'm glad we're leaving," Wade said. "I expect more bombs, and more fragmentation of the rebels. Bakri may be in for an even rougher ride."

"Good luck to him," Kyle said.

"Sergeant Monroe," Wiesinger said after a few seconds of quiet.

"Yes, sir?" he replied.

"You are an insubordinate, impudent, rude little jackass."

Kyle said nothing. It was all true, though "little" was only in comparison to Wiesinger's bulk. The laundry list of complaints he had about the colonel would take a book.

"But you did do a respectable job. I'm going to ignore a lot of what happened the last few days," the colonel finished.

"I appreciate it, sir. And I'm glad we were able to get the job done."

"I will expect a full after action review on events, specifying what you did against my orders and Army regulations, and why. While I won't charge you, I want you aware of what you did."

"I am aware, sir, and I'll give you that report." *And I'd do it again in a second, you pencil-pushing clown.*

"Very good. If there are any areas where you feel changes are needed, write them up as suggestions and I will forward them. That's how it is done. Sergeant Curtis, you also."

"Yes, sir."

"Will do, sir."

So Kyle was going to get buried in paperwork for his sins. He realized he was just happy to have it over and done with, and would go along with the program without feeling disgruntled.

Besides, he thought, it was just barely possible his recommendations would be accepted.

He let the issue drop. They were all on the same side anyway.

20

A **WEEK LATER, THEY WERE BACK IN THEIR SMALL,**
unassuming shop/office in a sixty-year-old building. It felt good,
Kyle thought. Be it ever so decrepit, there's no place like home. Far
better than cargo aircraft, decks of ships, trucks in jungles, huts in
jungles, or bare skies in jungles.

On the other hand, to be stuck here every day would be a sentence in hell. It was the contrast and variety that kept Kyle sane. You
had to leave to know how good home was.

The stop in Germany had been far too brief. Besides, he'd stayed
in hospital for follow-up tests that showed nothing. That was the
military. Afraid he'd develop something lasting they'd have to pay
for. They'd concluded it was minor, would heal quickly, and posed
no long-term threat. So he didn't get any German beer or sausage.
They weren't popular with Janie, either. She'd spent half the night
snuggled up to him in her waterbed, sobbing in relief and clinging.
The other half, she'd been incredibly passionate. He could still feel
her hair and skin touching him, her hands. It was good to be missed,
and to be welcome home. But he wasn't about to credit the Army
with that.

He sat at his desk, perfectly arranged with the pile of magazines
and tech manuals on the left, phone on the right, miscellaneous junk
on the shelf above the monitor and sick, twisted jokes printed out
from the Schlock Mercenary comic strip on the wall. It looked like
a mess to anyone else, but everything he needed was at arm's reach.
That was helpful. His foot throbbed even when elevated and despite
lots of Motrin. He wouldn't be walking much for the next week.

The in-box was stuffed, of course. Between receipts for all the
material and paperwork they'd handled so far, and routine memo-

randa, the stack was inches high. Same for email. Some soldiers could never get over the amateur habit of replying-all to acknowledge a letter. Some people felt compelled to report every minor event. Still others sent out jokes that were appreciated by most but triggered a wave of responses. Kyle groaned and started deleting, reading, filing, sorting, and signing. Wade followed suit at his desk, which was much neater, even obsessively so. Neither spoke much, though the occasional sharp tap on a keyboard indicated satisfaction or frustration with the load.

"Wiesinger returned most of the cash upon reporting back," Wade said.

"Figures. So Bakri got his trucks repaired in exchange for hospitality, food, lots of hours, risk to self, seven of his men dead, and a price on his head. Such a deal."

"Nothing we can do now, man."

"No," Kyle agreed. It sucked. Get over it.

He received an email from someone in intel. He read it.

"They think they got him!" he announced to Wade.

"Who?"

"Some scumbag who goes—went—by 'Agung,' who was the probable party behind the explosive shipments and was probably one of the ones the Kopassus killed in the raid. And we got the imam . . . so we may have batted a thousand."

"Will we ever know for sure?" Wade asked.

"Probably not. It's all extracted data."

"So don't sweat it, Kyle. We did our job, we came back in one piece, we saved a lot of people. Let the intel wienies worry about it."

"I guess so," Kyle agreed. It made sense. But, dammit, he wanted to know. That was the point of the scope to him; to be sure he got the kill.

But that was a rare situation. Guys in Iraq and 'Nam had swapped fire daily and never known if they hit anything. So he'd take the probable and be happy.

It was 1530, a half hour from the end of the duty day, when Wade snagged another document from the box and stared for a moment.

"Hey, check this out," he said. He waved two sheets of unit stationery.

"Whatcha got?" Kyle asked.

"We are each getting an Arcom for 'supporting the operation,' per Wiesinger."

Both of the last missions had been Bronze Stars with Combat V for valor. For this one, they were credited with "support," and getting an Army Commendation Medal, akin to that given to people who volunteered for deployments to Germany or Turkey to support the war.

Kyle was a professional. He didn't really care about the medals save as markers to point to his record. The acts spoke for themselves. Nevertheless, to see Wade and himself credited with so little was a slap in the face.

"So what did Weaselface put himself in for?" Kyle asked.

"A Silver Star."

"Shit."

"Yeah. Asshole." Wade's usual relaxed demeanor was dark.

"Well, we're still alive, the mission's a success, and we saved some civilians including a little girl. I say we call it even."

"You don't really believe that."

"No. But Robash is healthy again and we'll have things back to as normal as they ever get next time. Meanwhile, he might sort this out. You and I know what we did."

"Yeah." Wade sounded more than a bit disgruntled. Kyle knew it wasn't the Arcom that bothered him. It was the Silver Star for Wiesinger.

"Hey, buddy," Kyle said, standing and coming to attention, facing Wade. Wade stood and faced him, looking curious.

"You're the finest spotter and shooter I could ever be teamed with. Wiesinger may not say it, but I will. You rock." And he raised his hand in salute.

Wade snapped to attention that would credit him on parade and popped his own arm up. "Means more from you than any medal he can ever award, buddy. Thanks." The look in his eyes was probably a match for Kyle's own.

They both dropped back to attention, then relaxed again. It was a close moment, but also an embarrassing one, with the circumstances behind it.

"Screw it. Let's get my girlfriend and go watch civilian chicks dance without any fear of being blown up." He indicated the door.

"Sounds good. You're buying," Wade agreed, cheerful again.

"How come I always wind up buying?"

"If you don't know . . ."

It turned to friendly shoves as they headed out the door.

Author's Note

INDONESIA IS A FASCINATING NATION, AND I HOPE I'VE
presented it well. It has a chaotic past and its own current problems, but has some of the friendliest people and most beautiful
scenery on Earth. It's always hard to be critical of places one isn't
familiar with, and my Indonesian friends deserve thanks for helping
me build this story with some liberties on the political situation for
sake of entertainment value. There have to be bad guys and there
have to be heroes, but in the real world, things are not so black and
white.